Lew, I ca

Dio's voice was as clear
bedroom at Castle Ardais
over, Marja starts to scream ..... *up in a ball and*
hides her eyes, and I am afraid she will start having
convulsions or something!

I know, my love. I know! And I am sorry you have
to deal with it. She seemed fine when we left—a normal
child. But somehow her channels have been . . . tam-
pered with. I was only a mechanic, not a Keeper, but
it doesn't take a leronis to know that Marja has sus-
tained some sort of deep shock. She will probably grow
out of it, in time. Children are wonderfully resilient.

I don't think so, Lew. You don't spend as much time
with her as I do, so you can't really judge. . . .

I can't! Every time I look at her I remember Sharra
and how small Thyra looked when she was dead, and
how white Regis' hair was. . . .

I think we should take her back to Darkover, Lew.

No, Dio. I think going back would kill her! And it
would certainly kill me!

Margaret blinked. Had she actually overheard this
conversation, or was her excellent imagination playing
games with her? Her father had wanted to keep her
safe, even though the sight of her had caused him
pain. It must have gotten worse as she grew into womanhood, for she knew now that she had a strong resemblance to her mother, Thyra. How relieved he
must have been when she left for University. The Senator must have thought she would be safe there. How
could he have known that her work, so tame and simple, would eventually lead her back to the place which
was more dangerous to her than any known disease.
Well, he couldn't have, unless he could see into the
future, and no one could do that. Or *could* they?

A Reader's Guide to
DARKOVER

THE FOUNDING

A "lost ship" of Terran origin, in the pre-empire colonizing days, lands on a planet with a dim red star, later to be called Darkover.
  DARKOVER LANDFALL

THE AGES OF CHAOS

1,000 years after the original landfall settlement, society has returned to the feudal level. The Darkovans, their Terran technology renounced or forgotten, have turned instead to freewheeling, out-of-control matrix technology, psi powers and terrible psi weapons. The populace lives under the domination of the Towers and a tyrannical breeding program to staff the Towers with unnaturally powerful, inbred gifts of *laran*.
  STORMQUEEN!
  HAWKMISTRESS!

THE HUNDRED KINGDOMS

An age of war and strife retaining many of the decimating and disastrous effects of the Ages of Chaos. The lands which are later to become the Seven Domains are divided by continuous border conflicts into a multitude of small, belligerent kingdoms, named for convenience "The Hundred Kingdoms." The close of this era is heralded by the adoption of the Compact, instituted by Varzil the Good. A landmark and turning point in the history of Darkover, the Compact bans all distance weapons, making it a matter of honor that one who seeks to kill must himself face equal risk of death.
  TWO TO CONQUER
  THE HEIRS OF HAMMERFELL

THE RENUNCIATES

During the Ages of Chaos and the time of the Hundred Kingdoms, there were two orders of women who set themselves apart from the patriarchal nature of Darkovan feudal society: the priestesses of Avarra, and the warriors of the Sisterhood of the Sword. Eventually these two independent groups merged to form the powerful and legally chartered Order of Renunciates or Free Amazons, a guild of women bound only by oath as a sisterhood of mutual responsibility. Their primary allegiance is to each other rather than to family, clan, caste or any man save a temporary employer. Alone among Darkovan women, they are exempt from the usual legal restrictions and protections. Their reason for existence is to provide the women of Darkover an alternative to their socially restrictive lives.

THE SHATTERED CHAIN
THENDARA HOUSE
CITY OF SORCERY

AGAINST THE TERRANS

—THE FIRST AGE (Recontact)

After the Hastur Wars, the Hundred Kingdoms are consolidated into the Seven Domains, and ruled by a hereditary aristocracy of seven families, called the Comyn, allegedly descended from the legendary Hastur, Lord of Light. It is during this era that the Terran Empire, really a form of confederacy, rediscovers Darkover, which they know as the fourth planet of the Cottman star system. The fact that Darkover is a lost colony of the Empire is not easily or readily acknowledged by Darkovans and their Comyn overlords.

REDISCOVERY (*with Mercedes Lackey*)
THE SPELL SWORD
THE FORBIDDEN TOWER
STAR OF DANGER
THE WINDS OF DARKOVER

AGAINST THE TERRANS

—THE SECOND AGE (After the Comyn)

With the initial shock of recontact beginning to wear off, and the Terran spaceport a permanent establishment on the outskirts of the city of Thendara, the younger and less traditional elements of Darkovan society begin the first real exchange of knowledge with the Terrans—learning Terran science and technology and teaching Darkovan matrix technology in turn. Eventually Regis Hastur, the young Comyn lord most active in these exchanges, becomes Regent in a provisional government allied to the Terrans. Darkover is once again reunited with its founding Empire.

THE BLOODY SUN
HERITAGE OF HASTUR
THE PLANET SAVERS
SHARRA'S EXILE
WORLD WRECKERS
EXILE'S SONG
THE SHADOW MATRIX
TRAITOR'S SUN

THE DARKOVER ANTHOLOGIES

These volumes of stories edited by Marion Zimmer Bradley strive to "fill in the blanks" of Darkovan history, and elaborate on the eras, tales and characters which have captured readers' imaginations.

THE KEEPER'S PRICE
SWORD OF CHAOS
FREE AMAZONS OF DARKOVER
THE OTHER SIDE OF THE MIRROR
RED SUN OF DARKOVER
FOUR MOONS OF DARKOVER
DOMAINS OF DARKOVER
RENUNCIATES OF DARKOVER
LERONI OF DARKOVER
TOWERS OF DARKOVER
MARION ZIMMER BRADLEY'S DARKOVER
SNOWS OF DARKOVER

EXILE'S SONG

SONG

A Novel of Darkover

MARION ZIMMER BRADLEY

DAW BOOKS, INC.

DONALD A. WOLLHEIM, FOUNDER

375 Hudson Street, New York, NY 10014

ELIZABETH R. WOLLHEIM
SHEILA E. GILBERT
PUBLISHERS

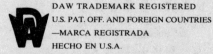

DAW TRADEMARK REGISTERED
U.S. PAT. OFF. AND FOREIGN COUNTRIES
—MARCA REGISTRADA
HECHO EN U.S.A.

PRINTED IN THE U.S.A.

1

◆

There must be some way to travel between the stars that doesn't nauseate me—some drug to which I'm not sensitive. If only I weren't allergic to so many things. If only I had chosen a career in agronomy or journalism.

The woman on the thrust couch smiled grimly without opening her eyes as she tried to ignore the nausea and dizziness. It was an old thought, one she had replayed many times. Years before, when she had left home for University, she had actually considered those two professions as career possibilities, along with accounting and several others she couldn't remember now. It had taken her less than a semester to realize that she had a rather black thumb, and hated the idea of reporting the miseries of others. She found she had little skill with words, and numbers were boring, although she had fine mathematical skills, and could have become, she thought, a rather successful embezzler. This made the smile widen into a grin, and a little of the tension in her face slackened.

Beneath the turquoise-colored cuff of her black Scholar's uniform, she could feel the itch of the patches on her skin. One was to supply her with the drug, hyperdrome, that prevented space sickness, and the other was to counteract her allergy to hyperdrome itself. Silly, really, that she was allergic. Her father was, too, so she must have inherited it from him. She really was his daughter, even if she didn't feel that way most of the time.

She moved her head back and forth against the vile-smelling cushions of her couch. The knot of very fine but abundant red hair piled atop her head chose that moment to escape from the pins that held it in place, and began to slither down her neck. She could feel the tension in her body and tried to will herself to relax. The faint smell of disinfectant that hung in the stifling, dry air of the third-class compartment was disgusting and made her squirm.

As long as she kept her eyes closed, she had the illusion of privacy and was a little less aware of the eleven other people who shared the cramped quarters with her. The presence of other people nearby, people as anxious as herself, made the terrible, grinding nausea she was trying to ignore even worse. It had always been this way, ever since that first voyage away from the place to which she was now returning. She had only a few, vague memories of her childhood, but that first trip was more vivid and powerful than the others. The smells and sounds of a space vessel, and of a belly which felt as if demons were dancing in it, were associated with something dreadful that she could not remember clearly. She never actually became ill, but hovering at the edge of nausea for endless hours was just as bad, or perhaps even worse.

Few people would believe that a Federation Senator's daughter would travel third class. They tended to think that such people lived glamorous lives of parties and diplomatic soirees. But she was a Scholar of University, and academicians rarely traveled any other way. She was a seasoned traveler now, ten trips and more than a hundred jumps, yet her body still refused to adjust to the drugs, and she had resigned herself to the discomfort. At least she was not forced to endure the agonies of steerage again—as she had on her first solo trip, from Thetis to Coronis in a sixteen-jump nightmare. And traveling first class, as she had once, was not much better— the air still stank and the drugs made her mouth dry.

I am like a fine wine—I don't travel well at all. I wish this drug really put you to sleep the way it's supposed to. There's Professor Davidson, snoring away like a baby, bless him. How does he do it? Will this be our port-of-call? I've lost count. Is this the sixth jump or the seventh? Mother of Oceans, let it be the seventh.

She began to play the Game. She and her stepmother, Dio, had invented it on that half-remembered first voyage, when she was very small. It consisted of naming every goddess and god she could think of. When Dio had taught it to her, she had only known a few—Zandru and Aldones, Evanda and Avarra. By the time they had reached their destination, she could name more than a hundred, and knew some of their stories. The list had grown as she had gotten older and learned more, until it included names of deities that dated back to the days when Terra had really been an Empire. She had added the names of deities learned from fellow students, names from planets she had visited and places she had never been. Sometimes she looked for rhymes in the names, or tried to put them in alphabetical order—anything to distract her from the rebellions of the flesh. She had never run out of names, but she was not sure whether this was through repetition or not. The exercise gave her something to focus on, rather than listening to the sound of the great ship around her and smelling the acrid scent of her fellow travelers.

The stomach-turning surge of the ship itself began to slacken. The machinery sounded different, the whine of something ceasing. The noise always made her tense because it meant they were leaving the void between the stars and entering the gravitational pull of some world. The steady boom of the planetfall engines kicked in—a slightly-out-of-tune A flat—that made her shiver.

The professor gave a sputtering snort on the couch beside her, coughed, and stirred. He was awake. Years of enforced intimacy with the old man had familiarized her with his every grunt and gesture. She did not need to open her eyes to know he was flexing his fingers over an imaginary keyboard.

How accustomed we have become to one another, she thought. *He likely knows all my little habits, too.* It was rather comforting to feel the easy familiarity of her companionship with Ivor Davidson, her mentor and practically her foster-father. His wife, Ida, had been like a mother to her, and she decided that in spite of the vile feeling in her middle, she was really very blessed. She was doing the work she loved in the company of a dear friend she respected. Who would dare to ask for more?

The loudspeaker above her couch whined and hummed, and Margaret winced. Damn her extra-sensitive ears! They made possible her studies, her scholarship, and her career as a musicologist. But damn—and double damn—the sloppy communications officer—who was probably

tone deaf—who had made the last three landfalls pure
agony. After some tinny clicking and a sharp squeal that
made her shiver with discomfort, a nasal recording, in
the heavy accent of some backwoods planet, began to
drone. It was old and needed replacement. She had to
force herself to listen and not just tune out the noisy
thing.

Then the recording switched off, and something resembling a human voice, speaking in Terran Standard
with a fearsome accent which drawled the words, started.
"We are now on final approach to Cottman Four,
called Darkover by the inhabitants." There was something almost disdainful about that word, as if the speaker
imagined Darkovans to be naked savages or some such.
Typical Terran arrogance. "Passengers are reminded not
to unfasten restraints until the all-clear has sounded. For
those passengers in steerage and third class in need of
assistance, a steward will be ready to assist you soon
after landfall." After the voice had given the instructions
to the passengers in Standard, it began to repeat them
in half a dozen other languages, those she was able to
recognize rather obviously mangled.

Darkover! Their destination at last. The planet of her
birth. But the sound of the word in her mind triggered
the strange apprehension she had felt ever since she had
found out she was going there. It was something akin to
dread, and it was completely illogical! She had been to
other planets with Ivor during their work, and never had
she felt such crawling unease.

Margaret took several deep breaths and made herself
relax. The muscles in her shoulders were tense, and they
loosened reluctantly. But her relaxation exercise worked,
slowly, and she gave a little sigh of relief and stopped
listening. Her attention wandered. She was accustomed
to being told everything a dozen times. As a Colonial,
she had a healthy contempt for the regimented and
closely-governed ways of the Terran Federation. While
valuing its technological achievements, which allowed
her to study music on a dozen worlds in a single lifetime,
she bore with Terran arrogance for the sake of her scholarship and the freedom it afforded her. But she did not
like it at all, and she thought she probably never would.

Her father would have been happy to send her to any

of several Colonial colleges, but the University on Coronis had not numbered among his choices. She remembered the row which had exploded when she first suggested it. To say her father hadn't approved was a masterpiece of understatement, and worse, he would never explain why. Dio, her stepmother, had intervened as she always did, keeping the peace between father and daughter as well as she was able, but she had endured what felt like weeks, though it was only days, of anxiety and brooding silences before the Senator had given his consent. She wished she understood him better—or at least understood his strange mixture of distance towards her and fierce protection of her. The Old Man (as she thought of him) and Dio were absent a great deal, being forced to attend Senate functions and do the business of the Federation. With his own allergy to hyperdrome, the Senator didn't come back to Thetis very often, and when he did, he avoided her as much as possible. It was almost as if he loved her and hated her at the same time.

For no reason she could discern, thinking of those dreadful days waiting for the Senator to give her permission to go to University, Margaret was suddenly reminded of another time, when she had been much younger, thirteen or fourteen. Dio had found her sitting on the shore of the Thetan Sea of Wine, weeping. She couldn't quite recall what she had been crying over, but the words she had said suddenly came back. "I'm ugly," she sobbed, as the older woman tried to comfort her. "Father never hugs me, or lets me go anywhere, and I know it is because I am ugly. Why can't I have pretty hair, like you. Why do I have skin that gets spotty in the sun? And you and Father are gone so much, and when you are home, he never touches me, or talks to me, or anything! What's wrong with me?"

The memory made her shiver all over as the ship gave out a huge roar. Then it made a sort of metallic sigh, almost as if it were tired, and she thanked the Goddess she was no longer thirteen, and subject to the horrors of adolescence. All those years when she had been convinced that the Old Man's attitude toward her was due to something she had done wrong, or failed to do, even though Dio told her it had nothing to do with her, and everything to do with the Senator himself. Dio did her best to comfort her, and said that Margaret was *not* ugly. The Senator *did* love her in his brooding way, Dio insisted. But she had somehow never gotten around to explaining why he was so distant, nor why she looked so unlike both of them. It wasn't until a long time later that she learned she was not Dio's child at all, but the Old Man's by his first marriage.

Margaret could still remember her utter shock at this revelation, just before she left for University. She had never imagined that her father had been married before. There were so many things she did not know about her own past and her father's. She started to shudder and stopped herself. She was not the heroine of some trashy romance, with dark secrets lurking in the background. So, why did she have the strong and terrible sense that there were not only things she did not know, but things she did not *want* to know. Foolishness! She was just tired from the long trip, and ill from space drugs.

No, it *was* more than that. She was returning to the planet where she had been born more than twenty-five Terran years before. Margaret had only the vaguest memories of it, and even thinking about it gave her a mild sense of discomfort, a slight headache and the sensation of the air just before a storm. There were so many troubling things about it. Her father was the Senator for Darkover, but he did not live on the planet, and, so far as she knew, he had never set foot on the place since he left over twenty years before. The mother she had known for most of her life was not really her mother, and Dio was adamant in her refusal to reveal more than the barest generalities about her real mother.

There was a moment of silence, except for the blessedly on-pitch chime of the all-clear. After this came the thumps of a clumsy technician inserting the landing announcement, and the chatter of half the compartment informing one another of the obvious fact of their arrival. It was almost as if they could not believe anything unless they told someone else about it.

"We have now arrived at Thendara Spaceport on Cottman Four and passengers with this as a final destination are cleared to disembark at their convenience. Our stop here will be brief, so passengers continuing to Wolf—Phi Coronis Four—are advised not to disembark but to remain in your restraints. Passengers for Sagan's Star, Quital, and Greenwich are requested to disembark here and consult a uniformed Spaceforce Attendant for the transit information to your final destination. Please prepare immediately for disembarkation. A Medic will enter your cabin at once to administer hyperdrome for all continuing and newly boarded passengers. Repeat; we have arrived at Thendara Spaceport; passengers for . . ." The voice went on and on.

Margaret ignored the mild headache, and her unspoken desire to stuff a rag into the loudspeaker. She ignored the itch of the dermapatches on her left wrist. Instead she started to unbuckle the straps which held her against the couch, eager to be away from the smell and sound of the ship as quickly as possible. Well, not as eager as usual. The sense of dread remained, just at the back of her mind, and she had to force her attention away from it. Once free, she turned to her companion.

Professor Davidson was fumbling clumsily with his restraints. His eyes were a little glazed from the drugs, and, as usual, he was slightly disoriented. She watched him struggle with one buckle and bit her lip. The first thing she had noticed when she first met him were his hands—beautiful hands, like those of an angel in some old painting. Now they were twisted and bent, hardly able to manage the simple chords on a guitar. It seemed to have happened overnight, but she was sure it had been slower than that. He could play almost any instrument developed for humanoids—and even some fashioned for nonhumans—but he had always been hopeless with simple things like catches and buckles, and he hated it if she reminded him of his clumsiness. Finally he gave her a look of helplessness, defeated by the stupid thing. She sat up—a little dizzily against the brief rush of postural hypotension—and reached over to help him as a steward came into the cabin.

"What would I ever do without you?" he asked, his seamed nut-brown face wrinkling in the smile that never ceased to delight her, even when she was aggravated with him.

"Hire another assistant, of course," she answered dryly. His ever-increasing dependence on her distressed her more than she wanted to admit. It was as if their

year-long sojourn on Relegan had drained away the last
of his vigor, leaving behind a dried-up husk of a man.
She forced herself not to show the sense of helplessness
and rage she always felt when she noticed his rapid de-
cline. She owed Ivor Davidson more than she could ever
repay. Not in anything so vulgar as credits, but in affection and loyalty. During her first, terrible year at University, while she had floundered in search of some
subject she could master without boredom or frustration,
she had met Ivor in the library. She had been singing
softly, much to the annoyance of some of the nearby
students—quite unconscious that she was doing so. He
had taken her in hand, tested her with a kind of savage
thoroughness, then brought her into his home. Ivor and
his wife Ida had nurtured her both as a musician and as
a woman, giving her a sense of confidence she had never
gotten with Dio and the Old Man. In the end, he had
arranged an open fellowship for her, made her first his
protegée, then his assistant. It was the sort of position
that was highly prized in University circles, and she
knew she was very fortunate.

She shivered a little as she remembered how insecure
she had been then. It had taken so much of her energy
to escape from her father's inexplicable combination of
distance and over-protectiveness. The pair of them made
her welcome, as they had done with generations of students during their lengthy careers. Ida had taught her
the manners of University culture, and Ivor had taught
her musicology, and his passion for his field. They had
both given her an unconditional affection that she had
never experienced before, and she had mistrusted it at
first. Their persistence had worked, and somewhere
along the way she had ceased to be a wild Colonial girl,
and become instead a respected scholar. It was not anything like she had imagined when she lived on Thetis,
but she liked her job, and she loved the old fellow.

For more than a decade the Davidsons had been her
family, and she felt blessed to have found them. Thetis,
her homeworld, she pushed into a back room in her
mind, remembered only when she had to fill out the
various forms to which the Terran bureaucracy seemed
addicted. She worked very hard at erasing all memory
of her father, that bitter, silent, one-handed man and

even those of her gentle, laughing stepmother who was so ready a foil for the Senator's moods.

...en she did recall her childhood, she usually remembered the pleasant things. The roar of Thetis' waters, rushing along the shore of their island home, and the smell of the flowers which bloomed in spring outside their door; the taste of the first-caught *delphina* of summer; the intense blue color of the azurines, the marriage flowers of Thetis, as they curled in the pale hair of couples. The color of azurines always made her throat grow tight with tears, for no reason she could discern. Margaret had rather a large store of such images, because she had been alone a great deal during her childhood. The Senator and Dio were gone for months at a time, much to her guilty relief. She was always so anxious when he was there. She still had only the vaguest idea what he actually did, and no interest whatever in it. Odd, now she thought about it. The few friends she had made at University all had a lively curiosity about their parents, and a great deal of pride in whatever it was that Daddy or Mommy did.

"No, I don't think so, my dear." Ivor Davidson's voice broke into her troubled reverie. "I don't think I could ever accustom myself to having someone new around me. I hope I do not have to. Selfish of me, I know. I should be thinking of you, of your future, not my own. A beautiful young woman like yourself should have a beau or several, should be bearing children instead of bearing with an old man's crotchets and grumbles. But the truth is I could not get along without you—and I am very glad you are here with me."

Margaret looked at him with a start of unease. She realized she had been avoiding seeing how old he had become, had been denying his increasing decrepitude. Old at ninety-five—like some Prehistoric. The last rejuvenation treatment hadn't taken, hadn't worked. His hands, his angel hands, were turning to stone and she could hardly bear it. *Ivor, please stop getting old. . . .*

"Nonsense!" She spoke briskly, to conceal her emotions. "That filthy hyperdrome always makes you melancholy. Let's get out of this flying coffin." This last remark unfortunately made in her full voice, the trained voice of a singer, earned her a dirty look from one of the continuing passengers. She felt herself blush to the roots of her red hair, and she lowered her voice, before continuing. "You'll feel better after a drink and a bath," she said. Cottman IV was described as primitive in the little information she had been able to get her hands on, but Margaret knew perfectly well that this only meant, in Terran bureaucratese, that there were not com booths on every corner, or a vid-deck in every home.

She had a sudden, very clear memory of a huge vat of a bath in a room that smelled of something she could not name. Through a door on one wall she saw a tall man step into the room. He was slender and his hair was pale, kind of silvery. There was something about him that made her stomach lurch, and she shivered all over.

Margaret forced herself to shut away the disturbing image and turned her energy to mentally cursing departmental politicking and academic funding for sending them to Darkover. They had only been back from a very tiring year on Relegan a brief month when the command had come from the head of the Music Department to dash off, ill-prepared and still exhausted, to save the department's bacon. All the work they had done among the Relags had had to be abandoned, or handed over to associates, just because their colleague Murajee had gotten himself involved in a scandal of some sort. The Department Chair, the overly ambitious and politically conniving Dr. Van Dyne, had sent them because there was no one else available with the credentials to do the job. It had been that or lose the funding, and Dr. Van Dyne never lost funding.

She had been frustrated at every turn, trying to get information about Cottman IV. It was most peculiar, and she had taken it rather personally. She kept finding the notation "Restricted" on files in the University Library, and even trying to use her father's access codes had not worked. She had sent word to Dio, asking for information, but no answer had arrived before they left.

It almost seemed to her that the computers were keyed to keep her ignorant. Which was ridiculous, of course. Margaret had managed to get a basic language tape, a disk on customs of the Trade City, and the printout of what she suspected was a piece of fiction, though it had come from the history section. At least *My Tour of Several Worlds* by Claudean Tont read more like a romance than anything else. She had discovered that Cottman IV was a Protectorate, not a colony *per se,* and that information about it was largely inaccessable. She almost wished she had paid more attention to the Old Man's occasional bouts of loquacity.

She was too tired to fuss over an insoluble problem. Margaret slung her flight bag, and Ivor's, too, across her right shoulder. Then she grabbed the seemingly skimpy all-weather cloaks—which weren't—in her hands. The only thing she looked forward to was getting out of her loathed Scholar's uniform and into whatever the locals wore. University frowned on its scholars "going native," but she was sufficiently experienced to know that the best way to do research in the field, here collecting samples of native music, was to appear as ordinary as possible. It was the reason she was there, and damn the stuffy rules.

They went into the green corridor. It spiraled down ahead of them, and her nausea returned in force, so she gripped the cloaks tightly in her hands. After what seemed like an eternity of stairs and slanted ramps, and corridors whose walls changed colors in some manner that had meaning only to the builders of the ship, they arrived at a portal and exited onto a broad expanse of tarmac.

A sudden blast of icy wind with a few drops of moisture in it stung their eyes, then died away. It cut through the cloth of her uniform, chilling her completely. Margaret stopped, ignoring the mutter of someone behind her, and draped Ivor's cloak over his shoulders. The impatient passenger who had followed them growled and stepped around them. She watched him stride away, toward the cluster of Imperial buildings across the tarmac, square and foreboding.

Beyond them lay an eerily familiar horizon. The huge red sun was just at the edge of the sky, but whether rising or setting she could not be certain. Her usually reliable sense of orientation seemed to be on the blink. She wasn't sure what time it was locally, although they had probably mentioned it during the disembarkation announcement. Stupid. She should have paid more attention!

The sun made a bloody blot in the sky and etched the nearby buildings in carmine. Margaret squinted at it, and the sense of *déjà vu* nearly made her stagger. Tears welled in her eyes and she blinked them away quickly, pretending to herself it was just the stinging of the wind against her cheeks that made them prickle.

Why not? I was born here after all. I haven't been back since I was four or five, but it's not so strange I should recognize the sun, even if I didn't expect to react. My father is the Senator from Darkover—how could I not have known this sun! The dull headache which was a leftover from the hyperdrome increased suddenly, so there were stabs of pain behind her eyes. She whispered a fine collection of curses, in the polyglot of tongues she knew, and hurried to catch up with the professor. Each step made the stabbing pain hurt more, and she glanced at the sun over her shoulder. It seemed to her that something within her troubled mind was afraid of that sun, as if it roused memories better left alone.

They found the Administration Building, and took their place in the line that had formed. "Hurry up and wait" was just as true now as in the dark days when the phrase had been coined. Out of the intermittent wind, and away from the sun, Margaret found her headache subsiding, and decided she must be even more tired than she had thought. A bored clerk stamped their permits and papers, and gave a wave toward yet another corridor, nearly identical to the others they had traversed.

Eventually she saw a sign that directed them toward the baggage area. Their sparse luggage and the foam crates containing Ivor's guitar and Margaret's small harp were sitting on a platform. She broke the seals and hauled out yards and yards of gray biodegradable packing plastic. It was awful stuff, but it was all that was allowed in or out of class-D planets. A few hours beneath even the fading sun of Darkover would reduce it to a few grams of clean-burning waste. She dumped it in the allocated bin, stripped the two drug patches from her wrist, and dropped them in as well. She handed Ivor his cased instrument and slung her harp in its cloth covering across her back. Then she picked up the two bags.

Ivor shifted his guitar from hand to hand as she made a pack animal of herself. She knew that even the minimal weight of the instrument was painful for him, but he would not give up carrying it. It was almost two hundred years old, made by the hands of a long-dead craftsman, and Ivor cherished it as another man might love a woman.

They followed corridors and arrows until they finally emerged into a cool dusk. She felt marginally better now that she had an idea of what time it was. Now to solve the problem of finding the place they were to stay in Thendara Old Town, before they rolled up the sidewalks for the night, without the nicety of ground transport. She knew from the tapes she had listened to that skycabs and motored vehicles were nonexistent here.

Ahead there was a high wall, made of Terran concrete blocks. Through an arched opening, she could see a cobbled area that flickered with torchlight, contrasting sharply with the bright, actinic glare of floodlamps. The two light sources crossed, making huge shadows, and the dread she had managed to force into the back of her mind returned, flooding her with apprehension. On this side of the wall, she knew who she was, but beyond it, Margaret suspected, she did not. She had a powerful sense that once she crossed that boundary, she would be different, and it was not an appealing prospect.

Then a gust of wind touched her, and she recalled her duties. This was no time to be standing around having the jitters! Margaret swallowed hard as her hair blew around her face. She dropped her burdens and thrust her wind-blown hair viciously into the collar of her uniform, where it tickled her neck. It was a relief to have something to be angry at—her flyaway hair! Then she regathered the bags and marched toward the gate, Ivor trailing beside her wearily.

2

◆

Beyond the gate, Margaret set the bags down again and put on her own cloak. She repositioned Ivor's again, and tucked it around the guitar as well as she could. She knew it would get much colder as the sun went down, and after the tropical warmth of Relegan, it was close to painful. Ivor looked at her with misery in every line of his face. She had never known him to look so old and tired and ill. She bit her lip and looked away.

Margaret looked around for some form of conveyance, a cart or pedi-cab, perhaps. This was where the taxi stand was at most spaceports. All she found were a couple of keen-eyed youngsters in tunics and trousers and calf-length cloaks. She found herself staring at them both with interest, and a cautious eye. The boys returned her stare with open curiosity.

"Hey, lady, you want some help with your stuff?" one shouted in Trade City pidgin, as if he expected that she was ignorant of his language and thought that speaking more loudly would bridge the gap. She managed to make out what he meant, though his accent was broader than on the tapes she had listened to. His companion grabbed him roughly and whispered something urgently, then came forward with an awkward little bow.

"May I be of service, *domna*?" This was more like what she had heard, and Margaret felt a little less helpless. The bow bothered her, as did the sudden change in attitude, but she was just too tired to think about it now.

"I was hoping to find some sort of conveyance," she stammered. The first boy, the taller one, seemed to find this very amusing. "A cart or a horse or something."

"You won't get one here," he stated with the finality of the very young.

Margaret felt foolish and a little angry. "No, of course not."

The second boy glared at the first. "I could go for a horse car, but it is easier to walk. The rest house is right over there." He pointed to the edge of the square. There was an ugly little cluster of buildings perhaps two hundred feet away. They were typical Terran architecture—fortresslike and forbidding.

"We are not staying at the rest house," she said slowly, forming her mouth into patterns that seemed to be right on the tip of her tongue, but were hard to get out. Once, she knew, she had probably been fluent, or as fluent as a five-year-old could be, but since neither the Old Man nor Dio ever used anything except Terran Standard on Thetis, she had nearly forgotten what she knew. Worse, she realized, when she listened to the language tapes, her mind seemed to resist grasping the words, and she had to struggle as she had never done before.

"Do you know the way to Music Street?" There was something wrong with her phrasing, she was certain, but the boy appeared to get her meaning. His eyes widened slightly. She could almost hear him thinking *Why are these people going there?* Damn her active imagination anyhow.

"Yes, *domna.*" The answer was polite, but she could see that the lad was very curious.

"Is it far? My companion is very tired. We have traveled a long way." Wasn't that a masterpiece of understatement.

"Not too far, if you don't mind walkin'. Pretty far, for Terrans. What would you be wanting in Music Street?"

A gust of wind crept under the nape of her neck, caught the loose strands of her hair, and the last of the pins beside her ears slithered out of it. Silky strands of red blew across her face in the chill breeze, blurring her vision. Margaret dropped the bags and grabbed for her escaped hair as the boys watched her with amusement. With a few small curses which she hoped they didn't understand, Margaret grabbed at the flying strands and yanked them back with chilly fingers. She coiled them into a knot, and one of the lads gathered the fallen pins and handed them to her. One of the few things her step-

mother *had* told about their home planet was that unbound hair was the mark of a common streetwalker, an
invitation to trouble. Odd, she thought, that Dio would
tell her that. "We are staying in Music Street with Master Everard. Do you know the way there?"

"We can take you." The second boy spoke. He was
courteous enough, but Margaret felt uneasy. Their bags
held few clothes, but all their disks and recording equipment. On a low technology world like this, they were
wealth beyond price. Not to mention the hell there
would be to pay if they were stolen. She and Ivor were
replaceable; their equipment would be a form-filled
nightmare to recover. The thought made her rage as she
often did at Terran arrogance and paternalism.

Margaret knew she was too tired to think straight, and
finally realized that her anxiety must be due to sleep
deprivation. It certainly wasn't hard to understand. She
had not really slept for days.

The second boy was dark and had an honest sort of
face, but after all these months with nonhumans, she
no longer trusted her own assessment of faces. And a
confidence man by definition had an honest face. It was
his stock in trade. It was growing colder by the minute,
and she couldn't stand there being indecisive. Ivor
couldn't bear it even if she could.

"Lead on, MacDuff," she said with more vigor than
she felt. She picked up the two bags herself, still wary
in case these seemingly nice boys were really thieves.

"Naw," the dark-haired one answered. "I don't know
any Macduffs. 'Tis MacDoevid. You know any Macduffs, Geremy?"

"Not me," Geremy said, and made a gesture toward
her luggage. "You want some help with those?"

"MacDoevid, eh?" Margaret ignored the offer out of
sheer pigheadedness. "Professor, is he a relative of
yours?" The old man forced a feeble smile. He was having trouble following the exchange of words between
Margaret and the boys, and it showed in his face.

Ivor didn't answer immediately, and then he seemed
to understand her question. It took time for the sounds
to make sense in his mind, she knew. "Perhaps. The
sons of David have always been a widespread tribe," he

said with a real grin, as if he found the whole thing enormously amusing.

The boy MacDoevid tilted his head to one side to stare at the old man. "What did he say?" There was a glint of interest in his eyes, curiosity and intelligence combined.

Margaret sighed. Ivor always had a terrible time at first in learning local dialects. One of the many ways in which Margaret was invaluable to him was her ability to pick up new languages quickly. She knew that what she had learned was basic and simplistic. The language disks had contained typical phrases that arrogant Terran tourists considered important to know: "Where is the Skyport? How much does that cost?" and other equally inane but universal matters. She had nevertheless been able to obtain a rudimentary knowledge of the common Darkovan tongue. Ivor had obtained a disk of complex musical terms, but she had not had a chance to listen to it, because of the haste of their departure. Besides, musical terms would be of little use with these lads.

Margaret drew a long breath, disciplining herself to go slowly, even though the chill of the sunset wind made her want to hurry. "Permit me to make introductions," she said, choosing the words with care. "Professor Davidson, meet young MacDoevid. You see, your names are akin." She emphasized the vowel sounds, so the youngster could hear them, and was rewarded by a widening of eyes and a nod that told her he had understood. Clearly a bright lad.

"Huh, wait till I tell my father 'bout that," responded the boy. "But what is 'Professor'?"

Margaret realized that for want of enough vocabulary she had used the Terran title. From the little she had learned thus far, she had not found any mention of anything like a college or university on Darkover, and realized that there was no immediate equivalent to use. Her weary brain fumbled with words for a moment, before she realized the answer was much simpler than she had thought. "He is a—a teacher. Of music." She was rather pleased with herself. It both answered the question and explained why they were going to Music Street.

Ivor gave her a tired and rather forlorn look. He never managed to master pidgin anything. For weeks he would mumble like an illiterate, expecting Margaret to translate everything. Then one morning he'd wake up speaking the language almost like a native, and chatter to make up for lost time. *But he won't be here long enough for that.*

Margaret scolded herself immediately. Where did that thought come from, anyway? She did not believe in premonitions; such beliefs were illogical and unscholarly. She was only tired and worried about her companion. And she was cold and hungry, too, which just made her dark thoughts worse. They were going to be on Darkover for a year or more, and Ivor would be fine, as soon as she got him to Music Street. If only she could shake the sense of dread she had that had been gnawing at her for weeks. If she had just been able to get in touch with Dio, she was sure she wouldn't be so apprehensive. Why hadn't her stepmother answered any of her costly telefaxes? She had always responded before. What if something was wrong with her—or the Old Man? *Stop borrowing trouble,* she told herself furiously.

They had left the wall around the spaceport buildings behind them, and now passed a gray stone structure that made her skin crawl when she looked at it. The windows were screened from the street, and it was squat and silent and hideous. "What is that? A jail?" As she spoke, she knew it was not. There was something utterly familiar and vile about the place.

"Na, that's the place where they put extra children. The Terrans are very strange. They put children there and leave them." Geremy answered her question, his young voice dripping with condemnation.

"He means, *domna,* that it is the orphanage." That was the MacDoevid boy, his voice a little deeper than Geremy's in the growing darkness.

Now she could see a lighted sign which read *The John Reade Orphanage for the Children of Spacemen.* Of course! She had lived behind those screened windows once, when she was small and alone and helpless. But her father was not a spaceman. He was an Imperial Senator. He had never been a spaceman either, as far as she knew, so it didn't make any sense. Why couldn't she remember? Her stomach tightened, and she had to swallow several times. Despite the chill of the air, she felt sweat break out on her forehead and under her arms. Why, oh why, had the Old Man and Dio been so secretive?

Stop this! There must have been reasons, probably good reasons, why they never told me anything about this world. And they never thought I would return to Darkover, did they? They don't even know I'm here now, unless they got my last communication. They probably think I am happily ensconced at University, or off somewhere doing music research. And they probably have no idea that I need them right now. The Old Man is busy with the Senate, and Dio is . . . no, I must be imagining something. Dio is fine, just fine. Despite her logical insistence that her stepmother was all right, Margaret had a nasty feeling that something was very wrong, at that very moment, and she did not like it at all.

"You idiot," MacDoevid said, shoving his companion on the shoulder. "Extra children, indeed! Stop showin' off or I'll tell Auntie how rude ye' were, and when she finishes skelpin' ye', she willna let ye' meet any more ships."

"Do you boys come here every day?" Margaret asked, too exhausted and disoriented to try to make any sense of this byplay.

"Na, *domna,* only when there's a passenger ship. Lots o' ships land here, but most of 'em aren't people ships." It took a moment for her tired brain to realize he meant cargo ships and transfer ships, which were more common and more frequent visitors to Darkover than the passenger ships. Darkover was well situated as a transfer point, but most people never left the spaceport. "We get money for luggin' stuff," he hinted broadly, gesturing at the bags she clung to stubbornly. "We have to be people the Officer knows. He tells us when one is coming, because he knows us, and knows we is trusty. Strange ones might be thieves," he added, as if he knew her reluctance to surrender her load was fear of just that.

She understood the boy's hints perfectly well, and wished she felt more comfortable about trusting them. Margaret had some local money in her belt pouch. She had cleaned out the University branch of Rothschild and Tanaka, Moneychangers, of their entire stock of Cottman currency. It was the equivalent of about twelve

standard credits. What that meant in the local economy
was anyone's guess. She tried to flog her tired brain into
useful channels. What should she give them for being
guides, always assuming they were not going to lead
them into a dark alley and rob them. She dismissed that
thought as unkind. Geremy would certainly not be bash-
ful about telling her if she was stingy, she decided. He
seemed irrepressible, and she envied his confidence.

Ahead, she saw another wall, a lower one this time.
It seemed to separate the loathsome orphanage from the
rest of the city. They passed beneath an arch where a
black-leathered guard lounged comfortably. He waved
to the boys as if they were a familiar sight, and gave
Margaret and the professor no more than an indifferent
glance. She guessed he saw all the few tourists there
were. Once beyond the arch, they were surrounded by
stone houses and cobblestoned streets that seemed to
run together at crazy angles. No wonder there were no
wheeled vehicles! These streets were too narrow for any
Terran car.

The cold was intense now and seemed to pierce her
bones, even through the cloak. The somewhat crabby
agent at the University travel service had grudgingly told
her it was spring on Cottman IV, which had conveyed
to her mind something warm and balmy, not this icy
reality. She envied the boys their comfortable wool tunics. *When I lived here, I must have worn that sort of
wool, and furs, too. I think I had a fur tunic when I was
very small—funny I never remembered it before now. It
was rust-colored, the color of my mother's hair.*

Margaret shook herself. How strange to think that her
tunic was the color of her mother's hair. The memory
was fugitive, faint, and maddening, and she shivered.
Then a small grin curled her lips for a second. She
wished she had a fur tunic now!

Margaret tried to dispel the unease the memory of
that tunic brought her. Instead, she remembered something Dio had said years before. "The Terrans can dash
between the stars, but they have yet to invent any synthetic which is as comfortable as wool or silk. I do wish
they would stop trying!" That made her feel better, even
as she cursed the clinging material of her Scholar's uniform. It was, in theory, comfortable in any climate or

weather. Like many theories, it worked better in the lab than in the field, and was typical of the Terran passion for technology, and their disdain for nature. All-weather was a concept, like "one size fits all," probably made up by some idiot who never left the weather-conditioned environment of a Terran compound. Despite her fatigue, Margaret started to feel a little better. There was something so satisfying about sneering mentally at Terrans and their fondness for the unnatural.

"How would you like to help me out tomorrow, Master MacDoevid? It would be after school."

Both lads looked at her, and she realized that they had the same last name. It was not the dark one who answered, but the fairer and taller boy. He had almost red hair in the flickering torchlight, and gave her a shy grin. "My father is Master MacDoevid, *domna,* I'm just Geremy. I dunna go to school, *domna,* but I'd be honored to be of service." He eyed her in the light that spilled from a nearby wineshop. She glanced up at the sign outside the place, and saw something like a tree wearing a crown. Until that moment the actual meaning of "preliterate," which was how the meager information she had described Darkovan culture, had not sunk in. It was one thing to know something intellectually, and quite another to meet the actuality.

Margaret was rather surprised at herself, realizing she had unconsciously assumed that young people went to school during the day, even though she knew that on many planets, this was not the case. She had become a scholar, and while she and Ivor had done a great deal of field work in the past decade, she still thought of things as a person from University, not a girl from Thetis or Darkover. And somehow she had imagined that the world of her birth would be more like University or Thetis. It was a profoundly disturbing realization, and she knew she was going to have to spend some time rethinking things.

Something was nagging at her mind, and she paused to try to figure out what it was. It took a moment for Margaret to realize that it was the persistent honorific the lad used; *domna.* She had learned *mestra* which was the equivalent of Ms. or Mistress. But the term Geremy had used meant something like "Noble Lady." Why was he calling her that? And why did it bring up such a peculiar feeling, as if she could almost remember someone else who was called by that title. Her brain was too weary to puzzle it out.

"I need to purchase some garments—warm ones, for myself and for my teacher. Do you know where I can get some?"

Now he grinned. "To be sure. We are both from Threadneedle Street, and we know about cloth." He sighed. "Our fathers are in the business. And I will take you to MacEwan's; he is the best tailor in Threadneedle Street. He will be proud to have your custom, *domna.*"

"He is also our uncle," the other boy muttered, so softly Margaret almost missed the words.

"A good merchant always keeps business in the family where he can," she said peaceably. She couldn't quite figure out the darker lad, who seemed intensely curious and antagonistic at the same time. Geremy seemed to be a friendly fellow, and his cousin—if they were both nephews to this MacEwan, cousin seemed the right relationship—quite another thing. She was just too tired to think straight. She could almost sense his emotions, like the wind stinging her skin, but she could not guess at its reason. His foxy features, the sharp nose and penetrating eyes, were wary and hopeful at the same time. Perhaps some woman in his family had been seduced or dishonored by a Terran. That was a scenario repeated all too often on human worlds. The Terrans were famous for their disrespect of local customs. Unwanted or unfathered babies were all too common all over the Empire's old territory . . . wherever Terrans could interbreed, they did. And low-tech worlds weren't noted for birth control.

"Geremy is a boot-licker," the foxy boy grumbled.

"And Ethan likes to argue. He'll probably end up as a judge."

"Oh, no," Ethan protested. "I'm going to be . . ." he stopped, Margaret saw the expression in his eyes, the look of hunger and longing. She had often seen it during her stint of student teaching. It concerned an ambition so precious that even to speak of it to an outsider was painful.

"Ethan is apprenticed to the cloth-dyers guild, but he

really wants to be a spaceman." Geremy got a wild punch on the shoulder for this disclosure.

Margaret did not laugh. It was obvious from Ethan's face that he had expected her to. They were nice boys, she thought, the sort of brothers she might have had if the Old Man and Dio had ever had other children. Although she had never wished to travel between the stars, she understood that the young man wanted something different than following family tradition. She had never imagined as a girl that she would end up collecting music on worlds she had never even heard of, yet she knew she had not wished to become a mother or a wife.

Margaret knew, too, that when she had been what she guessed Ethan's age to be, she would have died rather than admit her secret ambition to become a dancer or a famous actress. She could laugh at her younger self, but she would never laugh at this solemn boy.

"It is very difficult to become a spaceman," she said gravely. "The first thing you must do is get a good education, with special attention to mathematics." Ethan studied her cautiously, measuring her as she had measured him shortly before. He seemed to decide she was taking him seriously and stood up rather taller. A moon was rising, and it cast dark shadows beneath his eyes. The moon looked like an amethyst against the darkened sky, and she tried to remember its name. Her weary brain refused to cooperate.

Geremy studied her thoughtfully. "Are you Terranan?"

"Don't be silly," Ethan said, "Anyone can tell she is not Terranan."

"No, I come from a world called Thetis," she told them. "A lovely world full of waterfalls and great oceans. We live on islands where the winds blow warm and smell of salt and flowers." Margaret had a sharp wave of homesickness for the warmth of Thetis. It surprised her by its intensity. She found herself thinking of her father, staring out at the rolling surf with a goblet clutched in his single hand. In her mind, he turned his dark eyes away from the sea and looked at her, almost as if he felt her presence across the light-years which lay between them. She shook herself back into the present. Born on Darkover, yes, but the home of her heart was still Thetis.

"I don't even know which star it is in this sky. I have visited many worlds, though. I am a musician."

"You have been on lots of planets? Please, let me carry your bag. Would you—could you—tell me everything?" Ethan grinned up at her, and was transformed, his face aglow with interest.

Margaret surrendered her grips, forgetting her earlier fears in her exhaustion. She knew this wanderlust; sometimes it seemed to be some universal drive among the children of Terra. She had a touch of it herself, despite her loathing of the travel itself. At first she spoke haltingly, groping for the right words. Then she had a sudden leap of mind, as if she had discovered an unexpected cache of language lurking in the recesses of her mind, as if some barrier were breached. It was amazing, because she was using words which were not in the limited vocabulary she had learned from the disks. It was not the words which startled her as much as the rhythm of them which seemed to come so easily to her lips now.

After a few minutes, Margaret realized that she had more of a vocabulary than could be explained by living on Darkover for her first five years. This was not a child's lexicon, but that of an adult. At last, she understood that she must have heard Dio and the Old Man talking in the night—the walls of Thetis homes are thin and light, to let the breezes rush through them—while she slept, and learned the sweet rhythm of the language. It seemed likely that if she had had occasion to use it before, she would have been chattering like a magpie. Magpie. That was one of Ivor's names for her, a way he teased her out of her solemnity when she was in the dumps.

All these thoughts dashed across her mind as she spoke of Thetis, of the University world of Coronis, where she had gone to school, of Rigel Nine, and the Congress of the Confederation, where her father helped make the laws governing the Terran Federation. She told them about Relegan, the last planet she and Ivor had visited, and about anything else that rose in her tired brain.

The boy was so serious Margaret was not even tempted to "yarn" him. He fired questions at her concerning metals and mechanics, and she was glad for the first time that "Basic Technology of the Big Ships" was a required first-year course everywhere. Enlightened self-interest, of course. The entire Federation staffed its ships by feeding the curiosity of children like Ethan. She did not tell him that he could never leave his world without the tools of reading and writing which the simple signs outside shops led her to suspect would never be available to him.

The streets seemed a little wider here, the structures made of roughcut stone. Wooden doors were painted brightly, and there was a smell of damp stone and animal droppings and garbage. They passed an eating house, and the smell of the food was tantalizing. Margaret realized that she was now very hungry. The smell was familiar, too. She could almost name the dish, though she had not eaten it since she was tiny. Oh, well, they said the mid-brain—and the sense of smell was a very primitive part of that—never forgot anything. Perhaps it was true.

She ignored her hunger and her tiredness and forced herself to go on amusing, or instructing, the boy. Professor Davidson stumbled along beside her, listening mutely. Geremy had somehow managed to get him to surrender his precious guitar, and now also lent him his arm.

"Margaret, are we going much farther? I seem to be a bit short of breath."

"I don't know. Ethan, how close are we to Music Street?"

"Only one more street, *vai domna*." This was a new honorific. She vaguely knew it meant something like "Highly Honored Lady" and was the same one that would be used to a Princess or a Keeper. *What the devil is a Keeper?* She felt as if the answer were just on the edge of her consciousness, something vitally important which she could not seize in her near exhaustion.

"Just a little farther, Ivor." She spoke in Standard for the professor's benefit, then turned back to Geremy and spoke in her much improved Darkovan. "It will be good to be out of the cold and rain," she added, for an icy drizzle had begun in the last few minutes. "We just spent the last year on a very warm world, and it is hard for him, you see." *This place seems colder than Zandru's hells . . . He has whips or something, doesn't he?*

The half memories were maddening now. Margaret

could no longer tell what she was remembering and what
she had picked up from the language and culture disk.
She gave it up and wished her mind would let go until
she had had some good food and sleep. "It seems very
late. Will your parents be worried?" The lads looked
young to her, and the dark shadows of the streets
seemed alive with potential dangers.

"Oh, no. Cloth Street, where we live, is only a few
minutes away. It's not yet even an hour after sundown,
when we have to be indoors."

"And you, Ethan?"

"I live next door to Geremy; our fathers are brothers.
Hoy, we all know each other's name. Except you,
domna."

"True. I forgot to introduce myself. My name is Margaret Alton." She spoke her last name almost as if it
was spelled Elton, in the way it was pronounced on the
vid or at University, the way she had become used to
saying it for years.

"Alton. That's a good old name." He spoke the name
the way her father had, and Margaret felt a kind of thrill
at hearing it said correctly. Ethan also seemed to be very
impressed with it, and she wondered if he knew her father was the Senator from Darkover. It seemed likely.
She was just too tired to fuss over it.

I knew she was comynara—*I just knew it!*

The words whipped into her mind like a needle, startling her. That sort of thing had happened a few times
before, especially when she was tired, but never with
such clarity and distinction. Margaret looked at both
boys, but she could not tell which one had thought the
words, and she supposed it didn't matter. "Is it much
farther?"

"No," Ethan said. "Here we are." They turned the
corner into a narrow street, where signs with pictures of
various musical instruments hung outside nearly every
house.

"The Street of Musicians," he announced, making a
little bow, and waving his hand like a magician. He was
so pleased with himself that, in spite of her exhaustion,
Margaret laughed, and the lad laughed with her.

3

———— ◆ ————

There were houses on either side of the street, and the doors of most were painted with pictures of a bewildering variety of musical instruments. Margaret identified a kind of harp, an assortment of wooden flutes, and something vaguely like a violin. Its shape was different, more elongated, enough to be sure the tone would be subtly different than anything she knew. The street was poorly lit by flickering torches and the moon, but she could see wood shavings and small pieces of stuff scattered around on the rough cobbles. In a less damp climate, it would have been a terrible fire hazard, but she doubted the debris ever dried out enough to be dangerous.

It smelled good. The woods gave off pleasant fragrances, the mist which dampened the air was clean, and food was cooking behind the brightly painted doors. These were such homey scents, after days in the confines of the ship, that she felt ready to weep from the pleasure of it. Margaret could not remember ever reacting so strongly on any previous planetfall, and it was a little unnerving. Not unpleasant, precisely, but disquieting, as if there were memories hovering just out of mind, wisps she could not quite grasp.

From behind one door, or perhaps from the big shuttered window beside it, came the sound of a group rehearsing with stringed instruments. Someone hit a very sour note; Margaret winced. As if in answer, a huge bass voice roared angrily.

"That's Master Rodrigo," Geremy informed her, his earlier formality forgotten. "He's a terrible bully, but they say he'll be craft master after Master Everard, because he's a better musician than Everard's son Erald. He really *is* good; I heard him sing last Midwinter, and it made goose bumps all over my arms. He's almost the best singer in Thendara except for Ellynyn Ardais—and Ellynyn is *comyn* and an *emmasca*, so of course he has a wonderful voice."

Margaret considered these words. They had not been on the tape of Trade Language of Thendara City, but she was fairly certain she knew what *emmasca* meant. She had heard the famous castrati of the pleasure world of Vainwal, and could almost wish they were legal on other worlds. They had the reputation of being the finest voices in the Empire. Were they legal on Darkover? Or were they, whatever they were, born that way? The other term remained a mystery, because while she knew it, something seemed to be blocking her ability to understand its meaning.

Then she realized that Ivor was no longer beside her. She looked around, and found the professor standing underneath one of the street signs, studying the oddly-shaped violin on it. Margaret shook her head, retreated to him, and herded him gently down the narrow street. He was muttering happily to himself, asking himself questions and answering them almost immediately.

When they caught up with the boys, who were waiting very patiently, she asked, "The job of craft master is generally handed down from father to son, then?" Her brain might be tired, but it seemed her tongue ran on automatic and continued to ask questions.

The boys looked at each other and shrugged. It was Ethan who answered. "Sometimes. It depends on the son's skill or lack of it. The MacArdis, and the MacArans, have been craft masters in the Music Guild for a long time now. Just as the MacEwans and the MacCalls are master tailors, and the MacDoevids are the best weavers in Thendara. Erald MacArdis will not care, for what he likes best is to wander about and gather songs. My sister Becca is married now to Rodrigo's brother, so I hear a lot of music gossip when she comes home. Is that something like you do, *domna?*"

"That is exactly what I do. But, if you'll forgive me for asking—I don't know what's rude here—didn't your family want Becca to marry in the cloth guild? Why did she marry an outsider?"

"Why? Because she sings like a bird, is why. And the mess she makes with a loom! Why, I can weave better than she can—and I could when I was ten years old." *I wish I couldn't, so I could do what I want—but like Mama says, we don't always get what we want!* "But to hear her sing—that really is a treat."

"I hope to hear her, then," Margaret said and the boy grinned up at her in the flickering light. He was really quite nice-looking when he smiled. And the emotion behind his thoughts was very strong—even though she was probably imagining the whole thing.

"Da let her marry outside the guild when she threatened to run off and join the Renunciates if he didn't." Margaret wondered what kind of a threat that was, what the Renunciates were, and what they renounced. She let the question that rose to her mouth go unasked. Ivor was drooping again, and beginning to shiver, his previous interest in the strange instrument gone.

"Does Master Everard live hereabout?"

"Right there," said Geremy and led the way to a house halfway down the narrow street. It was a little larger than the rest, but gave no other indication to her eye of being different. The door had a painting of a stylized harp sort of instrument, and another of a bagpipe. Geremy put the bags down and bounced up the three steps. He gave a sharp rap on the door.

After a brief wait, a thickly-padded woman in her fifties opened the door and peered out nearsightedly. "Yes? Oh, it's you, young man. What d'you want now?"

"I have brought your guests from the spaceport. They are important people from beyond the stars," he announced, puffing up his narrow chest with pride. "Where is Master Everard, Anya?"

"What? *Now?* Are you certain?" She looked at Margaret in the flickering light from the doorway and shook her head. "That old fellow will forget his own name next! Come, come in! What a muddle! I wasn't expecting you for yet another tenday, but I'll manage, I suppose." Anya seemed rather doubtful for a moment, then remembered her manners. "Do come in out of the cold, *mestra* and . . . surely you are not Master Doevidson?" She gave the name the local pronunciation rather than the Terran one.

"No, I am his assistant." Margaret looked around and found that Ivor was still standing across the street, look-

ing at the instrument painted on the closed shutters of
a shop. His breathing seemed rather noisy, and she
hoped he was not coming down with a cold or something
worse. He looked so small and old in the flickering light
of the torches that her heart ached.

"She is Margaret Alton, Anya," Geremy said, evidently feeling that he must make the introductions. She
heard the words as she started guiding Ivor across the
street gently, and when she glanced up, she could see
that Anya was surprised at her name. And very curious—the way the boys had been when she said it a few
minutes before. She hadn't really noticed, but now, remembering their reaction, she wondered what it meant,
if anything. A good old name, Ethan had said. Probably
it was a common patronymic, and there were Altons all
over the place.

She could wonder about such things later. She guided
Ivor up the stairs, toward the light and warmth of the
house. He leaned heavily on her arm. "Come along now.
It's too cold to be standing out and looking at street
signs."

"Yes, yes, my dear. I am sure you are right—but are
those paintings an accurate rendering, or are they merely
stylized? You remember, on Delphin, we saw the pictures of the sacred horns, but the real things looked
quite different. I just cannot believe those eff-holes."

"Not tonight." She led him inside. "The eff-holes will
keep until tomorrow."

Like an overweary child, Ivor broke from her grasp
and turned around on the steps, starting back down
them. "But I've never seen anything like it; what kind
of tone do they get with star-shaped eff-holes? And what
sort of wood . . . ?"

She was ready to scream with weariness and impatience, and she nearly took a nasty spill as she grabbed
the edge of his cloak and virtually hauled him back.
"Not tonight! Ivor, do come in. I'm cold. You are cold.
You are going to make yourself sick, and then you won't
be able to do anything!"

"Moira! Raimon!" Anya shouted cheerfully. "Come
out here and get these bags. We have guests!" She made
it sound as if the absence of those she called was some-

how their fault. Margaret would have laughed if she had not been quite so tired.

The stoop was a little crowded, between Geremy and Ethan and the baggage, but it sorted itself out in a few moments. The lads handed the bags to the man who appeared—he must be Raimon—and Ethan carefully placed Ivor's precious guitar inside the door, out of the way of feet.

Margaret opened her belt pouch and fumbled in it for money. She drew out two silvery coins and handed one to each boy. They stared, and Geremy finally said, "*Domna,* this is too much."

She was too tired to haggle. "Nonsense. You are going to come back tomorrow and take me to see your uncle the master tailor. I may want you to take me other places as well. May I expect you after the noon meal?"

"Yes, we will both be here." He shook his head in wonder. "Whatever you need, we will help you find. Ethan's brother works for the finest bootmaker in all Thendara and . . . well, it will keep, won't it?" Then he shoved the coin into his pocket, and bounded to the foot of the stairs, where the other boy was waiting. "See? I told you she was *comynara* . . ." she heard as they raced down the uneven cobbles of the street.

That word again! She went into the house and closed the door, leaning back wearily against the heavy wood. Margaret pulled her hood down, and her red hair came tumbling out with the tug of the sleek fabric, damp and curling slightly. It clung to her neck and cheeks, and she felt like something the cat would not bother to drag in. Her skull pounded with a wretched headache, and the wonderful smell of cooking was enough to drive her wild with hunger. At the same time, she did not think she had ever felt so tired in her life.

Anya, plump as a pigeon, and the other servants were clustered in the doorway, staring at her as if she had suddenly grown two heads. Briskly, she made herself smile anyway, and prepared to deal with the business of getting herself and Ivor some food and a place to sleep just as quickly as possible.

Margaret lay in a bed large enough to sleep three or four comfortably and reveled in the utter luxury of it.

After several days on the narrow couches of the ship, or in the cubicles provided at stopovers, it felt wonderful. And it was much larger than the bed she usually slept in in her quarters on University. The Terrans might regard Darkover as backward, but in the matter of decent beds, they were clearly very civilized. She looked toward the small window that pierced the wall. The first red glimmer of sunrise had awakened her, brushing her eyelids like a soft caress. One of the few things her father had ever said about Darkover, she decided, was accurate. She had never really believed it, but it was true; the great red sun of Darkover really was the color of blood. "The bloody sun" was descriptive, not poetic hyperbole.

Now she tried to recall the events of the previous evening. There had been a warm, meaty stew, something that tasted like venison, but not quite, served with crusty bread, obviously home-baked. Margaret had eaten without tasting much, because in between bites she had to act as translator for Ivor and Master Everard MacArdis. The professor had clearly memorized all the musical terms that were on his disk, but his accent was dreadful, and she had a hard time figuring out his meaning sometimes. He did not have the natural musical line of Darkovan speech yet—he would in a few weeks—and his Terran Standard pronunciation was distressing.

Words kept filling her mind, things she must have learned as a child, or things she had heard through the walls from her parents, but they were jumbled up so she sometimes had to pause in the middle of a sentence for several seconds before she could continue. More, she was mildly disturbed by the places where she found words she "knew," yet could not really grasp. Why should she have a mental block on some words, but not on others?

The demands of being the middle of a three-part conversation held by two elderly musicians, eager to exchange information, had been exhausting, and Margaret had been extremely glad when Ivor nodded off abruptly. Master Everard apologized for his enthusiasm, and called Anya to take them to their rooms. She liked the music master immediately, and felt at home in his large, comfortable house.

Margaret let the pleasant memory of the previous evening slip away, and returned to her problem with the language. She did know it, and for the most part, understood it. She must have been fluent in it once—after all, it had been her first language. She knew that *casta* was descended from Gaelic, Spanish, and English—but was no more like those languages than English was like ancient High German. So, what was the matter?

Another memory curled up from her mind, like a snake stretching. It was rather vague, and also unpleasant. It had something to do with that ugly building— The John Reade Orphanage. She shrank away from the memory. It had not been a bad place, just very ordered and cold. And no one was supposed to speak Darkovan within its walls. Matron—she couldn't remember the woman's name, only that she was very stiff and stern— had been very determined about that. She washed out little mouths with soap if she caught them speaking *casta* or any other dialect. They were supposed to speak Terran Standard and nothing else.

She chuckled to herself. That must be the root of her difficulties—a sort of aversion to the very language of her childhood. Margaret could almost taste the soap. Well, she was no longer a child, and Matron must be long gone, either dead or retired. Satisfied that she had solved the puzzle, she let her mind wander onto more pleasant subjects.

Margaret thought about the wonderful hot bath she had enjoyed before going to bed. The great steaming vat of hot water was very like those in her memories, and she had soaked away the aches and disgusting scents of space travel. Gervis, an old servant she had not met at the door, had taken charge of Ivor, and with relief she saw that he knew just how to handle a weary, querulous old man.

The girl, Moira, had shown her to her room, and she had found her things unpacked. Her tiny recorder and the blank disks were stacked neatly on a chest, and a warm flannel nightgown was laid out on the bed. It was very clean but well-worn, darned neatly around the embroidered cuffs, and the collar turned. She had been happy to wear it, rather than having to sleep in her skin, or the horrid tube of Terran-made synthetic, considered appropriate for travel, she had packed in her bag. Clean, warm, and dressed in soft folds of flannel, she had fallen asleep—or rather, lost consciousness, almost before she pulled up the blanket.

Now, as the bloody sunlight set the room aglow, she sat up and looked at the embroidery around the cuffs. *Yes, my stepmother wore something like this when I was very small; it was embroidered with butterflies. No, it wasn't Dio—it was someone else. Why did I think it was Dio?* Everything was so terribly familiar and so alien at the same time. She shivered a little, for while the house was warm, it was still much colder than she was used to. Still, it felt rather nice—the sharp tang of the air, and the smell of the nightgown. There was some fragrance they used—she was sure she would remember the name in a minute or two—on linens, and it made her feel safe. Margaret knew the mind never really forgot anything, but she felt besieged by all these disordered fragments of memory, vague and fugitive wisps of remembrance, like gnats circling her face.

I used to dream of a sun as ruddy as this one. And Anya kept staring at me in the oddest way all evening, almost as if she knew me. But, why? I don't look very much like my father. The Senator is dark-haired and gray-eyed; my hair is red and my eyes yellow—"like a cat," he always used to say, when he was in his better moods—or drunk. It is not a physical resemblance, then, at least not to my father. Something about my name! Margaret found she did not want to pursue that thought. Something about it made her uneasy.

Who do I look like? Not my stepmother, of course. We aren't related at all, though she has always treated me as if I were her real daughter. Margaret let herself dwell affectionately on a mental image of Diotima Ridenow-Alton, a picture many years out of date. She saw a tiny woman, with pale hair like yellow silk, and laughing green-gray eyes. By the time Margaret was ten she was almost as tall as her petite stepmother, and had always felt like a great lummox beside her.

Her last night at home, years before, drifted into her mind. The Senator had been crouched in his great chair, looking across their lanai at the raging sea. Thetis was a tranquil planet, but sometimes storms came up and roared along the shore—beautiful and frightening. The Old Man had often watched the wind and water, fascinated. "I never saw anything like this until I left Darkover," he had muttered, curling his one remaining hand around his cup.

Margaret hated him when he drank, when he watched the sea rage, when he raged inside himself over some unspoken and unhealed grief. She could always feel it roaring inside the man, this stranger she called Father, and it made her skin crawl. He sometimes seemed as if he wanted to tell her something, and she knew somehow that she didn't want to hear whatever it was. It was almost as if she could read his mind, hear the words he had not yet spoken.

This train of thought made her too uncomfortable. Margaret pushed back the warm covers reluctantly and got out of bed. As she removed her nightdress, the chill of the room made her skin gooseflesh a little. She put on one of her other uniforms with mild reluctance, black trousers and the tunic that came to her knees. The material slithered against her skin, unnatural but warm. She pressed the closings into place and sighed.

Today she would find something more suitable to the climate and less obviously Terran. She didn't want to spend all her time answering questions for the curious. She brushed her hair and braided it, hardly glancing at her image in the mirror. She rarely liked to see her reflection, even in shop windows. There was something about mirrors that made her nervous, and had for as long as she could remember.

As she tidied the flyaway hair, Margaret wondered why she wanted so much to get into the local clothing. It was not just that she despised the synthetics—she had been wearing this garb for over a decade, and was extremely proud to be a recognizable Scholar of the University. It was a privilege she had earned, and she valued it highly—what it represented, not the thing itself. She did not want to be noticed here, she decided. It felt almost as if she were afraid to be seen, as if some danger lurked in the crooked streets of Thendara. Nonsense, of course, but she could not escape the feeling entirely.

Margaret coiled the braid into a flat chignon, covering the nape of her neck neatly, and pinned it into place.

This was how Dio wore her thick yellow hair. Once, when she had been about nine, she had yanked her hair up on top of her head, and the Senator had gotten enraged for no reason she could understand. Dio, ever the peacemaker, had explained that displaying the nape of her neck was considered unseemly, and she had blushed along her high cheekbones as she spoke, so that Margaret had been left with the impression of some naughtiness associated with both unbound hair and a bare neck. Later, when she went to University, she realized that there were literally hundreds of things that were taboo on some world or other—eating with the wrong hand or eating the wrong-shaped food. It did not have to make sense. Custom was custom.

At the same time, there had been no mention of this custom on the disks she had gotten. Indeed, now she thought about it, as she shoved in extra pins, there had been very little information about anything especially useful. She knew, for instance, that such government as existed on Cottman IV was feudal in its organization, but details of it were sparse. There seemed to be a king, or a regent of some sort, and there was mention of powerful families. The study disk she had viewed said more about Terran prejudices than it did about actual Darkovan culture.

Sighing, Margaret got out the recorder and her transcriber, and dictated notes on the conversation between Master Everard and Ivor the previous evening. She didn't think she had left out anything important, but she played it back just to be certain. Then she clipped the little machine to her belt and went downstairs.

In the kitchen Anya greeted her with the odd, almost deferential manner she had shown the night before, when Margaret had been too tired to do more than take mental note of it and add it to the ever-lengthening list of questions and puzzles. The woman had not acted that way toward Ivor. She put a bowl of fragrant porridge in front of Margaret and rubbed her worn hands on her apron, looking apprehensive. Then she bobbed her knees slightly.

Margaret's hunger made her curiosity fly away. She thanked the woman and fell to like a healthy young wolf. It was delicious.

Professor Davidson came downstairs as she was finishing a second bowl. He looked rested and fresh, but a little off-color beneath his Relegan tan. He had misbuttoned his Scholar's tunic, and forgotten—or failed, anyhow, to comb his thinning hair. When she had first known him, they had been almost the same height; their eyes had been level. Now, he was so stooped, he barely came to her shoulder. But he flashed her a smile, and she tried to ignore the little voice that told her that something was very wrong.

Master Everard arrived just as they finished breakfast. "I trust you have slept well?" he asked after greeting them.

"Very well, thank you."

"Room not too cold? Sometimes off-world guests find it so. As a boy I was schooled at Saint Valentine's monastery, and we would wake up sometimes, and find snow lying on our blankets. I resolved then that no guest of mine should ever be cold." His voice was a resonant baritone, and Margaret thought he must have been a fine singer in his youth. It was a surprisingly deep voice for such a slender man. He looked as if a good stiff wind might blow him off his feet. Still, he was tall and erect despite his years, not shrunken like poor Ivor. She had taken his measure in the first five minutes, for he was very like some of the academics she knew and whose company she enjoyed. He had a square chin and lots of little laugh lines around his pale gray eyes, white hair, and lots of *good* wrinkles, the sort that come from doing something that, however difficult, was deeply satisfying. She hoped she would look like that when she was old.

She was lost in her thoughts, and almost missed a question from Ivor. "Master Everard, that instrument maker across the street. I was struck by the shape of the eff-holes . . . damn it, you tell him, Magpie. I wish I didn't have so much trouble learning new languages!"

The use of his pet name for her touched her. He hadn't used it often since she stopped being an undergraduate. She regarded him affectionately as he spooned porridge into his mouth. How fortunate she was!

Master Everard was waiting for her to tell him what Ivor had asked, from the look on his face, with a slight degree of confusion. She sighed. She hoped it was not

going to be last night all over again. Margaret drew some
lines on the tabletop with her fingertip, showing how the
holes on a Terran violin looked.

"Are you sure, he asked, after a moment's thought.
"I never saw holes like that—does it make good music?"

Margaret laughed softly. "Well, the Terrans have been
making music with this configuration for several thousand years, so I think you could say so."

"Astonishing. I see that I will learn a great deal during
your visit. And that is a wonderful thing for me."

"What did he say," Ivor asked.

"He says he's surprised you can make good music with
eff-holes of that shape—well, he was more polite than
that. He likes his star-shaped ones. And he says he
thinks he will learn a lot from us. I think he is tickled
pink about that."

"Is he?"

"Well, he is no youngster, and he probably knows as
much about Darkovan music as anyone alive—so the
chance to learn new things might be very attractive."

"I had not thought of that." Ivor seemed satisfied, and
his color was improving as he ate. Margaret felt a sense
of relief, because she wasn't sure she could cope with
him being ill.

"When you have finished your morning meal, we can
continue our discussion," the Master said slowly. Margaret dutifully relayed this reply to Professor Davidson,
and watched him bolt the rest of his bowl, heedless of
his somewhat delicate digestion. It was good to see him
eager, but she still wished he would take it easier.

At last, when the porridge was gone, the warmed cider
drunk, Everard led them into a front room in his house.
It was a large chamber off the entry hall, and when Ivor
saw it, he almost beamed with delight. He was much too
dignified to clap his hands together and jump for joy,
but the glint in his eyes was almost the same. It was a
room to warm the heart of any musicologist anywhere
in the galaxy. The floor was polished wood, the walls
paneled and gleaming, and everywhere the eye went,
there were musical instruments. Margaret was almost
glad, for the first time, that Professor Murajee had gotten himself into trouble, since without that she would
never have seen this wealth of instruments. The room

was a veritable museum of the instruments of Cottman IV. Everard was evidently a man with a sense of history. He explained that the collection had been begun by his own grandfather, but modestly added that it had been more a muddle than a collection when he was a boy.

He began an unhurried tour of the room, and the professor submitted to being shown around with as much good grace as he could muster. Odd—she had never seen him quite so impatient, almost trembling with eagerness. She was kept so busy translating she hardly had time to enjoy the various instruments herself, and was sorry she had not brought the camera with her when she came down to breakfast. More, she regretted she did not have the opportunity to try the several lutes, or the small harp not unlike the one Margaret herself carried.

It became evident that Master Everard had a museum curator's attitude toward the collection, though not the stuffy sort that sometimes made visiting such places a boring experience. Each instrument was treated like an old friend. Margaret turned on the recorder and listened to stories of makers long dead, or stories of pipes carried into battles so long ago that Everard himself did not know if they were history or legend. She had never seen an actual bagpipe before, though she knew about them from courses in early music at the University. Here the art of playing them, she understood, was still known. It had died out on Earth, and nobody alive could play one. "It makes a hell of a racket," Master Everard told her. "I've heard they were invented to scare the foe away—and I reckon a war pipe played loud enough would scare off a banshee."

Margaret asked on her own accord for details of their playing. If she learned nothing else, this piece of scholarship would make their trip worthwhile. The bagpipe was the only wind instrument, however, except for a few wooden flutes; and there were no brasses except for a couple of Terran imports, clearly included because the Darkovans perceived them as exotic. It made sense that a world as metal poor as the teaching disks had insisted Darkover was would not waste any on tubas or trombones.

Much of the morning was gone, and the question of the strange eff-holes remained undiscussed, what with trying to describe the sorts of woods used to make the lutes, and how the tuning was arranged. At last Everard reached into a niche in the wall and took out a small harplike instrument which Margaret had been eyeing with curiosity. He called it a harp, but Margaret heard, like a whisper beneath his breath, that it was called a *ryll*.

"You know," he rumbled, "that they die if they are not played." He seemed to have forgotten that neither Margaret nor Professor Davidson knew anything of the sort, and realized he was speaking almost to himself lost in some remembrance. "You will, perhaps, think me a foolish old man. The old makers understood these things better than this generation does. They would tell you it is the spirit of the tree in the wood that gives life to the instrument. A tree is a tree, you might think. Perhaps— but wood is living stuff, not like stone or clay. Then the maker himself puts something into it, as well. And if it's associated with one person for a very many years, it takes on something of his touch also." Then, as if noticing them, he looked mildly embarrassed.

Margaret smiled. "Anyone who knows anything about instrument making would agree with you, Master. I am often certain my own harp is quite alive, and Ivor has a relationship with his guitar that would make his wife jealous if she were that sort of woman." She was surprised by her eloquence, but so pleased at her growing ease with the local language that she hardly noticed.

"My wife was jealous, too," replied Everard, sighing a little. "But she was born in Tanner Street and did not grow up with wood shavings in the soup, as the saying goes. Now, this *ryll* . . ." he used the native term in his eagerness to tell the tale, "is a real problem child. It once belonged to a woman of great talent, and more than a little madness—they say she was of *chieri* blood— a woman who has her own place in the history of our world. It is not a pleasant story. But that is the way of life," he went on, again lost in his own thoughts. "If you win, or succeed in what you try to do, you are a hero; if not, a villain. That is the way of history."

Chieri blood? The word was not one she recognized, but it made her feel peculiar. "But what is so strange about this—*ryll*?" Margaret asked, her fingers itching to caress the silky wood, and she banished her unease and curiosity at the same time. The instrument had fascinated her since she came into the room.

The old man gave another sigh. "This *ryll* was given to me by a student of mine, some twenty years ago by our reckoning. How he came by it I do not know, but he traded it for a wooden flute—an unequal exchange—and I was too eager to have it question him as I should have done—as I might have today, if he came again. I believe it was crafted by Josef of Nevarsin. He was perhaps the finest *ryll* maker who ever lived. He has been dead now for more than a hundred and fifty years, but I know Mestra Melora Alindair, who is one of our best lyric performers, paid a hundred *reis,* which is a very substantial sum, for one of his signed instruments. She is, after all, one of the MacArans, and they know musical instruments. Of course, I know that there are such things as forgers, even on our world. But if this was not made by Josef himself, it must have been made by one of his apprentices. Josef had a way of cutting the wood which is lost now, neither on the grain nor on the cross. See here." He pointed to the upright, where the grain seemed to spiral up as if it grew that way. "Anyone who could duplicate it today would make his fortune. It looks like the rapids running in the river. But for all of that, no one can coax a tune from it. I am no mean harpist myself, but it cannot be played. Oh, when there is a high wind it sighs a little, but so do many instruments; and if there is lightning, as there often is in summer, it moans— almost as if something were trying to get out."

He glanced hesitantly at them, but when Margaret made no sign of derision, or of disbelief he went on. "It makes the same uneasy chord, over and over, and it is quite unnerving to my students. Here—I will show you."

He laid the harp flat across his knees. His hands were old and a little stiff, but still flexible enough to pluck the strings. She now knew that he was upward of ninety, about the same age as the professor, and it hurt her to see that he could so easily do what Ivor could no longer manage. He pressed the levers at one end, and ran his hand across the strings; but although all the other instruments had quickly responded to his expert touch, this one made only a low droning noise. "See? Nothing but that—which isn't even a proper harp sound. Here, you try it.

Master Everard stood up and handed the instrument to Margaret. She sat down and studied it. The pale blonde wood was very beautiful, and the swirls in the grain, a little darker, made it more so. She stroked the wood, feeling for joins, and found nothing her sensitive fingers could distinguish. There were inlays of a darker wood in a decorative pattern on the sound box and under the bridge. The smell of the old wood pleased her with a faint familiarity, as with the spices in the stew last night. For a moment she saw the red-haired woman who sometimes haunted her sleep holding a *ryll* like this one. Then she ran her hands across the strings, pressed the levers and was rewarded with a sudden shower of cascading arpeggios, like a spring rain on Thetis.

Margaret forgot the two old men, both staring at her in astonishment. She strummed the strings, thinking of a lullaby she had learned on Zeepangu. They had an instrument not unlike this. Her hands moved involuntarily, almost—she could not help thinking—as if the *ryll* were playing *her*, and it was not the simple song she intended. She had a blurry vision of the silver-haired and silver-eyed man of her old nightmares, seated in a large carved chair, and the feelings she had about the man were, as always, a muddle of fear and excitement. For just a moment she saw the Old Man, with his hair not salt-and-peppered as now, but still all dark. Both his hands extended from embroidered cuffs. It was a flash, and it was gone.

Her throat closed slightly and her eyes stung with tears. Then words forced themselves out from between her lips. She swallowed, trying to push the words away, for they were elusive and not completely like anything else she had ever sung. Then, abruptly, resistance disappeared; she let the words flood out, simply because she could not stop them; the thickness in her throat vanished and she surrendered to the melody as if possessed.

> *"How came this blood on your right hand?*
> *Brother, tell me, tell me.*
> *It is the blood of an old gray wolf,*
> *That lurked behind a tree.*

*No wolf would prowl at this hour of the day,
Brother, tell me, tell me.
It is the blood of my own brothers twain
Who sat at the drink with me."*

The verses rolled out of her without volition, one after another. Margaret was like a woman entranced—captured by she knew not what.

An indefinite time later, Margaret found herself slumped over the *ryll*, with an overwhelming feeling of disorientation and foreboding, and the image of the silvery man wavering behind her eyes. *I know him; I have walked with him in my dreams, he used to carry me in his arms, he has kissed me and stroked my face. I was small enough to carry then. Who is he? And why am I sure he is old, much older than Daddy? He sang me a lullaby once. Dio caught me crooning it once to my doll and slapped me—and she never did things like that. Not even when I ate up the greenberry tart she had made for our guests.*

Margaret felt her muscles tense with an exhaustion that had nothing to do with the instrument now resting quietly across her body. She had a sense that she stood on the brink of discovery—though what she might be about to discover she could not guess. Her heart was pounding, and she waited for it to return to its normal rhythm. She wanted to cast the *ryll* onto the polished floor and run up to her room, shut the door, and scream until her throat was raw. It took every ounce of her hard-earned control and self-discipline to remain just where she was, looking to the two men, she supposed, like an ordinary woman. They could not guess the visions that haunted her, nor what the playing had raised in her, like a phalanx of ghosts.

Her mouth was very dry, and seemed to strangle her throat. She was taking very shallow breaths, because she knew if she breathed deeply, she would pass out. Questions swirled in her mind, painful questions that came up whenever she was distressed. *Why did my father always look at me as if the sight was painful? The older I got the worse it became. I was so glad to get away, and I still feel ashamed that I was glad.*

For just a moment she had the impression that the

Old Man had materialized in front of her, slightly transparent, but to her eye, completely visible in the room. He was staring at the stump of his arm the way he did, as if puzzled by the absence of his hand, and drinking. She knew it was a memory, even when the vision lifted its eyes from the arm, and looked right at her, appearing to look right through her. He could remain like that for hours, while she got more and more anxious, wondering what she had ever done to him.

In her heart, Margaret knew she had never done anything, that everything that had gone wrong, that had cost him a hand and something else she had no words for, was not her fault. She had been too little for any faults, except perhaps spilling her milk. She knew the image before her only existed in her mind, that it was memory, nothing more. Still, it felt as if her mind were shattering just a little. She knew she could not let that happen—she had Ivor to think of, to take care of!

Margaret forced herself to stop thinking about her father, or that other man, the one who frightened her. Instead, she gathered what remained of her wits, and said as calmly as she could manage, "Master Everard, I think your harp is haunted. The professor and I have observed a similar phenomenon once before on Ceti Three. There, of course, musical spirit possession is commonplace—an article of religion, as it were." She retreated into the safety of academic objectivity, quite forgetting that Master Everard had never heard of Ceti Three. "I don't know where I can have gotten that song. It's not in Child, is it, Ivor? There are several of a similar sort, to be sure . . ." Seeing the incomprehension on Master Everard's face, she repeated her question in *casta*

"Yes, an old student of mine did a post-doctoral paper on them," Ivor put in, "The revenge theme in Scottish, Irish, and Norse ballads. You remember her, Maggie. What was her name? Ah, yes—Anna Standish."

"But *I do* know the song," Master Everard answered, ignoring Ivor's comment. "It's known better in the Hellers than here. It is an old ballad called 'The Outlaw,' said to be based on the tale of Rupert Di Asturien, two centuries ago, who killed his whole family in a fit of berserk rage—except for one sister, and it was she who proclaimed him outlaw. Your accent is excellent, but I

noticed last night that you spoke our tongue better than
many Terranan who have been here for years. When I
heard you sing, I would have sworn you had lived here,
had I not known better. You used the accent of the
Kilghard Hills, where 'The Outlaw' is sung around the
fireside. Truly, you did. Sung like you had listened to it
a hundred times."

"If you say so. But, as far as I know, I had not heard
it before I began playing," she said. Then Margaret wondered if she should be so certain. The mention of the
Kilghard Hills had sent a strange shiver up her spine, a
sort of resonance not unlike the music itself. Perhaps the
Old Man had mentioned it sometime, in one of his rare
bouts of loquacity. Or she had seen mention of it on the
disk. That must be it. Relief flooded her body. She
wasn't going mad. Her mind was just playing tricks on
her, muddling her memories a little.

Just as Margaret had managed to persuade herself that
she was calm and entirely rational, she saw in her mind
a range of hills, surrounded by higher mountains,
shrouded in mists and snow, and her blood began to
thrum—now where did that image come from? It was a
very clear picture, almost as good as a holovid, but she
was sure she had never seen that place, or a vid of it
either. It almost felt as if she had snatched the picture
from someone's mind, and that was plainly impossible.
There was an ache in her now, a peculiar longing, a
hunger unlike anything she could remember. She wanted
to see those hills, as if she had seen them before, and
at the same time, she felt there was something there
that was frightening. Margaret firmly told herself she was
being overimaginative again, and turned her attention
back to Ivor and Master Everard.

" . . .but to play a tune on that particular *ryll* . . ."
Master Everard was saying, "I think it must like you; I
should give it to you. This is something really beyond
my experience."

"But you said it was historic . . ."

"Yes. It belonged—or is supposed to have belonged—
to a woman named Thyra; That is a *chieri* name, and
she was popularly believed to be half *chieri*. She died—
oh, some twenty years ago, it must have been."

Something in Margaret pricked up its ears. *Thyra—I*

*know that name, and it . . . there is something very bad
about it. Twenty years? That would have been about the
time my father left Darkover.* Aloud she asked, "You
knew this . . . Thyra?" She found she didn't even like
to say the name aloud, that her throat closed up.

"Gods forbid," Master Everard said. His old face
looked distressed now. "I was always a loyal subject to
Danvan Hastur, may the gods rest him. He came to
power when I was a young man, and I . . . it doesn't
bear thinking about. A very sad page in our history.
Many folk died then, and more lived and suffered, because—eh, well, *domma.* You wouldn't know about it,
and you are not likely to be interested. I dare say the
poor lady had her reasons, to have done what she did.
My son, Erald, could tell it better; he has spent almost
all of his creative life writing a song cycle about those
times."

Nothing he said conveyed any useful information to
Margaret, but she was much too polite to say so. "A
song cycle—how wonderful!"

Everard chuckled without merriment. "Hardly that!
My son won the distinction, at twenty-eight, of having
one of his songs proscribed, though whether it was a
political or artistic judgment I would not care to guess."
From the pained expression on his face, she suspected
he had some very strong feelings about the matter, ones
he kept to himself "Still, even I find 'Sharra's Song' a
very disturbing piece."

"Where is he now?" Margaret could feel the pleasant
buzz of curiosity stirring in her mind, and had a great
desire to speak to Erald, to quiz him mercilessly. This
was something she could get her hands on—a new song
cycle, but written in a conventional mode, most likely.
Even if it only made a footnote in her publication, it
was a find, a real find. *Proscribed. How interesting!* She
tried to persuade herself she was being a scholar, not a
snoop, and failed. After a moment she gave up the attempt as foolish. This was personal, but she was afraid
to admit it, even to herself. Some secret was wrapped
up in the *ryll* and this woman, Thyra, and the composi-
tion called "Sharra's Song." She knew it was going to
nag at her until she unraveled it.

"Oh, he's away in the Hellers." Everard shook his head. "My mother said to me, 'Don't marry a tanner's girl,' and perhaps she was right. We had three children, and only Erald has any musical gift. The two girls are all but tone deaf, and the grandchildren nearly so. Ah, it doesn't bear thinking about. My grandson is a good enough craftsman of instruments, but, truly, he hasn't a single song in him. So, Rodrigo MacAran will be craft master after me, and he is a great artist, for all he's difficult to work with. But only because he wants the best, not because he is mean, you know. Erald will never settle down, you see."

He gave a sigh, a small, regretful noise of unfulfilled dreams for his son. "What were we talking about? Oh, yes, that *ryll*. You're welcome to get anything you can out of that one, but don't take it near the Hastur harp." He pointed across the room. "The last time I did, it snapped six strings." The Master did not seem to think there was anything too strange about either a *ryll* which had a song in it, nor a harp that snapped strings, and Margaret wondered if he were teasing her. He appeared to be quite serious. And he clearly wanted to change the subject.

Margaret swallowed her disappointment. Erald, she knew, was off on a tour. The lads had told her that the previous evening. Well, perhaps he would return to Thendara soon, or she and Ivor would meet him when they went out into the countryside to do their own research. "Sharra's Song" would have to keep.

Then she noticed she was cold all over, that her arms beneath the slick fabric of her uniform were covered in gooseflesh. The nameless dread which had haunted her since she had found out she was coming to Darkover returned. But, why? That word bothered her. It reminded her of something she feared. She would have asked more, but she was too tense now, too frightened. Instead, she swallowed, her mouth dry and her lips hurting.

Everard moved away and continued speaking. "Master Ivor, you wanted to know about the fiols, didn't you? Here they are. The fiol, this is a bowed instrument, though it can be plucked as well, for certain effects . . . ." Margaret replaced the *ryll* on the wall. She knew it had

given her all it had to give, for the present. As she hung
it up, it gave a little sound, a soft rush of notes so quiet
she could barely hear it. Margaret laid her hand along
the sound box, and promised herself that she would
come back to the mysterious instrument someday, and
wrest its secrets from it. Then she felt a little foolish.

She followed the men to the display of fiols ranged
along the wall. She allowed her attention to wander,
knowing her recorder would pick up everything, and that
Ivor would not hesitate to demand her attention if he
needed it.

As she stood, not really listening, Margaret realized
that the name Thyra was not entirely unfamiliar to her.
Her father had shouted it sometimes in drunken nightmares, but it had been so many years since she had
heard one that she had almost forgotten. It always
evoked the same image in her mind. She saw a screaming red-haired harridan with claws for hands . . . and the
silver-haired man who would cry out "No, Thyra,
no . . ." just as her father screamed these words in his
restless sleep. She was torn between reluctance to know
more, and a burning curiosity. It was a knife-edge in
her mind.

Sometimes, in dreams, she found herself looking up,
and gazed, as if through a veil, into the face of that same
woman, or one like enough to her to be her sister, and
felt the warmth of a breast, and tasted sweet milk. It
was almost as if she knew the woman as a mother—
though she could not connect the screaming, wild woman
to any sort of mothering. Dio was all the mother she
had, or had ever wanted, surely.

Those dreams had faded after she left Thetis, except
for nightmares in hyperspace. Margaret remembered the
psych on University who had told her she was repressing
something, and had offered her deep therapy, but she
had rejected it. She had the right to refuse, as one of
her basic civil rights; she hadn't wanted to remember
anything. She still didn't. Under Ida Davidson's maternal
hand she had almost forgotten the chaos of her early
teens and the battles between her father and stepmother—mostly over her—which had finally driven her
away from home. The Davidsons had given her a new
home, and she had repaid them by submerging her own

career in Ivor's. She knew any third-year student could do what she did and do it as well. She had not known she was unhappy until the Davidsons had given her happiness, and she would never forget.

For a moment, Margaret wondered if somehow she had been coming to Darkover on some astral plane. Not that she believed in such things though it seemed more pleasant than space travel, for certain. The University had trained her to think rationally, to be logical and organized and to believe only in what she could hold and touch and feel with her flesh and blood hands.

The me of my dreams was a very small girl, or even a baby. But, damn, I do remember that fortress of a building, the Reade Orphanage. And Dio has always behaved as if she was my biological mother. I was an orphan, yes, but the Old Man is my father, isn't he? Dio and I couldn't have been closer if I'd been born to her. What a mess! This has got to stop—right this second! I won't have it. Whatever happened twenty-some years ago is the past, and it has nothing to do with me!

Margaret and Dio had lost a certain amount of intimacy during the many years they had not seen one another, though they still wrote long letters and spoke via vidcom several times a year. The Old Man never wrote, but Dio always sent his love, and Margaret was glad of that. She was, she decided, more than a little disturbed, and even almost angry, that she had received no answer to her last communication, the one she had sent shortly before leaving University. Oh, well. It was probably somewhere in the system, and would arrive on Darkover after she and Ivor had left for the outlands. So much for the efficiency of Terran technology!

Something nagged at the back of her mind, something important and maddening and frightening. Margaret frowned, knowing it was something she did not really want to think about. It all came back to her in a rush of feelings of desolation and rage. She allowed herself to shudder, and tried to hold the memory away, then surrendered, just to get it done with.

It was her last night on Thetis, after the Old Man had finally agreed to her choice. It had begun well enough, with a good supper, toasts of Thetan wine, and her favorite dessert. Margaret had let herself start to relax, to believe everything would work out. Dio had retired early, which she often did. She said the sea air made her sleepy.

Then the Senator had gotten ugly drunk and tried to tell her something that she had not wanted to hear. What had he shouted? "If you have the Alton Gift, if you are an untrained telepath, you are a danger to yourself and everyone around you. You are my daughter, and you probably have it! Gift! The Alton *Curse* is more like . . ." She hadn't understood what he meant, but the tone of his voice had made her blood run cold. And then something else had happened—and she realized this was what she did not want to recall. For just a second she had felt as if there was another person in her head, a woman, and a very nasty one. She had a soft voice, but it was very strong and authoritative. *You will not remember, and you will not destroy me!* It was this, and not the Old Man's ravings that sent her running from the living room, into the security of her own quarters. She had locked the door behind her, as if something were chasing her, and spent the entire night packing and re-packing her belongings, as if her very life depended on it.

It was *only* a memory, Margaret told herself. The strange voice in her head was probably due more to unaccustomed wine and the tension of leaving for University than anything else. There, she was fine again. She was a Scholar of University, not an overwrought adolescent!

Margaret forced her attention back to Master Everard's scholarly discussion of the fiol. It was clearly a relative of the Terran violin or viola, though the belly was deeper than any Terran violin, and the sound holes were formed like a many-pointed star. Professor Davidson plucked the strings and sighed.

"Would you fiddle it for me, Maggie? I'm afraid these old hands are beyond it."

"Mine, too," Master Everard said. "And I give you my word of honor it is possessed of nothing but a lovely tone."

Margaret tucked the fiol beneath her chin and adjusted the tuning strings. It felt comfortable and familiar, though the neck was a bit longer than a Terran violin.

Other than that she did not hesitate, for the Music Department on University made sure their students could handle anything constructed for eight fingers and two opposable thumbs. She began to play a little Bach gavotte from her student days, followed by one of Corbenic's variations. She had four thousand years of Terran music to draw from, but Corbenic remained one of her favorites.

Everard listened intently, his eyes sparkling. He smiled at her. "That was exquisite, my dear child. So crisp and clear, and yet there is deep feeling in it, at the same time. We must invite some of the other musicians in the street over for the evening. They would be delighted for the opportunity to hear you play that."

Margaret blushed. She knew she was no better than a good second fiddler, that her playing was not really concert quality, but his praise eased her fears and tensions. "I would be glad to do that."

Ivor made some mention of Mozart as a predecessor to Corbenic, and this demanded an exhaustive discussion, which strained her translating abilities to the utmost. She played the cadenza from the Fifth Violin Concerto, to demonstrate the influence of the earlier composer, and Everard nodded. The fiol did indeed have a lovely tone, despite, or maybe because of the oddly-shaped eff-holes.

By the time she had demonstrated the six fiols in the museum—three soprano and three alto—and the woods used to make them had been explained, with a discussion on technical acoustics that made her headache start up again, Margaret was ravenous and exhausted. Ivor was looking wan, his eyes glazed and his color dreadful. Still, he wanted to go on to the larger harps, and Margaret hated the look he gave her when she suggested they pause for the midday meal.

"Forgive me," said Master Everard. "I am a poor host, indeed. Of course we must eat."

"There is so much to see, to learn," Ivor grumbled.

"It will still be here after lunch and a rest, Professor." Margaret mustered her patience to persuade him.

"When you get to be our age, young woman, you will want to do as we do." Master Everard laughed softly. "The young think they have all the time in the world."

As they left the chamber, Margaret looked over her shoulder at the *ryll* standing in its niche in the wall. For an instant she saw slender hands, with an extra finger, play across the strings—ghost hands that both beckoned to her and repelled her at the same time. She was quite relieved to get out of the room and into the hall, banishing the vision and cursing her overactive imagination. It must have been a trick of the light. She told herself that, but she did not believe it.

4

◆

The two old men were clearly enjoying sharing their mutual interest in music, but Margaret was finding translating for the professor while she tried to eat more than a little wearing. She was almost relieved when Master Everard was called away from the table as they consumed their midday meal of thick soup and heavy bread, then felt guilty about it. The headache that had started in the music room did not go away as she ate, but she dismissed it as the remnant of the drug hangover from traveling. It was the sort of headache she sometimes got when storms blew across the Sea of Wine on Thetis, something to do with barometric pressure and other weather phenomena. It almost certainly meant nothing on Darkover.

Alone with Ivor, she found herself troubled as well by his frail appearance. His color was gray beneath the remnants of his Relegan tan, and she wondered if she should cancel her planned shopping expedition and try to convince him to return to the Terran Sector for a visit to the Medics. He loathed doctors, and would almost certainly resist her efforts, so she decided not to suggest it—at least for the moment.

"Are you feeling all right, Ivor?" Margaret asked, in spite of her decision. She tried to mask her anxiety and to sound light and casual.

"I confess I feel pretty tired, my Magpie-Maggie." This was the seventh or eighth time he had used his pet names for her, and she found it a little disquieting. "The older I get, the harder it is for my belly to settle into new foods, for one thing. These Cottman dishes are very tasty, but they sit in my belly like bricks. I really want something less heavy—clear soup and crackers—the kind that Ida makes." He sighed rather gustily, enjoying the thought. "I was really looking forward to the amenities of University—electric lights, the quiet of the library, catching up on my reading, and getting my notes on Relegan into order. I keep having this fantasy that I won't have a chance to do it, and some downy-cheeked kid with a diploma with damp ink on it will make a total mess of our work."

And where am I in this fantasy, Ivor? "I know," Margaret replied, ignoring the little prick of irritation his words gave her. She immediately felt dreadful and guilty because she realized *she* was not missing University at all. The sounds and smells of Darkover tantalized her, surrounding her with siren promises of comforts which had nothing to do with controlled heating, voice-activated light levels, and the many other benefits of an advanced technology. True, the flickering lamps, candles, and other primitive light sources in Master Everard's house seemed to her a bizarre affectation—why wasn't Thendara City electrified, she wondered? The Terrans had been on the planet for decades now, and still were confined to their little enclave around the spaceport. It didn't fit. It was another enigma that nagged at her aching head. She looked at the red sun streaming in through the high windows of the dining room, and at the small lamps that burned on the table, and found they did not hurt her eyes. In fact, now that she thought about it, the light from without seemed "right" as no light she had seen on any other planet had been.

"I think I got a bit of a chill during our walk here," Ivor continued, breaking into her thoughts. "At least, I can't seem to get quite warm.

"Ivor, no one can get really warm in these damn all-weather things the Service imagines are suitable clothing. Add to that the year we just spent running around nearly nude in a tropical climate—I'm chilled, too!" Actually, with the soup in her, Margaret was nearly comfortable, but she wanted to reassure herself that there was nothing wrong. "It's hard to adjust to such a radical climate change."

He chuckled. "I am just an old man, with an old man's complaints, child. It was fun, wasn't it, wearing flowers and feathers and beads instead of uniforms. But you know how the Service feels about getting too native—

the idiots. I know I looked quite foolish in my feathered finery—Ida had a good laugh over the holopics—but the freedom of it was wonderful. You know, this uniform isn't very comfortable, Magpie. I think it is too small across the back or something."

This time the use of her nickname chilled her right down to the marrow. He was not himself, if he was being so openly affectionate. Margaret knew Ivor, his moods and crotchets, and this was just not like him. She gave him a hard look, but he seemed ordinary enough—a small, elderly man, wrinkled and tired-looking, and perhaps a little off his feed, but he appeared to be the person she knew well, whose every maddening habit and season was familiar to her. There was no reason to be alarmed. She was jumping at shadows, imagining ghosts in harps, and mistaking fatigue for illness.

Darkover comforted her with its near-familiarity, but she found it disquieting as well. It was throwing her judgment off—that was all. One sound night's sleep just wasn't enough to restore her to her normal disgustingly good health, not after days of space travel and a total change of climate.

Ivor smiled at her, stretching his withered mouth across his big teeth. It looked entirely too skeletal in her present state of heightened senses, and she held back a shudder. "Are you sure you are all right? With all the shots they gave us, you shouldn't be . . ."

"Don't cluck over me, Magpie-girl. You go off with those young scamps and get some local togs. I know you are itching to get out of your uniform. If you see a good wool cloak—nothing fancy, mind you—that would suit me, get it. I'll have a nap now, and by suppertime, I will be perfectly fine." He gave another chuckle, and she knew he was remembering the black-and-white Thetis cape she had draped over her University uniform during her first lonely year there. That and her fondness for sparkling jewelry had given her the nickname, and it had stuck. Even in the hodgepodge of the academic community, she had remained different—a little strange and exotic for the hierarchies of the order that were the Terran way.

"I'm not clucking! I just can't help worrying about

you." Margaret tried to ignore the feeling of helplessness that suddenly threatened to overwhelm her.

"What a good child you are. You have been like a daughter to me—even though the first time I saw you in Relegan garb I had several unfatherly thoughts." Ivor smiled wistfully and sighed. "You made me wish I was fifty again."

"Did I?" She was fascinated by this admission, because the professor had never done anything to make her feel he knew she was an adult and a woman. There was a safety in his manner toward her, something which kept her from longing for the untidiness of love affairs and broken hearts which often seemed to be the bread and butter of her classmates. Not for the first time, but with a renewed sense of surprise, Margaret realized she had achieved nearly three decades of living without becoming sexually active. She was no prude, and she had heard the woeful tales of fellow students with curiosity and interest, but without the slightest urge to leap into bed with anyone she had ever met. She kept to herself, as if she were obeying some instinct or order. It struck her now that this was rather peculiar, but it didn't seem important. It wasn't as if she felt she had missed anything, was it?

"My dear—I am old, but I am not dead yet! You are an extremely lovely woman. The Relegans assumed at first you were my wife, or at least my concubine, and they were very puzzled by our sleeping in separate huts. The Relegans were fascinated by our behavior, or rather the lack of it, and finally the hetman asked me if you were taboo. I told them you were as a daughter to me, which made sense to them in light of their profound incest prohibitions. Isn't it funny how universal that one taboo is?"

"Not really; it seems to be hard-wired into our brains. With a few notable exceptions," Margaret answered, thinking of a few cultures she had studied where it was not forbidden. She knew that Ivor and Ida treated her like their child, but to hear it expressed moved her more than she could have imagined. She was warmed by the words.

She cleared her throat, thickened with a sudden surge of emotions she did not wish to have. To cover her feelings, she asked, "Do you think Kuttner will ever finish that study of incest taboos?"

"Possibly. If he doesn't go off the deep end and wind

up living in a grass shack on some God-forsaken planet on the rim of the galaxy. Anthropologists can be a little unbalanced."

"I know. Not like musicologists, who are entirely scientific and objective!" They laughed together at this old joke. The debate as to whether it was possible to objectively evaluate the disciplines of a non-Terran culture had been raging for centuries, and was no nearer to any solution. Margaret and Professor Davidson adhered to the belief that it was not only possible but necessary to study a culture within its own context. He had spent most of his academic career traveling to distant worlds to prove this thesis. His famous contemporary, Paul Valery, held that field work was, by definition, contaminated. Valery only stepped outside the comfortable Music Building on University to go home for meals. He had not been off-planet for decades, even to accept honors from other universities. On the rare occasions when the two men met in the corridors of the building, Valery would flare the nostrils of his narrow, aristocratic nose, as if he smelled something unpleasant and ask, "You still here, Davidson? Not off drumming with some ignorant natives?" Ivor always answered these barbed questions with a dignified silence, and swept into his own office. His reputation was excellent, and he felt no need to respond. Margaret, on the other hand, often had a desire to punch Valery on his overbred nose and leap to the defense of her mentor.

The professor pushed his bowl away. "Well, I'm off for a sleep, my dear," he said cheerfully. "Enjoy your visit to the tailor, Maggie, and be sure to keep your ears open for anything interesting. Weavers often have loomsongs that get overlooked in favor of other sorts of music. I have long thought there was a rich area of study in . . ."

"Ivor—go to bed! You need rest, not another area of study."

He left, laughing. The sound of his delight made her feel less anxious for several minutes, as she lingered over a hot cup of herb tea, savoring the taste of it. Margaret's worries came hustling back as she finally emptied the cup. Ivor looked "wrong," and it was more than just fatigue. She wished she weren't plagued with sudden flashes of premonition, and the ridiculous idea that she could somehow hear the thoughts of others. More, she wished the dread she felt in her bones would just go away and let her be. She was in a nice house, with good food, and there was nothing at all to worry about.

Anya bustled into the dining room, bobbing a little curtsy. She was rosy-cheeked from the kitchen, and her jowls quivered with her movements. "*Domna,* the boys are here to take you to Threadneedle Street."

"Oh, splendid! Anya, can you tell me what would be the correct amount to pay for a cloak and boots, and such garments as you and Master Everard wear? Not that the boys would mislead me . . ."

"No, they're good, honest boys, or I would never have let them in this house, far less let a noble guest go off with them. Let me think." While the housekeeper considered, Margaret wondered at the use of the word "noble." Why were people acting as if she was special? Could they have guessed she was the daughter of the Cottman Senator—she hadn't said a word, because she had found that mentioning her connections in high places made people behave oddly. She had never traded on her father's position in the Terran government, and often didn't think about it for months at a time. It had nothing to do with her. But "noble guest?" A political functionary was hardly nobility as she knew of it—which was nearly nothing. There weren't many nobles on University, unless one counted department heads and professors emeritus. It was just another Darkovan mystery she could not solve because she did not know the right questions to ask.

"I believe five royals should get you a fine outfit, though things cost more than they did when I was a girl. That's a blouse, three or four petticoats, a chemise and tunic. The underwear will be about seven sekals. A cloak of good spun wool, about three *reis,* one of leather about eight. Stockings, oh, four sekals or a bit more, unless you want spidersilk or something."

Anya gave a sniff of disdain. "That stuff you are wearing wouldn't keep a dog warm in the mountains. I can't understand why the Terranan wear it—it smells funny and it never seems to warm them. I've seen them, standing around looking down their noses at us, and pulling their clothes closer. What's the matter with a good wool cloak instead of those shiny things they wear? What are they afraid of—do they think that wearing stuff grown on the backs of animals will make them . . ." Anya shrugged and stopped speaking.

"There is just no accounting for taste, Anya." Margaret was not about to try to explain the attitude common in the Terran Federation, that a civilized person was evident by his clothing, and that meant synthetics, except among the very rich, where the wearing of natural fabrics was a sign of wealth. It would have been insulting, implying that there was something less than civilized about simple Darkovan garb—which indeed was how the Terrans regarded it.

"How true! I'm an old woman, and I have seen many changes here on Darkover—not all of them for the good! The boys want to go off and be star pilots, and the girls are full of ideas that don't include cooking and marrying. Now, let me think. Boots! Those will be two or three *reis,* high boots a few *sekals* more. You put yourself in Master MacEwan's hands, and he will have you fitted out right and proper in no time. And, if you need credit, Master Everard will stand surety for you."

"That's kind of you; but Master Davidson prefers— and the University prefers—that we pay as we go. Thank you for the advice."

She went up to her room to leave the little recorder and get her money. If she heard something worth recording in the clothing district, she would return later with Ivor. Across the hall she could hear Ivor snoring; he didn't do that unless he was really exhausted. She fingered the coins in her hand. One was of silver, the other some base metal; she knew these were iron sekals, worth about three Empire cents; the other, a *reis* or royal, was worth about three credits last she had heard. The clerk at Rothschild and Tanaka had not been sure, and after a year on a planet without any currency at all, she was unused to thinking of it. At University, of course, she never handled such things—everything was done with credit chips.

Geremy and Ethan were hunkered down on the steps, playing some kind of game with their hands. The gestures with open hand or fist or two fingers extended,

flashed rapidly back and forth. They jumped up as they
saw her, bowed and smiled.

"Good day, *domna.*" said Ethan.

"Good day. What were you playing?"

It was Geremy who answered, "That was 'Scissors,
Rock, and Leaves.' " As they went off down the street,
the boys explained the intricacies of the game. Margaret
had seen a dozen similar games played on a dozen different worlds, and said so. They were fascinated. Ethan
wanted to know more about space travel, but Geremy
told him he was being a bore, and, remarkably, this
seemed to silence the sharp-nosed boy.

The doors of the shops along Music Street were open,
but what she had thought were shuttered windows the
night before revealed themselves now as wide bays with
counters behind them. Beyond the counters she could
glimpse workmen busy at benches. The smells of wood
and oil and resin rose in the air, accompanied by the
sounds of chisels and files and the occasional sound of
an instrument: a whistle, a drone pipe, a harp, or a fiol
being played or tuned. The boys explained things to her,
and the walk out of Music Street passed quickly. The
ruddy sunlight fell across her cheeks, warming her. It
felt good, and the nagging headache faded away slowly.

A few craftsmen stared at her, and one even left his
bench and came forward to bow. Others frowned and
looked away quickly, as if embarrassed. These were men
close to her own age, or women younger than she was,
and she began to feel self-conscious.

"Ethan, tell me the truth; am I dressed in an immodest
way?" The uniform covered her body but far more tightly
than the clothing commonly worn by the Darkovan women
she had seen. She was sure her hair was covering her nape,
remembering the Senator's insistence on that. Her tunic
came well below her waist, falling almost to her knees, and
had been especially designed by the Service for planets
where dress and gender were almost the same. Of course,
the ideas of modesty that someone back on Terra had
often were complete failures in the field—a concept Federation employees seemed unable to grasp.

"Uh, not exactly. It's your hair, mostly." This puzzled
her and maddened her slightly. Why couldn't the Service
supply sufficient information? Why was the data on

Cottman IV so patchy, so full of holes. After the decades that the Federation had been on the planet, the ethnologists and anthropologists should have published enough monographs to fill a small library! Geremy went on, "And your uniform, too. Folk in this part of Thendara don't often see women from the Terran Sector—they keep themselves up in the buildings around the port. Black is an uncommon color here, because our dyers can't make a good, lasting black. And since we value our craft, we don't dye that color. Our Guardsmen wear black cloaks, but it is from wool that is naturally black. You know how people are, *domma*—they stare at anything different." He squirmed a little and looked uncomfortable.

"You just don't look like a Terranan somehow," Ethan piped up, "or a thesis—what you said. The planet where you lived. You look like a lady!"

Margaret held back a broad grin, while vowing to remember to share Ethan's mispronunciation with Ivor. In a way, all academics came by way of thesis, didn't they? "It's Thetis, Ethan, not thesis. But don't the other women at the port look like ladies?"

"Lands, no," Geremy answered. "They're just women." He clearly thought this was a complete explanation, so she let it drop. It amused her, as she thought it over, to realize that her own definition of what a "lady" looked like was based on appearance. Specifically, a "lady" looked like her stepmother, the Senator's Lady. That meant blonde hair, short stature, and a generous bosom. Her red hair and yellow eyes had never pleased her. Her inches had been a trial since adolescence, being about a foot too many in the vertical direction, and four or five inches too few around the chest. She was very tall compared to Thetan natives, and even at the University, she stood out. She would have liked dark hair, like the Old Man had before he began to gray, and dark eyes like his, or gray-green eyes and golden hair like Dio. Dismissing these futile thoughts, she listened to the two boys identifying the various shops as they entered what was clearly an area devoted to the fiber arts.

"There's the shop where my brother's apprenticed, but you don't want to go there. He makes bad imitations of Terranan cloth." Geremy pointed to a shop with a deep counter covered with bolts of stuff. It did not look

bad to Margaret's untrained eye, but she could tell that
Geremy was ashamed of the place.

"How does apprenticeship work here?" Margaret asked.

Both boys began to speak at once, flattered by her
interest, and in a friendly competition to inform her first.
She realized she was getting, effortlessly, information for
which a cultural anthropologist would cheerfully have
sold his mother, or taken out a mortgage on his soul.
What they told her seemed well-considered and fair, not
like some planets where the young were regarded as
slave labor or mere property. It was a shame she had
left her recorder behind in her room.

They turned into a street which appeared to be their
destination. The signs showed pictures of finished garments, or in one case, just a very bright golden needle
against a brown background, which she suspected indicated an embroidery shop. Where the bays in the previous street had been piled with bolts of cloth, now there
were shirts hanging, or tunics. There was a great deal
of embroidery on everything. She noticed fine chemises,
almost sheer, and heavier and more practical ones as
well. One or two of the shops boasted a dressed figure
in what was clearly festive clothing—shiny, transparent
stuff she guessed was the spider silk which Anya had
mentioned. The sight of it gave her an odd shiver, and
evoked a memory that was vague and disquieting. The
mental doorway in her mind, behind which lurked some
childhood fears, opened a little farther, and she felt her
headache returning.

Ethan opened the door of a shop and guided her inside. A big man with black hair was standing behind a
large cutting table, holding a bolt of cloth in his hands
as if considering how to drape it and cut it. He had an
abstracted expression on his face, the look of an artist
in the midst of creation, and she was reluctant to break
his concentration.

Her young guide clearly had no such reservations.
"Uncle Aaron, this is the lady I told you about. *Domna*
Alton, Aaron MacEwan."

The man gave a little blink of heavily lidded eyes,
then bowed gracefully. "Welcome to my shop, *domna;*
you lend me grace. How may I serve you? A spider-silk
gown for the Midsummer Festival in featherpod green,

perhaps?" He gestured toward a bolt of shimmering textile leaning against the cutting table. Then he picked it up as if it did not weigh an ounce, and held it near her face, so he could see if the color went with her skin.

That looked very expensive, and totally unsuitable, though her hands longed to caress the sheer stuff. Close to her face, it had a scent she knew—a wonderful, clean odor. Like so many other smells in the past few hours, it was evocative of the past. Was it the scent of the silk, or of the wearer which trembled on the threshold of her conscious mind. And what wearer—Dio or some other woman? She tried to banish the memory quickly because she could feel herself starting to tense and stiffen.

Margaret rarely attended any functions which required her to wear anything more dressy than her academic robes, presently packed in a chest back on University. She hadn't realized until that moment how often she had wanted to wear dresses like Dio did, for dinners with dignitaries, and the occasional ball the Old Man could be persuaded to attend.

She gave a little sigh. "Thank you, but what I had in mind was something practical and simple," she said. "I need some good sturdy warm garments, suitable for walking or riding. The kind of thing Anya wears, but for out of doors. Ethan?" she appealed.

Ethan looked shocked. "But—my lady—Anya is old." Margaret was surprised. Old? Anya looked fifty perhaps, which was not old by her measure. With the advances in rejuvenation technology, fifty was not even middle-aged. The life expectancy here must be much shorter than she had thought. Why? It didn't make any sense. Then she realized that Anya was a matron, and probably past the age of childbearing. Lots of cultures dressed girls and young women differently than mature, married women. How could she have been so dull-witted?

"Then the sort of thing Moira wears.

"A servant, *damisela*? But you cannot dress like a servant. Uncle, perhaps that russet outfit you made for *Mestra* Rafaella, that she did not like when it was done."

Aaron looked relieved. "The very thing," he said. "It is completely unworn, *domna*," he told her. "The *mestra* decided the embroidery did not suit her." His voice sounded thinner, and a little strained. Margaret gave him a hard look, and wondered if he were lying—and why. Then she decided she was being hypersensitive again. Really, she must get herself under control soon, or she was going to cease to function at all. Jumping at every smell and shadow. Enough!

"The two of you are of a size, and of like coloring as well." MacEwan continued, nodding as he spoke. "That boy is going to be a real help to me—he knows my stock better than I do. Manuella!" He did not notice the look of displeasure the comment brought to Ethan's thin face. Margaret gave the lad a smile, and he brightened up immediately. She could barely believe that only yesterday she had been suspicious of him, thinking him a potential thief.

The raised voice summoned a weary-looking woman in clothing similar to that worn by Anya, and she realized that she had guessed correctly. There was some distinction, invisible to her untrained eye, between what was appropriate for a married woman, and what was right for an aging spinster like herself. The thought startled her a little—she had not thought that about herself before.

"My wife, *domna.* Take her in the back, my dear, and show her the russet outfit we made for that picky Rafaella. You, Ethan, run up to the loft and get that green rabbit-horn wool. It is light, but very warm. Then step over to Jason, the belt maker, and have him send a good selection of ladies' belts and gloves. You, Geremy, go over *Mestra* Dayborah and have her send a good selection of undergarments for a lady—about the size of *Mestra* Rafaella."

Margaret found herself being tugged gently into the rear of the shop by a clearly embarrassed Manuella. "Please forgive him, *domna.* He is an artist, and sometimes forgets his place. He does not mean to order everyone about!"

"I think he was deep in the throes of creation when we came in."

Manuella gave the sigh of a long-suffering wife, then smiled shyly. "He's been mooning over that length of cloth for days now. He's a good man and never looks at another woman. But the way he is with a bolt of fine goods is almost more than flesh and blood can bear. How can I compete with wool or spider silk, or even

Dry Town cotton? Still, he is a master craftsman. Here is the russet made for Rafaella—as fine a garment as you'll find in all Thendara, but not good enough for that—cat! Those Renunciates! Can't behave like a decent woman. Yet she gives herself airs, just because her father was *coridom* to the MacLorans. Well, a *coridom* is still a servant, I say, and no better than an honest craftsman."

As she rattled on, the woman was shaking out the folds of the complex garment. There were three petticoats, each dyed a slightly lighter shade of russet, and embroidered about the hem with a pattern of green leaves, a blouse the color of the palest petticoat, and a tunic of very dark russet, which completed the ensemble. Worn all at once, it would be heavy and warm, and, Margaret thought, much more comfortable than what she had on at the moment.

"It's beautiful," Margaret said, "and just about my favorite color. But I think it's a little too—too elegant for what I had in mind. What I want is a working outfit." She somehow knew the correct word for what she wanted, as distinct from a garment suitable for a fancy occasion, and wondered how, because she knew she hadn't gotten it from the basic language disk. It just came to her, like the song had come out of the *ryll.* The garment, lovely as it was, was too elaborate, she thought, for prowling around in a maker's shop full of wood shavings or collecting songs in remote corners of this world, at once so familiar and so alien. "I really like it, but what I wanted would be something more like what you have on.

Manuella looked at her serviceable petticoats and plain gray tunic, then cast her eyes heavenward. Margaret had seen that gesture many times before, and it always meant the same thing—why were people so incomprehensible. She felt comforted by the very humanness of the look, and smiled a little.

"Dress like a tradeswoman? Would you shame your family? Please, *domna,* anyone can see what you are, and dressing below your station will not fool anyone." Manuella's voice was earnest.

Station? Margaret could not imagine what Manuella meant. Did these people know she was the daughter of the Cottman Senator, and what difference would that make? The woman was clearly distressed by the idea of her wearing the wrong clothing, but she had no idea why. She was about to ask when a wrinkled old woman came in, her arms full of soft garments. She paused, gaped at Margaret in wonder, then dropped a deep curtsy.

She heard a faint whisper of thought from the older woman as she was introduced to Dayborah, the lingerie maker. Comynara! *It is like the old days! When I was a girl. . . !* She caught a feeling of longing, a yearning for a bygone era when people knew their places, and shook herself free of the sensation of hearing the old woman's thoughts. Margaret was certain she was being mistaken for someone else, though she could not imagine who.

Suddenly too tired to argue about it, she let them bully her into buying what they considered the correct clothing. They tried on several pieces before Manuella declared herself satisfied. The clothes fit well enough, though the drawstrings at waist and neck left room for variations. Manuella pulled down the braid she had made, combed out her hair, and refastened it with a beautiful silver butterfly clasp, which appeared in Manu-ella's worn hand, like a conjurer's trick. It felt heavy against the nape of her neck, heavy though it was light, and familiar though she did not clearly remember seeing one like it. Most of all, it felt right.

As the two women conferred over belts, and chose a dark green one, Margaret had a disturbing sense of losing her personal identity. There was no more Margaret Alton, but instead an endless parade of strangers, garbed in layers of cloth, hair caught in butterflies, wrists banded with embroideries and bracelets. The smells of the textiles aroused memories she was sure were not hers! They aroused the disturbing image of that silver-haired man who sometimes haunted her dreams, and the screaming red-headed termagant. Suddenly she was assailed by a kaleidoscope of conflicting images. She struggled to remain in the here and now—in the present, not the dangerous past. But the previous night's memory of the orphanage came back, and she was suddenly afraid. She bit her lower lip, and made herself pay attention to the women fussing around her.

The green rabbit-horn wool was pressed into her nearly numb hands and she found herself mechanically agreeing to have a festival tunic made up, with a matching blouse of some cottonlike fiber. Surely it was too cold to grow cotton on this planet.

Margaret mentally clutched at her Scholar's credentials, as the questions grew and her sense of disorientation increased. She asked about the textile and found out that it was woven from the fibers of the featherpod tree. She heard about the hearty sheep that lived in the hills, and a great deal more. As she listened, she began to feel a little more focused, and Manuella took her back into the big workroom.

Aaron MacEwan brought out a length of the spider silk in a dark green-blue that was so beautiful it filled her with wordless longing. It was even nicer than the stuff he had shown her first, and her resistance wavered a little. He urged her to have it made into a ball gown. Margaret protested in vain that she had no use for such finery. They all smiled knowingly, and rushed on, overwhelming her feeble protests.

She caught a glimpse of herself in the long mirror at the end of the shop then, and her knees trembled. Margaret looked at the stranger in the glass, then looked away quickly. That was not her. She suddenly felt a desperate need to have her miserable old uniform back! She was afraid of the woman in the mirror. Margaret turned away, biting her lip and trying to still the shaking in her legs.

The faces of Aaron and Manuella and Dayborah began to take on the appearance of friendly demons, and her skull throbbed. Margaret struggled not to shrink away, feeling they were going to snatch and pinch at her at any moment. They all seemed to be speaking at once, and the words made no sense to her. There was a heady excitement in the room, one in which she could not seem to participate. It swirled around her, but did not touch her. Her shoulders ached with tension, and she listened for the sound of thunder. Surely a storm was going to start soon. But she heard only the meaningless chatter of the tailor and his wife.

Aaron sketched a drawing of the proposed garment, telling one of the boys to bring an embroiderer. Margaret summoned the last of her energy to put an end to the torment of voices around her. "Please! Stop! I don't need any dancing clothes. I am a scholar, not a princess." Then she fled into the back room, removed the garments and yanked her uniform back on.

When she returned to the workroom, Dayborah had vanished, and both Manuella and Aaron had puzzled expressions. Indeed, Aaron looked more than puzzled—he looked hurt!

MacEwan said, "But what about the Midsummer Ball?"

As firmly as she was able, Margaret replied, "I'm sure if there is a ball at midsummer, I will not attend. I do not move in those sorts of circles. What I want now is a good wool cloak, for a man perhaps this much shorter than you, Master MacEwan," she gestured with one hand, "and quite elderly. I really must get back to him soon—this has all taken too long."

"Well, if you must, you must, *domna*. We will have everything brought to the Castle later in the day, then." She sensed the confusion, and a mild resentment from them, as if she were deliberately robbing them of some pleasure. If only she could make sense of anything. Her brain felt filled with porridge, and lumpy porridge at that.

"Castle?" They had mistaken her for someone else. Suddenly her sense of humor asserted itself. It was like a very bad old story. She must resemble some local noble, and they must think she was slumming.

Young Geremy said, "The *domna* is staying with Master Everard, in Music Street. I told you that before!" He was red with embarrassment.

His elders all looked at him with that expression of disappointment that went with disbelief. Aaron MacEwan shook his head. 'If you say so, *domna*."

"I do say so," she said, exasperated. "Now, if you will just make up a parcel, I will take it with me."

"No, indeed; that would not be fitting," Master MacEwan answered firmly, clearly not believing either her or his young nephew. He was the picture of outraged dignity. "We will send it within the hour."

Margaret gave up. They refused to be convinced she was who she said she was, and stubbornly went on believing she was someone else entirely. "How much will this be?" Aaron stared off into the corner of the room, abstracted, while Manuella named a price which was much less than she had been prepared to pay. At least they were not overcharging her. When the awkward business of commerce was completed, MacEwan cleared his throat.

"*Domna*," Aaron said, "It is not our place to question you. But when young Ethan told me who you were, or appeared to be, I was truly honored that you had chosen my shop for your custom. Oh, I confess I did it for my own glory. I have little occasion to dress a lady of the *comyn*, for mostly they buy cloth and have their own servants make it up. It goes against the grain to think of untrained hands on my fine goods, but that is just how things are. I am not without a reputation, but one can only go so far with social climbers, lyric performers, and gleemen."

Her skull was now throbbing as if a thousand drums were beating within it, and her skin felt cold and clammy beneath her uniform. Summoning all the good manners she was able, Margaret replied, "Believe me, Master MacEwan, if I were going to patronize any tailor, it would be you. You have been more than kind. I know an artist when I see one. I don't know who you think I am, but believe me, I am not a member of this *comyn*. I've never heard of it before!"

As soon as the words were out of her mouth, Margaret knew they were not so much untrue as inaccurate. She knew the word, knew what it meant, but it was all connected to that place in her brain where she did not want to go. No, where she *must* not go, even if she wished to. The air around her seemed too still, and she listened again for the sound of summer thunder. She could see the looking glass out of the corner of her eye, and there seemed to be something in it, just the hint of a face. But it was a frightening face, and she turned her gaze away quickly.

Then a great weight seemed to settle on her chest. A huge hand gripped her heart and squeezed. She felt herself lean against the long cutting table, its edge pressing into her hipbones as a long swirling tunnel opened before her eyes. *Falling, falling!* She tumbled into the depths and everything vanished in circling darkness.

5

◆

Margaret opened her eyes and felt a hard, flat surface beneath her back. Overhead there were high beams, painted with intricate patterns that made her head spin and her stomach churn. Where was she? For a second she couldn't remember. She closed her eyes to shut out the sight of the beams. Something soft and heavy lay across her body. She closed her fingers around it, and felt the warm, rough kiss of a woolen blanket. She could smell it, the good, clean smell of mountain balsam. She shut her eyes and tried to breathe normally.

When she opened her eyes again, she found the dark, bearded visage of Aaron MacEwan watching her with anxious eyes. She could feel something beneath her head, and guessed it was a bolt of goods. "Be still, child. Manuella will bring you a cup of tea. You gave us quite a scare, fainting like that. I don't blame you. This hot spell we are having makes me giddy sometimes, too. The shop gets so stuffy."

Hot spell! She felt as cold as a block of ice. Her hands and feet ached with the chill, while her chest was drenched with frigid, clammy sweat. Margaret had an urge to scream or laugh with madness. She took a ragged breath, forcing a calm she did not feel down into her body. The events of the previous day swept into her memory, and she knew that by Darkover measure it was a very warm day indeed.

Margaret struggled to sit up, and the world spun. She sank back weakly, angry at her body's betrayal. Something was wrong, something so terrible she did not want to know it. She must! It was urgent. But her mind refused to cooperate.

Hands helped her to sit upright, tender hands, callused and work-worn hands, the real hands of real people. A mug of strong, scented tea rested against her mouth. She was so thirsty! She swallowed, scalding her tongue slightly. It was heavy with honey, hot and sweet. She gulped, then sputtered and coughed as a drop went down the wrong way. The terrible weakness began to leave her body, and she emptied the cup, draining it in huge, ungraceful gulps. The sugar hit her bloodstream like a drug, and memory flooded back.

Ivor! Something is wrong with Ivor! The certainty of it filled her with dread. She could not say how she knew, but for once she did not try to persuade herself that her imagination was at work. It was too real for that. Her teeth chattered against the rim of the empty mug, and she trembled all over.

Margaret resisted the urge to leap off the firm, supporting surface of the long cutting table and run back to Music Street. Only the sure knowledge that her knees would buckle at the first step made her remain where she was for a few minutes, breathing as slowly as she could. All the discipline of her academic training asserted itself, and slowly dizziness departed and a small sense of strength returned to her limbs.

"Please—I must go immediately!"

"But, *domna,* you are ill." That was Manuella, her small features creased with concern. Even in her roil of emotions, Margaret knew the concern was genuine, and she was touched. These people were strangers, and yet they behaved toward her as if she mattered. It touched a deep longing within her, something that was injured. She had not known it was there until that moment.

Gritting her teeth she pushed aside the urge to sink into the kindness of these people, pushed the blanket off her legs, and braced herself. "That does not matter. I must return to Master Everard's immediately!" She pushed her feet onto the scrap-littered floor, then staggered like a drunk. "Geremy! Ethan—take me back as quickly as you can!"

Both adults and children looked at each other helplessly. Aaron gave a shrug, as if to say "As you wish," and she straightened up. Margaret pulled her hated uniform tunic down where it had rucked up under her arms, and shivered all over. There was no real need to hasten, and in her heart she knew it. It was too late. But she wanted desperately to be wrong. She had one vivid impression from her spiral into darkness, the memory of a hand clutching her heart. Yet she knew it was not her heart, but that of Ivor which had been seized. She wished for it to be a dream, but she was certain it was as real as the hands which offered assistance now, actual and terrible.

Outside the shop, the light in the street was red. The great, bloody sun had slipped close to the low roofs of the houses, casting deep shadows between them. Her feet sped as she dashed down the lane, her heels striking hard against the rough cobbles, pushing the pace with her long legs, until both boys were gasping beside her. Her blood pounded like the death-drums of Vega VI, throbbing in her ears until she was nearly nauseous. One foot slipped, and she went down, falling on her palms and knees. The pain made her cry out sharply, cursing more fluently than she imagined she could.

The lads helped her up, and Margaret looked down at the cut across one palm as if from a great distance. She could feel a warm trickle seeping down her leg beneath her uniform. Her fine hair had pulled free of the butterfly clasp which remained in it, and fluttered against her cheeks as the boys watched her tensely. She tucked the wisps back impatiently, smearing a streak of fresh blood across her brow without realizing it.

Where were they? The streets seemed endless, winding and twisting beneath the rubidescent light of the lowering sun. How long had she been unconscious? Why had she left Ivor, when she felt he was not quite right? Her feet moved rapidly, mechanically. She focused her energy on reaching her destination, trying not to think, not to imagine what she already knew, though she could not say how.

The door to the house swung open before she could grasp the wooden knocker. Master Everard himself, pale and shocked, stood before her, his skin nearly as pale as his white hair, and his old teeth yellow against it. His blue eyes were damp with grief as he took in her disheveled appearance .

"Ivor . . ." she gasped, her heart aching in her breast.

"Dear child, I have sad news for . . ."

"He's dead, isn't he?" Her voice sounded blunt and crude in her ears, thick and rough like a jackdaw's call.

Everard nodded as he drew her into the house. "Yes, he is gone. The lad went to waken him and could not. He must have slipped away in his sleep."

"But he wasn't sick," she protested, her voice rising shrilly, like that of a weary, hysterical child. "He simply can't be dead," Margaret insisted stupidly.

Master Everard helped her to a seat, patting her hand kindly. "We don't know what happened, child. He was old. He was weary. When a man's time comes, it comes. His face is peaceful, and I do not think he suffered at all."

"I have to go to him!"

"No! You are in no condition to see him. Just sit still and calm yourself."

"But I have to see him—I have to be with him!" Helpless tears streamed down her cheeks.

Anya bustled across the room. She carried a bowl of steaming water and a soft cloth. Clucking gently, she wiped the tears off Margaret's face, and the blood off her torn hands. Margaret winced while the cuts were cleaned and rubbed with a thick salve that smelled of herbs, sharp and bracing. Behind the woman, the music master stood, twisting his hands before him, trying to help and being told to stay away.

Margaret wanted very much to push Anya's hands away, to yell at the two kind people who hovered around her. She lacked the strength to even form the words. She tried to get up, but her legs refused to support her.

Margaret huddled on the seat, wishing she could rouse from this nightmare. She knew it was real, but she felt so faraway, so distant. Her mind floated without direction, the smell of the salve making her feel drowsy. She remembered Ethan's mispronunciation of Thetis. *I never got to tell Ivor about the planet of "thesis." What a silly thing to think of, but he would have loved it.* Fresh tears welled in her eyes.

"Come along to bed now," Anya told her.

"I have to see him. Really, I will be all right, if only I can see him."

"You are in no . . ."

"Anya—take her to him. She can't rest like this."

Master Everard's voice was sharp, pained, and authoritative.

The housekeeper gave a grunt, looked at the old man, and nodded. She helped Margaret up the long stairs, and the two of them went into Ivor's room. Anya stood in the doorway while Margaret walked toward the bed, her feet hesitant now. There was no need to hurry.

The room was on the afternoon side of the house, as her own was on the morning side, and the rays of the sun came through the window, casting a glow on the figure in the huge bed. He looked so small. And peaceful. Just as if he were only sleeping, as she had seen him sleep hundreds of times before. But she knew he was not going to wake up.

"Ivor," she whispered, then repeated the word louder. *What could I have done? Nothing. So why do I feel this is somehow my fault?* "I'm sorry! Why did you have to leave me? What am I going to tell Ida? How am I going to go on without you?" The words sounded foolish in her ears, but she knew they weren't. They were just human words, what people said and thought when someone died.

"I loved you, old man. Did I ever tell you that? Did I ever tell you that you were a father to me, all these years, and that I would not have traded one second of it for all the credits in the universe?" Margaret reached down and took the hand of the man, twined her chilled fingers between his cold ones. She could still smell his familiar scent from the bedclothes, the odor of his face lotion and the stuff he put on his thinning hair.

Margaret stood for a long time, holding the cooling hand in her own, thinking of their years together, and his many kindnesses. At last her aloneness filled her senses. He was gone, and she would have to do the best she could, though at that moment, she wasn't sure she knew what that was. She put his hand down on his chest, smoothed the covers a little, touched his wrinkled cheek tenderly, and turned away. There was nothing more she could do.

Exhaustion hit her like a bludgeon then, and her knees buckled. She staggered against the side of the huge bed, hitting her shin so hard that dots of light danced in her eyes. Grimly, she shut out the pain. It would still be there later, she knew. It would always be there. She was empty of tears, empty of everything except pain and loss. Anya took her arm gently, and led her off to bed.

Walls; high walls; rose above her. Beneath her little feet, there were great squares of concrete. Margaret felt so small, so powerless. She looked at the great sculptures which stood around her. There was a long keyboard, like a curl of the sea, rising beside her. She stood on tiptoe and tried to touch one of the keys; and a soft chime sounded in her ears. It reminded her of something, but she could not remember what. The sound was the sound of fine crystal, and it made her shiver.

A bear, round and hefty, danced on a pedestal, friendly. Beside it there was a long sheet of metal, covered with intricate Ceti tri-model notation. Margaret tried to puzzle it out, for Ceti notation worked both as music and as language. It was a code, and she knew how to read it, but there was no sense to what she saw. She moved as if through some thick, invisible liquid, slowly and with difficulty. She stared into it as she circled the statuary garden and sought a way out.

A yellow sun, hateful to her eyes, glared at her, and escaping it became urgent. She walked along the walls, staring at the stones, looking for an exit. At last, she found a door, so small she had missed it before. As tiny as she was, it was smaller still, just over a foot high and hardly reaching her knee. She reached down a hand and twisted the little metal handle. It was locked. She beat small fists against the door, turning and twisting, as the statues seemed to mock her efforts. Exhausted, she put her head against the door and wept.

She opened swollen eyelids and felt the pillow beneath her head. The cover was damp. Margaret blinked her eyes, and cleared her vision. It was not very dark in the room. She turned toward the window, and decided it was about mid-afternoon, local time. Why was she in bed? She hated sleeping in the daytime. It left her feeling muzzy-headed and crabby.

Why had she slept in daylight? Margaret rolled onto her back, and looked up at the richly-painted beams above her head. Memory rose like a river, flooding her mind. The fainting spell in the shop, the terrible run back to Master Everard's, the spill on the cobblestones. She lifted one hand and saw the tidy gauze bandage which wrapped around her palm. No, she had not imagined it. Ivor was dead.

The tears came again, running into her ears with a maddening trickle. Her grief hardened into a kind of rage, a sense of having been abandoned again! She couldn't figure out where that came from, this emptiness within her that filled her with a senseless anger which seemed to have no particular object. She sat up and cursed fluently in several languages, expelling the rage with words, until she sounded like a lunatic to herself.

Margaret silenced herself abruptly, and let her mind wander purposelessly. She did not want to think, because thinking just filled her with pain. For a moment she wished for the oblivion of wine, and found herself thinking of the Senator in his bouts of drink. Was this why he did it? For the first time she almost understood him, and found the sensation disquieting. She did not want to understand her father—ever!

Banishing him to the place where she consigned her most hated memories, Margaret found herself recalling the intricate rhymed couplets of Zeepangu. On that mist-shrouded planet, death was seen as an incredible shirking of responsibility. The mourners never wept or showed any sorrow. Instead, they cursed the corpse and cast the two-lined poems into the grave. She almost understood, for a moment, their sense of outrage and loss. But she was not Zeepangese, and she had no desire to curse Ivor for abandoning her. She just desperately wished he hadn't died, as futile as that desire was, and that she was not so terribly frightened. How did anyone bear the pain of death?

Margaret had arrived at University a naive little Colonial of sixteen. It had been very strange, very alien, and she had hated it until Ivor had found her and given her both a home and a direction for her life. She had never imagined how ignorant she was until she began to meet the students from other worlds of the Federation, all with their own customs and assumptions. And every one

of them had been as provincial as she, as certain that
the way they did things at home was the *right* way.

The difference between Thetis and the University was
the difference between country and city. Margaret hadn't
suspected she was a country mouse, that even the daughter of a Senator could be an idiot under certain circumstances. What a revelation it had been! She had been so
frightened, and when she found Ivor and Ida Davidson,
they had made her so welcome. She could feel both the
terrible aloneness of that time, and the pleasure of being
rescued by the kindly Davidsons.

For a moment, she relaxed into the warmth and safety
of her treasured memories. But her sense of outrage
persisted, like a heated brick just beneath her sternum.
She couldn't hold the pleasant feelings in her mind, because her fury kept bubbling up, no matter how hard
she tried to prevent it. Why was she so angry? She was
a logical person, a trained scholar, wasn't she? Worse,
why did she feel angry at Ivor? How disgusting!

Margaret experienced a sense of urgency now, a need
to discover the source of her anger, to define it, package
it up neatly, and thrust it away from her. No one close
to her had ever died before. She was sure of that. She
sat up in the bed, put her elbows on her bent knees, and
rested her chin on her palms, frowning.

Except the feelings refused to allow themselves to be
nicely analyzed and tucked away. They seemed like a
bag of cats, all howling and scratching. And all of them
had a claw in her belly. It was more than Ivor, wasn't
it? Someone else had died, someone she cared for? Margaret thought, but she couldn't imagine who, except perhaps her real mother, her father's first wife. She rarely
thought about that woman. The few times she had, and
had asked Dio about her, the look of pain and distress
she had seen had made her wish she had kept silent. Or
that other woman, that Thyra person, whom she was
sure was part of the puzzle. Was she dead? Master Everard spoke of her in the past tense, so she supposed
she was.

Ugh! She stank of sweat and dirt and misery and the
Goddess knew what else. Margaret couldn't bear that a
moment longer, so she pushed the covers aside and
looked for her clothes. Her uniform was nowhere to be

seen, but the soft Darkover clothing she had purchased was hanging in the little closet. It felt wonderful under her fingertips, comforting and safe.

Margaret pinned back her hair and removed her sleeping clothes. She looked at the light, and realized she must have slept the clock around, and lost a day. She found her chronometer, and, indeed, a day had passed. No wonder she felt as if her head were stuffed with weeds. She shivered all over and pulled a robe out of the closet, tugging it across her naked skin, then headed for the huge tub she knew waited across the long hall. Darkover might lack electricity and landcars, but at least they were extremely civilized about bathing.

Margaret almost smiled, and found that the muscles of her face were so stiff that it was nearly painful. She never wanted to smile again! She felt stupid, then. She was still angry, and was probably going to be for a long time—even if she couldn't find a specific reason to be raging. It would not go away for wishing. And she would smile again, and even laugh—Ivor would have wanted her to do that. But not right now. For the present, she was going to have to cope with having several strong emotions all at the same time, and none of them very pleasant. She sighed deeply, and a part of her chided herself for being so very dramatic. She felt as if some stranger had invaded her body while she slept, some other Margaret that she had known was lurking in her mind, waiting for the opportunity to escape and take over her body. Foolish, of course, but that was the truth of it.

Sinking into the heated depths of the bath, she reached for a green jar that stood on the side of the tub. Pouring some of the contents into the tub, she was overwhelmed by the scent. It was sweet and flowery— and somehow familiar. That little door in her dream came back to her, vividly. She stopped moving, remembering. What lay behind it? It was not an actual door, but she knew it had some meaning.

She closed her eyes for a moment, and the sweet scent of the flowers seemed to calm her. She was small again, a child's body somehow superimposed over her own. She was sitting in a tub of warm water, scented with this same green mixture. Graceful arms had lowered her in.

Whose? Margaret was almost certain those arms belonged to the red-haired woman who haunted her nightmares. And there was someone else, too, someone she could not see. The silver-haired man?

And abruptly Margaret remembered another night before she left Thetis, a night she had shut away in her mental closet with all the others. For days before she left she had been too excited to sleep much, had packed and unpacked half a dozen times, trying to decide what to take with the small weight allowance permitted. At last she had gone downstairs to find something dull to read, to put her to sleep.

The Old Man was sitting before the fire, a glass in his hand. Her memory reconstructed every line of his face; the dark coarse beard, the deep furrows between his brows, and the scars he covered with flesh-colored makeup when he was outside his own house. She had often asked him, when she was small, how his face had become so scarred, but he had never answered her. Later, she had learned not to ask questions, not to remember, and never to disobey his strange orders.

He looked up and part of a smile touched his mouth. "Marja." He had always called her that. Her passport named her "Margaret," but Dio and the Senator always called her Marja.

"Excited?"

"A little. I couldn't sleep. I suppose I'll get some rest on the ship."

"I doubt it," he said. "When we left . . . when we came here, you were so sick. You appear to have inherited my allergies to most of the hyperspace drugs, though they have developed some new ones since then. Marja, do you remember anything at all from before you came here?"

For some reason, though he had spoken gently, the question made her chest tighten with terror. "Not much," she said, "I was almost a baby."

"But you weren't. You were nearly six, and that's old enough to remember a lot. Nothing? Not even in dreams?"

"Not really," she replied. Six? Surely he was mistaken. How could she have forgotten six years of her life? Margaret felt angry and cheated. It was an old and bitter anger, one she wished she did not have. It came up at odd times, when Dio tried to explain the odd ways in which the Senator behaved toward her, or when she asked questions and was told to be quiet. "Dreams? Of course I dream . . . everyone does."

"What about?" he asked instantly.

"Oh, the usual rubbish," she said casually. The few months of the year when the three of them were together, when the Senator was not away doing whatever it was that he did, they kept such distance between them that they had nothing like a family life. His question made her feel as if the privacy they had long established between them had been violated, and she squirmed and wished she had stayed in her room. "You know. Stuff. Symbolic things. Locked rooms. Doors, walls. Something very valuable is locked up behind one door."

His eyes brightened as she said this. "Like what?"

"A big—well, a jewel," she said uncomfortably. "Does it matter?"

"It might. Is there anything more?"

"No, not really." But there was.

Some awareness must have reached him, because he said, quite gently, "Tell me, child."

"Oh, nothing. Sometimes I dream about a little door that seems very dreadful. I cry and bang on the door, but I can't get in. Or maybe I cannot get out. Who knows in dreams. I'm very small, but the door's smaller, and then—" She stopped, overcome by an emotion she could not put a name to. "Then you and Dio are there, the way you always are." *But you weren't there when I was locked away!* It was remarkable how angry she felt when she thought about the dream. She hoped he had not heard her thoughts—sometimes it seemed as if he could—because she did not want him to know how angry she was.

Apparently he had not caught the strong emotions that rattled her adolescent mind, or he was too far gone with drink to notice. "Come. Sit here, Marja; on the floor beside me, as you did when you were very small."

For a second the offer was tempting. She had loved to curl up beside him before the fire when she was young, but now it made her feel stupid. "I'm not your puppy dog."

"No," he retorted, his quiet mood vanishing suddenly

and inexplicably, the way it often did when he was drinking. "You're a hellish redheaded bitch—just like your mother."

"That is a fine way to talk about your dead wife!" she flared. Then she shivered. It was dangerous to provoke him when he was like this.

The Senator looked startled. "Marjorie? Why would you think I meant her? I loved her more than words can say," he answered, a little more kindly. "But she wasn't your real mother, curse the gods!"

"Dio is all the mother I have ever known. But I thought my biological mother was your first wife, even though you never talked about her. I just thought you loved her so much you couldn't." The words spilled out, even as she tried to hold them back. Margaret knew how dangerous it was to confront the Old Man, and she was surprised at herself. Everything had become confusing since she had decided to go off to University. He still wasn't happy about her choice, but he would never say why.

Secrets sometimes seemed to fill the airy house with a vapor, the smell of ancient rage and sorrow. Margaret was so accustomed to it that she rarely asked questions. She tried to guess his mood, and failed, biting her lower lip and shifting from foot to foot.

"Marjorie?" he said unguardedly. "No. Your mother was Marjorie's sister, Thyra."

Margaret tried to digest this new, and unwelcome, bit of information. Who? She knew that name—sometimes he shouted it in his sleep. It always gave her the shivers. She wanted to leave the room now, but her curiosity got the better of her. "I've heard of some pretty weird marriage customs, but that is a new one! Is the first child always born by the wife's sister?" She was being sarcastic, and she knew it, but she would have died before she let her father know that she was interested.

He didn't laugh. "It wasn't deliberate," he said, looking bleak. Margaret was just old enough to think she understood and be embarrassed, whether for him or herself she was not sure.

"Does Dio know?"

"Yes, of course; I told her the whole thing when—when I found out myself," he said. "Did you know Dio and I once had a child?" The pain in his voice made her wince.

"No," she said, a little more gently. "I didn't know."

"It's why—Dio was so glad to have you."

"But why did you never have others?" She had longed for sisters and brothers, for the sorts of large, bustling families she saw among the Thetans. Margaret had always felt a little cheated in being an only child.

"I didn't dare," he said roughly. A terrifying picture flashed into her mind, of a wretched infant too deformed to survive. "I couldn't make her face that . . . again. No man would." He hesitated. "Dio said you should be told, but I've always been too cowardly. Our son—died. Then I found you. You were such a wonderful little girl, and Dio wanted a child of mine so much. I think she's been a good mother."

"She is. I never questioned that." *But where—and who—is Thyra—my own mother?*

"Dio should have had half a dozen children. She would have liked to," her father said, "but I just could not risk it." Margaret could not contradict him. But why was it a secret? And why had she always felt it was somehow her fault, some failure of hers, that there were no other children?

"No," he said gently, and she knew he had heard her, in that strange way he had sometimes. She had never been able to figure out how he did it—as if he could read her mind. She was sure that was impossible. Certainly it was unthinkable—people should not be able to invade the minds of others. "It had nothing to do with you—though at your age, I know that is really difficult for you to believe. When I was your age, I thought everything that went wrong with my father was my fault, and I expect you are the same." Since Margaret could not imagine her father as ever having been young, let alone being wrong, she had withdrawn before he said anything more. She remembered going back to her room, and then shutting his words away, making herself forget what he had said. She had done that other times, she realized now. Whenever anything frightened her, or was too painful, she sent the memory away into a place in her mind that was locked and hidden.

Now, in the warm waters of the bath, she wondered

if the red-haired, screaming woman in her dreams was this Thyra. If she was, Margaret hated to think about it. And who was that man she kept getting glimpses of? If only she had told the Old Man the truth, all those years before, about her dreams. But, she hadn't trusted him enough to disclose her dreams. And there was no use thinking about the past. It was gone, and it really did not matter to her.

Was the Thyra who had owned that *ryll* the same woman? It seemed likely, but there wasn't anyone she could ask about it. She noticed her fingers were starting to get all prunish from the water, and that was such a normal thing that she felt better in spite of herself. Margaret shoved aside this riddle she would probably never solve, and finished her bath.

If the woman in her dreams was the same Thyra whose *ryll* she had played two days before, if she was indeed her mother, then the Old Man had a great deal to explain. If she saw him again—no, *when*—she was going to tie him to a chair and not let him go until he told her everything! The resolve heartened Margaret more than a little, for she realized she was no longer a frightened girl. Well, perhaps just a little frightened, but certainly not a child any longer.

Bureaucracy, Margaret thought, was something invented by the devil to make the lives of people more difficult. After two days of wrestling with petty officials in the Terran Sector, she had been told that she could not send Ivor's body home because she was not a relative. He had to be buried on Darkover, and if Ida wanted to claim the body, she would have to come there and claim it. She had called the person behind the desk several colorful and unlikely names, then stomped off with the headache she was certain was going to become a permanent fixture in her brain.

She had telefaxed Ida—enriching the Federation's communications system considerably, but not with any sense of satisfaction for herself—and received a sad message telling her to bury the professor on Darkover at least for the time being. Margaret had found a coffin maker, with some help from Anya, and had chosen a nice casket. It had been an almost comforting experi-

ence, because the man had wanted to know all about
Ivor—what he did and what he liked. He showed her
designs from his book, and she chose a guitar to be
carved onto the top of the coffin.

Now there was one spot on her brow that throbbed
incessantly, and she had rubbed the skin almost raw—
as raw as she felt within. Filling out forms and answering
the same questions over and over had almost held her
grief at bay. But in the moments when she was not busy,
she felt lost and abandoned. Only the kindly presence
of Master Everard and Anya kept her from surrendering
completely to hopelessness. They behaved as if they had
known her and Ivor all their lives, as if he were a valued
friend, not a stranger who had had the poor manners to
die in their house after only two days' stay.

Master Everard walked beside her now, along the narrow streets. The coffin was borne along by four members
of the Musicians Guild, and the rest of Master Everard's
household walked behind it. Margaret carried the professor's precious guitar in one hand. Her palm was nearly
healed from where she had fallen in her wild rush to get
back to the music master's house, but the cut on her
knee was scabbed and painful.

As they approached the little cemetery which lay at
the edge of the Terran Sector, a number of people
stopped and looked at the procession. Margaret, deep
in her anguish, ignored the curious looks she got from
Darkovans and Terrans. She was dressed in the clothing
she had bought from MacEwan, for warmth and comfort, and it was all she could manage to put one foot in
front of the other. She kept stumbling in the unfamiliar
long skirt.

They passed beneath a handsome stone arch and entered the walled enclosure. There were a scattering of
headstones, trees here and there, and up ahead, a little
huddle of figures she thought were the statues from her
dream. Then one turned and she realized they were
quite alive. The breeze brought the clean scent of balsam
and stirred the garments of those who waited.

"I hope you do not mind, child. I asked a few people
from Music Street to join us." Master Everard was
weary, and he seemed apprehensive as he spoke.

"No, I don't mind. But they never knew him. It seems strange."

"True, but they would have wished to have known him. In the short time I had with him, I found him to be a very good man. I feel very gifted in that time, you see."

Margaret didn't, but there seemed to be nothing to add, so she moved onward, her eyes burning with unshed tears, her muscles aching with fatigue. Margaret came to the grave, looked into the faces of strangers, and saw—not strangers, but friends she had not known she possessed. It gave her the strength to endure as the Terran chaplain, in his gray clericals, a sober note between the greens and blues of the Darkovans, began to read the ritual words. Ivor had not been an adherent of any one of Terra's many faiths—if he had a religion, it was music—so the words were impersonal, almost without impact.

The pallbearers lowered the casket into the earth, and the chaplain read from his book, a worn volume, old-fashioned and probably valuable. The words, like the book, were well worn, ages old, formal and probably as meaningless to the Darkovans as they were to her. When he was done, he bent over, cast a handful of dirt into the grave, and withdrew, his duty done.

Stepping toward the open earth, Margaret bent and picked up a clod of dirt. As her fingers closed around it, she felt a disturbing tingle, as if the very soil itself could speak. She could not move for a moment, the sensation of the warm earth in her hand, as if Darkover were running along her blood. Then she dropped the bit of earth down onto the coffin, and went utterly still.

Margaret stood frozen on the spot until a woman stepped forward. Her hair was dark, her skin pale, and she was dressed in blue. She raised her arms and began to sing in a strong soprano that rang out between the trees and headstones. It was a mournful melody, heart-piercing in its beauty and purity. The words were of springs Ivor would never see, food he would never taste, and flowers he would never smell. All the senses were celebrated, and Margaret, her composure shattered, sobbed helplessly.

When the unknown woman was done, she stepped aside,

and a large man took her place. Margaret recognized the voice as that of the man who would succeed Everard as head of the Guild. She could not recall his name just then. He sang a beautiful song in a form of Darkovan that was archaic, and Margaret struggled to follow the words. The warm vigor of his baritone filled her with a sense of release, and she found she could stop crying and just listen in silence. She wiped her face on her sleeve, the sudden calm enveloping her so unexpectedly she hardly knew what to do.

At last, Margaret took Ivor's ancient guitar out of the case, tuned it carefully, and stroked the strings. Roughly at first, she sang, her voice hoarse. But as she warmed up, she forgot herself in the music, picking pieces which the professor had especially loved, old Terran songs, and drinking songs from the University. She sang love songs from a dozen worlds, and when she grew too weary to continue, she concluded with a dirge so ancient no one knew where it had originated. It spoke of a hero, fallen before his time, brave and fearless.

When she looked up, Margaret found that the little crowd of mourners had been touched by the music, weeping or holding back tears. She lowered the guitar and bowed her head. It was over.

Everard touched her arm. "Come. Let's go home now."

Home? Where was home? Where did she belong? All her sense of loss rushed back, gnawing at her and making her head hurt. "Thank you for everything, Master Everard. You have been so kind. But I'd like to sit here for a while, with Ivor. Then I will come back to the house. Would you be so kind as to take Ivor's guitar with you?"

"Certainly, but are you sure you'll be all right on your own?"

"Oh, yes. I know the way perfectly well now."

"I am sure you do. You are a very remarkable woman, Marguerida Alton." With that, he left her.

6

---◆---

Alone now, Margaret grieved. Birds sang on the branches of the trees in the cemetery; she heard them without really paying attention. At last, her body decided it was hungry and brought her back to the present with a start. It was irritating. Then she could almost hear Ivor chuckling and telling her not to be a complete idiot. She walked through the stone gates of the graveyard and started looking for someplace to eat.

She found a little cookshop just before the Terran Zone. Most of the patrons were Terrans, sporting their black leather uniforms and speaking in loud voices. She winced at the noise, and found a table near the back of the shop, where it was relatively quiet. She let her mind wander idly, feeling numb.

A plump girl in Darkovan dress came over and asked what she wanted. Too tired to choose, Margaret told her to bring something from the menu chalked behind the counter. Whatever it was, she was certain it would be good and filling.

The serving girl brought her a bowl of steaming rabbit-horn stew, a basket of bread still warm from the oven, and a mug of beer. There were large chunks of tender meat in a thick sauce, and lots of vegetables which tasted hauntingly familiar. The herbs and spices still tasted strange to her tongue, long accustomed to the blandness of University cuisine. She found herself smiling over the food, remembering her early experiences with food at the Commons. As one of her classmates had informed her while she gazed in horror at a bowl of flavorless cereal masquerading as breakfast, "University food offends no one, being without either taste or character." That pleasant memory made her chuckle softly.

The stew definitely had character. She tucked into it

without caution, or any thought of good manners. Despite Anya's best efforts and strenuous protests, she had been running on tea and nerves, longing for coffee occasionally, but without any real urgency. Now she felt like making up for it with a vengeance. She let the enticing flavors dance across her tongue as she became more full, and found herself thinking that she had eaten the dish before. For a moment it was as if there was a small child sitting on her lap, a child who could barely reach the table, spooning the same stew into a hungry mouth.

Margaret was almost finished when she noticed a man watching her. He wore the leathers of a Terran spaceport employee, but he lacked the physical attitude of a Terran. She puzzled over that realization for a moment, and finally decided he did not look as if he were slumming, the way most of the rest of the occupants did. She glanced away quickly, refusing to make direct eye contact, as she had been told was good manners, but she was aware that he continued to watch her. She began to be a little alarmed, and grew more so when he stood up and walked toward her table.

Without asking permission, he sank into the empty chair on the other side of the table and smiled in a way that almost stilled her fears. "I know who you are," he began without introduction. "You're Lew Alton's daughter, aren't you?"

Margaret could hardly deny her parentage, but she wondered how this stranger knew her. She didn't look like the Old Man at all. He seemed to sense her puzzlement and went on speaking in his friendly way. "My name is Captain Rafael Scott, but most people call me Rafe."

Margaret just stared.

When she didn't speak, he went on. "We are relatives."

"What?"

"I am your uncle. Didn't Lew ever mention me?"

Margaret wished she were not wearing Darkover clothing, that she were not so tired, and that people would stop talking to her as if she knew things she didn't. The man was about forty, and he seemed pleasant enough. But she was suspicious. The serving girl was watching them now, and several of the men from the spaceport were looking at them as well. She looked like a native, and she felt vulnerable as she would not have if she were still in her Terran clothing—uncomfortable as it made her feel. She did not want to be mistaken for a spaceport whore—it was one of the few things that Dio had actually told her about Darkover that she had understood.

"I am Lew Alton's daughter, yes. The only uncle I know of is my father's brother, and he has been dead for a long, long time." She wondered what her father would make of this strange conversation, and silently cursed the Old Man for never telling her the important things she needed to know. It was just like him—to leave her in the dark like this! Her anger, which had receded into the background while she ate, rushed forward in her chest.

"What do they call you?"

"Marguerida," she replied, using the Darkovan form of her name. "How can you be my uncle? I've never even heard of you!"

"Actually, we have met before, but I was still just a stripling then, and you were a very small child."

"I don't remember anything about it." She could hear the doubt in her own voice, and wished she were a better actress. Margaret decided this was one of the oddest conversations she had ever had, even though it seemed that every conversation on Darkover had a quality of strangeness. She wondered if he were telling the truth, and as she asked herself the question, she had the feeling that she knew he was. It was more than his open friendliness. She sensed his honesty across the table, almost as if she could read him like a book. *He is going to order himself another drink.*

A moment later Rafe Scott signaled the serving girl and gestured with his empty mug. Margaret squirmed, wondering how she had known that. If only she did not keep having these maddening episodes of near-clairvoyance or whatever the devil they were. It made her feel warm with blushing, as if she had pried into something private.

He turned his attention back to her. "I cannot believe Lew has never mentioned me. We were close friends, though I am much younger than he. I was older than Marius, Lew's brother, but not by very much. Marius would have taken his place on the Council when he was thirteen, if they had allowed it. All those damn conservatives, like Dyan Ardais, refused to let him." Margaret was surprised at the anger his voice held, old rage, ancient and hoary, but none the less vigorous for all that. And there was something else. That name—Dyan Ardais. She was sure she had never heard it before, but it made her want to hide under the table. She was so upset she almost missed his next statement. "He died before he was twenty. Your father was furious."

"What Council? What conservatives? *And who are you?!*" She snapped at the man, losing control of her frayed temper at last. It was a great relief to have something to be angry at, instead of having a bellyful of unexpressed rage eating at her. Shameful, too, because she was a grown woman, not a cranky child. Unfortunately, despite, or perhaps because of the hearty meal, Margaret felt very much like a small girl who needed a nap!

Rafe Scott regarded her calmly, quirking one eyebrow as if confused. The serving girl brought his beer, and he sipped at the foaming brew. "I am Marjorie Scott's brother Rafe. She was your mother, and that makes me an uncle. It's very simple."

Margaret studied her companion and newly discovered relative. Her first reaction was that it was rather nice to have family. She had always envied her neighbors on Thetis and her few friends at University for having brothers and sisters and aunts and uncles, just a little. It was an empty place inside her, one she rarely allowed herself to dwell on. But, at that moment, with the dirt from Ivor's grave still on her palms, it was oddly comforting.

Marjorie Scott's brother. The name of Lew Alton's first wife did not bring any strong feelings into her heart, for she knew that woman was not her mother. Dio was her mother, all the mother she wanted. But she found it interesting that he did not seem to know that Marjorie was not her mother, but that she had been born to that sister, Thyra. Of course, if Thyra was Marjorie's sister, as Lew had told her, then Rafe Scott was still her uncle. She thought about asking him about it, then decided not to. Something inside her did not want to talk about Thyra to anyone.

"But you are Terran, not Darkovan, aren't you?" She was surprised that she somehow knew this to be the truth.

"My father, Zeb Scott, was Terran. He married Felicia Darriell of the Aldarans, who was your grandmother." He sighed a little. "It was all a long time ago, and it was a sad page in Darkovan history. Marius died; your father lost his hand, and the Alton Domain . . . well, it is better not to dwell on the past."

Margaret resented his attitude. "It may all be in the past to you, but ever since I arrived here, people have been insisting I must know what they are talking about— but they never *tell* me anything. I feel as if I am trapped in the middle of a conspiracy of silence. And I am getting really tired of it!" Her voice rose, and several people at nearby tables stared. Her cheeks warmed again, aware of the attention she was drawing to herself, and she swallowed hard.

"But, surely, Lew has told you . . ."

"I have seen my father for only brief periods during the last decade, and he never told me much, on those rare occasions when I was favored by his presence." The bitterness in her voice was unmistakable. "I am here on a fellowship from the University, to do musical research. Until a few days ago, I was in the company of my mentor, but he died suddenly." Margaret stopped speaking, her eyes filling with fresh tears. "I have only just come from burying him! What I know about my history would be lost in a thimble!" She felt her entire body tremble and gritted her teeth in fury at her own weakness. If only she were not so tired!

Rafe looked aghast. He leaned forward and spoke softly, but with great urgency. "You mean you aren't here for the Telepathic Council?"

"For the what?"

"I am sorry. I assumed you were here with Lew, and that you had both come for the Council."

"As far as I know, the Senator is not planning to come here—he does not inform me of his movements, or of much else, it would appear." Margaret felt herself withdraw into an icy formality, distancing herself from both her father and the man across the table. Anger burned in her chest for a few seconds, and she tried to return to some semblance of calm. "As for telepathic councils—why would he come, or I, for that matter? Mind reading is as mythical as dragons."

Captain Scott leaned back in his chair, thoughtful now. "Damn Lew for a stiff-necked idiot," he said at last.

"I could not have said it better myself!"

Scott chuckled, and despite her fury, Margaret found herself responding to his laughter. "He was always as stubborn as a mule. But I don't understand how he could have kept you ignorant of your heritage!" *The Lew I knew was stubborn, but I never knew him to be plain stupid!*

Margaret ignored the words she heard, which did not leave the lips of her companion. She wished she could fly back to Master Everard's and fall into her bed for a week—without the intervening walk through Thendara. "I suppose he had good reasons. He never thought I would come to Darkover. And I never would have, if one of the professors at the University hadn't gotten himself in a pickle. It was completely unplanned and totally unexpected." She frowned. "Well, he did tell me to keep my neck covered and not to look people right in the eye—which he said was polite behavior here. But that was all. I can sort of understand the first, but I still don't know why I am supposed to avoid eye contact."

"The Alton Gift is forced rapport, and eye contact makes rapport less difficult. Not that Lew ever needed that."

"If you do not stop talking in riddles, I am going to pour the rest of my beer on your leathers! What 'Gift'?" She felt a prickle of apprehension start at the nape of her neck and crawl up her scalp.

"That would be a waste of excellent beer. I hardly know where to begin, and I am not sure it is my place to inform you. And this is certainly not the place—here, where there are a great many ears—to tell you what I know."

"It seems to me you have said quite a lot already! And none of it very informative." She had the satisfaction of seeing him redden. He looked at her directly, very hard, and she noticed that his eyes were remarkable, flecked with gold, like her own, but more penetrating. A moment before he had seemed safe, but now Rafe appeared to be somewhat threatening, as if he could look into her mind. Her father had looked at her like that, sometimes, and she reacted as she always had, by thinking of something neutral. Margaret focused on the score of a complex piece of music almost reflexively, and after a moment he looked away. For the first time she noticed his hands, and saw that he had six fingers instead of five.

The sight of his fingers brought a rush of memory, of another pair of hands, a woman's hands playing across the strings of a *ryll*. They, too, had an extra finger. Margaret held back a shudder and refused to remember more, for she knew those hands belonged to the red-headed woman, to Thyra.

The man shifted uneasily in his chair, and sighed deeply. "Your father is one of the finest men I ever knew, Marguerida, but he never could manage his personal life worth a damn! What a mess!"

"Personal life? I think he hardly has one, except for Dio."

"You are very hard on him, aren't you?"

"Not nearly as hard as I would like to be," she answered tartly. If she could have transported her father across the light-years at that moment, she would have cheerfully boxed his ears. The image gave her an immense amount of pleasure for a second.

Rafe smothered a laugh. It made him even more handsome than before. "We can't safely talk here. Under the circumstances, I think I had better escort you up to the Castle."

"I think you'd better rethink that, Captain Scott. I am not going to any castle with *you* or anyone else who waltzes up and tells me they know the Senator. I may be ignorant of Darkovan customs, but I know better than to go gallivanting off with a total stranger."

But Margaret could not help feeling rather curious, even as she also felt very contrary and exhausted. She wished that she could manage to have one emotion at a time, that she was not being pulled in so many ways at once. She remembered how MacEwan and his wife had assumed she would be going to the Castle, how people had deferred to her, just on the basis of her appearance.

Rafe leaned forward, pressing against the edge of the table, and lowered his voice. "Marguerida, you are a

very important person, whether you know it or not. You
have an obligation to fulfill and you are heir to the Alton
Domain. It is critically important to the entire future of
Darkover that you come with me."

For a moment she did not move, so compelling were
the man's words. "I think you must be mistaken," she
replied at last.

"No. I was young when you left Darkover, but not so
young that I was unaware that you had the Alton Gift
in great measure—even though you were only a child."
There was no mistaking the urgency in his voice.

"Are you trying to tell me I was some sort of mind
reader when I was little?" A memory nagged at her,
something about manners, and it was unpleasant. Someone had called her a snoop, though they laughed when
they said it. The voice in her mind was her father's,
though it was a more gentle tone than she ever recalled
him using afterward.

"Not 'some sort' but a very skilled telepath, child."

"Well, I must have lost it when I grew up, because I
certainly don't have it now!" Margaret was not sure she
believed what she said. It would certainly explain several
curious incidents. She did not *want* to believe it, she
realized. It made her think of the silver man, and the
redheaded woman, and death.

With a suddenness that made her almost sick, Margaret knew she had felt someone die, in her mind, long
ago. It was horrible, and she wished she could run away
from the unwanted memory. Something so terrible had
happened that she had locked it away in her mind, forever, she thought. She clutched the table reflexively and
tried to rise, flooded with terror.

But a strong, six-fingered hand closed around her
wrist. "It's all right. There is nothing to be afraid of."

Margaret could feel a presence within her, calming,
soothing. She gazed into the gold-flecked eyes across the
table from her and bit her lip until she tasted blood.
"Get out," she hissed, furious and helpless at the same
time.

The sense of invasion vanished, leaving her with the
ancient and familiar terror.

"Come on, Marguerida. Let's at least get out of here,

so we can talk." Rafe threw some coins on the table and stood up.

She rose, trembling, and followed Captain Scott out of the cookshop, hardly noticing the looks she got from Terrans and locals alike. She was dazed as she stood on the cobblestones. The late afternoon sun cast its bloody pall on the street, and everything felt familiar and eerie. The past she did not want to recall seemed only a breath away.

Margaret wished she could just walk away, to leave this man standing in the street and go back to Master Everard's. She wanted to take a long, hot bath, put on her cozy nightgown, and go to bed. She definitely didn't want to get involved with any more puzzles or councils. To her disgust, her mouth seemed to have a completely different plan, for she found herself asking, "What is the Alton Domain?" The words were out before she could censor them.

Captain Scott looked at her and gave a brief sigh. "The great families of Darkover, called the *comyn,* each possess ancestral lands and properties, which are called Domains. Since Lew left, there has been no one of the direct line at Armida, the Alton stronghold. *Dom* Gabriel Lanart Alton is from a cadet branch of the family, and he has been . . . never mind. Were Lew dead, the Domain would be yours. In any case, you are the heir of Alton, and in his absence, you must speak for it." He seemed quite certain of himself now.

"Stop! You are going too fast for me. I know Darkover is feudal in its cultural structures—the learning disks at least told me that." She frowned. "I have been to nearly a dozen planets, but I never came to one so miserably undocumented! It's an outrage! The only disk I could get my hands on was all but useless! It told me some geography, a small amount of history, and a few customs. Now you inform me that my family is powerful, and that I own a chunk of the planet. Is that right?"

"It is an accurate, if limited, summary."

"That is ridiculous! My father would have told me."

"Lew relinquished claim to his Domain when he left to become our Senator."

"Oh. So I *don't* own this estate, actually. That's a relief! I don't really want to be saddled with . . ."

"Marguerida—Lew did not give up *your* claim to the Alton Domain, only his own. Under Darkovan law no one can relinquish claims for a minor child—that would be wrong."

"Wrong? If you ask me, the entire planet is tilted on its mental axis, about thirty degrees off." She knew she was being stubborn, and that she was trying to avoid asking about the council and the other tantalizing things he had mentioned.

Rafe laughed, a good, healthy laugh, very human and very normal. "The Terrans have been saying that about Darkover for years."

"Well, I am an Imperial citizen, which makes me a sort of pseudo-Terran, and I don't want any part of your local politics. I came here to study folk music, and that is what I am going to do!"

"That does make things a little difficult, but I am sure it can be ironed out—your citizenship, I mean."

She glared at him. "Ironed out! I hadn't even noticed it was wrinkled. And what does it matter to you—you're Terran, aren't you?"

"It matters because Darkover is my home, and I love it. Yes, I work for the Terran Service, but my heart is here. And your presence is important. There are things going on even I don't quite understand. What I do know is that if the Darkovans don't do something, there is a good chance that the planet will be gobbled up by the Expansionists. If we lose our protected status . . . well, it doesn't bear thinking about. I can't imagine why your father left you in such ignorance about your heritage."

At least the Expansionists were something she knew about, which was comforting in this sea of confusion. When she and Ivor had been getting ready to leave University, she had heard that the Expansionists had won a majority in the Federation government for the first time in more than two decades. The newsfaxes had been full of speculation about what it meant, but she hadn't given it a great deal of thought.

She turned her attention to Rafe's last question, though, because she knew it troubled him, as it troubled her. "I think it was too painful for him to remember, to speak of his own past. Captain Scott, the man you knew is not the one I know. Whatever Lew Alton was when he lived here, he isn't that anymore. I think he tried to tell me something, the night before I left for the University, but we had never gotten into the habit of conversing, and it didn't happen. These days he is an angry, bitter man who drinks a little too much, and keeps his own counsel. And since he did not choose to inform me of my history, I have assumed there was a good reason for it. He's not an impulsive person."

"Then he *has* changed. At least, he seemed very impulsive to me. He was a loving husband to my sister—I never saw anyone so much in love. I can't believe you remember so little. Don't you remember Marjorie—you resemble her rather strongly—or the Alton house here in Thendara, or anything? I was sure . . ."

"What I remember or don't is none of your business." *Do I look like Marjorie or Thyra? And if the Old Man was so deeply in love with her, why did he sleep with her sister?* It didn't make any sense. Nothing made any sense to her—not Ivor's death or the way people deferred to her, or her sudden importance in something concerning the planet of her birth. Why hadn't she picked another place to eat?

Once again she had the impression that he could hear her thoughts, for he said, "So, you know that much, do you? You look like yourself, but you have a strong family resemblance to the Scott sisters—both of them. If we were seen together, in Darkovan clothing, we could be taken for father and daughter, I imagine."

"Is that how you recognized me?"

"First I noticed the red hair of the Comyn, and then the line of the nose, the bones of the face. It took me several minutes to realize that you must be my niece— that you had to be an Alton. And since Lew had only one daughter, I assumed you were also a Scott."

"You aren't telling me everything, are you?" She could sense he was holding something back.

"Only a fool empties his entire sack on the table."

Margaret was so annoyed by his words that she sat down on the curb and refused to go any farther. "And only a fool tries to stuff a horse back into his sack when it is halfway out."

He sat down on the curb beside her, leaning his arms across his knees. For a minute he did not speak, and when he did, there was a compassion in his voice that touched her deeply. "What has made you so wary, Marguerida?"

"Secrets. The walls of the orphanage, and something terrible I cannot remember." The words were out before she realized she was saying more than she wished to. His shoulder was close to hers, and she realized for the first time that he was a short man, a good three inches shorter than she was. Short and serious and probably trustworthy. The wind shifted, ruffling his hair and bringing her the scent of him. He smelled of Terran leathers, but more, he smelled of local soaps and the spices of Darkovan food. Captain Scott smelled *right*, not alien and antiseptic like most Terrans.

"If you will come with me to Comyn Castle, I think we can answer some of your questions—and get some of those secrets untangled."

"Are you reading my mind?" The sense of trust which had begun to form within her vanished.

"Not really. I am not a very skilled telepath; I have just enough *laran* to pick up the surface thoughts, but no more. And my small skills lie more in the area of foretelling, actually. I mean, I don't ordinarily frequent that particular cookshop, but today I felt almost compelled to eat there."

"*Laran?* What is that?" Margaret felt she almost knew the word, and that its meaning was very important, but she could not decide why. How could he talk about being a telepath as if it were the most ordinary thing, instead of something impossible?

Inside her, she could feel something stir, something dark and frightening. She knew it well, because it had always been there, a frightening face looking back at her from mirrors, telling her to keep herself apart from everyone. Now it wanted her to ignore this man, not to listen to what he said. It seemed to grip her brain, and the more tightly it held, the more she wanted to resist it. And the dread she had felt since she learned she was coming to Darkover rose in her, choking her breath a little.

"Come with me to Comyn Castle, and I promise . . ."

"Why can't you tell me now?"

"Because it isn't something to be discussed on a public

street." He looked distressed, and even though he was shorter than she was, she suspected he could force her to accompany him, if he decided to.

Margaret felt she was standing at some crossroads. If she went in one direction, events would go one way, and if she took the other, things would be different. It was almost as if she could see several futures winding away from her feet, all of them dark and vague. She had to choose, and she was so tired! If she walked away from him, something was going to happen that was bad. She was certain of it.

The internal struggle seemed to go on and on, though she knew it was only of a few seconds duration. That cold force that made her afraid of mirrors was trying to move her away from Captain Scott, and, feeling as contrary as she did, she decided to oppose it. And as soon as she reached that decision, the feeling of dread lifted a little, and the future no longer seemed as terrifying as it had a moment before.

Resolutely she set her shoulders straight. "Very well. I will come with you—but I am not going to turn into a feudal landlady, no matter what I find out."

Captain Scott just smiled.

7

$\blacklozenge$

Comyn Castle was the sprawling white building she had noticed when she looked up from the square next to the Terran headquarters. It had been a fairly long walk, and she had been standing and walking so much that day that her feet were protesting by the time they reached it. Margaret followed her new-found kinsman through the outer courtyard, observing the architecture like any tourist. It was impressive, but she decided she did not want to be impressed. It was not as if she had never seen a castle before, and as castles went, this one was neither the largest nor the most awesome she had seen. That distinction was still held by the old Imperial Palace on Zeepangu, a single building covering several square kilometers.

This place must be a maze to find your way around in. As she had this thought, Margaret "saw" patterns of corridors and rooms, layer upon layer, and knew that somehow she possessed an internal map of the place. There were secret passages and rooms no one had entered for generations. It was a place of plots, rivalries, and ancient feuds. *How do I know that?*

The nagging sense of another memory niggled at the back of her mind. Margaret looked up at a small balcony that jutted from one of the upper floors, and the memory of a large room with a richly-patterned carpet and heavy wooden furniture floated before her eyes for a moment. There was a large table or desk, and Lew, a much younger man than the one she knew, sat behind it. He seemed enormous, and she realized she was seeing him with a child's viewpoint, looking up from the floor. The patterns of the carpet coiled out from between her sprawled legs, and she could see plump baby hands tracing the curves. *I must have come here once. But that doesn't explain this feeling I have that I know my way around the entire building. When are things going to start making sense?*

Margaret looked away from the balcony, shutting off the flood of uneasy memory. Instead, she found herself staring at a tall tower to one side of the complex. Alone of all the great buildings, this was the one thing of which she had no clear image. It made her cold to look at it, cold and afraid. She wrenched her eyes away angrily. She was tired of feeling like some pawn on a chessboard, and somehow it was all Lew Alton's fault! Being furious at him helped, and she relaxed slightly.

They climbed several steps to a pair of great wooden doors, deeply carved with stars and other figures she could not immediately identify. Beside them stood two guardsmen in some sort of uniform. They wore swords at their sides, but no other armament. There was something about their stance which told her they knew how to use these archaic weapons, that they were not ceremonial at all.

The guards flung the closed doors aside, saluting Captain Scott as if he were well known to them, and ignored her entirely. Margaret had a strong sense of relief when she passed through the portals of Comyn Castle without eliciting comment. After all the years of having to present documents at every turn, due to the obsessive bureaucracy of the Terrans, it was rather pleasant to enter a building so easily.

The doors opened onto a grand foyer. The floor was carpeted with a fine rug, and her feet, hot and weary after the long day, felt refreshed by the softness of it beneath her soles. There were armorial banners hung along the walls, bright colors against translucent white stone. The fading light of the sun penetrated the stone and lent the chamber a curious ambiance. Margaret could not decide if it was sad or festive—or somehow both at once.

Rafe Scott led her through the foyer and into a corridor with several doors opening off it. The hall was wide, spacious enough for several people to walk abreast, and it smelled clean and dry. There were a few paintings hung along it, pictures of people for the most part, and more armorial banners. Comyn Castle, Margaret de-

cided, was not a cozy place. The height of the walls and
the starkness of the decor began to oppress her, and she
longed to be back in Master Everard's comfortable
house. Anya would be starting supper now, and there
would be the smell of food and the sound of music. Even
though she had eaten only an hour before, she found
she was hungry again, and terribly tired.

The corridor was very long, and she saw several people walking on their errands. Scott stopped one of them
and said something in a voice too faint for her to hear,
then pointed down the hall. The servant gave a nod,
glanced with some interest at Margaret, and then
walked away.

They finally entered a room that was arranged for
meetings. There were rows of chairs and a long table at
one end of the room. Rafe gestured her into one of the
chairs, and she sat down heavily. One of her feet was
developing a blister and the small of her back hurt. She
watched incuriously as he spoke into some sort of communication box on the wall, and waited upon events.
Part of her wished she had not come, and another part
of her wanted to get the meeting over with, so she could
get back to her old life.

While she waited, Margaret found herself reflecting on
her life. It seemed to her that she was being guided
along some invisible path, one she did not entirely wish
to explore. She remembered some of the philosophical
discussions she had heard from fellow students at the
University, on whether man was predestined or had free
will. In the thousands of years of human history, no one
had ever arrived at a plausible conclusion, and she suspected, no one ever would. Still, she wondered if her
meeting with Rafe Scott were destiny or coincidence. He
seemed to think it was the former, and she was not
happy to discover she almost believed him.

She was deep in these musings when two men entered
the meeting room. Their faces were no longer young,
and her first impression was that they were about the
same age as her father. Their movements confirmed this
guess a moment later, for they had a kind of certainty
that came with years. One of the men looked very familiar, and she realized she had seen his portrait in the hall.
They stood close to one another, and there was some-

thing deep and intimate in their stance. The familiar man was slender and well-formed, with the pure white hair that belonged on a much older man.

The man whose portrait Margaret had seen smiled at Scott and said, "It is wonderful to see you, Rafe. It has been too long since you paid us a visit. What is it—no problems, I trust?" He spoke in a good-natured and friendly way, without any formality, but beneath the words Margaret caught an undertone of worry.

Before Rafe could reply, the man caught sight of Margaret, and his eyes widened a little as he glanced at her, an indirect look that was no less penetrating for being so quick. His companion followed his gaze, and she felt somehow chilled when his eyes swept across her. She lowered her eyes to her lap and studied her hands for a moment.

"Why, you must be Lew Alton's child! I'd know that hairline anywhere, though you don't look like him otherwise. I used to envy him that peak, when we were young." He smiled at her with great warmth, and moved toward her. "Where is Lew?" He paused, as if he expected the Senator to be lurking under one of the chairs. Then he looked very disappointed. "He isn't here, is he? I thought, when he telefaxed us about his resignation, that he would be coming back immediately. I would have known if he had returned to Darkover, I think. He has a very strong presence. Has he sent you to take his place on the Telepathic Council?" As the man spoke, Margaret suddenly knew that his name was Regis Hastur—though how she knew it she could not imagine.

Resignation? She hadn't paid attention to the newsfax for weeks, and in all the turmoil around Ivor's death, she hadn't bothered to pick up her own messages either. Maybe that was why Dio hadn't answered her—they were in transit somewhere between the stars. For some reason, the knowledge that her father had left the Senate was disquieting. And, stubbornly, she didn't wish to appear ignorant. It put her at a disadvantage that she disliked. The big building seemed to press down on her.

"Whatever that is, he didn't," Margaret answered rather icily. Did *all* these people imagine she had no other purpose in life than to travel halfway across the galaxy just to attend some meeting? How provincial they

all were. The annoyance she had experienced while talking to Scott in the cookshop returned with a vengeance.
Darkover appeared to be peopled entirely with lunatics
who assumed she knew things she didn't, and never gave
a reasonable answer, or even introduced themselves before they began to plague her about this damned Telepathic Council! They were not only provincial, they had
terrible manners!

Rafe coughed, then spoke. "Regis, she doesn't know
what you are talking about. Lew never told her about . . .
well, anything, as near as I can tell."

Regis Hastur reddened slightly. *What?* "And I have
forgotten my manners. Forgive me. I am Regis Hastur,
and this is Danilo Syrtis-Ardais, my paxman." He made
a graceful gesture at the man standing beside him. The
mention of that name made her tense, as had Rafe's
earlier reference to someone called Dyan Ardais. She
wanted to turn away, anything to avoid his eyes, as if he
presented some threat to her. Still, he seemed ordinary
enough—just a slender man wearing a sword, standing
close to Regis with an attitude of watchfulness. So, why
was her skin crawling? This was utterly ridiculous, and
she chided herself for being a fool.

Then Margaret felt quite certain that both men had
sensed her thoughts, had felt her fear and confusion. She
was angry, her privacy invaded, and embarrassed that
she was afraid of a complete stranger. Just because he
had the same last name as someone she couldn't quite
remember, but feared, was not reason to be angry, was
it? All this nonsense about telepathy was just that—nonsense. Her imagination was running wild just because
she had a few random incidents that seemed like telepathy. Still, she felt herself blush all over.

"Regis Hastur? You are the Regent, aren't you?" At
least the disk had told her that much. "It is a pleasure
to meet you," she continued, wondering if she should
stand up and bow or something. Her legs felt like jelly
now, and her head began to throb.

"I have that duty, yes." He did not sound entirely
pleased with that. "And I am pleased to welcome you
to Comyn Castle. I have been anticipating Lew's return,
and I assume he sent you in his place? Why? Will he
arrive soon? Where are my manners? You are tired.

Dani—will you see to some refreshment?" *He must come, he simply must, else all my plans will be for nothing.* Despite the calmness of his words, he was clearly a little agitated, for his beautiful hands clenched and unclenched, and he shifted uneasily from one foot to the other.

For a moment, the paxman did not move. Margaret realized he was studying her with polite interest, as if he found her as puzzling as she found him. She had a sudden impulse to hide from him, and quelled it with difficulty. Then he turned away, a little reluctantly from the set of his shoulders, and went to a small cabinet against one wall. As soon as he turned his gaze away, she felt an enormous relief.

"I cannot say. I have not had any communication from my father or mother for some time. I did telefax them before I left University, but I received no reply," she answered. The retreat into careful formality made her feel less vulnerable, less subject to fits of imagination. Margaret still had the creepy feeling that all the men in the room could sense her thoughts, if she let them. That made her feel too powerless, and she determined not to permit anything of the sort. There was no such thing as telepathy, she told herself over and over. No matter how she felt, or what anyone told her. "The Senator had no plans that I know of to come to Darkover. Until just a few minutes ago, I did not know he had resigned his position."

In the silence that followed her statement, the paxman returned with a tray with several glasses on it. Margaret was a little surprised that he was acting as a servant. She thought he was something else—something more powerful and even a little sinister. He handed a glass to Regis, and they smiled at each other as their fingers brushed. She was nearly shocked by the tenderness of the look which passed between the two men. More, she was deeply embarrassed, as if she had glimpsed something entirely private. She dropped her eyes to her lap and pleated the folds of her skirt with restless fingers.

"Some wine, *domna?*" Margaret could see the strong legs of Danilo, and knew he was standing, waiting for her. She found herself very reluctant to raise her head, to meet his eyes.

"Thank you," she answered quietly, lifting her hand and head, but looking past the paxman at the wall beyond. At least she knew it was not rude to refuse to look directly at him, as it would have been at University or most places in the Terran sphere.

Regis Hastur sipped, then scowled. "Lew is my cousin—and my oldest friend, but he is the stubbornest and least predictable fellow I have ever known. We were brought up together at Armida. I cannot believe he never mentioned me." *She really does not know me. And her mind is locked up, blocked. I've never seen anything like it. She didn't know Lew had left the Senate—how very odd.*

Margaret felt that whisper across her mind and swallowed. Of course she didn't know—Lew Alton never told her anything! The bitterness of that thought made the wine taste sour in her mouth, but the alcohol eased it a little. It was just like him!

Margaret schooled herself to reveal nothing of her increasing distress, retreating into herself as much as she was able. "He never spoke of his past, unless he spoke to my mother. I would not even have a clue to who you were except for some research I did, preparing to come here on assignment for the University Music Department to collect folk music. I knew, in a vague way, that I was born here, but, in truth I remember very little." *And if I had my way, I would be happy not to remember anything at all—because everything I recall just makes things stranger!* "Perhaps he did not tell me things to spare me unpleasantness. As I have told Captain Scott, he is not the man you knew. When he is not doing his job in the Federation Senate, he stares at the ocean and broods." *And drinks,* she added silently.

Margaret sensed that what she said had increased Hastur's distress, not lessened it, and she wished she possessed more tact. It was the way in which she was most like her father—speaking her mind instead of being polite. She knew she could be rude, and never more so than when she felt vulnerable. She took another mouthful of wine, really tasting it for the first time, and found it was strong and flinty. It had a clean taste, and she let herself enjoy it and the softening of tense muscles that came with it.

Regis looked around the room, his brows knitting in thought. "Come. Let's walk out in the garden for a bit. It's not dark yet, and the gardens are quite lovely. We have things to discuss, and this room is too formal for my taste. Danilo, take Rafe to my study. We will join you there when we have had our talk."

Danilo looked alarmed. He tensed and his hand went to the hilt of his sword for a moment. Then he let it go. The paxman gave her a hard look, as if he wanted to probe her heart with his eyes. Did he think she was going to pull a knife and stab Regis Hastur? With sudden insight, she knew this was exactly what worried him, that as unassuming as he might appear, he was deadly and would strike at anything which threatened his master. And that was why he had served the wine—in case of poison! For an instant their eyes met, locked in silent combat, and then he looked away, apparently satisfied that she did not represent any danger to Hastur.

Regis took Margaret's elbow gently and ied her out of the chamber through a door she had not noticed, down a narrow corridor, and into a pleasant courtyard filled with sweet-smelling flowers. "I find myself at a disadvantage, and in something of a quandary, ethically speaking."

"Do you?" She was beginning to like this white-haired man, to feel almost comfortable with him, and that worried her. It was not that he wasn't friendly, but that he was clearly being charming for some reason. She was suspicious of that. She felt that he was preparing to maneuver her into something, to suit his own purposes, whatever those might be. She was so tired that her judgment was doubtful, and she knew it.

"Yes, Marguerida, I do. Lew chose not to reveal to you anything of his past, and you must know his past in order to understand some of the present here on Darkover. I am still shocked that he told you nothing."

"He tried, I think, to tell me something, just before I left for the University." *And when he did try,* she finished without speaking it aloud, *I didn't let him get very far.* "I think it was terribly painful for him to talk about himself, about his past, as if he had terrible memories."

Regis gave a short, bitter bark of a laugh. "I can see

how he might—he was very nearly the ruin of our world.
But he is also a hero, and a savior."

"A little hard to do both, isn't it?" Her breath was
coming in short pants, for Margaret felt she was on the
brink of learning something that she needed to know,
but was terrified of discovering.

"Your father is a complex man, perhaps the most
complex person I have ever known. And Darkovan customs brought him enormous griefs when he was still too
young to bear them. I've had years to think about it.
Whenever I look at the night sky and see the stars, I
think of Lew. I wanted to go to the stars, and he got to
do it, while I was left to tidy up an unholy mess and be
a king without a real kingdom."

"What griefs?"

Regis, still holding his glass, took a sip while he
thought. "Lew's mother was half-Terran, half-Aldaran,
and for that reason the Comyn Council denied him his
place. They called him a bastard, and that injured his
pride—the Altons are a proud family, and he has that
pride in full measure. He was never certain that he was
good enough. I know that doubt very well, for it has
plagued me as well. He tried to please his father, who
was a good man, but very stiff-necked and demanding.
He forced Lew to do things that both of them knew
were wrong, because he was determined to get Lew onto
the Council."

"Why? What was so important about being on the
Council?" Margaret demanded.

"It was not so much that a seat on the Council was
important—although it was—but Kennard wanted Lew
to be accepted as heir to the Alton Domain." He gave
a deep sigh. "It turned into an intolerable situation, and
it ended with Kennard Alton, your grandfather, taking
Lew off-planet, in direct violation of our laws, leaving
the Alton Domain without a leader. Kennard died out
there among the stars, and Lew came back six years
later, bearing a very powerful matrix which he had taken
into exile with him. And that resulted in another crisis,
in which many people died, and the entire society of
Darkover was altered."

Margaret turned and stared at the man, quite forgetting to avoid his eyes in her astonishment. "I would like

to say I understand, but, frankly, it is very hard to connect your tale with anything I know about the Senator.
You might as well be speaking of some ancient hero
from a myth, almost."

"You are very astute. In many ways it *was* mythic.
The events of the Sharra Rebellion were indeed mythic
in proportion; even the gods became involved. My hair
was as red as your own once."

"Was it?" She wished he would stop being so cryptic,
giving her hints, bits and pieces, but not a coherent set
of facts she could sink her teeth into. And that word
again—Sharra. It gave her shivers, even though it was
pleasant and warm in the garden. "Very well—this is
more of my father's history than I have ever known before. He is ambiguous—that has not changed." She felt
her mouth curve into something resembling a grin. "But,
if this is the story, then why was there nothing of the
matter on the disk I studied. The kindest thing I can say
about it is that it was nearly information-free. There was
no mention of any . . . Sharra, and if, as you say, it was
such a significant event, then why isn't it mentioned in
the Terran Archives?"

Regis seemed almost lost in his own thoughts now,
speaking without really paying attention. "Oh, it is there,
but it is not general knowledge. There are things we
believe are better not left about for public gaze. Darkover still has a few secrets tucked into her bodice, and
I think that is a good thing."

Margaret had a scholar's reaction to this calm statement of the suppression of information—she was livid.
It was a much stronger surge of emotion than it needed
to be—governments, she knew, often tried to keep secrets. She realized she was angry at this pleasant stranger
beside her, but angrier still at the Old Man. She clenched
her hands, then let them go. "Your little secrets have
nothing to do with me. I am here by accident, not by
intent, and I just want to get on . . ." She used her
coldest, most formal voice, for it made her feel less weak
and lost.

Margaret needed that, because she could feel a rising
helplessness, triggered by the sound of two harmless syl-
lables. A deep sense of dread almost overwhelmed her.
Sharra! Sometimes her father called the word in the

night, and whenever he did, she would wake up and
shiver all over. And when she returned to sleep, she
always dreamed of a great, shining jewel, full of light
and fire. The image burned in her mind for a moment,
until she banished it again.

"You sound so much like your father! And you look
very much like your mother, at this moment."

"Thyra?" she answered icily.

"Ah—well, at least you know about that. It's a bit
awkward for me."

"Awkward! Why? You didn't bed your wife's sister,
did you?" As soon as the words escaped, she regretted
them.

To her surprise and great relief, Regis did not seem
offended, almost as if he understood her anger and her
confusion. "No, I have not. I've done some interesting
things in my life, but not that one. I only saw Marjorie
Scott once, and I never met her formally, but since she
and Thyra were half-sisters and looked much alike, I
suppose I meant both. Technically, you are the daughter
of Marjorie Scott—even if she was your aunt. Oh, my.
I am making a complete muddle of this, aren't I? I mean
you are listed as her child in our records. You are like
all your parents," *and you have the same unholy sensitivity Lew has,* he thought, without speaking. Margaret
heard the unspoken words clearly, and flinched.

"It would seem that I have an excess of mothers—if
you add Dio into the mix. I find the entire thing confusing and unpleasant."

"What do you mean?"

"How would you feel if you found out that your
mother is actually your aunt, and your aunt is your
mother, and was so strange a person that no one likes
to mention her name."

"Hmm. I think I would be rather upset, now you put
it that way. But, where did you hear her mentioned—in
what context?" Regis glanced at her, and he looked both
interested and sincere.

"At Master Everard's, in Music Street. He let me handle this *ryll* that he said could not be played, and this
song came out of it . . . it was very eerie. Then he told
me a little of the history of the instrument, and I

realized . . . well, it doesn't matter." She held back a
shudder as she remembered her experience.

"You are getting cold. Let's go back inside." Hastur
took her hand gently and spoke very quietly. For a moment, he appeared to be listening to some interior voice,
and she could sense a light brush of awareness, as if a
feather had been passed across her brow. "So you do
have *laran,* and some of the Alton Gift, Marja."

Margaret held back a shudder. The word *laran* made
her blood seem cold, and she felt that thing inside her,
that voice that told her to stay apart and not ask questions, stir into life. She struggled to resist it. "Whatever
the Alton Gift is, I don't believe I have it. At least, I
hope I don't. Ever since I arrived, things have been insane for me, what with the feeling that I might be overhearing thoughts, and getting peeks into the future, and
meeting relatives I did not know I had! I don't like it!
And I don't want anything to do with spooky gifts or
Telepathic Councils or anything else. I just want to finish
my companion Ivor's work—our work for the University
and . . . I don't seem to know *anything*! And let me tell
you, for a scholar to know nothing is a very bad situation!" She could feel her frustration boiling up again.

"A scholar? At University?" His eyes lit up. "Tell me
what it is like. I always wanted . . . but this is not the
time for that. It must have been difficult for you to be
stumbling around Thendara—how long have you been
here?"

"About a week, I guess. I've kind of lost track, what
with Ivor's death and . . ." Her wail was that of a tired
child, for tears began to fill her eyes again.

Regis Hastur did not attempt to stop her tears, but
waited calmly, finishing his wine, until she ceased. When
she had wiped her face, he said, "I was certain you had
the Gift when you were a very small child. That was
why—"

At that moment the door into the garden opened, and
a woman came out, followed by Danilo. The lady smiled,
a warm, friendly gesture, and came forward, extending
her hands. She was full-figured, and had the cheerful
expression of someone who sees the world with delight.
Margaret liked her in an instant. "Ah, here you are!
Regis, it is too cold to be out in the garden now! And

stop plaguing the girl with your plots and schemes. You must forgive him, child. He thinks he must carry the weight of this world on his shoulders, and sometimes he loses perspective." Marja found herself clasped in a warm embrace, a light kiss brushing her cheek.

Regis said, "This impulsive creature is my consort, Linnea Storn, Lady Hastur. Linnea, this is Lew Alton's daughter, Marguerida." He seemed amused by his consort's words, and a subtle tension left his body in her presence.

Exhausted, Margaret asked, "Are you a relative, too?"

Lady Hastur chuckled and patted her cheek. "We are distant cousins, kinswoman, but I might have been your mother. At one time there was a plan to marry me to Lew—I was fifteen, I believe—but he declined and broke my maidenly heart. Which is just as well, for otherwise I would not have become Lady Hastur, which suits me very well, you see." She smiled at Regis, and he returned it with a look of real affection.

Linnea released her, and Margaret found herself being scrutinized again by the paxman Danilo. There was something in his gaze which disturbed her. It was not that he was overtly hostile, but there was a subtle menace in his look that chilled her to the marrow. She felt that if he gazed at her too long, she would cease to be Margaret Alton and become someone entirely different. But who? Fury and terror swelled in her breast, and she fought it off. She was imagining things again! There was nothing at all threatening in his stance or expression. Indeed, if she had met him under other circumstances, she would have thought him innocuous.

"I am sure it does," she answered weakly. She felt she was going to drown in too much information, and too damn many relatives all at once. And the worst part was, the more she learned, the less she felt she knew.

Fifteen! Margaret did not doubt Lady Linnea, but she still found that disturbing. Why so young? It was easier to think about that than about the other things, the ones that buzzed like bees in her brain, warring with a compulsion to be silent. "That seems very young to marry. Why do you have that custom?" Her tactlessness demon prompted the question before she could censor it, and she blushed to the roots of her hair. A slight breeze ruffled the silky stuff, sending her bangs tickling her forehead and cooling her blazing cheeks.

"We have both a high infant mortality rate and a low birth rate. I have been fortunate with my children, but many others are less so." Linnea answered her as if the question were perfectly appropriate. "We treasure our children here, and we want to have as many as we can."

Margaret had spent most of her life on planets of the Federation, where the populations were both limited and controlled, either by law or custom, and she found the idea of having lots of children rather appalling. It was only on backwater worlds, primitive worlds, where children were born in large numbers. And she knew there was no good reason for infant mortality, for Terran technologies made child bearing almost risk-free.

There were so many puzzles about this planet. It wasn't just the absence of motored vehicles, but something that looked as if they had rejected technology outright. "But did you *want* to get married at fifteen?"

"Certainly. It was my duty."

"Duty?"

Regis gave his consort a sharp look, and Linnea lifted her brows in response. "We possess certain talents, here on Darkover, and we have discovered, over the centuries, that the best way to conserve them is to marry young," she answered.

"Talents? You mean you have a sort of breeding program?"

Linnea made a small moue with her generous mouth. "You could say that—though I dislike the metaphor. It makes me feel too much like a brood mare."

Margaret was shocked. More than that, she was disgusted. She realized that it had something to do with these Gifts Rafe and Hastur had mentioned, and that these apparently friendly new relatives were probably thinking of marrying her off to keep her genes on the planet. No wonder her father had left!

"How interesting," she answered feebly. "I think I must go now. It has been a very long day, and I want to get back to Master Everard's before it gets too dark." *I can't take any more of this! If I don't get away quickly, I will start to howl.*

Lady Hastur looked distressed. "But, surely, you are staying here at the Castle, child."

Not on your life! Margaret wanted to escape the huge building as expeditiously as possible. She knew that there was a chamber above, with a carpet she could recognize, unless it had been changed in the past twenty years. It belonged to the Altons, to her father, and that there were probably servants scurrying about, changing the linens and airing the rooms. She could almost feel the bustle of activity, and knew that she could have found her way to the rooms almost without a guide. The knowledge made her shiver with discomfort.

From the expressions on the faces of Lord and Lady Hastur and the enigmatic Danilo, she realized that her feelings had been almost shouted. Margaret wanted to be polite, to be properly diplomatic, a credit to her family, while at the same time she wanted to run away as fast as her tired legs would carry her.

With meticulous politeness, she said, "I am sure it would be wonderful to stay here, but I am leaving Thendara as soon as I can arrange it. I do have work to do, and the death of my companion, Ivor Davidson, has delayed me already."

"Work? I don't understand," Lady Hastur responded.

Margaret decided that she had to take a firm line with these people. Otherwise they would continue to assume she was there to serve their ends, and not her own. She drew a ragged breath. "I am not here for your Telepathic Council or anything else. I am here to study and collect folk music as a Scholar of the University, and that is precisely what I intend to do. Nothing else!"

"Collect folk music?" Linnea sounded bemused. "I must have misunderstood." Lady Hastur gave her husband a helpless look, as if to say: "I tried, dear."

She could almost hear them, speaking in one another's minds, trying to marshal arguments to manage her. She wasn't having any of that! They could not understand her, and she did not feel she understood them. Her skull throbbed, and her knees ached, and she just wanted to get away.

"We certainly will not force you to stay here," Danilo said, speaking for the first time since he had offered her wine. There was something in the way he said it that made her think this was not quite true, that he could have forced her to remain if he had chosen to. "However, it would be a good thing for Darkover if you did. You belong here, whether you realize it or not."

Quite rudely, Margaret looked the paxman directly in the eyes. All she saw was a rather good-looking man somewhere between forty and fifty, with light-colored hair and deep lines along his mouth, as if he had suffered some great tragedy. There was, indeed, a kinship between Danilo's somber expression and that of her father. *But who was he to speak with such authority?*

She found she did not dislike him, but that she mistrusted him deeply. He was clearly devoted to Hastur, and something more. Margaret wondered if he was Regis' servant or his lover, and was mortified at herself. But she was certain that whatever his position was, Danilo would do anything necessary to protect Regis, even kill for him. "No doubt you believe that, but I don't." *I won't be involved with your local problems!*

Margaret could feel waves of incomprehension drifting across her, but she just didn't care. She knew she could have been more tactful to Lady Hastur and Danilo, but they were not listening to her. They were too involved with their damned breeding program and their Council to hear her. It was like trying to talk to Lew—he wasn't good at listening either. Maybe it was a racial thing. Perhaps all the inbreeding they had done for centuries had done something to their hearing.

The utter ridiculousness of this thought lightened her mood a little. *A year ago—hell, a week ago—the thought of meeting my father's kinsmen would have delighted me. Now it just makes me angry—no, scared. I won't be used again!* The image of the silver-eyed man rose in her mind, and made her tremble. *I just want to get away from these people, from feeling like they are walking around in my mind.*

"Thank you for meeting me. I regret I can't stay. Now, if you will excuse me." She gave a little bow, a clumsy movement which betrayed her fatigue, and started for the door. Margaret saw her uncle standing just under the shadow of it, and almost ran toward him to escape from Regis, Linnea, and the ambiguous paxman.

"I'll walk you back to Music Street," Captain Scott announced when she came up to him.

Margaret wanted to weep with gratitude. "All right—so long as you promise not to plague me with more duties and obligations I have no intention of honoring."

"You are determined to go on as if you were not the heiress of one of the Domains, then? To wander around doing this 'work' of yours, when Darkover needs you?" He sounded troubled and rather sad.

"Exactly!" The viciousness of her reply startled her a little. She was too close to the ragged edge of exhaustion to care.

"You are most decidedly Lew's child," he replied, with a somewhat sardonic smile.

" 'What's bred in the bone will come out in the flesh,' " she quoted tartly.

"If you only knew how true that was, Marguerida." Rafe gave a little sigh. "You are going to need permits to leave Thendara, you know. Will you at least let me help you get them?"

Margaret laughed a little, comforted by his steady presence. At last someone was behaving rationally! "I may be stubborn, but I never object to anyone making themselves useful."

8

♦

*T*he cemetery was clothed in mist, and she wandered between the worn headstones, looking for something or someone. It was night, dark and star-pocked, and a violet moon was rising from the horizon. Finally she came to a mound of fresh earth, banked with wilted blooms. She could smell the balsam in the air, and the scent of turned earth beneath her feet.

A wraithlike figure rose from the mound of earth, and her breath caught in her throat. Perhaps Ivor was not dead! What if he had been buried alive? What if he was suffocating in the neat, Darkovan coffin he was laid in? The features of the figure were shadowed and indistinct, and she peered at the head, terrified and curious all at once. It had its back to her, and all she could see was smooth hair along a long skull.

The figure turned and moved toward her. She waited, tensed to flee, expecting the bare bones of a dead man. For a moment the face was too shrouded in mist to see clearly, and then she saw the squared jaw and scarred cheek of Lew Alton. He looked at her and gave a crooked smile, then extended his hand to her.

Margaret sat up in her bed, her heart pounding and her breath ragged. Her throat ached with terror, and it was dry and painful. Images spun in her mind as she tried to tell herself it was only a dream. What was her father doing in Ivor's grave, and why was he reaching for her? She sank back into the pillows, fresh tears welling in her eyes, and pulled the blankets up around her. It was only a dream!

The morning following Ivor's funeral, Margaret presented herself at Terran HQ, dressed once again in her Scholar's uniform, and armed with all of the correct doc-

uments. Then she waited. It took two hours to get to
see a bored clerk who sent her to a computer terminal
to fill out forms. The smell of HQ gave her a nasty
headache, and the overwarm air made her sweat.

After she completed the forms, which were complex,
confusing, and ambiguous, she pressed the "transmit"
command, rose, and headed for one of the refreshment
machines. It accepted her credit chit without trouble,
and gave her a cup of lukewarm mud pretending to be
coffee in return. She was making a face over it when
she heard her name called. She returned to the clerk,
who handed her a disk and sent her on to another office.
There she waited again, to see another bureaucrat, mus-
ing that efficient and bureaucracy seemed to be mutually
antagonistic terms. She wished she had something to
read, but the office was empty even of posted notices,
let alone any publications. She was so bored she would
have read the latest proceedings of the Federation Senate if it had been at hand.

The thought of the Senate brought back the nightmare, and she began to sink into a morbid mood. Margaret stared at her boots and tried to shake it away, but it
seemed to have taken a firm grasp on her mind, and
would not be shrugged off. She almost didn't hear her
name when it was called, as she was coiled deep in
misery.

A stern-looking woman sat behind a metal desk,
drumming her fingers. She did not rise when Margaret
entered the office, and she did not look at all friendly.
A modest metal sign sat on the desk. It read "Major
Thelma Wintergreen," and looking at the forbidding
countenance, Margaret thought she was well-named.

"I doubt we can permit you to continue Professor Davidson's survey of native folk music, Miss Alton," Wintergreen began without preamble. "You are too young
to undertake such a mission, you do not have the proper
credentials, and besides, it is not a task for a solitary
woman. I cannot imagine why permission was given for
such an unnecessary and expensive undertaking in the
first place. The local music can be of no interest to anyone but the locals."

Margaret was outraged. Didn't have the proper credentials? Who did Wintergreen think she was? She held

in her temper by force of will and ignored the throbbing in her temples. "Are you a trained musicologist, Major?"

"Certainly not!"

"Then you are hardly in any position to make a judgment about the value of Darkovan music, are you?" Margaret forced her mouth into a smile that was, she knew, closer to a snarl. "Captain Scott led me to believe there would not be a problem transferring the grant to me."

"Who?" Wintergreen's mouth went pinched, and her eyes squinted.

"Captain Rafael Scott." She realized she should have tried to find him while she was sitting around and waiting. Her brain seemed stuffed with cotton. He had offered his help, and she had agreed on their walk back from Comyn Castle. But this morning she had just started off without him. Why was she so damned independent? Margaret realized she didn't even know what section he was in, or if he really had the influence to make it easier for her. On the other hand, the invocation of his name clearly carried a lot of weight with the woman.

The Major looked displeased, and tapped something into her terminal. Then she folded her hands in front of her on the desk and stared at Margaret. "Just how do you know Captain Scott?"

"We are related."

Wintergreen's jaw clenched. She tapped another command into the terminal, then stared at the screen with a look of fury that surprised Margaret. She could feel waves of rage and envy radiating toward her, and she could not imagine what cause the woman had to be jealous of her. "There is no record of it," the woman snarled.

"Captain Scott is my mother's brother, whether it is in your records or not."

As if his name had conjured him into being, Rafe walked through the office door. Margaret had rarely been so glad to see anyone in her life. He gave her a smile, patted her shoulder, then turned to Wintergreen.

"What's the problem, Major?"

Wintergreen looked apprehensive now, and, if anything, angrier than before. "This isn't any business of yours, Scott! I am not going to let this young woman go traipsing off into the hinterlands. Cottman is no place for a woman to go wandering around alone!"

"How would you know, Major, when you never leave HQ at all?"

"Why should I? There is nothing out there but a bunch of backward indigenes who don't even have the sense to want . . ."

"Thelma, your prejudice is showing." Margaret could hardly believe the tone of Scott's voice. It was hard and authoritative, quite unlike the pleasant and almost modest man she had met the day before. "You really should put in for a transfer, you know."

"You keep your nose out of my business, Scott!"

"Gladly. Just give her the necessary documents, and we'll be gone."

Something like malice shadowed Wintergreen's features. "I don't think so, Captain. She isn't a full professor, just a clerk."

"She is fully trained, and she has been in the field for years, on more worlds than you have ever visited. And she is a Scholar, not a clerk. Stop this behavior—it does you no credit whatever."

Margaret gave her uncle a glance. He must have called up her records after they parted in front of Master Everard's the night before. She felt the warmth of gratitude flood her limbs.

"How dare you!"

"Thelma, everyone in HQ knows you loathe and despise Darkover and the Darkovans. I expect even people who have never met you know it. You are the wrong person for this job, and if that gets into your records, you know, you can kiss your chances of promotion goodbye. Now, be a lamb and let Margaret get on with her business."

"It is out of the question. She knows nothing about . . ."

"I was born on Darkover, Major."

"There is no record . . ."

"If you look under the correct spelling, A-L-T-O-N, you will find out that my niece was indeed born here." Rafe cut in. He turned toward Margaret. "I noticed, when I logged on, that some idiot has used an E instead of an A."

Margaret shrugged. "That has happened before, but I thought I had it straightened out." *Sometimes I think that Terrans are spelling impaired.*

Precisely! "And the first name would be Marguerida, Major Wintergreen," Rafe continued dryly. Margaret hardly noticed, so stunned was she by the brief mental interchange. She knew she had not imagined it, and she only wished she had.

If looks could have killed, Scott would have been dead on the floor. As it was, Major Wintergreen grudgingly accessed something on her terminal and gave a small grunt as she read the display. "I suppose you think that being the daughter of a Senator gives you some sort of special privileges," she snarled.

"Actually, I don't. I've never used my father's influence. I have never needed to." Margaret had a kind of quiet pride in the truth of that statement.

The Major made a face as if she had bitten into a ripe fruit and found half a worm, hit a command key, and waited. A stack of flimsies popped out of the slot which concealed the printer in her desktop, and she almost flung them at the girl. "Take these to room 411. And don't blame me if you get raped and murdered out there in the hills!"

"What? And deny you the pleasure of saying 'I told you so'? I promise I'll come back and haunt you if anything happens to me," Margaret replied, allowing her dislike of the Major to spill from her tongue.

Scott escorted her to 411, leading her through several corridors and up lifts and down two flights of stairs. "You never would have found your way alone," he assured her.

"I can see that. This place is a worse maze than Comyn Castle. Why was she so hostile?"

"I don't know the whole story, but she screwed up badly on her last posting, and it made her bitter. Darkover is not the sort of place that Terrans want to come to—it's become a kind of demotion to come here, during the past few years."

"Is everyone here like her?"

"Hardly. We have a lot of very good people here,

dedicated people who have the best interests of Darkover at heart. At least they think they have the best interests—which is bringing Terran progress to Darkover. Regrettably, what the Darkovans want and what the Terrans imagine is good for them are not always the same thing. I have a foot in both places, and like you, I am a citizen of two worlds. That isn't easy. The Terrans made some dreadful blunders in the past, and the Darkovans did, too. One of the things your father undertook to do was heal some of those wounds, by keeping Darkover protected but not excluded from the Federation."

Even though it was obvious now, Margaret had never thought of the Senator as a servant of the planet he represented. She felt not only ignorant, but stupid because she had paid so little attention to his work. She knew it was not entirely her own fault, that she had been rebuffed in her own attempts to make contact with her father. The dream came back, and she felt a cold hand clamp her heart. What if he were dead?

She shook her head to clear it, and her hair began to uncoil against her neck. Damn silky stuff. It was only a dream! Ivor's death had disturbed her; he had been like a father to her, and it was not really surprising that his passing had brought up her fears of loss and abandonment. Besides, Margaret and the Senator had abandoned one another years before. Hadn't they?

Room 411 was unlike the narrow offices she had spent the morning sitting in. It was furnished with comfortable couches, draped in native textiles, and it smelled of Darkover. There were some fine masks hung against the walls, and she frowned at them. One in particular disturbed her—a woman's face with flames rising from the scalp in place of hair. She felt herself tremble and forced herself to look away. Margaret frowned at her reaction. She had seen masks before, and they had never given her gooseflesh.

A man rose from behind a carved table. He blinked, his eyes hidden by a pair of spectacles that belonged in a museum. His hair was grizzled, and he sported a patchy beard that looked as if it grew at random along his sunken cheeks. But he smiled, and that gave his ancient features an animation and a friendliness which took away the nasty taste of Major Wintergreen, which she had not known contaminated her mood until it was gone.

"So, you are Margaret Alton! How delightful to meet you! I am Brigham Conover, Head of Ethnology here."

"Professor Conover." Margaret extended her hand in a friendly fashion. "I read your paper on the Dry Towns wedding customs. It was one of the few things in the archives about Darkover that wasn't restricted." They shook hands and grinned at each other like naughty children looking for mischief. Conover reminded her of Ivor, in his younger and stronger years. Now she was close enough to him, she could see his blue eyes had a lively twinkle and there were deep laugh lines around them.

Rafe cleared his throat. "I'll be off now, Marguerida. I'll come back in about an hour, if that's all right, and get you some lunch."

"Thank you, Rafe. You've been wonderful."

"Sit down, sit down." Conover gestured toward one of the couches. "Would you like some tea?"

"I would. My throat feels like ten miles of bad road. The air is so dry in here." She watched him bustle about, and felt the tension in her body begin to dissipate. Maybe now she could get some straight answers. He brought two steaming mugs and gave her one.

"Now, how can I help you?"

"I intend to complete the work that Professor Davidson and I came to Darkover to do, and every time I turn around, I run into stone walls. At least, that is what it feels like. When we got posted here, I couldn't get data from the central files, which was very odd. Why is that?"

"You want a simple answer to a complex question. I will do my best." Conover paused and stared into the vapor rising from his mug. "You know that Darkover is a protected planet, neither a full member of the Federation nor entirely apart. The history behind that is before my time, but I know a few of the facts. Twenty years or so ago there was a rebellion here, in which a number of people died, important people. Your father was part of it. He went away to become the voice of the planet to the Federation, and Regis Hastur started to try to bring Darkover into some sort of agreement with the Federation. That has not been easy—Darkovan culture resists any kind of change. And one of the things that occurred was that a great deal of information about the planet that would ordinarily have been accessible became restricted."

"Why? Surely Darkover presents no threat to the Federation."

"There is no way to predict what is perceived as a threat, Miss Alton."

"Oh. Won't you call me Margaret, please."

"Certainly—if you will call me Brigham. I can see by your expression that you are not satisfied. The problem is that there is a great deal about Darkover which remains a mystery to us here at HQ, and mysteries and secrets always create distrust between nations. So, the Federation classified much of what was known about Darkover and chose a waiting game. Those who make such decisions—and let me assure you, most of them have never even been here—believe that eventually Darkover will capitulate, open its doors, reveal its secrets, and become just another Federation member. At the same time, the Darkovans remain obstinate. They don't want to accept everything Terran and give up the way they have lived for thousands of years. I am in the middle. My job is to be an ethnologist and gather data for use by the Terran Federation."

"What kind of 'use'?" She sipped her tea and tasted the honey in it. Margaret was not sure she liked the sound of any of this. With a small start she realized that her father had probably held the Federation at bay all those years, and now that he had resigned, she worried about what might happen. What an idiot she was, not to have paid better attention, to have appreciated that her father might have been doing something worthwhile!

Conover paused a moment before answering. "What they really want is to discover what weaknesses exist in the Darkovan culture which can be manipulated to the advantage of the Federation. I confess I have enormous reservations about wholesale interference with any local culture. I've seen the results too often. The history of Terra is a history of cultures destroyed by progress and arrogance.

"So, what do you do? Surely you don't *suppress* data?" The very idea scandalized the scholar in her.

"That is one sin I have so far avoided, Margaret." He gave a sharp bark of mirthless laughter. "No, I don't hide data—I am just very careful what subjects are studied. You see, I am in charge of giving the grants which allow research. So, we learn about Darkovan music and marital customs and other fairly harmless matters, but we do not delve too deeply into the essential Darkovan mysteries."

"Such as?"

Conover reflected for a moment. "There are no learned treatises on the Alton Gift or the other peculiar talents which have been observed, Margaret."

"I still don't understand why." She was startled. He knew about the Gifts. It seemed as if everywhere she turned, people knew things she didn't. Well, it didn't matter. Margaret was not going to get involved in local matters, and as for her supposed Gift—to hell with it. If she had the occasional bit of telepathic interchange, as she had with Rafe earlier, it wasn't going to bother her. She would keep herself apart, as she always had. She ignored the cold, sad feeling that rose in her chest at that thought.

"There are people within the Federation who would exploit those talents, and I do not believe that that would be in the best interest of Darkover. It is a difficult path to tread." He gave a little sigh.

"But if it's such a big secret, how do you *know* about the Alton Gift. I never even heard of it myself, until yesterday."

"Your father was kind enough to grant me several interviews before I came here, and he was not reticent, once he had taken my measure. That is how I recognized you when you came in—he has a portrait of you in his office."

"He does?" Her head was beginning to ache again.

"Yes, and he is very proud of you."

She made a face. "It's a pity he never mentioned that to me." She hid her fury as well as she could. Lew was confiding in Conover when he hadn't had the consideration to tell her things she needed to know about her own heritage. Didn't he trust her? How could he—they barely knew each other.

Margaret took a long, slow breath and tried to calm herself. She shifted her body on the couch into a more easy position and forced herself to let go of her rage. It was a struggle, and her anger almost won out. She found her eyes were moist with unshed tears, and she blinked them away.

"So, tell me, Brigham, what is the best way for me to go about finishing the work I came here to do?"

"You will need a guide, since you will be going into the Kilghard Hills. It is rough country, and the people are not entirely friendly. You have the advantage that one look at you will convince them you are a native of Darkover. But you will need more than that, I think."

Margaret laughed. "I have already encountered that— when I went to the clothiers, they acted as if I were royalty. I nearly went nuts. They kept insisting I needed a ball gown for when I went to the Castle, not working clothes. I haven't owned a ball gown since I got my degree at the University, and I couldn't understand it, nor why they kept calling me *domna* instead of *mestra*. Then Ivor died, and I was too busy trying to arrange burial to think about it. You can imagine my surprise when I bumped into Rafe Scott yesterday and found out I was some sort of heiress and that I had relatives all over the place. He took me up to Comyn Castle, and I met Lord and Lady Hastur—who both turn out to be some kind of cousins of mine. And then they expected me to stay there, and they were rather hurt when I insisted I was going to finish Ivor's work. They were very courteous, but I felt as if I were smothering."

"You are used to the relative freedom women enjoy in the Federation, Margaret. Darkovan women are more confined, and except for the Renunciates, rarely travel."

"Renunciates? What are those—nuns?"

Conover grinned, and his eyes lit up. "No, not nuns, at least not in the sense that you know that word. The Renunciates Guild, or Free Amazons, are a group of women who have chosen to remove themselves from the restrictions of Darkovan culture. They do not marry, which is almost unthinkable here, and if they bear a child, they do so without giving the child his father's name. They began by functioning as guides and escorts, and then expanded their role to include educators and midwives. They have become the principal agency of spreading Terran knowledge on Darkover during the past twenty-five years. Remarkable women."

"Free Amazons? Do they call themselves that?"

"Very astute of you. No, that is a name that has become attached to them—most women on Darkover wouldn't know an Amazon from a rabbit-horn. The Renunciates are something of a cultural anomaly, independent females in a very patriarchal society. They learn to read and write, which is still unusual on Darkover, and they bow to no man in any matter. Thus the nickname Amazons. They study everything from martial arts to medicine. Several Terrans have even become Renunciates—much to the displeasure of people like Major Wintergreen."

"You mean they've gone native?"

"Essentially. There is something about Darkover that speaks to some of us—I can't explain it, but it happens. Genetically, Darkovans are human, but they are more than that. They have something extra, and that either attracts you or repels you. If you feel at home on Darkover, there is a good chance you will want to remain here, and that makes people like Thelma very uncomfortable."

"What about you, Brigham?"

"I have a Darkovan wife and two children. If I were a little younger, I would have gone over the wall. Instead I have chosen to follow the example of Magda Lorne and some others, like Captain Scott, and tried to become a bridge between our worlds. It isn't easy, but it is, in some ways, the most satisfying thing I have ever done. Now, let's get down to the business at hand!"

By the time Rafe returned, Margaret was ravenous enough to eat the tasteless food in the HQ cafeteria without a fuss. She had learned a great deal from Conover—important things about the danger of forest fires in the Kilghard Hills and the continuing problem of brigands. He had given her copies of maps, and answered most of her immediate questions. It wasn't until she sat down at the table in the cafeteria that she realized she had not asked him about the Telepathic Council or any details about the mysterious Alton Gift. It was as if she had already entered into the conspiracy of silence that surrounded so many things Darkovan.

"I'll show you the way to Thendara House," Rafe announced when she had finished eating. "They will supply you with a guide, and help you get the supplies you will need. By the way, can you ride a horse?"

"As a matter of fact, I can. I had a horse when I was growing up on Thetis, and the only sport I pursued at University was riding. It has been a long time, of course, but I think I can manage." The mention of horses brought back the memory of riding along the surf, the wind against her face and the smell of salt rising in her breath. "The horses they had at University were pretty tame, and I couldn't afford to get a better mount."

Rafe seemed amused. "Did you go in for dressage?"

Margaret shook her head. "No, I did some jumping— and a lot of cross-country racing. I love to give a horse its head. It's like flying!"

"Agreed. But don't try too much of that in the Kilgh-ards. The ground is too rough for racing—though they used to have proper races at Armida at Midsummer, when I was a boy. The Armida horses are famous on Darkover—worth a king's ransom."

She barely heard him. "I'm finished. Let's go. I can't stand being in here another minute! The air smells funny, and it makes my throat hurt."

Thendara House was a large building a few blocks beyond the boundaries of the Terran Sector. From the outside it did not look special, and certainly not like what Conover described as a "cultural anomaly." It looked exactly like the houses on either side. It was constructed of local stone, and it gleamed in the afternoon light, a plain, strong building with no windows on the ground floor that faced the street. Only the plaque above the doorbell gave any indication that it was more than a private home.

Rafe took her as far as the stoop, bade her farewell, and patted her on the shoulder again. Margaret watched him as he walked away, his back straight in his dark uniform, and tried not to feel forlorn. As he moved away, she had the sense that he was hiding some strong feeling, a yearning of some sort, which was puzzling. Surely he did not want to go off and help her with her research! She wrenched herself out of her confused emotions, and rang the doorbell.

The door was answered almost immediately by a cheerful-looking woman in her late teens or early twenties. She did not bow or curtsy, as had most of the Darkovans Margaret had encountered so far, but looked the visitor directly in the eye, taking in her Terran garb with a swift glance. The young woman's hair was short, in contrast to the other women Margaret had seen. She had a rag in one hand, and a smudge of dust darkened part of her forehead. She looked happy and well-fed and friendly as a pup. It did not go with Margaret's mental image of people who called themselves Renunciates, which made her smile slightly. She was making too many assumptions—which a Scholar must never do.

"I have come to see about hiring a guide," Margaret said. She wished Rafe had not taken himself off so quickly, then reminded herself sternly that she was on her own, and that was how she wanted it. She didn't need anyone, did she?

"Come in," the girl answered. "I'll go find *Mestra* Adriana for you—anything to get out of dusting! I joined the Renunciates because I wanted to be independent, but I am still doing housework."

"Technology has never solved the problem of dust," Margaret answered dryly.

"You mean Terranan women do housework? I always thought they had machines to do everything."

"No, not quite everything."

"I'll put you in the parlor until I find Mother. I'm not really supposed to answer the door, but I was right here, and it seemed silly to wait for one of the others." She ushered Margaret into a pleasant room and hurried away, leaving her to puzzle over why the girl was not supposed to open the front door.

Margaret looked around the room while she waited. It was well furnished, if a little shabby. There were thick rugs on the stone floor, deep chairs with upholstery rubbed shiny by use, and on the wall, there were some posters. Margaret examined these with interest, for they

were clearly made on a printer's press with movable
type. The ink was heavier in some places than in others,
and the paper had never seen the innards of a box. She
looked curiously at an announcement of a midwifery
class, and realized how much she took for granted that
childbearing was a simple matter. She noticed another
poster. It described the history of the Bridge Society,
founded by someone called both Magda Lorne and Margali n'ha Ysabet. She remembered that Conover had
mentioned Magda Lorne, and wondered if she were still
around. She might be able to answer some of Margaret's
questions. Deep in her reading, she almost did not hear
a gentle cough behind her.

A woman in her forties stood in the parlor. She had
dark hair and green eyes and a chin that spoke of deter-
mination. She was dressed in dark green, and she looked
both friendly and formidable. "Welcome to Thendara
House. I am Adriana n'ha Marguerida. I understand
from Jillian that you wish to hire a guide." She spoke
Terran as if it twisted her tongue.

Margaret answered her in *casta*. "I am Margaret
Alton, and, yes, I wish to find a guide to take me into
the Kilghards. I have all the necessary permits and papers and . . ."

"Papers! Pah! Where would the Terranan be without
their permits? They think a bit of paper means something, as if a person could be measured by it. What foolishness! You must excuse me—I get very weary of forms
and passes and permits. And tact is not one of my virtues. My poor mother often remarked upon it."

Margaret warmed to this forthright woman. "I am not
very tactful, either. I have just spent the morning at HQ
trying to work my way through the layers of paperwork,
and I share your distaste for it."

Mestra Adriana nodded and smiled. "They don't seem
to realize that Darkover got along just fine for centuries
without a thousand clerks making pieces of nonsense
called permits. Now, sit down and tell me why you want
to go the Kilghards." She paused while Margaret took
a seat. "Alton?" She looked at Margaret intently for a
moment. "You are not a Terran."

"No, I am not. I was born here, but I left when I was
very young." *Not so young I don't remember the smells*

and colors of Darkover, she thought grimly. The House smelled good, of woodsmoke and rich stews. It smelled right, as the house on Thetis never had. Even when Dio cooked, it had never smelled quite this nice.

"I see." *Mestra* Adriana studied her again, and Margaret was sure that very little escaped those penetrating green eyes.

Margaret stifled a sigh and prepared for another frustrating recital of her parentage. But *Mestra* Adriana asked no personal questions, thus belying her claim of tactlessness. "You speak the language well," was all she said.

"Thank you. It seems to come back to me in great lumps. And sometimes I still don't understand half of what people are saying." She leaned back into the armchair.

"Now, what is your purpose in going to the Kilghards?" *Alton! Is she going back to Armida? What a nosy old woman I am!*

Margaret heard these unspoken thoughts quite clearly, and felt a blush rise along her throat. She felt as if she were prying. And, worse, she felt as if she had no control over it. Her stomach clenched around the dreadful meal from the cafeteria, and she wondered if she were going to be sick.

Armida. Rafe had mentioned that it was the Alton stronghold, and that she was the heir to Alton. Likely it was in the middle of some village where there were lots of Altons, and everyone spoke in riddles. Even if they had the most beautiful horses in the civilized galaxy, she had no intention of going there! She brought herself back to the task at hand.

"I was sent to Darkover by University to do research and collect music—folk songs and ballads. I came with my mentor, Professor Ivor Davidson, but he died suddenly. I intend to complete his work. We had planned to spend some time here in Thendara, then go into the back country. I decided that I want to take advantage of the season, and do the rural work first, since, if what I have been told is accurate, travel will become more difficult after the summer is over. The people at HQ tried to talk me out of it, and there was this Major Wintergreen who decided it was too dangerous. But I got the things I needed anyhow." *Thanks to Rafe! Did I remember to tell him how grateful I was?*

Adriana chuckled. "Dear old Thelma! She is a prickly one. She has done everything she could to destroy the work the Bridge Society has done. A most dislikable female, to be sure."

Margaret hesitated for a moment. "She certainly seemed quite disagreeable to me, although we were only together for a brief time." She decided that it was a good thing Rafe had intervened when he did, because she would probably have lost her temper completely.

"She gets worse with further acquaintance, believe me. Folk music? Odd sort of reason to go tramping around the hills, *Domna* Alton." There was a tone of disbelief in her voice, and beneath it, suspicion and wariness.

"Not if you are a musicologist, *Mestra* Adriana. To me it seems like the most logical thing in the world."

"Have you done this before?"

"Yes. I have been on several planets with my mentor, studying the musical forms of the local people."

"How very peculiar. I don't think I will ever understand these things. We had a woman here, a time back, who was wanting to know all about the Renunciates for some book she was going to write. Said she was an anthropologist, but I thought she was looking for scandal. I don't know if she ever wrote her book—she went away after a while and I never found out what happened to her. It just seems very impractical to me."

"I am a Scholar, and collecting apparently useless facts is what I do. Besides, I love music, and I love my work."

"You must, if you dared the dragon Wintergreen in her den and escaped to tell the tale. How did you manage it?" The green eyes glinted with intense curiosity.

"I had some help from Captain Rafael Scott, who is a kinsman of mine."

Yes, he would be. "Very well. Let me see if I can think of someone suitable to accompany you."

Margaret heard the thought and the spoken words at the same moment. Did everyone on Darkover walk around with genealogies rattling in their brains? She stood up, restless from too much time sitting in chairs, and returned to reading the Bridge Society history on the wall while *Mestra* Adriana cogitated. She was a little surprised that the woman did not consult a list, and realized that despite the printed posters on the wall, this was not a culture that relied on the written word so much as on memory.

"Ah! Rafaella is just the person!" *Besides, she needs the work. Maybe going about with a sober-sides like this young woman will settle her down a bit.*

Margaret heard the underthoughts as clearly as if they were spoken, and wondered why the unknown woman needed settling down. "Is she a good guide?"

"Certainly. It would not reflect well on the Guild if I gave you someone who could not do the work. But I chose her because she sings fairly well and will perhaps understand your work better than some of our other people. She was born in the Kilghards, and has kinsmen all over the hills."

"That sounds good," Margaret answered. "Where do I find her?"

"Go to the Horse Market tomorrow morning, and she will be waiting for you."

"How will I know her?" Margaret felt anxious again, having no idea where the Horse Market was. Oh, well, she could probably get someone to show her the way. Maybe young Geremy would be pleased to escape for a morning.

"We have a stall in the Horse Market—just ask for the Guild booth. You won't be able to miss her. Rafaella n'ha Liriel is unmistakable."

9

◆

When Margaret left Thendara House, she felt tired, but not as weary as she had during the previous days. She decided to visit Threadneedle Street on her way back to Master Everard's and see if either Ethan or Geremy could take her to the Horse Market the following morning. She now knew her way around much of central Thendara fairly well and did not hesitate in finding her way to the clothiers.

Aaron MacEwan was standing in the middle of his shop supervising the cutting of a garment by one of his apprentices, and Manuella was rolling up a bolt when Margaret came in. They both greeted her eagerly, with smiles and offers of tea, and she felt warmly welcomed after the sterile corridors of HQ. She told them she was going into the Kilghards, and they exchanged a look which spoke volumes.

"You will need some warm garments for that, *domna*. And that dress we sent you will not do for the hills. You will want a riding skirt, and a heavy tunic." He glanced with a measure of distain at her Terran garments.

Margaret was rather startled at this, because she had not really thought through the matter. She had planned to ride in her wretched uniform, hated though it was. So, before she knew it, she was bustled into the robing room by Manuella and offered a fine garment that covered her limbs but would allow her to ride astride. It was dark brown, very generously cut, warm, and extremely comfortable. A tunic of a paler brown slipped over her head, and once more she had the sensation of correctness she had felt when she touched the earth of Darkover at Ivor's grave.

She concluded her transactions, and asked if one of the boys could show her the way to the Horse Market

early the following morning. Manuella promised that
Ethan would be at Master Everard's at first light. She
gathered her purchases and set off for Music Street, well
content with a good day's work.

*The darkness of the void was broken by the swirl of
the galactic wheel, a spin of stars against the night She
floated between the stars effortlessly. This was the way to
travel, without drugs or smelly space ships! A figure
began to coalesce, first feet, then legs and torso, arms and
shoulders, and, at last, a head. Lew Alton, made of suns,
glared at her from the void. His single hand reached for
her, and his mouth moved as if he were trying to speak.
She felt her hands extend to him, and was caught in an
icy grasp. It was so cold she could not bear the touch,
and wrenched herself away. The stars winked out, and
she was alone in the blackness, screaming in the night.*

When the first light of morning touched Margaret's
face, she sat up, the remnants of the dream fading as
she opened her eyes. She shook herself free, and climbed
from the warm covers into the chill of the room. Everything except her toiletries and the clothes she was going
to wear had been packed the night before. She brushed
her teeth, and washed her face. Then she scrambled into
her clothes, eager to be gone. She slipped the russet
tunic over her head, and pulled the riding skirt on, yank-
ing at the drawstring waist. Margaret brushed her hair
until it was smooth, then coiled it into the butterfly clasp.
She only gave the mirror a quick, sidelong glance, to
make sure she was reasonably neat, biting her lower lip
in unease. She really hated reflective surfaces.

Satisfied with her appearance, Margaret slipped her
belt around her narrow waist. She grabbed her things
and went downstairs with as much haste as her baggage
allowed. It was not until she reached the ground floor
that she realized she should have left the task for Raimon, or one of the other servants. She shook her head.
She was used to helping, not being helped.

Anya was already up, and the house smelled of porridge. She found the housekeeper in the kitchen with
young Ethan. He was tucking into a large helping of the
cereal, his sharp features concentrated on the task at

hand. Margaret suspected that it was his second breakfast, and remembered that there had been a time when she had eaten with such appetite.

Margaret sat down at the big table in the kitchen, and Anya brought her a cup of tea and a bowl of porridge. There was honey and a pitcher of rich cream in the middle of the table, and Margaret shamelessly added both to her breakfast. She and Ethan smiled at each other as they ate, and she was grateful for his silence. She hated chatter first thing in the morning, and was impressed by his sensitivity. Lads his age only seemed to stop talking when they were asleep.

Master Everard came into the kitchen as they were finishing, his white locks tousled from sleep. He looked like some old tortoise, blinking in the morning light that streamed through the narrow windows. He sat down stiffly and Anya brought him a mug of tea.

"So, you are away to the hills, *chiya*. It has been a long time since I wandered there—years and years. My late wife was from the Kilghards. I met her when I was visiting there. She was so lovely." He gave a small sigh. "I shall miss you—it has been a great pleasure to have you in my house. My son is up there, and perhaps you will meet him on your journey. He is a good man, but he dislikes city life, and I see him all too rarely."

Margaret was touched by Everard's use of the endearment *chiya*, but it brought back an unwanted rush of memories. The red-haired woman who was her mother had used it, but without any affection, and that haunting man with the silver hair and eyes had called her that when he had left her at the orphanage. It was the first time she had recalled that incident so clearly, and it made her feel small and frightened. And angry, too, though she suppressed the feeling as quickly as she could.

"I will miss you as well, Master Everard. I have enjoyed my stay in your home, and trust I will return before I leave Darkover."

"Leave?"

"Well, yes. When I have completed Ivor's work, I will go back to University, of course." She said the words, but she did not believe them. At the same time, Margaret could not imagine remaining on this world for the rest of her life. It might be the home of her heart, but she was too much a citizen of the Federation to think of living on this almost primitive world. Not that she *needed* hot showers and computers, but she was used to them.

"But, I thought . . . well, I confess I assumed after your visit to Comyn Castle that . . ." Everard trailed off, confused and embarrassed.

Margaret looked at him for a long, silent moment. Did everyone in Thendara know about her meeting with Lord Hastur? It seemed an intolerable invasion of her cherished privacy for a second. Then she realized what a small community it was, really, compared to cities on other worlds. Thendara was more like a small town than a city, despite having a spaceport and a Terran sector.

"I am going to the Kilghards to complete Ivor's work—he would have wanted me to, I am certain—not to make any claims to the Alton Domain, no matter who tries to convince me otherwise." The crispness of her reply bordered on rudeness, and she felt dreadful as soon as the words were out of her mouth. At the same time it seemed terribly important to distance herself from the seductive whispers of Darkover, lest she find herself embroiled with matters she was certain had nothing to do with her. The sense of suffocation she had experienced in the castle garden returned, and she tried to breathe deeply. To conceal her discomfort she tried to think of something pleasant to say.

"I see." Master Everard looked sad. "Well, no man can make another's destiny, and all the wishing in the world will not make it so. You must follow your heart— though I think that perhaps you are running away from something, instead of running toward it."

"You may be right." Margaret had the feeling he had seen through her, and knew that she had been running away from things for most of her life. She had run away from Thetis to escape her father's sorrow, not knowing what it was, and she had become Ivor's musical assistant to avoid becoming close to anyone her own age. The thought of marriage made her skin crawl, and the idea of children was simply too dreadful to contemplate. There was some memory, deeply buried but powerful, that made her shrink from intimacy or physical contact.

She did not know why this was, but she knew it to be true.

"What shall I do with your master's instrument?" Everard asked.

"Ivor's guitar?" She had all but forgotten about it since she had let Master Everard carry it home after the funeral. Should she arrange to ship it back to Ida? That did not feel quite right. "Will you keep it for the present? I think Ivor would like that. And if his wife is able to come and claim his body, then she can take it home with her. I don't want to entrust it to the spaceways without an actual person going with it—silly of me." Her mind, she realized, was not really on the matter, and she didn't have time to go over to the com center and send a message, then wait for a reply. She wanted to get out of Thendara and away from people mistaking her for someone she never wanted to be, and she wasn't going to let anything prevent that.

The old man looked pleased. "I will be honored to keep it for as long as is needful, for it is a wonderful instrument. Do you think that the *Mestra* Doevidson will come here?"

"I don't know. She might, but it would be very expensive. Thank you for everything. I have loved staying here so much." She could barely manage to contain her impatience now.

"We have enjoyed having you—and, frankly, I will miss you. This house needs young people in it, and Erald is so rarely at home." He seemed a little sad, but he cheered up so quickly she could not be sure.

A few minutes later, she bade Anya and Master Everard farewell, and set out, with a stuffed and rather subdued Ethan. The lad carried one of her bags, and she carried her harp and the other. They were three streets away when Margaret noticed he was carrying a clumsy bundle in his free hand.

"What have you got there—your lunch?" Margaret asked with more humor than she felt.

"Naw." He gave her his friendly grin and hefted the lumpy object. "This would be too much for even my belly. Mother says I eat enough for three, and that I will beggar her before I grow up. She said the same to my older brother Jacob, so I don't mind much. If mothers cannot scold you for something real, they invent something, don't they?"

Margaret thought about this, and found no answering experience. Dio had never commented on her eating, her dress, or even the state of her room, which often appeared to have been the scene of one of Thetis' more violent hurricanes. The only scolding she had ever received was for pulling her hair up on top of her head and exposing her neck, or for looking directly—rudely, Dio said—into the eyes of others. "I suppose they do," she replied indifferently. "But you still haven't told me what you are carrying. Of course, if it is a secret, that is a different matter. I always keep other people's secrets."

"I know. You didn't say a word to Uncle Aaron about me wanting to be a spaceman."

"No, I didn't. It wasn't any of my business, and I thought he would not be pleased to hear of your ambitions from a stranger. I suspect he would not approve if he knew."

"Too right, *domna!* Aaron thinks the world begins and ends in Threadneedle Street. Do you know, he has never been out of Thendara in his whole life?"

"No, I didn't know, but I am not surprised. He loves his work, as I love mine, and I can see that he can't imagine doing anything else. It is often that way."

"Does it get better when you get older?"

Margaret thought about that as they trudged along streets so narrow that the morning sun had not yet warmed them. The little harp slung over one shoulder bumped against her hip with each step she took, and her bag was becoming heavy. She wondered how much farther it was to the Horse Market. She thought about her Uncle Rafe and Lord Hastur and their expectations that she would instantly become the holder of the Alton Domain. She thought about Lew Alton, who, she believed, had never really approved of her musical career. He had never spoken of it, but she knew he had hoped she would pursue politics or journalism instead.

"I don't think so, not really. No matter how old you get, there are always older people who think they know better."

"I thought so. My grannie is always after my father for being in trade instead of bettering himself."

My lord, the sociological implications of that, Margaret thought, trying not to wince. She supposed that all parents had plans for their children, and were often disappointed. Why hadn't humanity learned better after all these millions of years?

They turned into a broad square, where the pungent smell of horse manure, leather, and damp straw rose from the stones. There were dozens of booths made of heavy canvas ranged in ranks across the open square. Even at this hour, there was a great deal of activity— voices raised in the pleasant sound of commerce or just gossip.

In the center of the Market she noticed an open-air kitchen. As they passed it, Margaret could see a woman cooking crisp crullers in a cauldron of oil, pulling the hot pastries out with wooden tongs and spreading them on a cloth. A man in full trousers tucked into crimson boots and a brightly colored woven tunic offered her a coin, and the cook handed him two of the things. Margaret noticed the strange hat he wore, a turbanlike thing, and decided he must be a Dry Towner.

Despite having risen from the table a short while before, Margaret found her mouth watering. She remembered a pale hand offering her a pastry like that, and saw her own plump hand closing around the treat. She could taste the sweetness, and she found her throat tightening at the memory. Once she had known the name of the pastry, but now it eluded her.

Ethan led her toward a cloth stall on the other side of the Horse Market. Several women dressed in trousers and tunics were tending the horses which were stabled there. They had short hair, like the girl who had answered the door at Thendara House, and they wore belts with knives on them. Their faces were bronzed from working out of doors, and they looked both capable and formidable.

"Which one is Rafaella n'ha Liriel?" Margaret asked quietly. Not quietly enough, apparently, for a woman stood up from where she was bent over cleaning a horse's hoof and looked at them. She had remarkably red hair, as if her head were ablaze, and looked to be younger than Margaret by a few years. She took in

Ethan and Margaret in one quick glance, a look that spoke of a headstrong nature, and stepped forward.

"Just what the devil are you doing wearing my blouse?" she snapped, pointing at Margaret's garment.

"Your blouse?" For a moment Margaret was confused, and then she remembered that Manuella had told her that the clothes she had purchased on her first trip to Threadneedle Street had been made for someone named Rafaella. It had never occurred to her that the person who had been hired as her guide, was the *same* Rafaella, for she knew that it was a common name in Thendara. "I was given to understand it did not please you when it was done."

"I have changed my mind!" She lifted her chin, making her cap of curls toss merrily, and tried to stare Margaret down. Unfortunately, she was a bit shorter than Margaret, and she had to crane her neck. "I went away, and while I was on the trail, I decided that I liked it. But when I returned, MacEwan told me he had sold it. He made some excuse about how he couldn't afford to have things hanging around the shop—as if my mother and grandmother had not given him their custom for years and years."

Ethan scowled, and his fair skin reddened. "Uncle can't be expected to read minds. He don't have *laran, Mestra* Stuck-Up. *Domna* Alton got those clothes fair and square, so don't you go putting on your airs." The boy spoke firmly, though his adolescent voice cracked slightly in mid-scold. Beneath the words Margaret sensed something more, an emotional quality for which she had no immediate term. *No one talks to my* domna *like that!*

Then the word fealty sprang into her mind, and she realized something important about Darkovan culture she had not really understood before. She had sensed it in Regis Hastur's paxman, Danilo, and then again in Rafe Scott. It was not a blind, unthinking loyalty, as she had first believed, but a profound pride in the form of rule represented by the Comyn and the Domains. No wonder the Terrans had not been successful in converting Darkover into another colony of the Empire. For reasons of its own, the Terran Empire had decided that participatory democracy was the only tenable form of freedom. Margaret knew that there were many forms of

government in the Federation, and that they worked as
well as anything involving millions of people could. Still,
the Terrans tried to impose their ideas on all their member planets, often with sorry results. Clearly, the Darkovans liked the way things were and couldn't see any
good reason to change them.

Rafaella appeared as startled by this vigorous defense
as Margaret was herself. She glared down at the young
man. "You keep your tongue behind your teeth, Ethan
MacDoevid, or I'll buy my clothes from old Isaac next
time. Your uncle wouldn't be pleased to lose my
custom."

"Isaac," Ethan sneered. "He can't cut on the straight
with a rule. You will look like you were dressed by . . .
by a chervine."

The image this created in Margaret's mind was very
odd, and Rafaella seemed to find it amusing, too, for
she began to laugh in spite of herself. She ran her fingers
through her fiery hair, and looked, if anything, even
younger than she had before. Margaret wondered if she
was experienced enough to be a guide, and decided that
the trip must be much less dangerous than anyone had
suggested, if they would let her go off into the wild
with Rafaella.

"Everything has gone amiss this past tenday," Rafaella complained, as if to excuse her earlier rudeness.
"My horse got killed on my way south, and the one I
got to replace her turned out to be a sluggard. I was
late in completing my contract, which cost me dear, and
then I came back to find my new outfit had been sold
to a stranger. I designed the embroidery pattern myself!
And I had hardly gotten here when *Mestra* Adriana sent
word she had hired me to a Terranan." She paused in
this recital of woe and blushed slightly. "Don't think I
mind working for the Terranan, but they can be very
hard to please."

"She is no more a Terranan than you are," muttered
Ethan, still flushed with temper.

"Humph! Well, I am not sure I am better pleased to
work for a *comynara* than a Terranan." She said this to
Ethan, and seemed not to care if she offended her employer. "Now what am I going to do for a dress for

Festival?" *And I didn't even have a chance to see* him! *Drat Mother Adriana for being an interfering busybody.*

Margaret had no idea who *he* might be, but clearly being a Renunciate did not preclude romantic adventures, as she had assumed it did. She was beginning to understand what *Mestra* Adriana had meant by "settling Rafaella down." She was not at all sure she wanted to go out into the hills with such a quick-tempered female. Just what she needed—an emotional guide in the throes of love!

"I am sorry if it has caused trouble, but Master Mac-Ewan acted in good faith, I am certain." Margaret spoke peacefully, but her belly was full of flutters, sensing the strong emotions of the guide without wishing to.

Rafaella gave a pert sniff "No doubt he prefers *comyn* customers to mere Renunciates." She seemed determined to hold onto her sense of ill-usage for as long as possible. "Surely he knew I would pay for it, or if anything happened to me, the Guild would."

Margaret was suddenly weary of the whole matter. If one more person commented on her imaginary status, she thought she would scream. "I am not a member of the *comyn,* just a Scholar. Besides, I don't see what that has to do with anything," she protested, her patience wearing all too thin.

"Not *comyn*—I like that! You stand there in my clothes, with the very air of a *leronis* and you expect me to believe you! Oh, the color looks as well on you as it does on me, but I designed it for a very special occasion," *for a very special person to see me in,* "and I don't want anyone else wearing it! It isn't fair—the merchants are greedy and . . ."

"And you are a very rude young woman. Perhaps I had better return to Thendara House and inform *Mestra* Adriana that I wish to have another guide." As she spoke, she found that Captain Scott's face came into her mind, and felt her eyes widen a little. Was it possible that Scott was the "he" this girl had not had time to see while she was in Thendara? Why, Rafe was almost old enough to be her father! *It is none of my business! But when he left me at Thendara House, he acted . . . love-lorn! Well, maybe he was only ill from that wretched lunch—sometimes I have a hard time telling the differ-*

ence. I just don't understand all this love nonsense, and I never will It is better to keep myself apart, to remain unentangled, to not inquire too closely into things.

The thought was unnerving, and Margaret was puzzled. It was almost as if someone in her head had just told her to be alone, no matter what. She felt cold all over, despite the warmth of the Horse Market and her comfortable clothing.

Rafaella blinked and looked wretched. "No, don't! I really need the job. Losing that horse and . . ."

Margaret decided she had had enough whining and complaining. "If you need the job, then start behaving like a professional. I have no intention of hiring a spoiled brat!" Ethan snickered at her words, and Margaret looked down at him. "And don't you go stirring up any more trouble."

"She started it!"

"That is not a good reason for you to have provoked her, Ethan. If you acted like that to a commanding officer, you would end up in the brig before you knew what hit you." Margaret was not certain of that, because most of what she knew about how starships operated was from watching the occasional vid-dram, but the lad needed to learn not to let his temper run wild if he hoped to succeed. And, suddenly, she wanted very much for young Ethan to realize his ambitions.

"Oh!" The boy subsided and clutched his clumsy package against his chest. Then he looked up at Margaret worshipfully. "I'm sorry."

Rafaella ignored this byplay and looked at her almost rudely. "Truly, you are not *comyn*?"

Margaret could not imagine why it was so important to the girl, but she decided to get matters settled immediately. "If I understand it right, my father was indeed *comyn*. But he left Darkover years ago. I was born here, but I left Darkover before I was six years old. I was educated far away, and have lived on Empire planets for as long as I can remember. Several people have mistaken me for one of your aristocrats, but I am here only as a musical scholar from University. I was not raised here, and I have no interest in being anyone but *myself*. Now, if we can stop discussing my personal life and yours in a public square, perhaps we can get on the road before tomorrow!" She had spoken in a voice of authority, one she usually reserved for getting Ivor settled or when giving orientation lectures for new students. The sound of it issuing from her mouth was startling, as if she had been overpowered by a strength she had never quite realized she possessed. Disquieting as well.

Recalled to her business, Rafaella said, "I suppose Mother Adriana picked me because I am a good singer, then. Loud, anyhow." She gave a feeble grin. "I was not good enough to be trained as a performer in the Musician's Guild, and it wouldn't have suited me anyhow. When I am traveling, I sometimes sing in taverns for a round of drinks."

Margaret listened to this, and hid her dismay. A tavern songstress was hardly what she had hoped for. "You have a strong speaking voice."

"And I love the sound of it," Rafaella answered tartly. Ethan gave a sharp snort, then covered his mouth and turned it into a cough. "And I *do* know lots of people in the hills who know the old songs."

"That is wonderful," Margaret said with a greater warmth than she felt. "Do you play any instruments?"

"I can manage a guitar, and I always take my wooden flute when I travel. Do you play instruments?" Rafaella seemed to have forgotten her hostility for the moment.

"I play many instruments," she said, "but none of them so well that I would wish to perform in an orchestra. I am more of a scholar than a performer." She remembered her encounter with the haunted *ryll* at Master Everard's, and how she had played it as if she had been practicing for years. She said nothing of her own singing, which she had done all during her childhood, for the sound of it had always made her father scowl. For a moment she remembered how she sang to herself in the spare cubicles at the orphanage, and could almost recall the lullaby she crooned to herself, to keep away the loneliness. She was sure that red-haired mother she hardly recalled had sung it to her, and now she knew why it must have been painful for the Senator to listen to.

With an effort she banished the memories. "It will be very useful to have someone who knows the local people, Rafaella. Shall we get started?"

"I'll see to the horses and the mule," the guide answered.

"*Domna,*" Ethan said timidly, reminding her of his presence.

"Yes, Ethan."

"This is for you. My auntie sent it." He thrust his bundle toward her, turning red along his cheeks. "It's a gift."

"Why, Ethan, how nice of her." Margaret bent her knees and squatted so their eyes were level, ignoring the horrified expressions of several locals who had been observing them with interest.

"All the merchants are not greedy, no matter what that cat says." He was determined to defend the honor of his family.

"I know they aren't, Ethan. And your uncle is an artist, and everyone knows that artists don't understand money, do they?"

The boy gave a little laugh and looked at her intently. "Do you really think I can go to the stars?"

"Since I don't have a crystal ball, I can't see into the future, Ethan, but I think that if you work at it, you can do whatever you wish to. But it is very difficult, and you will have to learn things you never imagined." Where, on Darkover, Margaret wondered, could a merchant's boy get the education needed to go into space? And did she have any business interfering in his life? His parents and his aunt and uncle probably would not like the idea one bit. They expected him to live life as they had lived it, not go off into the void.

As if he followed her train of thought, Ethan nodded. "I am not afraid of hard work—I've done it all my life. But where can I learn the things I need to know?"

Margaret chewed her lower lip for a moment, then stood up. Her writing materials were all packed away in her bags, but across the Horse Market she saw a booth where a public scribe sat surrounded by the tools of his trade. "Come along," she told the boy, and walked toward it.

"I wish to have a letter written," she informed the scribe.

"To whom will it be directed, *domna*?"

She held back a flinch—there was that honorific again!

She could not seem to escape it. "To Captain Rafael Scott, Terran Headquarters."

The scribe perked up, looking curious now. He took a sheet of paper from a fine wooden box, and she could see that it was of a better quality than the stuff on his table. He picked up his pen, dipped it into ink, and wrote the name in the curling letters of Darkover.

"Greetings," Margaret began dictating, glad her command of *casta* had improved enough during the past days to allow her to write a letter. "The bearer of this letter is my friend Ethan MacDoevid. It is his earnest wish to travel between the stars. I will be grateful if you will aid him in this ambition, and help him to get the education he needs." She paused for a moment, wondering if she should add more, then decided not to. "I remain, your respectful niece, Marguerida Alton." Having not the faintest idea as to the proper form of such a document on Darkover, she used what she had learned at University, and decided that Rafe would understand. What good was it to have well-connected relatives if you did not take advantage of them? With this bit of sophistry Margaret persuaded herself that she was doing the right thing and felt rather pleased.

The scribe appeared nearly beside himself with interest, casting a glance at both Margaret and the boy. He dusted the ink with fine sand while she dug into her pouch for some coins. "How much," she asked.

"Three sekals, *domna*." Ethan was stunned into silence for once, but his eyes were large and the start of a grin was playing around the edges of his mouth.

"I will give you five if you do not share the contents with the entire bazaar."

The scribe turned an unlovely red and nodded. "To be sure, *domna*. I hope I can have your custom in the future."

"You can, if you can keep your nose out of my business." She gave the man the coins, took the letter, folded it, and reached for the scribe's pen. "May I?"

He looked astonished, and Margaret realized that most women, even those in the aristocracy, were not lettered. But he nodded. She wrote Rafe's name and rank across the folded letter, then added "personal" and wrote her name, Margaret Alton, below it in Terran script. She dipped her thumb into the inkpot and put her print beside her name, so that if there were any questions asked, Terran records would know it was authentic.

"Now, Ethan, take this to one of the guards at the port—one that knows you—and show it to them. They will find Captain Scott for you, and he will see if you are clever enough to do the work."

The boy was blinking back unmanly tears. "Thank you, *vai domna.*" He rubbed a rather grubby hand against his jacket and took the letter as if it were made of gold. Then he handed her his bundle. "Can you open it, so I can tell Aunt Manuella if you like it?"

"Certainly." She wiped the ink off her thumb with a cloth from the scribe, and untied the strings that bound the oiled paper. What appeared to be a wad of dark brown wool emerged from the fold. Margaret lifted it up, and the folds of a heavy cloak fell against her arms. Something else slipped out, almost falling to the cobblestones of the market. Ethan caught it, grinning. It was the blue-green spider silk, made up into a soft gown, which Aaron had tried to persuade her to take on the first visit. Silver leaves had been embroidered around the neck and sleeves. "Oh, Ethan! It is absolutely beautiful—but I will never have occasion to wear it!"

"Auntie said you might need it, next time you go to the Castle."

Margaret could not help laughing. "Well, if I go to the Castle, I'll wear it." Everyone on Darkover seemed to be conspiring to make her into that other Margaret, the one called Marguerida who was heiress to a Domain, whether she wished it or not. She gathered her finery into her arms. It was too great an effort to resist the kindness of the MacEwans, and, besides, she had always had a secret yearning for the sort of garments Dio wore for state dinners and other formal occasions.

They crossed the square, back to the booth where Rafaella was tending the horses, in contented companionship. Ethan and his cousin Geremy were her first friends on Darkover, and she knew she would never forget them.

It took a few minutes to open a bag and fold the gown away. Margaret tied the cloak behind the saddle,

fingering its thick warmth tenderly. The horse waited
patiently, and when she was done, she went to the
horse's head to make its acquaintance. The big bay
looked at her nervously at first, rolling its eyes and shifting from hoof to hoof. Margaret crooned to the horse,
as she had to other horses on Thetis and at University,
and let it take her scent. It gave a wet snort, as if confused by the mixture of Darkovan smells with something
exotic. She stroked the muzzle and watched the sharp
ears prick.

"I see you are good with horses," Rafaella commented. "That's a relief—I've taken a few jobs where I
swear my employers didn't know one end of a horse
from the other—and cared less. There was this one, a
Terranan woman who came to Thendara House with
such questions! We all thought she was a fool, but we
wanted to be polite. Well, we didn't really want to be
polite, but Mother Adriana told us to be. She was a
scholar, like you, but it was clear she had never been on
a horse in her life. She wrapped her arms around the
horse's neck in terror and wouldn't let go! We had to
stuff our sleeves in our mouths to keep from laughing."

"Horses are not common on Terra, Rafaella."

"I suppose everyone rides in aircars." She gave one
of her speaking sniffs, showing her contempt for me-
chanical vehicles.

"Not everyone, but, yes, there are a lot of aircars, and
slidewalks and other things." Margaret decided she
didn't want to argue about it.

"Well, we are as ready as we can be. Shall we go?"

"Yes, please."

When they had ridden for about an hour along a well-
maintained but fairly primitive road, they left Thendara
behind them and came into a countryside filled with or-
chards and farms. The air was crisp and fresh, and the
smell of growing things was everywhere. Margaret was
still getting her riding skills back, and also learning the
habits of this particular steed. She had not been on a
horse in several years now, but it seemed to be coming
back to her fast enough. Her legs were going to ache,
and her knees were already informing her that she was

abusing them, but she ignored it all, glad to be on the
road at last. If only Ivor were with her!

"I am sorry if I was rude back at the Market," Rafaella said, breaking into Margaret's rather morbid reflections. "There's an old saying that not everyone with red
hair is *comyn*. My father was a *nedestro comyn*, but he
didn't give me any of *Dom* Rodrigo's *laran*. That's a
good thing or we would be up to our ears in *leroni*."

Margaret untangled Rafaella's words for a moment.
Laran and *leroni* had not been on the disk she had studied, but she knew them in a vague way. They had something to do with the Gifts Rafe and Lord Hastur had
mentioned, though the connection was not clear to her.
Why hadn't she pursued the matter when Rafe mentioned it the day before? Again, she had the feeling that
she must not ask too many questions, and also the sensation that someone in the back of her mind commanded
it. She dismissed the matter, because wondering made
her head feel almost woozy, and she didn't want to get
giddy on horseback. Instead, she tried to decipher the
meaning of the rest of Rafaella's words. *Nedestro* meant
"bastard" though there didn't seem to be any onus
attached to it. At least the guide did not appear embarrassed that her father was illegitimate. At last she asked,
"did you want to have this *laran,* then?"

"Once, when I was young and silly. They tested me,
and I haven't a drop. Between ourselves, I have never
missed it. It is a great burden to see the future or hear
the thoughts of others, whether you wish to or not. And
the sickness! Ugh! I was spared that. I watched my
younger sister go through it, and it was not a pretty
sight. I am happy that I got brains and a good voice
from him, and not powers that would have made me ill."

"Illness?"

"When the *laran* comes into you, there is this sickness
that comes, too. Some people die from it. You get terrible headaches, and fainting spells, and you can't keep
food down unless you take medicines that make you
rave."

"It doesn't sound very appealing. Why does anyone
do it?"

"If you have *laran,* you either get through the threshold sickness, or you die. No one chooses it—it's just born in you or it's not."

"When does this happen?"

"Oh, when you are twelve or thirteen, sometimes a little older, but not much."

Margaret felt a great relief. She was much too old for that problem! So much for Lord Hastur's insistence that she had the Alton Gift! "What happened to your sister?"

"She went up to Neskaya and studied to be a matrix mechanic for a while, and then she came back and got married. She has a fine brood of children now, and she seems content enough."

"And you became a Renunciate?"

"I didn't want to be tied to a man or a house, not ever." Rafaella fell silent for a second. "Now I am not so sure."

Margaret "saw" Rafe Scott's face in her mind again, for just the barest flash. It was a strong impression, and not her imagination. She had guessed right, but she found she wished she hadn't. What kind of life could they have—with Rafaella going all over Darkover, leading travelers, and her uncle tied up at HQ. And, now she thought about it, they would make a very odd couple. Rafe was so sturdy and dependable, and Rafaella was, well, rather impulsive.

"Can you be a Renunciate and still marry?" she asked tactfully.

"You can have a freemate, but you do not take his name and your children don't have it either. And some people frown on that. My mother wasn't too thrilled when I took the Renunciate's Oath, and she would not really like it . . . oh, well." She paused, looking a little uncomfortable. "How are you on mountain trails?"

This abrupt change of subject let Margaret know her guide did not wish to discuss her personal life any further. "I don't know." She glanced at the horizon, beyond the rolling farmlands, and saw the outlines of hills, and beyond them, just at the edge of sight, were mountains still cloaked in snowy whiteness. "I've never been on a world with much in the way of mountains."

"Really? It is hard to imagine that. Even out in the Dry Towns there are lots of hills. What is it like, Terra?"

"Oh, I have never been to Terra. I grew up on Thetis, which is a lot of islands and big oceans. It's pretty flat. I used to ride my horse along the beach."

"Well, if you want to find songs, we will probably find some in the Kilghards, but the best ones are up in the Hellers. Those are the mountains you can just hardly see out there. They are days away, though they look close," said Rafaella, pointing to the horizon. "The trails there are narrow and difficult, with sheer drops and cliffs. It's rough country, not counting the chance of bandits and banshees." *And, besides, I don't want to be away from Thendara so long!*

"I don't have a good head for heights, to be truthful." Margaret ignored the overheard thought.

"There are women in the Guild who knew the founder of the Bridge Society, Margali n'ha Ysabet. She was long before my time. They say that she was an acrophobe," she used the Terran word, and went on in Darkovan, "but she mapped a good bit of the Hellers in spite of that. They even say she traveled to the Wall Around the World, but I don't really believe it. Margali n'ha Ysabet is something of a legend in the Guild."

"Why is that?"

"Oh, because she was brave and did remarkable things, but mostly because she never returned from her last trip," Rafaella said, laughing. "She went into the Hellers, and she never came back. Some people think she found a way into . . . never mind. Most likely she fell off a cliff and died. She was like you, Darkovan born, but educated somewhere else." Rafaella seemed bored with the whole subject.

Margaret remembered the poster she had been reading at Thendara House when *Mestra* Adriana had interrupted her. It had mentioned a woman named Magda Lorne who was also called Margali n'ha Ysabet as the founder of the Bridge Society. She found herself both curious and slightly disapproving, as if part of her found the exploits of Magda Lorne less than appropriate. What was going on with her? She never had thoughts like that! Margaret felt invaded, as if some new personality was emerging in her mind, and a very unpleasant one at that. She scolded herself silently for being so edgy, and made herself forget about Magda Lorne. "I want to get as much research done as I can, but I don't think breaking my neck will actually enhance my contribution to learning."

Rafaella laughed so hard she nearly lost her seat. "We will plan a journey that will not be too hard for you, then," she said, when she had caught her breath. *And one that won't keep me away from Thendara past Midsummer!* "You ride well enough, but you are going to be sore by evening."

"A small price to pay for a ballad," Margaret answered, and her words set Rafaella off laughing again.

"You said you knew some songs, Rafaella. Why don't I get out my recorder, and you can sing as we go along?" The guide smiled at her, and blushed with pleasure to the roots of her fiery hair.

They camped in the open the first night, and Margaret was very glad of the warm cloak Manuella had given her. She used it for an extra blanket, wondering what it must be like in winter here, if summer was this cool. The thought made her shiver all over, and huddle closer to their small fire. Her sleep was disturbed by another vision of Lew Alton. He seemed to be very angry with her for coming to Darkover, and, in her dream, she was angry, too.

By sundown of the third day, they turned off the well-paved road and began to climb into the hills, traveling east, as near as she could guess, Margaret's legs had finally stopped aching, but now her lungs hurt as they climbed to a greater altitude than she was accustomed to. They rode across a stone bridge that spanned a rapid river, and Rafaella told her it was called the Kadarin. The name made her skin go gooseflesh, just as the name Dyan Ardais had a few days before. She tried to think why, and again found her mind resistent to inquiry. She felt troubled by this until they were away from the sound of its waters. Then the tension eased, and she simply studied the countryside.

"I think it is a good thing you are coming up here to hear these old ballads," Rafaella commented as they rode into a sleepy hamlet.

"Do you?" It was the first direct reference her guide had made to her work.

"The old people are dying off and some of our music is getting lost. We don't have libraries like the Terranan, except for the *cristoforos'* archives at Nevarsin. I never thought about it before."

Margaret wondered what else had been lost on Darkover. The people she had met had been intelligent enough, but they seemed to lack the sort of curiosity which she had found at University. Was this oral tradition because of some taboo she did not know, or for some other reason? It was just another puzzle to frustrate her—like the bits of memory that continued to plague her awake and asleep.

"We will spend the night here, I think. If old Jerana hasn't died, she will be glad to sing for you. She was once the best lyric singer in Thendara and knows many songs. But she married a farmer and gave up her music, which I think she regrets. Now she is a toothless old granny, but when I came here last, her voice was still fine."

Margaret asked "Does the old lady know much about the Terrans?"

"Enough not to think of them as having horns and tails like some demon," said Rafaella peaceably. "Besides, no one would take you for a Terranan."

Margaret was more relieved than she could say. She didn't want to be mistaken for a devil, or have her precious equipment perceived as soul-stealing devices. She had never actually encountered that situation, but the Music Department abounded in horror stories of scholars who had gotten killed out of ignorance. *I was born here*, Margaret thought. *And nobody could possibly be afraid of me.*

They drew their horses up before a well-kept cottage, and an ancient woman waddled out. She was bent and toothless, but her eyes were bright, and her speaking voice was clear and strong. She greeted Rafaella warmly, then looked at Margaret with a lively curiosity.

Rafaella introduced her to old Jerana, and the woman bobbed a stiff curtsy at the sound of her name. "An Alton! Why, there hasn't been an Alton here in many years. You have the look of the old man, that Kennard, and his father before him. Poor man. He went away and died somewhere, some planet. I don't know. My mind gets muddled these days. I was born the year the Terra-nan came to Aldaran."

Margaret knew that Darkover had been rediscovered more than a hundred Terran years before—the history disk had grudgingly disclosed that much. She regarded Jerana with wonder, because few people in the Federation were this old without taking the treatments which extended life.

"*Domna* Alton wishes to hear you sing, Jerana, and to make a record of your singing."

"Really? Why, I haven't performed in decades! It has been thirty years since I sang in public, if it has been a day!" She looked pleased. "Come in, girls, come in!" She rubbed her gnarled hands together. "Alan! Alan, where are you, lazy boy! My great-grandson. Here come tend to these fine horses!" She herded them into the cottage, and seated them beside the hearth while she gave a steaming cauldron a stir and kept up a stream of reminiscences.

After a hearty meal of stew and bread, Jerana settled on a stool while Margaret sorted out her recording equipment. The old woman was completely at ease after the things had been explained to her, grinning and show-ing her gums. Margaret could tell she was tickled by all the attention, and felt pleased to give the old woman a treat.

Rafaella took a guitar down from the wall and tuned the strings easily. It was an old instrument, the wood polished by years of use, and belonged in a museum. Jerana chuckled over it. "That boy of Everard's was here a time back, and he wanted to take my old friend back to Thendara with him, to put in that collection that Everard has. I told him that since my husband died, it's the only lover I have."

Then she began to sing in a clear, steady voice which belied her years. Margaret was lost in the music, so lost she did not notice when tears began to roll down her cheeks. The words bought some emotion welling up, something nameless and precious, and when that song was done, she felt at peace for the first time in days.

It was late when Jerana ceased her singing, and Mar-garet had recorded two dozen pieces. The old woman showed them to a large bed in the back of the cottage, and Margaret hid her discomfort at the idea of sleeping with another person. It didn't matter. She could hardly keep her eyes open. Rafaella was yawning, too. She pulled off her boots, yanked off her tunic and trousers, and climbed under the covers, so Margaret did the same.

Sleep came almost immediately, and, for once, she did not dream.

10

———— ◆ ————

Margaret woke at first light with a feeling of oppression and a sound like bees buzzing in one ear. Still muzzy, she shifted beneath the soft covers, and found that Rafaella had rolled over and pillowed her head against Margaret's shoulder. She glanced at the fiery head resting upon her, and smiled a little. Rafaella was snoring ever so delicately. Gently she rolled the woman away, and the slight sense of suffocation left her. *I guess it is a good thing I've never married, since sharing a bed makes me so uncomfortable.* As soon as the thought came into her mind, Margaret knew it was not entirely true. She had not really minded sleeping with Rafaella the night before.

There were sounds from the main room of the cottage, and Margaret heard the voice of Jerana lifted in song. The good, warm smell of porridge wafted in the chill morning air, and she felt a lassitude in her limbs. She was enjoying the sensation of relaxation when Rafaella snorted abruptly and stopped snoring. A moment later she sat up, pulling down the covers with her movement.

"I smell breakfast," she announced.

Margaret laughed at this. Rafaella had a healthy appetite, and she wondered how the woman maintained her slim figure while eating so much. "Yes. I can hear Jerana." The cool air made her shiver, and she pushed away her covers, rose, put on her discarded garments, then pulled her hair into a semblance of order. Her clothes smelled of horse and sweat and the trail now, and she thought longingly of the huge tub at Master Everard's house, scented with balsam and hot enough to redden her skin.

While they ate breakfast with old Jerana and her silent great-grandson Alan, the ancient singer pondered aloud on her career as a performer, the inadequacy of present-day vocalists, and scandals of the past. Margaret was sorry she had not kept her recorder out, for it was fascinating to hear old gossip told with a lip-smacking glee.

When they were done, Alan and Rafaella went out to see to the horses, and Margaret sat and sipped the last of her morning tea. She felt grubby and longed for clean clothes and a bath, but her belly was full of hot porridge, and her heart felt feather-light. She was quietly happy, and realized she had not felt that way in a very long time.

"I think," Jerana interrupted her thoughts, "that if you go to the village over the hill, you might find Gavin useful."

"Gavin?"

Jerana gave her disquieting cackle and nodded her head. "Gavin MacDougal was a good singer in his day, though he never joined the Guild. He is a bit cantankerous, but he does know music. Now, don't you tell him I said so! He's proud enough without that. And I warn you, he does not like your Rafaella at all."

"But why?"

"Gavin thinks a woman's place is by the hearth, and he disapproves of the Renunciates. As if they needed his approval! He was a stuck-up youngster, and now he is an arrogant old man. He wanted to marry me once—he is only ninety now, and I thought him too young at the time—and he has never really forgiven me for picking my Padric instead. You wouldn't think it to look at me now, but once I had all the men after me. I was a real beauty. Oh, I ramble these days. Let me tell you, Marguerida, age is a blessing, but it is also a curse. Some days you almost can't remember your name."

Margaret thought of Ivor, getting feebler before her eyes, and nodded. "Yes, my teacher was like that. He was sharp as a whip when it came to music, but with day-to-day things, his mind was getting very . . . I don't know. Muddled?"

"The very word! Where is he, your teacher?"

"He died last week, right after we arrived." She found tears welling in her eyes and blinked them away as quickly as she could.

"That is terrible! I can see you miss him greatly.

There, there, lambie, you just cry all you like. It is healthy to weep!"

"I did so much crying that I feel as if I should have used up all the tears I have." But Margaret found herself weeping again, the old woman's kindness releasing her still fresh grief. She mopped her face with her sleeve after a few minutes, and snuffled noisily. "We had been traveling together for many years, going to planets to study the indigenous music. He was very precious to me."

"Death is a path we are all on, though so far I haven't reached the end of it. I have outlived a husband, two sons, one daughter, and three grandchildren. Now Alan is married, and when his wife has her child, I will be a great-great-grandmother, and here I still am. Sometimes I think it is unnatural to live this long."

Margaret decided it would be rude to mention that citizens of the Federation often lived two centuries, with the help of treatments. It seemed unfair that Ivor had not been one of them. "So, Gavin is cantankerous?"

"Hmmph! He is a crabby old man, but then, he was a crabby young man. He knows a lot of songs. I have to give him that. And there is an inn in the village, too, so you can be at your ease."

Margaret reddened and wondered if Jerana knew how she longed for a bath. "I cannot thank you enough for your hospitality, Jerana."

"Pah! It was my pleasure. Singing last night made me feel seventy again!"

Rafaella and Margaret set out a little later, their food-bag stuffed with a fresh loaf, some cheese, and salted meat, Jerana's parting gift. They had gone about an hour beyond the tiny hamlet when Margaret began to feel queasy. Her stomach roiled, and her head ached, but she said nothing to her companion.

They paused beside a gurgling creek for a midday meal, and Margaret dipped her wooden cup into the water and drank thirstily. Then she sat on a rock and did not move for several minutes, feeling achy and tired. She dragged herself to her feet and nearly stumbled.

"Are you all right, Marguerida?"

"I think the altitude must be affecting me. I have lived

most of my life at sea level, and even though these hills are not very high, my body is reacting. I can't seem to catch my breath."

"You look pale."

"Don't worry about it. I'll be fine after I eat some bread and cheese."

But she wasn't. They had not gone a mile from the creek when her stomach rebelled and spewed up her lunch and much of her breakfast. She barely managed to dismount before it happened.

"You are sick," Rafaella insisted as Margaret stepped away from her mess. The guide looked very worried.

"No, really. I am fine now. It is just the altitude, or maybe my belly didn't like something I ate." She rinsed her mouth out with some clear water, then pulled herself back onto the horse. "How far is it to this village where Gavin lives?"

"Another three hours, at least. Perhaps we should camp here instead."

"No. I feel better now." That was true. She was very thirsty, but having emptied her stomach had made her feel less breathless and weak somehow.

The trail wound higher and higher, growing narrower and rougher for a while. Then it broadened out, and Margaret realized they were on the ridge of the hills. She glanced back the way they had come. The River Kadarin was a serpentine flash of silver in the distance, far below. The ascent had been so gradual she had not really noticed.

It was close to sunset when they arrived at the village. It was much larger than the one Jerana lived in, with several roomy houses of stone between humbler cottages. The inn was marked by a swinging sign with a picture of a deerlike beast painted on it. They brought their horses to a halt before it, and a sharp-eyed boy ran out to greet them.

"Ho, Rafaella! Welcome back!"

"Thank you, Valentine. You have grown two inches since my last visit."

The boy puffed his chest out and grinned. "True. I am now in Tomas' hand-me-downs, but his old boots are already too small."

"And how are your parents?"

"Last winter was hard on Ma—her joints hurt something dreadful. But she perked up when it got warmer, like she alwus does. And Pa is Pa. Come in. I will stable the horses, and Ma just cleaned the front bedroom."

Margaret dismounted, her head spinning. She took some deep breaths, then waited for the giddiness to pass. She had been feeling less and less well during the past hour, but she had not said anything to Rafaella. She didn't want to spend the night on the trail. She wanted a bed and a bath! And supper. No! The thought of food made her queasy again. All she needed was some sleep, and she would be fine again.

Inside the inn was a deep-beamed taproom. Several men in rough tunics were drinking mugs of beer and lounging around tables, talking quietly. Margaret could hear their voices, but their dialect was so thick she could not follow it. They looked at her with mild curiosity, but no more than that. Two or three of them greeted Rafaella in a friendly way, and Margaret was glad her guide was well-known there.

The room was smoky from the large fireplace, and the smell of burning wood and beer nearly overwhelmed her. She willed herself to stand up straight and ignore her spinning head. She had disgraced herself once that day, and she did not intend to do it a second time. She was grateful when they left the taproom, climbed a narrow staircase, and were shown to a large, airy room on the upper floor.

Margaret sank onto the bed, leaned back on the pillow, and let her body go slack. Distantly she heard the voice of Rafaella and another woman, probably Valentine's mother, but she felt too weak to listen. Strong hands tugged her boots off, and she felt her tunic being pulled over her head. She tried to protest, but she couldn't get the words out.

"I just need to sleep," she mumbled, and closed her eyes.

A wide plain of snow spread from horizon to horizon, and the sky was white with clouds. The smell of cold seemed to freeze her bones. The clouds separated, and a white moon shone in the sky for a moment. Two women walked toward her, like and unlike at the same time. Each had red hair, but one's was lighter than the other's. They moved as one, their slender arms swinging in time, their long legs moving easily across the snow-clad landscape. Their garments were soft and flowing, the white of the snow, and their hair was unbound across their shoulders.

The women stared at her with gold-flecked amber eyes, and reached for her with white hands. She felt herself shrink away from their touch. "Child," said one. "Marja," the other spoke. She knew they were sisters and that one was her mother, but she could not decide which was which, so similar were they in appearance.

Suddenly a man appeared between them, strong and dark-haired. He put his hands on their shoulders and pushed them apart. Then he seemed to grow taller, until his head brushed the clouds in the sky. Margaret stared at her father as she had never known him, two-handed and powerful, unscarred and handsome. "I tried to warn you! I told you that a wild telepath was a dangerous thing! Why didn't you listen to me? Get up! Stop running away from your duty! Stop trying to avoid your Gift!"

Margaret sat up in the bed, her head throbbing. She stared at the whitewashed walls and the heavy wooden beams above her, and felt disoriented for a moment. Then she remembered that she was in the inn with the sign of the deer outside it, and not trapped in some snowy landscape with her mother and her aunt and a furious Lew. Relief flooded her, and she felt her hands unclench. Her rapidly beating heart returned to normal after a few minutes.

She looked around and found that Rafaella was asleep on a mattress on the floor beside the bed. A large gray cat was curled in the curve of her legs, and it looked up at her and yawned. The sheer ordinariness of it all calmed her. She swung her legs from under the covers and found that she had been undressed completely, and Darkovan nightclothes had been put on her. The pungent smell of the trail still clung to her skin, though, and she longed for a bath.

Rafaella prized an eye open and examined her. "There is a bathing tub two doors down the hall, and *Mestra* Hannah washed your clothes. They should be dry by now. How do you feel?"

"Much better, thank you. It must have been the altitude."

"I am glad. I was very worried. Go bathe while I get a little more sleep. You must have had some fearsome dreams—you kept whimpering—when you weren't screaming."

"I am sorry if I disturbed your sleep, Rafaella."

"Not me—I can sleep through anything—but the horse merchants in the next room might have lost some." She grinned, showing all her teeth. "They deserved it—if they are horse merchants, then I am a rabbit-horn." With this cryptic comment, she turned over and went back to sleep.

Bathed and dressed in the outfit she had originally purchased from MacEwan, Margaret felt almost herself for the first time in twenty-some hours. The sense of a headache just a breath away persisted, but her stomach seemed to be the reliable organ it usually was, one which could consume almost anything without discomfort. She decided not to overdo it and ate a light breakfast with several mugs of tea.

Rafaella joined her as she was sipping her tea, rubbing sleep from her eyes. "I talked to old Gavin last night in the taproom, and he is expecting us later this morning," she announced. "He wasn't glad to see me, but I promised him a few *reis* for his song, and told him you were a Terranan."

"Why did you do that?" Margaret was surprised, because she had been to some effort to appear as a Darkovan.

"The man is very selfish—egotistical, I guess. He was ready to say he wouldn't sing until I told him his songs would be heard in far places. They will, won't they? I wouldn't want to have lied to him."

"Certainly. My recordings will go into the archives on University, and students of music will listen to them. And after that, who knows?"

"What does that mean?" Rafaella asked, helping herself to a huge bowl of porridge.

"A few years ago some popular musicians got hold of some folk songs from New Hispaniola and turned them into hits."

"Hits? Did they strike people with the songs?"

Margaret nearly choked on her mouthful of tea. The Darkovan word she had used meant a "blow" and lacked any other meaning. She coughed and recovered her breath. That would teach her to try to translate Terran into Darkovan without thinking first!

"No, nothing so violent. What I meant was that the songs were recorded and much acclaimed—played over and over until everyone in the Federation got totally sick of them. They call that a hit."

"Oh. Why didn't you say so?"

At mid-morning the two women approached the cottage of Gavin MacDougal. It was still cool, and the street was a little muddy from rain the previous night. Margaret carried her precious equipment in a bag over her shoulder, and looked around with interest. She had been too ill to notice much the previous afternoon.

MacDougal's cottage was something of a hovel. The little garden beside the building was full of rank weeds and a few drooping bushes, and the walk to the door was littered with oddments. Margaret saw a broken plow, a saddle which had sat out in the weather for several seasons, and several other things she could not immediately identify.

Rafaella opened the poorly-hung wooden door and entered without knocking. It was dark and fairly ripe within. It smelled of old man, wood-smoke, cooking, and dirty clothing. Margaret was shocked. Somehow she had created an image in her mind where all Darkovan homes were clean and smelled of balsam and freshness. How did the old man live in this filth?

A form crouched beside the hearth stirred, and as her eyes adjusted to the dim light, Margaret saw Gavin. He was small and wizened, his head entirely hairless and his shoulders stooped with age. He coughed and hawked into the fireplace, and the sound of sizzling broke the silence for a moment.

"Welcome," he muttered gruffly. He peered near-sightedly at the women. "I thought you told me she was Terranan."

Rafaella scuffled her boots on the floor and looked slightly uncomfortable. "Well, she is, and she isn't."

"Don't you try to riddle me, girl. I may be old, but I am not senile! She is one or the other." He moved closer, and she could smell ancient sweat on his garments and beer on his sour breath. He looked at her closely in the poor light.

Margaret was annoyed at being discussed as if she were invisible. "In truth, I am both. I was born on Darkover, but I have spent most of my life . . ."

"Forgive me, *domna*," he interrupted. "Even these old eyes can see you are of the *comyn*. You honor my house." He glared at Rafaella. "What are you playing at—trying to pass this woman off as a Terranan to me? You are a bad girl, and you will come to a bad end. And none too soon either. Dashing around like a hoyden, instead of behaving like a proper woman."

Rafaella bristled and was about to answer in her forthright and heedless way when Margaret spoke. "My father was *comyn*, *Mestru* MacDougal."

"I knew it! Think you can fool me! May I know his name, my lady?" He managed to combine spite and servility in a way Margaret found extraordinarily distasteful. She could see why Jerana had not wished to marry him, for she was sure he had been an extremely unpleasant young man.

"My father is Lewis Alton, the Imperial Senator for Darkover." She saw the look of startlement on Rafaella's face, and realized that somehow she had never mentioned her father by name before. It didn't really matter that he had resigned, because he would always carry the rank of Senator. Besides, these people probably never thought about the Senate, or the Terran Federation, if they were anything like the back-country people she had encountered on other planets.

An expression of distaste came across Gavin's face, and he pursed his wrinkled mouth. "I wish you nothing but good, *domna,* but if I were you, I would not be too quick to claim that lineage here in the hills. There are many who are old enough to remember the burning of Caer Donn, and some of them bear old grudges."

"I know nothing of that," she replied abruptly, silently cursing the Senator for being a close-mouthed old— She cut off that thought. "I don't even know what Caer Donn is."

"Was, *domna,* was. It was one of the oldest cities in the world. The Terranan came there and built their first spaceport, making pacts with those blasted Aldarans. I visited there long ago, and sang my songs, but it was never a generous place. Those Aldarans hardly give a man a drink for his song. And some years back, it was destroyed."

"I am sad to hear that, but since I was not yet born, I can't see it has much to do with me. I can't be held responsible for something that occurred so long ago."

Gavin MacDougal gave a snort. "That is Terranan thinking, for sure. We in the hills have long memories, especially for that time. Here, the very name Alton will remind many who do not wish to be reminded of the burning of Caer Donn and of the Forbidden Tower."

"You are croaking like a raven of ill-fortune, old man," Rafaella replied.

"You are too young and too headstrong to know what you speak of, so keep your tongue behind your teeth. Your father Lewis was part of the reason Caer Donn was destroyed, though he was only a child when the last members of the Forbidden Tower were slain. We make no songs of those times, but we remember."

Margaret tried to imagine what role her father might have played in the events old Gavin referred to, but could not manage it. The mists of Darkovan history were too thick, too impenetrable for her. Then she remembered her dream, and how her father had come between the two women, and had still had both hands. She held back a shudder with a great effort.

"I came here to listen to you sing, *Mestru* MacDougal, not to hear old tales." This was not entirely true, but that part of her which was cold and distant insisted that she quell her curiosity. It was a frustrating feeling, for the questions formed in her mind, but did not seem to be able to get to her mouth. She felt silenced, as she had as a small child, and outraged.

Margaret realized she was extremely interested in this story, but at the same time, she did not *want* to know what had happened. She remembered how Lord Hastur and Brigham Conover had hinted at terrible events in the past, and realized now that they had not told her everything because they knew it would only distress her.

I will record this old man, and then we will turn back for Thendara! Rafaella will be pleased, and I will escape from . . . leave the work unfinished? No, I can't do that. I have to go on, for Ivor's sake!

"Well, if it is song you want, then song you will have." He waddled over to the wall and took down an ancient bowed *ryll,* caressing it gently. "Let's go out into the sunlight."

They sat on some stones in front of the cottage, and Gavin tuned his instrument while Margaret set up her equipment. He had a thready voice now, the remnants of a good tenor, but his memory was capacious, and by the time the sun was descending, he had considerably enlarged Margaret's store of Darkovan music. Her bottom ached from sitting on a rock, and she was glad to stand up and stretch.

She thanked the old man and offered him payment, but he shook his head. "I would take money from a Terranan as quick as a rabbit-horn, but it goes against the grain to accept payment from an Alton. You mind yourself, young woman, and don't you let Rafaella get you into mischief." Then he walked into his hovel and slammed the door.

Margaret put away her equipment in the bag, and she and her guide started back to the inn. "Tell me about this Forbidden Tower," she said, ignoring her sense of fatigue and a sudden rush of dizziness, just managing to get the question out before her interior censor silenced her again. Her heart pounded, and her blood seemed to reverberate in her ears. *You will not ask questions!* She swallowed hard, to keep her stomach from rebelling again.

Rafaella walked beside her in silence for several minutes. Then she said, "It is better not to speak of those times, Marguerida."

Margaret still felt like protesting, but when Rafaella was this determined, she had already learned it was not much use to argue. And the urgency she had managed to summon up a few minutes before was gone, leaving her empty. She shifted her bag against her shoulder, and let it go. The excitement of hearing new songs faded, and her body began to ache. When the inn came into sight, she was delighted. She would spend a little time transcribing some of the songs and making notes, and then she would go to bed. In the morning they would turn back to Thendara, and she would leave her exhaustion and the feeling of oppression behind her. Someone else could finish the work. She was going back to the security of University on the first ship she could find!

There were buildings all around her, the dull, square buildings typical of Terran architecture. It was night, and the moons had risen. There was a kind of quiet all around. Then the buildings began to redden, and in a moment there was fire everywhere.

Morning found her feverish and giddy, her head spinning like a top when she tried to sit up. Margaret sat up, then sagged back onto the pillows, swallowing with difficulty. Her throat was parched, and her stomach heaved. She tried to get up again, but found she could not.

Rafaella bent over her, smoothing her hair away from her face. "You are ill, Marguerida. You must stay in bed today."

"Altitude," she muttered. "I must go back to Thendara."

"You aren't going anywhere today. You rest, and I will bring you something cool to drink."

Margaret felt too weak to argue, so she lay beneath the covers and tried to breathe slowly, to relax her body. She closed her eyes wearily, and the face of Danilo, the paxman, swam behind her lids. He looked down at her, and somehow she was certain he had something to do with her illness. Then she realized how ridiculous that was. *I am behaving like a superstitious idiot. Before long I will be thinking I have been bewitched by a man who is hundreds of miles away. I'll just lie here for a few minutes, and then I'll be fine!*

The morning passed, but she was not fine. Her skin got hotter and hotter, until it felt as if it were shrinking into her muscles. The weight of the covers was too much to bear, so she pushed them aside, then lay shivering, exhausted by the effort. Her skull pounded with a dull throbbing that seemed to increase every second. She tried to drink the stuff Rafaella brought her, but it refused to stay down, and she was sick repeatedly into a bowl. She felt cool cloths pressed onto her brow, and all sense of time faded.

Margaret began to shiver, and clawed at the covers with a hand that felt cold and dry. She cried out sharply. Every movement was an agony. She felt a gentle hand touch her cheek, and the covers were drawn up around her. "Dio—Mother!" She felt she was falling into a vast void, and closed her aching fingers around the bedclothes.

Whiteness! She had never seen such whiteness. It filled her from toes to head, and it was cold and barren and terrifying. There was nothing in it but emptiness. It seemed to press against her chest, stealing her shallow breath, sucking the life from her body. She struggled to get free of it, and fell somehow deeper into the cold.

Then there was something in the dreadful lightness— no, someone—and she tried to cower and vanish. Someone was looking for her, and she was afraid. Was it the silver man? Or red-tressed Thyra? The dead were seeking her, trying to draw her into themselves!

A face peered down at her, like no face she had ever seen before. The angles of the bones were wrong, not human. The skin of the being shone against the whiteness, and the eyes looked at her with infinite compassion. She was going to die! She was going to join Ivor and Thyra and Marjorie Alton and the grandfather she had never seen. The face was distressed, as if it knew her thoughts, and there was a slight shaking of the head, as if to deny her death. The face bent closer and closer while she tried to get away, and, at last, she felt thin lips pressed against her brow. The terror vanished as if it had never been, and she lay, calm and cold, waiting for the end.

How long she waited she could not guess, but after a time, she saw the Senator walking toward her. He was old, stooped and lame, and he peered into the whiteness like a blind man. Margaret wanted to call to him, but her voice had lost its power.

At last he saw her, and he looked angry. "Get up! You cannot be sick now! I will not have you dying! I have lost too much. Don't you dare to die on me, Marja! Get

*up!" Something swelled in her breast, a bubble of some
emotion. It rose into her throat, and burst.*

"I'll die if I want to!" Then she laughed at him.

Margaret was extremely surprised to waken in the bed
at the inn, her fever broken for the moment. She felt
more tired than she could believe, but her mind was
clear. She pushed herself up on both hands until she was
sitting in the bed. Carefully she reached for the cup of
water that waited beside the bed, guessing at the time.
Then she noticed she was alone, and wondered where
Rafaella was.

She had a sudden fear that the Renunciate had abandoned her in the nameless village, but then she heard
the sound of Rafaella's voice in the hall. A moment later
she came in, frowning. When she saw that Margaret was
awake, the worry lines between her red brows smoothed
away, and she seemed to breathe a sigh of relief.

"How are you, *chiya?*"

Margaret heard her term of endearment, and it made
her feel like a child again. She felt her mind protest for
a second, then decided it was not so bad after all. "I am
fine, really. A little weak, but some soup should cure
that." The mention of food made her queasy immediately, and she swallowed hard.

"Are you certain?"

"Of course I am." Margaret wasn't certain of anything, but she didn't want Rafaella to know that. She
was too weak to get out of bed, and she could not imagine how she had gotten so sick. She had been fully im-
munized against everything anyone had ever thought of
before she left University. It must be the altitude. It just
had to be!

"Humph! I don't think you know how you are. You
are as white as your nightgown, and I think you still
have some fever."

"Perhaps. But I am sure I will be completely recovered by tomorrow. I am sorry if I worried you—I didn't
mean to get sick!" She sounded like a cranky child to
her own ears.

"There, there. I know you didn't mean to get sick—
what a silly thing to say! Do you think you can get out

of bed, so I can change the sheets? You've soaked them through."

"I'm sorry!" To Margaret's surprise, she burst into tears. Great sobs rose out of her chest as tears spilled down her face. "I didn't mean to make a mess," she whimpered. "I tried to be good, really, I did."

"Of course you did," Rafaella soothed her, the frown returning. She bent forward and put her arms around Margaret, drawing her against her chest. "It's all right, *chiya.*" The Renunciate stroked her sweat-soaked hair as Margaret continued to weep and apologize.

The door of the room opened, and the owner of the inn came in, a sturdy woman with a no-nonsense air of competence about her. She had a pile of clean sheets on one arm, and a gown draped over the other. She shook her head slightly, put down the sheets, and came over to the bed. Margaret tried to make herself stop crying, and nearly succeeded. Instead she got hiccups which almost made her retch.

Between them, Rafaella and the innkeeper managed to get Margaret out of the bed. They put her into a chair, and pulled the covers away. They stripped the bed efficiently, and Margaret could smell the crisp freshness of the new sheets, even though her nose was very stuffy from weeping. She could also smell her own body, stinking of sweat and sickness, and she shrank from it. She needed a bath.

Then the two women removed her nightgown gently but relentlessly. She tried to protest, embarrassed at being naked in front of strangers, but they ignored her. Rafaella brought a bowl of warm water and a cloth, and washed Margaret's face and body as if she were an infant. Her skin felt like parchment, dry and crackly. The innkeeper noticed it, left the room, and returned with a container of balm. She massaged it into Margaret's aching flesh, and, to her surprise, it felt very good. It must have some herb in it that eased the aches. Then they put a clean nightgown on her, and helped her back into bed. Margaret fell back against the pillows, too exhausted to move, and heard the voices of the women from very far away.

"I don' like the look of her, I tell you, Rafaella. She's

skin and bone, and she's going to get another fever, or my name's not Hannah MacDanil."

"I know."

"We need a healer woman, but we've not had one here since old Grisilda died last winter."

"There has to be someone!" Margaret could hear the near panic in Rafaella's voice, and she wanted very much to reassure her that there was no need for a healer. She could just imagine being dosed with local herbs! Why had she ever come here? Why had Ivor died? It just wasn't fair. If only she had not been so stubborn, if only she had not insisted on finishing the work. She had no business being sick out here in the middle of nowhere. Maybe it was psychosomatic, brought on by the shock of Ivor's death. Perhaps her dreams were making her ill. Or maybe she had that Trailman's Fever that was mentioned on the disk. No, that couldn't be right. It had a cycle, and this was the wrong year. Her skull began to throb again, so she stopped trying to think. It was simpler just to lean back and enjoy cool, clean sheets and a fresh nightgown.

"I think you'd better ride to Ardais and bring back help. I would send the boy, but I really cannot spare him just now. I don't trust those horse traders any farther than I can toss 'em, and I don't want to be without a man about the place." The innkeeper gave a sigh. "If Emyn were another sort of husband—well, no good wishing for what you haven't got!"

Margaret heard Hannah's words from a great distance, but the mention of Ardais almost roused her from her weakness. She wanted to protest, to beg Rafaella not to leave, not to go to the place where the Ardais dwelt, but she couldn't seem to get her mouth to form the words. All she knew was that she was terrified, as well as ill.

"I'd better go immediately. It is a fair ride, and I don't really want to do it in the dark."

"Fine. I will look after the *vai domna* until you return."

Hours passed. Margaret faded in and out of lucidity, slept, dreamed, and tossed. She tried to remain awake, to avoid the voices which troubled her. She could hear the Senator urging her to get up, and Ivor telling her that he needed her. And there were women's voices, too—arguing or weeping. But sleep kept coming upon her, troubled and white. And the voices rose like a storm, howling and shrieking.

At some point she woke, briefly, and heard the sound of wind and rain against the shuttered windows. The innkeeper was sitting in the chair beside the bed, knitting by the dim light of the candle. "Where is Rafaella?" Her voice was a croak. "I'm so thirsty."

Hannah gave her some liquid, water with something in it, by the taste. "Rafaella has gone to fetch a healer." She glanced toward the window. *I hope she got to Ardais safely! Our mountain storms are so terrible.*

"Oh." She drank, and before she slipped back into her dreams, Margaret shuddered. She knew she had heard Hannah's thoughts, that no words had been spoken. And she knew that something awaited her, something she did not wish to meet. She could almost feel the tug of it against her aching muscles.

Light touched her face. It hurt! She raised a hand to shield her eyes. Then she felt a rocking motion beneath her, and clutched for the bed-frame. There was none, only a thick staff of wood on either side of her protesting body. She could hear hooves, and smelled the scent of horses. Her support swung back and forth, and she felt her body rebel again. Her stomach protested, but it had nothing to release, so she just lay there, heaving.

Rafaella's face hovered above her. "Marguerida!"

"Where are we? What is happening. Oh, I hurt so much!"

"I know, *chiya,* but we will be at Ardais soon, and have you back in bed, I promise."

"Why is the bed swinging?"

"You are in a horse-litter. Do not worry. You are safe. We will be at Castle Ardais soon."

"The light hurts my eyes!" Rafaella's words penetrated her mind. "Ardais! Oh, no! Don't let Danilo hurt me!"

She heard a male voice, deep and troubled. "What is she raving about?"

"I don't know," Rafaella answered. "She seems fright-

ened of something. She's been doing this off and on for
the last couple of days."

"We'd better tie her more tightly on the litter, *mestra*.
Otherwise she's going to fall off and hurt herself."

Nothing they said made any sense. All she could think
of was the quiet paxman of Regis Hastur, and her irra-
tional fear of him. *He will make me into someone else!*
That was the last coherent thought she had for a long
time.

11

◆

The bone-racking jostle of the horse litter changed, and Margaret was just aware enough to realize that they had left the rough terrain and gotten onto some smoother ground. She heard the hooves fall on stone, a deep, resonant sound, and forced her eyes to open. The harsh light had faded, and it was close to sunset, cool and crisp. A bird sang, and she wished she could enjoy it. Around her the sounds of boots and hooves on stone and voices was painful, and she held back a wince as she turned her head toward them.

They had come into a broad courtyard, and around it, spreading like the open arms of a mother, was a large building of pale gray stone. It seemed to fill the landscape from horizon to horizon, its several-storied height reaching toward the clouded sky. Lichen grew across the stones, and the windows in the lower floors were narrower than those higher up.

Bone-weary and slightly feverish though she was, Margaret still found herself trying to make mental notes on the architecture of the place. The habits of a scholar were not easy to break, she mused, as she studied the place. It was quite different from Comyn Castle, more like a fortress. She wondered what they had to protect themselves against. Brigands? She was relieved to find she seemed to have no previous memory of Castle Ardais, despite her strong aversion to the name, and decided her strange fears were silly.

When the men removed the litter from between the horses, gentle as they tried to be, Margaret could not help but cry out in pain. She bit her lip to stifle the cry, but it escaped despite her efforts. They carried her to the entrance of Castle Ardais, and into an entryway which rose above her more than two stories. From her position on the litter, she could see light streaming down from the upper windows, filling the chamber with the fading light of the day. It reminded her a little of the cathedral at University, except in that place, there were no shrill voices, as there were here. She could hear Rafaella arguing with someone nearby, and she wished they would all be quiet. There seemed to be several voices involved, mostly female, and the pitch of them hurt her ears.

A firm-sounding male voice cut suddenly through the gabble. "What, may I ask, is the meaning of all this?"

"I was just telling this person that Ardais is not a public house where you can bring . . ."

"Enough! *Mestra* Rafaella and her companion are expected, Martha, and it is not your place to question it. If you had not been down in the village with your daughter, you would have been aware that we have anticipated the arrival of these people." He seemed quite calm and very authoritative, and Margaret wondered vaguely if this were the master of the castle.

"She was near her time, Julian, and I could not just leave her alone!"

"She is in good hands with the midwife, who I am certain, did not appreciate your interference."

"Interference! I like that! You are only a man—you do not understand such things." Martha, whomever she was, did not sound as if she were going to give up the argument.

Margaret saw a man's face as he bent toward her. "I welcome you to Castle Ardais." She could see an expression of puzzlement in his features. "I am Julian Monterey, *coridom* to Lady Marilla."

Margaret tried to remember what the term meant, flogging her weary brain. It was something between a major-domo and a foreman, but the exact distinction was impossible to fathom in her present state. "Thank you for your welcome," she croaked, "and forgive me for coming in such an untidy manner. I did not mean to be sick."

"Of course you didn't," he answered gently, as if visitors arriving on horse litters in a high fever were a commonplace occurrence.

"Why is my entrance hall full of gossips?" a sweet

voice interrupted him. "And, why, might I inquire, is our guest still waiting here? I ordered a bedchamber prepared. Has it been done?" Despite the soft tone of the speaker, Margaret suspected that she had a will of steel.

"*Domna* Marilla, I was not informed that we were expecting guests," Martha whined, "and I did not know that a room was to be prepared."

"Excuses will not get our visitor into bed," Marilla replied. "And *Mestra* Rafaella has had a wearisome journey, for she has been thrice upon the trail, with no sleep and little to eat. Now, stop hanging about and go to your duties. Julian, I wish to speak with you."

Margaret heard the murmur of Julian's conversation with his mistress and the swish of skirts as the various servants hurried away to their tasks. Her two stretcher bearers waited patiently, holding the litter between them. Margaret could see the back of the one at the front. A concerned Rafaella bent down over her. She touched Margaret's wrist, then clasped her hand tenderly.

"How are you?"

"Dreadful." She noticed the dark circles beneath the guide's bright eyes and the strain around the generous mouth and felt guilty for complaining. Her usually shining curly hair was dirty, and clung to her skull, as if she had gotten wet recently. Had it been raining? She could not remember. "I keep fading in and out, and having these terrible visions. My throat hurts!"

"I am not surprised. You screamed loud enough to scare a banshee most of the way here. But now you will be taken care of."

"I worried you, didn't I?" Margaret seemed determined to make the worst of a bad situation. "This isn't fun—you didn't bargain for a nursing job. I'm so sorry, Rafaella."

"Don't be foolish. None of this is your fault. I have never seen anything quite like this fever you have. If you had not assured me you were no *leronis,* I would swear you were having threshold sickness."

"I am much too old for that," Margaret replied. "Aren't I?" A cold fear clutched her now. Rafaella had told her enough about threshold sickness during their travels to make her extremely uneasy. It was a child's sickness, and she was no child, but she was not really certain that her age gave her any immunity. And Margaret now knew that it presaged the onset of that mysterious *laran*. She knew what that meant, in a vague way, and she knew she wanted nothing to do with it!

A fair woman of some fifty years came to the other side of the litter. She had sharp features, pretty once, now honed with age to a narrow jaw and a vulpine nose. "Welcome to Ardais. I am Lady Marilla Lindir-Aillard." She patted Margaret's other hand. "Rafaella—go to bed! You look ready to drop in your boots! I will see to your companion. What is your name, child? Rafaella told us nothing but that her companion had fallen ill with some unknown malady."

"I am Marguerida Alton," she whispered so softly that she could barely hear herself.

"What? Say again. I am slightly hard of hearing." From the expression on Marilla's face, the immediate frown and the slight pursing of lips, Margaret was certain she had heard her well enough, but did not believe her ears.

"This is *Domna* Marguerida Alton, *Domna* Marilla," Rafaella answered.

The fair woman lifted her head slightly and looked at the guide. "I believe I told you to go to bed." *So, this is that child of Lewis'! It can be no one else. I thought she had died during the Rebellion—no, I remember, that was another. Lew took her away when he left. Yes, she has the look of her family—I hope I am doing the right thing, having her here Zandru! She could be Felicia Darriell's twin!* As Lady Marilla had these thoughts, Margaret saw a face, aged gently, that mirrored her own so closely she felt a shudder. She had no idea who Felicia might be, but there was no denying that they were very alike.

Rafaella hesitated, clearly reluctant to abandon her charge, yet nearly trembling with exhaustion. "As you wish, *domna*," she finally said. The Renunciate reluctantly released Margaret's hand and vanished. *She looks so terrible—I don't want to leave her, but I'm nearly dead with exhaustion myself. Why do these things happen to me? She has gotten to be like a sister, but I know she'll be in able hands now. It won't do anyone any good if I get sick as well!*

Lady Marilla smiled, showing what seemed to be a great many sharp teeth. "Rafaella is a good woman, but she does not take orders at all well. Now, let's get you settled into bed and find out what is wrong with you."

"I am sorry to be such trouble," Margaret whimpered. She was feeling hot once more, and her head was starting to spin. Her skin felt as if it were tissue-thin; it seemed as if the very light from the high windows could penetrate through her body. It hurt so much.

"Nonsense. You are no trouble at all. Take the lady up to the Rose Room, lads, and be careful about it!" *Trouble! The Altons have been nothing but trouble for generations. Poor thing. Threshold sickness, and she has to be at least twenty-six! This is beyond me. I hardly know what to do, and I always know what to do! Always! That's what I get for being so proud. I am going to need more than a healer, and quickly.*

Time lost all meaning. There were voices, several different women, and terrible tasting drinks which made her gag and spew. There were cool cloths pressed against her brow, and others which washed her limbs. The hands that held them were gentle, but Margaret still cried out at their touch. And, shadowing it all, there were the nightmares. She saw Lew and the two sisters, Marjorie and Thyra, and, behind them, Felicia whose face she seemed to wear. They all seemed to want something from her, something she could not grasp. This made them all angry, and she tried to remain awake to avoid them, but her body betrayed her again and again.

During the few lucid moments she had, she saw the ancient crone who forced her to drink foul-smelling draughts and Lady Marilla and Rafaella. They all appeared anxious, and she tried to tell them she was all right, but her throat was too raw to make any sound but terrible croaks.

At last she heard a voice clearly. "I am sorry, my lady, but this is beyond my skills as a healer. You will have to send for a *leronis*."

"I have, Beltrana, but she will not arrive today. Do what you can. A pity that she came here—it would have been so much simpler if she had gone to Armida." Lady Marilla's voice was weary, and more than a little bitter.

"Now, now, my lady. It does no good to be wishing after what isn't. You should know that by now—but you always were one for wanting what you hadn't." There was a rusty chuckle, and, surprisingly, an answering laugh.

"Yes, I am. Still, after all these years, and all my disappointments. She is starting to come around. I think you'd better give her another dose."

"Very well. But I don't like it."

"Nor do I, Beltrana, nor do I."

The turmoil of her mind faded, and Margaret found herself in the center of a wide bed. She looked at the embroidered hangings around it, and wondered, for a moment, where she was, and why she was tucked up so tightly. Then it all came back, the sudden fever and the wretched trip in the litter. And with those memories there were also her terrible dreams.

Margaret felt very weak, but her head was clear for the first time in several days. At least she thought it was days, because she seemed to recall changes in the light beyond the bed curtains, days and nights and days again. Carefully, she pulled herself up into a sitting position and saw a woman sitting in the wide seat of the window. She was very old, and her skin was like parchment, but she looked up sharply at the movement on the bed.

"Good day, *domna*. I am Beltrana the healer. How do you feel?"

Margaret didn't answer immediately, but listened to the steady patter of the rain against the window. She was so sensitive that it sounded like kettle drums to her ears, though she knew it was only an ordinary noise. So this was the woman who had given her all those dreadful-tasting drinks. She supposed they must have done her good, but she could still find the flavor of the most recent one in her mouth, and it was foul. "I feel like ten miles of bad road, actually, but I am hungry. Is that good?" Then she realized that she had spoken in Terran, not *casta*. She licked her cracked lips and made a face. "I think I am actually hungry," she said slowly in *casta*. "Is that good?"

The crone nodded and chuckled, looking relieved. "It is a sign of returning health. That last remedy I tried seems to have broken your fever."

"Remedy?" Margaret had a sharp memory of struggling while another draught was forced down her throat. "You mean the stuff that tasted like bird droppings?" She thrust out her tongue and grimaced. It hurt! Every muscle in her body seemed to be tender.

Beltrana nodded, and the white hair that crowned her old head shone like a halo in the light. Margaret dropped her eyes, for the movement of the healer's head made her dizzy. "No one has ever described it that way before, but yes."

"When can I get up?"

"Not for some time, *domna.* You have been in a high fever for three days and nights, and I nearly despaired. Now you must rest and eat and regain your strength."

"But—I've been resting!" Margaret knew she was behaving badly, but whenever she had been sick as a child, she had always insisted she was fine and wanted to get up immediately. Actually, just the act of sitting up had exhausted her again, but she refused to admit it to anyone but herself.

"*Chiya,* you have been extremely ill, and you cannot just leap from the covers. You do what Beltrana tells you, and you will be fit again." *I don't like the look of her yet. Her color is too high, and she will throw another fever if we do not watch her—so headstrong and willful! She is not out of the forest yet—and I want her to be better when the* leronis *arrives.*

Margaret heard the unspoken words, and they made her shiver. *Why is this happening to me? Why can I suddenly pick up things that aren't said? I did it a little, before, but now it seems like I am hearing more. Damn! It's not right, or fair! I don't want to be sick or hear thoughts. I don't want a* leronis, *whatever that is! I want to be back in my rooms at University, or anywhere but here. If Ivor hadn't died . . . . I wish I had never come to Darkover!*

Tears welled up in her eyes, then began to trickle down her face. Her skin was so tender that it hurt to feel the drops against it. Margaret sank back into the pillows.

Beltrana rose stiffly and came over and tucked the

covers in again. "I know, I know, little one. But you let old Beltrana take care of you, and you will be up and about quick as a flash."

"I take care of people, not the other way around," she sobbed. "But I didn't take care of Ivor, and he died! It's all my fault!" She balled one hand into a fist and struck the pillow feebly.

The old woman patted her arm gently, but not so gently that it didn't hurt, and Margaret winced. It was infuriating—crying like a baby and being sick. But she could not seem to stop, and after a few minutes, she stopped trying.

"Rafaella, I am totally sick of being sick," Margaret complained the following morning. "I want to get out of bed!"

The guide smiled at her. "If you are being bossy, I guess you must be better. You gave us a terrible scare, Marguerida. I thought Lady Marilla was going to pop her buttons—as vulgar as that is to say of one of the Comyn." Rafaella looked rather worn, but her eyes were their usual mischievous selves. Her hair was bright with a recent washing, and the circles under her eyes were not as dark as they had been when they arrived.

Margaret shifted under the covers, trying to find a comfortable position, and failed. She envied Rafaella's cleanness. She felt very grubby, even though she knew she had had several sponge baths, and that her nightdress had been changed more than once. The thought of a bath was extremely desirable, but she was so weak she would probably drown if she tried to take one.

She wished she was better at doing nothing, and resting afterward. After a few moments, Margaret decided that she was bored, as well as restless. There was probably nothing to read in this enormous house, and she wasn't sure she could have done that anyhow. She cast about in her mind for something to discuss, and decided she wanted to hear more about her hostess. After all, she was taking up a bedroom, and probably causing a lot of bother for the servants. "Tell me a little about her, will you? She seemed very formidable, from the little I can remember."

"That's a good word for it. She had to be, to endure

Lord Dyan Ardais. They were fond of one another, which is odd. He was . . . well, different." Rafaella seemed extremely uncomfortable now, her voice low and tense. "He died before I was born, so I don't know most of the story. People don't like to talk about him. And it is not proper to gossip in someone's house." The guide's face was conflicted as she spoke, but at least all Margaret heard were the words. That was a great relief. Maybe she was not much of a telepath after all. Perhaps she had only heard things she thought people were thinking. *Stop that! Stop trying to convince yourself that you are imagining this stuff! Be the scholar you pretend to be, and accept the facts.*

Then what Rafaella had said sank in, and Margaret shrank into the pillows. Her mind recoiled, as if it were trying to escape itself. She *knew* that name, and she possessed the memory of a face to go with it. She could see a hawk-faced man, handsome and fierce. And the name Dyan Ardais triggered another memory, of a cold room, and something . . . *"You must not remember, and you must not question. I will not let you destroy me—you are sick, and soon, you will not be sick any longer. You will be free of pain and fear, little one. Just do as I say, and soon it will all be over."*

Margaret did not know who spoke in her mind, but she found she was trembling all over. The voice was peculiar, familiar and yet not. There was something about it that made her think of mirrors, and how she disliked them. She didn't want to think about it, or about that man, that Dyan person. He had picked her up, hadn't he, and taken her to a cold place. The memory frightened her even more than the one of the silver-eyed man did, and she wanted to run away. Only her legs were child limbs, too short to escape from the peril.

A familiar vision erupted before her eyes, one she had seen many times, and each time she had managed to bury it away deep in her mind. Margaret could see a battle, with light and swords. It had gone on and on, and yet it was actually very brief. Her tired brain could not deal with the contradictions, so she stopped trying to figure it out.

The events played themselves out, like some ancient vid-dram, and when it was over, he lay dead, the man called Dyan Ardais. She was certain of it—that she had actually witnessed this memory. He looked quite harmless in defeat, nothing to be frightened of. But now Margaret knew why she had been so uneasy when she met Danilo at Comyn Castle. It had nothing to do with Regis Hastur's quiet paxman, except that he bore a name which disturbed her.

The body of Dyan lay on the floor, and beside him there was another body. In memory, the face was turned away, but the wild red hair spread on the stones told her it was Thyra. She had not seen her mother die, but she had seen her dead, and for a moment she was furious. Why hadn't she been protected from that? Where was Lew in all this—she was certain he was nearby, but her memory told her nothing. The empty husk that had been Thyra, who had terrified her, seemed now a tragic thing, a broken vessel.

She wanted to reject the memories, but now she knew that she would never again be able to stamp them out. It was pointless to even try. She sighed a little, and noticed Rafaella watching her with some alarm in her weary face. Margaret shrugged. "It is all right. I was only remembering something I wanted to forget."

"Oh. Your face got so white—I didn't think it could get any whiter, and then it did. You looked like you wanted to faint."

"No—I am not going to faint, though that would be something of a mercy just now."

For the first time she wondered what else she had deliberately forgotten, and now she wondered why she had done it. She had been very small, very young and vulnerable. People had moved her from room to room, and if they were not cruel, neither were they kind. It was almost as if she were not important except as some sort of bargaining piece to make her father do something. He wasn't the old man then, but younger than she was now, and already one-handed, and probably just as uncertain of himself as she knew herself to be.

Her thoughts unwillingly returned to Dyan Ardais, so tall and stern. He had been, she realized, quite an attractive man, but very remote and cold. What had made him so? She could remember his movements, how he never hurried, and how hard and strong his hands had been when he picked her up. Why had he done that? There was something . . .

He had taken her to a place which was both empty and occupied, a narrow room with blue glass in the walls. But it was not glass, it was stone, and the light came through it. It was not only the walls either. The high ceiling and the floor beneath were made of the same stuff. It was like being inside a blue diamond—quite impossible, of course. The room was incredibly cold, and she had shivered because she was only wearing a nightdress. And because she was frightened.

Margaret felt impressions bob about in her mind more than actual memories now. The room seemed quite empty, except for a high-backed chair, carved of gray stone, placed at the center of the chamber. It was like a throne, she thought. She wanted to look away, but her eyes seemed drawn to the vacant seat. She could almost make out a presence, the figure of a very small woman with eyes that ate light and sound and, most of all, feeling. When the strange entity looked at her, she had felt empty, no longer Marja, but a small nothing without identity.

The name Ardais had triggered a wisp of memory. So why did she still have the feeling that there was something dangerous about Danilo Syrtis-Ardais? It was quite a distinct emotion—something different from her remembered fear in that crystalline chamber. Was it because he would do anything to protect Regis Hastur? That had nothing to do with her, did it? Perhaps he was no threat at all, but simply a man who reminded her of what she did not wish to be reminded. She knew that since she had come to Darkover the sounds, and particularly the smells, had conjured up all the things she had hidden away in the recesses of her mind. Something had occurred which she did *not* want to remember, something to do with that little woman shimmering on a seat of stone. Where was that room, that crystal place? She did not want to know, and yet she knew she must!

It was more than not wishing to recall the past, she realized with a start. That voice! The cold voice that told her not to question, not to remember! It wasn't Dyan nor was it that other man, the silver man, who haunted her dreams. It was a woman's voice, she was certain, and it had something to do with the blue crystalline chamber. It made her dizzy to think about it.

"Marguerida, what is it?" Rafaella shook her wrist.

"I guess I am not as well as I thought," Margaret murmured.

"You eyes rolled back in your head, *chiya,* and I thought you were going to have another seizure."

"Another what?"

"A seizure—you had several during our journey here. Small ones, to be sure, but frightening nonetheless."

"Did I? I am sorry if I frightened you." Margaret spoke calmly, refusing to express the terror which gripped her heart. She had never shown any evidence of epilepsy before, but who could say what this strange illness might provoke. After a moment the fear subsided a little, and she thought that it was a pretty pickle to be ill so far from Terran medical aid. *I really got myself into it this time, didn't I?* "Fevers sometimes cause fits, you know."

"Do they?" Rafaella seemed reassured by Margaret's apparent sanguinity. The frown lines between her light brows smoothed, and her mouth relaxed a little. Margaret looked at her, and found she felt a great fondness for her guide. She had never had many friends her own age. Her fellow students at University had been nice enough, but she always kept her distance from them. It was almost as if she were unwilling to get close to anyone. The Davidsons had been more than friends, but they were both two generations older than she was, and it was not the same.

Margaret let herself sink into the sensation of friendship in silence, clasping Rafaella's callused hand. It was a new feeling to her, as fresh as spring blossoms, and she wanted to savor it. She knew, somehow, that she could trust Rafaella completely, in any situation.

No! You will keep yourself apart!

She flinched as she heard these words spoken in a soft but unyielding, female voice which belonged to no woman she knew. It was not Dio, nor Thyra. For a flash she saw the glass room once more, and she knew that the woman whose invisible presence occupied the throne there was the speaker. How she had created this barrier to any intimacy when Margaret was too young to protect herself, she could not guess. But she knew that this had happened, that it was real, not imagined. She felt herself being drawn toward the empty throne, sucked against her will to move toward the thing, and she almost screamed.

Then the vision was gone, and she was once again in the bed, tucked beneath warm covers and as safe as she could be. So long as she did not remember, and did not allow anyone to come too close, she was safe. Her mind was full of locked rooms, full of doors that must remain shut. But every moment she remained on Darkover, she was certain, the chance that she would remember what she *must not* grew greater. She could not escape from this terrible presence in her own mind as long as her body lived. That was what it had meant when it said she would be free soon.

Margaret felt despair rise in her throat. She was going to die. She almost wanted to die, rather than continue being a prisoner of her own mind, of elusive memories, and that thing which dwelt within her. Another part of her, however, was outraged. For a moment she understood that her many angers, so strange and powerful, came from this part of her. And that part not only wanted to live, but it wanted to revenge itself on . . .

She was still too weak to manage these conflicting emotions. She wanted to cry, scream, leap out of bed, take an ax to something, faint, and several other actions she lacked the energy to put names to. Instead of trying to deal with her turmoil, she said, "I think I'd better take another nap now. Even if I feel as if I have been sleeping since forever."

"Yes, I think so, too. Your pulse is racing, and Beltrana will have my hide if anything happens while you are in my care." Rafaella leaned forward and kissed Margaret's cheek very tenderly.

Margaret was startled by this affection, startled and moved. She felt awkward. Clumsily she returned the gesture, then turned her face away, into the pillow, so that no one would see the blush that colored her cheeks.

Poor thing. I wonder what she would have done if I had given her a proper hug?

12

◆

The following morning, Margaret was feeling somewhat better, but her pulse still raced if she tried to get up, and her knees were like jelly. This unpleasant discovery had presented itself when Rafaella had helped her out of bed while two maid servants changed the bedding, and she had cursed until she was too tired to continue. She also found that whenever she was alone in the room, she panicked.

Luckily, Rafaella seemed willing to stay with her, and she was almost able to convince herself that sudden attacks of fear when she was alone were due to her illness. She had the feeling that there was something she had remembered the previous day that was bad, very bad, but she couldn't recall it now, and she was almost relieved that it was gone again.

To pass the time, she asked the guide to tell her about some of the things she had done on her other journeys, and the Renunciate, after a show of modesty, began to regale her with tales of snowstorms and great cliffs, brigands and the other dangers of the road. It was interesting, but it made Margaret feel that her own life had been rather dull by comparison. Not that she had particularly wanted adventures, of course—she was not that sort of person.

A soft rap on the door interrupted a quite good story concerning an encounter with a banshee, and Rafaella rose to answer it. Margaret heard the murmur of voices, and then the sound of two sets of boots moving toward the bed. One of the voices was male, and she hastily pulled the covers up over her chest and tucked her tangled hair down into the collar of her nightgown.

"*Domna,* may I present Lord Dyan Ardais," Rafaella said, her body stiff with outrage. *For shame! He knows he has no business barging into the room where a single female is sick. Just like an Ardais to claim a right that violates good manners!*

The sound of the name made her want to shiver, but she knew this was not the man in her memories. He was dead, wasn't he? She had seen him dead! She could just feel the shimmer of memory, hovering at the edge of her mind, and she forced it back into the recesses with every strength she possessed. This must be a son or grandson, or even some relative of Danilo's, and no one to fear. There were probably ten people called Dyan Ardais running around Darkover. It was probably a very common name! So why didn't she believe that?

Despite her wariness, Margaret found her curiosity stirring. She heard Rafaella's thoughts with some disquiet. Since no further incidents of overhearing people's thoughts had occurred during the morning, she had almost managed to convince herself that it was not a very important matter, that it was only a small talent, like the ability to juggle. Now she wondered why it came and went, why it happened sometimes and not others? Was it strong emotions that did it? There had to be a logical explanation, if only she could find it. Yet, as much as she wanted to ask, something inside her kept her silent and raging.

She was starting into another headache, trying to figure it out, so she made herself let go of the problem. Instead, she wondered what the Renunciate would have thought if she had seen Margaret with Ivor on Relegan, garbed in a few feathers and some large blossoms. Rafaella would have been scandalized, probably, even though Ivor was old enough to have been Margaret's grandfather. From what she had managed to gather about Darkovan customs, that might have been all right. She was not sure. They seemed to have some very odd ideas about the relationship between the sexes, and she didn't quite understand it yet. She felt herself quite old enough not to have need of any chaperone, but it was clear that Rafaella was ready to defend her honor, and if she had not been so weak, she would have laughed out loud.

The man who looked down at her from between the bed curtains was of moderate height, flaxen-haired and startlingly handsome. He appeared to be her own age or a little younger, and his eyes were so pale as to be nearly colorless. He did not resemble that othe. ^van, the one of her memories, for that man had had dark hair, hadn't he? He looked away, dropping his eyes hastily, and Margaret remembered that it was considered very rude to look directly at members of the opposite sex on Darkover.

For just a second she saw the older face of Dyan Ardais superimposed upon the young man, and she began to tremble a little. They were very alike in their bone structure, but otherwise the newcomer looked more like Lady Marilla. There was none of the forcefulness she remembered from that other Dyan. This man had an arrogance about him, but no confidence in it. His chin was narrow, like Lady Marilla's, and rather weak. He moved restlessly beside the bed, back and forth, and looked at the walls and curtains anxiously, as if he did not enjoy being indoors.

"*Dom* Dyan," she said quietly. "I cannot thank you and your mother enough for taking care of me."

He took hold of one of the bedcurtains and began to pleat it between his fingers. "Are you really Marguerida Alton?" The question burst from between his lips as if he could not prevent himself. *She has the look of an Alton—too much nose for beauty. I do wish Mother were less ambitious. If she tells me it might be an advantageous alliance one more time, I will fall on my sword and be done with it!*

"So far as I know, I am." Margaret wanted to ignore these highly-colored underthoughts, intrusive as they were. *"Too much nose for beauty,"* indeed! It was a good thing Margaret wasn't a vain person. He was, she decided, purposely distracting her from her own thoughts and the anxiety that played along her muscles, a very dramatic young man, still under his mother's thumb.

"And have you really taken the Big Ships to Terra?"

"Well, I've never actually been to Terra, but I have visited a number of worlds, yes."

"Oh." He shifted his feet uneasily. "I wanted to do that, but I can't, you see, because I have to stay here."

"That must be difficult for you."

"Here, now," Rafaella interrupted. "You told me you

wanted to see if *Domna* Marguerida was on the mend, not gabble on about places you can't go."

"I . . . I'm sorry. I hope you get better soon. Rafaella says you are a musician, so perhaps when you are feeling better, you could sing for us. My grandfather was a fine singer, they say. I never knew him. I don't seem to have inherited the talent, but I love to listen to music."

"That will be quite enough," Rafaella said sternly. "You go off right now! She's too weak to be pestered." *Especially by the likes of you!*

Apparently the young Lord Ardais was accustomed to taking orders from women, for he made a little bow and exited hastily. "What was that all about?" Margaret asked when he was gone.

Rafaella gave one of her telling sniffs. "Men! They think every woman is just panting to get married and have their children—as if we had no other purpose in the world!"

Margaret was highly amused, but held back her smile. "All men, or just this one in particular?"

"Him! He has three *nedestro* sons, but he can't seem to get himself a wife so far. He nearly married one of the Lanart-Hastur twins a few years back, but she had *laran* and went to a Tower instead. I can't remember if it was Ariel or Liriel—I never can remember which is which, though for twins they are as unlike as milk and wine. He is foster-brother to Mikhail Lanart-Hastur, and he grew up with those girls. The *comyn* are a little wary of marrying an Ardais, ever since the Sharra Rebellion." Her eyes narrowed, as she was suddenly aware of having said too much. "That's old gossip. It has been a long morning for you. Why don't you take a nap, and I'll bring you a tray with some soup soon."

The term foster-brother rang a distant chime in Margaret's mind. In a vague sort of way, she knew that it was a common practice on Darkover to foster one's children to another family. She could remember that the Senator had once or twice mentioned his own foster-brother, and she suddenly realized that he must have meant Lord Regis Hastur. It seemed to her a very strange custom, to give one's children to relatives or strangers to rear, but she knew it was not an uncommon practice in other human societies. The idea seemed to be that strangers could discipline teenage children better than parents, that they were more objective. Margaret had definite opinions about the entire subject of objectivity. She thought it was fine for the sciences, and utterly silly for real people.

There was something in what Rafaella had said that she did not want to think about—that her mind seemed to avoid deliberately. Whenever she tried to concentrate on it, her brain refused to cooperate. There was a word, only a word, that insisted on slithering away, and this infuriated her. It was bad enough that her mind was full of locked rooms without single words provoking mental discomfort. Margaret suddenly thought of the old tale of Bluebeard, the man who killed his wives, and how he had given his last spouse the keys to the castle with the admonition that she must not open a particular room—which, of course, she had, being humanly curious.

What was the word? She groped in her mind for a moment. Ah, yes—Sharra. No, it wasn't. It was another word, very similar, but another word entirely. It had something to do with that huge jewel she had dreamed of—or was it the jewel with the chair inside it? She felt herself shudder all over as she struggled to grasp fragments of memory.

What she had remembered the previous day returned, less vividly than before, so that she was able to think about it without doing more than tremble a little. The chair and the presence who sat on it in that icy chamber was her personal Bluebeard. She felt certain of that. People seemed to be pressing keys into her hands, but she did not know what rooms they opened, and she was afraid of what she might find behind them. To her it seemed much worse than the corpses of dead wives.

She would have wished that she had never come to Darkover, but it was much too late for that. Margaret forced herself to accept the present without regret. She did not like it, but she had to deal with it, no matter what. If only she hadn't gotten sick.

Everything around her, the scent of the bedclothing, the sound of the rain pattering down, the very air, spoke to her heart of the home she had never found elsewhere. Her safe life as Ivor Davidson's associate was fading into a kind of dream, and she resented that. It had been a happy, simple life, full of interesting intellectual puzzles and strange planets, without the complications of family.

Family! That word meant a great deal on Darkover. For the first time, she had an actual family that she had never known about. She had discovered an uncle who, like her, had a foot in the Terran Empire and on Darkover, and she suspected that Rafe was only the tip of an iceberg. It seemed as if everyone on Darkover—or at least those families in the Comyn—was related to everyone else, either by blood or by loyalties. What about Dio's relatives? She might have a dozen aunts and uncles and hundreds of cousins she had never heard of, and while these would not be blood relations, they would be "family" as well.

For the first time she thought of the Senator and his lady as the exiles they were, cut off from the culture they had been born in, away from all the connections which bound the *comyn* into a body both politic and social. Margaret had never considered that her parents might be unhappy, that Lew might have drunk to excess to forget the smells and sounds of Darkover. And what about Dio? Margaret had never heard her complain, but sometimes she had sat looking into the fireplace in the evenings with an expression of sorrow in her features. She would poke the burning wood and sniff, and now Margaret knew she must have been yearning for the pleasant scent of burning balsam which seemed to linger in every place from Gavin's hovel to the halls of Comyn Castle. If she responded to these remembered odors and noises so strongly after leaving Darkover when she was five or six, how dreadful it must be for Dio and Lew who had lived for so many of their years on the planet?

Margaret dwelled on her newfound empathy for her parents for a time, but after a while she acknowledged she was still absolutely furious that she had been kept in such ignorance of her heritage. It didn't make any sense! There had to be a reason, some rational cause, for the silence. Her father had represented Darkover in the Senate, but he never discussed the planet at home.

Lew, I can't stand it! Dio's voice was as clear as if she had been in the bedroom at Castle Ardais. *Every time I mention Darkover, Marja starts to scream! She curls up in a ball and hides her eyes, and I am afraid she will start having convulsions or something!*

I know, my love. I know! And I am sorry you have to deal with it. She was fine when we left—a normal child, if a little aggressive. She was too little to know how to be a polite telepath, wasn't she?

I'll never forget it! The little minx watched every time we made love—she was worse than impolite; she was damned intrusive! But, you know, I'd give a lot to have her like that again, instead of this remote adult in a child's body. What has happened to her?

I think the voyage out was traumatic—her allergy to the space travel drugs—but I think there is something more. Somehow her channels have been . . . tampered with. I was only a mechanic; not a Keeper, but it doesn't take a leronis to know that Marja has sustained some sort of deep shock. She will probably grow out of it, in time. Children are wonderfully resilient.

I don't think so, Lew. You don't spend as much time with her as I do, so you can't really judge . . .

I can't! Every time I look at her I remember Sharra and how small Thyra looked when she was dead, and how white Regis' hair was. . . .

I think we should take her back to Darkover, Lew.

No, Dio. I think going back would kill her! And it would certainly kill me!

Margaret blinked. Had she actually overheard this conversation, or was her excellent imagination playing games with her? Her father had wanted to keep her safe, even though the sight of her had caused him pain. It must have gotten worse as she grew into womanhood, for she knew now that she had a strong resemblance to her mother, Thyra. How relieved he must have been when she left for University. The Senator must have thought she would be safe there. How could he have known that her work, so tame and simple, would eventually lead her back to the place which was more dangerous to her than any known disease. Well, he couldn't have, unless he could see into the future, and no one could do that. Or *could* they?

At that moment she felt in no immediate danger of dying, though a few days before she would not have believed she would live through whatever odd bug had

plagued her. It seemed Lew's worst fears were not to be
realized. But she did feel threatened, mostly by the tricks
her mind was playing. There were things lurking inside
her which, if she could not remember them soon, would
drive her crazy. What did they do with madwomen on
Darkover?

Sharra! The word echoed in her mind, like some great
bell tolling doom. Her father had used it when he spoke
to Dio, too. Brigham Conover had mentioned it in connection with some rebellion. What was that? It sounded
like a woman's name, but there was no accompanying
memory of a person attached. Wait! There was something else; that word tried to wriggle away in her mind.
She nearly had it! Sweat beaded her forehead. Almost,
almost! Similar sound. She was a musician and she dealt
in sounds! So, why the devil couldn't she . . . *Ashara!*
That was it! It was a place and a person all at once. She
nearly sobbed in her triumph.

For a flash she "saw" the indistinct figure which was
enthroned in that terrible, cold room. Then her stomach
clenched and her heart staggered in its beat. Margaret
curled her hands into the blankets, hanging on for what
felt like dear life. The words she had reclaimed with
such effort sank down into her mind, and the feeling of
a great hand seizing her heart passed away. *I hope they
have a good place for madwomen here,* she thought as
she slipped into the safety of unconsciousness.

By early evening, Margaret was almost herself again.
Rafaella had awakened her with a bowl of soup and
several slices of bread. She had gobbled them down so
quickly she had nearly been sick, but once the food was
settled, she began to feel nearly normal. Strength was
returning to her limbs, and she knew if she had to stay
in bed another minute, she would scream.

"I'm getting up," she announced.

"I can see that," Rafaella answered disapprovingly as
Margaret swung her legs over the side of the bed. "Are
you sure?"

"I need to move around. If I stay in bed much longer,
I will start counting the stitches in the embroidery on
the curtains out of sheer boredom! There isn't even any-

thing here to read. I would almost sell my unborn children for a trashy novel and a box of chocolates."

Rafaella looked scandalized. "What a thing to say! You don't mean it, do you? Only Dry Towners sell children."

"Of course I don't mean it literally. Where are my clothes?"

"Oh." The guide looked immensely relieved. "I'll fetch them. Terranan do not sell children, do they?"

"No, Rafaella, they neither sell children nor eat them. At least not on civilized worlds. There are a few places I've heard of, very primitive planets, where that happens."

"How horrible." Rafaella handed Margaret her garments, disbelief strong in her voice. They were well washed and scented with balsam. She lifted her tunic to her nose and inhaled deeply. Then she noticed her own smell. Even with the frequent sponge baths, she was still pretty high. "I want a real bath first."

"Very well." Rafaella sounded extremely doubtful. "But I'd better come with you. You might drown otherwise."

The Renunciate took back the garments, then offered Margaret a warm robe and a strong arm. They left the chamber where she had lain for days, went a few feet down the hall, and entered the steamy confines of a bathing room. By the time they got there, Margaret's ears were ringing, and she had to sit down for a minute. She wasn't nearly as well as she thought.

Rafaella helped her off with her bedclothes, then got her into the great tub. She leaned over, looking dismayed, trying to keep a hand on Margaret. Finally she shrugged, removed her own clothes, and climbed in as well.

"Umm . . . this is so nice," Margaret murmured. The hot water was boiling her aches away, but she was glad that Rafaella was in the tub with her. The heat was making her slightly dizzy.

"Yes, it is. Do you want me to scrub your back?"

"That would be fine." She felt more relaxed by the second, and even the presence of another woman so near did not manage to disturb her. After all, they had already shared a bed, so why not bathe together. Still, it was a little disquieting to be so close to another person unclothed.

"You were saying something about some planets where they sell children, before."

"Was I?"

"Yes. I am curious—if you don't mind telling me."

Margaret shrugged and felt the warm water move across her shoulders. Rafaella took a large sponge from the side of the tub and began to scrub her back gently. When Rafaella was through, she handed Margaret the soapy sponge to wash the rest of her body. As she scrubbed, Margaret felt so relaxed that it was difficult to think clearly. She would have liked to have melted into the water completely. "I don't mind in the least, but it is a bit hard to explain to someone who has never been on another world. Anything, and I mean anything which is forbidden on one world is sure to be customary—or even compulsory—somewhere else. One of the wonders of the Terran Empire is that so many planets manage to get along with so many different ideas of what being human is. There are some places—not many—where a man has to marry one of his sisters or close cousins in order for his children to inherit property. There are others where a woman has to marry someone who isn't related to her in any way at all. There are scholars who spend whole lifetimes going around researching social customs and writing papers about their findings. Everyone assumes that the way they do things at home is a universal way to behave."

"How does anyone bear it?" Rafaella sounded puzzled and distressed. Margaret looked over her shoulder at the other woman. "Marrying your sister—that's dreadful." She put some soap on Margaret's hair and began to shampoo it gently.

"More dreadful than breeding for *laran*?" Now where had that come from, she wondered. Ah, yes, that conversation with Lady Linnea at Comyn Castle. She sighed. That all seemed to have happened in another lifetime, to some other Margaret. She shut her eyes to keep from getting soap in them, took a slow breath, and continued. "Some long-ago scientist said that the entire purpose of the human species was the conservation of zygotes," she went on, using the Terran word, for no Darkovan equiv-

alent existed that she knew of, "and nothing else mattered. He said Nature didn't give a damn about love or
duty or anything—just keeping the race going."

Rafaella gave a nervous little laugh. "He couldn't have
been from Darkover. What's a zygote?"

Margaret thought for a moment. "The beginning of
a baby."

"I see—well, maybe he was a little Darkovan. But not
very much, because duty is very important. And love,
too, though less so." She turned an interesting shade of
pink beneath her fair skin, and Margaret did not need
to be a telepath to guess that Rafaella was thinking of
the "him" she had not had time to see before they left
Thendara. She wondered if she dared ask the other
woman if she knew Rafe Scott, then decided it was really
none of her business.

Then, as if he were in the room, she heard Lew's
voice, raging and thundering. *I've done my duty, all my
life! I tried to make my father happy, and I have tried
to protect Darkover from the stupidity and greed of the
Federation. I've had a crawful of duty, Dio, and I don't
know if I can stand anymore!*

Margaret could not tell if she remembered these
words, or if they were being said as she heard them. But
there seemed something in them that had an immediacy,
a nearness. It rattled her badly, more than it should
have. She wondered if she were ever going to get used
to these intrusions into her mind, or if they would go
away and leave her be. She hoped for the latter, but
there was a nagging suspicion in her mind that she was
going to be very disappointed. "I think we'd better get
out of the tub now—I'm starting to feel pretty woozy."

"Let me rinse out the soap first." The Renunciate
poured hot water over Margaret's head while she held
on to the side of the tub. "Here, now, I'll get out first,
and then I'll help you." Rafaella climbed out of the tub,
dripping, and dragged a huge towel from a shelf. She
tossed it calmly over her shoulder, and reached out for
Margaret. She put her hands under Margaret's armpits
and lifted her half out of the tub, while Margaret managed to get a leg over the side, and almost stand. For
just a moment she rested against Rafaella, with nothing
separating them but the folds of the towel. She felt the

pulse of the other woman, smelled her clean skin. Then
Rafaella wrapped the towel around her and reached for
another for herself.

Her head swam, then cleared. Margaret felt something
within her, a strength that had nothing to do with bone
and muscle. She wasn't even sure the strength was her
own—there was something almost cold and remote
about it. Her legs, wobbly moments before, seemed firm
again. She breathed the heated air of the bathroom, and
realized she had been holding her breath, as if she were
afraid to be too close to another person, as if touch
were dangerous.

"I can dry myself," she muttered, drawing back from
contact. Rafaella looked doubtful, but just nodded. Margaret rubbed herself dry, wincing a little where her skin
felt tender. By the time she was done, the rush of
strength was gone, and she felt ready to fall down again.
Rafaella was already putting on her clothing, and she
noticed Margaret's distress.

"Here, now, sit down." She took Margaret's arm and
guided her to a chair which stood near the wall. "Silly
goose," she added cheerfully.

Margaret smiled at this, and realized she needed help,
even though she wasn't comfortable with it. She permitted Rafaella to pull her chemise over her head, and help
her get into her underclothes. "I am sorry I am being
so much trouble."

"It is not the trouble I mind, but the worry."

"Worry?"

"Marguerida, *chiya,* I have been half out of my mind
worrying about you for days and days. Everyone has.
Trouble I can manage—my life seems to be full of it.
Here—raise your arms so I can put your tunic on!"

"I feel like a baby!"

"I know. And you are so independent that I'm sure
it sticks in your craw. But one of the things we learn in
Thendara House is that there is no shame in needing
help—that we are sisters, and sisters must help one another. And, believe me, it isn't always easy—because the
sort of women who join the Renunciates are either
plucked chickens who cannot make up their minds, or
bossy roosters in skirts."

Margaret had to laugh at this description. "And which type are you?"

Rafaella shook her head, and sent her unbound hair flying. "No one has ever plucked me!" *I wouldn't permit it, and anyone who tries is going to come to grief. But, you make me feel like a broody hen with a nest with one egg in it. A rooster egg! Oh, dear!*

"I should think not." Margaret struggled to her feet, so she could get her petticoats and skirt on more easily. "Do you enjoy being a Renunciate? I mean, there seems to be a really strong emphasis on Darkover toward marriage and family."

"Yes, but my sisters are my family. And children are welcomed in Thendara House as much as in any other. I just don't need some man telling me what to do." *And "he" gives me the feeling that he wouldn't! Oh, I hope I can trust him—men are such odd creatures.* "Now, let's go back to the room. You need to lie down a bit. If you are feeling strong enough after a rest, then we can take dinner at the table."

"That sounds wonderful. I have almost forgotten what eating at the table feels like. And I am very hungry all of a sudden."

"That's a good sign, and it eases my mind a great deal." Rafaella grinned. "You were a good patient, except for insisting that you wanted to get up every other second."

Two hours later, Margaret descended the long staircase, leaning on Rafaella's arm and gripping the banister tightly with her free hand. Her energy seemed to ebb and flow, without any pattern, so that she felt well enough one second and weak the next. She gritted her teeth, glad of Rafaella's strong arm supporting her, and uneasy with the physical touch at the same time.

Julian Monterey, the *coridom*, was waiting at the bottom of the stairs when Margaret and Rafaella reached the lower floor. "It is good to see you up and about, *domna*," he told Margaret. "We have been very concerned."

"I am sorry if I caused anyone to worry—a fine way for a guest to behave!" She made a face, and was pleased when he chuckled.

"I will show you to the dining hall."

"Thank you. Something certainly smells delicious."
Now that they were off the stairs, Rafaella released her
hold on Margaret's arm, but remained beside her, ready
to support her if she faltered. She was a comforting presence, dependable and strong, and Margaret gave her a
warm glance.

Julian led the way across the entry hall and into a
large chamber where a long table was set for the evening
meal. A pleasant fireplace blazed in one long wall, and
there were a set of tapestries hung on either side of it,
one of a man holding a blazing blade and the other of
a woman with a sparkling jewel in her hands. Their faces
were masterpieces of the weavers' art, and they seemed
to gaze serenely down from the threads.

Two men stood before the fireplace, warming their
hands. One was the young Lord Ardais who had invaded
Margaret's bedroom earlier, to Rafaella's displeasure,
and the other was a stranger. They turned at the sound
of footfalls, and looked at the newcomers with careful
sidewise glances, to avoid the rudeness of direct gaze.

Dyan Ardais stepped toward them and opened his
mouth to speak, but Julian Monterey interrupted him.
"Ladies, may I present Lord Dyan Ardais and Mikhail
Lanart-Hastur, his foster-brother and paxman. Gentle-
men, this is *Domna* Marguerida Alton. You already
know her companion Rafaella n'ha Liriel, of course,
Dom Dyan. But, *Dom* Mikhail, I do not know if you
have encountered her before." The tone of his voice
made it clear that he expected the proper formalities to
be observed. He almost certainly knew about Dyan's
intrusion into her chamber, and did not approve.

Dyan gave the *coridom* a swift look of mild rebellion,
then schooled his features into a sort of arrogance that
made Margaret wince. It was too like her memory of his
father. "*Mestra* Rafaella and I have already met, but I
am pleased to welcome the Lady of Alton to Castle Ardais." He gave a little bow, and Margaret thought that
he might be a spoiled brat, but he had exquisite manners
when he chose to show them.

She barely noticed him, however. It was the other man
who drew her attention, and drew it more strongly than

she was comfortable with. She almost stared, then dragged her eyes away with difficulty.

Mikhail Lanart-Hastur bore some resemblance to Lord Regis, but he was taller and, she guessed, about her own age. He had fair hair that curled across a wide brow, a mouth made for laughter, and eyes of a remarkable blue. At the same time, there was something hesitant about his posture, as if he were not certain where he stood. Still, she instantly liked the look of him, for there was something very steady about him, a quality utterly lacking in Dyan Ardais.

"I am delighted to meet you," he said, in a fine tenor voice, but he did not sound very pleased.

Margaret felt mildly rebuffed, and that increased her interest. Then she chided herself for being a silly fool. What was it about him? She had seen handsome men before, for University was not lacking in comely males, and several much better looking than Mikhail Lanart-Hastur. She glanced at the full mouth, so wary in spite of its generosity, and the eyes which had a quiet sadness in them. She watched him move from foot to foot, restlessly. She did that, too, when she wasn't certain of herself.

Lady Marilla came into the room then, smiling, and interrupted her thoughts. "How good to see you up and about, Marguerida. I trust you do not mind me speaking to you so familiarly—it seems so silly to use forms and titles at a family dinner. We are quite modern here at Ardais, you know. I have had my son educated in the Terran manner, and the women of my household have been instructed in their letters by one of Rafaella's Guild—from the Neskaya House. Not that it has done much good! They cannot see the use of education yet. But we are so isolated here, and I thought it would be good to be better informed. Lord Dyan—my son's father—must be turning in his grave. He disapproved of all things Terran." She rattled on as she motioned everyone toward the table. "Besides, I am old enough to be your mother. My, how tall you are. I had not realized." *What a pity she is a handspan taller than Dyan!*

Margaret ignored this unspoken comment. She had long given up feeling miserable about her height, though when she had been a girl, it had been a dreadful burden

for her. "My father is tall, so I suppose I take after him."
She felt a sudden doubt that she could sustain an entire
meal of pleasantries like that. Her mouth was dry, and
she had just the hint of a headache now. Maybe getting
up hadn't been such a good idea after all.

Margaret found herself seated between Marilla, at the
head of the table, and Mikhail on her left. Rafaella sat
across from her, and Dyan sat beside her, an arrange-
ment which pleased neither of them from the sour expressions on their faces.

"Julian, please have the food brought in," Marilla
said.

A few moments later, a servant carried in a tureen of
soup, holding it aloft, as if it were a grand occasion. He
quite spoiled the effect by rolling his eyes toward Margaret, as if he were very curious about her. A slight clear-
ing of Julian's throat brought him back to his senses,
and he set the tureen down beside their hostess. A second server appeared with a tray with blue and white clay
bowls on it, and held it while the first man ladled out
the soup, then placed it gravely before each diner.

The vapors rising from the soup smelled wonderful,
and it was with some difficulty that Margaret restrained
her hunger until Lady Marilla picked up her spoon and
began to eat. It was delicious, and it was not until she
had nearly emptied the bowl that she really looked at
the china itself. It was finely made, and Margaret realized it was the first time she had seen nonwooden
eating ware.

"These are beautiful bowls, Lady Marilla. I haven't
seen anything like them on Darkover." It was a polite
thing to say, but Margaret, heartened by the excellent
soup, really meant what she said.

"Thank you very much." The little woman was nearly
brimming with pride.

"Oh, no," Dyan muttered. Margaret glanced at him
with surprise. "Now we are in for another . . ."

"This service was made in our own kilns, right here
at Ardais," Marilla interrupted, as if her son had not
spoken.

"You will have to forgive my mother. She has an obsession about clay. Such common stuff." He sniffed, as
if he were embarrassed about something.

Margaret was beginning to think that young Lord Dyan needed to mend his manners. She felt Mikhail stir beside her, and gave him a quick glance. He was a little rosy across his fair cheeks now, and was looking at Dyan with a stern expression on his pleasant features. "On the contrary, Lord Dyan, on some planets fine china is valued above jewels or precious metals. I am not an expert, but these bowls are very beautiful, and the pattern is excellent. And original, as well."

Marilla tried to disguise her delight and failed, for her face was alight with pleasure. It took several years off her age, for some of the lines in her brow smoothed, and her mouth relaxed as it had not before. "It is just an old carving pattern, but I am pleased you like it. You must have eaten off much better pieces than this, surely, being the Senator's daughter."

Margaret laughed and shook her head so that a few wisps of hair escaped the butterfly clasp nestled at the nape of her neck. Rafaella had dressed it for her, but the silky stuff still had its usual bad habit of slipping out of any restraint. It tickled her cheeks in a maddening way. "Perhaps my father has, but for the most part I have dined off unbreakable plastic horrors—when I was not eating off of leaves on some strange world." She put down her spoon, realizing that if she ate another drop she would be too full for anything else.

"Leaves?" Dyan stared at her across the table, then dropped his eyes. "Is that some new custom in the Empire?"

"No," Margaret replied calmly. "Despite my father's position, I have not moved in the more rarified circles of the Federation. That is because I have spent most of my adult life going to places in the galaxy where people had not yet invented, or did not wish to invent, such things as fine china. A broad leaf is a good plate, for you do not have to wash up after supper." She could sense the mild disbelief around the table, except from Rafaella. But at least she heard no thoughts, and that was a relief.

Julian Monterey took a seat beside Dyan Ardais as the next course was brought in—fresh fish lightly battered and fried to perfection. Margaret was glad that the heads had been removed—she hated to eat anything that looked back at her. The servant filled glass goblets with wine, and she sipped a little. It was nicely dry, a good accompaniment to the fish, and she wondered where on Darkover it was warm enough to cultivate grapes. She almost asked, but it was too great an effort.

There was no conversation for several minutes, as everyone concentrated on removing the small bones, then eating the delicate flesh. Margaret was starting to become rather full, and decided her stomach must have shrunk during her illness, for normally she had a healthy appetite, when she remembered to eat. Often she got so involved with her work that she skipped a few meals, then made up for it later. She let her mind wander in the stillness, and was becoming quite relaxed with the wine and the warmth of the room.

Mikhail shifted in his chair beside her, and she raised her eyes from her food to look at him. He looked back, his eyes narrowed and almost hostile. He opened his mouth, closed it, then opened it again, clearly deciding to do something that he thought he should not. "So have you come to throw my aged parents out of their home?"

Margaret was so startled that she nearly dropped her fork. "What? Why would I do that?" She could sense he was in some distress, some conflict, but she had no idea what was causing it. She hated arguments, and usually withdrew at the first hint of a quarrel, unless it was one involving the Terran bureaucracy. Like most people in the Federation, she felt she had a duty to thwart bureaucrats whenever possible.

For once, however, she had no desire to retreat from provocation. In fact, Margaret decided, she almost *wanted* to argue with this stranger. All her suppressed anger seemed to want to find a focus, something to hit or snarl at. And, for no reason she could discern, it felt quite safe to dispute him. It was an intriguing sensation, as if he were not quite a stranger, but someone she almost knew. Ridiculous, of course. She wanted to like him, and she could not imagine why. She felt a warmth toward him, for a moment, and then a rush of chill. *You will keep yourself to yourself—no matter what!*

"Armida is yours, by rights, though my father has been maintaining it for years and years."

Margaret was too distracted by the sudden intrusion

in her mind to answer at first. She felt cold all over, cold and threatened, though she was not sure if it was her sense of the alien presence within her, or the man bristling beside her. Both, perhaps. There was something a little intimidating about his look, for he was staring directly into her face, against good manners. Margaret dropped her eyes, because there was something in his that tugged at her heart in a very disturbing way.

She lifted them again, after a moment, unable to continue to look at her lap any longer. Who was this fellow, and why did she feel as if she knew him? How dare he pull at her heart that way—she was much too old to have her head turned by a handsome profile and clear, blue eyes.

"Your father?" she sputtered at last. "Pardon me, Lord Mikhail, but I haven't the slightest idea what you are talking about. Or do I call you Lord Hastur-Lanart?"

He seemed quite puzzled by her reply, as if her ignorance had taken him off guard. Mikhail shifted his shoulders, as if marshaling himself. *Damn! She has the most beautiful eyes I have ever seen! And that jaw—never thought I'd see a square jaw that looked so fetching on a woman. She probably thinks I am a complete oaf—and I have no one to blame but myself!*

"You really don't know, do you? Amazing." He turned his gaze away, took a deep breath, and continued, as if reciting a lesson which he hated. "I am the youngest son of Gabriel Lanart-Alton, who is kin to your father, and Javanne Hastur, who is elder sister to Lord Regis Hastur. I have two brothers, Gabriel and Rafael, and the three of us are called the 'Lanart Angels,' because we have the names of those *cristoforo* archangels." As he said this a self-mocking edge of sarcasm colored his voice. "We also have two sisters, Ariel and Liriel." He stopped and glanced at her, expecting some reply.

"How nice for you. I always wished for brothers and sisters. Are your sisters angels as well?" Margaret felt like an idiot as soon as the words were out of her mouth, but she still could not make any sense of what he had told her. She was aware of Lady Marilla beside her, continuing to consume her fish in dainty mouthfuls, and Dyan, watching her with bemusement. Only Rafaella seemed to be aware of anything out of the ordinary, for she gave Margaret a look with lifted brows, and a quick grin of reassurance, as if to say, "Don't worry."

Mikhail chuckled, and she felt his tension ease. "Well, my mother wouldn't say that *any* of us were in the least angelic."

"Mothers rarely do," Lady Marilla put in dryly. She cast a look at her son, as if unhappy that he was not talking to Margaret, and letting Mikhail hold her attention.

"I still don't understand anything," Margaret complained, starting to feel both tired and a little annoyed at her dinner companions. "Should I be impressed, awed, or just plain humble?"

"Oh, all of those would do nicely," Dyan said somewhat maliciously.

Lady Marilla silenced her son with a single glance. "I did not realize that you knew so little about the Altons, Marguerida."

"Little? Sometimes I am not sure I know that much!" She was rewarded by mild laughter.

"Confess it, you have made a muddle of things, Mik," Dyan offered, ignoring his mother.

"I suppose I have."

"Why don't you begin at the beginning, then," Margaret said, taking pity on the man. She could sense his embarrassment, and she had not forgotten that he liked her eyes. No one had ever admired them before, and she found she rather enjoyed being admired. It was an odd feeling, though, and she noticed the restless stirring of the cold presence within her.

"Oh, Lord! The beginning?" Mikhail paused, gathering his thoughts, and she waited for him to continue. "I don't really know what I can say."

She could feel his conflict, though his thoughts were not clear enough to make any impression on her mind. Margaret found she was glad of that, since there was something about Mikhail that she decided she would rather not be privy to. "You accused me of planning to throw your aging parents out into the snow, like some landlord in a melodrama. Then you trot out your lineage, as if that would explain everything. Well, it doesn't—so I am still waiting to hear whatever it is you want to say." She was trying to be calm and reasonable, but she was still feeling too weak to keep her voice from rising shrilly. Rafaella looked at her, a little alarmed, and started to speak.

Before she could, however, Mikhail asked, "But what are you planning to do about Armida?" as if it were a question she could answer.

"Why should I do anything about Armida at all? And why does everyone assume I am going to claim something that doesn't even belong to me? My father is still very much alive, as far as I know, so Armida is his business, not mine."

"He gave up his own claim, but not yours," Mikhail interrupted.

"You may call yourself an angel, but your manners are hardly angelic, Lord Mikhail. What would I do with it? I know almost nothing of agriculture or horse breeding. I am a Scholar of the University, not the interloper everyone insists on making me out to be." She felt her face flame in her fury at being misunderstood. It was not fair.

"Forgive me if I disbelieve you, *damisela.*" *I want to believe her, but how can I? And Father will not thank me for looking out for his interests—I can't do anything right! She simply cannot be as ignorant as she pretends— that is impossible!*

"You can believe anything you damn well please," she hissed. Margaret could feel Lady Marilla's eyes on her, watching her in a manner that seemed more suspicious than solicitous. Her head was starting to throb again, and her stomach churned, though whether it was from the lingering effects of her strange illness or from trying to talk to Mikhail she could not decide. If her legs had been steadier, she would have gotten up and walked out of the room, and dealt with the consequences later.

The rage boiled in her body, and she tried to silence it. Margaret pictured her father's face in her mind, trying to direct her anger at him, since she believed he was the author of most of her troubles, but she failed. Instead, she saw Mikhail's fair countenance, deliberately being impossible, for his own reasons. She experienced a desire to punch him right along his strong jaw, just to relieve her mixed feelings of attraction and repulsion.

Before anyone spoke again, there was a heavy knocking at the front door, and Julian rose calmly and left the dining room. In the silence which followed his departure, Lady Marilla leaped into the breach almost anxiously. "Do you think our china would find a market in worlds where people are eating off leaves, Marguerida?" There was something in Marilla's voice which suggested that she thought Margaret had been pulling her leg on the matter of the leaves, a hint of humor she had not glimpsed in her hostess before.

"It is very beautiful and well made, and there is a great demand for such things on many worlds," she answered. It was a relief to be able to understand a question and make a rational answer. Really, these people were very peculiar. What could she expect? They knew virtually nothing about her except that her father was Lewis Alton, and that she was technically the inheritor of a Domain. Of course they would not believe she didn't want the thing—it was out of their realm of experience.

Margaret could hear two voices in the entry, Julian's and a woman's. She tried not to eavesdrop, but she couldn't seem to help herself. The skin at the nape of her neck started prickling, and she was certain that the newcomer was someone she wanted to avoid.

Julian returned, accompanied by a small woman robed in a travel-stained cloak over a crimson gown which seemed to throb in the light of the dining room. Despite her diminutive stature, she had an air of enormous authority about her. Her eyes swept the room, coming to rest on Margaret. Their eyes met for an instant, and Margaret flinched.

"The *leronis* Istvana Ridenow, my lady," the *coridom* announced.

13

———— ◆ ————

Margaret took one look at the small woman, and the remnants of her appetite vanished. There was something uncanny in the steady gaze of the gray eyes, something stern about the set of her narrow shoulders. Only the too-wide mouth in the oval face gave any hint of flexibility, for there were lines around it which spoke of old laughter.

Then her mind repeated the woman's name—Istvana Ridenow—and Margaret began to see a slight resemblance to Dio, her stepmother. Dio was perhaps an inch taller, but just as fine-boned. The hair above the high brow was pale, silver now, but with that yellow tone that previously blonde hair gives in age, and it grew in the same pattern as Dio's did. It had been a long time since she had seen Dio and she had no recent picture. She was probably gray now, too.

For a flash Margaret had an impression of Dio's face, pain-worn and incredibly tired. She looked old, really old. She felt herself shudder and grasped the edge of the table with icy fingers.

Lady Marilla rose from her seat at the head of the table, spilling her napkin onto the stone floor. A genuine smile softened her rather foxlike features, and she moved across the room to greet the newcomer. "Isty! I did not expect you before the morning! Julian—take her cloak, and have another place set. You must be exhausted."

"Oh, do stop fussing, Mari. You know I am never tired." The voice was deep, a fine alto, strong and authoritative and used to being obeyed. "Lord Ardais, Lord Hastur." She acknowledged the men briefly, but her eyes were focused on Rafaella and Margaret.

"Oh, Isty. Still the same as ever." Marilla Aillard did

not seem in the least intimidated, and shook her head, as if recalling some pleasant incident. "If you aren't tired after your journey, you should be. Horses are ever so much more wearying than working the relays." She rose and gave the other woman a light kiss on the cheek, and the gesture was returned gracefully.

"I came as quickly as I could. Your message was rather urgent." Istvana sounded as if she suspected that she had been dragged from wherever she had come from for no good reason, and was prepared to be annoyed.

Marilla appeared just a little anxious now. "It *was*, Isty." *A pity she arrived now, and not tomorrow, as I expected.*

"And it is no longer urgent?" There was a quality in the voice of Istvana, a tension, that belied her claim not to be weary from her journey.

"You must judge for yourself," Marilla hedged, looking anxious and much less the grand lady than she had before. "I must present you to my other guests, Istvana." She drew the now uncloaked woman to the table where a servant was bringing out a clean plate and utensils.

"Don't tell me you are still the same flighty girl you were at Neskaya so many years ago, Mari." The *leronis* said the words gently, and Margaret could hear the quiet affection in them.

Margaret could see Mikhail and Dyan both trying not to laugh at this comment, their fair cheeks reddening from repressed guffaws. She did not blame them one bit. Flighty was hardly a word she would have chosen for her hostess.

Marilla ignored both the byplay and the criticism. "Istvana, I would like to present *Domna* Marguerida Alton and her companion Rafaella n'ha Liriel."

Gray eyes swept across the two women, and Margaret felt she had been examined and found wanting without a word. Then she wondered if the woman knew who was whom. She and Rafaella were alike in coloring, age, and height, like enough to be mistaken for one another. No, the shorter hair of the Renunciate was likely to inform Istvana. Then the *leronis'* words banished her question from her mind. She looked directly at Margaret and spoke. "I am honored to meet you, Lady Alton. This is . . . unexpected. You have been ill?"

"The honor is mine," Margaret answered stiffly. "Apparently, the immunizations the Terrans give are not as effective as they are promised to be, and I have reacted to some local organism. Either that or I have had a bad response to the altitude." She did not believe her own words, and she felt weak and ill, but she was determined not to show it for an instant. Her head pounded, and her mouth started to taste like she had eaten iron filings, not excellent soup and fresh fish.

She watched as Istvana and Marilla exchanged a speaking look. It made her skin clammy, and she looked down at her plate. The remains of her fish were cold now, and she felt her throat clamp shut. The idea of eating another bite made her shiver. The urge to to get up from the table and return to her room as quickly as possible was enormous, and only the knowledge that she lacked the strength to make it up the stairs unassisted kept her in her seat. Instead, she folded her hands into her lap and tried to make herself invisible as she had often done when she was very small.

Evidently, Istvana had decided that eating was a good idea, for she took the place that the servant had set. Margaret tried not to look at her, but kept finding her eyes drawn to the stranger. Her unfinished fish was removed, and a plate of grain, vegetables, and a slab of some meat was put before her. She gazed at it in horror, and bit her lip.

The *leronis* ate daintily but steadily, making inroads on her food that Margaret decided were remarkable. Where did she put it all? Enormous silences punctuated little gusts of conversation that seemed to perish almost before they began, and the meal dragged on and on. There was an air of wariness around the table, the earlier easy cheer and her dispute with Mikhail banished by the presence of the newcomer. It was clear that all of them were trying to pretend that there was nothing out of the ordinary in the arrival of the *leronis,* but Rafaella had told her just enough during their travels that she knew it was rare for Keepers to leave their Towers, whatever those were. Margaret knew the woman's presence had something to do with her, that somehow Istvana and Marilla were conferring without a word being spoken. It made her skin crawl, but she couldn't think of anything she could do about it. She had rarely felt so helpless in her life.

Lord Dyan, after a look from his mother, manfully attempted to liven up the conversation. He asked Rafaella something about horses, and the Renunciate answered him. Then Mikhail chimed in, and the three of them discussed some famous bloodlines. It was all incomprehensible to Margaret, but she was grateful that she was not expected to participate, because she could barely keep her breath going, let alone speak. Margaret revised her earlier opinion of Dyan as a feckless youth, then felt Mikhail stir beside her. She gave Mikhail a fast glance, and met his eyes unexpectedly. It was an unreadable look, and she dropped her gaze hastily, regarding the disgusting stuff on her plate with growing queasiness. It had almost looked like pity, and she could not stand that! How dare he! He was an oaf. And if he looked at her again, she was going to smack him!

Margaret could feel her temperature starting to climb again, and she gulped some water thirstily. The thought of wine was loathsome. She longed for her bed, for silence instead of the clatter of utensils on pottery. The noise of it seemed to go right through her aching brain, like slivers of glass. If only she had not insisted on getting up!

Istvana Ridenow put her napkin beside her plate abruptly and rose. Hastily, they all pushed their chairs back and stood with her. Margaret was slow to move, and she found that Mikhail was watching her in a concerned way that both warmed and annoyed her. Standing, she was swept with a dizziness that made her sway. Rafaella moved around the table with surprising swiftness and took her elbow, steadying her gently. Then the Renunciate glared at everyone accusingly, and Margaret felt the woman's strength and loyalty surround her like a warm blanket.

"You can use my sitting room, Istvana," Lady Marilla announced. "It has not changed much since your last visit." Margaret looked from Istvana to Marilla, and found their faces carefully neutral. She was sure they had been talking to each other—even though she tried to tell herself that they could not have been. She had not picked up any hints, for which she was grateful. She should be glad she had not overheard their conversation, shouldn't she? Now she could escape to her room and go back to bed. And as soon as she was well enough, she would return to Thendara and . . . . her head ached too much to think beyond that.

Her hope was quickly dashed. "*Domna,* if you will come with me," Istvana said calmly, "we will see if we cannot find the cause of your illness."

"I told you it was just . . ."

"You must trust me, *chiya.* I know what is best." The *leronis* spoke in a way that brooked no argument, and Margaret did not feel strong enough to try to disagree. *Why does everyone think they know what is best for me? They don't even know me! And, worse, I no longer know myself. I wish I had never come here. Why did I have to get sick? And who is she to be ordering everyone around, including me? I think they are all a little afraid of her— I know I am. But why?*

Rafaella helped her out of the dining room and down the hall. They followed Istvana into a modest room where a fire crackled comfortingly in the grate. There was a soft couch, several armchairs, and an embroidery stand with a half-completed work stretched on it. The colors of the room were soft blues and creamy whites, and it was a cozy place. Margaret would have enjoyed it if she hadn't felt so wretched.

"Leave us," Istvana told Rafaella. Then she gave the girl a kindly look. "Marguerida will be quite safe with me, I promise."

"Don't tire her, *vai domna.* She has only gotten out of bed today." Then the Renunciate left the room reluctantly, and Margaret sank into one of the chairs, exhausted by the short walk from the dining room. *Damn interfering woman! If she makes Marguerida ill, I'll* . . . The thought was unfinished, as if Rafaella could not decide what she would do. Margaret felt alone and afraid without her companion.

Istvana Ridenow sat down facing Margaret and arranged the folds of her robe across her lap. A silence grew between them, interrupted by one of the servants bringing a tray with a pot of tea, cups, and a slender bottle of what looked like a liqueur. It was a startling

blue, or else the glass was, and Margaret eyed it warily.
She definitely did not want any alcohol.

"I confess I never imagined I would find Lew Alton's
child when I came here," Istvana began, pouring some
tea into a cup and offering it to Margaret.

She took the tea because she was infernally thirsty.
"You and everyone else," she nearly snapped. "Ever
since I got off the ship, people have been coming up to
me and bowing and scraping and trying to give me ball
gowns and . . . I don't know. It has been very confusing.
I don't like being confused!"

"That seems quite reasonable to me," the *leronis* answered with a surprising mildness. "I don't know anyone
who does enjoy being bewildered. Perhaps I can answer
some of your questions."

"That will be a first," Margaret answered bitterly. "No
one on Darkover seems willing to give me a straight
answer to a simple question—they just speak in vague
terms and tell me it is better not to discuss 'such things.'
Or they assume I already know everything, or they tell
me they are my relative. Honestly, I could just scream,
except my throat won't allow it. Am I related to *everyone* on Darkover?"

Istvana laughed. "Essentially, yes. At least you are
related by blood or marriage to all of the families of the
Domains, which in your case is what counts."

"It doesn't count with me," Margaret contradicted. "I
prefer Rafaella to any of these 'new relatives,' if you
must know the truth."

"I see. Then I probably should not tell you that Diotima Ridenow is a niece of mine, should I?" There was
a sparkle in the older woman's eyes, and some of Margaret's tension eased.

"You didn't need to—you look very like her. And
you have the same family name. Does that make you
my stepaunt?"

"Why, yes, it does. I hope you do not mind *too* much."
Istvana's voice was chiding, but not unkind.

"It wouldn't do me any good if I did. It doesn't matter
anyhow, because I am going to go back to Thendara as
soon as I can ride and then I am going back to the
University where I belong."

"Marguerida, do you know about the Gifts of the Domains?"

"I know of their existence—though my belief remains dubious. Lord Regis Hastur and my uncle Rafe Scott made reference to the Alton Gift and Uncle Rafe mentioned that it was 'forced rapport,' but neither of them bothered to explain it very well. Does it come in a nicely-wrapped package?" *Not that I gave them much opportunity, did I? I was afraid to hear all they might have said, and that . . . person in me . . . I must not think about it! Keep myself apart! Yes, that's what I must do.*

Margaret felt that somehow she must prevent the conversation from becoming too serious, and now that she had the opportunity to hear the answers to some of her many questions, she found that did not want to know them. She sensed that there was some danger to her, that the knowledge would alter her in a fashion she would not like at all!

Istvana ignored her joking question. "The Gifts are mental talents which, over the centuries, we have refined. The Ridenow Gift is that of empathy, so I have some idea of how you are feeling. I can't help it, so please don't feel I am intruding. One of the problems in a telepathic society is that of privacy, and we try very hard not to put our noses in where they don't belong."

A telepathic society? How could this woman just sit there as if she were speaking of something ordinary and simple? Empathy? Well, Dio had a lot of that, though Margaret was not sure she would have called it a gift. She realized now that Dio had tried to help her, to reach her, but she had been too angry all the time, hadn't she? And cold. She wondered what it felt like to an empath to be around a furious adolescent, and decided it was probably dreadful. She wanted to weep for her past, but she held herself back from it.

Istvana waited patiently for Margaret to speak, and if she heard any of the thoughts rushing through her mind, she gave no indication. "I guess I've figured out that much, even if I didn't really believe it. I find I keep 'hearing' bits and pieces of people's thoughts. I thought I was going crazy. I can't seem to help it."

"Did that happen before you came to Darkover?"

"Occasionally, but not as much as it does now. And I always told myself I was just imagining things."

"And Lew never told you about the Gifts?"

Margaret emptied her cup. "That's another thing! Everyone seems to assume that my father told me all sorts of things . . . well, he never did! We hardly ever spoke at all, and we certainly didn't have any intimate conversations, mental or otherwise. We just tried to keep out of each other's way when he was home."

"That must have been very lonely for you."

Margaret flared at this. She could not stand being pitied! Then she dragged a breath into her aching lungs and told herself not to get upset. The woman was trying to help, wasn't she? "Not really. I learned not to be lonely almost before I could walk. In the orphanage. And to be brutally honest about it, I can't say it has been a bad thing. All those things that happened when I was little—the things no one wants to discuss—have left me mistrustful." *I keep myself to myself and I am very good at it!*

"Yes, I can sense that about you. But just because you are wary of people does not mean you like being alone. So, you *do* know that the Alton Gift is forced rapport. But can you imagine what that means?"

"The capacity to make contact with people whether they want it or not? That isn't a Gift! That would be a curse, and I am very glad I don't have it."

"Uncontrolled, it would indeed be a curse. We have learned over the years that these talents, *all* talents, must be trained. Your father was very remiss in not teaching you how to use . . ."

"I don't have any Gift!" Margaret shouted at the *leronis* and watched her flinch as if she had been struck. "I *won't* have it! I don't want to know what people are thinking or feeling. I just want to get off this damn planet and go somewhere where I don't have any relatives who want me to—"

"*Chiya,* it is already awakened. You cannot turn back now. Either you learn to use your Gift, or you will indeed go mad. We must test you to determine the strength of your talent, but you cannot turn away from it. I am afraid it is already too late for that."

"You can't know that!" Margaret felt desperation choking her.

"But I can. *I do.* I can sense the Alton Gift even as you sit there, weak from as bad a bout of threshold sickness as I have ever encountered. Usually that happens when one is younger, in adolescence. Do you remember anything like this from when you were a teen?"

"No. I was a perfectly normal child and I never . . . When I was very little, there was something. I can't remember." *She told me not to remember!*

Who told you not to remember, Marguerida?

The mental exchange was over in a flash, and Margaret felt the sharp stab of pain above her brows. She blinked her eyes against it. Her breath came in short gasps, as if she were running, and she felt hot and sweaty. She was terrified, not of the small woman across from her, but of something else.

Istvana Ridenow reached beneath her gown and drew out a small bag which was suspended from a cord. Margaret glanced at it and shrank away. She saw a small hand, a child's hand, reaching for another such silken bag, and heard a voice telling her not to touch. She knew there was something in the bag that was more dangerous to her than poison.

The *leronis* reached within the bag and drew out a shining stone. It was blue and faceted, and it reflected the flames leaping in the hearth on its sparkling surfaces. Istvana cupped it in her hands, so the flames colored her skin with an orange light. Margaret looked into her lap and clenched her hands, driving the nails into her palms so deep they cut.

"*Chiya,* do not be afraid. Lift your eyes and look into the crystal. Do not try to touch it—just look into it."

Istvana's voice was low and compelling, but Margaret refused to move. She looked at her hands and watched a line of blood creep out from beneath her nails while her skull pounded like all the demon drums of Algol at one time. She narrowed her attention so that all she saw or thought of was the way she was driving her nails into her palms.

Moments passed. Margaret heard the faint crackle of the fireplace, the soft patter of rain against the windows and the rustle of trees beyond them. She smelled the

fire, the clothes against her skin, the old stones of Castle
Ardais, and the faint perfume of the silent woman across
from her, waiting with infinite patience for her to look
into the crystal.

She tried not to think about the crystal by concentrating on the notes of a piece of extremely complex music,
but despite her efforts, she found her mind moving into
a cold chamber with a throne inside the crystalline colors
of the walls. The dreadful presence on the throne waited,
then reached toward her with nearly visible hands. Tiny
hands, but terrifying. *You will keep to yourself!*

Margaret felt the voice echo along her bones, more
than heard it. It was like the chime of quartz and metal
brought together—a sound so powerful she wanted to
quail away. But she could not—it was inside her! If only
she could stop seeing that room in her mind! If only
she could escape the voice ringing in her flesh! It was
too late!

*"Put away your bauble before I destroy it and you with
it!"* Margaret spoke the words aloud, yet it was not her
own voice which commanded, but that of another, a
stranger.

She felt something change, a subtle alteration in the
sitting room. The fire was the same, the rain and the
trees, but the energy around her was now charged with
strength, as if a stone tower had grown up around the
leronis. Margaret felt as if she were caught between two
forces, equal in power, warring over possession of her
aching body.

"Stop it! I will not be a bone between two dogs!" It
was her own voice now, but thin, like that of a child,
small and piping. For all of that it had a curious potency,
and the snarl of tightness in her chest eased just a little.
She swallowed hard and took several trembling breaths.
The air seemed to sear her lungs. "I think you had better
put that thing away, because I think if I look at it, it will
shatter." The child Margaret was gone now, replaced by
the voice she used when addressing classes at University.
This was the one she was accustomed to, that she knew
best. She felt a vast relief at the sound of her normal
voice, neither that of a stranger nor of a small child.

There was a rustle of fabric across from her. "I have
hidden my matrix, Marguerida. Now, please look at me.

Tell me, if you can, what you felt or saw, and who spoke with your mouth."

"I don't know." Margaret's shaking hand reached for her cup of tea. She stared dumbly into its empty depths, then poured herself more, and drank deeply. "Or, rather, I do know, and I am not able to tell it." She felt something release, a kind of tension that she had always carried inside, but she was just too weary to pay it any attention.

"Have you always known?"

"In a way. It was kind of fuzzy, a dream thing, but while I was sick, it got a lot more distinct." She frowned. "I think Dio knows about it, or that something troubled her about me, when I was little. She told my father, and I remember him saying something about 'channels,' whatever those are. When I had the fever, I heard them talking a lot, in my imagination, I think. I can't remember much of it now, but something happened to me after we left Darkover." Part of Margaret did not want to talk, but another part of her was compelled to discover the secrets hidden in her mind, no matter what the cost. Istvana Ridenow was not the person she would have chosen to disclose her secrets to, but some deep sense trusted the small woman, and she knew she would have no better opportunity than this. The tight place inside her gave another movement, a kind of uncoiling, and Margaret decided she was doing something right at last. She found she didn't care about Gifts and Domains at all, but she did want to find out what secret was buried within her. It was the most important thing in the world at that instant.

"Your father knew your channels had been tampered with, and he did nothing?" Istvana sounded extremely angry now, outraged in a way that warmed Margaret and made her feel protected for a moment.

"He thought I would grow out of it."

"Then he is an even greater fool than I thought! You don't 'grow out' of such a thing—it must be mended, attended to." She paused. "I think the best solution would be for you to return to Neskaya with me for a time."

Margaret caught an impression of a tall stone tower gleaming against the night. Within it there were people moving about, and she could see great crystals set in arrays, their many facets shining. She began to shudder violently. It was another room of glass, a trap of crystal. Her hand shook, spilling warm tea over the cuts in her palms and causing her to cry out in pain.

No! Don't make me go back into the mirror! I don't want to die there!

Istvana Ridenow flinched as if she had been struck in the face. She rubbed her brow and flexed her narrow shoulders, as if to shake off some burden. "Can you tell me about the *mirror,* Marguerida?" the *leronis* asked at last.

"Mirror?" Margaret looked around the room, dazed, then set down her cup and wiped her hand against her skirt, smearing tea and blood over the russet fabric. "There isn't any mirror in here, is there?"

"No, there isn't. But there is a place in your mind, a place full of mirrors or glass, and it terrifies you. Doesn't it?"

"Yes."

"And my matrix crystal reminded you of it?"

"I guess." She was so tired. Why couldn't they leave her alone?

Because you are a threat to yourself and everyone else, until this matter is resolved. This was stern, but not unkind.

"Tell me what you are able to remember, and stop whenever you feel threatened."

"I feel threatened all the time. But there are words, specific words, that are the worst. And mostly I can't remember the words, but can only go around them, like barriers. Rafaella mentioned something today, about some Rebellion, and that set it off. For a little bit, I could nearly remember, but then. . . . *she* made me stop. Not Rafaella, but someone in my mind." *It's so cold in the mirror, so cold.*

"You have a very powerful mind, Marguerida, for which we can be grateful. If you were less powerful, you would have gone mad a long time ago. But that very strength is injuring you now, and we must find some means to help you heal yourself. What did Rafaella say, exactly?"

"I can't remember, but it was something about the

Ardais—Dyan came up and talked to me while I was still in bed, which made Rafaella furious. I think his mother wants him to marry me or something. And when he left, she said that all the *comyn* were wary of the Ardais, since that Rebellion thing, and then she said it was better not to talk about it."

"Very good!" Istvana sounded extremely pleased. "I suspected it was the Sharra Rebellion she meant, but now I am certain. I was a young woman at the time, but I was old enough to hear things. That was a terrible time for Darkover. But I did not know you were involved— you could not have been more than four years old then."

"I was five, almost six, I think, when we left Darkover. It depends on whose calendar is being used." Something struggled up from the depths of her mind, something so dreadful that she did not want to know. Margaret tried to resist it, but it was too strong for her. *Sharra killed my mother and the silver man. Why didn't she ever love me? Why did she send me away to the orphanage?*

"Yes, your mother died at the end of the Rebellion, *chiya*." Istvana sounded very sad as she spoke. She seemed to gather herself then, setting her shoulders back firmly. "When I spoke the word 'Sharra,' your body reacted, just as it is reacting now. And when you thought it, just a moment ago, all your throat muscles tensed and I could feel your voice being throttled. Let me tell you, feeling strangled is not a pleasant experience for an empath!" Istvana wiped her brow with her sleeve, and Margaret realized that both of them were sweating, though the room was not overly warm. It was such a normal gesture, so simple and human. *I guess telepaths aren't supermen if they still work up a sweat.* It was a comforting thought, and right then, she needed all the comfort she could find.

Then she was aware that this thought had been nearly shouted, and she quivered with discomfort. She could feel the difference now, between the endless chatter of the mind to itself, and those other thoughts that somehow communicated themselves to these people. How did they bear it? "I'm sorry. I didn't mean to think so loud."

The older woman laughed. "With the Alton Gift you really cannot help it, and actua!ly, for an untrained tele-path, you do a very good job of limiting your broadcasts.

Are you certain your father never told you how to behave?"

"Oh. I guess when I was real little, and I intruded on their privacy, they told me not to. Yes, Dio complained that I . . . well, you know, when they were making love." She found her cheeks blazing with embarrassment. There was something subtly virginal about Istvana Ridenow, and Margaret was sure that she had violated some unknown taboo.

"The energy of passion, *chiya,* is like nectar to the bee for a telepath. It is especially so when the people love one another. But let me see if I understand this correctly—you were five when you went off Darkover, but you could already 'hear' the thoughts of those around you. And, later, you lost the ability in some fashion?"

"That's pretty close to it. The Senator thought maybe it was the space travel drugs—he's allergic, and so am I."

"What a facile explanation," Istvana said dryly. "How like a man to think it was some simple cause, without examining all the facts."

"I think it caused him pain to remember, *vai domna.*"

"I'm sure it did and does, but that is no excuse for putting his brains in a sack! Your father is a great man, and he has served Darkover well in the Imperial Senate, but that does not change the sad fact that he has never had the wisdom to think before he acted in personal matters. I would gladly box his ears if I could reach them."

"Hmm. Dio has said the same thing many times. He is maddening, isn't he? I always thought it was just me, something I did that made him . . . the way he is."

"Lewis Alton was a troubled man before you were ever born, Marguerida. I never knew him, but I know what he did. The family was not entirely pleased when Diotima decided to marry him, but she has always followed her heart. Has she been happy?"

Margaret found her eyes were filled with tears. "I don't know. I know she has tried to be, but I don't know if anyone can be happy with my father. I always wanted them to be. There were some families on Thetis, our neighbors, and I visited them when my parents were off planet, and they seemed so . . . serene, I suppose. Those people were very kind to me, and I often wished the Senator and Dio could be like them."

"You never call him by name, do you?"

"Rarely. You have to know someone to do that. I don't know my father, and I never have."

"I think you know him better than you imagine, perhaps better than anyone, but I think you do not like what you know."

"It could be that way, too," Margaret replied, feeling her exhaustion flood her body. There was something more than weariness, though, a kind of comfort and ease. She thought for a moment and realized that Istvana was gently wearing away at her defenses, that her kindness and understanding and resemblance to Dio was infinitely soothing and very pleasant. She was starting to trust the *leronis,* and that was a very frightening thing.

I trusted Ivor, and he died!

"I know how that feels," Istvana said.

"What?"

"To trust someone, and then have them die. My father, Kester Ridenow, has been dead for almost twenty years, and sometimes I still get angry that he left me. And it was not even his fault—he was assassinated. But I still think, sometimes when I am feeling low, that he could have managed better."

Margaret found herself laughing at this. Then she sobered. "Am I being difficult? I mean, I know you came a long way to see me, and I feel as if I am not being very cooperative. So much has happened to me since I got here, that I feel lost, and when I feel lost, I get very stubborn. It's as if I am going on a picnic, and it starts to rain, and I just sit on a rock and refuse to budge until the sun comes out again. I stop caring how wet I get, or if I am risking pneumonia—I won't move until things are going the way I want them to."

Istvana smiled and nodded. "You are not being difficult, but you have become very strongly buttressed. You have managed your talents as well as you could by becoming willful and very determined. That is a good quality, but it can get in your way, too. A fortress is only useful if you can walk away from it when you choose to. And your barriers are not of your own making, but come from that place with all the mirrors that you try not to remember."

"What can I do, then? You wanted to take me to that Tower, but I think that would be a mistake." She shuddered a little. The idea of being locked up anywhere was intolerable—and there was something about a tower that made her think of a prison.

"Now that I know more about you, I agree. It would be extremely disruptive, and dangerous as well."

"Dangerous?"

"Not dangerous to you, but to others. This is a situation, indeed! I can't permit you to go wandering around Darkover half-awake, an untrained telepath, because that would be irresponsible. Leaving Darkover would not solve the problem either. But if you think you could trust me, we might be able to do something to release you from that room you fear."

"No crystals!" She could still sense the jewel which was hidden beneath Istvana's garment.

"No, no matrices. Whatever happened to you has made you very sensitive to mirrors and glass and matrices. I believe, and this is only a guess, but I think it's a good one, that you were trapped within a matrix, although I don't have any idea how. Trap matrices are not unknown in our history, but no one has used them in decades." Istvana made a face, as if she smelled something foul. "I confess I am feeling my way here. I have never seen anyone react as you did to a matrix."

"Tell me what they are, will you?"

Istvana looked at her for several seconds. "We have found over the years that we can use certain crystals to focus our minds, to enhance our native talents, and enlarge the scope of the Gifts. A matrix is not absolutely necessary, but it is extremely useful. The matrix is a tool, and each one is keyed to an individual."

Margaret was not sure quite what to make of this explanation, but accepted it for the moment. Actually, it was easier to believe in crystals than to accept telepathy. Except, while the idea of telepathy terrified her, it did not make her skin crawl the way the sight of Istvana's matrix had. "What can I do, then—if I can't go to a Tower without causing trouble, and you can't use your matrix without . . . that thing in me poking its head out.

Sit here and wait for the next episode of this threshold sickness to finish me off? I mean, I won't equivocate about it—there were a couple of times when I nearly died last week, and more when I really wished I could!''

Istvana pursed her lips, considering something she clearly did not like. She looked at the pretty bottle of blue stuff that sat on the tray. "We have other resources. Over the centuries we have developed certain substances which aid in reducing mental barriers. They are not without their own risks, but I cannot think of any other way to discover what is blocking your Gift. Do you think you would be willing to try that approach?"

"You mean drugs?" Margaret frowned. "I tried a few things during my first year at University, and it was not a lot of fun. I had visions, I guess, that left me feeling very . . . vulnerable. I haven't thought about that for ages, but I think now that maybe I remembered what I was not supposed to remember when I took them. I never experimented with anything again."

"You are a very sensible young woman."

Desperately as Margaret needed Istvana's approval, she couldn't agree. "Am I? I don't feel sensible, just stubborn and rather stupid."

"We never live up to our own impossible standards, do we? Now, what I propose is that you get a good night's rest, and in the morning, we will try some *kirian* and see if we can't clear up some of those channels of yours." It all sounded very simple and practical, but Margaret could feel the tension in the other woman, and she sensed it was much more complex than it seemed.

Margaret considered this for a long time. "I'm afraid to wait. I'm afraid that if I go to sleep, I'll be trapped in the mirror. That part of me—the part that spoke earlier, that threatened you—is much closer than it was before, like it is waiting to jump out and gobble me up. I can keep it silent while I am conscious, but I'm not sure I can control it if I go to sleep again."

"You are a very brave woman, Marguerida Alton. In another time they would have written songs about you and sung them for generations."

"Brave?" She laughed uneasily. "I just want to get this over with, so I can get on with my life." Margaret thought about some of the ballads she had heard, and wondered if she were really worthy of a song.

"You are your father's daughter, to be sure. Very well. We will try the *kirian,* a very small dose, and see what transpires. Just a moment." She closed her eyes and leaned back in the chair. "There. I have asked Marilla to monitor—she was quite good at it when she was in the Tower—and she has agreed."

Margaret looked toward the door, expecting Lady Marilla to walk into the room. When no one came in, she raised her eyebrows at Istvana Ridenow. "Where is she?"

"In the next room. She does not need to be physically present. I thought it would be better if we remained alone."

"Thank you. You are very kind."

"Perhaps." Istvana leaned forward and picked up the bottle from the tea tray. She poured a minuscule amount into a tiny cup, so small it was like a child's toy. The liquid that spilled out was a remarkable blue, and it had a slight perfume that wafted out into the room, mingling with the smells of fire and rain. Then she handed the cup to Margaret. "Now, try to compose your mind, and banish your fears. Breathe slowly and deeply, and when you feel yourself calm, then drink. Do not hasten."

"What is this?"

"It is a plant distillation, one we have used for generations to release the grip of the conscious mind."

"That is exactly what I want to avoid." She felt her fears welling up, and forcibly banished them, as well as she was able. Her will felt like a feeble reed, a fragile thing that could be broken with a breath. "Oh, well. Nothing ventured, nothing gained." She spoke with more confidence than she felt. "What will happen?"

"I cannot predict exactly—everyone has a different reaction. With the dose I gave you, you should go into a light trance. You may see places that are strange, but you will be safe. It will be a waking dream."

Safe? It sounded wonderful, but Margaret doubted that it would be so. She took several shallow breaths. "All right. I've had a few of those, so I know what to expect." She closed her eyes and tried to think of something soothing. The guttering fire disturbed her and she tried to shut it out. Part of Margaret wanted to discover why the sound of the fire bothered her, but she silenced the question almost before it rose. The steady patter of the rain against the stone walls of Castle Ardais was pleasant, and she listened to its fall as she began to breathe deeply. She imagined she was warming up to sing, not preparing for anything alarming. She felt a little giddy at first, and realized how shallowly she had been breathing. Her throat opened, relaxing, and she thought of the words to a sweet serenade that Ivor had been fond of. That was safe and familiar.

After a time the muscles of her body slackened, and her mind was focused on the sound of the rain and the music that ran within it. Why, there was a language in the rain . . . no, she must not get too distracted. With an enormous effort, she lifted the tiny cup to her mouth and drank. It tasted of flowers and sunlight.

Time slowed, the moments stretching out into eternity, so that she could hear each drop of rain as it fell. She moved down a corridor, each step more slow than the one before, passing doors, until she reached a stairwell that curved up and up. For a long time she stood at the foot of the stairs without moving, then set her foot on ancient stones.

One step, then another, and suddenly she was speeding upward, her feet not touching anything. She was flying, and it was wonderful. She did not want to stop, but something held her, gently and tenderly, as if her hand were clasped in a kind embrace. She looked down, and saw a ghostly, gleaming hand entwined in hers. A fear she had not been aware of, that she would fly off into nothing, departed as she watched the hand in hers.

Then she came onto a featureless plain, a vast stretch of emptiness all around her, and paused. She seemed to be standing on an invisible platform that looked out in all directions, and it was cold. She started to shiver, and then a warmth came into her limbs, and she looked again. The plain was not empty, as she had thought at first, but full of tall structures made of starlight, beacons in the night.

One in particular drew her eye. It was old, and the starry stones which made it were crumbling, barely held together by the mortar. But for all its appearance of decay, it was full of energy and power. It beckoned her and frightened her at the same time, and she made herself be still even as she longed to rush toward it. There was a presence in that Tower she could feel, old and weak, but still strong enough to threaten her. And, as if it knew of her regard, it seemed to brighten while she watched. The stones grew denser and the mortar thickened.

"Come!"

The command rang in her mind, stern and peremptory, and she quailed before it, fighting and struggling to remain where she was. But though she didn't move, the distant building began to move toward her, the stones shining with an uncanny light that hurt her eyes. They were like mirrors! She felt her heart stagger and her throat began to close. Closer and closer it came, hurtling toward her through the limitless reaches of time and space.

Then the Tower was beside her, looming over her, dragging her toward the shining stones. The power of it pulsed along her blood, halting her heart and stifling her breath for what seemed like an eternity. She was going to be consumed! She was so little, and the Tower so huge.

She felt her right hand clasped more firmly, and the terror abated for a moment. She waited. It took all her stubborn will to remain still, and she felt her jaws clench in the effort. The Tower began to lean down toward her, bending like a snake.

"Come!"

"No!" The refusal seemed to take forever to speak, and it was a child's voice which spoke. To her astonishment, the building halted. "You don't exist!"

"Look into the mirror, Marja!"

The stones of the Tower reflected into her eyes, and she could see herself a thousand times. So many Marjas looked at her that she felt herself lost among them. She wished she could close her eyes, shut out the endless multiplication of her image. There must be something else to look at but herself!

What was this Tower, and who or what occupied it? It was so old, and had perhaps existed before anything else in this peculiar realm. She swore she could sense the age of those stones, and knew they possessed something that gave power to the voice which tried to command her. The *secret is in the stones,* whispered something in her mind, someone who had crept in beside her, like a mouse.

It vanished before she could think about it, so quick she almost believed she had imagined the whisper. She could feel rising panic in one part of her, and a cold calm in another, as if she had separated into two people. The frightened part was close to overwhelming, and she held it at bay with effort. The other portion, the cold part, was frantically seeking some clue to the stones themselves.

When she finally found the single stone that did not show her face in its facets, she was astonished and more frightened than she believed possible. A countenance gleamed on its surface, a small, moon-round face with eyes like empty wells. Except for the eyes, there was nothing remarkable or even frightening about the face, but Margaret still wanted to scream with fear. She tried to drag her eyes away from the face, from the reddish hair around it, from the little mouth that grinned at her. There was nothing in that smile of warmth or humanity. She stretched small hands toward Margaret, old hands like claws.

"Now I have you! Now I will live again!"

"Live again? What are you?"

"I am Ashara, and I anticipated your coming. You cannot destroy me. I will return, and I will regain my power!" The hunger in these words seemed to eat her very bones, and the empty gray eyes grew larger and larger.

"Let me go!"

Margaret dragged herself away from the grasp, away from the eyes like dark mirrors which tried to trap her, and felt the claws leave her arms. Her own image in the rest of the stones shrank. The thing called Ashara became less distinct, less present, as she leaned backward in her attempt to escape. The secret was in the stones, and in the eyes! If only she could think of something to do! She was panting now, and cold sweat dripped down her sides. She drew her gaze aside, and looked out across the plain at the other Towers in the distance. Time slowed, almost stopped. She did not move, and she could feel someone hovering beside her, guarding her, and pouring strength into her.

Then, slowly, reluctantly, Margaret looked once more at the mirrored Tower, and saw herself many times, pale

*and shaking. The small woman stared back at her from
a single mirror upon the face of the building, gray eyes
ravenous, and hands clawing as if she, too, were trapped
in the myriad reflections. Margaret moved with her hands
to defend herself, and found the right one held firmly in
a ghostly grasp. With agonizing slowness she lifted her
left hand and extended it toward the mirrors. She leaned
forward toward the shining Tower.*

*She leaned into emptiness and stretched until she felt
her fingers close around the single stone which showed
the Ashara-thing so clearly. Margaret pressed her palm
over the face, digging her ghostly fingers into the empty
eyes, her thumb into the unholy mouth. She felt resistance,
but no feel of flesh or bone. There was a sound, a pale
scream, as her fingers closed firmly around the single
stone, squeezing. She could feel nothing in her hand, and
yet Margaret knew she was holding onto something, and
that she must not let go.*

*Now what? She couldn't just hold onto the stone for-
ever. She was so tired. Margaret felt her own semi-visible
fingers start to slacken, and she sensed a purr of triumph
from beneath her palm. Her own face, pale and sweating,
reflected all around her, seemed to mock her.*

*She summoned her strength, commanded it to return to
her, and began to pull on the stone. It resisted and she
knew she could not pull it out alone. She was all alone,
and she would be eaten by this terrible thing as, she suddenly realized, others had been consumed before her. Despair ate at her, sapping her energy. The stone screamed
in her hand.*

*Then, from beyond the edges of that place, Margaret
felt a burst of power. It felt odd, alien, not like the presence of Istvana at all. There was something very male
about it. It hardened her muscles, warmed her hands and
icy limbs.*

*"Pull, damn you! Pull!" She did not recognize the
voice, but it was not Istvana.*

*She tugged at the stone in her hand, and felt it yield
just a little. The screaming sound in her mind increased
as she drew the stone from the walls of the Tower of
mirrors. She was terrified she would lose her grip, and
determined not to. It was like dragging something through*

a heavy liquid, something so heavy it was like a whole mountain.

NO! NO!

Pain! Anguish shot into her palm, up her arm, and into her breast. Her heart ached, and she wanted to let go. It was like a cold knife in the palm of her hand, and in her heart as well. Her mouth rounded in a scream that seemed to shake the mirrored structure and the misty plain beneath it. Then the stone in her hand pulled free with a great burst of energy, and she nearly fell backward.

"Stop! Stop! I am As . . . As . . . har . . . ah!"

She staggered back, and suddenly she was away from the mirrored place, on the platform where she had emerged, clutching the stone in one hand while the other was grasped tightly in a ghostly embrace. She felt weak and exhausted, but she dared not let go of either the stone or the hand.

"You do not exist!" *The words streamed from her bitten lips like a great wind, as the stone burned coldly against her flesh. She was filled with despair and terror, panting and trembling. She squeezed the stone between her fingers with all her remaining strength. It seemed to resist forever, but after an eternity, it began to yield and shattered. There was a rush of sound and light then, and the rest of the shining Tower shot up into the void, exploding in a whiteness that blinded her for a moment. And far away, somewhere Margaret could not name, another Tower rocked on its foundations.*

Margaret fell away from the destruction of that strange Tower, plummeting down, held firmly by only a ghost of a hand. "Good girl!" *roared the unfamiliar male voice in her mind, and then that, too, was gone.*

She was in Lady Marilla's sitting room again, soaked with sweat, tears dribbling down her cheeks, and shaking in every muscle of her weary body. Istvana Ridenow slumped across from her, hardly seeming to breathe, her silver hair plastered against her brow.

The door opened, and Lady Marilla rushed in, her eyes wide and her breast rising and falling rapidly. She bent over the *leronis* carefully, not touching her. "I never should have let her do this!" She glared at Margaret for a second, then softened.

Margaret wanted to shrink away from the look, but

she was so tired she could barely move, let alone protest her own innocence. Her brain felt bruised, and her thoughts were swirling. In spite of this, she found she had a hundred questions, if only she could have formed them in her dry mouth. *They probably won't answer them anyhow. And who was that man in my mind?*

Not tonight, chiya. *Be patient a little while longer.*

"Never should have let me do what, Mari?" Istvana's voice was thready, but steady for all that. "Get me something to eat!"

Lady Marilla looked from one to the other, shook her head, and shouted, "Julian—wake the cook! At once!"

The *leronis* brushed the hair off her wide brow and took several long, staggering breaths. "By the gods, I pity anyone who was in the overworld this night."

"What happened?" Margaret asked weakly.

"You broke the mirror, *chiya,* you broke the mirror." Istvana and Marilla were looking at her, disbelief and exhaustion written on their faces. Why?

She looked down at her hands and found they were the same familiar ones she had known all her life. Her right palm still bore the cuts where she had driven her nails in, but the left was smooth, as if something had burned away the wounds. She held it up to the fire for a better look, and saw, riven into her flesh, the outline of a many-faceted stone.

14

---◆---

Margaret never remembered getting to bed, though she tried. All she could recapture were a few fragments—strong male arms lifting her up, though whose she never knew, and voices speaking, lots of voices, none of them identifiable. All she knew was profound exhaustion, and the feeling of a hangover without the drunk before.

She slipped in and out of normal consciousness, into a sleepless state that was unlike anything she had ever experienced. When she was "awake," there was physical pain, as if every cell in her body were rebelling against something. She could have endured that, but for the terror. She was afraid of something, and she couldn't stop it, or name it either.

The other state was almost worse, for while the pain was diminished, the fear was even greater, and she struggled to remain awake, in order not to drown in terror. She almost welcomed the pain of her body, because she could focus on it and make the fear a little less.

Time became meaningless, and nothing except fear and torment remained. There were a few moments of lucidity, when her mind seemed clear, and the fears receded. During these, she knew she was having fevers and chills, that she was once more in the grip of the threshold illness, and that the people around her were trying to help. She tried to cooperate, but the foul brews they put down her throat came back up, and she could feel the despair around her, the fears which fed her own. She knew she was having more seizures, and that these alarmed everyone. She couldn't manage to tell anyone that these were actually small blessings, because in the fits there was no fear or pain—only emptiness. Her body seemed to rest, to relax after the violence, and she almost welcomed them.

When she was in the near waking state, everything hurt, and she kept trying to burrow into the soaking pillows to escape her terrors. Sometimes she knew she was in the Rose bedroom, in Ardais Castle, on Darkover, but at other times she was sure she was back on Thetis, or even on her cot at the orphanage. And wherever she imagined she was, Margaret still felt the presence of her terror, and the being which had created it.

The gentle touch of hands was an agony, and the nearness of several women was more threatening than comforting. She attempted to remember that none of these females was the small woman with the hollow eyes who had almost destroyed her, and she nearly succeeded. Slowly she realized that it was not all of the women who felt threatening but only the one called Istvana, the *leronis*. There was something about her which reminded Margaret of the other, the Ashara, though she knew this was foolish.

In the rare moments of coherence, when her mind seemed almost clear, she was certain she was going to die, like Ivor. It was a tempting prospect, to escape the suffering of her body, but part of her rejected it angrily. *I haven't gone through all this to die! I won't. Damn that Ashara-thing!*

The anger was cleansing, almost refreshing, though it left her even more exhausted. And the fevers followed it, which she noted in a remote way, as if they were some form of peculiar music which demanded her attention. If she could just stop getting furious, the fevers would leave her, she was certain.

But there seemed to be a great deal to be enraged about, as if she had postponed all the anger of her life until now. Occasionally she heard the thoughts of the *leronis* agreeing with that, which was both comforting and frightening. She didn't want anyone in her mind— not ever again! Margaret shouted at her when this happened, though she was never sure if she spoke from her aching throat or from her aching mind.

Sometimes she listed all those she was angry at, because it seemed to keep the fear away. There was her father, and on him she brooded. She thought of several things she was going to tell him if she ever saw him again—none of them either nice or respectful. But,

oddly, she discovered she was not as mad at Lew Alton
as she was at others—at Thyra, at the silver-eyed man
whose name she did not know, at that Dyan Ardais who
had delivered her to her tormentor, Ashara, and, most
of all, at Ivor, for dying and leaving her. She hated being
angry at Ivor, even though she knew he was beyond
being injured by her fury, but she couldn't seem to
help herself.

It was impossible to keep the rage going, and when it
left her, Margaret was terrified again. It was an endless
cycle, one she could not seem to break. She was sure,
despite Istvana's reassuring voice telling her otherwise,
that the Ashara-thing was going to return and trap her
again. She resisted sleep with all her will, for sleep meant
dreams, and she did not wish to dream. What logic remained in her troubled mind told her that she had destroyed the being in the Tower of Mirrors, but the rest
of her did not agree. How could one destroy something
that only existed in that other place, the overworld? She
was too sick to believe anything except the worst.

Even sound, her trusted ally, became a foe, for the
slightest noise made her whimper. The whisper of the
rain against the windows, a pleasant sound she liked,
reminded her of the voice of Ashara in her mind. The
hushed voices of Istvana or Rafaella in the room sent
her wild with terror, until they finally gave up trying to
talk quietly, and just spoke in normal tones. That helped,
oddly enough.

"Please, Marguerida, please, try to rest."

"Don't let her get me!"

"There is nothing to fear."

"She is going to come back and hurt me again."

"No, no, *chiya,* she is gone, gone forever!"

"I don't believe you. Oh, make it stop hurting."

"You are hurting yourself with your fear. Try to rest.
Try to sleep."

"If I sleep, she will get me."

There were a number of such exchanges. During her
infrequent calm periods, Margaret knew that old Beltrana and Istvana were correct. But she could not seem
to stem the flood of terror that rolled through her whenever she started to relax even the smallest bit. It almost
seemed to her that it was some last trick, some final

attempt of the Ashara-being, that if she could not control Margaret, she would kill her.

Isty—what is happening? I have seen a few bouts of threshold illness, but never anything like this.

Neither have I, Mari. I am not sure what is happening, but I feel that whatever it is, it is a normal thing.

Normal? She hasn't slept in three days. She has had seizures that would have killed another person. I know you are an empath, but surely this cannot be normal!

Yes, I know. But this is an incredible situation—she's an adult going through what a youngster does. We just don't know what that does to the body.

She's dehydrated and raving! There was a strong sense of outrage in these words, and Margaret, despite her pain, agreed silently that it was outrageous. She found herself starting to warm toward Lady Marilla, then remembered that she must keep herself apart, that people died if she let them near her. That thought threw her into fresh terror, and she struggled to banish it. She let herself go back to listening, even though she felt mildly guilty, like a sneak. *How can you talk about normal. Really, Isty! Sometimes you can be utterly maddening. Isn't there something we can do?*

She's terrified—and I cannot blame her. I only saw Ashara through her eyes, and it scared me silly. And she has been walking around with that presence in her mind for twenty years! Can you imagine what it would be like to be a little girl of five or six, and be overshadowed by the will of a dead leronis? If we could just break the cycle of terror, I think she would start to recover.

Well, none of the things we have given her stay down long enough to do a bit of good! And I don't think her poor body can take much more of this. She has lost a great deal of weight, and she wasn't heavy to begin with.

I know we must do something, but I just do not know what. Still, there is something. . . . Her channels were interfered with when she was so young! We have always theorized that during threshold sickness, the channels were somehow impressed in the mind. My best guess is that what we are seeing is the creation of new channels, ones that have not existed before. It is something to do with those peculiar marks on her hand.

New channels? That is impossible, and you know it!

Nothing is impossible! I would never have believed that the spirit of a long-dead Keeper could reach through the centuries to bend the will of one of her line, but that is exactly what happened. Mari—you are exhausted. And you are no help to me when you are half out of your mind. Send Rafaella to me, and go and rest.

But she cannot monitor! I'd ask Mikhail—he's the only one in the house who has had that training, but it wouldn't be proper!

<Laughter> This is hardly the time to be worrying about scandal, dear friend. Send Rafaella. I have noticed that Marguerida is quieter when she is present, and I think that she trusts her as she cannot trust us. They have ridden the trail together, and that makes a bond nearly as strong as that we learn in the Towers.

Margaret heard their "discussion," and wished she had the strength to tell them that she very much wanted Rafaella nearby. Her cracked lips were too swollen to form intelligible words, and her throat hurt. She felt her aching body, and noticed that her mind was clear for the moment, neither angry nor fearful, and she savored it.

There was something else, if she could just get her brain to remember what it was. It was something concerning her baggage. She felt a damp cloth against her face, and the moisture on her mouth was wonderful. It didn't hurt nearly as much as she expected. She felt her eyelids being washed ever so tenderly, and actually managed to get her eyes open.

The light was painful, and she almost shut her eyes again immediately. Only the sight of Rafaella's face made her keep them open, for it was exhausted, and there were deep lines between the brows. She didn't want Rafaella to worry!

"I am going to put some salve on your lips now, *chiya*, and it may hurt a little. But it will help the cuts heal and reduce the swellings. I will try not to hurt you, really."

"Fine." It hurt to get that word out, but Margaret was beyond caring. If just one part of her could be less painful, she would be glad. She winced as Rafaella spread something across her lips with a cautious fingertip, and almost immediately her lips felt better. "Wha' is?"

"Well, to be absolutely honest, it is something we use

on horses, for swellings and bruises, only I mixed up a slightly different kind."

"Good. Put all over?"

"It's got numbweed in it, so I am not sure. Don't lick your lips, or your tongue will go to sleep."

Numbweed. Margaret's weary brain fastened on the word, and she remembered that she had been trying to think of something in her baggage. "Medkit," she slurred suddenly.

"What?"

She had licked her lips in her thirst, and her tongue was suddenly gone, as if it had vanished out of her mouth. Margaret strained to get the words out. "In pack. Medkit. Patch." She sounded like a drunk in her own ears, but apparently Rafaella understood, because the guide left her side and vanished from view.

Margaret closed her burning eyes against the light, but she heard talking on the other side of the room. There seemed to be a great many birds just outside the window, and all of them were chattering at the top of their voices. She wanted to tell them to be quiet, but she couldn't even summon up the energy.

After a time, she opened her eyes again and found both Istvana and Rafaella bent over her, hovering above her like anxious angels. She had no idea how long they had been there, because she had been trying not to listen to the birds, and the rustle of the wind against the stones of the castle, which gave her the shivers.

"We found your medkit," Rafaella told her.

"Patch," she repeated. Her tongue seemed a little less leaden now, and she supposed the effect of the numbweed was wearing off. They could have been bending over her for hours, and she would not have known.

"What does she mean," the guide asked Istvana? "There are not scraps of cloth in it. Unless she means these gauze things?"

Marguerida! Tell me what you mean! She sensed the urgency in Istvana's unspoken words, but she shrank back from the contact.

Don't get in my mind!

I will leave you alone as soon as you tell me what you want from this kit!

Margaret flogged her brain, and pictured the familiar

contents of the medkit. It was standard issue for all Terrans when traveling. She had completely forgotten about
it, which was stupid, since it contained a variety of anti-
biotics, dressings, bandages, and even a foam-splint that
could be used to set a broken limb. She could sense
Istvana observing her mental images without real intrusion. It was almost as if the *leronis* were standing some
distance away, watching her mind without making her
want to scream with fresh terror.

Most of the medicines were in the form of small
squares which were intended to be applied to the skin,
the same way hyperdrome was administered for space
flight. One of these was a euphoric which would, she
knew, ease pain and bring a deep and dreamless sleep.
She did not want to sleep, but she knew that if she didn't
soon, she was going to die. So she pictured the patch,
and the lettering on it, and then showed it placed on her
arm. The effort was exhausting, and she felt her brow
bead with sweat in the effort, but she decided it was
worth it.

There was the sound of the contents of the kit being
sorted through, with occasional mutterings from Istvana
and questions from Rafaella. Margaret was not able to
follow this conversation, because the terror was creeping
back, and it was all she could do not to scream and
thrash around. She held her body still, telling herself that
soon she would feel different, if not better.

"Ah, here it is. I have never before regretted that I
do not read the Terranan script, but this is what she
pictured."

"But, *domna,* she is so confused! What if it is something deadly, some poison?"

"The image is very clear, Rafaella. Now, what do I do
with it? Ah, I see—what a clever thing this is."

"What is it?" There was a sound of plastic being torn.

"From what I was able to gather from Marguerida's
mind, this little thing contains a drug of some sort which
enters the blood through the skin—which is very useful
when one cannot keep anything down. See, it is sticky
on one side, which goes onto the arm, thusly." Istvana
sounded extremely pleased, and relieved as well.

Margaret felt the patch being pressed against her skin
very tenderly, and she winced a little. Then she waited.

First her arm seemed to become numb, then her hands and shoulders, and after what seemed like an eternity, the rest of her body. The ever-present terror began to fade, to recede into some mental distance, and she fell into soft and blessed sleep.

Wakefulness came suddenly. One moment she was floating in whiteness, and the next she was in the bed. Margaret's eyes opened, and she stared at the hangings. It was very quiet in the room, with only the flutter of the hearth making a soft and pleasing sound. Her first thought was that she didn't hurt, and her second was that she was very thirsty.

The room seemed very dim, and she decided it must be night. What night she could not say, for she had no sense of how much time had passed during her illness. It didn't seem to be very important. Nothing was important except not being a mass of pain. And fear.

The thought of that made her yelp, and brought the sound of footsteps across the room. Istvana Ridenow emerged from the shadows around the great bed, looking worn. In the dim light, her family resemblence to Diotima was much greater, and Margaret's heart lurched. She hadn't known until that moment how much she wanted her stepmother.

"Thirsty," was all she said. She wanted to say more, but her throat was too dry.

Istvana laid a small hand over Margaret's brow, a gesture so like Dio's that Margaret wanted to cry. Indeed, tears filled her eyes, as the *leronis* bent forward and helped her to sit up. Then Istvana held a cup against her lips, and she drank a mouthful, then another.

"Not too much at first. Yes, yes, I know. You want to drink the Kadarin dry. What? You shuddered all over."

Kadarin!

Istvana flinched in spite of herself. "You needn't shout, *chiya*. And it was not kind of me to use that river, I realize. I confess I am not at my best just now. There, lean back, and I will give you more water in a few minutes, when we are sure this will stay in your belly. Your fever is gone, thank goodness, and your eyes are clear enough. You have given us quite a time."

"Sorry." Her brain didn't feel up to making long sentences, though she understood Istvana well enough.

"There is no need to be sorry, for you certainly did not do it to trouble us. I think you are past the worst of it, though you may have a small relapse before you are done."

"No!"

"You are as willful as your father, which is good. I think you would have died if you had been otherwise." She patted Margaret's hand. "I cannot say how grateful I am that you managed to remember your med-kit, and to show me what you needed from it. That patch thing turned the tide. I think a bit more liquid is in order now.

Margaret realized how weak she was, when the effort of swallowing left her feeling limp. But she could feel the water soothing her throat, and her body seemed to enjoy it. Although she knew it was impossible, she imagined she could feel her individual cells drinking up the fluid, or whatever cells did.

Istvana kept up a small flow of chatter while she continued to give Margaret more water, a bit at a time, until she found her thirst was quenched. She barely heard what the *leronis* said, concentrating her mind on her body.

She could feel the terror still lurking, ready to leap out and envelop her. If only she was not so weak. How could she fight against her fears now? "Ashara!"

Istvana gave her a long look. "She is gone."

"I'm afraid."

"Yes, you are, and you will be for some time to come. I will not pretend otherwise. But right now you need to get your strength back. I have some strong chicken tea, and I am going to get you a cup now."

You can't make tea from a chicken!
Tell that to the chicken.

Margaret didn't remember falling asleep after the tea, but she did, and woke again, refreshed and untroubled. It was daylight now, and by the slant of the sun, afternoon. She felt fretful, restless to get up, and too weak to do it.

Rafaella was sitting on a chair beside the bed. She looked tired, but she smiled at Margaret. "Well, lazy bones, how are you?"

"I think I am hungry."

"*Domna* Istvana said you would be. Oh, Marguerida! You gave me such a scare. I have never felt so helpless in my life." The brows of the Renunciate drew together, making deep lines between them, and the corners of her mouth turned down.

"Me either," Margaret answered. "But I am fine now. Stop frowning! It makes you look like a dried fruit, and Rafe . . ." She stopped abruptly, and felt her cheeks flame with embarrassment.

Rafaella's face mirrored her own, red with blush. "What do you know about him?"

"I didn't mean to pry, really. It's just that a couple of times I sort of heard you thinking about him, and since he is my uncle, I knew who you were thinking about."

"Your uncle! Well, of course. Why didn't I make the connection?" She almost jumped out of the chair and bustled away from the bed, muttering to herself almost happily. When she came back, she had a bowl of soup and a slice of bread on a tray. "I try not to think about him much, but it doesn't seem like I do a very good job of it." She put the tray across Margaret's lap, then started feeding her like a baby. The inclination to protest was drowned in the first mouthful, and Margaret decided she wasn't up to feeding herself yet. "It doesn't matter, for likely nothing will come of it."

Margaret swallowed her mouthful. "Why not? If you like him and he likes you—what's the problem? You could be freemates, couldn't you?"

"I don't know. We haven't gotten that far yet," Rafaella said doubtfully.

The door of the bedroom opened, and they both started, and looked at one another, as if they had been interrupted at something unseemly. Rafaella's expression was so peculiar that Margaret almost choked on her soup, holding in her laughter. Ouch! Her ribs were very sore, and laughing hurt.

Istvana Ridenow approached the bed, her face serene and almost rested. She smiled and bent over Margaret from the other side of the bed, peering at her eyes, and brushing her forehead with a swift stroke. "So, *chiya,* you are awake again. How do you feel?"

"Pretty well, everything considered. I would like a

bath as soon as possible! I know I would feel much better clean!"

"We'll see," the *leronis* answered. When she saw Margaret's scowl, she added, "Perhaps late this afternoon. I don't want to have you having a relapse from trying to do too much too soon. You have been a lot sicker than you can imagine."

"Maybe. It is just that I have never been very good at doing nothing. And I think I have slept enough to stay awake for weeks now." *I still don't want to sleep, do I? Who was Ashara?*

"Rafaella, I will take over here. You go get some rest."

"Yes, *domna.*"

"I don't think I can eat any more right now," Margaret told Rafaella. The guide removed the tray, and she left the room quietly.

When she was gone, Istvana took the chair beside the bed, and looked at Margaret for a long time. "You have a great many questions, some of which I can answer, and many of which I cannot. But I think you need to know as much as is possible."

"This isn't going to be another time when I just get bits and pieces, and no real information is it? Because, if that is what you are going to do, I will probably go into a high fever again!"

"Ah, threats. A sure sign of recovery." The *leronis* looked almost pleased. "I shall try to answer your questions, but the problem is that I may not always know the answer. You see, there was a time in the history of Darkover which our historians call the Ages of Chaos, and properly so. We have lost many records of that time, because of the wars that occurred, and some of the tales we have are closer to myth than to history. It is hard to tell which is which, you see.

"That is true on many planets, Istvana. I've heard a lot of stories during my travels, where some perfectly human fellow has gotten turned into the sun god because he did some remarkable things, some things that didn't seem possible for a mere mortal."

"Forgive me. I keep forgetting that you are educated in a way I cannot comprehend. Very well. I will tell you what I know about Ashara Alton—and it isn't much!"

"Alton? You mean she was some sort of ancestor of mine?" For some reason, Margaret did not like that at all.

"You are certainly descended from members of her family, but since Ashara was a Keeper, you are not related to her directly."

"Why not?"

"At the time when she lived, Keepers did not marry or have children. It was thought that virginity was necessary for the job. It was not until recently that this was disproved, and the disproving of it was a painful episode in our history." Istvana seemed troubled, as if the memory of those times disturbed her.

"But I thought that in order to preserve these Gifts, women had to marry and have children, or at least have children."

"That was certainly the rule, but Keepers were the exception to that rule." Istvana cleared her throat. "Ashara Alton was the Keeper at Hali, which was at the time the principal tower of Darkover, and, by all accounts, she was the most powerful *leronis* of her time, or any other. Now, under normal circumstances, a Keeper remains in her Tower for life. Even when they are old, and no longer quite in their correct minds, they stay in the confines of the Tower. But Ashara did not remain at Hali. I do not know the details—no one does. But she was expelled from Hali."

"Just a second! If she was so powerful, how did they make her leave?"

"Marguerida, I just don't know. My guess is that she was dislodged by the concentrated effort of several telepaths—but that is only a guess. What records existed were destroyed, and all we have are a few tales and fragments of stories. I do know that they did not kill her, because we know that she retired to Thendara, and became a recluse in a tower of her own construction. It was when they were just starting to build Comyn Castle—not the one you have visited, but an earlier building which is concealed within it today."

"The Maze!"

"What?" Istvana looked quite startled.

"When Captain Scott took me to see Regis Hastur, and we came into the courtyard of Comyn Castle, I felt

as if I could 'see' a pattern of . . . well, light is the best
description, running through the building. There were
places where it ran into walls, but the light just went on.
I thought I was crazy at the time. And on one side there
was this tall tower that gave me the creeps, and the light
seemed to start there. All I can say for certain is that at
that moment, I think I could have found my way around
the castle blindfolded—if I could have walked through
a few walls."

"I see. Well, there is indeed a legend that some sort
of labyrinth exists within Comyn Castle, though I never
heard of anyone who knew what it looked like."

"If this . . . ancestor of mine was there when the first
castle was being built, and she was as powerful as you
say, then maybe . . . could she have influenced the archi-
tects?" Margaret could feel her terror, hut it was a distant emotion, because she was intensely interested in the
story. It was all in the past, and the past was safe. No, it
wasn't! She felt her agitation start again, and swallowed hard.

Istvana gave a laugh that lacked any merriment, a
sound of discomfort. "With the Alton Gift, *chiya,* influencing others is not difficult. It is the nature of forced
rapport to be able to do so. And what little we do know
about Ashara Alton is that she never hesitated to use
the Gift as she wished."

"So, what happened to her?"

"Being mortal, she eventually died. Her body, that is.
The rest of her lingered in her tower in Thendara, and
we know that she overshadowed several Keepers from
time to time."

"Overshadowed? I've heard that word several times,
but I am not sure exactly what it means." This was not
entirely true, because Margaret had a very good idea
what was meant, and she did not like it. But her scholar
self had taken over now, and she wanted data, hard data,
if she could get it.

"It is difficult to describe, but it means that the personality of one person is shoved down, bottled up, you
could say, and dominated by that of another."

"Is that what she did to me?"

"Yes, it is, though why I cannot imagine. You were
only a child!"

"How evil! I am glad I . . . killed her!" Margaret's breath was coming in little pants, and Istvana looked alarmed. She reached out and touched Margaret's right hand, and calm started to return. Dio had done that sometimes, just touched her and made her fears go still. It must be some empathic skill. "Can Keepers see the future?"

"What a peculiar question. There are those who can, but it is not an Alton attribute. Why do you ask?"

"It might be nothing, but I had a dream or something, and I could swear I heard her voice saying that she would not let me destroy her—as if she knew I was coming or something. Probably just my imagination again. I mean, it was a long time ago, wasn't it?"

"Hundreds of years, Marguerida." Istvana thought for a moment. "There is mention of a handmaiden who came from Hali with her, of the Aldaran line, and their Gift is foretelling."

"But she is gone forever now, isn't she?" Margaret found she was desperate for reassurance, that she was afraid that Ashara would somehow return and seize her again.

"She has not existed in the material world for centuries, Marguerida, but only in the overworld. And when you took the stone from her Tower there, you destroyed the place where her spirit dwelt. She cannot hurt you any longer. But I do wonder how much of her memory remains with you."

"I wish I could believe you, that she was gone for good. And for the other, I can't say. I don't have any way to sort out my own memories from hers, if I have them. At least, right now, when I think about it, I don't have any, so I am going to assume that I don't. But, there is something else. When you mentioned Kadarin— that's a river, isn't it—I got very scared. It was a different scared than from Ashara. Why is that?"

"Robert Kadarin was part of the Sharra Rebellion, and was the lover of your mother," Istvana replied, her mobile mouth pinching.

"What did he look like?"

"He was quite tall, I understand, and had hair of silver, and shining eyes.

"Ah—so that's it!" She felt a great relief. "He is dead, isn't he?" Margaret hoped he was.

"Yes, he is. But why does it upset you?"

"He was always there in my dreams, with her, Thyra, and there was something unnatural about him. He was like some nightmare, because he seemed kind to me, as if he cared, but there was also a way in which he used me! He took me to the orphanage . . ."

"Stop! You are getting upset, and you must not."

She sank back against the pillows, realizing the good sense in what Istvana said. Then Margaret looked down at her left hand, at the blue lines that traced along her skin. It was covered with some soft bandages, but they had slipped, and the strange lines across the palm were visible. She held it up toward Istvana's face. "What is this?"

"It is a puzzle which will have to wait for another time, *chiya*. I think you have talked enough for now, and heard more than perhaps you should have."

Margaret pushed the bandage away, turned her palm toward her eyes, and looked at the lines intently. She felt herself become dizzy, and all the strength started to drain from her limbs, as if she were being sucked into the figure on her skin. The lines felt hot and alive. She tried to look away, and couldn't.

Istvana shook her shoulder, but Margaret continued to stare at her hand, growing feebler and feebler by the moment. Finally, the *leronis* grabbed a damp towel that was sitting on the bedstand and threw it over Margaret's head. The slap of wet cloth hit her cheeks, and energy returned to her body.

She lowered her hand and burrowed it into the bed-clothes, then plucked the towel off her face with her other hand. Margaret found Istvana standing next to the bed, tense and alarmed, bending toward her. "'We need to get you to a Tower as quickly as possible. This is beyond my ability to deal with alone!"

"No, I don't think so. Just get me a glove or something to put over my hand, and I think I can manage. Whatever it is, it is . . . powerful, but only if you give it attention. I think it is her last trap, and I will be damned if I will let her win!"

15

◆

Some days later, Margaret was up and about, and becoming thoroughly sick of being fussed over. She could eat, dress herself, and climb up and down the stairs without becoming exhausted. But everyone insisted on treating her like an invalid, until she felt like a baby chick with a whole troop of hens following her around and clucking. She needed privacy, complete privacy. It was remarkable how difficult that was to achieve, even in a building as large as Castle Ardais.

Part of the problem was her own independence. She had spent too many years being on her own, or at least being Ivor's assistant, to take to being told what to do easily. The other was that everyone seemed to assume she would let them make decisions for her, that she would be an obedient woman. Istvana and Marilla wanted her to go to Neskaya Tower, and nothing she could say could convince them that she would not. Margaret looked down at her hand, now concealed in a soft leather glove that was not entirely comfortable, and tried to think why she was being so stubborn. It was as if she just *knew* that she wasn't going to Neskaya or any other tower. Where else she might go she could not imagine, except back to Thendara and away from Darkover. And that, she knew in her bones, was not her path either.

She had explored the ground floor of the castle, trying to find a bolt hole where she could be alone, and stumbled upon the room which served as a library. The existence of such a place in Castle Ardais pleased her enormously, for books were still her favorite companions. Even though most of her reading at University was from disks on computer, she had grown up with bound volumes. The Thetans made a fine paper from seaweed; there was a small industry devoted to the production of

beautiful books for collectors of such things. Margaret
had always enjoyed the feel of a book in her hand, for
unlike people, books were safe.

As libraries went, it was a pretty sorry one, but she
was glad for the quiet of the little room, and the slightly
musty smell of books and leather bindings. It felt cozy
and secure and familiar, and she found she could think
her own thoughts, and not dwell on the overworld and
the terror it still held for her.

On one wall, there was a small grate with a fire flickering in it. A single bookcase stood opposite, and another smaller one sat on the wall beside the fire. Aside
from the two bookcases, the room was sparsely furnished, suggesting that it was not much used by the inhabitants. There was one large and comfortable chair,
where she now sat with a blanket over her legs. The
only other place to sit was in the window, on a cushioned
bench that ran beneath the panes of glass. It faced the
rear of the castle and overlooked a small garden full of
flowers and some rather noisy birds. It was good to be
able to hear birdsong again without discomfort, and she
spent many pleasant hours sitting on the window seat,
staring out at the flowers, thinking of nothing in particular. The walls were bare, except for a rather moth-eaten
embroidery that hung above the grate, so dark with smut
from the fire that its subject was nearly invisible.

From the amount of dust on the shelves and on the
forty-some volumes scattered there, Margaret deduced
that the Ardais were not great readers. Still, it pleased
her to see any reading material, for these were the first
books she had found since she arrived on Darkover.
When she studied the titles she realized why the books
were not used much. Most of the books were transla-
tions of standard Terran textbooks of a highly technical
sort. This was clearly a working library, not one designed
for pleasure. She tried to imagine young Dyan Ardais
delighting in *Nitrogen Replacement Fertilizers in Temper-
ate Climes* by C. J. Bandarjee or Lady Marilla reading
the four hundred pages of *Midwifery: A Survey,* and
smiled. Just looking at them made her sleepy. But she
found some sort of reminiscence, and she decided that
would be good to read.

What she really wanted, she knew, was a concise history of Darkover—or better, a several-volume work with lots of footnotes. Margaret could not quite understand why such a thing did not exist, for she was sure that if it had, Istvana would have told her about it. It wasn't that the Darkovans had no sense of history, for clearly they did, but just that they hadn't written it down yet. Or maybe there were records locked up in that monastery, St. Valentine of the Snows, she had heard mentioned a few times. Where was it? Ah, yes, Nevarsin, wherever that might be. There were maps in her bag, but she was too tired to look at them. Still, she reminded herself that she must get them out soon.

Margaret flexed her left hand, now covered by the soft leather glove that Rafaella had given her, sensing the lines on her skin. Both Istvana and Lady Marilla seemed to find those lines intriguing, but worrisome as well. And they agreed that the strange design should be covered, that the lines were related to the matrix crystals they wore, though neither of them would hazard any guess about what it might mean.

She did not want to think about the lines on her hand, or the strange adventure which had produced them, but she had a very hard time concentrating on anything else. She glanced down, and for an instant she could "see" the lines, right through the soft leather. This was troubling, and she wondered if there might be some material that would prevent that. Leather was not the answer, although it allowed her to touch things without disturbance. The palm seemed hot and itchy, and her skin was still very tender.

Margaret forced herself to ignore her hand, and looked down at the page of the book she had finally selected. It was *Memoirs of a Vagrant Scholar* by Paula Lazarus, and had seemed promising. But it proved to be so dull and stiff that she had only managed to get to page seven after most of an hour. She stared at a paragraph she had already read several times without either pleasure or understanding. Then her eyes went to the moving flames in the small grate, and she let the book fall into her lap. Her eyes itched, even with all the sleep she had gotten in the past few days, and she closed them wearily. She wondered if she would ever feel rested again. Then she drifted off into a light doze.

Heavy footfalls echoing in the corridor roused her abruptly. The door was behind her chair, and she heard it open. A chilly draft swept in as she leaned out of the chair to see who it was. She expected Dyan, or perhaps Mikhail, for both of them had paid her brief visits in the little library, or even Julian Monterey, though his feet were never that heavy.

Three men entered the room, two in uniforms of gray and green. They had the look of policemen everywhere, for their eyes went to the corners, and their backs were straight with purpose and vigilance. The third man was thickset, broad of shoulder and strong-thewed, and had the square jaw of one used to imposing his will on all and sundry. Not really fully awake, Margaret wondered if the guards had come to arrest her for practicing unlicensed telepathy or creating a mess in the overworld. She would have been amused at this whimsy, but the seriousness of the three men kept her from enjoying her own thoughts.

The heavyset man stood before her and studied her for a moment. He had rusty red hair, going gray at the temples, and a neatly trimmed beard. His eyes were blue, cold, and penetrating. He studied her very directly, in a way she knew was rude by Darkovan standards, and Margaret had to work to resist the impulse to take an immediate dislike to him. She did not meet his gaze, but looked at the embroidery on her cuffs instead.

"*Domna.*" He made a half bow, a grudging movement. *Look at her—arrogant brat. Just like her father! She fairly reeks of* laran, *and doesn't she just know it!*

Arrogant? She couldn't understand why he thought that of her, but the comparison to her father seemed to be at the root of the matter. Odd. She had thought a great many unkind things of Lewis Alton, but arrogance was not one of them. "*Vai dom,*" Margaret replied as mildly as she was able, mimicking the manners of Lady Marilla while trying to ignore his agitated thoughts. She sensed he was a little afraid of her for no reason she could guess, afraid and hostile. Worse, she suspected that laughter was foreign to his personality.

"Your father is not here? What did he do? Send you to take his place?" *I won't have it! I've held Armida for twenty years, and I won't be ousted by a chit of a girl, no matter who she is.*

As she often did when she felt threatened, Margaret retreated into mockery. "He is not hiding under my skirts, for certain," she replied, and was pleased at the shocked look from one of the uniformed men. She waved a hand toward the bookshelves. "You might seek him among the dusty volumes there, if you like."

"Did he send you to take his place?"

"I cannot imagine anyone who could take my father's place, and certainly not me." She was alert now, her mind clear of sleep, and getting more annoyed by the second.

Arrogant and smooth-tongued as well. Why did Javanne send me on this fool's errand? Damn all women! "I am your uncle—your only living uncle—Gabriel Lanart-Alton, and I want to know what you intend to do about Armida!" He spoke with effort, laboring under powerful emotions, and Margaret concluded that he was a man of action, not words, and that he was as uncomfortable as she was.

Ah, he was Mikhail's father, the aged fellow he had assumed she intended to cast out into the snows of the mountains. He was not aged, obviously, nor the least bit feeble. Why had she had the impression that Mikhail's parents were old? Her resistance to disliking him weakened. "How lovely for you, though I believe Rafael Scott would dispute your claim to be my only living uncle."

"He doesn't count," Gabriel almost sneered. "He's Terranan." *She is trying to confuse me—this is not going as I planned! She's probably clever like her father, and I was never that.*

"Really? As a brother of my mother, he counts a great deal to me. As for Armida, why should I do anything at all about it? For no reason I can discover, half the people I meet assume I am going to rush over there—wherever it is—and insist on the keys to the pantry immediately." Behind Gabriel, one of the guards was having a dreadful time keeping a straight face.

"Why else would you come to Darkover—and what the hells are you doing here at Ardais, for that matter?" Gabriel had the harassed expression of a man driven to the edge of his endurance by things beyond his control.

Javanne will have my liver for lunch if she marries Dyan Ardais!

"I came to Darkover as a Scholar of the University, to collect folk music, quite unaware that I was some sort of heiress. As for my presence here at Castle Ardais, I think that is my own business, not yours." Margaret was beginning to take the measure of this new uncle, and suspected he was not a thoughtful man, but one who bulled his way through things. She also believed that he had a grudge against her father, though she could not imagine why.

Gabriel's face reddened, and his eyes bulged with barely suppressed frustration. *Didn't know you were an heiress, I'll believe that when Zandru's hells melt! What is Lew playing at? He was always up to some mischief! Even when we were lads, and friends together. Why hasn't he come himself?* "As my kinswoman, *domna,* anything you do is my business. I can't have you dashing around the Hellers and . . ."

"I have hardly been dashing anywhere, *Dom* Gabriel. I arrived at Castle Ardais because I was ill and needed medical attention, and it was the nearest place. Lady Marilla has taken excellent care of me, and I am deeply in her debt."

I'll just bet she has, all the while putting forward that spineless son of hers. There isn't a mother in the Domains who wouldn't want this girl for her son, no matter how ill-born she might be. If only I had not been flat on my back with the fever, all of this might have been avoided. "I have come to remove you to Armida immediately."

"*Dom* Gabriel," Margaret began, attempting to be conciliatory with the man who looked as if he might have a stroke if he became any angrier. "I realize you are accustomed to giving orders and having them obeyed, but I am not someone you can bully into obedience. I had not planned to visit Armida at all, and I see no reason to change my plans." The idea of getting on a horse and riding off was almost more than she could bear, for she still ached in all her muscles and bones. The guardsman behind him nearly disgraced himself entirely. *I never knew anyone to stand up to the* Dom *but Lady Javanne! If I tell this tale in the barracks, no one will believe it.*

"You listen to me, young woman! You are here, and your father is not, and that means that you will do ex-

actly what I say, with no back talk. I am your legal
guardian in the absence of Lew Alton."

They glared at each other for a second. "Precisely how
are we related?" she asked mildly.

"My mother was your grandfather Kennard Alton's
sister. What does that have to do with anything?"

"I was just curious. Ever since I arrived on Darkover
I have been meeting relatives I never knew I had, a
family I never imagined. But I rather doubt that you are
my guardian, legal or otherwise. When I saw Lord
Hastur, he made no mention of it, so I think you are
presuming something you have no right to."

"I am the holder of the Alton Domain, and that gives
me the right."

"You come in here and demand to know if I am going
to claim Armida and throw you out of your home. You
don't want that—no one would. You won't believe me
when I tell you I have no intention of making any claim.
You wish me to accompany you there, but you don't
want me there at all. In short, you are behaving very
badly, and we are getting off on the wrong . . ."

"Hold your tongue!" He swelled up once again, and
Margaret tried to feel sorry for him, but could not manage it.

"I am not a child, nor am I your chattel. Perhaps you
can order your wife and daughters around, but I am neither your wife nor am I your daughter." She felt her shoulders tense with unexpressed fury. The man was maddening,
and she wondered how "Javanne" put up with him.

*She's Kennard all over again, as stubborn as a mule.
Plus whatever she got from that be-damned mother of
hers. Why did she have to return?* "As you are my niece,
domna, you might as well be my daughter. I will excuse
your rudeness because I realize you do not know our
ways. Here on Darkover you are still considered a child,
since you are unmarried, and you are my child inasmuch
as I hold the Domain."

"Nonsense! Either I am an heiress and the Alton Domain is mine by right, or I am not, but your dependent
I will never be. Now go away. You have clearly just
arrived, and are likely tired, as am I. I think we should
continue this matter at a later time, don't you?" Margaret was surprised at the strength with which she spoke,

a quality of voice she had not known she possessed. It did not seem to be her own voice, but that of another, and she quivered a little. She hoped it was her imagination, and not some remnant of Ashara, for she did not want anything of that dreadful woman to remain within her.

To her surprise, he moderated his tone a little. "You cannot remain here at Ardais."

"As soon as I am fit to travel, I intend to return to Thendara and leave Darkover." This was a blatant lie, but she was past caring.

"Leave Darkover? You can't do that!" *It would solve my problem for now, but it would be the wrong thing. Damn Lew Alton for creating this mess, and leaving me to clean it up. Where is he? He resigned his post, without so much as a by your leave and . . .*

"Just watch me," she replied savagely.

Gabriel gathered himself, breathing heavily and squaring his broad shoulders. "You don't understand. You must come to Armida. There are people you must meet." *I have botched this badly, and Javanne and Jeff will be furious. Why couldn't she have been a sweet girl instead of this flaming vixen!*

"Must?"

Dom Gabriel Lanart turned and stormed out of the library, slamming the door so it boomed as he went. He had left his guardsmen, and one of them opened the door and followed him while the other looked at Margaret for a moment and grinned so hard he nearly cracked his face. Then he went, leaving her alone and exhausted.

Perhaps an hour later there was a knock on the door. "Come in," Margaret answered, expecting it to be Rafaella or Lady Marilla. Instead, Mikhail Lanart-Hastur entered the room, looking hunted. Her heart gave an unexpected flutter as she looked at him, and she chided herself. She was much too old to be moved by a handsome face.

"I hear my old man has arrived to bear you off to Armida," he began hastily.

Margaret blinked, a little dazed. "Old Man? Oh, you mean *Dom* Gabriel? Funny. I call my father the Old Man, too. Not to his face, of course."

Mikhail laughed, and the harried expression on his face faded. This was a shame, because laughter made him even more handsome, and she found herself feeling drawn to him. She felt as if she already knew him, although she knew that was impossible. She felt the familiar coldness within her, a desire not to be close to anyone, to keep herself apart. Istvana had told her that this was part of the spell Ashara Alton had put on her when she had overshadowed the child Margaret, and she bit her lip, because she hated the sense of separation. At the same time, it was safe, and she was accustomed to it now.

Miknail was doing a fine job of disturbing the quiet of her mind, without, she suspected, having any hint of her feelings. Which was just as well, she decided. He probably wasn't anything like the man she imagined, the man she felt she knew already. Margaret wished she could shake the feeling, since it kept her off-balance.

"No, never to his face. My father hates getting older. He used to be able to ride for three days without stopping to eat or sleep, or anything—if you believe his stories. Now a day in the saddle leaves him worn out and irritable. And he has been sick, too, and since he is a man who never gets ill, he is simply furious at the failure of his body to obey his commands. He would have been here days ago, but for that."

"That explains how he behaved. And I have to say I am grateful he didn't arrive sooner, because I think he would have burst into my bedchamber and demanded that I get up and follow him to Armida, like a good little girl."

Mikhail sighed, then shook his head a little sadly. "Was he very rude?"

"Well, he did seem used to having his own way."

"He's always like that whether he has been traveling or not." Mikhail clasped his hands behind him and looked into the fire. *I have to work to keep from looking at her! It is intolerable. I have never been so drawn to anyone in my life! She caught me with a look, and I followed her to that place.* "He was Captain of the Guard until last year, and he got into the habit of commanding. Or maybe he was always like that. We aren't close, because of me being Lord Regis' heir for so long. I was raised at Comyn Castle, and was there for quite a few years. After Lady Linnea had her son, young Danilo, I was no longer first in line, and I returned to Armida. But since I was made Dyan's paxman, I don't spend much time there. I mean, he's fond enough of me in his way, I suppose." *If he is, I don't know it. He always looks at me as if he would like to strangle me.* "So, when are you leaving?"

Margaret was so busy sorting out the thoughts that came to her unbidden, his conflicted feelings of attraction and his distance from his father, that she didn't answer immediately. When she did, all she said was, "I'm not."

"What?" Mikhail looked directly at her for an instant, then dropped his eyes. The look made her quiver with a longing she had never before experienced. "You mean you actually defied him? That must have put him in a rare temper."

"He slammed the door so hard he nearly broke the hinges. He seemed to think that I would just do what he said automatically. He gave me some song and dance about being my legal guardian in the absence of my father. I tried to point out that I wasn't a child, but he didn't really listen."

"Father is a good man, but he doesn't listen very well. He just makes up his mind and forges ahead. I'm sorry."

"Don't be. We can't help how our parents behave. Tell me, please, if you can, why he wants me to come to Armida. I mean, he's afraid I'll claim it or something, so why does he want me there? And who is Jeff? And Javanne? I feel as if I wandered into the middle of a Russian novel."

"What's that?"

"A Russian novel? A story where there are thousands of characters and all of them have at least four different names."

Mikhail laughed again. "That sounds confusing."

"Believe me, it isn't any more confusing than trying to keep track of Darkovan bloodlines."

"Oh. I've lived with those all my life, so they don't seem confusing to me. But I can see how it might be difficult for you. Javanne is my mother; Javanne Hastur, sister to Lord Regis."

"Ah, that explains something. I mean, I knew she was your mother, but somehow I forgot she was Lord Regis' sister. You gave me the impression she was old, and so was your father, at that dinner I never got to finish. It's been days, hasn't it? My brain is still a little muddled, and all these relatives I never knew about before don't help." A faint memory niggled in her mind. "I think my father actually spoke about her once—something about a party and a scratching match. No, not scratching—biting! He has a little scar on one arm, and when I asked him where it came from, he told me that Javanne bit him. Is it the same person?"

He laughed again. "Mother loves to tell that story—she was about nine at the time and already hot-tempered. She and Lew got into some childish argument, and she insisted he take back whatever he had said, and when he wouldn't, she threw him on the ground, sat on his chest, and bit his arm when he tried to unseat her. It was most unladylike, but Mother was a bit of a hoyden, if Uncle Regis' accounts are true. In fact, he once said it was a damn shame she had been born female and he male. He was a little tipsy at the time, so I didn't credit it much."

"Your mother sounds pretty formidable. Or have the years mellowed her?"

Mikhail grinned widely. "Not to notice. She's rather wonderful, but strong-minded, you know."

"I can guess. And with your father being pretty stubborn, I assume they get along perfectly."

"If shouting at each other and banging on the table is love and harmony, then they have it."

Margaret was surprised at how comfortable she felt with Mikhail now, as if she could say anything to him. It was a new experience for her and she relaxed into it. And then the chill returned, that feeling that she must keep herself apart, that she must never allow anyone to come close to her. It made her feel pulled in two directions, torn apart by conflicting desires. She could always say anything to Ivor or Ida Davidson, but this was different. This was an attractive man her own age, and she had never felt comfortable in that circumstance before.

Then she felt, more than heard, an answering emotion from Mikhail, as if he, too, were comfortable with her

as he had never been with another person. It was a wonderful sensation, but very disquieting for both of them.
*He could be my friend! I have never had a man friend
before, except Ivor, and that was different. But I must
not. Something will happen, something terrible, if I allow
myself to be drawn to him.*

For a moment she tensed, waiting for something. Then
she realized that the voice in her head which had always
isolated her from others was missing, and the full import
of her labors with Istvana Ridenow during her slow recovery began to trickle into her conscious mind. It did
not make for comfortable awareness. Indeed, she felt
deeply angry, because something in the presence of Ashara within her had caused her to miss having friends, the
way other people did.

To distract herself from these troubling thoughts, she
asked, "And who is Jeff?"

Mikhail began to pace in front of the fire. "Jeff is
Lord Damon Ridenow," he began, as if that explained
everything.

"Ridenow? Not *another* uncle!"

"I'm afraid so. But we tend to count uncles and aunts
as being those people of the immediately previous generation, and Jeff is from the one before that. He is twice
your relation, because he is descended from Ellemir Lanart, who is in the Alton line, and from Arnad Ridenow,
who is related to your father's wife."

"You know, I am starting to regret I am not the sort
of person who can go off into hysterics all the time. All
these new relatives are driving me crazy. But if he's Lord
Damon, why is he called Jeff?" Confused as she was,
Margaret was still extremely curious. And, she discovered, she wanted Mikhail to go on talking to her, because she wanted to be near him for just a little longer.
At the same time, part of her wanted to be alone, so
that she would not have to feel drawn to the man.

"Has anyone mentioned the Forbidden Tower to
you?"

"Istvana might have said something when she was answering my questions."

"What did she tell you?"

"Let me think. It was about seventy or seventy-five
years ago, wasn't it? That's where I heard the name

Damon Ridenow before! I knew it was familiar. But this Jeff can't be the same person—he'd be more than a hundred now!''

"No, they are not the same people. Damn! It is an old story, and not a happy one." He gave a brief sigh. "For centuries all Keepers have been female, and also celibate. Damon Ridenow was the first male Keeper since the Ages of Chaos. He was married to Ellemir Lanart, but he had a daughter by another woman, Jaelle n'ha Melora.''

"N'ha Melora? You mean she was a Renunciate, like Rafaella?''

"Yes, and please don't interrupt me, because the story is complicated enough without."

"I'm sorry." She wasn't really, because he wasn't the least bit annoyed with her, and that made her quietly glad.

"Leonie Hastur, who was *leronis* at Arilinn Tower where your father trained was very distressed, because she and Damon were very close, and she felt betrayed, both by his becoming a Keeper, and then by his fathering children. The Keepers wielded an enormous amount of power, about the only power women had then, and they were rather protective of it.''

"I can see how they would be, considering how women are shuffled off into marriage so young.''

Mikhail grinned at her, then shook his finger like a schoolmaster chiding a naughty student. "I don't want to get into an argument with you about how we treat our women, Marguerida.''

She thought her name had never sounded so pretty as when he spoke it. "No, of course not. I didn't mean to criticize." *From what Rafaella told me on the trail, there is a lot to criticize, but it is none of my business. No one is going to rush me into any marriages!*

"Anyhow, Damon Ridenow established a functioning tower at Armida, with his wife, her twin sister Callista, and a Terranan called Ann'dra Carr. This did not set well, but there was not a great deal that could be done to prevent it, not without a lot of bloodshed. The daughter of Damon and Jaelle was called Cleindori, and she was supposedly one of the most beautiful women who ever walked. If the one painting of her that exists is

Marion Zimmer Bradley

anything to judge by, that is true. She went to Arilinn and became a *leronis,* and started to create a formal science using matrices, which we had not had for centuries." He sighed. "We lost a lot during the Ages of Chaos, a lot of knowledge, and we still haven't entirely recovered it."

"Why? I mean, I don't understand these matrices to begin with, although I know they work like focuses. I would think that if the Darkovans have been using them for centuries, they would have developed a formal science a long time ago."

"You are quite right, but the destruction that happened during the Ages of Chaos made us very wary—there was a lot of misuse, and we were afraid to return to the ways of our ancestors."

"So what happened to Cleindori?"

"She broke the rules. I guess she took after her father. She married Arnad Ridenow, which was unheard of for a Keeper to marry. That was bad enough, but she kept her *laran!* And that did not go down well, because it had been established for years that only a virginal woman could have a Keeper's *laran.* She was just as powerful as before, which upset everything."

"I can tell you are uncomfortable discussing this, and I don't know quite why."

"Well, I have never discussed virginity with a woman my own age, and it feels really odd. You aren't embarrassed?"

"Should I be? It isn't like I don't know about sex, Mikhail. I mean, I've been to University," she added playfully.

He laughed, throwing back his head so the fire glowed against his golden hair. "Of course! You are a sophisticated woman, and I am a backwoods yokel."

"Don't be silly! You are clearly intelligent, and that is what really matters."

He smiled and gave a little sigh. "Yes, I am the clever one in my family, which is perhaps why my father and I do not get along. The Old Man is very suspicious of clever people."

"People like my father, you mean."

"Precisely!"

"Why? I have the impression that your father and mine were friends once, a long time ago."

"They were, indeed. But my father was always in Lew Alton's shadow, and he resented it. That is my own guess, not anything that I know for certain. My father never anticipated holding the Alton Domain, and he got it because your father left Darkover, so he has always felt that he got second prize, as it were. And you coming back has upset his cart a bit. Please, try to be patient with him. He is a good man, but he is very set in his ways, old-fashioned as they are."

Margaret was not entirely sure she knew what he meant by old-fashioned, but she discovered she wanted to please Mikhail. It was a surprising feeling because, other than with her musicology, she had never wanted to please someone, not since she was a child and had felt rejected at home. "I will do my best. But you still haven't finished explaining this Jeff person, who is my uncle once removed, or my cousin, or both. Are all Darkovan families this complicated?"

"Mostly they are, yes. Remember, we have been intermarrying for generations, so all the Domains are connected to one another by blood, as well as by loyalties. Thank you for being willing to be patient with my father. I know how trying he is, but he is completely devoted to Darkover, and that sometimes makes him narrowminded." He gave her a wide grin, as if they were partners. "Where was I?"

"You had gotten as far as Cleindori and Arnad."

"They had a child, another Damon Ridenow, named after his grandfather, who was later adopted and taken to Terra, where he was called Jeff Kerwin, Jr., after Cleindori and Arnad were murdered by some fanatics who could not see that it did not matter whether a Keeper was virginal or not."

"How sad."

"It was worse than sad! It was stupid and tragic!" He was outraged, as if the event had just happened.

"Yes, I can see that."

"Some years later, Jeff returned to Darkover and discovered who he was. He found he had very strong *laran* and went to Arilinn to be trained, but he kept the name he had grown up with. Because of his descent from the earlier Damon, he was the legal heir to the Alton Domain. He renounced that claim in favor of your father, because he wanted to remain in Arilinn. After the Sharra Rebellion, when your father left Darkover to become our Senator, he also renounced his claim to the Domain, because our laws state that the head of a Domain must reside on Darkover. That is how my father ended up with Armida. And he has been a good husbandman to it, and loves it, so your return makes him very uneasy. Technically, Jeff could assert his claim again, though he wouldn't. Basically, it is all a terrible tangle, and your being here makes it worse."

"I think I liked it better before you explained. It sounds as if there are too many people with a claim on the Alton Domain, doesn't it? My brain feels battered." She frowned. "Where does the Lanart name come from?" Margaret was trying to make some sense of all this geneology and failing miserably.

"The Lanarts are a cadet branch of the Alton line."

"So, that's why your father is a Lanart-Alton?"

"Yes."

"But it sounds like this Jeff isn't actually related at all—he is the grandson of that Jaelle and the older Damon Ridenow, not of his wife Ellemir Lanart. Is that right?"

"As far as it goes, yes. But Marcella Ridenow married Esteban Lanart, and their daughters were Callista and Ellemir and . . ."

"Stop!" she protested, suddenly very tired. "My brain won't take another fact! I'll just accept that this Jeff—Lord Damon Ridenow—is kind of my uncle, except he isn't. If I didn't know some of the kinship patterns in other cultures, I would think you were all crazy!"

"I never realized how complicated it was until I tried to explain it to you." Mikhail paused. "Pity there is only one chair in here. My legs are getting tired." *If she were anyone else, I'd just sit on the floor. But that wouldn't be good manners. Funny. I only met her a tenday ago, but I feel as if I have known her for forever.*

"I know. This is a funny room, isn't it—so few furnishings? I still don't understand why your father thinks I need to meet Lord Damon, though. For that matter, I don't understand half of what has happened since I arrived." She ignored the trickle of thoughts, which were just as puzzling as his explanation of the intricacies of the family. Why shouldn't he sit on the floor?

"My Old Man is a stickler for protocol, when it suits him. So he has probably invited Jeff to come from Arilinn, to observe all the proprieties, and as a disguise for his actual intention."

"And what might that be?"

"To marry you off to one of my brothers as quickly as possible."

"Your brothers? Not you?"

"My father tries not to think of me whenever possible, except when he orders me to do something I don't wish to. As I said, we have not been close since Lord Regis made me his heir. So he and Mother would want you for Gabriel or Rafael." *I am not even considered—I am the outsider. If Regis had not had me educated, perhaps it would have been different. The Old Man doesn't trust me. Damn!*

"Why?" Margaret could understand the logic in Regis Hastur making one of his sister's sons his heir, until he had children of his own. With the Darkovan obsession with keeping the Domains intact, anything else would have been thought insane.

"I'm the youngest."

"But you are my age or thereabouts! So your brothers are older and still unmarried? Isn't that rather unusual?"

Mikhail almost scowled. It made his face look strong and interesting, rather than otherwise. "It is practically a scandal, if you must know. Every time I go to Thendara, Lady Linnea has a sweet girl of good family just panting to meet me, or Regis tactfully suggests I might wish to meet this lass or that. I have been hunted by women most of my life, for as long as I was Regis' heir, for my position or potential one. It has given me a very poor opinion of them, because I never know if I am being sought for who I am or for my connections. And if anything happened to Gabe and Rafael, I'd have also inherited the Alton Domain. Now that you are here, everything has changed."

"Do you want the Domain?"

He gave a shrug. "I know it is difficult for you to understand, because our ways are extremely complex—

even for me, and I have known all these stories since I
could toddle. Regis vowed that he would give his regency to a child of Javanne's, and I was chosen over my
older brothers. Uncle Regis trained me in statecraft and
a great deal more."

"What do you mean—more?"

"Regis got the regency almost by accident. A lot of
things happened that no one anticipated, and when the
dust settled, he was all that was left. So he wasn't trained
to the job, and he didn't want that to happen to me. My
father was none too pleased since Regis made me learn
a lot of things that were not Darkovan. I've read a lot
of Terran history and philosophy because Regis felt it
was important. My father thought it was all a lot of
nonsense."

"But it didn't work out."

Mikhail shook his head, and shifted from foot to foot.
"Regis found Linnea, and they had children, so while I
am technically the heir, because Uncle Regis has not
officially made his eldest son, Danilo, the heir yet, the
plain fact is that I am a man trained to rule, but I don't
have a kingdom. And my very existence is bothersome.
There is too much potential power in my hands, and it
makes people—not just my father—very uneasy."

"Well, why hasn't Regis Hastur fixed things—made
his son the heir? It seems pretty untidy to me!"

He chuckled. "That's a good word for it. I don't know
why Regis hasn't made Dani his heir. He has not consulted with me, and it would be very impolite to ask.
My uncle is not a man who reaches decisions quickly.
But if anything should happen to him, I would be the
designated regent, and if anything happened to my father and brothers, I would have a real claim to the Alton
Domain. Well, I would have had, before you showed up.
It is about the balance of power, Marguerida. I don't
particularly want the regency any more, and I never really think about the Alton Domain because it is such a
remote possibility. But no one, especially my father, believes that. They imagine I am just longing to be backed
into the throne or the Domain. They have no idea what
I really want."

Margaret watched him. She liked his candor and his
sense of humor and the way he kept his thoughts to

himself, except when something leaked out. And she could sense his passion for Darkover. He was, she decided, a disciplined and admirable man, totally unlike anyone she had ever met before. "And what might that be?"

"To go off-world and see other places. Regis promised me he would arrange it, after young Danilo was made the official heir. He understood, because he always wanted to go to the stars himself but he couldn't. I don't want to stay here and marry a nice girl and father a bunch of children—even though I know that is my duty. It makes me feel like . . ."

"Like a stud animal?"

Mikhail blushed, and Margaret realized she had hit the mark. "That sums it up nicely, yes. I've read a few Terranan novels, and I know about romance. Let me tell you, there is no romance on Darkover, at least among the families of the Domains. We don't marry for love, and often we don't even meet our spouses until the wedding day. Well, there have been a few exceptions, but they only make it worse because they tend to muck matters up. Your father and Majorie Scott, for instance, are held up as a bad example of what happens when people fail to do their duty!"

"Oh. Was it romantic? You see, I don't know anything about that. My father never mentions her, and neither does my stepmother."

"I'm not sure, but it seems to have been something quite dramatic. The usual way, until my generation, has been that the parents arrange a good match, and that is that. Mother married Father when she was fifteen, and she had only seen him twice! And she didn't have a thing to say about it. Sometimes love happens—I know that Jeff really loved Elorie, his wife. She died and none of their children survived. The entire idea of romantic love is regarded as . . . rather peculiar here. Children are what matters most."

"It all sounds very impersonal to me. Not that I am any fancier of romance myself—I've read a few novels, and I thought them rather silly. And Darkover isn't that different from a lot of other worlds because arranged marriages are common in some places. But not for children, I think. For power and property."

"That, too. The Domains have run Darkover for generations, and they don't see any reason to change things."

Margaret fell silent for a moment. "Would I like your brothers?"

"Gabe is the Old Man all over again, stolid and forthright and very sure of himself." Mikhail made a face. "We try to avoid one another."

"And Rafael?"

"He loves to hunt and is devoted to horse breeding."

"Neither of them sound like they would be suitable for me."

"You don't mean you are seriously considering . . ."

"What does it matter to you either way?"

Miknail considered her question, his face thoughtful and a little perturbed. "I don't think I would want you to be unhappy. You seem like a . . . well, you aren't like anyone I ever met before. You are smart, and you don't hide it. You are educated and know about 'Russian novels' and kinship on places I've never heard of. I think being married to either Gabe or Rafael would be pretty miserable for you. Gabe couldn't stand to have a woman who was more intelligent than he was, and Rafael isn't much of a talker." *And you are too independent, too much like me. Why couldn't you have been ugly and stupid! It would make everything much easier.*

Margaret felt an imp of mischief seize her. "So why not you?"

Before he could think of a reply, they both tensed, as if some alien presence had entered the library. Margaret could feel something stirring and after a moment she knew it was not in the room, but somewhere nearby in the castle. The walls prevented her hearing any voices, but she knew that an argument was occurring, and a fairly vigorous one at that.

"Damnation!"

"What?" Margaret asked.

"I think the Old Man and the *leronis* are having a shouting match. I wonder why?" *The old fool. Why pick a fight with Istvana?*

"I suspect I am the cause, Mikhail." She gave a great sigh. "Your father wants me to go to Armida, and Istvana wants me to go to her Tower for training—and neither of them cares what I want!"

"And what do you want, kinswoman?"

She could feel him distancing himself from her, and it left her feeling more alone than she ever had before. "I don't really know anymore. Things are so muddled. Part of me wants to leave immediately, but another part wants to remain on Darkover. I don't really have any skills for living here—what would I do, become a farmer or an innkeeper? No one on Darkover needs a music scholar, do they? I don't really want to marry, which seems to be the main occupation of women here, unless they become Renunciates."

"You could try mushroom farming," he answered, and she caught a glimpse of a twinkle in his blue eyes. "I don't think that takes any special skills."

"Now, there's a thought," she replied, anxious to enter into the spirit of the thing and to avoid discussing more serious matters. "What a good idea! But I have no skill with plants, you see. I confess I have never given a thought to mushrooms before—where they came from and how. I just eat them whenever I get the opportunity. In fact, I am quite greedy about it. I always thought they just grew, grew like, well, mushrooms." Her mouth was babbling because she did not want him to stop talking, because she wanted to return to their earlier camaraderie. He was disturbed by the distant argument, but he had withdrawn a little into himself as well.

"There are several mushroom farms in the Kilghards. I could probably find you one that has been abandoned. I think it is pretty simple—you find a dead tree and gather ye mushrooms while ye may. I mean, I never knew anyone who planted them, so I guess they just happen. You wait for them to get ripe—or whatever mushrooms get—harvest them, and that's it. No weeding, no beating off birds."

There was a sharp, sarcastic tone in his voice, as if he were fighting with himself about something. She was nearly tempted to use her newfound *laran* to discover why, but she resisted. She wondered then how the Darkovans managed to keep out of each others' minds. She must remember to ask Istvana.

"And no running out to the stable to deliver a foal in the middle of the night either."

"Exactly! You will need a sharp knife and some baskets and . . ." They both started laughing so hard that tears formed in their eyes.

The door to the library opened and Gabriel Lanart-Alton and Istvana Ridenow entered, both in high color, and looked at them. Margaret felt as if she had been caught doing something naughty, and Mikhail turned red to the roots of his fair hair. They exchanged a swift glance, which was a mistake, for the look nearly set them off laughing again.

"What are you doing here?" Gabriel almost snarled to his youngest son.

"I was just telling my kinswoman about the delights of Armida," Mikhail answered stiffly, his humor vanishing.

"That's no business of yours! I'll tell her all she needs to know. Now take yourself off."

Mikhail stiffened at this crude dismissal, gave his father a look that was empty of affection, and left the library. *I won't argue with him! Even if it kills me!*

Margaret heard the thought and felt the rage simmering beneath it. She wanted to do something, to leap to Mikhail's defense and tell the old tyrant to do something anatomically unlikely. The strength of her emotion startled her. It was almost as if she and Mikhail were allies. It was more than mere liking, she realized, feeling the cold within her rise in response to the sense of kinship that had nothing to do with blood. The heat of her yearning to defend Mikhail warred with the habitual remoteness which had always kept her apart, and neither had the upper hand. She bit her lip, then glared fiercely at her uncle. She sat silent, her hands clenched in her lap, until Gabriel began to squirm with unease.

"I want you to come to Armida, Marguerida, and I want you to come as quickly as possible." Gabriel began to speak in a calm voice, but it rapidly turned into a barking command.

"I think that would be a very bad idea," Istvana said. "You really need to come to the Tower and learn how to use some of your talents. It is true that we have removed the major impediment to your Gift, but without training, you are still as helpless as a newborn babe. And dangerous, to boot. I have explained this to you, and I thought you understood. Then *Dom* Alton informs me that you are removing to Armida immediately and . . ."

Margaret looked from one to the other. She liked the *leronis* and, more, after their days and nights together, she trusted her. She felt almost safe in the presence of Istvana, as safe as she had ever felt with Dio. She did not like Gabriel Lanart-Alton one bit, though it was possible he had some hidden virtues lurking in his great chest. She was inclined to favor Istvana's suggestion, but only to spite her high-handed kinsman. At the same time she knew that would be extremely stupid, because within her there was some quiet knowledge that her path did not lie toward Neskaya. If only there were some impartial person to talk to. If only Ivor was still alive! What would her beloved mentor have made of all this?

She considered discussing her problem with Rafaella, for she trusted the Renunciate now, trusted her and valued her companionship. She knew, intuitively, that Rafaella would follow her to the ends of Darkover, but Margaret was also aware that her friend was young and headstrong. *Almost as headstrong as I am,* she thought wryly.

"There is no need for Marguerida to go to the Tower at Neskaya," Gabriel informed the *leronis,* once again swelling with the indignation of having his will thwarted. "My daughter Liriel and my kinsman Lord Damon Ridenow can take care of her. She's over the threshold sickness now, and I see no reason to pamper her as if she were . . ."

"I have nothing but respect for *our* kinsman," Istvana interrupted, emphasizing her own relationship to Lord Damon, "but he alone is not a full Tower circle, and neither is Liriel, excellent technician though she is." She paused, then continued. "You cannot imagine what Marguerida has been through, nor do you know what sort of care and training she needs." She gave Margaret a motherly look and smiled. "Surely even you can see the sense in her coming to Neskaya, Lord Lanart."

Margaret observed this restrained insult, aware that in using a lesser title, not *Dom* Alton, Istvana was subtly putting the man in his place. She made it sound as if Gabriel barely had the sense to come in out of the rain, and he bristled. "Marguerida belongs with her family! She has to learn our ways, and do her duty as an Alton."

"While the two of you are busy planning my future for me, neither of you knows nor seems to care wbat I want." Margaret spoke quietly and found both of them looking at her as if she had suddenly grown an extra head. "It doesn't seem to occur to either of you that I have my own life, my own plans and ambitions, and that those may not include either Armida or Neskaya."

"Not this damn foolishness about leaving Darkover again! I won't have it! You belong here, and you are staying here!" *I'll have my men put her under arrest, if I must. I don't want her going off with this witch—laran is a curse!—and I dare not leave her here.*

Margaret realized that her kinsman was doing what he believed to be best, and that he really could not understand why she was resisting him. He was not stupid, just very determined to have his own way, from his own sense of right and wrong. With a slight shock, Margaret realized that Gabriel really meant well, that he wanted to do the best he could. A small, grudging admiration for the man started to form, for she knew that it was not easy for him to stand up to Istvana.

The *leronis,* on the other hand, was concerned that having unblocked her potential, she might come to harm through her own vast ignorance. Poor Gabriel sincerely believed that she belonged at Armida, married to one of his sons and bearing a child as often as possible. He did not know any other proper way for a woman to live, and she could sense that he regarded any choice but marriage and motherhood as unnatural.

What did she want, then? Mikhail had asked her that and she realized what an important question it was. She had very little idea what sort of life living in a Tower might be like, but it didn't really sound appealing. She knew it involved using matrices, and she found even the thought of them unnerving.

The Renunciates were an alternative, but she knew she was no Magda Lorne, and that living the circumscribed life of a Free Amazon was not a path she wished to pursue. As for marriage and children, she had never really thought about it before now, but did not think she was really suited for it. With the right person, it might

be fine, but she had never met anyone yet who seemed
a good match. She would like someone as learned as
Ivor, as strong as her father, but also someone who could
laugh a great deal. Powerful and playful seemed like an
impossible combination. She had traveled widely, and
she was fairly certain she could never be completely
happy to live only on Darkover.

Marja!

Her nickname seemed to echo in her mind, and for a
moment she thought that either Gabriel or Istvana had
thought her name. Then she realized that neither of
them would call her that—that it was too intimate for
these near strangers, despite their kinship to her. Dio
would, and, more rarely, the Senator. But it was not a
woman's voice she had heard.

For the first time she could remember for years, Margaret *wanted* her father. She found herself thinking of a
moment when she had been very small, when she had
sat in his lap, leaned her head against his chest, and
listened to the steady thump of his heart with total trust.
He had a certain smell that was comforting.

There was a vast vacancy within her which longed to
be filled, not by the man she had known on Thetis, but
by that other Lew Alton who had existed when she was
a child. She knew she could never be a girl again, snug-
gling into his arms, but that did not mean she did not
want to. She wished he were there, not light-years away.
Although she had no direct experience of his strength
and wisdom, she was sure he would be able to tell her
what to do.

Time seemed to still for a second, and she forgot the
presence of the man and the *leronis* in the library with
her. Instead, she remembered a fragment that had come
during her illness, the sense that Lew was in the room,
talking to her. She had thought it was some fever dream,
but now she was not sure. Maybe he was not somewhere
on the other side of the galaxy.

Margaret recalled the surprise she had encountered
from more than one person that Lew was not on Darkover, as if he were expected momentarily. There were
things going on which she knew nothing of. And the
sense of his presence was very strong. She did not need
laran to sense it. She could almost smell him.

Marja! Go to Armida! It will be all right. Chiya, *it will be all right at last!*

The effect of these words was nearly overwhelming, for they were accompanied by such a great flood of feelings, of longing and affection, that Margaret felt her heart would break. She did not believe that the Senator's thoughts were coming to her from far away. Logic, her faithful servant, then suggested that he must already be on Darkover. But, surely, Gabriel and Istvana would know if he were.

No matter. She was sure it was Lew Alton whose voice she heard. She had asked for guidance, and he had given it, as a father should to a daughter, however undutiful and headstrong. For an instant she resented that she was being told what to do again—that another person was deciding what was best. He had wanted her to leave home, because he could hardly bear to look at her as she grew into womanhood, and now he wanted her to go to Armida. But it all seemed to make a crazy sort of sense, somehow. She had no words to describe the rightness she felt at that moment.

Gabriel Lanart was preparing for another one of his commanding performances, and Istvana was restraining clear annoyance with the blustering man. Before he could speak, Margaret nodded.

"I will come to Armida. I am sure Rafaella can escort me there."

"Nonsense! You will accompany me."

"I will come in my own time, Uncle."

"But . . . oh, very well." He seemed prepared to make the best of it, and she was pleased to see he did not gloat over his apparent victory. "I am happy you have at least shown the sense to do as you are told, and stop talking about leaving Darkover or going to a Tower or any other foolish notions you might have in your mind." His sturdy body relaxed, and for the first time she saw his resemblance to Mikhail. He must have been very handsome when he was young. "We'll see you settled before Midwinter."

Margaret gave him a half-smile. "I am not doing this for you, *Dom* Gabriel, and I doubt you will ever see me settled, by Midwinter or any other time. You have no authority over me, and I hope you will disabuse your mind of the idea that you do."

"We will knock those foolish Terranan ideas out of you, and you will do as you are told."

"Please, don't make me regret my choice," she answered with more mildness than she felt. She was suddenly too tired to argue any further. "I will do as I wish, no matter what you believe."

Gabriel Lanart raged silently for a moment, then stormed out of the library once again. Istvana looked at Margaret. "Be careful. Gabriel may look like a stuffy old fool, but he is both canny and powerful, Marguerida."

"I know, but it just makes me furious the way he behaves. I'm not used to being meek and mild, to doing what I am told the way he clearly expects me to."

Istvana gave a small chuckle and nodded. "*Dom* Gabriel is of the old order, and he refuses see how much Darkover has changed since your father left. I am not entirely at ease with the changes myself, but I do know that change is inevitable, no matter how we would wish otherwise. And believe me, I often wish otherwise."

"Why?"

"Half the youngsters who come for training are full of ideas about leaving Darkover, and the rest are hoping for a return to the past. It makes it very difficult for all of us."

"I can see that. Do you think I made the right choice?"

Istvana hesitated. "I heard him, too," she answered. "I suspect that half the *leroni* on Darkover heard him." She rubbed her forehead, as if she wanted to remove an ache. "I am concerned, but I think you are doing the right thing. I trust that Jeff will see you come to no harm. You can depend on him."

"Thank you, for everything."

"I did my best, my duty, but I admit I rather enjoyed it. When I am an old woman, in my dotage, I will no doubt bore the young with my tale of Marguerida Alton and the Tower of Mirrors." She gave a little shiver. "It will take me until my dotage to recover from the experience!" Then she chuckled and looked years younger. "I wish you all that is good, *chiya*. You deserve it."

16

◆

Margaret decided that sitting down to dinner with *Dom* Gabriel Alton and Istvana Ridenow looking daggers at one another would not suit her digestion. She pleaded weariness and retreated to her room, where a servant brought a tray to her. The leather glove made for clumsy eating, and she removed it. Although she could not hear the voices from the lower floor, she could sense two conflicting energies and was glad she had chosen solitude over company. Besides, she had a great deal to think about.

Her first thoughts went to Mikhail, and she scolded herself for being an idiot. She could not seem to help herself. The man managed to get past her defenses, and he was both charming and intelligent. It was perfectly clear that he had a few of the same feelings, but there was some reason why he could not follow them.

What had he said? Something about keeping the balance of power intact? Of course! If she was heir to the Alton Domain, and he was still in line to take Regis' place, then the two of them together would be in a very nice position. She indulged in a fantasy of running Darkover, of establishing schools and hospitals and other features of Terran civilization for a moment. The only problem was, she didn't want that sort of life, and she knew it.

What would happen if she simply renounced her claim? That would please *Dom* Gabriel. And probably Lady Javanne as well, from the impression of the woman she had gotten from Mikhail's mind. After all, she really knew very little about Darkover, and she wasn't fit to be the holder of a Domain, no matter what everyone assumed. No, the Old Man would not like that, and she was, at that moment, more interested in pleasing him than these strangers. She didn't have enough information, and, as a scholar, she knew the danger of theorizing without sufficient data. Besides, just because Mikhail liked her was no reason to believe he wanted to be married to her, was it?

Something else nagged at her mind. It was something Mikhail had said . . . no, it was a vagrant thought. Margaret had a great deal of difficulty keeping what she heard with her ears and what she heard in her mind separate. Something about following her. What did he mean?

Then she remembered the final moments in the overworld, when she had wrestled with the keystone whose lines now colored her skin. There had been someone there, someone who was not Istvana nor that Asharathing—a man. Could that have been Mikhail? She wanted to ask him, but that would have meant going down to dinner instead of keeping to her room. It did not seem very likely, though—why would he help her, and how did he get into the overworld? It was all too confusing, and it really wasn't important, was it?

Reluctantly, she made herself stop thinking about Mikhail. He was a very nice person, but he likely had several bad habits which she would find intolerable when she knew him better. So why did her chest have this odd ache? *Stop this!*

Margaret turned her mind to the mental message she had received from her father, still a little wary of it. Why did he want her to go to Armida? There had been an urgency in the words, and beneath them, some strain, some stress that troubled her. Again, she did not have enough information. She was becoming frustrated by her own ignorance, and by the way in which people managed not to answer her questions directly.

She wanted to know more about the Gifts, her own and the others. Istvana had been maddeningly oblique and vague on that subject, except for explaining the nature of the Alton Gift. Even then she had not been given very much useful information, Margaret realized now. She had been too ill to notice that her questions were only half answered, or put off until another time. Istvana had just kept telling Margaret that she would learn more when she came to the Tower.

She knew that the Alton Gift was that of forced rapport, but those were only words. What did it really mean? Margaret now knew that the Ardais Gift was that of catalyst telepathy—that had slipped out at some point. This was the ability to cause another person to wake up to their own telepathic capacities. But young Dyan Ardais did not have it, as near as she could tell, and Lady Marilla was an Aillard, not an Ardais. Margaret remained in maddening ignorance of whatever Gifts her hostess had, except that she knew how to monitor. That seemed to be one thing that anyone who trained at a Tower learned something about. But Istvana had explained that her feelings of unease around Danilo Syrtis-Ardais most likely had to do with his ability to catalyze unawakened talents. She had said that Danilo was the most powerful catalyst telepath alive on Darkover.

And the Ridenow Gift was empathy, which she had seen well demonstrated during her recovery under the *leronis'* watchful eye. She understood a little better now why it had been so difficult for her and Dio to remain in close quarters for any length of time. It must have been exhausting for Dio, to be around a raging girl with a mental block that made her cold and hostile.

Tomorrow she would ask Istvana about the Gifts again. With that decision, Margaret felt better, finished her supper, and yawned. And tomorrow she would find Mikhail and talk to him again!

Her tidy plans did not come to be. First, she slept very late, weary from the previous day. When she finally arose, bathed and dressed, and descended the stairs, she found the entry full of baggage and activity. Both Istvana and Gabriel were preparing to leave.

The *leronis* came toward her, smiling gently. "I must return to Neskaya and my duties there, *chiya,* but I am glad you woke before I left."

"You mean you would have gone without saying good-bye?" Margaret was stunned, and more than a little hurt.

Istvana shrugged. "We have said all we need to say, for the present." There was a slight tremor in her voice, as if she was not happy to be leaving. *As if I would have used my influence on her! Damn* Dom *Gabriel for a suspicious old fuddy-duddy. But he would have dragged her off if I had not agreed to depart. I know how he is. He respects no opinions but his own. I will have to trust Mari to look after her, and pray that she has no further problems.*

That, at least, explained things, and made Margaret look at *Dom* Gabriel's broad back with a glare. She felt abandoned by Istvana and disappointed that the woman had lacked the strength to stand up to her uncle. Still, she understood, in a way. And she still had Rafaella and Mikhail and young Dyan, if she wanted him, so she was not entirely alone. So why did she want to cry?

"But I still have so many questions," Margaret protested.

"They will have to keep, *chiya.* " Istvana turned away and seemed to make her mind a blank.

Margaret had to make a very deliberate decision not to become enraged. She was being shuffled off just as she had when she had been left in the orphanage. She was just a tool, a pawn in the scheme of others, not a person of any importance, no matter how many Domains she might be heir to. It was all "go here, go there, do this, do that." It would serve them right if she went back to Thendara and took the first ship to anywhere.

Furious and frustrated, Margaret turned to go back to her room. Before she could make her escape, *Dom* Gabriel stepped into her path. He looked at her, his blue eyes meeting her golden ones. "You are looking much better today, Marguerida. Perhaps I will delay my return to Armida, and escort you myself, tomorrow."

"I doubt I will be fit to travel tomorrow, *Dom* Gabriel. I still tire very easily."

"But I am sure that if you just . . ."

Go back to Armida, you interfering old man! I don't want your escort! Just leave me alone! She pushed past him, refusing to notice his shock, and marched back up the stairs, her feet thudding against the treads. Her mouth tasted of iron, so flooded was she with anger. It lasted all the way to the top of the stairs, and she turned and gave a look downward.

Gabriel and Istvana were staring at her, their upturned faces pale. She hated them both in that moment. No, she would not go back to Thendara. Instead, she would go to Armida and throw Gabriel and Javanne out—it was a shame it was summer and not winter, for she wished it would be snowing when the scene was played out. But Mikhail would not forgive her for that, and she knew in her heart that she would never do something so rash. But she wanted to, burned to. She was really tired of being pushed around.

That afternoon, when she had recovered somewhat from her pique, Margaret came back downstairs, looking for Mikhail. She checked in the empty dining room, the great hall, the library, and several rooms whose purpose she did not know. Finally, she came to the door of the parlor where, more than a week before, she had gone out of her body into the overworld, to do battle with a long-dead Keeper. The thought of Ashara still gave her the shivers.

Margaret could sense that the room was occupied, so she knocked on the door. A soft voice bid her "Enter."

Lady Marilla was bent over an embroidery frame, and when she saw who it was, she smiled. "Well, Marguerida, this is a pleasant interruption. Come in, come in."

"I was looking for Mikhail. I wanted to ask him to tell me more about Armida." It was not entirely a true statement, but it would have to do.

"He has gone, I am afraid."

"Gone? Where?"

"I have no idea. He left suddenly, before dinner last night. I think he wanted to avoid any further confrontations with his father." Marilla sighed and put down her needle. "They can hardly be in the same room for five minutes without starting to glare at each other, so I was quite relieved, in truth. Dinner is so much more digestible without fuss, isn't it?"

"He just left? He didn't say where he was going, or when he might return?" She tried to stem the feeling of loss, of abandonment so fresh from Istvana's departure, and the rage that always seemed to accompany it.

"He might have mentioned his destination to Dyan, but Dyan has gone off to see to some of the outer farms. We are having a small problem of cats attacking the cattle."

"In summer?" Margaret could not hold back the disbelief in her voice. "I thought the cats only bothered livestock in the winter when game was scarce." Now where had she picked up that tidbit. Ah, yes, Rafaella. She was almost afraid to ask where the Renunciate had gotten to, for fear that she also had departed without even a word of farewell. But, no, she sensed her companion nearby—out in the stables talking to the horses. This was more reassuring than she would have believed possible.

Lady Marilla shrugged, as if she knew she had been caught in a fib, and did not care. "We will just have to make do with one another, *chiya.* Sit down. You have been so ill since you arrived that I have hardly gotten to know you."

"I do wish that everyone would stop dashing off into the morning," Margaret said, more vehemently than she intended. Then she sat down on a small settee, not the chair where she had confronted Ashara. No power in the world would make her sit there again! "Have I thanked you for your hospitality?" she asked, trying to make amends for her burst of ill-temper.

"Several times, Marguerida. My goodness, but you are a wary one. Do you know that you look at everything with suspicion, as if it might bite?"

"I wasn't aware of it, but I think I have good reason. I've always thought that vigilance was a good survival trait. And there have been a few times when it has come in very handy. Like on Relegan; they had an intertribal war—if I hadn't been on my toes, Ivor and I would have walked right into the middle of it, and probably not lived to tell the tale."

"It is very difficult for me to imagine how your father allowed you to go wandering around into such dangerous circumstances, Marguerida. For a son, perhaps, but a daughter needs to be protected and kept from harm." She bit off a length of thread with her small teeth, and began to put it into a needle.

"No one thinks of a musicologist as being in any danger. It looks like a very safe occupation, and it is, unless you do field work. But I like field work, and my father has never intereferd." *Besides, I wouldn't have let him!*

"Well, once you are settled here on Darkover, you will be safe."

Margaret wanted to argue, but decided not to. "Can

you answer some of my questions—some that Istvana never got around to?"

Instantly, Lady Marilla looked wary and uneasy. "Perhaps."

"I know a little about the Gifts—about the Alton and Ardais and Ridenow ones. Oh, and yes, the Aldarans can foretell, can't they? But I would like to know more. Is there, perhaps, some book I could read?"

"There are some writings, but they are kept in the Towers. It is not the sort of thing that could be left lying about, you see."

"No, I don't."

"If the real extent of our powers were known by the Terranan . . ."

"Well, yes, they would want to exploit them. I can see that. What is the nature of the Hastur Gift?"

"When fully realized, the Hastur can work without any matrix, as if their flesh were all that was needed."

"You mean, like this . . . this thing on my hand?"

"No. That is something entirely new, beyond our knowledge. Neither Istvana nor I know what to make of it." Lady Marilla was becoming more and more agitated by the second, and Margaret was picking up her discomfort. She felt sorry for the older woman. It must be hell to have a house guest with an unknown and untrained power.

Margaret decided that she wanted information more than she wanted to disturb her hostess, so she returned to the previous subject. "Is there more to the Hastur Gift?"

Marilla looked very relieved. "They can, in some cases, manipulate minds—though this is quite unethical, of course. It is akin to the Alton Gift, in some ways, and very different in others. And since I possess neither, I cannot really tell you anything more."

Margaret digested this, recalling her sense of unease while she walked in the garden of Comyn Castle with Lord Regis Hastur. She remembered how she had felt she had to be very careful, that he was trying to manipulate her. Had he been, or was she only being cautious. She sighed softly and let the matter drop. "What about the Aldaran? Everytime I mention them, people react as if I just said something . . . sordid."

"That is a good word for it. They are not to be trusted, none of them!"

"But, aren't they one of the Domains?"

"No longer! They can just sit up there and rot, for all we care!" *What am I saying—why did Istvana go away and leave me alone with this remarkable woman? She frightens me, and I do not like to be frightened! I don't know what to tell her, and what not to! Isty is right—I am a flighty woman, for all that I manage Ardais as well as any man! But thinking of the Aldarans always makes me nervy, and she is Aldaran on her mother's side. Oh, dear!*

She tried very hard to ignore the thoughts she was hearing, knowing she had upset Lady Marilla without intending to. She liked her little hostess, who was usually very calm. Beneath all the agitation, Margaret got the vague impression of a massive pile of a castle, and snow-capped peaks, and strong redheaded men and women. The topic was clearly a touchy one, like so many others. She willed herself not to become frustrated with Marilla's obliqueness, and regretted again Mikhail's unexplained absence. He, she suspected, would answer her questions better, and with less distress.

Margaret leaned back in her chair. How exactly, she wondered, was she related to the Aldarans, and why did everyone get hostile at the mere mention of their name? Well, considering the rate of intermarriage among the Domains, she was probably distantly related to all seven of them, in some fashion, and it did not really matter.

"I do not mean to distress you, Lady Marilla. Try to understand that I am a trained scholar, and that asking questions is my occupation."

"Yes, of course. And I am sure your curiosity is very unsatisfied." Lady Marilla was becoming her usual calm self again, as if she sensed the danger was past. "But you will have to wait a little longer for answers. Perhaps when you go to Armida, Lord Damon will explain matters to you." *And it cannot be too soon! I have never been so uncomfortable with a guest in all my life!*

Two more days passed, each one seeming a little longer than the one before. Margaret ate and slept and regained some of the weight she had lost. She took short walks in the garden with Rafaella, visited the horses in the stables, and went with Lady Marilla to the porcelain manufactory she had established. She still became tired easily, but her sleep was peaceful, and she did not have any recurrences of the threshold illness.

The third night, young Dyan returned from wherever he had gone, and the meal was quite festive, as if he had been absent for a month, not three days. Clearly, Lady Marilla doted on him. After the meal was done, her hostess asked if Margaret would sing. Her throat was no longer a mass of raw tissue, so she agreed, glad to have something she could do to repay their hospitality.

As they retired to the great hall, Margaret mentally sorted through the music she knew. She chose one of the ballads she had heard Jerana do—she had been listening to the recording of it that afternoon, so it was fresh in her mind. Dyan brought out a wonderful guitar, which had belonged to Kyril-Valentine Ardais, his grandfather, and she began to tune it warily, remembering the *ryll*. But the instrument was not haunted, just a good guitar that needed some playing. Rafaella went upstairs and got her own guitar, and accompanied Margaret very well. When the Renunciate was asked to sing, she did so in a good, clear mezzo, untrained but strong. Dyan then performed a rather naughty song, much to his mother's chagrin, and finally, Julian Monterey, the *coridom*, sang a dirgelike piece in a rumbling basso profundo. It passed the evening, but Margaret found she missed Mikhail, for she was sure he would have joined in the music.

The following morning she declared herself fit to travel, and, indeed, she felt very much like her old self Rafaella sighed in relief. "We have about worn out our welcome here, Marguerida, though Lady Marilla would bite her tongue before she would confess it."

"We did that days ago. She will be glad to see the back of us, won't she? And, truthfully, while I am grateful for her hospitality, I think I would rather sleep under the stars, or even the clouds, than in that room again. I find rose a depressing color."

Rafaella went off to see to the baggage and the horses while Margaret sought out Lady Marilla and informed her of her decision. It was accepted with only slightly disguised relief and the offer of aid in packing. Margaret thanked her, but said there was not that much to gather, and got into her now very clean traveling clothes with more delight than she would have imagined possible.

As Margaret started down the great staircase for the last time, she saw Mikhail coming into the entryway. His tunic was soiled and rumpled, even from that distance, and he looked as if he had not slept in several days. When she reached him, the smell of beer wafted from his clothes and skin, and she wrinkled her nose.

"Whew! What have you been up to?"

"What. Oh, yes, I must be pretty ripe. I had to get away, before I did something unforgiveable to the Old Man, and I just lost track of time."

"Where have you been?" Margaret wanted to scold him, but decided she had no business doing it.

"Oh, there is an inn a morning's ride away. I went there."

"Do they have any beer left for their regulars?"

Mikhail grinned, and her heart did irregular things. "Not much, nor wine either. Dyan tells me the Old Man charmed you into going to Armida." He brushed a tumble of golden curls off his brow in a gesture that would have looked casual, if he were not so clearly agitated.

They glared at one another for a second. "*Dom* Gabriel didn't charm me into anything," Margaret said severely. "Something else entirely made me decide to go."

"It hardly matters," he pouted. "You will end up doing what he wants. He always wins."

"Nonsense! No one wins all the time." She was angry at him for running away and getting drunk, for it reminded her too much of her father. At the same time she could barely stand to see him so despondent.

"You don't know him as I do!"

"For that I am extremely grateful, Mikhail, for I cannot imagine we will ever be in the same room without making each other furious in about ten seconds. I may, in time, come to respect your father, but I will never like him."

This remark seemed to perk the man up a bit. "He really is impossible, isn't he?"

"I think parents are always impossible, even the best of them."

"I warn you, if he doesn't bend you to his will, my mother will. She gets her way, too."

"You still think they will marry me off to one of your brothers?"

"It is my mother's chief joy in life, after spoiling Ariel's brood. She says often that she is very happy to be married to my father, though you might not believe it when they shout at each other."

"I take it that you do not normally try to drink all the beer in town?"

"No, I don't. I am, actually, quite abstemious. You may not believe it, but this is the first real drunk of my life."

"I am relieved to hear it. Now, before I depart, tell me a little about your mother, will you?"

"She is a force to be reckoned with." He looked at his scuffed boots for a moment. "If my father does not persuade you, she will, for she *never* allows her will to be thwarted. She is very managing, and it is a wonder that Ariel alone, of all my siblings, is the only one wedded and bedded."

"What are they like, your sisters?"

"I can hardly say, for I do not know them very well any longer. She matched Ariel up as soon as she let her skirts down, and when Ari complained she could not marry a man she did not know, Mother just said 'you will get to know him soon enough.' I suppose she really did know what she was doing because Ari is so happy with Piedro, you would have thought she had chosen him herself." He gave a small sigh, and Margaret could feel that he was extremely fond of his sister Ariel, in spite of his pretence of not knowing her. "But Ariel is rather nervous and prefers to have others make decisions for her. She doesn't have more than a scrap of *laran,* even less than Gabe, which is saying a good deal."

"And Liriel?"

"Ah, yes, Liri! She is like my mother in many ways. I would play the occasional prank on Ariel, but I never dared with Liri. Mother tried to marry her off, too, but she is quite willful, and insisted on going off to Tramontana Tower instead. She is, I think, more like you, though I hadn't thought about it before. But, trust me, Javanne will have you arm-shackled before . . ."

Margaret shook her head. "If she tries to make a match for me, I will be happy to inform her I am of no mind to marry. I am an adult, not fifteen. I imagine she would have a hard time finding anyone on Darkover who would want to marry a woman so ancient." She did not really believe what she said, but she wanted to cheer him up. She wanted to see him smile again.

Mikliail gave her a wan grin, and Margaret felt rewarded for her feeble efforts at playfulness. "Oh, I don't know. I can think of a couple. And with Armida as your dowry, there are many who would be willing to overlook your age and the way you look directly at people." *Her eyes are like an eagle's, and they go straight to my heart!*

"I know! I don't mean to be rude, but it is a hard habit to break." Margaret tried to ignore his thoughts, but it was very difficult.

"I don't mind. It is rather refreshing, after all those girls of good family who droop over their laps whenever we meet. But lots of people will find it uncomfortable, you know. So be careful. They will think you are trying to read them, even if you are quite innocent."

"I will try to behave better," Margaret answered, restraining a sudden impulse to laugh. She couldn't understand it, but every time she was with Mikhail, a bubble of laughter came into her throat.

"If I am not mistaken, they intend you for my brother Gabriel." A little frown creased his brow.

"From what you told me in the library, I don't think we would suit at all!"

"True but irrelevant, cousin. Suitability doesn't enter into it at all. But if you really want Armida—"

Margaret said quickly, "But I don't! I wouldn't have it with all of the Kilghard Hills thrown in for good measure. And why do you assume that your parents will want me to marry one of your brothers? What about you?"

"I do not like that kind of joke."

He was so serious, so determinedly glum, that she could not help but tease him. "Why should I be joking?"

Mikhail stiffened. "I am not in consideration, *domna*. I cannot be." She could feel his emotions, and they were very intense and confused. "If it is Armida you want . . ." he began.

"Why can't you get it into your thick head that I don't want Armida?" The man was being purposely obtuse, and she could not understand it.

"You'd best pick old Damon, " Mikhail continued as if she had not spoken. "He never remarried after Elorie died, but he isn't too old to father a few children. That would really infuriate the Old Man," he added with a sort of savage satisfaction. "He gave up his claim to the Domain, but I think that could probably be reinstated."

"That might be, but it doesn't sound as if be wants a wife. You call him 'old'—so how old is he?"

"Old enough to be your father, no—your grandfather!" Mikhail said angrily. *It's obscene to even think about! But not as obscene as Rafael or Gabe!*

Margaret couldn't understand his fury, but sensed this was an area which was taboo to discuss. She had enough experience to know that local customs rarely made sense to people who had not grown up with them. "Why are you in such a hurry to get me married?"

"You have to marry someone! You won't have any choice."

She could barely endure the powerful emotions he was experiencing. "Mikhail," she said, "I haven't even set eyes on old Jeff—or Damon or whoever else you imagine. I assure you I wouldn't marry him if he were the last unmarried man in the civilized universe. Even if he is rich as Croesus, or whatever expression they may have on Darkover for the richest man around."

"We say 'Rich as the lord of Carthon,' " he answered. "If you won't have Jeff, then you had better resign yourself to one of my brothers."

"I am not resigning myself to anything!"

A small gleam of something like hope shone in his blue eyes. "Promise me, then, that you won't let my father—or my mother—marry you off."

"Nothing is easier. I am visiting Armida for my own reasons, and I am not thinking of marriage at all."

"I don't care what you are thinking of," Mikhail said with a queer, precise literalness. *Just don't do it.*

17

◆

After four days of steady but gentle riding, Margaret and Rafaella came into the lands of the Alton Domain. Margaret did not realize they had crossed some unseen boundary, for it looked very much like the lands they had ridden through the previous days. There were small villages where the children ran out to stare at the strangers until their mothers shooed them into the houses. There were larger communities, with inns for the occasional traveler, or isolated farmhouses where chickens scratched in the yards and chervines grazed. But when Rafaella informed her that they were now in Alton lands, she looked around with renewed interest.

It was hilly country, but there were plenty of growing things, shrubs and plants. Now it was green, but Rafaella told her it would be tinder-dry in the height of the summer season. There were fields, well cultivated, and stands of trees that did not look wild, but planted with some purpose. Ignorant as she was of rural life, Margaret could see that the trees had the lower branches trimmed and the ground cleared of brush. Her uncle Gabriel might be a stuffed tunic—she laughed at this to herself—but he appeared to be a good landlord. She had been on worlds with social systems not too different from Darkover's, but where the land owners had not husbanded the resources, had taxed the peasantry or left undone the things which preserved the land, and she was quietly happy to see the family estate in good order. She could not think of it as her own no matter who insisted that it was.

"Look! There is Armida," Rafaella announced, abruptly rising in her saddle and pointing into the distance.

Margaret squinted against the bright sunlight and

looked. She saw a large structure of gray fieldstone and wood, lying in a fold of the Kilghard Hills like an egg in a nest. It was much smaller than Castle Ardais, smaller and plainer and lacking in any pretensions. Rail fences bounded it, containing grassy fields full of horses. She counted about twenty, mares with some foals, and several older animals, clearly out to pasture or waiting to be ridden. They rode up the broad dirt path that ran between the fences and watched the younger horses run about and kick their heels.

It was very beautiful, and at first she felt nothing besides curiosity and general interest. She had never been here before, as far as she knew, and no memories disturbed her. But the shape of the house seemed very familiar, and she guessed that perhaps she had picked up impressions of it from her father, when she was still very small and before she had been blocked. He loved this place, and some of his ancient emotion stirred her. A slight prickling in her eyes told her she was more moved than she knew, and she looked away from the house, not feeling able to cope with strong emotions yet.

Instead, she looked at the horses that were capering about in the field on one side of the road. One steed, a large gray animal whose muzzle was white with years, thrust its wedge-shaped head across the fence and looked at the women. Margaret looked back, and the horse nickered at her. She leaned out a little and held her hand out, and the horse snorted at her. Then it turned away and raced across the field in a manner which gave the lie to its age. "I guess I must smell wrong or something," she told Rafaella.

The Renunciate chuckled. "No, Marguerida. I think you smell *right*. I think that old gelding was glad to see you. Just look at him!" Rafaella had stopped using any titles now, and they were on extremely friendly terms. Margaret was glad of that, because being "*Domna* Alton" still made her feel extremely odd.

But Margaret was distracted. At the far end of the enclosure she saw a graceful mare the color of pewter, with mane and tail as black as night. She was not a large horse, like the gelding, but medium-sized and very dainty. Her hooves almost danced across the pasture as she ran, and she came to the fence and pricked her ears toward Margaret. Stamping her feet impatiently, the mare stared at her and blew its heavy lips. She had never seen an animal quite so beautiful, and wondered who she belonged to. Margaret wanted to ride her, weary as she was. She knew that the little mare would run like the wind, that her hooves would hardly brush the ground. How foolish. Surely she was too old to have horse lust.

Suddenly, Margaret realized that if she were the heiress of the Alton Domain, the horse would be hers. For only a moment she actually considered accepting the Domain just to get the horse, and then she laughed merrily at herself. It was not a thing that anyone could understand, she supposed. Besides, horses were even worse space travelers than Altons, which was why they had been transported to very few planets in the Federation. And she wasn't going to stay, was she?

"What is so funny," Rafaella wondered.

"I have just fallen in love with that horse. Ridiculous, isn't it?" Margaret gestured at the dark gray animal, and it whinnied. "Sorry, dear, I am fresh out of carrots," she informed the mare.

Rafaella nodded. "Everyone covets the Alton horses, *domna*. They are the best in the Domains, except perhaps those of the Serrais."

Margaret looked at her companion affectionately. Serrais? Istvana had mentioned that—it was the place where the Ridenows had their Domain. There was so much she did not know yet. "What's that? I thought we had agreed you were going to call me Marguerida."

The Renunciate made a little face. "I do not think that Lady Javanne would like to hear me . . ."

"Rafaella, I will observe Darkovan customs as much as I am able, but if you start kowtowing to me, I will be very hurt. Frankly, I don't really care what Javanne thinks, or anyone else, just now. She sounds like a very interfering person, and I don't like interfering people! I mind my own business, and I expect other people to behave with equal courtesy."

Rafaella smiled. "I know. But you had better prepare yourself to be annoyed because I think everyone in that house will try to mind your business, whether you like it or not. They think it is their right."

"I am afraid you are correct, but I don't have to like it, do I?"

"No, you don't." *Poor Marguerida. She has no idea how to be a great lady, and they will expect that of her!*

They arrived at the forecourt of the house and dismounted. Two young boys dashed out to take the horses and help unload the baggage from the mule, grinning as they worked. Margaret took another look at the house where her father had been born and lived during his youth. Now that she was closer to it, she could see that some of the stones from which it was built were translucent, a wonderful clear color that was nearly silver.

Just as the lads were taking the animals away, a sturdy man descended the front steps. He had dark hair, but otherwise was a younger version of Gabriel Lanart. Margaret judged him to be in his mid-thirties, and guessed he was one of her cousins, the brother of Mikhail and one of the Lanart Angels. If he was an angel, he was a dark one, and she assumed that Mikhail had gotten his fair coloring from his mother. He appeared a very sober and serious fellow as he strode toward her.

"Welcome to Armida," he began, and she found he had a pleasant voice, deep and resonant. "I am Rafael Lanart, and you must be my cousin Marguerida." He bowed toward her and ignored the Renunciate, but Rafaella did not appear to notice. "Father told us to expect you."

"Thank you for your welcome," she answered formally.

"We are glad to see you. My brother Gabriel is out riding the boundaries, but he should be back soon. You will meet him tonight. And Mikhail has been sent for—but you already met him, didn't you? At Ardais?"

"I did." Margaret did not think it would be good manners to tell him that Mikhail would not be coming. "He was kind enough to attempt to explain all the ramifications of the Alton family, but I am not sure I understood everything."

"Did he now? I never knew Mikhail cared much for that." He tensed slightly. *Probably trying to steal a march on me and Gabe! It doesn't matter. Father won't have it!* He finally realized that he had ignored Rafaella, and he gave her a stiff half-bow. "*Mestra,* welcome to

Armida. I am sure you will be glad to have my cousin in the bosom of her family, and be relieved of the responsibility of guarding her."

Margaret was first outraged at this near dismissal of her friend and companion, and then amused at her cousin's high-handedness. He was not as rude as his father, but clearly cut from the same cloth. "Guarding me? From what?" she asked, laughing. "Rafaella has been guiding me, and she took care of me when I was ill." Despite the laughter in her voice, Margaret made it clear that she did not appreciate Rafael's interference.

The Renunciate watched the exchange with bright eyes and repressed a grin with some difficulty. Margaret suspected she was enjoying seeing Rafael Lanart put in his place, though she was much too well-mannered to let it show. Then she looked at Margaret for a moment and winked. *Be careful, Marguerida! Dragons often smile before they dine!*

Margaret held herself stiff to keep her surprise from showing. It was the first time Rafaella had deliberately spoken to her mentally, and there was an undertone of affection and loyalty in it that moved her deeply.

Rescue from Rafael appeared in the form of an attractive middle-aged woman. She was not tall, but she moved with the air of one used to authority. Her once-dark hair was faded to a dull rust-brown color, and elaborately styled, as if she had taken great pains over it. The throat of her gown was ruffled, so that one did not immediately see the square line of the jaw that intimated a strong personality. She held out a pale hand toward Margaret, and it had six fingers.

The resemblance to Regis Hastur was quite unmistakable, and Margaret suspected she would have known Javanne Hastur Lanart-Alton as his sister no matter where she had encountered her. Determined gray eyes met hers for an instant, and then she found herself enfolded in a scented embrace, her cheeks brushed with a light kiss and her shoulders hugged gently. The smell of her perfume was heady and almost overwhelming.

She released Margaret enough to hold her at arm's length and looked her up and down, as one might examine a piece of horseflesh before one bought it. "Welcome to Armida, kinswoman. I am Javanne. My Gabriel has told me so much about you."

I'll wager he has, Margaret thought rebelliously, *and none of it to my credit* She took measure of her aunt before she spoke, noticing how Mikhail resembled her and differed as well. She noticed that Rafael had inherited her good bones, but his father's rather porcine eyes. "Thank you for inviting me."

"There, there. Don't be stiff. You are with your family now, where you belong. I can hardly wait for you to meet my daughters—they are about your age. It will be quite delightful." There was neither warmth nor enthusiasm in her voice, and Margaret suspected she was not particularly happy to have her there. The inner conflict was well-contained, but enough of it leaked out to make her very wary. The ease she had enjoyed on the journey evaporated, and she felt the tension return. "Come in, come in. You must be weary from your journey. Rafael, don't stand there like a statue. Take Marguerida's things."

Margaret started to protest and then saw that Rafaella had slung her precious harp over her own shoulder, and had picked up the bag with the recording equipment, leaving the hapless middle son to deal with the rest of the luggage. She grinned at the Renunciate behind Javanne's back, and got a nod in return.

Beyond the doors there was a wide entry hall with benches on either side. Javanne led them through it and into a large, comfortable room where a fire roared. The fireplace was large enough to roast an ox, and after the mild day outside, it was quite warm. It was even a little uncomfortable, with her body heated from riding, but she tried to disregard it.

There were several couches set along the walls, upholstered in dark greens and grays. She noticed the tapestries hung on the walls, and wished she had remembered to ask Lady Marilla about the two in her dining room. That at least would have been a topic that would not have upset the woman, as had the conversation about the Gifts. She observed four or five large chairs, and the legs of someone occupying one, his feet thrust toward the roaring hearth, his body hidden by the wings of the chair.

She watched the legs retreat as the sound of their footfalls left the hardwood of the entry and came onto the thick carpet. Strong hands pushed against the arms of the chair. In a moment, Margaret found herself looking up at a remarkably tall man, burly and grizzled. His once red hair was almost gray, but his eyes were bright and alert. He moved a little slowly, though he seemed to be no older than sixty, and took her hand gently in his.

They stood looking at one another, and Margaret felt a remarkable flood of emotions at his touch. There was something about him that reminded her of her father, not his appearance, but some quality she could not name. As she curled her fingers into his, Margaret felt all her repressed longing for the Old Man swell up in her throat. She swallowed hard and told herself not to be an idiot. It was just being in her father's house that was getting to her.

It was an experience of kinship, like that she had found with Mikhail, but quite different in quality, she decided. There was no heart-tug at his touch, just the sense of strength and utter trustworthiness.

"How do you do? I am your kinsman, Jeff Kerwin—or Damon Ridenow, if you prefer. Welcome to Armida, Marguerida Alton." He studied her closely, as if seeking some resemblance to her father. "You have that widow's peak of Lew's, but otherwise you do not much resemble him. And I never met your mother, so I do not know if you look very like her."

"I try to look like myself," Margaret said more tartly than she intended, still swamped with emotions. Then she gave Jeff a shy smile. "Lady Marilla thought I looked like my grandmother, Felicia Darriell, but I can't be sure. I've never seen a likeness of my mother, and memory is not always reliable, is it?"

Jeff nodded and sighed. "No, it isn't. People I remember as tall are often much shorter when I see them again!" *And Elorie grows more beautiful each year she is gone.* "Lew did not return with you, did he?"

Margaret was now heartily sick of people behaving as if she had her father stuffed into one of her bags. She almost wished he was—though the idea of her large father shoved into one of her duffles was absurd. But since she had heard his voice in her mind at Castle Ardais,

she, too, had begun to anticipate his presence just a little. It was almost annoying that he was absent. Where
the devil was he? He had seemed so near when he told
her to come to Armida, and yet no one knew where he
was. And she was damned if she was going to show
anyone that it was important to her. "Oh, I had him in
my pocket, but he fell out when we crossed the river,
and I have no idea where he is now."

The old man laughed, while Javanne, beside her,
looked slightly scandalized. "You are a disrespectful
minx," he said in Terran, "and very much your father's
child." Then he chucked her beneath her chin with a
long finger.

Margaret liked the sound of his laughter and wished
her father had been less sober and more playful. She
would have liked to have had someone like Jeff for a
father, she realized, and felt disloyal. She wondered why
she felt as she did, and decided it was because Jeff
seemed the sort of man she could talk to, as she had
never been able to with the Senator.

She ignored the mild turmoil she sensed from Javanne, feeling Rafaella's quiet steadiness instead. It was
reassuring to have at least one person she felt she could
trust. And, perhaps, in this new relative, another. Margaret was uneasy as she had not been at Ardais. There
were undercurrents that she knew she did not understand, and all her training was frustrated by them. She
was not only ignorant, she did not even know what the
right questions were!

Yes, you can speak to me, if you wish to. Aloud, Jeff
said in Terran rather than *casta,* "Try not to be too hard
on Lew. He never was any good at sharing counsel with
others, and least of all with women." *I am sure you are
a good daughter—if any of my own had lived, I would
have wished them to be as strong and independent-
minded as I suspect you are.* There was sorrow in that
thought, and great fondness as well. Margaret felt hot
with embarrassment, uneasy with an affection she did
not feel she had earned.

Then she heard Javanne clear her throat and realized
that it was very rude to continue to speak in Terran,
although she suspected her aunt could understand perfectly well. It was just that it was so good to talk in

Terran again, where she didn't have to worry about saying something impolite. Her *casta* was fluent enough now, but there were subtleties that eluded her, from time to time, and she wondered if she would ever be able to speak without also minding her tongue.

Margaret could feel her rising ambivalence again. Part of her wished to get off on the right foot with her new-found relatives, and another wished to be free of formalities, to be the woman who had arrived with Ivor weeks before. She knew that was impossible, but that did not prevent her from wanting the simplicity she had enjoyed with her mentor and friend.

"I know you are my kinsman, but are you an uncle or a cousin? Mikhail tried to untangle it for me, but it didn't make a lot of sense, truthfully." She could feel her aunt's mood darken at the name of her youngest son, mingled with deep affection, so it was extremely confusing. What was wrong with Mikhail, that both of his parents bristled at the mention of him?

"Strictly speaking, I am your cousin." He took her lead politely, and Margaret felt Javanne relax behind her. "We are both descended from Estaban Lanart, who was a great-great-grandfather to Lew. But we are almost two generations removed, which makes me more of an uncle."

"Why is that?"

"Cousins on Darkover can marry; uncles and nieces generally do not."

"And here I thought Arcturian kinship was complex!"

"Have you been there?" He appeared genuinely interested and quite unmoved by Javanne's increasing restlessness.

"No, but I've read papers about them." *I wonder why uncles and nieces don't marry here?*

In the past, chiya, *any man old enough to be your father just might be!*

This response was confusing, because Margaret had the idea that women on Darkover were carefully kept, that the obsession with bloodlines made the sexual license Jeff had just implied quite unthinkable. In the past, he had said. That must explain it. She remembered what Mikhail had told her about the Forbidden Tower, and saw that things were not quite as organized as she had imagined. Sex between the generations was taboo. Satisfied that she understood the problem, she now felt she knew why Mikhail had reacted so violently at her playful suggestion that she would solve the problem of the Domain by wedding the tall man before her. No, it was more than that. Mikhail found her attractive, and for some reason she did not understand, he did not want to feel that way. Why, he almost behaved as if he were jealous. Margaret did not have any first-hand experience with jealousy, so she was not sure. And there was nothing she could do about it anyhow.

She forced her thoughts away from Mikhail, from the puzzle of his seeming attraction and her own to him. It was not a good idea to have such musings in a room with telepaths in it. Javanne was already hostile, spoiling for some sort of fight. If she found Margaret thinking fondly of her youngest son, she would be displeased. And, Margaret realized, she had no real idea of how much of her thoughts were audible to others, although Istvana had said she did not broadcast very much.

She just had to hope that she was keeping her mind sufficiently opaque to preserve her own privacy. For once her lifelong habit of keeping to herself, that foul legacy of Ashara, now seemed an asset. And fussing over things was not going to help. Instead, she tried to enjoy the sense of security she found in the presence of Jeff. She felt as safe with him as she had with Ivor Davidson. "I must not monopolize you, Marguerida. Javanne wishes to see you settled." He released her hand a little reluctantly.

I'll just bet she does—settled with one of her sons! Margaret was fairly certain that her aunt could hear that, but she was suddenly too tired to care. She was not going to be pushed around if she could help it. "Of course. There will plenty of time to talk later."

Jeff bent forward and kissed her on the cheek, and she smelled his clean skin. "And, until your father arrives, I shall be as a father to you, and you may come to me with any questions. Are we agreed?" He spoke very quietly into her ear.

Margaret was so surprised by what he said that she could only nod mutely. She could feel Javanne's annoyance and heard her think, *Interfering old man! Gabriel* was a fool to have invited him! I could have managed things much better without him, for he will side with her. "I should be pleased to have you stand in for the Senator. I am certain he would wish it, if he knew."

Why did the Old Man send me here? What is going on? This is all so muddled. Why did I ever come to this crazy planet? God, but I am so tired!

Margaret turned and followed Javanne Hastur out of the big living room, toward the stairs. She did not need to be a telepath to know her hostess was seething inside. One look at the set of Javanne's shoulders told her all she needed. As she climbed the stairs behind the older woman, she realized that by establishing a child/parent relationship with old Jeff, whose claim to the Alton Domain was as valid as her own, she had effectively put herself outside Gabriel Lanart's control. This was not what Javanne had intended. Her new aunt was up to something—or was she? Margaret tried to tell herself she was being needlessly paranoid, and that her kinsmen must have her best interests at heart, but she did not entirely believe it.

By the time they reached the door of the bedroom, Javanne had calmed down enough to try to be gracious. "I hope you don't mind sharing the room," she began. "I know that Terranan are accustomed to living in little rooms all alone, which I think is extremely odd."

Margaret glanced around the large chamber. There was a bed large enough for four, a wardrobe for clothes, and a washing stand. Two straight-backed chairs stood against the wall, and there were another pair, red wing chairs, close to the small fireplace. The red chairs did not go with the overall blueness of the room, and she wondered if they had come from another chamber.

The bed was hung with blue linen curtains, embroidered with a stylized figure that might mean mountains, and covered with several quilts and a figured spread of silvery leaves. There was a large window which overlooked the pastures in front of the house. In all it was a pleasant room, but Margaret was wondering if Rafaella was going to share her bed again. She was ambivalent about that prospect. She had not found sleeping with the Renunciate uncomfortable at Jerana's house, and the bed was certainly large enough.

When Rafaella bent down and pulled a trundle bed from beneath the curtained one, and put Margaret's bag of recording equipment on it, Margaret felt relieved. The Renunciate had become like a sister to her during the journey, a sister she had never had and always longed for. But she was still in a mind set which demanded privacy, and getting close to others, either physically or otherwise, remained uncomfortable. This, too, was part of her legacy from Ashara, as Istvana had explained to her, and while part of her resented it, there was still a strong impulse toward keeping herself distant from people, even people she loved and trusted.

"Rafaella and I have been sleeping in the same room for some time now, Lady Lanart, and we are used to each other's habits. When I was on Relegan and several other planets with my mentor, Ivor Davidson, we often shared lodgings that were much less comfortable than these."

As soon as the words were out of her mouth, Margaret knew she had said something shocking. Javanne colored under her fair skin, and Rafaella quickly busied herself with sorting out the rest of the luggage. The maid who had carried the bags upstairs, a fat woman in her sixties, looked very interested, and Margaret did not doubt she would be gossiped about in the servants quarters before the hour was out.

"What sort of lodgings, Marja?" Javanne mastered her outrage, and her curiosity overcame her sense of scandal. She was not actually interested in the details, but she clearly wanted to know more. Probably she wondered if Ivor had been her lover as well as her mentor. Under the circumstances, she realized, no one on Darkover would be able to understand a young woman dashing blamelessly around the Federation with a male.

Margaret was distracted by the use of her childhood name for a moment, then wondered whether she should tell the truth or dissemble. "Oh, single room huts made of grasses—that sort of thing," she answered, deciding to be provoking. If she disgraced herself sufficiently, perhaps Javanne would abandon her plan to have Margaret marry one of her sons and the entire visit would be less unpleasant.

The maid gasped, and Javanne rounded on her in a

fury. "Put down those things and go about your work! And don't you go wagging your tongue either. I won't have the *domna* gossiped about!" Then Javanne fixed Margaret with a steely gaze. "I don't know how you behaved on other planets, but I expect you to remember your place and act like a lady while you are under my roof."

"Ivor was an old man—in his nineties, and hardly . . ."

"Enough! I can excuse your manners because you do not yet know our ways, but that will change immediately. Do you understand me?"

Margaret was tired, and her frayed temper finally snapped. This order was more than she could bear. "Tell me, Aunt, is everyone on Darkover so filthy minded?"

Javanne turned red beneath her cosmetics, her cheeks and throat blushing furiously. She trembled all over and then left the room, banging the door as she went. *Damn the chit, coming here and acting like a common whore!*

"I wonder there are any doors still on their hinges at Armida, with both *Dom* Gabriel and *Domna* Javanne given to slamming," she commented, enjoying her foolish victory.

Rafaella roared with laughter, trying to muffle the sound in her sleeve and failing utterly. Small tears trickled from her eyes. "It was very naughty of you to provoke her," the Renunciate said when she had recovered her breath.

"She puts me in here in a room with a bed large enough for an orgy, and expects me to not consider sex. That makes no sense at all."

"She is very proper, Marguerida, and she does not want people to talk. And in the past . . ."

"Don't do that! If you tell me it is something not to be discussed, I will scream. Why is she so sensitive?"

Rafaella gave a long sigh, then shrugged. "When the Forbidden Tower was here, at Armida, there were some things going on that were very shocking."

"You mean like Damon Ridenow fathering a child on a woman not his wife? Mikhail told me all about it. What's so dreadful about that—men have been having children by their mistresses since time immemorial, Rafaella. Even good men, decent men." *Even my father,* she thought.

"Yes, but you see, it is a very sore point for her."

"Why? Tell me so I won't make any bigger mistakes than I already have."

The Renunciate thought for a moment, looking torn. "Very well. You see, *Dom* Gabriel is descended from Ellemir Lanart, who was wife to old Damon Ridenow, and from Ann'dra Carr, the Terranan who was part of the Forbidden Tower. That is very improper!"

"Why? Because Gabriel's father was *nedestro,* or because he is part Terran?" She remembered her uncle's unspoken hostility to Terrans, and wondered if this was the reason. It would certainly explain a great deal.

"Both, I think. But I believe that Lady Javanne is very conscious that there were goings-on at Armida that were very shocking, you see."

"No, not really. That was years and years ago. *Dom* Gabriel is a legitimate descendant of the Lanarts, or at least as legitimate as I am. Is everyone afraid there is some sneaky gene for sexual misbehavior lurking around?"

The Renunciate opened one of her bags and began to pull out her clothing. "No, but . . . it's very hard to explain. It's all about *laran,* really. For many years, hundreds and hundreds, *laran* was only in the Comyn families. And that was fine for the *comyn,* and not so bad for everyone else. So, the *comyn* intermarried to keep the *laran* strong and to preserve the Gifts of the Seven Domains. Some of these customs have changed a little since the Terranan came, about a hundred years ago. But it is still not proper for a married woman to bear a child to someone other than her husband. It is . . . very irregular."

"I see, I suppose. But if Comyn lords were dashing around fathering *nedestro* children on this woman or that, it sounds like the *laran* was bound to spread out into the general population. Like your sister."

"Yes, but it still isn't considered right."

"Right? It sounds damned convenient for the men, and perfectly dreadful for the women."

Rafaella gave a shrug, as if to say that was just how things were, went to the window and looked down. "Here comes young Gabriel, riding his horse too hard. And there is Mikhail with him."

"What?" Margaret rushed to the window and peered out. Why, he must have set out the same day as they had, or else ridden harder. Probably the latter, since she and Rafaella had not pushed themselves, due to her tendency to become exhausted. She looked down at the tumble of golden curls, the set of his shoulders, the way he sat his steed. *He had a good seat.* Then she blushed, realizing she was not thinking of Mikhail's seat on a horse at all.

He had told her he would not come to Armida, at that parting in Castle Ardais, yet here he was. Margaret remembered that Rafael had said he had been "sent for," and she felt a mild disappointment. Perhaps he was not quite the man she assumed, if he came when called. He must be more under his father's thumb than he pretended.

She told herself not to judge him too hastily, and found she was very glad he was there, for whatever reason. She allowed herself a moment of speculation that perhaps his presence at Armida had nothing to do with obedience or duty. Maybe he just could not keep away from her. The thought shocked Margaret more than a little, and she shook her head. But, she reflected, she rather liked the idea. There was no pleasing her, was there?

It did not matter one bit, did it? She was only paying a courtesy visit to the family home, and only because the Senator had told her to. She was not there of her own choice, was she? While she watched, she saw the pewter-gray horse run across the pasture, nickering loudly enough for her to hear. The mare reared up as she reached the fence, and Margaret saw Mikhail wave at it. The horse must be his own, then, or else she ran to greet everyone. She watched the sun sparkle on the dark mane of the mare. That really was a beautiful horse. And watching helped to keep her from speculating about Mikhail.

The two riders vanished around the side of the house, and Margaret sat down on the bed with a thump. Damn the Old Man, and Mikhail, and all men everywhere, she thought. They either order you around, or lie to you, or die on you. Why did women put up with such unreliable creatures? She thought of Dio and how she had patiently

endured all of the Senator's black moods and his drinking and decided that it must be some flaw in the female character.

When Margaret and Rafaella came down the stairs at
dinner time, they found most of the family gathered in
the large room where she had encountered Jeff Kerwin
earlier in the afternoon. Javanne had changed her gown,
and now wore a less modest garment. It still had the
throat-concealing ruff beneath her chin, and Margaret
decided her aunt was very vain. Well, just because she
was not very vain herself was no reason to judge the
woman, she chided herself, realizing that she *wanted* to
dislike Javanne. It was not a pretty admission, and she
did not feel good about it.

Javanne rose from her chair as they entered, smiling
with rather too many teeth, and studying Margaret with
steely eyes. "I trust you are rested and refreshed, Marja-
chiya. Do you have everything you need?"

Bathed and dressed in the garments she had first purchased from MacEwan, Margaret felt more at ease than
she had on her arrival, but she was still extremely wary
of almost everyone in the room. Jeff Kerwin dozed beside the fireplace, and Mikhail and Rafael were discussing something intensely. She could tell that Mikhail
was trying not to look at her, was desperately paying
attention to whatever his brother was saying. Very
well—two could play at that game.

Dom Gabriel stood with his eldest son, so like in appearance that they might have been twins, but they were
silent. They looked slightly uncomfortable, as if their
rather formal clothing was too tight. On one of the couches there was a woman, small and slender, surrounded
by what appeared to be a herd of small children all demanding her attention. She might have been rather
pretty once, but now she was drawn looking, her skin
dry and pale, her hair a mousy red. Margaret guessed
the woman's age to be close to her own, but she looked
nearer to fifty.

Another woman rose from a chair, wearing a full
green gown that billowed around her like a tent. She
was as tall as Margaret, with large bones concealed beneath firm flesh. The impression of grandeur, strength,

and dignity was enormous. She was carrying about
twenty extra kilos, by Margaret's quick estimation, but
it looked good on her. The eyes that shone from the
round face were intelligent, bright with interest and
some of the same humor she found in Mikhail. Her red
hair was thick, not fine like Margaret's own, and fell
past her shoulders, clasped at her nape with a heavy
butterfly ornament.

Javanne followed her eyes. "Marguerida, I wish to introduce you to your cousins. I believe you have already
encountered Mikhail, and also my son Rafael." She drew
Margaret toward the couch. "This is my daughter Ariel,
and my grandchildren. Ariel, stop fussing over Kennard
and greet your cousin."

Reluctantly, Ariel turned from the demands of her
children and offered her hand to Margaret. She hardly
looked at her, glancing with lackluster eyes, then turning
back to the youngsters who were squirming and wiggling
and pushing each other. Margaret found the hand was
limp and dry, and with its touch she felt so powerful a
sense of anxiety that it nearly made her gasp. "Welcome
to Armida," Ariel whispered, then drew her hand away
and returned her attention to her fussy children.

In the shadows behind the couch, Margaret realized,
there stood a man clothed in such dark colors he was
nearly invisible. He, too, hovered around the children
with a look of uneasiness, as if he expected her to snatch
one away or something equally unlikely. "This is my
son-in-law, Piedro Alar." The man gave a formal bow,
but made no move to otherwise greet her. Margaret
could not help wondering how two such worried people
managed to get out of bed in the morning, but she held
her tongue. It was unwise to judge on appearances, and
likely they were more cheerful when they were out of
Javanne's view.

"Now, Marguerida," Javanne said, drawing her away
from the depressing couple, "this is your cousin Liriel.
She and Ariel are twins, though you might not believe
it."

"So you are Marguerida Alton." The large woman
smiled, and her face lit up. "Where did Mother put you?
I hope it isn't the blue bedroom—the roof has a leak,
unless it's been fixed since I was here last. Mother puts

people there when she doesn't want them to stay very long."

Javanne glared at her daughter, and Margaret knew immediately that the two of them did not get along well. She remembered that Mikhail had described this sister as the spirited one, the one who would not marry. For that reason alone, Margaret was inclined to like her. She seemed so sunny compared to her sister, and friendly into the bargain.

"I don't know which room it is, but it seems quite comfortable," Margaret answered politely. The room did have blue walls, she realized, and the hangings around the bed were blue as well. She looked at Javanne, and so did Liriel, and the older woman flushed unbecomingly. "I had no idea Armida was so large."

"Oh, have you been shown around?" Liriel asked. "I had the impression that you arrived and went directly to your room."

"True, but it looked quite large from outside." She felt herself drawn to this new cousin, and they exchanged a look of mutual amusement. There was mischief in the blue eyes, as well as intelligence.

She drew her generous mouth into a more sober line, as if containing some secret jest. "Appearances are often deceiving," Liriel said with sibylline solemnity, and then Javanne almost dragged Margaret away from her daughter.

"Marguerida, this is my son Gabriel," Javanne said, and the man standing beside *Dom* Gabriel gave a stiff bow. The older woman spoke with pride, and Margaret was certain her eldest child was the apple of her eye. He was stocky like his father, and had the same sort of bulging eyes, and she suspected he had a similarly choleric disposition.

"Welcome to my home," he said gruffly.

"Greetings, Cousin Gabriel. I am glad to meet you at last." Margaret knew she did not sound in the least glad to meet the man, but hoped no one would notice.

Javanne was apparently exhausted from her duties as a hostess and turned away, leaving Margaret and Gabriel staring at each other. She tried to think of some topic of conversation that might be interesting to them both, but nothing sprang to mind. *Dom* Gabriel looked from one to the other, waiting for them to be sociable, and when the silence continued, he grunted.

"I've invited some singers for after dinner," the older man announced with the air of someone offering an enormous boon.

"I am sure that will be delightful," Margaret replied, and wondered if she was going to be able to endure an entire evening of polite nonconversation. She wished she had the nerve to plead a sudden headache and retire. Mikhail appeared at her elbow, smiling pleasantly. "So, cousin, how do you find Armida, so far?"

Grateful to be rescued from trying to converse with either Gabriel, she turned to him happily. "What I have seen is very lovely. The horses are wonderful. I was quite taken with the one that has a dark gray coat."

"That's Dorilys. She's a fine steed, if a little feisty."

"What a pretty name." Margaret thought her tongue would cleave to her palate before she got to the dinner table if she had to continue making meaningless noises. Was this what Dio had to endure at state dinners? Her admiration for her stepmother rose another notch.

"She was born during the mother of all thunder-storms," Mikhail answered. "I know, because I was in the foaling barn for her arrival. It isn't quite a proper name, for it means 'golden,' but there was a woman, long ago, called Dorilys, and she could call the storms, they say. Since I was midwife to the filly, I had the privilege of naming her, so Dorilys she is. I am glad you like her."

"I did more than like her. I think I fell in love with her. Is it possible I could ride her, while I am here?"

"Dorilys is no horse for a young woman," growled *Dom* Gabriel.

"But, Uncle," Margaret answered as sweetly as she could, "I am not a young woman. And I have been riding horses for years."

Fortunately, the *coridom* announced dinner before the older man tried to tell her what to do, and they all re-tired into a dining room which looked large enough to feed an army. Margaret hesitated, not sure where to sit, and she saw that both Javanne and *Dom* Gabriel were unsure as well. The places at the head and foot of the table were theirs by custom, but with the eldest member

of the Alton clan present, in the form of Jeff Kerwin,
things were not quite normal. Before everyone dithered
until the meat got cold, the old man solved the problem
by taking Margaret gently by one elbow and leading her
to the head of the table.

"This is your place, *chiya*."

"Surely Lady Javanne . . ."

"Must yield."

Margaret swallowed a giggle. "I can't imagine her ever
doing that, Uncle Jeff," she whispered hastily.

"It is high time she learned, then. Everyone must yield
from time to time. It is never pleasant, but it is a necessary life lesson." He held her chair out and helped her
into her seat, then took the one at her right, while the
rest of the family looked on with a kind of horrid fasci-
nation. Then there was a scraping of chairs as everyone
got settled, and the food was brought.

The presence of the Alar children made it a noisy
meal. The food was good and simple, and rather less
formal than the meals she had eaten at Ardais. The clatter of utensils and the passing of dishes was a dreadful
din after the quiet of the road, and Margaret exchanged
a glance with Rafaella. The Renunciate nodded at her,
then went back to whatever she was discussing with Liriel Lanart.

At last it was over, and the table cleared. Ariel gathered her herd of children and took them away to bed,
and Piedro followed her, looking glum and anxious.
Their departure lightened the mood of the gathering,
and a few minutes later the singers arrived, four sisters
so alike they might have been quadruplets, and a brother
who limped badly.

They tuned their instruments, a *ryll* and a plucked
object that seemed an uneasy hybrid of harp and guitar,
and began to sing. Several of the songs were now familiar to Margaret, but others were not, and she was sorry
she had not brought her recording equipment down with
her. Then she realized how shocking it would have been
if she had, and smiled a little to herself. She might be
an heiress, but she would never break the scholarly habits she had acquired during her time at University.

They began another song, and Margaret listened,
while gooseflesh formed along her arms.

"How came this blood on your right hand, Brother, tell me, tell me . . ." She had sung it herself, on her first full day on Darkover, rousing it from the haunted *ryll* that had once belonged to the mother she had never really known. She had not thought much about Thyra since she had left Castle Ardais, and she found the listening very uncomfortable.

"That is hardly a good song to sing before brothers and sisters," *Dom* Gabriel growled, but it was clear he was glad to have something to relieve his growing frustrations on. "It is not a fortunate tune."

"We are not superstitious here, Father," Liriel answered. "At least, I am not, and Ariel has left the room." *The ninny starts at falling leaves.*

One of the sisters gave a shrug, and the brother said, "We will sing another song if you wish it, *vai dom.*"

Margaret looked at Liriel. "I've heard the song before—sung it, actually. Is there some story attached to it?" Her scholarly instincts were aroused and she ignored the look she got from Javanne for her question.

Liriel Lanart laughed, a healthy belly laugh, and said, "It tells of a family curse, here in the Kilghard Hills. Some say it is unlucky for a sister to sing it in the hearing of a brother. We have many superstitions in the mountains. But where did you learn it? They do not sing it at Ardais, for certain."

Margaret frowned. "When I was in the house of Master Everard in Music Street, he showed me an old *ryll* he said no one could play. It is a beautiful instrument, made by a famous luthier, according to him, and I picked it up . . . with my usual curiosity. The song just came out, as if it had been left on the strings by the last person to use it." She hesitated for a moment. "Later I found out that the *ryll* had belonged to Thyra Darriell, my mother."

Dom Gabriel scowled and Javanne glared, while Jeff looked thoughtful. A dreadful silence spread through the audience.

"I will sing a song even more forbidden," Mikhail said, standing up and rushing into the stillness. "Wars have been fought on Darkover for less than this, but I am not superstitious."

He took a breath, squared his shoulders, and started to sing.

> *"0, my father was the Keeper of the Arilinn Tower*
> *He seduced a* chieri *with a* kireseth *flower*
> *From this union there were three*
> *Two were Comyn and the other was me . . .*

He had a good voice, untrained but strong and deep, and Margaret was grateful to him for distracting everyone from the mention of her mother. It was clear from Javanne's expression that this was not to be talked about! That was fine with Margaret, because she had no wish to discuss Thyra either. Why had she mentioned the haunted *ryll* at all?

Liriel chuckled. "You are behind the times, brother. That is not forbidden, just in terrible taste. I learned that song myself, within the walls of Arilinn when I trained there." She glanced at Jeff. "I suppose you did also, cousin."

"Of course! We have begun to learn to laugh at ourselves, and that is a very healthy thing."

"Did your father ever sing that one for you, Marguerida? He is remembered at Arilinn as one of the best technicians ever, as I know to my regret." Liriel made a face. "It is very depressing always to be compared to someone you never even knew."

"No, not a note. The Senator was too busy with his duties to tell me anything," she said, dissembling slightly. As for Arilinn Tower, or any other, the very thought of them gave her the creeps after her adventure in the Tower of Mirrors. "In fact I never knew he was trained in a Tower until recently." *He failed to inform me on a number of matters, and I am looking forward to taking him to task—soon, I hope!*

"He never told you . . ." Liriel looked shocked and angered, much as Istvana Ridenow had. "Do you mean to tell me you have been walking around for all these years with the Alton Gift, with *laran* almost dribbling out your ears, if I may be so blunt, and . . ."

"I don't mean to tell you anything," Margaret snapped. It was *her* business to criticize Lew Alton, not that of people who had never even met him! This reaction surprised her, because Margaret had not known until that moment that in spite of rejection and abandonment, in spite of everything, she had a deep, abiding loyalty to her father. If only she had the affection to go with it, she thought, she might be completely content.

"Forgive me, cousin. I have the Alton lack of tact," Liriel said, and Margaret knew she was sincere. She liked Liriel more for being able to admit a fault, and decided that tact was largely absent at Armida, that a stiff politeness was used because everyone was both volatile and blunt to a fault. Both *Dom* Gabriel and Javanne looked to be the sort of people who spoke their minds, no matter whose feelings got injured.

"It is a little close in here, isn't it," Javanne announced suddenly, as if she wanted to steer the subject away from Lew Alton quickly. "You look a trifle warm, Marja. Rafael, why don't you show your cousin the fragrance garden?"

This suggestion was met with a sullen look from the middle son, and a twinkling glance from Mikhail. "Of course, Mother. You may need a wrap—it is quite cool outside."

Margaret rose so quickly there was no time for Jeff to help her with her chair. "That sounds delightful." She wanted to get out of the room, with or without a shawl. Rafaella grinned at her, and Margaret nodded back. She could depend on Rafaella to keep her in a good mood.

A servant produced a finely-embroidered wrap, and Rafael took her down a hall and out into the clouded night. There was the smell of rain yet unfallen in the air, and then a scent that almost overpowered the senses.

"I am so used to seeing the stars," she said in the darkness, aware of her cousin's nearness, "that I do not know if I could ever get used to so many clouds all the time."

"I've heard Terranan say that before. What shall I call you—cousin or Marguerida, or Marja?"

"Anything you wish, but I think I am rather too old for Marja. Cousin seems safe, doesn't it."

"Very well." He seemed at some loss for words.

"What is that ravishing smell?" Margaret drew the shawl around her.

"This is Mother's fragrance garden. Many years ago,

before the Terranan came to Darkover, there was a
Keeper at Arilinn who was blind. She made herself a
garden of all sweet-smelling things, both those which
smell by day and by night, for it was always night for
Fiora, and Mother liked it so much, when she was training there, that she made one for herself."

"It is very wonderful." The clouds parted, and one of
the moons gleamed. "I would like to see all four moons
in the sky at once." Some faint memory rose in her
mind, and she could hear her father and Dio laughing
about things which happened beneath four moons. From
her present adult perspective, the tone of their words
was so clearly sexual that she knew that she had probably said something regrettable. To conceal her discomfort she continued, "I suppose it is a rare astronomical
occurrence."

"Yes." He shifted his weight back and forth. "We on
Darkover do not talk about it . . . damn! We didn't
come out here to talk about the weather or the moons
or if the rain will hurt the grain crop!"

"Yes, I know." Margaret sensed his discomfort, but
could not think of any way to lessen it.

Rafael took a long breath and exhaled mightily, like
a man under a heavy burden. "Mother isn't very subtle,
is she?"

"No. But I would have thought . . ."

"Cousin, I am unmarried and healthy," Rafael interrupted, as if he had to keep talking. "Therefore I am
free, and I would count it a great honor if you would
reunite the branches of our family by marrying me."

Margaret stared at him. "You cannot mean that," she
said. "We never set eyes on each other till this
afternoon."

"On Darkover that is not important. Mother and Father married the day after they met. It would be a good
thing and . . ." His voice faltered.

Margaret said forthrightly, "I wouldn't even think of
marrying you. I don't care what the customs are. Marriage is too important a decision to be made by people
other than the ones who are going to get married." *And
the way your parents mistreat doors does not speak well
for not meeting until the day before the wedding!*

No, it doesn't! Rafael laughed, a little uneasily and

said, "Thank you very much. I did promise my mother I would try. I don't think it would be so terrible, but you are . . . rather strongwilled, like my mother, and I suspect that would not suit me. Can we be friends?"

"Your mother is a very interfering woman," Margaret answered severely, liking Rafael for his honesty, and resenting her new aunt more by the second.

"Perhaps. She does her duty as she sees it. And she really does want to see the Altons one family again."

"She will have to manage that without me. It is getting cold. Let's go back in—or do you want to escape without facing the music?"

"It doesn't matter. One look at your face, and she will know you refused me."

"Then I think I will go right to my room! I really don't have the energy for another hour of watching my words, or my face!"

"As you wish, cousin."

18

◆

Margaret woke at first light and rolled over in the huge bed. The soft, steady sound of Rafaella's snoring from the trundle bed was a soothing, normal noise, and she rather wondered how she could sleep without it. That made her laugh silently. She could hardly take the Renunciate off Darkover. What a thought! She wondered how Rafaella would behave, and decided she was adaptable enough to cope with almost anything. How had they become so close, so quickly? She was not sure, but she certainly liked having a woman nearby she could trust, and felt safe with. Unlike her new relatives, who made her feel threatened despite their clearly good intentions. And, if by chance she actually became freemate to Captain Rafe Scott, then she would be Margaret's aunt! That was too much, and she laughed aloud. She rather hoped they would, just so that she could enjoy the absurdity of the situation. At least they would be happy.

Margaret contrasted Rafaella with the Alton clan, and decided that the difference was that the Renunciate had no plans or ambitions for her. There was nothing she wanted from Margaret, and that made her safe. She found herself feeling mildly lost, and sternly told herself not to get into a mood.

She stared at the ceiling and noticed a large dark spot in one corner. It was moist, though not dripping. Evidently the leak which Liriel had spoken of had not been tended to. Margaret started to get slightly angry. Her uncle Gabriel was so busy minding other people's business he had let Armida fall into disrepair. Her house! No, not her house—but she still felt a kind of attachment. How annoying! The vehemence of her thought startled her, and she exclaimed, "Damn!"

"Burrf? Huh? What?"

"Oh, Rafaella, I am sorry. I didn't mean to wake you.

"No matter. My bladder would have gotten me up soon enough." She pushed her covers away, got out of the trundle bed, and left the room. When she returned a few minutes later, Margaret was sitting on the side of the bed, trying to sort out her feelings. She wriggled her bare toes in the chilly morning air and coiled a strand of hair around one finger.

"Are you thinking or brooding," Rafaella asked.

"Both, I suppose. Rafael asked me to marry him, while we were in the garden last night, and I expect that sometime today young Gabriel will do likewise."

"What did you say?"

"I told him no, of course. What did you think I would say?"

"He wouldn't be the worst husband in the world, and I thought maybe you would take him as the least of several evils." Rafaella laughed. "Ever since you mentioned Rafe Scott, back at Ardais, I have been thinking that I could have a freemate, if I wanted one," she went on. *And perhaps I do.* "I never really considered it until now. I don't know if it would work. But you would have to marry *di catenas,* and I don't know if you could abide that."

"I'm not sure I follow you."

"Did you notice that heavy bracelet that Javanne wears? And the one that Lady Ariel has?"

"I did notice Javanne's, but not Ariel's. Why?"

"That was placed on her arm when she married *Dom* Gabriel, and it will never be removed, not even in death. He wears one, too, but it is smaller, and you don't notice it, because on men it is usually hidden by their sleeves. *Di catenas* is forever, and it is how the Comyn marry. It means a woman belongs to a man, not to herself."

Margaret scowled. "So *Dom* Gabriel can go around fathering *nedestro* sons all over the landscape—though frankly I have a lot of trouble imagining that—but Lady Javanne has to be a good little wife and keep her skirts down?"

The Renunciate roared, and her laughter seemed to bounce off the roof beams and brighten the entire room. "That is pretty close," she added when she finally got her breath back.

"No, I don't think that would suit me one bit. My father and Dio are very married and, as far as I know, faithful to one another, but Dio never belonged to anyone but herself. How can a woman 'belong' to a man? She isn't property, like lands and horses."

"But she is, almost. A lot of women in the Comyn, and the other classes, for that matter, are just property, just for making sons. That is one of the reasons why the Renunciate's Oath forbids any form of marriage except that of freemates—because we do not wish to be some man's property."

"Oh. Well, that has nothing to do with me. You are quite right. I could not abide being some fellow's brood mare. Speaking of mares, I wonder if I will get a chance to ride that dark gray, Dorilys, while I am here." She changed the subject because she was extremely uncomfortable with talk of marriage. It seemed to loom over her, like a closet-monster, waiting to leap out and grab her by the throat. The sense of chill which had been absent for several days returned, and she felt an echo of Ashara which made the average closet-monster seem quite nice by comparison. Even with all Istvana's assurances that she had bested the shade of the ancient Keeper, she was not certain that the manipulations of Ashara were not influencing her in some fashion, and she hated it.

"Marguerida, if you remain on Darkover, you will be married, whether you wish it or not. And changing the subject won't change the circumstances! Really, for an intelligent woman, you can be very silly!" There was impatience in her voice, but affection as well, and Margaret felt her fears of Ashara begin to fade again.

"That's why I am not going to stay here. Probably I will just renounce my claim to the Alton Domain. Then I will go back to University, where I really belong." She was whistling in the dark, and she knew it, but Margaret was determined not to get more enmeshed in the strangeness of Darkover, in heavy bracelets that made a woman a chattel and all the rest of it. What she would do about the problem of being a functional telepath she did not know. If only it would just go away!

"Are you sure?"

No, I'm not, and damn you for seeing it! "Let's get dressed and find some breakfast. I'm ravenous."

The dining room was empty except for Liriel. She had an empty bowl in front of her and was looking at it as if she were considering another helping. She looked up when Margaret and Rafaella entered the room and smiled.

"Good morning. Did you sleep well?"

"Very well, thank you, but I think there is still a leak in the ceiling."

Liriel chuckled. "Mother wanted to murder me for mentioning that. Mother often wants to murder me, which is one reason I chose Tower life. It keeps us out of each other's hair. Ariel lives about twenty miles away, and she and Mother are always visiting back and forth. But then, Ariel gets along with her, and I never did. We are alike, Mother and I, and two strong-minded women under one roof is a recipe for misery, isn't it?"

"I never thought about it before, but I think you are right," Margaret replied. She liked her cousin more and more, and thought she could become close friends with her if she remained on Darkover. And until she found some way to live with her telepathy, she was going to, however much she wanted otherwise. They sat down and a servant brought cereal and fruit, and Liriel held out her bowl for another serving.

"I had hoped to talk with you alone," Liriel said, after cleaning her bowl in record time. She gave Rafaella a quick glance, and the Renunciate returned it. "You must remain, Rafaella—by alone I mean without my meddling family."

"You seem to have your wish," Margaret answered warily. *I hope she won't plead the suit of one of her brothers because I don't think I could stand that.*

"By no means," Liriel said, clearly picking up her thought. "I am sure you will have enough of that before the day is out." Her tone was dry, but the look she gave Margaret was a sympathetic one. "I went to the Tower to avoid just such a forced marriage—they wanted me to marry young Dyan Ardais, Mikhail's liege. You must have met him at Castle Ardais."

"I did, and I think you were wise not to have taken

him. He seems . . . not up to your strong character. Perhaps I misjudge him, since I did not really talk to him much, and then mostly about ordinary things."

"That's a kind way to say I would have made breakfast out of him, and wanted a side of meat to finish with." They all laughed, and Rafaella got some cereal down the wrong part of her throat. Margaret pounded her vigorously between the shoulders, glad to have an outlet for her conflicting emotions.

"Are you all right?" Margaret asked.

"Oh, yes, but please do not try to be funny when I have my mouth full."

"I know that it is very hard for you to understand our ways," Liriel continued, "but they have worked well for centuries. You regard my mother as an enemy, and you should not. She does her duty as she sees it, which does not always suit me or my brother Mikhail. Even though I am firmly engaged in my technician's work at Tramontana, she keeps suggesting it is not too late for me to wed and bed and have lovely children."

"Everyone on Darkover seems to have marriage on their minds," Margaret answered darkly. "I keep expecting a priest to leap out of the corners and marry me without a by-your-leave."

"That is a misplaced apprehension. We have good reason, from our history, for our customs, Marguerida. Many of the Comyn, including my father, refuse to realize that times are different now, that Darkover is different than it was in the past. But I don't want to discuss our colorful history—though I can see you are interested. I had a long talk with Uncle Jeff last night, after everyone had retired. We are both aware that you have the Alton Gift, and have it in full measure."

"How do you know that?" She felt uneasy, as if someone had seen her without the protection of her clothing.

"*Chiya*, to any telepath it is as obvious as the color of your hair. Jeff and Istvana Ridenow also discussed it, so we knew before you arrived that you were in possession of the Gift."

Hell! Talking about me behind my back, and there's not a thing I can do about it! So, there's more to Javanne's wish to marry me off to one of her sons than Armida—they want to make sure this cursed Gift doesn't get lost in the genetic drift. I feel like a prize, like I did on Mantenon, when that chieftain offered Ivor a herd of cows for me. Then it was funny; now I want to scream bloody murder.

Margaret mustered her emotions with an effort that robbed her of the rest of her appetite. "I know you are right, but I don't think it is really any of your business," she said stiffly, her previous feeling of friendliness vanishing.

Liriel looked stern, and it gave her round face a startling grandeur. "*Laran* is the business of anyone on Darkover who possesses it. It is not like other talents, like being able to paint or compose music, which one may accept or ignore. If you have it, you must deal with it and learn to use it properly. Otherwise you are a danger to yourself and to everyone you might encounter. This is particularly true of the Alton Gift, because the ability to force rapport with another is like walking around with a loaded crossbow. If something startles you, you might fire without realizing it is not a deer, but your own kin."

"I can see that, and I promise to be very careful. But where is this leading?"

"Jeff believes it would be wise if I monitored you. Istvana has already tested you, but she feels that your channels are not really clear as yet. She believes that during your illness, you were actually creating new channels—a remarkable theory. She did as much as she dared in the time she had with you."

"I know she did. She wanted me to go to the Tower with her, but I can't. I can't explain it."

"There is no need to explain it, cousin." Liriel gave a deep sigh. "I wish, myself that you had gone to Neskaya, as she suggested, for I have an enormous respect for her skills as a *leronis*. Jeff could do what needs to be done, of course, but that wouldn't be at all proper." She gave a laugh that was too nervous for humor.

"And Heaven forbid we should do anything improper!" Margaret felt trapped, as if there were not enough air in the room to let her breathe freely. Everyone either wanted to get her married to any man on two legs, or take her off and shut her in a Tower, to keep her from harm.

Liriel flushed. She said, "Our customs seem strange to you because you have not lived in a telepathic community, Marguerida. We have many rules that make little sense except on Darkover. Monitoring is intimate, and it is not a thing a male does with a woman who might be his daughter."

"You mean you never talk to your father except vocally?"

"Don't I wish! He and I have had any number of arguments without a word being uttered. But he would die of embarrassment before he would monitor me. Mind to mind is not so different than face to face, but monitoring is much more."

"I am starting to see now. I thought Istvana asked Lady Marilla to monitor me, that night at Ardais, because they had worked together before, or maybe I just assumed there was no one else in the house that could do the task. But Mikhail could have done it, couldn't he?"

"My brother is a good enough telepath for that, but he would no more have monitored you, in those circumstances, than he would have disrobed in your bedroom. In a Tower it is otherwise, for when one works in a Circle for a long time, many of these rules do not apply. Jeff is too like a father to do the job, and Mikhail . . . well."

Margaret blushed to the roots of her hair. She remembered again the sudden intrusion of some male while she wrestled with the stone of Ashara's keep, and how it had felt as if he were holding her, had his arms around her waist. She suspected that must have been Mikhail, though she could not imagine how he got into the overworld or why. And she was wary of asking. She and Mikhail had exchanged thoughts, but there had been a caution, a constraint in it, and while it had come close to intimacy a few times, it had not gone into anything really private. They would draw together, then apart, as if both of them were afraid of the feelings they were having.

She wondered what it must be like to be close to someone who was able to read one's thoughts deeply. How did *Dom* Gabriel conceal his annoyance and chafing from Javanne? For that matter, how did Javanne hide her temper from her husband? She decided there must be self-restraint, and realized that her father and Dio must have a great deal of this virtue.

At last she had an understanding of why, when she had begun to be a young woman, her father had seemed to withdraw from her. It had hurt, and she found it still hurt. When she was very little, she had adored Lew, and then, without any reason she knew, he became cold and remote. She had been afraid she had displeased him in some manner. Why hadn't he told her what was going on? Why hadn't Dio?

Dio, we can't handle this without a Circle, dammit! I can't go mucking about in her mind, not when she's shut down like this, not just the two of us. And we can't go back to Darkover. I took this job, and I am going to see it to the end, no matter what. At least I will have done one thing in my life that was right!

The sound of the Senator's voice ran along her nerves, and Liriel heard it as well, for she gave a nod. "You must have been picking up bits, little snatches."

"How? I had the impression from Istvana that I was locked up tighter than a drum?"

"Even people with no *laran* catch thoughts spoken under strong emotions. We think now that it is a normal human trait, perhaps from before we possessed formal language. The Terranan are skeptical, but we have more understanding than they do." Liriel gave a little snort which conveyed her low opinion of Terrans perfectly clearly. "True, for generations we believed that *laran* was a special thing, limited to the Comyn and their kin, but we have found in the past hundred years that many individuals possess these talents to some degree."

"But I still don't see why you want to monitor me." Rafaella was almost squirming with discomfort beside her now. Margaret gave her a little nod, and the Renunciate left the table hastily. She was not happy to see her friend leave, but she understood that Rafaella must feel that she was intruding.

"You were over-shadowed very young, and while some of those channels are now clear, damage remains. Jeff and I think it is very important that we keep an eye on you, to see that you are healing."

"Healing! I was left alone in an orphanage until I was

useful, and I was kept in ignorance because the Senator decided it was more important to take care of Darkover than to take care of me! Then Fate or Destiny or something brings me here, and all of a sudden I am the most marriageable woman on the damn planet, and you want to make sure . . . to hell with all of you!"

To Margaret's surprise, Liriel did not appear at all distressed by her outburst. "It is for those reasons, those exact reasons, that I want to monitor you, Marguerida. You are very angry, and you have cause. But can't you see that this anger is dangerous, not just to you, but to anyone who might release those feelings by a word or look. I am trained, and I am well shielded, but others, like your friend Rafaella, are not. You could literally kill her with your anger."

"I would never harm Rafaella. She is my friend—like the sister I always wanted." She took a shaky breath. "I am sorry. I didn't mean to be so self-pitying. I know no one meant to hurt me, not intentionally."

"Marguerida, do you know what happens when you put water in a closed vessel and set it on the fire?"

"What? I know enough physics to know that if there isn't somewhere for the steam to go, the pot is going to explode, most likely."

"I wouldn't have called you a pot, myself. You are more like a finely made alembic, clear and fragile but also strong. But if you stop up the opening on an alembic, it will shatter."

"Yes, and to continue your metaphor, it will cut hell out of anyone in the neighborhood. I wish I had never come to Darkover."

"But, as you said, it was your destiny. You like it here, even though you find us very odd."

Margaret sighed and was silent for a long time. "That is true. I've always wanted something that I couldn't name, and when I saw the sun setting behind the city and smelled food cooking, it had a name. It was Darkover. I have been an exile most of my life, and now I've come home. If I had known, I might have come here long ago, but . . . but, Liriel, I don't want to be a telepath!"

"That is no longer a thing you can want or not. It is what you are. And for your own sake, and that of others, you will need frequent monitoring. Because now that the Gift has been awakened, it will grow and increase and change. And *you* will change. I am sorry, but that is just how it is."

"You aren't half so sorry as I am! Very well—do whatever you need to. I'll be a good girl." She didn't feel like a good girl at all, but more like a storm about to break.

"Let's go to my study. Mother keeps it for me, rather grudgingly, so I can be alone. No one will interrupt us there."

"They don't need to. They can just poke their noses in without . . ."

"Marguerida, don't be foolish." The big woman rose with a flutter of green cloth. "My father, who is very strict and correct, won't even remain within doors while we work, and Jeff is not at all snoopy."

"What about your mother?" Margaret was repelled by the idea of Javanne being aware of her thoughts.

Liriel grinned. "She will be curious, because that is her nature, but she will not intrude."

"Why not? Good manners?"

"Partially. But it is more like good sense. You are so strong you could knock almost anyone into the next tenday if you felt threatened."

"I could?" Margaret followed her cousin down the hall, considering this. The idea that she had the power to injure people without lifting a finger was even more terrifying than that of being a telepath.

The room they entered was modest in size. It had one window overlooking an open court which was different than the one in the front of the house—the stones were laid out in a circular rather than a rectangular pattern. Before she could really have a good look, Liriel drew the curtain across it. Margaret looked around then, and saw plump cushions piled on a thick green rug, and along two walls, shelves of books. The paneled walls reflected the light of lampions and she moved toward the shelves.

"Is this your personal library?"

"Yes, it is. I started it from books that were left in the house, some of your father's, and of Grandfather Kennard's, though he was not really much of a reader.

There are books here that Ann'dra Carr had imported when he lived here, in Terran, and others I ordered from Thendara. Mother always told me I would ruin my eyes with reading, but so far I have not."

It was an eclectic collection, from volumes of children's stories to works on mapping and surveying, and novels from all over the Federation. Margaret saw a collection of poetry dating from pre-space Terra, the work of Rupert Brooke, and another by Gala Montaral who had lived and died on Tau Ceti V two hundred years before. Since she loved Gala's verse, she thought well of Liriel for giving it a place in her library. From the shininess of the spine, it had been read often and, from the lack of dust on it, recently, too. "I was starting to think no one on Darkover read."

"Well, as a general thing, it is not so common a pastime as singing or sewing or hunting, but we are not all illiterate bumpkins."

"I never imagined you were, but I was rather surprised by how little reading matter I have seen. There were some books at Ardais Castle, but these are more interesting. That's all."

"Come, sit here by the brazier."

Margaret did as she was told, ignoring her unease. She felt as if she were visiting the doctor, where she would be probed and measured and tested, and she did not like the sensation at all. She tucked herself onto one of the large pillows and watched Liriel toss a handful of what looked like weeds into the tiny brazier. They hit the glowing charcoal and burst into flame, sending up a cloud of pale smoke. A sweet smell arose, a drowsy scent, like herbs under a hot summer sun.

She noticed that some of her uneasiness seemed to be fading. "What is that you are burning?" she asked Liriel.

"Just some dried flowers. They have a calming effect, rather like incense. It is my own creation, and I admit I am a little proud of it. One of the books there is an old herbal—Koolpipper—and it gave me the idea, so I went out and gathered things, and consulted some of the local old wives who use herbs, and experimented until I got the effect I wanted."

"Koolpipper? Oh, you mean Culpepper."

"Is that how you say it? Do you know the book?" The technician looked pleased as she smiled at Marguerida.

Margaret was rather startled. Her cousin was a continuous source of surprises. She had never expected to find anyone like her on Darkover. "I know of it. I took an exotic botany class while I was at University, to fill part of my science requirement, and Culpepper was part of the optional reading list. That's an old book, you know, from long before the Terrans went into space, but for some reason it keeps being reprinted and translated. Am I supposed to feel as if my body is light as a feather?"

"Well, you should feel relaxed," Liriel answered, looking a little concerned.

Margaret gave a little laugh. "If I were any more relaxed, I would be asleep. I *am* a little sleepy, but not too much. I just feel as if nothing in the world matters. Is that relaxed enough for you?"

"That's good. You are a very tense person, Marguerida." Liriel paused. "Watchful is perhaps the best word. Overalert? Do you know why that is?"

"I can guess. When I was Marguerida Kadarin . . ."

"When you were *what*?" Liriel looked startled, then a little peculiar.

She did not answer at once, filled with strange feelings, all a little removed and not immediate. "In the orphanage, that is what I was called. Funny. I didn't remember until you asked me why I am always anxious. There was a girl there, my age but bigger, and she liked to pinch and scratch and bite. And she seemed to enjoy pinching me a great deal. And then, when I went from the orphanage, and I was with . . . with my mother, she was cheerful one minute, and screaming the next. I would try to make myself very small, so she wouldn't see me." She gave a shaky laugh. "I used to believe I could make myself invisible, if I just tried hard enough." *And he was both kind and uncaring—Robert Kadarin.*

"I see. You did some of that at dinner last night, didn't you? Becoming invisible."

"I suppose I did. Your family is rather overwhelming, all at once."

"Our family, Marguerida. And, yes, they are, particularly when Ariel has all the children about. She cannot bear to have them from her sight. I don't know what she will do when they are grown and want to leave home. She and Piedro Alar watch those brats as if a hawk were going to carry them off. We are twins, but we are most unlike in disposition. She is always droopy and worried, and I am generally cheerful. It has always been like that."

"I know you have a high infant mortality on Darkover. Did Ariel lose children—is that why she is so fussy?"

Liriel shook her head and set her long hair flying. "My sister has been extremely fortunate, and all her children have survived and are as healthy a pack of brats as I have ever seen. But she sees no value for herself, I believe, except as a mother. I don't think she knows how Piedro adores her. My mother may have made that match, but she chose well for Ariel. She is pregnant again, though you can't see it yet. A daughter, at last. I hope she will stop when this one is born, because she is killing herself having a child every two years."

"How do you know it is a girl?"

"I'm a technician, Marguerida, and Ariel and I spent months together in Mother's belly before we breathed the air of Darkover. I always know when Ariel has conceived, and I know the sex of the child as well. It's part of my *laran*."

"I guess I don't really understand all this *laran* business. It's more than just telepathy, isn't it? Istvana Ridenow told me her gift was that of empathy, and while I think I understand that intellectually, I don't have any emotional grasp of it. And I was too sick and upset to really pay attention to anything she said, unless it was about me. How selfish!" She would have wanted to sink with shame, but the incense made all her emotions seem vague and distant.

"Yes, it is more than telepathy, cousin. Each family of the Domains has a Gift, which is to say a talent that runs in the blood. The Alton Gift is that of forced rapport, which means the ability to enter the mind of anyone, whether they are telepaths or not. For that reason we have always been suspect by the other Domains. Forced rapport can kill, which is why Jeff and I feel it is so important to monitor you. The Ardais are catalysts, and can awaken the *laran* of another. The Aldaran have the Gift of precognition, and you may possess that as well."

"Oh, great. It isn't enough I can poke into people's minds whether they want it or not, now I am able to foresee the future. Wait a minute—why would I have the Aldaran Gift anyhow? Lady Marilla thought something when I asked her about the Gifts. She didn't tell me much, and she got very agitated when I asked about the Aldarans."

"Thyra Darriell's father was Kermiac Aldaran, and your father's mother was Yllana Aldaran, who was half Terranan. So, you have Aldaran bloodlines not once but twice."

"I see. Well, I guess the Aldaran Gift missed me, anyhow. If I had had any precognition, I would never have come to Darkover." Even as she said this, Margaret realized it was not quite true.

"The ability to see the future is not the same thing as being able to avoid it, Marguerida. Now, let us start." Liriel drew a cord from beneath her robe and Margaret saw a small pouch similar to the one Istvana had worn. She pulled something out, and removed several layers of wrapping until a crystal was revealed.

Margaret held back her impulse to stand up and bolt from the room, so great was her terror of the shining stone in her cousin's hands. She tensed her shoulders and clenched her teeth, waiting for the hated and familiar voice which had possessed her at Ardais to speak. When, after several minutes, it did not come, she relaxed slightly. "I have to tell you, Liriel, I don't like those things."

"Yes, I know. But just look at it calmly. Don't try to touch it. You must never touch the keyed matrix of another person. It can throw them into deep shock, and even cause death."

Instead of looking at the crystal, Margaret opened her left hand and slowly removed the glove she was wearing. Then she studied her palm. She could sense Liriel's surprise at her action, surprise but no alarm.

The blue lines that had traced themselves on her skin seemed a little faded now, but she could still make out the pattern. If only she could understand what the lines meant. She felt a faint pulsing beneath her skin, as if some energy was moving that was not entirely from her body. Margaret shivered as the lines seemed to darken, to become bluer and bluer.

The room around her became vague, a place of shadows, and the technician seated across from her seemed not Liriel, but an image of faint light, lines of energy without any flesh around them. Then, abruptly, even that vanished, and she was plunged into her own mind, into a dark vision.

A twisted corridor yawned before her, and somewhere a woman screamed. It was a terrible sound, and she knew that its source was that woman, that unknown female who was Thyra Darriel, her mother. There was madness in the scream, and she felt herself shrink, becoming small and anxious and altogether wary. A voice, a man's voice, rang out "She's mad—she's out of control!"

There were more shouts, and she recognized Lew Alton's voice, and that of another—the silver man. She knew him now, knew he was Robert Kadarin who had given her his name for a time and sent her to the orphanage to protect her from Thyra's instability. She remembered crossing the river which was called Kadarin, and how it had made her uneasy, and at last she knew why.

What if I am mad like my mother?

Abruptly, the darkness of her mind vanished, and she was back in the cozy room, sweet smelling and book-lined, with her cousin Liriel. Her skull pounded for a minute, and then the headache disappeared, as if it had never been. She discovered she was panting a little, as if she had been running, and she deliberately slowed her breath, her singer's training coming to her rescue once again.

The question of madness lingered in her mind, and it was even more frightening than her fear of Ashara's ghost. She shuddered and hunched her shoulders, looking down at her ungloved hand with hatred and rage. If only she had not wrested the keystone from the Tower of Mirrors! None of this would be happening if she had left it alone. But if she had not, then Ashara would still be there, commanding her to keep herself apart, preventing her from being touched or touching others.

When she finally looked toward Liriel, she found the technician was putting away the matrix. She could see a sheen of sweat across Liriel's broad forehead, and the sag of wide shoulders spoke of great weariness. "You are too strong for me, Marguerida."

"I didn't mean to wear you out." Margaret felt ashamed, but still so brimming with conflicting emotions that her sorrow was more a grace note than anything else. She wanted to run away, to hide, to die. Anything to escape the oppression of so many feelings, none of them good, and all of them opposing each other. It was a terrible sensation, to be caught in the trap of feelings that she could neither control nor suppress.

"You didn't. I'll be fine in a bit. But you are too powerful—you *must* go to a Tower and receive some training."

The idea made the breath die in her lungs, and Margaret felt trapped and closed in. "I can't!" *If people don't stop telling me what I have to do, I am going to go crazy, and there won't be any doubt about whether I am like Thyra!*

As if she had not spoken, Liriel continued. "Arilinn, I think, is the best choice. Jeff works there, and I am certain I could get permission to . . ."

"I am not going to any Tower!"

"Your father was at Arilinn, you know."

"Didn't you hear what I said!" Margaret shouted. "I am not my father, and I am not going to a Tower. I won't be Rapunzel!"

Liriel looked at her blankly for a second, and then a slow smile spread across her features. "Rapunzel! Why, it has been years since I read that one, and I had forgotten that she was locked up in a tower. No, no, Marguerida— this is nothing like that. I am not suggesting you be locked up and have to grow your hair down to escape. You need to be trained, to learn to use your talents."

Margaret burst into tears. "I know," she sobbed. "But I just can't stand the idea of being closed in again." She felt her heart release something, a foreign mote of energy, a frozen bit that she had not even guessed was there until it was gone. She could feel a slight easing of tension, and she struggled not to relax. All that was holding her together was that stiffness, that tension of mind and muscle!

"Again?"

The Tower of Mirrors stood upon the Plain, cold beneath the starless sky. Once more it twisted toward her, and once again it shattered into shards.

"I won't go back there!"

"Marguerida, that place is gone. It exists only in your memory—though as loud as you were broadcasting I think every telepath on Darkover bears its image now. You destroyed that construct, and you need have no fear of it any longer."

Margaret held up her left hand and turned the palm toward Liriel. "Can you see the lines?"

"I see some faint blue tracings, yes. What are they— a tattoo? Did you get it on some other world? I noticed the glove you wore last night, and wondered. It seemed an odd sort of thing, with your pretty gown."

"No. When I came back from the overworld, I had these marks on my hand. They were more intense then, but they are exactly like the facets of the stone I pulled from the Tower of Mirrors. You mean Istvana didn't tell you about this?"

Liriel brushed a strand of hair off her face and looked thoughtful. "It is even more than I imagined. I misunderstood, I see. Certainly Istvana informed me, but she did not say that the thing had a physical form. Perhaps she was not certain what it was then." She fell silent, but Margaret was fairly certain that she was conferring with someone outside the room. "You have done a remarkable thing, cousin," she said at last. "You have brought a shadow matrix from the overworld."

Margaret rubbed the tears off her cheeks with her sleeve. "Just what I always wanted—a shadow matrix. It isn't bad enough that my mother was a lunatic and my father can't stand the sight of me, and I have the Alton Gift, but now . . . How can I get rid of this thing?"

"I don't think you can. I think you have to learn to live with it, and use it. Unless I'm mistaken, what you have is all that is left of Ashara Alton."

"Istvana told me a little about her at Ardais. Not enough to satisfy my curiosity—but nothing ever is. I've spent years with that Ashara-being inside me, and now you tell me that even though I sort of destroyed her, she is still around, right on my skin, on my hand. I'll cut it off!" Margaret felt her hysteria rise in her throat.

"Being one-handed is almost a tradition in the family, isn't it," she added bitterly.

"Stop that!"

"I don't *want* a shadow matrix! I don't want any sort of matrix at all! I hate the damn things! I don't want to be a telepath or anything except Margaret Alton, Scholar!"

"Believe me, Marguerida, I do understand. This is all very new to you, and you cannot see that it is not a burden, but something that . . ."

"Stop trying to convince me this is some sort of boon! It is a curse, and I know it." She could feel the anger boiling along her bones, and she was surprised, and a little pleased, that it did not appear to disturb Liriel at all. Margaret had always feared her own rage, and it was a new experience to find anyone who could put up with it without either telling her to be quiet, or abandoning her immediately.

"No, *chiya,* it is not a curse, though it may be some time before you realize that it is not. But you cannot be rid of it, and you had better start to accept that idea for your own peace of mind."

"Peace of mind! I've forgotten what that is, if I ever knew." The persistent smell of Liriel's incense and the calm of the technician herself forced Margaret's emotions to begin to dissipate, as if they were smoke rising from the brazier. A remnant of serenity stole into her mind, despite herself. "Tell me more about Ashara, at least. I think I might deal with this better if I knew more—my scholar's mind wants data, and lots of it."

"I am afraid that I do not know a great deal more than Istvana already told you. We have so few records of that time. She was a Keeper, centuries ago, in the times when *leroni* were virgins. She was exiled from Hali—the reasons are lost—and removed to Thendara. She died, but somehow she managed to continue to . . . she kept going after her body perished by overshadowing other Keepers. We all thought that Callina Aillard was her final vessel."

"Who?"

"The Keeper at Neskaya during the Sharra Rebellion," Liriel answered, not really paying attention. "I can't manage this. Jeff will have to take you to Arilinn immediately."

Chiya! Don't let them stampede you! Stay at Armida. And do not be afraid, my Marja. Do not be afraid.

The abrupt intrusion of Lew Alton into her mind startled her, for he seemed very near, and yet not. It was so comforting, so reassuring, that after her initial surprise, Margaret felt a vast relief. It was almost as if he were in the room, or just outside. She believed him, and she felt protected. He was her father and, for no good reason, she was sure he would make everything be right again. She cursed herself for a delusional idiot—Lew Alton had never taken care of her before. Why should she trust him now?

Margaret considered all her options, as clearly as she could with a pounding heart and a mind filled with conflicts. She could leave Darkover, and risk forcing rapport on some stranger who happened to annoy her—which seemed a likely outcome without some real training. She understood the need for formal discipline—she had not learned music in a day or a month.

She could go to a Tower and risk injuring someone like Liriel with the energies she now possessed, quite unwillingly. She knew that Liriel had no idea how much raw power she had in the palm of her hand. Margaret didn't either, but she guessed it was potentially tremendous. She could marry some suitable Darkover man, and hope her *laran* would vanish with her maidenhead, as it seemed to have in the past. Or she could trust the Old Man.

Of these uniformly repellent possibilities, trusting her father seemed like the least distasteful. He might have been a poor parent, but she was certain that he always had her best interests at heart, for he would never see her as a path to power, as a prize to be owned and used. For the moment, it was the best she could do, and having sorted out the matter as well as she could, Margaret had a sense of clarity. Things were beyond her control, which she loathed, but there was no help for it. She would just have to make the best of a dreadful situation.

"I won't argue with you, Liriel. Your mind is made up, and so is mine—and they don't agree! Unless you plan to have a bunch of your father's entourage stuff me into a bag and haul me off to Arilinn . . ."

"Marguerida! We would never do such a thing!" Liriel was shocked and dismayed, and rather hurt as well. "How can you think such terrible things?"

Margaret laughed suddenly, and felt her chest loosen. "Enough! I read too many trashy novels, and I have a very low opinion of humanity at the moment. Let's get out of here, before I lose my temper again, shall we?" She pulled the leather glove back on as she rose from her cushion.

"You are right. We cannot do anything more." Liriel looked sad, her blue eyes in her round face shadowed with sorrow. *We Altons are such a stubborn lot I can't imagine why I thought she would agree immediately. I'll just have to hope that Jeff can persuade her to do the right thing.*

19

◆

When they entered the hall, Margaret noticed that she was both ravenously hungry and thirsty. She did not want wine or herb tea or beer. She wanted, more than anything, a pot of strong coffee, laced with heavy cream and lots of sugar. Margaret laughed at herself and Liriel gave her a quick glance, unsure of the cause of her burst of merriment. The closest source of coffee was in Thendara, a good, long ride away.

"I don't suppose any of you folks can teleport me a pound of Aldebaran Black Mountain coffee, can you? No one has mentioned a Gift like that—but I don't know about all of them yet, do I?"

"No, you don't, but I think Jeff might have brought some coffee with him. He never quite lost his taste for the stuff—nasty, I call it, but there is no accounting for preferences. I know he would be glad to share it with you." Liriel did not answer the question about teleportation, and Margaret decided to let it go for the moment. It wasn't important, as long as she didn't start doing it.

Margaret lifted her arms above her head and stretched. She heard her spine pop. "I don't want to go to Arilinn, cousin, but for a cup of coffee, I might actually consider it."

Liriel looked at her, her eyes twinkling. "Odd. I would not have thought you could be bribed."

"That's because no one ever tried to bribe me before."

The two women moved down the corridor, laughing together, in the harmony of shared experience and mutual respect. Margaret liked her cousin almost as much as she liked Rafaella, and that was a great deal. As they drew closer to the dining room, the warm scent of fresh coffee greeted them, and Margaret grinned.

There were a number of voices from the dining room, several of them high-pitched and Margaret knew her cousin Ariel was there, with her many children. She sighed and shrugged. She wished she had as friendly a feeling toward Ariel Lanart-Alar as she did for Liriel, but it could not be helped. The droopy female gave her the creeps, and the children were ciphers to her.

The table was set for a meal, and the children were stuffing their mouths and talking. Margaret noticed the absence of *Dom* Gabriel and his sons at the table, and wondered where they were. She felt a sharp pang of disappointment that Mikhail was not there, and wondered if he had left again. She hoped not.

Then the demands of her body sent all thoughts flying. She examined the board, very pleased at the selection. There were trays of cold meats, platters of fruits, and loaves of bread, and the appetizing smell, combined with that of coffee, made her mouth water. Javanne was presiding from the head of the table, but when she saw Margaret, she began to rise. Margaret shook her head at her aunt, and Lady Javanne settled back.

Margaret took an empty chair between Javanne and one of the small boys. He looked to be about seven or eight, and he had the same dark hair as his father. Around a mouthful of fruit he said, "I am Donal Alar."

"Don't talk with your mouth full, Donal," Javanne chided in so gentle a voice that Margaret was amazed. She never suspected her aunt of being so tender.

He swallowed quickly. "I'm almost seven," he announced with pride. "I can ride a horse—well, a pony."

"Good for you," Margaret answered, a little unsure how to talk to the young man. She had encountered small children on many worlds, but she had never learned to be comfortable with them. Now she wondered why, yet suspected that something about her overshadowing by Ashara was the cause. She had a lengthy list of bones she would have enjoyed picking with the ancient Keeper. It felt rather good to be able to imagine shaking a finger at the monster and giving her a good scolding. Maybe, someday, she would actually stop feeling afraid.

Jeff came in carrying a tray, and Javanne looked unhappy. A frantic servant trailed behind him, attempting to take it from him, but Jeff ignored her. He set a mug in front of Margaret, and the smell of coffee wafted around her. He set down a pitcher of thick cream and a pot of honey, and grinned at her. "It isn't Black Mountain, I'm afraid—have you really drunk that? Sometimes I think it is a myth, so fantastic are the stories about it. This is New Kenyan, and I think it will satisfy your palate. No sugar, I'm afraid, but thyme honey is a good substitute."

"Thank you, Uncle Jeff. I love New Kenyan."

"Then I shall make certain there is always a supply here at Armida for you."

"That's very kind of you, but it assumes I will be here, doesn't it?" She gave him a hard look, and he had the grace to turn away. "And, yes, I have actually drunk Black Mountain—once. There was a huge formal reception at University, with a dinner that went on for hours. They served it after the meal, and it is really as remarkable as the stories say. It's like no other coffee I have ever tasted, and it makes you feel . . . I can't describe it. When they served the coffee, the hall went quiet. An old emeritus professor, Doctoran Hildegard, who was famed for his agnosticism, sipped his and announced that he now had evidence of the existence of the Deity." Margaret laughed, remembering.

"It was that good, was it?" Jeff chuckled. "I am glad to have someone in the family who shares my pleasure in good coffee. At Arilinn they all behave as if I have some secret vice for drinking it."

Margaret poured cream and honey into her mug and stirred it. Then she drank. It was delicious, dark and rich, and perfectly brewed. "You make excellent coffee, Uncle." She began to pile some meat onto her plate, her hunger enormous though it was not three hours since she had eaten breakfast.

"Thank you, Marguerida."

Donal tugged at her sleeve. "Can you ride a horse?"

"Yes, I can, Donal."

"Don't bother your cousin while she is trying to eat," Ariel chided, bouncing a small boy on her knee. "Kennard, you have had enough to eat! You will make yourself sick with another sweet cake, and I will not be pleased." The child on her lap looked about two or three, and he gave his mother a look of disdain and leaned out for the tray of pastries with one chubby hand.

"How do you manage so many children?" Margaret asked, trying to find some common ground with Ariel.

"So many?" She looked at her offspring with an expression both smug and anxious. "There are only five—Kennard here, who is two, and Lewis, who is named for your father, is now four." She pointed at a sturdy lad beside her and tried to take the pastry away from the youngest child at the same time. "Then there is Donal, who is next to you, and Domenic and Damon. They are eight and ten. The next one is sure to be a girl, or so I hope. Or two girls, perhaps. How sad it is for you that you are my own age and have no children. You should get married as quickly as possible, you know. There is nothing more important to a woman than having children."

Margaret could think of no reply that was not rude, so she ate some meat and drank more of her coffee. She was tired from her time in Liriel's parlor, and the coffee restored her. She could not imagine that anyone with five children would wish for more, even with nurses and servants to help with caring for them. From the way Ariel clucked over her sons, Margaret suspected she refused help and wore herself out fussing over them.

"So which of my brothers are you going to choose—Rafael or Gabriel?" Ariel asked in complete innocence, apparently unaware that Margaret had already refused Rafael's suit. She noted the absence of Mikhail's name, experiencing a small prickle of anger. They all treated him as if he did not exist, and she wondered why he put up with them. He was clearly more dutiful than she was. It annoyed her that no one ever mentioned Mikhail as a possible husband for her, and while she vaguely understood the reasons, she still found them stupid. "They are good men, steady and dependable, you know," Ariel continued, apparently ready to extoll the virtues of her brothers at length.

"I am sure they are both extremely virtuous, Ariel, but I am not thinking of marriage."

Ariel looked shocked. "But your duty is clear. You must marry, and quickly, or else you will be too old to have healthy children."

Javanne, beside Margaret, appeared ready to explode, and she glared at her daughter, but Ariel seemed unaware of her mother's ire. "Duty?" Margaret asked quietly, restraining her feelings as well as she was able.

"Of course! Lewis, don't pinch Kennard! Mother says you have the Alton Gift, and you must have children so it will not be lost. Now, which of my brothers do you like better? I admit Gabe is not much of a talker, but you seem to be, so perhaps a quiet man would suit you."

That was just too much! "Does anyone on Darkover ever think about anything but conserving *laran?* You seem obsessed with it," Margaret snapped.

Ariel recoiled as if she had been struck and Margaret felt like an ill-mannered lout. Of course her cousin was annoying, but that was no reason to snarl at her.

"I did not intend to offend you, cousin. But, indeed, I do not understand your behavior." *Obsessed with* laran—*how dare she! Is she making fun of me because I have so little? I could kill her, sitting there with her golden eyes, looking at me like a bug. Why is everyone against me?*

Ariel spoke with more force than Margaret would have imagined she was capable of, and her pale cheeks flushed with passion. She seemed almost transformed, a different woman entirely. There was a glitter in her eyes that made Margaret want to cringe, for it was not entirely sane. Then her cheeks paled again, and she went on, "I suppose you are just like your father, selfish. It must be your Terranan blood! If you had been raised properly, you would already be married and have children, and know your place."

"Ariel!" Javanne spoke very sharply, and the crepey skin beneath her determined jaw quivered above the apricot-colored ruff around her throat. *I should not have invited her here! No one can control her when she gets like this!*

"*What?* I am sick and tired of everyone tiptoeing around and treating Marguerida like some princess. If no one else will explain her obligations to her, then I will. She is little better than a spoiled child. It is time she started behaving properly, instead of jaunting about the hills with a Renunciate and listening to old people sing. That isn't a proper occupation for a woman. Jeff says she is a scholar—what is that? Reading books and thinking thoughts that mean nothing!''

Margaret could feel her cousin's outrage, though she could not imagine why Ariel was so provoked by her. After a moment Margaret realized that whatever was bothering her new cousin, it probably had nothing to do with her. She looked around the table, trying to discern any solution to the puzzle. Jeff looked troubled, and Javanne appeared ready to murder, though Margaret couldn't decide if she was the intended victim, or Ariel. The children grew still and anxious at the tone of their mother's shrill voice. Only Liriel seemed unmoved, as she continued to eat steadily.

Uh-oh—Mama's having another of her spells. Margaret thought that came from Donal, but it might have been one of the other children.

This is my fault! There was no mistaking Javanne's mental voice, nor the deep sorrow in it. *I should never have tried to comfort her for being nearly* laranless *with the nobility of bearing children. I believe that, but Ariel's mind is so fragile. I tried to be a good mother, but . . .*

Margaret would have given a great deal not to be picking up these scraps of thoughts, but the emotions of her aunt were very powerful, and she did not know enough about telepathy to block them out. At the same time, she found herself retreating into her academic habits, evaluating the information she was receiving. She felt sorry for Ariel. How dreadful it must be to lack a talent that was so highly valued, and present in the other members of the family.

No one understands me! They all think I am stupid and worthless. But I have children, and they are what really matters. If anything happens to my children . . .

This fear was so strong that it made Margaret's gorge rise. She knew it was something that haunted Ariel every waking moment, and probably in her sleep as well. No wonder she looked so old and worn. It wasn't child bearing that had aged her prematurely. It was fear. That, at least, was something Margaret understood, and even empathized with.

But why? The boys seemed remarkable hearty—just normal children of the sort she had seen on many planets. And on a planet with high infant mortality, five healthy lads was a wonderful accomplishment. And Liriel said she was pregnant again, this time with the girl child that Ariel clearly wanted. Why was she borrowing trouble?

Margaret's eyes went from child to child, and came to rest on the face of Domenic Alar. He had large eyes and pale skin with his father's dark hair. He seemed to have inherited something of his parents' fretful dispositions, though, for he looked at his mother with an anxious expression. It could not be easy for the boys, living with a woman who clung to them all the time, she decided.

Without really being conscious of what she was doing she glanced between him and his brother Damon, and knew, in that moment, that Domenic would never grow to manhood. It was a shocking sensation, not unlike the way she had felt when she looked at Ivor, the day he died. Margaret was unsettled by the feeling, and when it turned to vision, abruptly, she wanted to run out of the room. As she looked at Domenic, he seemed to wither. For a moment she saw his pale skin spattered with blood, and then as Margaret watched with horror, he became a skeleton, his little hands turning to bones with no skin to cover them.

She heard Liriel's sharp intake of breath from down the table at the same time Javanne spoke. "Ariel—it is not your place to be speaking of such matters. Your father will decide these things."

"Lady Javanne, *Dom* Gabriel will do no such thing!" Margaret was glad to focus on her aunt's statement in order to distract herself from the terrible vision. If she had to, she decided, she would provoke a fight with her formidable aunt, just to keep from thinking about what she had imagined. It must be that, mustn't it? Of course! Ariel's anxiety had caused her to see something, and that had triggered a remembrance of Ivor, and all the sorrow she still carried within her about his death.

"Liriel! Marguerida saw something, didn't she. Tell me instantly." Ariel's voice overrode both Margaret and Javanne. "You tell me right now what you saw, you . . . you *monster*. You have the Aldaran Gift, don't you? *Don't you!* And you are going to hurt my babies because I was the only one with the courage to tell you . . ."

"Stop!" Liriel's voice was deep and commanding. "You are making yourself hysterical, Ariel."

"No, I am not! She saw something! Make her tell!"

Margaret sighed. She longed for the quiet of the road once more, with Rafaella. There, at least, meals were not interrupted by all the strains of relationships. "Cousin, I would not harm your children for anything." *Liriel! I just imagined that, didn't I? Tell me I only imagined it—please!*

No, you did not I assure you that I can tell the difference between a foretelling and imagination. Marguerida, you do possess the Aldaran Gift. We suspected you might, of course. You did see truly, but I thank you for trying to calm my sister. Domenic will not live to father children. Let me handle this, please.

Thank you, Liriel. I'm certainly out of my depth here— the Aldaran Gift as well as the Alton Gift! Cousin, this is quite more than I can handle. I would trade it all for a fast ship to almost any destination! Shall I leave the house? Would that help?

There is nothing that will help Ariel now. When she becomes upset, she loses what little sense she has. It has always been so. Mother hoped she would become calmer when she was settled with her children and Piedro. We thought she would grow out of these fits.

Grow out of them—I know that song and dance all too well!

Yes, I know, cousin.

Margaret was surprised at the ease with which she and Liriel conversed, and she felt a great comfort in her cousin. She seemed to be so steady and sensible, unlike her twin. It pleased her, even in her growing agitation at the emotions rolling across the table from Ariel, that there was someone on Darkover who could answer some of her questions, and who might even understand her feelings.

Ariel, unaware of this exchange, rose and began to scream. "Do you think because I have many children I can spare one? Piedro! Where is Piedro? I will not spend another moment beneath the same roof with this monster."

"Stop behaving like a superstitious peasant," Liriel snapped.

"Ariel, you know perfectly well that the first experiences of *laran* are unreliable." Jeff spoke with the calm authority of age and experience, but Ariel was not listening.

"No, I don't know that! Liriel got all the *laran* between us." *She stole it in the womb! It isn't fair! She's set for life, there in Tramontana, and I am the only one in the family without* laran. *But I have children, and no one is going to curse my babies. It is all her fault, Marguerida's. She should have died. I know Piedro only cares for me because I give him children, and I have to watch over them . . . .*

"Stop being foolish, sister."

"Can you swear to me that her vision is false? She's evil. She is full of ideas, of *Terranan* ideas, and she is evil." Ariel leaped from her chair, sending the child on her lap almost onto the floor. Javanne grabbed her youngest grandson as Ariel began to bang her small fist on the table. Her uneaten plate of food went onto the floor, and the goblet followed it.

"Ariel, sit down." Javanne spoke firmly. Her eyes were large and full of despair, as if she were holding herself together by will alone. *I can't stop her! I never could! I was always terrified of her, when she got upset, and now I feel too old to control her. She was such a sweet baby!*

Piedro hurried into the dining room, looking harried and worried. "What is it, my darling?"

"Marguerida foresaw something terrible, and she will not tell me what it was! Get the coach. We are leaving right now! The children will ride inside with me, so I can take care of them." She leaned to her mother, snatched Kennard away, and glared. Then she turned on Liriel, her face white and furious. "Which one did she see, Domenic or Damon? Tell me!"

"Beloved," Piedro began gently, taking his wife's arm. "There is a storm coming in over the hills. We should not set out now. Come, you must not overexcite yourself. Think of the child you bear within you."

"Get the coach ready!" Ariel was desperate now. "I am not going to sit here and wait around for Marguerida to foresee something else, or to deign to pick one of my brothers. You are all conspiring against me. Piedro saw the futility of trying to reason with his wife, and grasped her arm more tightly, shaking his head.

"No one is conspiring against you, *chiya*," Jeff said quietly. *I had no idea it was still so bad. Poor woman! Her fears will be the death of her.*

"I know what you think of me, that I am a stupid woman fit only for bearing children. I need no *laran* to know that you all despise me."

Javanne looked truly shocked by these words, and hurt as well. "Ariel, that is not true. How could you think such a dreadful thing?"

"You never cared a bit for me, so don't pretend. You couldn't wait to get me out of Armida! And you!" She rounded on Jeff. "I am not surprised you take her side. For all that you have lived on Darkover for years, you are still a lover of the Terranan. If she had foreseen the death of one of Elorie's children, would you be so calm? Can you swear to me that her vision is false?"

Jeff looked old and sad and weary. "Only God knows our fates, Ariel."

Ariel's eyes narrowed, filled with hate and desperation. "You will never know how much I despise all of you!" She hugged Kennard against her breast with a viselike grip, then grabbed young Lewis with her free hand. Tearing herself free of her husband's embrace, she started to herd her other children away from the table and out of the room. The sound of her shouts up the stairs echoed back into the dining room, where Margaret, Javanne, Jeff, and Liriel remained in a stunned silence.

"I never realized," Javanne said at last, "how deeply she resented having no *laran*. Not until this moment." She looked older than her years, weary and a little haggard now. "Marguerida, I apologize for my daughter's foolish behavior. She was a nervous child, and I thought that being married and having children would steady her. I never wished to be rid of her, though it seems that she imagined I did."

There was no insincerity in her apology, and for the first time Margaret felt a near liking for her aunt. "There is nothing to apologize for, Aunt. I should have kept my face under better control."

"No, Marguerida. It was not your face which told the

tale, but my own and Liriel's. Your only mistake was not being able to shield your thoughts more closely." Javanne shrugged. "I will go and try to calm her down. I don't think I will succeed. Ariel is very stubborn, once she makes her mind up.

She left, and Margaret wished herself light-years away, on some planet where *laran* was unknown. If only Ivor had not died! If only she had never come to Darkover! If only the Senator had not told her to come to Armida. There was no help for her feelings, and she knew that she just had to endure until she could leave—though where she would go she had not a clue. If only there was someone she could talk to, someone to advise her.

Margaret glanced at Liriel and shook her head. Then she looked at old Jeff and found him watching her, his eyes sad. She had the impulse to trust him, to talk with him. Then the habits of her life resumed, and she withdrew, made herself go cold and distant. She was going to keep herself apart, where she could not injure anyone. So why did her heart ache? And why did she want to cry so badly?

20

◆

Within the hour, Ariel, with a remarkable show of organization for a woman who seemed nearly out of her mind with worry, had marshaled the servants and gotten the baggage packed. She marched her children out the front door, while a desperate-looking Piedro trailed behind her. Outside, there was an odd-looking coach of a sort Margaret had only seen in museums. It was square and high, mounted on six wheels, and pulled by four strong horses. The children climbed in with reluctance, the older ones looking over their shoulders, and the younger howling in protest.

Luggage of all sorts was piled atop the coach, and it didn't look very stable to Margaret's untrained eye. Two men sat on a seat at the front, looking uneasily at the clouds gathering above the hills. She was not sufficiently weatherwise about Darkover to guess how long the storm would be in coming, but she thought it would hit long before the Alar family rode the twenty miles to their home. Margaret sighed, shaking her head, as she listened to Javanne pleading with Ariel to reconsider her rash behavior. But Ariel just slammed the coach door in her mother's face. Piedro Alar, looking even more despondent than usual, mounted a fine horse. She didn't think he was a very good rider, for his seat was poor. If only she hadn't had the vision!

Javanne, her expression fierce, stood on the steps and watched the coach start away. It seemed to sway from side to side beneath the load on the roof. Unbalanced, Margaret thought, just like its occupant. Then she cursed herself for being judgmental, and hoped no one had heard her. The coach lumbered down the drive, and a little dust rose around the wheels.

Javanne turned abruptly and started up the stairs. She

noticed Margaret was standing just inside the open door, and her expression changed from fierce and worried to just worried. "You must not blame yourself for this, Marguerida. You will, of course, being your father's child." *Lew always imagined himself much more important than he was. Trying to be someone he wasn't! Kennard should never have forced him on the Council! He should have made my Gabriel his heir, and then we would not be having this problem at all! I know it is not your fault, but I cannot help how I feel! He was a morbid, prideful child, and you are very like him.*

The older woman brushed past her, leaving Margaret stunned and stung by this biting comment. She was puzzled by the resentment she felt from her aunt, and while she told herself it had nothing to do with her, still she was hurt. It wasn't her fault Lew was impossible, was it?

Margaret watched Javanne Hastur as she swept up the stairs to the second floor, like some minor goddess. She could see the pride in the way her aunt's back was held, but she could also sense the despair and rage within the other woman. She was worried about Ariel, and clearly frustrated at her inability to manage her daughter. Javanne, Margaret decided, was not a woman who liked to have her will challenged by anyone. Perhaps that shed some light on the way in which she viewed Lew Alton. Whatever his other faults, she knew her father always did what he thought was right, and she suspected that he and Javanne had probably disagreed on several matters she knew nothing about.

Margaret was going to follow her aunt up the stairs and seek the security of her own chamber when she heard the thump of boots coming down the hall from the rear of the house. Mikhail emerged from beneath the shadow of the stairs, whistling cheerfully and smelling a little of the stables. His face lit up when he saw her, and her heart skipped a beat in her chest. No matter how she argued with herself, what good and logical reasons she gave herself, she still could not help finding the sight of Mikhail Lanart-Hastur delightful. "Marja! Just the person I was looking for!" he began.

"Don't call me that." Her father's nickname for her on Mikhail's lips was disquieting. "It makes me feel like a child!"

"Forgive me, cousin, for presuming. What shall I call you, then? Marguerida is such a mouthful." He grinned a little, and his blue eyes twinkled. "I always feel like a child in this house, so why should you be different?"

"I'm sorry. I should not have snapped at you. It has been one hell of a morning. First Liriel wanted to monitor me, then she said I had to go to Arilinn, and then something happened in the dining room, and Ariel has taken her children away for fear I will put the evil eye on them." She sighed.

"'I heard about it while Piedro was getting the coach ready. He is fit to be tied, poor fellow. I regret that my sister is so silly—no *laran* and enough emotion for six people—that's Ariel. But I came to find you, to see if you wanted to ride with me around Armida. I'll even let you ride Dorilys," he teased.

Margaret thought of the pewter-gray mare, and the start of a smile moved her lips. "I would love that! In fact, a good ride would help me shake off the feeling I have that . . . I have done something dreadful. But *Dom* Gabriel didn't seem to think she was a proper mount for a 'mere' female. And there is a storm coming, too." She had a mild pleasure in the very idea of doing something her uncle would not approve of, and more so in doing it with Mikhail.

"I know. But we won't be gone long. And my father thinks all women, including my mother, should ride weary old nags who couldn't gallop if their lives depended on it. But he is not here, so let's take advantage of his absence and get into mischief." He smiled at her broadly. *She's so beautiful, and I don't think she knows it!*

This thought distracted Margaret from wondering where *Dom* Gabriel was. No one had ever called her beautiful before. Indeed, while she worked with Ivor Davidson, she rarely thought about her appearance except to be clean and tidy. Her aversion to mirrors had kept her from spending much time in front of them, and she always thought that Dio was the epitome of beauty, not herself. "While the cat's away . . . I think some fresh air would do me a world of good. I'll go change. Where will I meet you?"

"Go to the back of the house, past Liriel's lair, and

there is a door opening onto the Stable Court. I'll be waiting." *I've been waiting all my life—what's a few minutes more.*

Margaret didn't permit herself to dwell on Mikhail's thoughts. They were too disquieting, for she knew she felt an answering emotion, a tender, new-born desire for her cousin. What a mess! Things were in enough of a muddle without adding that!

When Margaret entered the bedroom, she found Rafaella sitting on the trundle bed, her eyes streaming and her nose a glowing red. "What's the matter?"

The Renunciate snuffled. "I have caught a dreadful cold, I think."

"Then get undressed and go to bed! I'm going riding with cousin Mikhail, but I won't be long."

"It looks like it is going to rain soon, Marguerida. Are you sure?" *Riding with Mikhail? That will put the cat among the pigeons! Oh, dear, I should go with her! Lady Javanne will have my head, if she learns about it. But I ache all over.*

Margaret pulled her riding skirt out of the closet. "I am sure that if I stay in this house much longer, I will go stark raving mad. It will do me good to get out. I miss the road, you know. A little rain won't hurt me, and it might just cool my temper. What a morning!" She gave a sharp laugh as she put on her skirt. "I never thought I would willingly forgo the delights of roofs and convenient bathrooms for the out-of-doors, but right now, I would be glad if the two of us were going about as we did before I got sick. You are splendid company, Rafaella. Now, get into bed."

"Am I? No one ever told me that before." The Renunciate sneezed enormously. "My head feels three sizes too large."

"I'll find a servant and ask for some tea for you before I go out."

"Thank you. You are good company, too, Marguerida." *Please, be careful!*

Ignoring the risk of infection, Margaret bent down and gave Rafaella a long hug. She brushed a strand of hair off her companion's brow and patted her shoulder comfortingly. Then she hurried out of the room.

*　　　*　　　*

When Margaret reached the Stable Court, she realized it was the place she had seen from the window of Liriel's room. What had Mikhail called it? Her lair? A good name for it. She could smell the pleasant scent of horses, dung, and wet stones as she crossed the open area. Grooms and hostlers were busy with their tasks, currying horses and checking hooves. It was a vast relief from the tension of the house, from the demands of her new family and all they expected of her.

A lad in a russet tunic led Dorilys out of the stable, and Mikhail followed behind. The mare was fairly dancing on the stones, clearly looking forward to the expedition as much as Margaret was herself. She approached the horse and let Dorilys take her scent, speaking to her in a low voice which made the animal prick up her ears and snort, pawing the paving stones impatiently.

Another groom led out Mikhail's horse, a fine bay with a white star between its eyes and two white socks on its fore feet. Her cousin came to her, to help her mount. As he reached for her hand, Gabriel appeared from within the stable, his face sullen. He pushed Mikhail roughly aside, grabbed Margaret's arm, and said, "Be off with you, Mik. It isn't your place to show Marguerida around." *He won't take my place!*

Margaret pulled away from his touch. "I prefer to mount myself, thank you," she said coldly. "And my plan was to go riding with Mikhail, not with you."

She could feel Mikhail seething before his brother's abrupt dismissal, and she realized there was something more going on. Margaret caught a wisp of thought from the younger man. *I never thought I would want anyone so much. No woman has ever . . . I might as well wish for the moons! I can never have what I want, neither woman nor kingdom. Though just now I'd forgo the kingdom for . . . it doesn't bear thinking of.*

"I don't care what your plans are, cousin. I and no one else will show you Armida! Take Dorilys back into the pasture, Asa. You must be mad, Mik, thinking of putting a mere woman on her. She's too . . ."

"Gabe, your manners are shameful." Mikhail spoke quietly, but his voice echoed against the stones. There was a kind of authority in his tone, a sureness she had not heard before, something of his mother or his uncle

Regis. She was startled at this, and pleased. She began to suspect that Mikhail Hastur was much more his own man than anyone imagined, and thought it was a dreadful shame he was the youngest son and not the eldest.

"I wish to ride Dorilys," Margaret said, before either brother had a chance to speak. They were sure to get into a fight if she did not prevent it, and she had had quite enough of exalted tempers for one day. She wondered how they managed, with everyone being so touchy all the time. "Mikhail has said I may, and, if I understand it, she is his to give."

Gabriel sulked and glared at his brother. "She is too much horse for anyone, let alone a softy like you, cousin. *I* know best. You must trust to my judgment. As for Mikhail, he is interfering where he has no business."

"You know nothing about me, Gabriel, nothing whatever." With that, Margaret set her foot into the stirrup and mounted the dancing Dorilys, and looked down at the two brothers. The horse nickered with pleasure and tossed her head merrily.

Gabriel looked ready to explode. Instead, he shoved Mikhail aside with a great push, knocking him to the stones of the court, and mounted the bay horse. "You had better learn to do as you are told, cousin!" He bellowed at her in rage, and Margaret could feel his roiling emotions as she turned the horse away.

Margaret was so angry she wanted to scream. Why couldn't she be left alone, to have a little peace and quiet. She had been looking forward to seeing Armida with Mikhail, and Gabriel had spoiled everything. Then she felt the horse respond to her emotions and decided that she had better calm down. She breathed deeply and slowly, and let Dorilys have her head a little. The mare broke into a trot and whickered with delight. The black mane tossed.

Margaret could hear the sound of hooves from the horse following her, but she ignored them. Gabriel was swearing at his mount, and she turned and looked over her shoulder. The bay was fighting his rider, and seemed reluctant to catch up with her. Did *laran* apply to animals? Or did the big bay merely dislike his rider?

She came to an earthen trail that led across wide pastures toward the hills, and she could see the clouds gath-

ering above them. It was beautiful. The air was clean
and fresh, and even the distant threat of thunder did not
lessen her delight in the freedom of the open country.
She could see thick stands of trees beyond the cultivated
fields of pasture and grain. This was rich land, fertile
and well cared for by her Uncle Gabriel. He might be
formal and much too full of himself for her taste, but
she was reminded, yet again, that he knew how to manage the land. He obviously took his responsibilities
quite seriously.

Margaret saw a wider track and turned Dorilys onto
it, still refusing to acknowledge Gabriel's pursuit. She
found the rhythm of the horse and matched it as they
moved into a good canter. Dorilys was well-gaited, a
smooth, light-mouthed filly, though Margaret knew she
had a mind of her own. Still, they were moving together,
as one, and after the horrors of the morning, that was
all she asked.

She was so deeply involved in the pleasure of the ride
that she was startled when a strong hand seized the reins
and yanked. Margaret heard the protest from the horse,
and matched it with her own. "Stop that!" Dorilys
reared slightly, and she turned on Gabriel. "If you have
cut her mouth, I will . . ."

"What?" He was breathing heavily, and his eyes were
glaring. "What do you think you can do to me, you
little cat!"

"Get your hand off the reins!"

"You had better get used to doing as I say, cousin. It
will make our marriage much less difficult."

"Marriage? If you were the last man in the known
universe, I wouldn't have you."

"You won't have any choice," he answered smugly.
"Mother and Father have decided that you will marry
me. I can't say I really like the idea any more than you
do, frankly. I don't want a woman who doesn't obey
orders. But I know my duty, and you will learn yours."
It's the only way to keep Armida!

Margaret wrenched the reins out of his hand, and her
horse capered away, giving a nervous whinny. She set
her heels into the horse, and Dorilys leaped forward like
a bolt. In a moment they were galloping along the
packed trail, heading for the closest stand of trees. Mar-

garet leaned forward across the horse's neck and smelled the warm scent of the animal. Not too far behind, she could hear Gabriel swearing and cursing, trying to catch up with the flying hooves of the pewter mare.

She rode into the trees, and she could tell that Dorilys knew her way. The branches were high enough to pass above her head easily, and the horse turned this way and that. Clearly the little mare thought this was a fine game, and was determined to have the best of it.

The light between the trees turned from gold to silver quite suddenly, and Margaret looked up toward the sky. The clouds she had seen over the hills had moved, and the sky was dark and threatening. She could smell electricity in the air, and a moment later she heard the ominous boom of thunder. She was going to get soaked, but just then she did not care. If she caught Rafaella's cold, she could go to bed and avoid the entire family!

A flash of lightning brightened the sky for an instant, and she heard the pounding of Gabriel's horse nearby. Dorilys whinnied and flickered her sharp ears, but she did not seem much disturbed by the storm. Still, she slowed to a trot, and Margaret stroked her neck. What a wonderful animal!

Gabriel, puffing and snorting, drew up beside her. "That was a stupid thing to do! You might have broken your neck."

"That would be very convenient for everyone, wouldn't it?"

"Is that what you think of me—of me and my parents? You must be as mad as your father! Not to mention your mother!"

"You leave the Senator out of this! And keep your hands off this horse. I won't be ordered by you, Gabriel. And I certainly will not marry you." She ignored the reference to Thyra, but it upset her more than a little. She was damned if she was going to argue with this man, this stupid man! How dare he!

"You don't understand. You have to. You don't have any choice."

"No, it is *you* who doesn't understand. I am not a piece of property to be handed around. I belong to myself, not to you or your stupid parents, or Armida or anything else." For an instant she had an image of cou-

pling with Gabriel, and it was so revolting she nearly
jerked the reins against the bit. Better to die a maiden
than to have him touch her.

Gabriel gripped her arm painfully, almost as if he
were hearing her thoughts, and dug his strong fingers
into the muscles. Margaret gave a small yelp. "You see,"
he gloated. "You don't really have the power to deny
me." *And I will get what I want, at last! I will best my
sneaky little brother and have Armida for my own!*

Margaret turned and looked at his triumphant expression in disbelief as rain began to pour down on them.
"So what are you planning? Are you going to try to rape
me?" She could not keep the disdain from her voice, nor
the anger. If she had been on foot, she would have used
the self-defense techniques she had learned at University, but horseback was no place for that. She struggled
to contain her emotions. Dorilys tossed her head and
danced, jerking away so that Gabriel lost his hold on
Margaret's arm.

The man gave a gasp, and all the color faded from his
face. "Of course not." He looked horrified, as if he had
just realized how his actions might be construed.

"Good. Because I really wouldn't want to test my
laran on you."

He swelled up again. "Do you mean to tell me you
would actually . . . that is disgusting! You bitch! You
misbegotten, underbred bitch! I am going to break you,
and I am going to enjoy it!" *I could kill you!*

Margaret had no idea what was driving the man, what
forces in his past had made him lose control like this.
She tried to think of some way to calm him, but nothing
came to mind. The tension in her chest was almost unen-
durable, and it found release in laughter, much to her
astonishment and shame. "How? You are a fool, Gabriel. I am sure that a well-mannered telepath would
never think of defending herself with her Gift, but I am
not constrained by your rules. Do you think you can
beat me into submission? Are you really so blind that
you imagine you could?"

Gabriel's hand whipped out and slapped her face. Her
skin stung, and Margaret felt something arise within her,
something strong and previously unknown. Her temples
pounded, and the distant thunder seemed to roll along

her bones. She wanted to kill him for touching her, for striking her.

A woman's face, twisted with rage, loomed above her, and small, strong hands slapped her face back and forth. Then someone dragged the woman away, screaming in fury, and she saw the silver-eyed man holding her. Thyra and Robert Kadarin wrestled, the man trying to control the woman without injuring her. She heard her own sobs, and felt her child-rage. She had wanted to kill the woman.

There was a flash of lightning and the vision vanished. Ancient rage warred within her for a second, and then she turned Dorilys aside, putting a little distance between them. The rain roared down, and the thunder boomed. "If you ever touch me again, I'll burn your brain to cinders!" She had no idea if she could actually accomplish such a terrible thing, but she was so furious she almost imagined that she could.

The man flinched. "I'm sorry, Marguerida. I must have been mad." The rain flattened his hair against his skull, and he looked utterly miserable. "I was going to be nice, and ask you nicely to marry me. I don't know what got into me." *Mikhail! This is all his fault, the little swine. Pushing in where he doesn't belong! I have to fix this, somehow, or Mother will be furious. She has to choose me, because she has already rejected Rafael, and there isn't anyone else.*

"It wouldn't have done any good, Gabriel. You could have been the nicest man on Darkover, and I still wouldn't have said yes." *And you aren't, by a long piece,* she thought .

"Why are you being so stubborn? Don't you see that you already belong to me, by right. Why can't you stop being so damn . . . do you really think we are going to let you do what you please? If he must, my father will go to the Comyn Cortes and have you declared his ward, and then you will find out that you can't do as you wish, but only as you are told. You are much too independent, and you don't know what is good for you. I do. I am older than you are, and wiser. It will be much easier if you just do as you are told, and stop trying to avoid your duty."

Margaret wondered if he might be right about that. The laws of Darkover might force her into marriage no matter what. "Gabriel, you don't have enough wisdom to fill a thimble. You can't threaten me in one breath and then tell me you know what is best for me in the next."

Another flash of light illuminated Gabriel's face, and she realized that he thought just that. There was a look in his eyes, an inward gaze, that suggested to her that he rarely listened to anyone but himself. She had seen this sort of solipcism before, in academics enamored of some pet theory or other, but never in a healthy, strong male. There was something more, too. Margaret sensed something unstable, a kind of willfulness that denied anything which did not agree with what she imagined was correct. He was not as stupid as she had thought, she realized, but like his sister Ariel there was something amiss within. Whether it was too much inbreeding for too many centuries or just a dreadful narcissism, she could not guess. All she could be sure of was that he was not a man who could accept her rejection mildly. Sitting astride Dorilys in the rain, Margaret sensed a whiff of desperate madness in Gabriel. It was in his eyes, and in the way he bent toward her as if nothing had happened, as if he had not threatened her and she had not spoken at all.

"Listen to me, Marguerida." His voice was loud above the roar of the storm. "I am going to be your husband, and you had better accept it. I'll have you and I'll have Armida, and that is that!" He was shouting above the storm, and the bay shifted restlessly beneath him.

"I'll see you in hell first!" Lightning struck a tree not a hundred paces away, and Dorilys decided she had had enough. She reared slightly, then started through the trees, sending clods of mud flying in all directions. Margaret clung to the reins and coiled her left hand into the mane, leaning forward against the neck of the animal. The mare bolted as the trees became fewer, and she hung on, pressing her chilled knees into the horse. She had no further thought for her unhappy cousin, but could only focus on staying in the saddle as the horse almost scraped her off beneath a low-hanging branch, then raced into the open.

Once on clear ground, Dorilys lengthened her stride, so her hooves hardly seemed to touch the earth. The wind whipped the rain against Margaret's back like a lash, drenching her completely. It was terrifying and exciting all at once, and Margaret just hoped the mare knew where she was going and didn't step into any holes. As the thought crossed her dazed mind, she felt a smug assurance beneath her, as if to say "I know exactly where I am going."

The thunder paused for a moment, and she heard other hoofbeats. Gabriel must be pursuing her, and Margaret found she was frightened. She knew she could protect herself, but she also knew that she was a danger to the stubborn man who rode after her. She actually *could* burn his brain to cinders, she suspected, but she didn't want to! And Gabe was too angry to realize what a danger she was to him.

Damn my father for keeping me ignorant, and damn Liriel and Jeff and Istvana for being right. I don't want to go to a Tower, any Tower! I don't want to be an heiress! I don't want to be a telepath—but I am. It's no one's fault. It's me, it's who I am, and I have to find a way to keep myself from harming people! I can't go on like this! I could have killed him, back there, and Gabriel's too obtuse to realize that I either have to get off Darkover immediately, or learn some way to control my Gift. And that probably means going to a Tower.

Dorilys gave a snort, bringing Margaret back to the moment. Clouds had settled at ground level, and the mist around her was so thick she could not see more than a few feet ahead of the horse. The mare shifted back and forth. *Take me home*, Margaret told her, and they moved into the mist at a moderate pace.

Between the thunder and the cloaking mist, sound became distant and diffuse. It was very dim, a twilight, all around her, and Margaret was shivering from the cold rain and from her fear. If Gabriel caught up with her, she didn't know what she would do.

A riding figure loomed ahead of her, and Margaret's heart pounded with terror. She hoped the mist would conceal her. Then Dorilys gave a piercing whinny, the sort of sound horses make to greet their friends. Margaret realized that the bay Gabriel was riding was stablemate to the mare, and her heart sank. Horses were wonderful, but they weren't smart enough to know friend from foe when it came to riders.

She clenched the reins, now slippery and treacherous from the rain, and prepared to try to outrun the man. She was determined to avoid any further confrontations with her stubborn cousin, even if she had to ride all night. The rider drew nearer, and Margaret could see his outline against the mist, cloaked and rather ominous. A flash of lightning dazzled her eyes, but not before she saw the fair hair of the rider. Relief flooded her as she realized it was not Gabriel, but Mikhail who emerged from the mist.

I have never been so glad to see someone in my life!
Yes, but would you say that if you were dry?

Margaret heard his pleasant laughter even above the storm, and felt herself relax a little. Her heart was pounding, and she could feel the rush of adrenaline in her blood. Mikhail drew abreast of her. "I started to get worried when you didn't come back."

"How long have I been gone?"

"Not very long—an hour at most—but in this rain . . . I can't imagine what Gabriel was thinking of. He is usually very sensible."

"We had an argument."

"I see." Mikhail turned his horse, a great black animal almost invisible in the storm, back the way he had come, and Dorilys fell into step beside him. "I suppose he informed you that you were going to be his wife, and you had the bad judgment to object."

"That is a fairly accurate picture. I threatened to turn his brains to oatmeal if he touched me again, actually, and I don't know who was more frightened, him or me. Everyone has been telling me for days that an untrained telepath is dangerous, but I didn't realize just how dangerous I could be until that moment. It made him hesitate, but . . . here he comes! I don't think I convinced him that I wouldn't marry him, because he seems to think I am his by right or something. I knew I should have taken the Amhax chief up on his offer." She was determined to ignore the squishy hoofbeats of the approaching horse, feeling secure in Mikhail's presence.

"What?"

She laughed in spite of herself, releasing the tension

in her body with the sound. "A few years ago, Ivor, my mentor, and I were on Mantenon, and I was pretending to be Ivor's daughter. Depending on the local customs, I went as his wife, his sister or his daughter, and once, when we were with a tribe where the men counted for very little, as his owner. But, on Mantenon, we were studying the Amhax musical system, which is remarkably complex for such a primitive culture, and the chief offered Ivor forty head of cattle—they were blue, with two tails and curly horns—for me. It was a very handsome bride-price among the Amhax—a forty-cow woman is a social superior, and all the women of the tribe were jealous."

"You are making that up, aren't you?"

"Mikhail, I would never lie to you!" As soon as the words were out of her mouth, Margaret knew them to be true. It was a strange sensation, she decided, to be certain that she would always try to speak the truth to this man, and she was not sure what it meant about her. But it was a comforting realization, and right then, she wanted all the comforts she could find.

Gabriel caught up with them, reined the bay viciously, and glared at his brother. He was puffing hard, as if he had had to fight the horse. He frowned at Margaret and reached toward the reins of her horse. "What are you doing here, Mik? I knew Dorilys was too much horse for Marguerida. She ran away with her." He was totally soaked, and in a very foul temper, his thoughts chaotic, so that she got no precise impressions, just a lot of mixed emotions.

"Please, cousin, stop it! Dorilys and I ran away together, and with good reason." Margaret pulled her mare's head aside, out of Gabriel's reach. "This is no place to have another argument. Let's get back to the house."

"We didn't have an argument," Gabriel roared, as if he thought he could undo his own mischief.

"And it isn't raining cats and dogs," Margaret snapped back.

"Mikhail, I order you to leave us! I will take Marguerida back to Armida."

"I think not, Gabe. Our kinswoman does not appear to wish your company."

"Damn you! Damn you both!" Gabriel kicked the bay hard along the flanks, and the horse darted forward.

"He'll break his fool neck if he isn't careful," Mikhail said, urging his own horse to follow.

"I would be surprised if he did," Margaret commented sourly as she followed her cousin. "Men like Gabriel rarely come to the ends they deserve."

The rain had slackened a little when the three riders came into the Stable Court, but it was obvious it was merely a pause in the storm. Booms of thunder echoed behind them as two grooms collected the soaking animals and led them away to be wiped down and cared for. Margaret dismounted and stepped into a fairly deep puddle. It seemed an apt end for a completely maddening day.

It isn't over yet. There is something coming . . . and it is not just the storm. Something's coming—something terrible! No reasoning could make her shake off the sense of impending disaster rushing toward them, something she had no power to control or change.

They entered through the rear of the house, their hair and clothing streaming. Mikhail bent down and began to pull off his soaking boots, and Margaret decided to follow his example. Gabriel, stiff-backed with outrage, strode down the hall, leaving wet bootprints behind him. The *coridom,* Dartan, appeared as if he had been summoned, looked at Marguerida's soaked clothing and Mikhail's dripping cloak, and shook his head.

"I wonder if Liriel would mind if I slipped into her room," Margaret told her cousin. "I don't really feel like facing the family right now."

"I think she would, Marguerida. You might ask her, but no one goes in there without invitation."

"Ask her?" Margaret stared at him blankly for a moment, then realized that the technician did not have to be present for her to communicate with her. She wasn't used to the idea of telepathy, and she wondered wearily if she ever would be. And how did one speak to a specific person? It was infuriating to have an ability and have no idea how to utilize it. If only there were a manual, a book of instructions!

Before she could marshal her thoughts, however, Javanne appeared, looking concerned rather than angry. "Come along, Marja. We must get you into some dry clothing immediately, or you will take a chill and get ill. You should never have taken her out in this weather," she said to Mikhail.

"I didn't. And if I had, we would have been back before the storm." He met his mother's eyes sternly. "I am afraid that Gabriel mishandled matters in his usual ham-handed way."

"What do you mean?" Javanne's concern vanished in a flare of mild temper. She looked from one to the other, and her pale brows knitted together in a deep frown.

"He means that Gabriel knocked him down in the Stable Court and tried to propose to me—if you can call being told I was going to marry him whether I wanted to or not a proposal—on horseback. Is he always so stupid, or just when the weather is foul?"

Javanne gave a sigh. "Gabriel makes his own weather," she answered in a voice that boded no good for her eldest child. "I am sorry, *chiya.*"

"Sorry he asked, or sorry he failed? It doesn't matter, Aunt. I have had quite enough of my loving family to last me a long time. As soon as the weather clears, I will go back to Thendara."

"But your companion is ill!"

Margaret had quite forgotten that Rafaella was down with a miserable cold. She set her jaw, determined not to remain at Armida past the morning, even if it meant going alone. It was not far, she knew, and she was sure she could manage it. A day's ride, or a little more, and she could be back in the Terran Sector, where no one would plague her with marital demands or tell her she had to go live in a Tower. "I'll get there somehow," she snarled, frustrated and feeling more trapped than she ever had before.

Javanne gave Margaret a look of intense dislike. Then she shrugged. "This is no time to be making decisions. Come along. Let's get you some dry clothes and a cup of tea."

"You aren't going to change my mind."

"We shall see." *I hope that Gabriel has reached Thendara by now, and that Regis will agree to make the girl our ward. We can't have her running around without a chaperone. Why is she so difficult? And why did my son have to be such a fool? I have to do everything myself as usual.*

Margaret heard these thoughts, and found herself furious. So Gabriel had not been imagining things when he had told her that a Darkovan judge might make her into a legal child, award her to these kinsmen who only wanted her for the children she might bear. They had gone behind her back, all of them. She had never felt so betrayed in her life. Liriel had distracted her while her father went to see Regis Hastur—who would almost surely hand her off like a sack of laundry.

She followed Javanne down the corridor, biting her lips. She could sense Mikhail behind her, seething, and she realized that he was nearly as outraged as she was. More, he was ashamed by the way his mother and father were behaving.

"Javanne!" Margaret's word stopped the older woman in her tracks. "Don't imagine you can force me with your judges. I am a Terran citizen, and if you try to hold me against my will . . ."

The woman spun around and faced Margaret. "This is Darkover, not Terra! You will do as you are bid. You don't have any rights here except . . ."

"I think the Terrans will take an extremely dim view of one of their citizens being detained against her will." Margaret continued.

Javanne's lips curled in a sneer, and her face reddened beneath the carefully applied cosmetics. "Not even the Terranan would be so stupid as to start a war over one girl."

"When you find a company of Imperial Marines camped in your pasture, you may think otherwise." Margaret was only half bluffing. There had been a few rare incidents where the Federation had moved to protect one of its citizens with sufficient force to topple a planetary government. It was almost always in the interests of the Federation when such things happened, and it was always hushed up afterward. Margaret did not know if the Federation was looking for a way to alter the status of Darkover, but if they were, this was a perfect excuse.

"I don't believe you! You are being spoiled and willful, and I won't have it! This is my house, and you are

my niece, and you will do as we tell you." With that she
turned and stomped down the hall, and Margaret trailed
after her.

When they reached the entry hall, Margaret, enraged,
said, "No, this isn't your house. It is mine! Your very
thoughts and actions support this truth. My father relinquished his own claim to Armida, but he did not relinquish *mine.* Why else would you be so desperate for me
to marry one of your sons?" Margaret was aware of a
kind of energy simmering along her nerves, a terrible
rage that was incredibly dangerous. She tried to lessen
her anger, breathing heavily as Javanne just stared at
her—shocked into a stony silence. She was afraid of
what she could do, but her aunt was even more so.

*Ariel was right—she is a monster. What am I to do? I
have never seen such raw and powerful* laran. *And she
knows! When Gabriel comes back we must force her to
go to a Tower—it's the only way we'll be safe from her!*

The two women glared at each other in silence, and
then the sound of heavy hooves could be heard from
the Manor courtyard. For a moment Javanne looked relieved, and Margaret wondered if *Dom* Gabriel had
managed to get back from Thendara already. No, that
was too far, and Javanne's face fell as she realized that
her husband was not coming to the rescue.

The sound of men's voices, shouting, and horses wild
with terror, came through the closed door. Above it all
there were the screams of a woman, harsh and hysterical.
Heavy blows thudded against the wood of the door, and
it rattled on its hinges until Dartan opened it.

Ariel stood in the doorway, holding something and
howling. She stepped into the hall, and Margaret could
see the still form of little Domenic draped across her
cousin's outstretched arms. Behind the woman the faces
of the other children were white with terror, their eyes
enormous.

"You tried to kill my child!" Ariel screamed.

21

◆

A dreadful silence followed Ariel's words, and everyone in the entry seemed to freeze for a moment. The child in her arms stirred feebly, one arm flexing slightly. Then everyone began to speak at once, and chaos followed. Ariel trembled and shivered, then began to scream in greater hysteria while Javanne and Piedro tried to calm her. Margaret felt as if her feet had rooted to the floor until Mikhail touched her elbow. She felt battered, and more, she was angry. At that moment she would gladly have consigned the entire Lanart clan, root and branch, to the farthest reaches of hell, and not been at all contrite.

"Be quiet!" Old Jeff came into the entryway from the living room and bellowed these words, and everyone stared at him as if he had grown horns and a tail. "What is going on?" He was angry, and Margaret was so glad to see his stern face that she wanted to cry. She was sure Uncle Jeff could get things calmed down.

"She killed my baby," Ariel howled. She clutched the now limp body of Domenic, and Margaret heard a little cry of protest. Javanne tried vainly to get the child away from her daughter, but that made Ariel even more hysterical. Piedro tried to speak, but the voices of his wife and mother-in-law were too shrill.

"What happened?" Jeff shouted.

Piedro drew away from trying to comfort his wife. His voice trembled. "The storm. I knew we should not leave. This is my fault, not Marguerida's."

"I doubt it is anyone's fault, Piedro," Mikhail said.

"We were driving toward home," Piedro went on, as if his brother-in-law had not spoken, "and it began to thunder. Lightning struck a tree just as the horses passed under it, and they bolted. Jedidiah tried to stop them, but they pulled him right off the coachman's bench, and onto the ground. He fell beneath the wheels, and that overbalanced the coach, and it rolled onto its side, while the horses continued to run. They must have dragged the coach three hundred feet before they stopped. I could hear Ariel and the children screaming, and I could do nothing. My son is injured, and Jed, my coachman, is dead." Tears poured down Piedro's face.

Piedro stopped speaking, and his shoulders shook with sobs. His frightened children looked at him, and the eldest, Damon, rubbed the tears off his own face and straightened his little shoulders. "We were all inside with Mother," the lad said, "when the coach fell over. It was dark, and the rain came in through the window. It was broken, and there was glass all over." He held up a small hand, and Margaret could see it was cut in several places.

"It seemed like it was all right when the horses stopped. Father came and opened the door, and I handed Kennard out to him, then Lewis. Donal climbed out on his own, and I reached over to give Domenic my hand. It was still warm, but he felt weird."

Piedro nodded. "His neck is broken, I think. When the coach overturned, he must have fallen wrong."

"Then we must get him into bed immediately," Jeff announced. "If his neck is injured, having his mother clutch him will not do him any good."

Margaret wanted to shrink into the shadows, to be away from this horror. She wondered what could be done for a broken neck with Darkover's fairly primitive medical technology. Herbs and simples were fine for stomach upsets, but this was beyond that sort of remedy. If only she could think of something to do to help, so she could escape the choking feeling that she was responsible for the accident.

Then she remembered the foam splint in her medkit. It came with instructions for immobilizing broken bones, didn't it? Of course it did—the Terrans had instructions for everything. It was how they did things! But the chances of relaying that information in the midst of the uproar, or getting close enough to the injured child to apply the tool, seemed impossible .

Ariel had continued to moan all during this, and now

she began to scream again. "I fell on him! I felt him underneath me. But it isn't my fault. I love my children! You did this, *you . . ."* She pointed an accusing finger at Margaret.

Margaret shrank against the wall, devastated.

Liriel appeared from behind the group in the entry, rubbing her eyes as if she had been napping, and took in the scene. As her sister screamed, she walked forward and slapped Ariel smartly across the face. "That is quite enough! If you hadn't dashed out of here when a storm was coming, none of this would have happened."

"She frightened me," whimpered Ariel "Marguerida frightened me. This is her fault, not mine."

"Accidents are not anyone's fault, Ariel," Jeff said sternly. "We know you love your children, *chiya,* and that you care for them. This is a terrible tragedy for everyone."

Instead of calming down at Jeff's words, Ariel turned red with fury. "What do you know, old man. You are on her side. Everyone is against me! Everyone thinks I am just a silly woman, but I know things you'll never know! I know you can't understand what it is to be a mother." Ariel's tirade degenerated into sobs. "My baby . . . my baby . . ."

Liriel pursed her generous lips and looked at Jeff for a moment. *She is going to lose the child she bears if she doesn't calm down, and that will finish her. We have to get her into bed before she gets sick. My poor sister. If only I had realized how unhappy she was.*

Margaret felt her continued presence was more of a hindrance than a help, and started to withdraw from the entry. Mikhail's hand on the small of her back stopped her. *Don't leave yet.*

Why not? It is just upsetting Ariel to look at me.

I don't think so. I know she is blaming you, but I think she knows that Domenic's injury is as much her fault as anyone's. She sensed his strength beside her, his strength and clear-headedness. It was wonderful—or would have been if she had not felt quite so shattered.

Liriel thinks she will miscarry if she doesn't calm down, and I can't see how standing here is going to help, Mikhail. Besides, if I go upstairs, I can get my medkit. There is a splint in it that just might help.

Really? It is good to know that someone is thinking about doing something—instead of having a fit of hysteria. I'll get it—I have the image of the kit in my mind now.

But I can find it faster.

No, cousin. I can be back quickly. You should stay here—trust me. Liriel is right that if she loses the child in her womb, she will never be sane again. She is close to breaking. Can you bring yourself to say something to her—anything at all?

Of course—but I think it is likely to upset her more. I'll do anything to help.

Mikhail turned and charged up the stairs, taking them two at a time, and Margaret swallowed, trying to think of something she could say. Why her? She didn't know Ariel very well. She heard the thump of his bootless feet on the wood of the floor above, and shook her head to clear her thoughts.

Liriel tried to get her sister to let go of the small, limp body. Domenic gave no further protest, but Margaret knew the boy was not dead, not yet anyhow. If his mother didn't let go of him, he would be, though. Ariel resisted, continuing to insist that her family hated her, that she was misunderstood and a great deal more. It was pathetic, but it was also painful, for Javanne looked close to tears, and Jeff seemed helpless.

Margaret swallowed hard, her mouth very dry, and close to tears herself. She moved closer to Ariel, carefully, so as not to frighten her. "Cousin, you must think of the child within you," she said quietly. The words came from some deep, caring place within her, someplace she had never known she possessed. "You would not wish to harm her, would you?"

"Her?" Ariel's voice, raw from screaming, was feeble and raspy.

"Yes, it is the daughter you have longed for."

"How do you know?" Ariel's eyes were completely unfocused, and she did not seem to be aware that she was speaking to the woman she believed to be the author of her sorrow.

"Liriel told me earlier today."

"Did you?" Ariel turned to her sister, and her arms began to sag.

Liriel took rapid advantage of this, and slipped her arms beneath the still form of the boy. His chest rose and fell slightly. "Yes, I did. I would have told you, but you ran off before I could." She clasped Domenic's body against her generous bosom. Then Jeff took the child from her in his long arms, supporting the lolling head with care.

"A girl. At last I will have a girl to love me." Ariel seemed to steady then, and began to stroke her still flat belly, caressing it sensuously. "I have always wanted a daughter to love me."

"And you will have her," Liriel answered, giving Margaret a quick glance of approval, "but you must be calm for her."

Suddenly, Margaret had the sense of vision she had experienced at the dining table a few hours before. "She will be beautiful," she said, not thinking of the consequences of her words.

Ariel, who had been almost dazed a moment before, looked at Margaret intensely. "What do you see? Tell me!"

"I don't think that would be wise," Margaret answered, though nothing in her vision was at all alarming.

"I don't care what you think!" Ariel's voice rose. "You must tell me, right now! ' '

"She will be beautiful and she will be healthy—what more can a mother ask for?"

"I don't care if she's beautiful," Ariel whispered. "I just want her to love me."

At these words Margaret saw her cousin's unborn child as a young woman, tall and russet-haired and striking. She had something of Javanne's look, the same strong jaw and fierce eyes, and there was something powerful in the gaze that stared back into Margaret's inner eyes, powerful and willful. "Of course she will love you. You are a good mother, and she cannot help but love you." As she spoke, Margaret knew she lied. Ariel was doomed to be disappointed in her daughter. She wondered if there was some way to make things better, to keep this unborn babe from becoming the wild, passionate, troublesome woman she foresaw. "You will name her Alanna, after your grandmother." *Not an entirely felicitous choice. She should be Deirdre for all the sorrow she will bring to Darkover.* Perhaps she was wrong. Margaret hoped she was, because what she could see of that future told of a woman who could not love Ariel as she longed to be loved.

Javanne gave her niece a sharp look. *I thank you for being kind to my little daughter, and I hope you are wrong in your vision. I never knew she felt so . . . unwanted and unloved until today.*

Mother, it is not your fault! Liriel's mental voice was firm and clear. *You did the best you could for her. You always did the best you could for all of us.*

It is kind of you, Liriel, to say that, but I do blame myself. I am a mother, and I should have known how unhappy she would be without laran. *Or, perhaps, the fault is in valuing that overmuch. And, in truth, I was not entirely pleased to have twins. Perhaps I did not want her enough.*

Stop whipping yourself, Jeff's command startled Javanne. *It is a complete waste of time. You did the best you could, and you could not have done more. Regret will not change anything,*

I hate it when you are right, Javanne replied with something like her normal vigor. *But, we must see to the child. He may not have taken as much hurt as we imagine, but the danger now is that he will get an inflammation of the lung.*

I have monitored him, Mother, as well as I was able, and one of the bones just below the neck is very bad.

I sent Mikhail for my medkit, and he should be back in a moment. There is a device in it that might be useful. Margaret felt anxious at holding out hope, but she knew it was the right thing to do. Indeed, Javanne looked at her with more favor than she had since she arrived.

Piedro had taken his wife's hands and was talking to her very softly, so gently that Margaret felt something like envy stir within her. As he drew Ariel toward the stairs, she wondered if she would ever arouse such a fine tenderness in another person. She watched them move upstairs, and felt exhausted and miserable. Her wet garments clung to her skin, chilling her, and she noticed that she had dripped a large puddle on the floor.

Mikhail nearly crashed into them, rushing down the stairs, but neither Ariel nor Piedro seemed to notice his descent. He had the medkit in his hand, and his face was rather rosy with embarrassment. Of course—Rafaella was asleep upstairs! If she hadn't been so tired and upset, Margaret would have been amused.

In a moment, Jeff had laid Domenic on the floor of the entry and stretched out his small limbs. His head rested crookedly above his slender neck. "This is no place for a field hospital, but I do not want to move the boy around any further," the old man said. "Someone fetch some warm blankets—he is shocky, and that will do him no good. Now, Mik, give me that kit. Lord, it has been a long time since I saw one of these. Hmm. They seem to have added some things." He started to sort through the contents, and Margaret knelt down beside him.

The remaining children watched these activities with stricken eyes. Javanne seemed torn between wanting to follow her daughter up the stairs and caring for her grandchildren. At last, she bent down and patted Damon on the shoulder. "Your mother will be fine now. But your father has to take care of her, so I expect you to help us with your brothers." Her voice carried above the renewed roar of the storm outside, and, for once, she did not sound too certain of herself.

Damon puffed out his little chest and looked proud. This brave gesture made the remaining adults smile, in spite of the circumstances. "Yes. I can do that." He turned to Donal. "Get Lewis, and I'll take Kennard."

Donal gave his brother a look of momentary rebellion, then shrugged. Of all the children he seemed the least upset, and Margaret found herself envying his resilience. "Come on, Lewee. You have to get some dry clothes or you will get sick, and Nurse will make you drink kamfer tea." He reached for his younger brother's hand, and the child took it, making a face which said that he would do nearly anything to avoid the threatened remedy. *Now I am second, and I will learn to read, like Dom did, and be very learned like Mikhail and Marguerida.*

Javanne was clearly shocked by this childish opportunism, but Mikhail almost laughed. "He can't help it, Mother. Being third is no fun at all."

Margaret had pulled the foam splint out of the kit, and was reading the instructions that came with it. It seemed easy enough, but she was terrified that now they would do more harm than good. If only they could take Domenic to a real hospital! If only they could call a plane or a helicopter to come and take him to Terran HQ! Her fingers were cold, and she dropped the splint into her lap, then snatched it back, swearing.

Jeff, beside her, was very calm, and that steadied her. But there was a kind of thundering in her mind that had nothing to do with the storm outside. It felt like the hoofbeats of some enormous equine coming closer and closer, and that, plus the general uproar in the entry, made it very hard to concentrate. Margaret wished she knew a way to block out the spillover of thoughts. Dartan, the *coridom*, returned with a pile of blankets. He and Jeff got one under the small boy, and wrapped it around him.

She thought she understood the instructions now, and while Jeff lifted the little head, she slipped the device under Domenic's neck. He looked so small and so helpless that her heart clenched. After they had positioned it as well as they could, with some advice from Jeff, who was able, she supposed, to somehow see where the lad was injured using his *laran,* she pressed the tab on the side of the splint. It expanded slowly, surrounding the neck without putting any pressure on the throat, lifting Domenic's head up from the floorboards a couple of inches. Jeff thrust a rolled-up blanket under the head, and everyone breathed a sigh of relief. Now, at least, it would be possible to take the boy to a bed without further damaging his spine, and that was the best she could manage. It did not seem like nearly enough.

Suddenly there was a tremendous banging at the door. Margaret looked up as Dartan rose from his knees on the other side of the child and hurried toward the booming noise. She felt something tug at her heart, something strong and wonderful and unexpected.

Before she could wonder what it was, Dartan pulled the huge door open, and a dripping figure moved into the light of the entry. It was cloaked and hooded, and the wind from outside blew the folds of wet cloth against the stranger, shoving the hood down over his face. Then an arm without a hand thrust the cloak away below the breast, and she jumped up and flew across the floor, heedless of the puddles.

Margaret nearly slipped twice in the short distance to the door. Then she flung herself against the soaking form of the newcomer. "Father!" was all she could say, and then she burst into tears.

Lew Alton pushed the hood back, sending a shower of drops down on her head, and drew her against his chest with both arms. Margaret could feel her aunt stiffen behind her, and a wave of mixed emotions flooded from the older woman. She was angry, shocked, displeased, and resigned all at once.

Oh, do stop being such a high-stickler, Javanne. I haven't seen her for more than a decade! Customs be damned!

I know, but I still don't like it. And I still don't like you, Lew.

Isn't it a mercy, then, that we never married!

Javanne, despite her mild outrage, laughed at this. "You are still a rascal, and a storm crow."

"Now, Javanne, surely you cannot blame me for Darkovan weather! There, there, Marja. I know you are glad to see me—you *are* glad, aren't you?—but you are strangling me! A fine welcome home. Why is everyone standing around dripping in the foyer?"

Margaret hardly knew what to make of the man she clung to. He was making jokes, and the Lew Alton she remembered did not do that. He was teasing Javanne, and she was not a woman who seemed a good candidate for that. More, Javanne actually seemed to be enjoying it. He felt different under her hands—almost cheerful. And yet, beneath it, she could sense a kind of deep sorrow, not an old one, but something new and fresh. "Of course I am glad—what took you so long?"

Lew chuckled and ruffled her still damp hair. He had not done that since she was a child, and the touch of his fingers nearly overset her again. Instead, Margaret snuffled against his shoulder. He smelled of rain and Darkovan cloth, but most of all he smelled *right*. She had not known, until that moment, how much she missed the scent of him, the sound of his strong voice, and the feel of his arm around her shoulders.

"If I could have been here sooner, I would have, *chiya.*"

"I know. You kept telling me, but I couldn't quite believe it was real. So many strange things have happened . . ."

"I have been a pretty sorry excuse for a parent, haven't I?"

"Yes," she whispered. "But I know you couldn't help it."

Lew Alton looked down at his daughter's head against his shoulder. She could feel his regrets welling up in his chest. *You have a generous heart, Marja. I can't imagine where you got it—not from me and not from* . . . He could not let himself think of Thyra.

I think it was Dio, Father. Where is she?

She stayed behind in Thendara, with Regis and Linnea.

Margaret could feel him holding something back. His arm around her tensed slightly, and even his mental voice seemed strained. After a second she was sure it was the source of that deep sorrow she had sensed a moment before, and her heart went cold. She shivered with chill, both physical and emotional. *What's wrong? Is she ill?*

Yes, chiya, *she is very ill indeed. It was the last straw, and I brought her home, though I never thought to see the sun of Darkover again.*

The last straw?

Later, chiya. *I should not call you that, for you are a woman now, but you will always be my little Marja.*

They drew apart reluctantly. "I want dry clothes, hot food, and I want them now." Lew announced this as if he expected the items to appear instantly. He seemed to Margaret like a monarch, used to issuing orders, and she had never really seen him like this before. "Then you can tell me why you are all standing around looking like drowned rats."

Dartan was supervising two servants who were lifting the small form of Domenic from the floor, using the corners of a blanket, and moving gingerly, so as not to jostle the patient. Lew took in the situation as he removed his dripping cloak and hung it from a nearby hook. *What happened?*

Margaret told him, without words, about the accident,

and who the child was, more rapidly than she would have thought possible. She confessed her own unwitting participation in the matter, and Lew gave a deep sigh. *Things have not been easy for you, have they, child? This is as much my fault, for not telling you about your history, as anyone's. We must just hope the child will make a full recovery.*

But they don't have any idea how to fix a spinal injury.

There are things about matrix science that would astonish you, Marguerida. I've known them all my life, and they still surprise me.

"Mikhail, take Lew to your rooms, please. I think something of yours will fit him." Javanne was calm now, almost resigned. "Did you meet Gabriel on the way? He was riding to Thendara."

Lew goggled at Javanne. "No, and I cannot say I am sorry. We have not seen eye to eye in many years, though once we were friends."

He went to get Regis to make me his ward, so he could marry me off to his namesake—who is a blooming idiot. Margaret's mental snarl contained all her frustrations and anger at the events of the afternoon.

Then he will be both wet and disappointed. Lew answered calmly. He seemed steady in a way she had never known him to be, and even though she knew he was worried about Dio, Margaret felt herself become quiet within.

Half an hour later, the adults gathered in the dining hall. It was a subdued group, and the pleasant smell of cooked meats and pastries did nothing to relieve the unspoken gloom.

Once again there was a hesitation while everyone considered where to sit. Lew, his silvered hair dry and curling slightly, appeared quite at ease as he seated himself at the head of the table, as if it had never occurred to him to sit elsewhere. He wore a rose-colored tunic with silver mountains embroidered at the sleeves and throat and a pair of blue trousers. He glanced around, completely confident. Margaret had never seen him in such command of himself, or the situation, and she felt both vastly relieved and mildly angry. Her earlier pleasure in his arrival was now mitigated by his air of assurance. How dare he waltz in looking so damn cheerful!

She sat down in the chair beside him, and Jeff took the place opposite her, across the board. Javanne seated herself at the foot of the table, with her sons, Gabriel and Rafael, on either side of her. It was as if the table was the battleground of two opposing armies, with Javanne as the general of one side, and Lew Alton on the other. When Mikhail took a place beside Jeff, silently allying himself with that side of the wordless conflict, Javanne gave her youngest son a look that spoke of betrayal.

Liriel came in then, her wide shoulders drooping a little. "'I have Ariel calmed down, and I sent Piedro to bed. The children are in the nursery. I don't think it has quite sunk in, yet, what has happened. Our old nurse is looking after Dominic for the moment, and I cannot think of any better hands to leave him in. That thing you put on him seems to have relieved the pressure, Marguerida, and the worst danger now is pneumonia, not his spine. We will need to transport him to Arilinn as quickly as he is able to travel." She sat down beside Mikhail, apparently unaware of her mother's hostile gaze.

Liriel glanced around the table, and her eyes stopped at Lew Alton. They widened. Then she turned back to face her mother. Whatever words they exchanged they kept private, but it was clear to Margaret that Javanne was understandably more concerned with her daughter and her eldest grandson than she was with the sudden appearance of the Old Man. Still, Javanne looked hostile, and Margaret was sure that she wished Lew Alton anywhere in the universe but sitting opposite her, at the other end of the table.

Donal appeared just as Liriel sat down, his hair tousled and wearing his night robes. He climbed into the empty chair next to Margaret. "I don't want porridge," he announced, and smiled at her winningly.

"Of course you don't," she told the charming child. "I never liked porridge for dinner myself."

"They make you have it when you are sick, and I am not sick."

The presence of the little boy seemed to ease the tension around the table somewhat, and the food was brought in by the servants. There was a miasma of worry that seemed to effect everyone except the child, so rather than talk, they gave their attention to a thick soup followed by roast meat and a custard side dish that was heavy with dried fruits. Margaret was surprised by her own hunger, and a little ashamed as well. It didn't seem right to be so hungry with that child lying upstairs with a broken neck. If he lived, he would probably be paralyzed for the rest of his life, and she could not bear that. She could not imagine what the life of a cripple would be like on Darkover.

Then she noticed that everyone, including her aunt, was tucking into their suppers with a good appetite, and felt slightly less guilty. It was not, she decided, that they were unmoved by the accident—not in the least! It was only that they had done what they could for the present, and needed to keep up their strength for whatever lay ahead.

Jeff finally broke the silence. "We never thought to see you back on Darkover, Lew."

"I never thought to return myself—but never is a word that almost always comes back to haunt me. I am finished with trying to be a diplomat. I was not very good at in the best of times, and now, with Dio ill, it was intolerable."

"Dio is sick?" Jeff's voice expressed concern, but Lew just gave him a head shake, as if the matter was not to be discussed for the present.

"But, Lew, who will represent us in the Senate now?" Javanne asked the question with real interest, and gave Mikhail a look as if she imagined that he might be sent to fill the spot. Margaret almost choked on her food. She could guess at her aunt's train of thought, without needing any telepathy at all. Well, it would certainly solve the problem of what to do with her third son, wouldn't it? Get him off the planet—which Mikhail would like, she knew—and out of her hair. But Margaret didn't like the idea at all, for some reason.

It took her a minute to unravel her own turmoil. She knew now that she must spend some time studying in a Tower, no matter how she felt about it. But Mikhail was her friend, and she wanted him to be on Darkover if she was. It was so simple and, at the same time, so complicated.

"Herm Aldaran, who has been sitting in the lower house for six years, is taking my place. He's sound, experienced, and he knows how to deal with the Terrans better than I do. He is also young enough to do the job. I was getting stale and frustrated."

"An Aldaran in the Senate!" Javanne looked quite alarmed, but Margaret was immensely relieved. "He will hand Darkover to the Terranan on a platter. Are you mad?"

"On the contrary, Javanne. Herm may be the only man in the galaxy who can save us from that just now."

Margaret gave her father a sidewise glance from beneath her lashes. She had never heard of Herm Aldaran, but guessed he must be some sort of relative, like everyone else. She knew that the Aldarans were mistrusted by both the Ardais and her aunt and uncle, but she did not know why. "Save us?"

"During the most recent election the Expansionist Party got control of the lower house."

"What's that?" Rafael asked quietly, before his mother could speak.

Lew stared at his kinsman for a moment. "The government of the Federation follows an old Terran form of a two body system. The lower house, the Commons, formulates policy, and the Senate makes sure they don't run wild with it. There are a number of parties in the Federation at present, but the largest are the Expansionist Party and the Liberals. For the past several decades, the Liberals, who believe that planets should choose the sort of government they wish, have been the majority in both houses. Now this has changed. There are just barely enough votes in the Senate to prevent the Expansionists from changing policy so that the needs of the Federation take precedence over the wishes of any individual planet. If the Expansionists have their way, no world will be safe from the greed of the Terrans."

"And you left in the middle of that! You are a greater fool than I ever imagined, Lew! You should have stayed and protected us, not left us in the hands of an Aldaran. I know of Herm. I was opposed to his appointment to the lower house when Regis sent him six years ago. Even though we have almost no contact with the Aldarans, we have to keep an eye on them. He seems a decent enough sort, for an Aldaran, but hardly . . ." Javanne was nearly sputtering with fury.

"Javanne, whatever you may think of Herm, he has the interests of Darkover at heart. This situation has been growing for a long time, and Herm has the advantage of knowing many men and women in the Commons well." Lew gave a little chuckle. "He's a better horse trader than I ever was."

"Humph! Likely he'll trade Darkover for an aircar, then. Surely there are more able men, older men, more experienced men, from among the Domains. I cannot think that Regis would have agreed to this insanity. The Aldarans are cowards and cheats!"

"Mother, I don't think you really know what you are talking about," Mikhail replied. "Herm Aldaran is one of the best men I have ever known."

Javanne did not take this rebuke gracefully, and her always ready temper flared up, now that she had a target to direct it at. "What do you know about it! Just because you can read Terranan does not make you an expert on anything!"

"I trust Herm." Mother and son looked daggers at each other, and to Margaret's surprise, it was Javanne who dropped her eyes, not Mikhail. Her aunt's hand closed around a slice of bread, and she proceeded to crush it between her fingers.

Donal, oblivious to the tensions around the table, pushed his plate back and gave a small belch. He rubbed his belly. "What's for dessert?"

Liriel looked at her nephew. "Where will you put any?"

"I always save room for dessert," he answered calmly. "Do they have good desserts in the Trade City?"

"Not really," Margaret answered. "Why do you ask?"

"Because if Domenic dies, I am second, and I get to learn to read and be educated like Uncle Mikhail. I always wanted that—well, since last Midwinter, anyhow." He seemed to think something about his place in the family gave him certain rights, and was determined to have them. "I want to go to Thendara and learn everything!"

Javanne shook her head. "Donal, first of all, I'll have no talk of Domenic dying! And secondly, your mother would never let you go to Thendara, not now. You are going to Neskaya as soon as you are old enough, and even that will be very difficult for her. You will learn everything you need to know there."

"No, I won't!" He turned and looked at Margaret. "Aunt Liriel says you can read all the books in her library. Is that so? She says you can read them all, and a lot more."

"I can read, and have read, a great many books, yes."

"I won't have you encouraging the boy, Marguerida," Javanne interrupted angrily. "You don't know anything about our ways, and I don't want you interfering any more. I think you have caused enough trouble for one day." *Trouble is all Lew ever brings, and his child is like him! I know I am right! We must maintain the Domains as they have always been. We never should have let the Terranan get a foothold. If I had been Regis . . . why was I born a woman!*

Do they think I don't know what is going on? I see how my son looks at Marguerida—it will not do! There must be some way to get Herm Aldaran out of the Senate, and Mikhail into it. That would be best. I will speak to my brother, and he will listen to me. I will make him listen.

"My father cannot read very good," Donal said in his high boy voice, "and my mother cannot read at all. Domenic wanted help with some hard words, and they . . . they couldn't do it. They say it is not useful, but Domenic told me that it was wonderful, to read and learn things!" His voice broke a little as he spoke of his injured brother. "I always wanted to be like Dom, and now I am going to, whether he gets better or not!"

Margaret was mildly shocked. She knew that literacy was rare on Darkover, but somehow she had assumed that at least the members of the Domain families were able to read. She realized that she took literacy for granted, except on the most primitive planets, and she felt slightly ashamed that the place of her birth seemed to have chosen deliberate ignorance over formal education. Why, Rafaella probably read better than most of the people at this table!

Gabriel decided to put in his oar. "I have heard all of

Liriel's arguments that reading makes you wiser, and I think it is nonsense. There is no reason for people to addle their brains learning what they will never need to know."

"There speaks the voice of a man who can hardly sign his name," Mikhail muttered, loud enough to be heard by Margaret, but not so loud as to carry to the other end of the table.

Jeff said quietly, "We are getting well ahead of ourselves. First we must hope that Domenic will make a complete recovery, that Marguerida's quick thinking about the splint will make the difference. On the other hand, it is obvious that Donal is quick of mind and that he will need to be properly educated. It is in the best interests of Darkover that our sons and daughters are educated. Ariel will resist, but we must not let her tie her sons with apron strings. It is neither healthy nor wise." *The Towers have served us well, but they are no longer enough. We must change with the times or perish.*

"Best interests?" Gabriel snarled at his uncle. "I like that! Half the young men are mad to go out to the stars, and some of the women, too," he added darkly. "The old ways are good enough for my father, and they are good enough for me, and for Donal as well. He is too young to know what he is talking about. He would be bored to death in a tenday."

"I would not," the child protested.

"You don't know what is good for you," Gabriel insisted, his skin darkening and his eyes narrowing. He looked to his mother for support, but Javanne appeared lost in her own thoughts.

"Gabriel," Margaret said sharply, "you seem to think that you know what is good for everyone—and you don't!"

As they glared at each other, Jeff tried to be reasonable. "We cannot change Darkover in a day, or even a generation, but if our children are not educated, they will not be able to make sound decisions about the future of our world." He sighed softly. "I have long wished we had some plan, some program, to teach the young more than can be learned in the Towers or among the *cristoforos.*"

Margaret looked at the older man, and realized that

he was speaking both to himself and to her. He, like herself, was a man of several worlds, and he loved Darkover as she was coming to love it. They both knew that without education Darkover was very vulnerable to forces like the Expansionist Party, which saw planets other than Terra as collections of resources to be exploited, not as the homes of human beings with their own aims and ambitions. She knew enough about the Expansionists from her occasional forays into the newsfaxes to understand the threat they posed, not just to Darkover, but to some of the planets she had visited— Relegan and Mantenon just to name two.

So, my Marja, would you like to remain here and create schools? I "heard" you as I rode toward Armida, wishing to run away, to be anywhere but Darkover, and I did not blame you in the least. But now your mind seems to have changed a bit.

I don't know. Between Istvana Ridenow, Liriel, and Uncle Jeff trying to drag me off to a Tower, Javanne trying to force me to marry one of her dreadful sons, threshold sickness, and Ivor's death, I have barely had time to think. She felt Mikhail flinch mentally at her thoughts. *Don't be an idiot, Mik. I didn't mean you! And you know it perfectly well, too!*

Thank you, cousin. I was beginning to fear that Gabe's bad behavior had rubbed off on me.

Don't be silly! You are quite sensible, for a Lanart.

Damned with faint praise. It is all that I can expect. His tone was mocking in her mind. Beneath the casual pleasantry, though, there was an undertone of feeling that was both attractive and frightening. What would she do if Javanne succeeded in getting Mikhail sent off planet? It did not bear thinking of.

The Senator was following this byplay with an interest Margaret found disquieting, and she felt her cheeks redden. He studied Mikhail curiously and lifted one eyebrow at the younger man. Then he looked at his daughter, and his eyes widened slightly.

Father, don't you go getting marriage-minded on me, dammit! I have had enough of that to last two lifetimes. Do you know that young Dyan Ardais came into my bedroom to plead a suit! Rafaella was horrified. She felt almost trapped, and her breath came in short pants.

Who? Lew's voice was curious, and her panic started to subside.

Rafaella n'ha Liriel, my guide and my good friend. She's upstairs with a terrible cold.

A Renunciate? You have been busy, haven't you, child? Having more adventures than I realized. I am not in the least marriage-minded, having been somewhat unfortunate with women in my early years. Still, anyone can see you are clearly on excellent terms with your cousin, which rather surprises me, since you are not fond of your Aunt Javanne. He gave a slight shrug. *I barely know you, do I?*

No, but it doesn't matter now. Just don't hand me off to the first fellow who approaches you for my hand, because I am quite fussy. I don't want to spend the next thirty or forty years slamming the doors of Armida off their hinges like Aunt Javanne and Uncle Gabriel.

Lew Alton smiled at his daughter, a face-splitting grin that took a decade off his age. Margaret stared at him, because she could not remember him ever smiling so broadly before, or at all. *We must, of course, consider the doors of Armida.*

Margaret dropped her jaw. Her father was teasing her! He was sitting there and making jokes as if he had never been a depressed drinker with a terrible temper. She was caught between the urge to hug him and another, equally strong, to smack him right across the face. *Could I start some sort of school on Darkover, do you think? I have been thinking of that, from time to time, when I wasn't busy battling dead Keepers or throwing up.*

What? Lew seemed stunned.

I'll tell you everything later.

I certainly hope so, because I am now very curious. But, I believe you can do anything you choose to, daughter. I never could stop you, once you made up your mind, you know.

You couldn't? No, I didn't know that.

Donal was bored with the sudden cessation of talk around the table, and the absence of dessert. "Would you teach me how to read, Marguerida? I would ask Liriel, but she has to go back to her Tower soon."

"I don't know, Donal. I have never tried to teach anyone to read before. It is not as easy as you think."

"Uncle Jeff said I was smart, so it should be real

easy." Donal gave her another winning smile, and she thought the boy was going to be altogether too charming when he grew up.

Before she could reply, Javanne spoke. "I think we have had enough of this nonsense for one night. Gabriel is right—Donal is much too young to know what he wants. He just thinks reading is exciting because Domenic can do it, and he has no idea what he is talking about."

Jeff shook his head. "Javanne, closing the door after the horse has run away is futile. We on Darkover must choose our destiny, and perhaps sooner than you imagine, and we will need all the young Donals to be as well-informed as they can be, lest we be eaten up by Expansionist politics or something worse."

Javanne Hastur seethed, but for once she held her tongue. She contented herself with glaring at Jeff and Lew and Margaret. After a moment, her face cleared, and Margaret was certain she was plotting at something again. Her dislike of her aunt increased, and she had to force herself to think of something else, just to keep her mind from boiling over with rage.

The dessert was finally brought in, a thick red pudding in clear glass bowls, and a tense silence settled around the table. Margaret hated this energy simmering just below the boiling point, for she could sense Javanne's feelings, and Gabriel's as well, though not their thoughts. They were angry and, she decided, dangerous. The sweet pudding tasted like acid in her mouth, and she pushed the bowl away unfinished.

Margaret leaned back and reflected that the two sides of Darkover were arrayed around the table. Javanne, her eldest son, and her absent husband stood for the past, but she was not sure that she represented the future. She felt trapped again by forces she could not control. The chill, the desire to withdraw from all human contact, grew in her, and she could almost feel the remnants of Ashara setting claws into her mind. Despair began to grip her throat, and she fought back the tears that rose in her eyes.

She glanced at her father and saw that he was very tired. Margaret knew it was not just from the long ride from Thendara, but from the years of his exile. She had never thought of her father as brave, had never seen him as anything but her troubled Old Man, but now she realized that he was many things she had never imagined he could be.

But the effects of a very long and tiring day made themselves felt in her body. Margaret found she could barely keep her eyes open, and that her legs ached from the wild ride. She shivered, not with cold, but with fatigue, and decided she could not stand another minute with her family. Without a word, she stood up and left the dining room.

Halfway up the long stairs, Margaret realized she was not alone. She turned, expecting to see her father, or perhaps Mikhail, and found to her surprise that Donal was trailing behind her. He looked very serious and determined.

"What is it, Donal?"

"Grandmother told me to go to bed."

"Well, come along, then. Does your nurse know you came downstairs?"

"Naw. She fell asleep in her chair right away. She's not very clever." He tucked one rather grimy hand into Margaret's and grinned again.

"You know, I always thought my nurses were not very clever as well."

"Did you?" His grin faded. "I don't care what Grandmother says, or Gabe, because everyone knows how silly he is, but I am going to learn to read and write and do everything."

"That's a fine ambition, Donal, but not tonight. You have had a very long day, and so have I."

"Will I get tired fast when I am old, like you?"

"I don't know," she answered dully. No one had ever called her old before, but just then, she felt it. Between getting soaked in the storm and the return of her father, she had had enough excitement to last for years. She took the little boy to the door of the nursery, then turned toward her own room, her feet all but dragging along the floorboards.

22

◆

Margaret got dressed for bed, glad that Rafaella was sound asleep, because she did not want to answer any questions. She climbed under the covers, then tucked her knees up and watched the fire flickering in the hearth. The movement of the flames was mildly hypnotic, and she found herself slipping into a light trance and shook herself out of it.

In spite of her exhaustion, she was too keyed up to go to sleep immediately. Margaret thought about her father's arrival, and how she had not been surprised, and smiled a little. What had Aunt Javanne called him? Storm-crow? She wondered about Diotima, and how ill she was. She longed to see her! It was a rather new feeling, for she had not wanted anyone except Ivor Davidson for so many years, she had nearly forgotten how it felt. Now, she wanted to see Dio, but she also found that she wanted to see more of Mikhail, and wished he were some other man, some more ordinary man, who could be her friend without provoking his parents.

But most of all, she thought about Lew Alton, the one who had sat through the difficult dinner, managing to keep the kettle at a simmer without letting it boil over more than once or twice. All the boiling had been on Javanne's side, not on his. She had never respected her father as a diplomat before, but now she realized that he had skills she barely even imagined. Tomorrow, she decided, she would get him alone and have a very long talk. And she would not let him get away until her questions were answered! Satisfied with this plan, she leaned back into the pillows and slipped away into slumber.

Moonlight half-woke her, and for a moment she did not know where she was. She had been dreaming about her rooms on University, and she had been looking for something. Then she heard a noise in the hall, and thought it was one of the servants, and began to close her eyes.

A fluttering scream brought her upright, muzzy with dreaminess, and she saw a white figure rising at the foot of the bed. It wavered and wobbled in the moonlight, and the terrible noise was repeated. In the thin light of the moon the specter was insubstantial and threatening at the same time. Her heart thudded in her chest, and she wondered vaguely if Armida had any ghosts.

Then Margaret heard a little giggle, and realized that there was no ghost at the foot of her bed, but only one of the Alar children trying to scare her. She was angry now, furious at being awakened and frightened. "Get out! Get out of here now!" Her voice vibrated in her tense throat and she knew she had done more than speak with force. It was an echo of that voice which had threatened Istvana with death at Ardais, and she shuddered.

The small form turned at her words and went back to the door. It moved slowly, clumsily, an almost machine-like movement, and she felt a flutter of alarm along her overtaxed nerves.

"She didn't scream," said a voice outside the room, which she recognized as young Damon Alar's. He sounded very disappointed. "I knew you couldn't scare Cousin Marguerida!" A thumping sound followed. "Ouch! Why did you knock me down, Donal?" She heard footfalls in the hall, moving away from her room. "Hi, you silly donkey, where are you going? Come back here!"

The words increased her sense of wrongness, and Margaret pushed the covers aside and went into the hall. It was dim with only the light of a couple of small lamps on the walls, and for a moment she did not see anything to worry about.

Then Damon, in his nightclothes, stood up from a deep shadow, rubbing one arm. He gaped at her, then looked toward the stairs. "What did you say to him, cousin? He pushed me down—I never knew Donal was so strong—and ran out of here as if all the devils were chasing him." The sound of the big door at the front of the house shutting echoed in the stillness.

"I told him to get out," Margaret answered, confused. "He startled me out of sleep, and I snapped at him." She bent down and picked up a discarded sheet. "Playing ghosts! Aren't you a little old for that kind of thing, Damon? It wasn't funny."

"It would have been, if you had screamed, like you were supposed to." Damon squirmed uncomfortably as he spoke. "But why has he gone outside? He was weird—like he didn't know me."

From the near end of the hall behind them, there was the sound of steps. Margaret and Damon turned at the sound, and Jeff, in a dressing gown, came out of the shadows. "What's going on? Can't an old man get a good night's sleep?"

"I'm very sorry, Uncle Jeff," Margaret said. "'Donal decided it would be fun to play spook in my room, and I told him to get out. He did, but he went outside. I don't know why."

"Out? You mean, out of the house!"

"Yes."

"What did you do—use command voice on the boy?" Jeff did not sound very alarmed, which eased Margaret's fears a little.

"The what?"

"The command voice." Jeff looked at her, took in her confusion, and shook his head. "It is part of the Alton Gift, Marguerida. It puts a compulsion on the listener to do as they are told."

She felt appalled. "You mean that I can make people do things they don't want to, just by commanding them? That's obscene!" She could hear, in her mind, the voice of Ashara Alton, telling her not to let anyone close and to forget, and she wanted to scream. "I just said 'Get out of here.' How could that be a compulsion?"

"*Chiya,* you have the full Alton Gift, and you don't know how not to use it. I don't blame you, since you were startled out of sleep. It was very naughty of you and your brother, Damon. You both knew better than to startle people. I'd better go after the boy before he walks into the lake or something worse." Jeff started for the stairs and paused. "Now do you see why you must come to Arilinn and get some training? What if you had told him to drop dead?" *I know she can't help it, but if anything happens to Donal, Ariel will come unhinged. It isn't her fault, but damn Lew for not sending the girl home years ago! I'm not even sure that Tower training will help now.*

Margaret was dismayed, then furious. She had never asked for the Alton Gift, and at that moment she would gladly have traded it for a sweet cake if she could have. The anger boiled in her chest. No one, not Istvana nor Liriel nor Jeff had ever said a word about voices. That was inexcusable! It was all very well for them to say they had asked her to go to a Tower, but they had failed miserably to tell her things she needed to know. Like her father!

All her ancient furies, her old hurts, rose up within her throat. She had the ability to force her will on anyone, to hear their thoughts or command them to jump in the lake, and all anyone could think of was a way to make sure her capacities were not lost to the family. Darkover needed more than schools and literacy, she decided. The whole planet needed to get some common sense! Genetic engineers could produce teeth that never rotted, and arteries that never clogged, but she doubted anyone had ever discovered a way to breed for good common sense.

Margaret followed Jeff down the stairs, her bare feet cold on the treads. Just as the old man reached the door, it opened. The moonlight shone on the figure of a man holding something across its arms. It was so like Ariel holding the injured body of Domenic that Margaret almost screamed. Then the burden wiggled, and she felt relieved that Donal was all right.

Lew Alton shifted the child clumsily. "I saw the boy outside, and when I reached him, he did not seem to know me. When I touched his shoulder, he went limp, and I realized he was entranced. I've never seen a child so deep in trance." He sounded puzzled and tired.

"Marguerida used the command voice on him when he startled her from sleep, Lew," Jeff answered.

"What did you say, Marja?"

"I told him to get out. That's all." How could those few words have had such an effect? She shifted from foot to foot as the chill of the night swept in through the open door.

"Hell! Close the door, Jeff, before we all take a chill. I think you sent him out of his body, daughter."

"Out of his body?"

"Into the overworld." Lew spoke very quietly, and Margaret felt her heart go chill.

The overworld! It was remarkable how a single word had the power to turn her knees to jelly and make the little remaining heat in her body vanish. She liked Donal, and the idea of the bright little boy all alone in that terrible place was almost more than she could bear. She knew the overworld frightened her, but until that moment she had not known the extent of her fear. Istvana had tried to explain that the realm of the overworld was not terrible, just a different place, but Margaret had not really believed her. She never wanted to return to it, and it was one reason that entering a Tower made her squirm. Istvana had told her that it was a normal part of the work of those in the Towers, to move about the overworld from time to time.

"Let's get Donal someplace warm. It is not cold, for the time of year, but he could take a chill, and then we would really be in the soup," Jeff said sensibly. He sounded calm, but Margaret could tell he was worried, and she shivered all over. "Damon, you go back to bed right now."

"But my brother . . ."

"Donal will be taken care of. You cannot help, and you will be very much in the way. Now, off with you!"

Damon looked at the faces of the adults and started up the stairs reluctantly. Margaret wished she could follow him, could retreat to her room and listen to Rafaella's comforting snores. But this was her mess, and she had to clean it up. It seemed a fitting climax to what, she decided, was the worst day of her life.

Nonsense! Lew's voice was brisk in her mind. *You don't know what* worst *is,* chiya.

Stop trying to cheer me up!

All right. Now, let's get this limb of Zandru into the living room before he gets deathly ill. And don't think it is only your fault, Marja. I spent much of my life thinking that I was the author of the ills of the world, and all that got me was some extremely bad hangovers, and a lot of self-pity. Dio tried to tell me not to be so hard on myself, but I never listened. And I don't suppose you will either.

The tartness of her father's thoughts was bracing. Margaret could sense his tension, his own feeling of responsibility for things over which he had no control. There was sorrow, too, in him, and much of it was about her and how he had distanced himself from her when she was younger. She felt even more ashamed for thinking about herself, for feeling sorry for herself at all. She wasn't important. Donal was important, and Dio, and her father.

Do stop being a complete ninny, Marja! This is no time to take a vow of selflessness! Liriel's wry thought startled her, and she turned and watched the technician descending the stairs. The woman wore only a nightgown of pale linen, but there was nothing self-conscious about her cousin. Instead, she looked moderately annoyed at being awakened after a long and demanding day, and also ready to deal with anything. What a woman! She liked and respected Istvana, but Liriel was steady in a way that the Keeper of Neskaya never seemed. Margaret guessed Jeff must have called her without waking the rest of the house, and decided that telepathy had a few advantages she had not thought of. She still didn't like it, but she could see now that it was extremely useful.

Just as Liriel reached the bottom of the long staircase, Mikhail appeared at the top of it. His light-colored hair was tousled, and he blinked down at them, then began to come down the stairs. "I heard voices. What's the matter?"

Margaret felt herself relax at the sight of her cousin Mikhail. Once again she felt very glad to see him, and less uncertain of herself. It was almost as if his presence gave her a confidence she lacked otherwise, and while she knew this was unlikely, she still enjoyed the feeling. And, she admitted to herself, she was more than just glad to have Mikhail present.

At the same time, her pleasure in the presence of Mikhail made her uneasy. The years of Ashara's mental dominance had taken a toll she was only beginning to understand. It was almost a reflex to keep herself apart from other people, and she found she had to struggle to overcome it.

Jeff explained what had happened while Liriel came and took Donal's limp body from Lew. They moved into the great living room, and put the child on the couch closest to the fireplace. Liriel wrapped the boy in a throw that hung on the back of the couch, and settled him into a comfortable position. Lew stirred the fading embers of the fire into life, Jeff added wood to it, and Mikhail lit the lampions. They were efficient and calm, as if this was an ordinary occurrence, not something terrible or frightening.

She knew that their outward appearance hid deep concern. She had sent Donal into the overworld with a few ill-chosen words, never suspecting she could do such a thing, and it was not a trivial matter. How would they get him back? Margaret wondered what she could do. She was still half tempted to withdraw, since she lacked the training to be of any help.

"No, Marja. You sent Donal out of his body, and you must be the one to call him back," her father said. *Poor child. If I had sent her here instead of letting her go off to University, all of this might have been avoided. Or if I had brought her home . . . ah, well. It is too late for that now. We just have to do the best we can.*

"I have to call him back? How?"

"We have to get to the overworld, find Donal, and bring him home," Liriel answered, as if she were suggesting a picnic by the lake. "I understand your reluctance, Marguerida. But the Tower of Mirrors is gone, and there is now nothing in the overworld to fear. It is a good thing you have a personal relationship with the boy—that will make it simpler."

"Easy for you to say, Liriel."

"Uncle Lew, can you still work as a technician?"

"I am pretty rusty, but I think I can manage." His scarred face softened. "I have not forgotten my years at Arilinn—it was a happy time for me."

"Good. I will monitor, then, and you and Jeff can make sure Marguerida does not blunder."

"Don't leave me out, sister," Mikhail said quietly. "I have not had your extensive training, but I did my time at Arilinn, and I am able."

"I know you are, Mik, but . . ."

"I know it isn't quite proper for me, outside a Tower,

but I think Marguerida and I are good enough friends that I can be useful." *She can depend on me, and she already does, though I don't know if she knows it yet. It's a damn shame I am the wrong son, but nothing can be done about that. We are friends, and whatever happens, we will always have that much. I just wish it could be more.*

Friends? Margaret felt a kind of relief at his words and his thoughts. Some of her fear began to dissipate. But the chill within her, the fear of intimacy, still plagued her. It was one thing for them to exchange a few verbal ripostes, to tease one another, and to make pungent comments about other people. That was something they could have done without telepathy, given a little privacy. It was quite another to enter into the sort of closeness she had experienced with Istvana Ridenow during her first foray into the overworld. Although she knew that the Keeper had been very discreet, Margaret was aware that there was almost nothing about her that Istvana did not know, after the battle with Ashara.

The idea of her father or Jeff getting inside her head in so intimate a manner was difficult enough to contemplate. The idea of Mik being there as well was different. It was simultaneously desirable and threatening. She did not want him to know how she felt, how she trusted him and loved the sound of his voice, the way his curls fell on his brow, and how his mouth curved when he smiled. She especially didn't want him to know how her body warmed when he was near.

After her session with Liriel, she knew she could depend on her completely. Had it only been that morning? Jeff, she decided, was also trustworthy, but she did not know him, and her father was almost a stranger to her. How peculiar. She had known Lew Alton all her life, but she did not really have any idea of his character. She felt more certain of Mikhail, whom she had known less than a month, than she did of anyone in the room except Liriel. Mikhail's presence would be reassuring, steadying, she decided, struggling with her conflicting emotions.

Margaret realized that everyone was looking at her, waiting for her to say something, and respectfully not hearing her jumbled thoughts. She could sense the ambivalence in the room, as if it were a palpable thing. "I think it would help if Mikhail . . . I have very little idea how a circle works. Istvana tried to explain it to me, but I was so determined not to go with her to Neskaya that I . . . just didn't listen! Still, it seems like more people would be better than fewer." *So long as the more does not include Aunt Javanne,* she thought.

Margaret felt her father's mental laughter. *Believe me, Marja, we all wish to keep Javanne from joining us. She is quite capable, but she does not like you, and that would present a problem.*

I know. I tried to be good, but she just made me cross all the time.

Javanne could make a cristoforo *cross, chiya. In fact, I would not be surprised if she already has. I think you remind her of me, and we never got on well.*

No, I think you do my mother an injustice, Uncle Lew, Mikhail replied. *Despite her strong sense of family loyalty, and her wish to welcome Marguerida as a daughter, she cannot bring herself to warm to my cousin. It has nothing to do with you, Lew, and everything to do with another strong-minded woman under the same roof.*

Enough chitter-chatter! Let's get on with this, Liriel announced.

"What should I do?" Margaret asked. "The other time I went into the overworld, Istvana gave me *kirian.* I'd rather not use that again. It made me feel extremely strange."

"You hadn't realized your Gift then, Marguerida," Liriel replied calmly. "From what I monitored of you earlier today, I think you can throw yourself into trance easily enough. The major problem is your fear."

Margaret gave an uneasy laugh. "That has always been the problem." She looked at Lew, and saw that he looked serious and distressed. "Some of that incense you make would help—it settled me right down this morning."

"I must have left my wits on the pillow," Liriel said. She left the room in a flutter of her voluminous gown, and Margaret shivered. Her bare feet were icy. She looked at Donal, stretched out on the couch, and bent toward him. She took one of his hands in her own, and realized he was cold, too. She wanted to pick him up and hold him against her, to warm his flesh with her own.

He seemed so small, there on the couch, and she felt quite helpless. If only she had not had that dreadful vision, and Domenic had not been injured so badly. Why hadn't someone bothered to tell her she might be able to compel people to do things with the force of her voice alone! She was a trained singer, so it was logical that her voice would be powerful, wasn't it? Everyone kept telling her she was dangerous, but no one seemed willing to tell her what she needed to know about her newly-arrived talents. They just patted her on the head and told her she could learn what she needed to know in a Tower! Jeff, she realized, had wanted to talk to her alone, but there had not been time.

What if she could not call him back? She knew she would never forgive herself, if this was the outcome of her ignorance. But she was not entirely to blame, was she? She glared at Jeff and her father, waiting for Liriel's return and warming their backsides in front of the fire. She liked Donal more than she had realized. She liked his cockiness and his intelligence. He was so self-assured for one so young. Margaret wondered if she had ever been that self-confident, and doubted that she had.

Lew returned her gaze with a solemn expression. She blushed furiously, and wished she had not looked at him so hard. Without being aware of it, Margaret tried to become invisible, as she had when she was a child. She might have managed it, but for the presence of her father and Mikhail. The younger man stood a few feet away, but she felt as if he were right beside her, so close she could smell him, and it was a very disturbing sensation. Her skin seemed too small for her body, and she felt close to bursting with tension.

What a royal mess she had made of things. The Lanarts had made her as welcome at Armida as they were able, but she had insisted on being headstrong. If only she could have liked Gabriel or Rafael better, or if the family were not so dead set on her marrying one of them. Now, if Mikhail had been her suitor, it might have been different.

Margaret was so surprised at this turn of thought that she nearly choked. She was certain the Lanarts would be glad now that she had not chosen to marry one of their sons. Javanne would be delighted to see the last of her. Having Aunt Javanne for a mother-in-law would be awful, anyhow.

If you had chosen either of my brothers, cousin, I think she would have softened. But she is not used to not getting her own way.

I still don't understand why . . . .

Why I am not one of your ardent suitors? Believe me, I would be, in an instant, if I could. We laugh together, and that is a fine thing.

So, what is holding you back? Surely you are not afraid of your parents!

Consider. My mother is sister to Regis Hastur, and if she set her face against a match, I think she would prevail. And my father and brothers would likely not forgive me. They have been envious of me ever since Regis made me his heir. I have grown up knowing that my father did not like me, and that my brothers felt that I had somehow stolen something which was rightfully theirs. Well, Rafael doesn't as much, but Gabe . . .

I know. He is the sort of fellow who always feels he doesn't have enough, no matter what he has.

That is a fair estimate. And now that your father has returned, it makes it even more difficult. By right, Armida is his, which puts my father back to being the sort of poor relation he was before Lew left Darkover. You cannot imagine how he has envied your father all his life.

But my father wouldn't throw them out! He's not like that at all. Margaret glanced at her father, but he was now deep in quiet conversation with Jeff and did not appear to be paying any attention. She wasn't sure that Lew wouldn't dispossess *Dom* Gabriel and Lady Javanne, now she thought about it. She did not know him, and he might do anything.

I think you are right, Marguerida, but my parents are suspicious of your father. When my mother calls him a storm-crow, she is not entirely wrong.

I still don't see why it would be right for me to marry your brothers, but not you.

I thought you did not wish to wed.

I might decide to change my mind. I am a woman, after all, and women . . .

I know you are a woman, Marguerida. That fact has hardly been out of my mind since I first saw you, and knew that I was the one man on Darkover who could not have you. My father wants Armida for Gabe, and my mother has always favored him over the rest of her children.

That's ridiculous! Gabe is like your father, and she doesn't like him one bit. She hesitated as Liriel came back with a small bag in one hand. *I don't suppose you could bring yourself to run away with me, could you?* She felt her cheeks warm at her forwardness, but she was not sorry for it. It was the first time in her life that she had felt bold before any male, and she savored the emotion.

What a shocking idea! I would do it in a flash, but for the consequences. He did not sound in the least shocked, but rather pleased at her suggestion. Indeed, he seemed to be laughing gently. Margaret felt warm in spite of her cold feet and her fear of what awaited her.

Lew and Jeff stopped talking, and Liriel told everyone to sit down. Then she cast her herbs into the fireplace. The heavy, sweet smell billowed out into the room, and Margaret began to feel less frightened. She was also less tired, as if the stuff had energized her. She closed her eyes and heard the sound of rustling fabrics. Without opening her eyes she knew that blue crystals were being unwrapped, and she felt the little group begin to grow close.

It was a curious sensation, warm and intimate, like arms welcoming. As it increased, Margaret knew she had always wished for such closeness, that its absence in her life had been an emptiness within her. She felt her father, strong as some ancient oak, a power she had never suspected him of possessing. There was more than strength in him. How could she not have known what a passionate, caring man he was? She had never known him! Why had they had been estranged for so long? Sorrow and loss seemed to overwhelm her, and she nearly cried out.

I know, my Marja, I know. But I am here, now, and we must find a way to make up for the past.

The smell of the incense softened her emotions. Reluctantly, she removed the rather ruined glove from her hand. The dampness had not done it any good, and the leather had dried stiff and hard. The almost invisible tracery of blue lines on her left palm began to feel warm, then hot beneath her skin. It was not a pleasant sensation, but it was not painful. What had Liriel called it? A shadow matrix. As Margaret thought these words, the pattern of lines on her hand seemed to hover in her mind's eye in a misty way. She tried to concentrate on it, and the lines grew more solid, thicker and stronger.

Within the facets of the pattern, she "saw" her father and Mikhail and old Jeff; not their faces, but something energetic, like light without any source. Lew's energy was strong, but somehow damaged, and Jeff's was so clear it almost hurt her inner eye. But it was the light of Mikhail which held her attention most.

It seemed to Margaret as she watched that her cousin's energy was strong, as strong as either of the other men, but it was clouded by such doubt and disappointment and a kind of loneliness that she could have wept. The fumes of Liriel's herbs had calmed her so no tears came, but the desire to cry made her throat feel closed and choked. She wanted to touch the light of Mikhail and make it clear, but she knew she could not. She had to let it be, even as she yearned to heal his hurts.

Outside the pattern shimmering in her mind, Margaret was aware of Liriel, guarding the silent little group. Her light was soft, like the moon she was named for, but so clear and focused that she felt even calmer than before. She relaxed into Liriel's secure grip, and let her awareness of her body fade. For a moment, nothing happened, and then she felt herself moving upward . . . upward . . . toward the plain of the overworld. One instant she was on a couch, and the next she hovered over the vastness beyond.

The overworld spread out in all directions, and Margaret could see the gleaming Towers of Darkover reflected in the light of that other place. Here and there dreamers moved, picking their way toward unknown goals. It was so huge an expanse that she wondered how she would find anyone, let alone a small child exiled from his body.

Where would Donal have gone? What did "out" mean to him? Margaret scanned the astral Towers, seeking the little boy, but she could find no trace of him. She looked at the dreaming wanderers, but even untrained she knew they were not what she sought.

Despair began to gnaw at her, despair and guilt. If she had gone to a Tower, as Istvana had wished, none of this would have happened. If, if . . .

Calm down, Marja. You are doing fine.

Lew's voice startled her slightly, because she had forgotten that she was not alone. It was a terrifying feeling. Margaret had been alone so long that the sensation of closeness was alien and threatening. Not just close, but close to her father for the first time. It was the end of an exile she had not known she bore, and it nearly overset her precarious emotional balance.

I know, child. But look now where you have been before.

What?

This is not your first visit to the overworld. Look where you have been before.

But I destroyed the Tower of Mirrors.

In the overworld, nothing is ever entirely destroyed.

The fear she had held at bay rushed in at the idea that some remnant of the dreadful place where, in one sense, she had been captive for so many years might still exist. The last thing Margaret wanted was another encounter with the shade of Ashara Alton. She froze, and the overworld seemed to still.

Then she felt something touch her fears, something calm and strong, and she knew it was not her father, but Mikhail. It was like the brush of a kiss upon her brow, and while there was nothing erotic in the touch, there was such passion in it that she felt her heart leap in her breast. And now, as she felt the energy of her cousin move around her, she was certain it was he who had come with her that other time, and urged her to pull the keystone from the Tower of Mirrors. Margaret knew that she would always remember that moment, that it was the most precious intimacy she had ever experienced.

She felt joy race along her blood, and the pounding of her heart seemed too loud, too fast. Then she felt Liriel slow it again, and she was grateful to her cousin. To both her cousins. Mikhail had eased the burden of her terror, and Liriel had steadied the beat of her pulse.

Bracing herself, Margaret once more scanned the plain. She ignored the dreamers and the phantom Towers, and sought the one place she had no wish to go. At first it was a fruitless search, for the Plain seemed empty. There was not a scrap of mirror to be found. This eased her still present fears a little more.

Magpie—Maggie—over here!

Ivor's name for her, for no one but he had ever called her that, was shocking. Margaret turned toward the sound, but there was nothing to see. She drifted in the direction the voice had come from, and the overworld rushed by beneath her, becoming a blur.

Ivor! Margaret called with a voice that was not a voice, and air that was not air moved in her lungs. *Where are you?*

Well, I can't say I am entirely sure. I think I am in limbo, but the music here is very fine, so I do not mind.

Dammit, Ivor, this is no time for games.

I know. But I never gave myself time for games before, you see. Ah, you are getting closer now.

Why can't I see you?

That I don't know. I can't see myself so maybe that is the problem. I've been drifting around here for a little while, listening to the star song. I always knew there really was a Music of the Spheres, and now I have found it!

Ivor, if you can't see yourself, I can't find you. Margaret was not sure how she knew this, but she felt certain she was right. Worse, she wanted desperately to "see" her mentor once more. She had not said good-bye, and now she had a chance to do that. She nearly forgot about Donal and her purpose in being in the overworld, so eager was she to see Ivor again.

That's very sensible, Maggie. But Ida always says I can hardly see my hand before my face when I am in the music. My, this is quite difficult. I feel even more vague than I usually do. Ah, there's my hand now—odd. I seem to have gotten over the arthritis.

A single hand shone in the light of the overworld, and then a figure began to form around it. A little misty, Ivor Davidson shimmered. He was not the old man who had died and lay buried in the Terran cemetery in Thendara. A man in his thirties appeared, hair dark and back straight and strong. Margaret had never known him at that age, but she knew him now. He was smiling at her, and she smiled back. Somewhere, far distant, she sensed a prickle of some dark emotion, envy or something like it, but she shut her awareness of it away.

I never guessed you were so handsome, Ivor.

How do you think I captured a prize like Ida? Are you lost? Am I lost? I've tried to find my way back to Everard's, but I can't seem to get there. I like this dream, but there are things . . .

Ivor, I am looking for a small boy. Somehow she could not bring herself to tell her beloved mentor that he was dead, not dreaming. *He's six or seven, with dark hair, and he's wearing nightclothes.*

What do you want with a boy? It doesn't matter. You always were looking for something, all the years we spent together, I knew you were looking for something. But I never thought it was a boy.

Ivor, this is a lost child, and if I don't find him and take him home, he will die.

That's different. Have you found what you are seeking—that other thing? I hope so, because I always wanted you to be happy.

I'll be happy once I get Donal safely back in his bed.

Did I tell you I was glad to see you, Maggie? I am. You were a light in my life.

Oh, Ivor! I am glad to see you, too.

Now, now. Donal? Can he sing?

Not that I know of. Ivor's obsession with music was maddening. *He's just a little lost boy, Ivor, and I really need to find him.*

Try in that direction. The figure pointed. *There's some rubble over there, and I think I saw something moving. It is hard to be sure. Direction doesn't seem to make much sense around here.*

Ivor! For a moment words failed her, for she could not find the right ones to express her affection and gratitude to the man. Then something steadied her again, something firm and certain, and she knew it was Mikhail. *You were the finest friend I ever had, dear Ivor. You gave me so much!*

Had? Ah, now I see. That's why the arthritis is gone—I'm not in my body any longer. What a shame! I was so looking forward to writing a paper on the Music of the

Spheres. It is quite interesting, because this is not what I expected death to be. How is Ida?

Sad, of course. She misses you, and I miss you more than I can ever say. I'm so sorry! It was a child's wail.

Never be sorry, Margaret. It's a waste of time. Now, go find your Donal. They've begun another song, and I want to listen. You have no idea of the complexity, do you? A pity, because you could make a monkey out of old Verlaine, when you got back to University, if you could tell him about it. But no one would ever believe that the dead can hear the stars in their harmonies. I am very happy here, my Magpie-girl. The music is incredible.

Thank you, Ivor. Thank you for everything. Good-bye. Then he was gone, and she was alone once more. She felt the absence of her mentor like the cold blade of a knife in her heart, for just an instant. Then it was gone, and she knew that she would never see Ivor again except in memory. She felt her sorrow crumble as she realized that her mentor was having an afterlife that was as perfect as anything he could have wished for, that he was quite content, and only regretted that he would not be able to publish his findings. A true academic to the last. It was a comforting realization, and she felt someone watching her, amused and touched. Her father, or Jeff, she guessed, for it did not feel at all like Mikhail.

Bringing her attention back to the task at hand, Margaret moved in the direction he had indicated, and agreed that the overworld was confusing. After what could have been a moment or an hour she spotted what seemed to be some ancient stones, foundation stones, which looked as if they had been thrust apart by a giant hand. Her palm throbbed, and she knew the hand had been her own. It was not an easy feeling, and she tensed all over, in spite of the influence of Liriel or the incense.

When she reached the ruins, she knew it was the place she feared, but also the place she sought. Shards of glass rested between the stones, reflecting stars that did not shine overhead. Margaret kept her eyes from direct gaze, because she was sure that the scraps of mirror were dangerous. The remains of Ashara's astral Tower seemed empty, but the matrix lines on her hand pulsed beneath her phantom skin. She half expected the ghost of the small woman to rise from the rubble and speak to her.

Donal! Donal Alar—come here right now.

I'm scared. The answer was weak, and Margaret could not tell where it came from.

I am here, and you don't need to be afraid, Donal. She wished she had more experience talking to little boys, and that she was not quietly terrified herself.

Are you still mad at me?

No, Donal, I am not angry with you. I am worried about you. This is not a place for either of us. Come here.

I'm sorry I scared you, came the voice, and with it the vague figure of the boy. He seemed to materialize from a point in the glassy rubble, and he looked frightened.

It's all right. There was no real harm done, except that you ended up here instead of in your bed, where you belong.

I didn't know where to go.

Of course you didn't, Donal. Now take my hand. That's right. Margaret drew the little ghostly form against her breast and held him close with her unmarred hand. She sensed that touching him with the other one would be fatal. She could feel her heart pound, and the exhaustion coursed along her veins like some subtle poison. *How do I get out of here?* she wondered.

Margaret looked around the Plain and saw the Towers. For a moment there seemed to be nothing but these, and she felt lost and alone. Then, at last, she saw a kind of coalescence that was not a Tower, but just a clump of light. She knew it was her family in Armida, supporting her and waiting for her.

She drifted in the direction of that light, speeding and barely moving at the same moment, and then she had the sensation of being tugged by strong hands, firm hands and loving. She felt Jeff's resoluteness, and her father's power, but most of all what drew her and held her was her sense of Mikhail Lanart-Hastur. It lacked the strength of her father and the surety of Jeff but what it had in great measure was the love she had not even known she longed for, until she felt it.

23

The overworld was gone abruptly, without any transition, and Margaret found herself slumped on the couch next to Donal. Ringed around her were the concerned faces of her family; her father, grave and serious, Jeff, looking tired, Mikhail smiling and meeting her eyes quickly, and Liriel, her expression unreadable. *When he smiles,* she thought, *he does look like an angel after all.*

Margaret sat up slowly. Her face was wet with sweat, and her feet and hands were icicles. The cloth of her nightgown clung to her breasts with cold wetness, but she had no thoughts of modesty. Her mouth tasted foul and stale. She shivered and wished she had put on her robe before beginning, but it was too late to think of that now. Liriel vanished, and returned a moment later with a large woolen shawl that smelled of lavender, and she hugged it around her closely. It was a real comfort, like the people around her.

Then she looked down at her left hand, curious. The lines there were dark, but fading, as if they were retreating into her skin. Margaret hated the thing, that shadow matrix, even though it gave her something she had never had before. Reluctantly, she drew the disgusting glove back over her hand.

Donal sat up and looked at the adults, rubbing his eyes, and apparently none the worse for his adventure. "How did I get here? I'm hungry!"

This made everyone, including Margaret, laugh. "You are always hungry, it seems. Do you remember what happened?" She flexed her hand against the stiffened leather. *There must be something I can use that isn't so dreadful,* she thought.

"I 'member spooking you, an' that's all." He rubbed his eyes again. Then he leaned against Margaret's body trustingly and snuggled up against her. She looked down at his tousled locks and felt something she had never known before. He smelled clean and healthy, not as if a part of him had just been wandering that place. What a dear boy! Perhaps motherhood was not as bad as she had imagined.

When she looked up from Donal's head, she found Mikhail watching her indirectly, an unreadable expression on his weary face. All the energy she had seen in him seemed gone now, or banked away. She remembered how he had seemed to her when her eyes were closed, how fine and troubled. Then she wondered how she appeared to him, and to the others, not her disreputable physical self, but that other Margaret she hardly knew yet.

You were splendid, cousin! Mikhail's answering thought warmed her, even as she chided herself for vanity, for needing approval.

"I'm hungry! Can I have something to eat?" Donal's piping voice broke into her thoughts, and Margaret realized she, too, was ravenous. She wondered if she would ever have a private thought or feeling again. Margaret looked over at her father. He lifted his arms and stretched, and she could hear the pop of spinal bones. He seemed different, and it was not the same difference she had noticed during dinner. What had changed?

I now know you as I have never known you before. The answering thought was filled with calm affection, and a certainty she found delightful. It was an intense sensation, simultaneously intimate and deeply respectful. She liked the closeness she had felt in the circle of her family, but it was rather overwhelming at the same time. She was so accustomed to being alone and separate, so unused to being known and, more, accepted. *Will I ever be comfortable with this?*

"Among those of us with the Alton Gift, I am afraid," Jeff said slowly, answering her unspoken question, "what you regard as privacy is almost unknown. When I was first married to Elorie, I used to resent that terribly. Not that it did the least bit of good. Things are as they are. You get used to it, or you don't. You just learn to live with it. Period."

"Swell," Margaret commented, too tired to be polite.

Jeff chuckled. "Life is not fair, Marguerida, and it is never easy. Think how boring it would be if it were."

"I would settle for about ten years of being bored just now, really. I have had enough adventures since I came to Darkover to last me the rest of my life. I'd even learn to embroider if I could just be sure my life would not be exciting any more."

Liriel laughed at her. "Marguerida I never heard anyone long for dullness before."

"Right now, I would trade Armida and the Alton Gift for a good hot bath and the promise of constant tranquillity."

Lew looked at her, a half smile playing across his mouth. "The bath you can get for free, my Marja, but the other—I don't think so. I have a strong feeling your adventures have only begun."

"Humph! I will thank you to keep any Aldaran foretellings to yourself Father! They have caused enough trouble today already. Come on, Donal, let's go raid the kitchen before we faint from hunger."

As she rose and took the child out of the room, she was aware that Liriel, Jeff, and Lew were talking about her silently. She forced herself not to "hear" the discusion, because it would only have made her angry right then. She knew perfectly well that she had very little choice but to go to a Tower for training, whether she wanted to or not. She wondered if she would be a good technician, like Liriel or her father, and what it would be like to work intimately with a full circle. Margaret shied away from the idea, for while she could manage it with her kin, she was not sure she would ever be easy with the thoughts of strangers.

Then she chuckled at herself. A mere month before she had thought the whole idea of telepathy was ridiculous, and now she was trying to find a means to adjust to it.

Mikhail caught up with her as she and Donal entered the great kitchen. It was an immense room, with two fireplaces, a hive-shaped oven, and three long tables set across the middle of the space. Polished cooking vessels hung along the walls and were stacked on counters, and the whole place smelled of cleanness and the lingering odors of cooking.

"Did you mean it when you suggested we run away, cousin, or were you teasing me again?"

The question surprised her, but it was a pleasant surprise. Mikhail walked across the room and opened a cupboard on one wall. He pulled out a plate of meats left over from supper and put them on a table, then filled a pot with water and set it in the still hot fireplace. Donal sat down at the table and looked eager as he pulled a slice of meat off the plate and began to wolf it down.

"I wasn't teasing, Mik, but I was speaking in jest. I know it would create a lot of problems, and right now I don't know what I want to do with my life."

"Except learn to embroider and have a dull existence. How I envy you. You have been to other worlds, so now you can think of settling down."

Margaret was a little alarmed at the tone of his words. She was too tired to want to discuss the future, any future, except eating and getting back to sleep. Her eyes itched a little. She tried to focus on something that had no particular importance, that had no emotions attached to it. She did not want to think of how he had seemed to her in the overworld, and how she might have seemed to him. "Mikhail, if you had ever seen my sewing, you would know that I would never be able to learn to embroider well. Dio tried her best to show me, but I never could make a French knot, and my cross-stitches were never even." The maidenly arts of needlecraft were as safe a subject as she could think of, and she was grateful for that.

"I know what a cross-stitch is, for Liriel and Ariel did that when they were younger—Liriel insisted they were called "cross' because they made one crabby. But I never heard of a French knot. What is it?"

Margaret sat down beside Donal, and tried to recall the thing. It seemed he also wished to speak of something neutral. She glanced at him and she realized that Mikhail was not asking her this because it was safe, but because he was really curious. His blue eyes were alight with interest. What a splendid scholar he could have been, if he could have gone to University. And what a contrast he was to his father and brothers who seemed to have no interests beyond horse-raising and child-

making. It occurred to her that very few people she had
encountered on Darkover were interested in things they
did not already know, and she knew that Ariel and
Gabe's illiteracy was not about reading, but about a lack
of curiosity.

"You take the needle and bring it up, then wrap the
thread around it a couple times, and push the needle
back down very close to where you came up. Only I
always went back into the first hole, and my knots un-
wound. It is a maddening thing."

"Oh, that. We call that The Keeper's Stitch." Mikhail
put some leaves into a pot for tea. Then he put several
empty plates on the table, and brought out bread and
honey and thick cream. "Liriel hated it, too, but Ariel
loved it, and made thousands of those things." As he
spoke, Lew and Liriel came in, with Jeff behind them.

The expressions on their faces were solemn and
slightly conspiratorial. Margaret watched them as she cut
off a slice of bread and slathered it with honey. "So have
all of you decided what you think you will do with me?"
She let herself sound challenging because it was true.
She might go to a Tower, but it would be under her own
power, of her own choice. She needed to have that much
control left in her life! Lew and Liriel exchanged a
glance while Jeff looked fairly sheepish, as if he had
been caught with his hand in a cookie jar.

Lew rubbed the back of his neck with his one hand.
"No, we have not, but we have discussed the matter."

"Would some coffee keep you awake, Marguerida?"
Jeff asked before she could answer her father.

"Nothing would keep me awake, and some coffee
would be most welcome. So, Father, am I to marry
young Gabriel or go to a Tower and be locked up?"

Lew settled down next to her at the table. "Your pen-
chant for the dramatic has not lessened over the years."

"By all accounts, I come by it honestly! From the
stories I have heard since I came here, you were pretty
dramatic yourself, before you left Darkover." Istvana
had given her some account of the Sharra Rebellion,
and her father's part in it, very censored, she suspected,
but there were still enough details to make her think
Lew Alton must have cut quite a figure in his youth.

He sighed and looked all his years with weariness.

"And you still have the unsettling habit of speaking your mind, I see. No, we don't think that you should marry Gabriel—for the sake of the hinges of the doors, of course." Margaret giggled; her father went on. "Jeff make enough coffee for me, would you? I wish there was someplace on the planet where coffee could be cultivated. But we do think that it would be completely irresponsible not to take you to Arilinn for training, yes."

"Well, I agree, but I'm not sure about Arilinn."

"What?" She could not tell if Lew was surprised by her sudden capitulation or her reluctance regarding the Tower where he had trained.

"I agree I need to be trained. I never, never want to make anyone do something they don't want to again! The overworld scares me. Being a telepath scares me. I'd rather have really curly hair or a grander bosom, if I had any choice." This remark made everyone at the table laugh, except Donal who was too busy trying to consume all the meat on the plate in two bites.

"But why not Arilinn? It is the principal Tower of Darkover, and everyone goes there."

"So I have heard. But I just have this feeling that I should start at Neskaya with Istvana Ridenow." Margaret paused and frowned. She had not known her feelings until she spoke, but she knew that she was right. "Is that against the rules?"

Jeff turned from the counter where he was spooning ground coffee into a paper filter. "It is not against any rules, Marguerida, though it is slightly untraditional. Frankly, none of us even thought of it. Do you have some objection to training with me?"

"Absolutely not, Uncle Jeff." Margaret chewed her bread for a moment. "But I think it is that the Alton Gift is so forceful, so strong, that I believe that working with an empath would make it wiser." *And I have a kind of bond with Istvana now that I do not have with anyone else.*

A silence spread across the kitchen. Jeff took the boiling pot from the fire and poured it into his coffee pot. The sweet smell of it filled the air. Mikhail brought more food to the table, looked at Margaret, and gave her a wonderful, supportive smile. *Neskaya is not so far from*

Ardais that I could not see you when your duties permitted.

You could see me even if my duties didn't permit, you dolt!

How can I resist such tender thoughts?

What makes you think I want you to resist them?

This pleasing byplay went unremarked by everyone except Liriel. She looked from her brother to Margaret, knitted her brows in a frown, then shrugged. *That is how the wind blows between you, is it? We should have known, have guessed, of course. I confess I am rather pleased, and distressed, too, for our parents are not going to be at all willing to support such a match, Mik, and you know it.*

Yes, I do know it, but what can I do? It is not my fault that so much power rests, potentially, in my hands, and in Marguerida's.

You are being logical, Mik, the way you often are, and this is not a matter of logic one bit! Liriel managed to sound severe. *Our father has never let his logic guide him, and our mother—well, you know that she was set on keeping Armida in her hands. She is almost obsessed with the place, as if it were her ancestral estate and not her husband's.*

I can explain it, I think, Lew chimed in. *Javanne is ambitious, and she was ambitious as a young woman. She wanted to run things, even when we were children. But, there being very little opportunity for female rulership on Darkover, she was forced to make do with marrying into the most powerful family she could manage. Which she did. But she would trade Armida for Comyn Castle in a second, if the chance were offered. It is not good, as I have discovered during my time in the Federation, to keep one sex confined and let the other do as it pleases.*

You make her sound as if she wanted Regis' position, which is impossible! Liriel's mental voice had a snap in it.

In imagination, Liriel, anything is possible—anything!

The room was quiet now, and Jeff served out the coffee. Donal, gorged and sated, gave a profound belch without the least self-consciousness. He wiped his mouth with the back of his hand and stretched out on the bench. Then he pillowed his head against Margaret's thigh and fell into a deep sleep.

"Marguerida has something, you know." Liriel spoke quietly, as if she had set aside the disturbing thoughts of her mother and turned her mind to something she could grasp. "Istvana is the most innovative Keeper we have had in years—since Cleindori, really. I know you have tried to change things, Jeff, but you have been swimming against the current. How do you feel about it, Uncle Lew?"

"I feel as if I had been pulled through a knothole backward, if you want the truth. The ride from Thendara took more out of me than I imagined—it has been a long time since I spent much time on a horse. But how do I feel about Neskaya rather than Arilinn? I have been gone too long to be able to judge. And frankly, I have been so out of my mind with worry about Diotima that I don't trust my judgment any further than I can toss it. I would like to discuss this with Regis." He patted his daughter lightly on her shoulder. "But my Marja may be right, and a wiser Alton Gift sounds to me an excellent idea. I wonder why no one has thought of it sooner."

"Thank you." Margaret could not remember her father ever praising her before, and she wanted to cry with gladness. She stroked Donal's hair softly and felt more content than she had ever imagined she could.

"Marguerida can leave for Neskaya . . ." Liriel began.

"I am not going anywhere until I have seen Dio!" Now that she had decided her course of action, she wanted to put it off as long as possible.

"Of course you must see Diotima, *chiya*." Jeff nodded, as if he approved of her feelings. "While you are in our company, I think you will come to no harm. So, tomorrow—well, it is already tomorrow—but after we have rested, we will go to Thendara, then." Jeff sipped from his mug. "Something is bothering you, Lew, something that has nothing to do with Diotima's illness."

"True, but it will keep. I am so used to the urgency of the Senate, where the fate of worlds is decided in hours, that I forget how slowly time moves here at home." *Home! My exile is ended, and it is nothing like I imagined. My daughter is a woman grown, and she is*

*the future of Darkover. I am the past, yet I am home at
last. But I want to get back to Dio. And soon. I will have
Marja and Dio together for the first time in so long—
my family!*

When Margaret finally pried her eyes open, it was late
afternoon and she was very hungry. She rubbed her eyes
and reflected that she seemed to eat a great deal more
on Darkover than she ever had before, but it didn't seem
to show around her waist. She wondered where the food
was going, and decided it must be used up by *laran*.
Margaret looked for Rafaella, but she was nowhere to
be seen, so her cold must be better. She tried to sort
out her memories of the previous night, then gave it up
and headed for the bathroom.

When she had bathed and dressed, Margaret started
downstairs. She could hear voices, and they were angry.
As she climbed down the steps, she could hear her father
and Lady Javanne going at it hammer and tongs, with
old Jeff and Liriel attempting to play peacemakers.

"You promised you would never come back, Lew, and
you have broken your word. You can't just dance in
here after twenty years and expect to take up where you
left off!" Javanne sounded tired, as if she had been arguing for a long time.

"The last thing I would wish to do is take up where
I left off, Javanne. I remember more vividly than you
can imagine what events precipitated my departure."

"That is not what I meant, and you know it! Even
you are not so great a fool as to bring another rebellion
to Darkover. But you can't reclaim Armida. I won't have
it. We've taken care of it for all these years, and, frankly,
you don't deserve it."

"I don't remember asking to have Armida back," Lew
said in a voice which Margaret recognized as a dangerous one.

"Mother, I think you are being unreasonable."

"Be quiet, Liriel. I can't imagine why you are so disloyal, but it is no more than I expected. You were always willful!"

Margaret walked into the great living room, where
some hours before she had left her body and gone to
the overworld, and looked at the gathering. There were

more people in the room than she had expected, for
Gabe stood before the fire, glowering, and Piedro Alar
sat in one of the chairs, looking tired and miserable.
Then she saw Mikhail, half hidden in shadow at one end
of the room, and her heart quickened.

"Good afternoon," Margaret said. "I seem to have
slept the day away."

"Good afternoon, cousin," Mikhail answered, smiling
at her. "I trust you are well-rested."

Javanne glared at her and stiffened. She seemed uncertain what to do. "You do not appear any the worse
for your adventures in my house, Marguerida."

"Oh, a little rain doesn't bother me," she replied, giving her aunt a maddening smile.

Javanne's determined jaw squared above her conceal-
ing ruff. "I was not speaking of that, and you know it
perfectly well."

"Yes, I do. I know you do not like me, that you would
not have me for a daughter but to keep Armida, and
that you believe you know best for everyone. Well, you
don't. No one does."

There was a shocked silence at this bald statement,
and Margaret reddened slightly. There was no use in
pretending, she felt, that things were well and that Javanne would ever like her. She could sense Mikhail tens-
ing, and she was sorry she had upset him, but she would
not take her words back.

"I have nothing but kindness toward you, Marguerida.
But your very existence presents a problem—a problem
I believe can best be solved by your marriage to Gabriel
as quickly as possible. Then your father's claim to Armida can be disposed of."

"The years have not lessened your high-handedness,
Javanne," Lew said, laughing. *The terrible thing is that I
can even see her viewpoint—I am the interloper, just as
I was when I was a boy. And she never could see that
her way was not the only way. I'd feel sorry for her, if I
didn't want to wring her neck.*

"That would be a good solution for you, Aunt, but it
would never do for me, and it would not be kind to
Gabriel either. I would make a very poor wife for him,
and you know it. We would be ready to murder each
other inside a week."

"I am certain that if you tried, you would realize what a good man my son is."

"Mother, I can speak for myself!" Gabe frowned and shifted his weight from foot to foot. "And I think Marguerida is right. I don't think it would take as much as a week!"

Javanne looked ready to argue, but her eldest son gave her a shrug of his broad shoulders, and she held her tongue. "Then, I suppose, we should all leave for Thendara as quickly as possible. We will let the Cortes settle the matter, both of who owns Armida, and the problem of Marguerida's marriage." She looked suddenly smug, as if she knew something no one else did.

Piedro Alar stirred. He looked miserable and uncomfortable, and his eyes were dark with lack of sleep. "You great folk are very busy worrying about land and marriage, but what about my son?" There was a stubbornness in his weak jaw, as if he knew he was speaking out of turn, but was determined to have his say. "And my wife, whose mind is nearly overset."

Everyone except Gabe looked embarrassed, and Margaret bit her lower lip hard. She had almost forgotten about the injured little boy lying upstairs, and his mother as well.

"I monitored him before I came downstairs," Liriel said slowly. "He is resting—indeed, he seems to be sleeping well. But I think he must be removed to Arilinn as quickly as possible. I believe it will be safe to move him tomorrow." *I do not like the sound of his breathing at all.* "It will be best, I believe, if Mother and I take Domenic and Ariel to Arilinn."

"But . . ." Javanne protested, looking as if she had suddenly had an advantage snatched from her grasp.

"No one can manage Ariel as well as you do, Mother," Liriel interrupted. "And she will need your support, for you know how she becomes anxious at the least thing."

"At first light, then, tomorrow, we will return to Thendara," Jeff said calmly. "I want to see Diotima before I myself return to Arilinn, so I will accompany you. Will that suit you, Marguerida? Lew? And you, Mikhail?"

"What? Mikhail has no reason to go with you!" Ja-

vanne was outraged, but Gabe gave his youngest brother
a slight nod, as if he were relieved. "I won't have it!
Mikhail must go back to Ardais."

Margaret gave Mikhail a quick glance, because she
could not decide why Gabe's attitude had changed so
abruptly. He was not a man to give in to reason, she
believed. What had happened?

*I told Gabe about our little adventure with Donal, and
pointed out that unless he thought he could keep you
gagged, he would have to live in fear of the Voice for the
rest of his life. And, considering how the two of you ag-
gravate one another, it would be a brief one.* Mikhail's
voice in her mind had a tone of satisfaction, as if he had
paid off several old debts in a single moment.

But, Mikhail—I wouldn't! Well, I don't think I would.

*I know that, and you know that, but since my brother
cannot imagine having any advantage and not using it,
he took my suggestion very much to heart.*

Mik! Aren't you ashamed? Margaret could barely contain her laughter.

Not in the least. I did it for his own good!

"This is intolerable," Javanne began, "and I will
not . . ."

"Mother, stop making a fool of yourself," Liriel said
firmly. "I think events are well outside your control, and
the best thing you can do is accept that. This is more
than a matter of lands and marriages now. Much more."

Javanne stared at her daughter, her mouth gaping
slightly. She looked so angry and thwarted that Margaret
almost felt sorry for her. "I don't understand any of this!
I just don't know what Darkover is coming to." *I cannot
stand by and let this happen! Why did Ariel have to rush
off and get my grandson hurt? Was ever a woman more
tried than I? Oh, my! I must not lose my senses—I am
behaving very badly, as badly as Lew ever did. And he
knows it, curse him!*

"I believe that Darkover is coming into the future,
Javanne," Jeff said, "and I think it will be very exciting."

24

◆

It was the warmest day Margaret had seen since she had arrived on Darkover, as if the storm had blown away the cold and left a blessed heat behind it. While Jeff complained a little of the heat, she was enjoying it. And being out of the sour influence of her aunt helped immeasurably. Javanne had continued to present arguments all during a long dinner and into the evening, until everyone was heartily sick of it, even the usually loyal Gabe.

The sky was clear, a rosy bowl above their heads, and a little breeze moved around them, ruffling Margaret's unruly hair pleasantly. Rafaella rode beside Margaret, looking pleased to be on the road back to Thendara. Lew and Jeff rode ahead of them, talking quietly.

Although they had planned to set out all together, Liriel and Javanne had remained behind. Ariel had proved more resistent than anyone had imagined, and she had been torn about leaving her younger children in the charge of their nurse. It would be several hours before they left for Arilinn, and Margaret was not unhappy at this change of plans.

She was unhappy, however, that Mikhail was not part of the company. Javanne had been utterly adamant that he not go to Thendara, and had ordered him to return to Ardais immediately. She had looked as if she wished he had never been born, and Mikhail, his face red with rage, had ridden off from Armida even before she had left. He had said no farewell, just gotten on his big bay horse and thundered away, as if the devil were on his heels.

Instead of dwelling on his absence, Margaret concentrated on enjoying the warm day, and the quiet pleasure of once more being on the road with Rafaella. The Renunciate was still sniffling from time to time, and seemed disinclined to talk much, but she smiled at Margaret occasionally, sharing the good mood which was almost irresistible under the open sky.

"You will be glad to be back in Thendara, won't you?" Margaret asked.

"You know I will! I have been in a few tight places—with hill bandits and avalanches and the occasional banshee looking for a meal. But, Marguerida, I confess that I would take all of those combined rather than sit through another meal at Domna Javanne's table. I have never been so uncomfortable in all my life!"

She laughed. "That makes two of us. Even my father, who is a formidable opponent, was rather . . ."

The sound of rapid hoofbeats behind them made Margaret pause and turn around in her saddle. Mikhail, a little red-cheeked from riding, came into view, and slowed his horse to a trot. His eyes danced with mischief, and his hair was tousled from the slight breeze. She was surprised to see him, but not that surprised. He had a talent for turning up unexpectedly. He grinned at her, and she grinned back, as if they shared a secret delight—which, she decided, they did indeed. Margaret felt a little guilty in her pleasure, but not greatly.

Mikhail reined his horse in beside her, with Rafaella on her other side. "Greetings, cousin. How nice to see you again so soon. And to you, Mestra Rafaella. I trust your cold is improved."

"And greetings to you," she answered, enjoying the game immensely. "Somehow, I had the impression you were being an obedient son and were on your way back to Castle Ardais."

"One must never judge by appearances." He forced his merry face into an attitude of seriousness that fooled no one. "If I gave Mother the mistaken impression I was returning to Ardais as she directed me to, then she was deceived. I feel perfectly dreadful for deceiving her, as well I should." He did not look at all ashamed, but appeared to be enjoying himself enormously. He stroked his horse's neck and the broad grin came back.

Jeff and Lew had noticed the new arrival, and dropped back to greet him. "She should know by now that you always do what you wish," Jeff answered peace-

fully, as if Mikhail's appearance was no surprise to him
at all. "I would think, after all these years, that she
would stop trying to bring you to a sense of your duties
and just let you go your own way."

"What a sad reflection on my character, Uncle Jeff,
that I am undutiful and disobedient as well. Perhaps she
will disown me, and I will have to learn to live by my
wits or something." *There is always mushroom farming
to fall back on, I suppose!*

Margaret was nearly overset by this last. She was glad
that Mikhail had the strength to stand up to Javanne,
even though she suspected it was going to cause trouble
in the future. She knew it was not the first time he had
done so, and she suspected he had always been much
more independent than his family liked. She wondered
where it came from, that ability to quietly rebel, and
guessed it might be from his exposure to Terran ideas.
No wonder his father and mother disapproved of him so
much. How it must have chafed him to remain Dyan
Ardais' paxman, when he had been promised something
more, without, it seemed losing either his curiosity or
his sense of humor. She decided she approved of those
qualities in her cousin, and wished she had more of them
herself. Then she laughed at herself a little. Mikhail did
not need her approval.

*No, I don't, but I rather bask in the glow of it anyhow.
Snoop!*

No, you were broadcasting rather forcibly.

*Damn! I am starting to feel like a comsat, sending out
stuff whether I mean to or not.*

*For one who has had no training, Marguerida, you do
quite well in keeping your thoughts to yourself. I think a
few months in a Tower will show you how to control the
Gift. I'm rather rusty, as I discovered while we were looking for that brat of Ariel's, and I think I should go back
and study* laran *a bit.*

*Rusty? I could feel you while we were working, and
you seemed fine to me.*

Using laran *requires a lifetime's study, Marguerida.*

*Oh, I hope not. I don't want to spend my years locked
up in a Tower!*

What do you want?

This was the third time he had asked her that question, and Margaret mused over it once more. When she had been in her teens, she had only wanted to remove herself from the home where she felt unloved and unwanted. At the University she had tried journalism, thinking she wanted to be a writer of some sort, and discovered Ivor Davidson and music. She had chosen music, but she knew now she was never actually consumed by it, not with the passion that Ivor had felt for his work. It was just something she could do well, that she enjoyed doing, but only a job, not a calling.

Ashara's interference with her mind had prevented her from wanting either a husband or a family, had forced her to be alone whether she wished it or not. Now that restriction was gone, and it had left a vacuum in her, an empty space where the forceful personality of the long-dead Keeper had held her captive. There had been too much else going on for her to think about what she might like to do with her life. And it was still very difficult to let anyone close, much as she longed for intimacy.

With a mild start Margaret realized that the cause of some of her antipathy toward her Aunt Javanne stemmed from her feelings toward Ashara. They were not at all alike, really, but they both thought they could control her and command her for their own ends. She realized she had very little tolerance for being dominated ever again. By anyone, even Mikhail.

For a moment, she felt she stood on a knife-edge. She could no longer deny her feelings for her cousin, could not pretend she merely liked him. Everyone, including his mother, was quite aware of her actual feelings for Mikhail. She knew she loved him, but did she love him enough to be subservient to him? Wasn't that what would be expected of her, if she married him or any other Darkovan man? She had only just gotten free of Ashara, and she didn't want another master in the place of the dead Keeper. Not even one as good as Mikhail.

I must remain on Darkover, I suppose, and study my Gift.

You don't sound very thrilled at the prospect!

You have lived in a telepathic society your whole life, Mik, but for me it is a brand new thing, and not a wonderful one. I had my life planned out, until Ivor died. I

*was going to be his assistant, and in some foggy future,
I would become a full Professor on my own, and just
continue to do research. It is difficult for me to just drop
all that and turn into a nice Darkovan girl who does what
she is told!*

*I was not suggesting anything of the sort, and you know
it! You are no better at being obedient than I am! What
are you good at, besides music?*

I suppose I excel at running away from things.

*Taking the way of least resistance, you mean? I do that,
too, you know. I never have pushed Uncle Regis to make
a decision, because I was afraid of the outcome. I know
he is waiting for young Dani to show whether he has the
Hastur Gift or not. Shameful as it is, I confess I have
occasionally wished that he doesn't have it—terrible of
me!*

*No, just very human. I guess I have this idea that tele-
paths ought to be some sort of supermen, and am rather
disappointed that they are still totally human, full of passion for power and glory, just like anyone else.*

*I love it that you will say things no one else will,
Marguerida!*

What?

*One of the features of living with other telepaths is a
degree of repression—a kind of dishonesty in order to
keep things from coming to blows.*

*Really? I would have thought that everyone would have
to be totally honest, all the time, no matter what!*

If that were the case, he laughed in her mind, *then no
one would be alive today, for we would have all killed
each other off centuries ago. And we nearly did, too, with
our passions. We don't want to remember the Ages of
Chaos because we behaved very badly a great deal of the
time. It has only been through struggling with the problem
that we have come up with ways to be who we are without
destroying one another.*

*I see I have a great deal to learn—which does not ex-
actly make my heart go faster with delight.* Margaret
paused, reflecting, aware of Rafaella's calm presence on
her left. The Renunciate seemed lost in thought. Her
father and Jeff had ridden ahead again, as if they wanted
to leave her with some vestige of privacy, and she was

grateful. *I suppose I would just like to do something meaningful, whatever that is.*

Wouldn't we all!

What?

Do you think waiting around for Regis to die, or being paxman to Dyan Ardais has been anything meaningful?

I hadn't thought about it, but I guess it would be pretty empty.

That's a good word for it. Not that I was ever conscious of feeling empty. I just went around being discontented and a real pain in the behind to the family.

You can say that again! Jeff's mental voice interrupted then, his thought full of friendly laughter. *Your sister, Liriel, was the fortunate one. She wanted to go to a Tower, and she did it—though not without a lot of fuss from Javanne. I have always thought it a shame that your mother was not a sufficiently powerful enough telepath to become a Keeper, for nothing less would have satisfied her ambitions.*

Margaret was a little startled by Jeff's intrusion, and felt mildly embarrassed at having a conversation with Mikhail that she had thought was private. Still, she hadn't thought anything terrible, so she guessed it was all right. She didn't think she would ever get used to telepathy, however, no matter how long she trained in a Tower.

Then she looked toward her father's back, strong and straight, as he rode beside Jeff, and decided that if he could manage to be a telepath, so could she. As if he heard her, Lew turned on his horse and gave her such an encouraging smile that she had to work hard not to weep. Why couldn't he have been like this, she thought angrily, when she was younger.

The travelers stopped at a little inn at midday. The innkeeper, a fat man in his fifties, greeted Lew Alton cheerfully, but with a kind of deference that made Margaret want to squirm. As she ate fresh bread and cheese and fruit, she wondered if she would ever be able to feel like an aristocrat, like a *comynara*. She had spent so much time in the relatively democratic environment of University—where deference was given on merit, not birthright—that she found all this forelock tugging more than a little distasteful. No doubt, in time, she would become accustomed to it, and even expect it, but she hoped she would not.

They continued their journey after lunch, and Margaret felt more relaxed the farther they got from Armida. Rafaella pointed out various features of interest along the way, but did not tire her with endless chatter, so Margaret was able to just enjoy the ride and think her own thoughts. It was the first time in days she had had any peace, and she reveled in it. Even Mikhail seemed to realize she needed quiet, and he kneed his horse ahead, until it caught up with the men. She looked at the three strong backs—at three generations of Darkovan men, and found herself experiencing pride in her birthright for the first time in her life.

After a time, Jeff dropped back and rode beside her. She could feel his gentle protection, and she smiled up at him. He added an occasional bit to Rafaella's mention of the passing sights, and Margaret listened to the two of them exchanging versions of old stories. It seemed that every foot of Darkover had some history attached to it, and at any other time, she would have been fascinated. But the warmth of the day made her feel pleasantly unfocused, and she had a great deal to think about after her conversations with Mikhail. For once, her academic mind seemed to be taking a holiday.

Toward the end of the afternoon they came to a lake, vast and a little misty in the soft sunlight. It seemed odd that there should be mist on such a fine day, and she stood up in her stirrups to see it better. In the distance, Margaret could see a tall, white Tower gleaming, its stones uncolored by the sun. It looked very like the places she had seen in the overworld, except it seemed more solid and real than anything in that strange place.

"Is that Arilinn, Uncle Jeff? Where you live?" She pointed toward the building.

Jeff turned to her in surprise. "What?" He looked where she was pointing. "Marguerida, what do you see?"

"I see a Tower like the ones in the overworld. Is it Arilinn?"

"No, *chiya*. This is Lake Hali. In that direction stood the Hali Tower."

"Oh. No one has mentioned that one before. No; wait—Istvana said that Ashara was Keeper at Hali Tower. Can't you see it?" She could not keep from shuddering at the very mention of the name of her dead tormentor, and she felt her breath grow thin and tight.

He shook his head. "Hali Tower was destroyed, a thousand years ago or more, in a war during the Ages of Chaos. It was never rebuilt, though I don't know why."

"But I can see it, just as plain as my hand before my face." Her voice was shrill, and her blood felt like ice. She wanted to turn away, but she was riveted. It was very beautiful, and it seemed to call to Margaret. But it was like a siren's call, and terrified her to the bone.

"I am sure you can, but I assure you, there is nothing there except the ruins now. It is a sort of memorial of that war. You might call it a ghost of a Tower," he added playfully, but Margaret could tell he was disturbed.

She was cold all over, despite the warm sunlight against her skin, and she shivered. She could see the Tower quite clearly, and it looked very real and solid and extremely ordinary. "What would happen if I went up and knocked on the door?"

Jeff looked at her for a long, shocked, silent moment. "I don't know, and I don't think I want to find out. That you are able to see Hali is troubling enough without you banging the knocker, Marguerida. I wouldn't advise it."

"But what would happen?" Beneath her glove, Margaret felt the traceries on her left hand begin to pulse, and she felt possessed by some demon of curiosity. No, it was more than that. It was almost a compulsion, and she wondered if, somehow, Ashara had set another trap for her.

"To my knowledge, other people have seen Hali from time to time, but no one has ever attempted to enter the ghost Tower, so I just don't know what would happen." Jeff looked worried, as if he thought that she just might dash over and try to enter the illusory building. "If you went in, we probably wouldn't be able to follow you, Marguerida."

"Uncle Jeff, you're frightening me—you sound as if you're talking about fairy tales or elf-mounds or something." They continued to ride, and he did not respond to her comment immediately.

"That is not a bad analogy," Jeff said slowly as he turned his horse away from Lake Hali and they continued down the trail. "I haven't thought of elf-mounds in a long time—I loved the stories of them when I was a young man, back on Terra. The Kerwins were of old Irelandic stock, and my adopted father's mother had a great store of tales—about Oisin and Fionn mac Cool and King Arthur, whom she insisted the British had stolen from the Irish. Called them 'shee hills.' It really takes me back."

The steady drone of the old man's voice calmed her, and her fears began to vanish as she listened. She knew some of the stories he mentioned, and a great many more, for it seemed that wherever humans settled, they carried tales of other races, of fairies and elves and dwarves, with them, and they often lived in places where time was somehow different.

Margaret turned in the saddle and looked back over her shoulder. The Tower was gone as if it had never been. All she could see were the ruins of the foundation stones, not white as she had seen, but blackened, as if they had been struck by lightning. It was not the craziest thing that had happened to her since she came to Darkover, but it was surely one of the most unsettling.

"It's gone now," she said with deep regret. "Like it never was. But I have a very odd feeling about this place."

"And what is that?" Jeff asked reluctantly.

"I can't quite say—except I think someday I *will* bang on the door of Hali. Why do you think I can see it, when you can't?" Despite the absence of the thing she had seen a few minutes before, Margaret felt a tremendous pull, a tug that seemed to fill her chest. She wondered if she would find Ashara there, a woman still made of flesh and blood . . . or merely find herself standing in an empty room.

"You have a strong part of the Aldaran Gift, Marguerida, and that is precognition."

"I know—and I wish I hadn't! But that's seeing into the future. I was looking into the past! That's totally different."

"Metaphysics was never an interest of mine, so I can only guess." He mused for a moment. "Just because we think time is a past, present, and future doesn't mean time thinks in those terms. But I trust you will not do anything foolish, *chiya,* and leap off your horse and dash over there, will you?"

"No, I won't. I think I have had enough adventures already, without going into ghost Towers. But for someone who pretends not to be a metaphysician, you seem to have a pretty good grasp of the matter." She gave a little laugh, but she did not feel merry. "Time as a matter of viewpoint reality—I studied a bit about that at University—is enough to drive you crazy, there are no reference points, nothing makes sense. Has any Aldaran seen into the past?"

"Well, now I think on it, I do know of one occurrence." He stopped speaking and looked troubled.

"Are you going to tell me or just let me die of suspense?" She teased him, feeling the need to break the mood. She looked toward her father, riding a few lengths ahead of her, talking to Mikhail. She wondered if she would ever be able to tease Lew Alton this way, the way she had sometimes done with Ivor, the way she already did with Mik. She found she wanted to, that it was an easy way to express affection.

They had drawn closer during the time at Armida, but the habits of a lifetime kept them still somewhat formal and distant. Lew would be almost cheery at times, then fall into his usual brooding silences. Margaret knew he was very worried about Dio, and was upset that he would not talk with her about it. She remembered that Jeff had said her father had a great deal of difficulty in opening up to other people, and she knew her uncle was right. But, for all of that, she still yearned to be at ease with her formidable parent, and she found herself impatient for that closeness. She shook away her thoughts, and turned her attention to what Jeff was saying now.

"My grandfather, old Damon Ridenow, whose name I am proud to bear, entered into Timesearch during the era of the Forbidden Tower. He was successful, but it was very dangerous. You will need a great deal of training to attempt such a thing, and I hope you never will."

I don't want to search time—I want to go into Hali

Tower, and I don't know why. What would I do if Ashara was there? Maybe I've already been there and met Ashara! Maybe that was why she was so determined to over-shadow me. Damn. I wish I had never seen that place, now.

"*I saw it, too, Marguerida! That's never happened to me before, and I've ridden along the lake hundreds of times. I hope you aren't planning to do anything . . .*"

Mikhail had seen Hali Tower? She was so stunned that she did not respond for a moment. Then she felt annoyed. *Don't you dare say "stupid," Mikhail. I am not going to rush over there—besides, it's gone now—but, someday, someday, I will go there. I just know it! I can feel it in my bones, and it scares me to death.*

Maybe I'll just come along with you . . . . He sounded happy—his usual playful self.

Margaret wondered what Mikhail and Lew had been talking about as they rode. *I thought you wanted to run off and see the stars!*

I did. I do! But Darkover seems more interesting to me these days than it used to. I can't imagine why.

Margaret caught the subtle undertone in his words, and knew he was flirting with her. It was a very odd sensation, and she wished she had had more experience with men. There had been a couple of young men at University who had tried to get her attention, but the hidden presence of Ashara, she now knew, had made it impossible for her to do more than draw away abruptly. Most of her knowledge of flirting came from books, and it had always seemed silly and rather embarrassing to her when she read it. Now it filled her with a strange warmth and excitement. Maybe Mikhail *would* come to Hali Tower with her some day. Beneath his teasing tone, there was an element of seriousness. *I would follow you to the ends of the world, Marguerida. Never doubt that.* She had her answer now, and it thrilled her in ways she could not describe, and she had no idea what she should do about it.

25

The party came into view of Thendara the following morning, after a pleasant night at an inn. Margaret could see the tip of the great skyscraper in the Terran Sector, and it brought back memories of her uncle Rafe Scott, the old ethnologist Brigham Conover, and Ivor Davidson. She wondered if he was still in the overworld listening to music, or if he had passed beyond to some other place.

It was midday, but the sky was overcast, and a chill wind swept down from the Kilghards, across their backs. Margaret watched Jeff struggle to conceal the pain from his aching joints and a desire for a hot bath, and felt Rafaella brighten up as she rode beside her. The Renunciate had become more and more quiet the closer they came to Thendara, and also quite tense. Margaret had missed her usual cheerful chatter, but she knew that her friend was thinking of Rafe Scott, and how she would resolve whatever stood between them.

As they approached the gates of the city, Rafaella began to look eager, and her eyes sparkled. It was clear that she was looking forward to returning to Thendara House, and to seeing Captain Scott. Margaret wished her own situation was so easy to resolve, because Rafaella could choose to be a freemate, but, because of the social strictures of the *comyn,* if Margaret remained on Darkover, she herself could not.

"Rafaella—how is courting done on Darkover?"

"Huh?" The guide, deep in her own thoughts, looked puzzled for a second at this question. "It *isn't* very much, at least not among the *comyn.* Even the merchants and traders arrange those matters for their own profit, not for love or romance. Oh, at balls and such there is a bit of flirting, I have heard, but we don't have much actual courting, I think."

"Yes. I should have guessed, what with all the marriages being what they are." Margaret sighed. She knew what she wanted now, and she knew what Mikhail wanted as well. She knew, as well, that Gabriel Lanart and Javanne Hastur would oppose her marriage to their youngest son, and she rather doubted that her father had enough power to influence the outcome. His position was, as she understood it, extremely ambiguous, since he had given up his claim to the Alton Domain long ago. She did not know enough about Darkovan law to guess what would happen, and it was fairly pointless to speculate.

It seemed hopeless, and rather ironic. She had finally found the man who captured her heart, and he seemed to be the one person she could not have.

As they passed beneath the wide gates of the city, Margaret looked at her father, riding ahead, lost in his own thoughts. She could tell he was very worried about Dio, and was eager to get back to her. How selfish she was being, worrying about Mikhail when Dio was sick. She was disgusted with herself.

Lew Alton had been very close-mouthed about Dio's illness, and that made her afraid. Until she left for University, there had never been anyone she loved or trusted more than her stepmother, and so soon after Ivor's death, the mere idea that Dio might die was unthinkable. She tried to harden herself, to make herself strong and able to face anything, but inside she wanted to crumple up and cry.

She very much wanted to talk to her father, but after that wonderful dinner at Armida when they had seemed so easy with one another, Lew had withdrawn from her again. It was not as bad as when she was a girl, but it was so reminiscent of the past that she hesitated to ask him the many questions that plagued her night and day. Her problems, right now, were unimportant beside the health of Diotima Ridenow Alton.

Margaret was used to keeping her own council, and now she realized that it was a habit she had picked up from her father, and that it was both good and bad. It made it very difficult to ask for help, to ask questions

of a personal nature at all. She thought he liked Mikhail
well enough, but though he had indicated that he understood her feelings about her cousin, he had showed neither approval nor disapproval. Maybe he wouldn't like
the idea any better than Javanne had or perhaps he was
genuinely indifferent.

She cursed herself for a fool. Lew Alton was never
indifferent. He might be a near stranger to her now, but
Margaret knew that he was a strong and passionate man,
who did what he did for what he believed were good
reasons. She would just have to depend on him to be
her advocate—he owed her that at least—and stop fussing over things she could not control. She gritted her
teeth. It was so hard to trust him, or anyone, it seemed.

They rode through the narrow streets from the city
gate, and approached the great bulk of Comyn Castle.
Margaret was now in a state of grim despair over her
own future.

Margaret was so deep in her own thoughts that she
hardly noticed Rafaella begin to draw her horse away.
"I think I will leave you now and return to Thendara
House. I'll fetch the mule back from the Castle stables
later."

"Must you?" Margaret felt lost without her friend.
Suddenly she did not want Rafaella to leave her, and
loathed herself for being stupid and selfish.

"I don't have any business at the Castle." *My business
is elsewhere, and it has been delayed long enough!*

"No, of course you don't. I wasn't thinking clearly.
Please give my regards to Mother Adriana, and tell her
you were an excellent guide and a good companion. I
don't know what I would have done without you." Margaret felt tears form in her eyes. *I do know. I would
have died, but for you, Rafaella.* She blinked hard. "Say
hello to Rafe Scott for me, won't you." She forced her
face into something like a smile, but it hurt.

Rafaella, knowing her expressions well now, was not
fooled. "Oh, Marguerida. Don't be sad."

"I will miss you!" *I wish you every happiness, and I
wish the same for myself!*

"And I will miss you—but I am not going away forever! You can always find me by leaving word at Thendara House." She leaned out of her saddle and gave

Margaret a firm hug across the shoulders. Then she turned away and put her heels into the horse's flanks, riding into one of the narrow side streets.

Margaret was left bereft by this abrupt departure, and she swallowed her feelings and straightened her shoulders. Mikhail rode up beside her, his big bay snorting. "Where's she gone off to?"

"Home." The word seemed to express all that Margaret would never have, and she struggled to cheer herself up. She realized she was tired, for the journey had been pleasant, but still wearisome. She was glad for Rafaella, no matter what. But it still was very painful. "I think she has someone she wants to see very much."

"Really? People say a great many unkind things about the lives of Renunciates, as if they were not quite civilized. So, does this mysterious lover have a name?"

"Can you keep a secret?"

"Of course!"

"I believe she and my uncle, Rafe Scott, are . . . becoming fond of one another." She knew she was expressing herself awkwardly, but it was a private thing, and she felt oddly embarrassed in sharing it, even with Mikhail. "Do you know him?"

"Rafe? Of course I do—but are you sure? I mean, he's much older than she is and . . . well, it does seem unlikely. An odd romance."

"I was not sure to begin with. It all started when he escorted me to Thendara House, to meet Mother Adriana and hire a guide. As he walked away, I heard him thinking about someone in the house with a great deal of . . . yearning. I didn't think much about it at the time, because I was not entirely sure that I was picking up thoughts, and besides, I was still in a state about Ivor's death and all the rest. So much had happened! You have no idea how peculiar it is to set foot on a planet and have total strangers bowing and scraping at you, or announcing they are your long-lost uncle that you didn't know you had!" Her sense of outrage pressed forward again, and she frowned. It was fine to have a focus for it, even for only a moment.

"Has anyone mentioned how much more golden your eyes get when you are angry?"

"Stop that!" Margaret felt out of her depth with Mikhail when he was in this playful mood, for he knew how to flirt, and she didn't. *Well, he has probably had a great deal of practice,* she told herself, flushing and trying to regain command of her thoughts. She had always hated her odd colored eyes, and to have them complimented was a new experience. Pleasant, but it threw her emotional balance off, and she was already in a mild state of disorder. She sensed something ahead—a premonition—and she didn't like the feeling of it at all.

"Forgive me, cousin. It is only that I have never seen anything quite like the way your eyes almost flame. I wonder what causes it. Some chemical, perhaps?"

That was better. Chemicals were safe. No one could flirt with biochemicals! "I would guess that adrenaline is the agent, but I don't know a great deal about body chemistry. I took the basic courses at University, and memorized enough to get through the tests, but, frankly, I have forgotten most of it."

"You know more than I do about such things." There was a wistfulness in his answer, almost as if he envied her knowledge. It occurred to her then that it must be very maddening for an intelligent and curious man to be limited by a culture that did not place a high value on education as she understood it. He had received the best that Darkover had to offer, but it was nothing like spending a decade in the halls of University, or even a few years at a minor planetary college. "So, tell me more about this romance of your guide's."

Margaret hesitated, but the cat was already out of the bag, and she decided that the guide would not really mind. "When I met Rafaella, she was annoyed that she was not going to be able to see someone before we left the city, so I put two and two together and came up with five. I did not ask her for quite a while, but when I was getting over the threshold sickness in Ardais, and we had become quite close, I finally did, and she admitted that Rafe Scott was very much in her thoughts."

"You are much tougher than I am, then, because I wouldn't have been able to resist asking for more than a day. Uncle Regis always said I wanted to know everything. I was always plaguing him mercilessly with questions about Terranan and Darkovan history, while he was trying to be a good ruler. It must have made him glad to be rid of me!"

Margaret was surprised at the bitterness in his voice. "But, why? Curiosity is a healthy trait in a youngster. You are quite intelligent, so I am not surprised you wanted to know things. Why would you think he wanted to be rid of you?" She had only met Regis for a brief time, but he did not strike her as a person who would dislike curiosity in his heir. Perhaps he wanted Mikhail to be interested in only the things he needed, not in everything in the universe.

"I . . . when Regis and Linnea had young Danilo, and the matter of the Hastur lineage seemed settled . . . I became just an extra. I think I was rather spoiled, because everyone had paid attention to me because I was Regis' heir. I resented Danilo—which was so petty. He was only a baby, but his birth changed everything! I felt very unwanted, in the way, and quite unnecessary." *I have never told that to anyone before in my life, not even Dyan! What will she think of me—I sound like a whining child.*

Margaret found herself remembering when she was still Marja Kadarin, in the John Reade Orphanage. She knew what it was to feel unwanted, to be abandoned and alone, and while she now knew she had been loved and wanted, it did not change the hurt at all. She noticed that now she could recall these events without so much pain, but she suspected that it would always make her sad. She allowed herself to feel a quiet ache for Mikhail, and realized they had much more in common than she had previously imagined.

"Cousin, I think you might have misjudged things." She wanted so much to comfort him, to ease his sense of loss. She would have held out her hand to him, but he was riding on her left, and she did not like to touch anyone with her left hand, even when it was safely gloved and shielded.

"Why do you think that?" He gazed directly at her for a second, and she could see the need in his eyes, the need to feel useful and cared for. Then he looked down at his horse's mane, and the moment passed.

"I always thought Lew could not bear the sight of me, and now I know that was not true. I was wrong. I interpreted things from an adolescent point of view, and have been walking around for years thinking my father did not love me at all. How old were you when Danilo Hastur was born?"

"Hmm. About fourteen or a bit older. I try not to think about it."

"There, you see! The same thing—being a crazy teenager! There you were, beginning to be a man, hormones raging, probably dealing with threshold sickness, and suddenly you were no longer the center of attention. I am sure that Regis did not change whatever feelings he had for you just because he had a legitimate heir."

"You are probably right. I just feel so useless sometimes. Yes, I was young when Danilo Hastur was born, but not so young that I had not made plans for what I would do when I took Regis' place. And you are right about the hormones—though it is not polite to speak of such things. I learned to be paxman to Dyan Ardais, but I cannot pretend my heart was ever in it. It is not a very challenging position. You don't need brains to be a companion, just infinite patience."

"And do you have such patience?"

Mikhail roared with laughter, and Lew, ahead of them, turned in his saddle and looked back. "No! I always chafe like a half-broken horse, wanting my carrots and unwilling to bear the weight of a rider. I'm one of those people who demand that the gods give them patience, and then add, 'And I want it right now!' "

Margaret laughed at this, and Mikhail beamed at her. Once again they had managed to dispel one another's dark moods. It was as if they were two halves of something, as if they balanced one another perfectly. It reminded her suddenly of how Lew and Dio were together, and the thought of her stepmother threatened to put her back in the dumps. Resolutely, she set aside conjecturing about Dio's illness. "Odd. It seemed to me that you were fairly patient, back at Armida. I wanted to scream at people half the time. I have always hated it when anyone told me they knew what was best for me, especially when they didn't know me at all. There was a counselor my first quarter at University who was completely convinced I should pursue the study of economics. It was her own specialty, and she liked to get others interested in it. And it is a very popular course of study, because the Terrans seem to have a constant need for people who can prove, with numbers, that there is a need for more grain from the farmers—even if the bakers are letting flour rot because they have no customers for their bread. It is a very gloomy subject, and I didn't want to study gloom." She glanced at Lew as she said this.

"So what did you do?"

"I told her I did not want to be an economist because I truly hated arithmetic, and that statistics seemed to me to be a means to lie in a large way. She was extremely put out with me, and assigned me to another counselor. It was a vast relief—for both of us."

"I wish I could have done that—told anyone that I didn't wish to do what was given to me, but wanted to do something else. But my father always thinks he is the wisest man, even when he isn't. I had most of what passes for a good Terran education in Darkover. It falls far short of your own training, but it was better than many others have received. But I never got to complete it, because once Regis had an heir, my parents could not see the need. They hustled me off to Ardais, as if they didn't want to have me hanging around Armida, and I felt very much in the way. Regis would have let me go off-planet, but my mother and father would not allow if. If they had, I might have met you on University." *Now wouldn't that have been a proper muddle.*

"But, I thought Regis was . . . well, the King of Darkover!"

"Yes and no. Technically, he is occupying the seat of the king. But our kings traditionally come from the Elhalyn Domain, not the Hastur. It is all quite complicated, even for me, and I have lived with it all my life."

"Elhalyn? Are there any? I think someone mentioned the name—I'm sorry, but I get rather confused with all these families."

"There are still Elhalyns, but the last male of the line, Derik, died before he achieved the position. All that remains is his sister, Priscilla, and her children. They were always an unstable lot, and, by all accounts, Derik was more than a little mad. If we still had the Comyn Council, Priscilla would sit on it, because the Elhalyn allow their women that power. I know them, of course, have known them all my life, but they keep to themselves. Priscilla has a retiring disposition, and after Derik, no one was really enthusiastic about letting any Elhalyn have much authority."

"I see, I suppose. But that still doesn't explain why your uncle is not quite the king. I was puzzled about that when I read it on the history disk."

"We are a very traditional planet, Marguerida. We let go of our customs reluctantly, if at all. We have had Elhalyn kings for centuries. They are a minor branch of the Hasturs, but sanctified by tradition. Regis had to make many changes, after the Rebellion, and then after the World Wreckers came in and assassinated members of the Domains right and left. Several of Regis' children were killed. It was a terrible time—babies were murdered in their cradles in an effort to upset the balance of things, so that the greedy people behind the Wreckers could take over. So, as he explained it to me, he took the position of regent, rather than king outright, in order to preserve something of our past while still keeping us moving into the future. Even that is traditional; the Hasturs have served as regents for Elhalyns for generations."

"You say you know these children of Priscilla Elhalyn. Are they legitimate inheritors to the throne?"

Mikhail shrugged. "They are not from the male line directly, but since the custom of the Elhalyn is to permit *comynara* status to their women, they could be. It is a sticky legal point, you see."

"And Regis is sort of waiting around, hoping one of her children will be sound enough to take the throne?"

"So it would seem. Regis is canny. He has to be to keep things going. And he does not like to rush into decisions. He prefers to let things go until the situation sorts itself out—unlike my mother, who likes to cause things to happen. They love one another, but they are often on the outs, because she always thinks she can make him do what she wants, as she could when they were young. And she certainly had enough influence to keep me here on Darkover."

"Really? Somehow I didn't have the impression that Regis Hastur was easily influenced, except perhaps by his consort or his paxman." *But that explains why she thought she could send Mikhail off to be Senator instead of that Herm Aldaran, whom everyone but my father seems to regard as some sort of monster. What will I do if she manages that trick?*

What? Where did you get that bit of . . .

When my father announced that he had given his seat to Herm, your mother became very angry, and I could hear her thoughts, just a bit. She was thinking that if she got Regis to send you to the Senate, it would solve all her problems. Can she do it?

So that is why she looked like a cat with feathers in her maw! I should have known, for she is a famous intriguer, Marguerida. Especially since all of us grew up, and she had nothing to turn her intelligence to but trying to arrange our lives. It is actually a pretty clever idea, now I think about it, for it would let me go off-planet, which I have always longed for, and it might be too tempting to resist. The only problem is that I don't have the foggiest idea how to be a Senator, and Herm does. And, frankly, I no longer want to go to the stars as much as I did before. Unless . . .

I went with you?

Yes.

I can't. I know that now. I have to be trained in a Tower, and I have resigned myself to that, even though it makes me shudder whenever I think about it. I can't leave Darkover until I learn how to control my Gift, and I have no idea how long that might take.

Years. He sounded incredibly gloomy again. *And when you were done, they would marry you off so fast your head would spin. They would strap the Alton Domain on your back, and never let you leave the planet!*

Then we had better hope my father has a few tricks up his sleeve!

There is that. I like him, Marguerida. We've talked a good deal during the journey, and he seems to me to be completely unlike the stories that are told about him. In the tales I've heard, he was headstrong, but he isn't. He's very thoughtful, and I don't think he gave Herm the seat on some whim, though I know Javanne would disagree with me. The problem is she still thinks of him as he was twenty or thirty years ago, as if nothing had happened to him during that time, as if he had not been changed by working with the Terranan all those years. And, likely, he still thinks of her as the bossy girl he knew when he was a young man.

That's very astute, Mikhail. He isn't the man I remember, and I have to keep reminding myself that he isn't. It is very hard!

Mikhail gave a brief sigh. "Do you know, all the way along the road, I kept having this feeling that something was happening that was going to . . . be important to me. And to you, and everyone else. It kept getting stronger, and since you saw Hali Tower yesterday, and I did as well, it has become enormous. It is like a headache that hasn't quite arrived!"

"I know! This foresight business is the very devil. Not that I have had the slightest bit of a distinct impression, like I did when I set Ariel off, and poor Domenic was hurt."

"That was not your fault! Stop trying to take responsibility for things that aren't your concern. Ariel has always been pretty hysterical, and never more than when she's with child. It's odd, really, because pregnancy is supposed to calm a woman. But it never has with my sister! If there is a fault, it is with my mother, for not preventing her from dashing off like an idiot!" He paused. "Yet I still think something is just over the horizon, and I hope it will be for the good, not for the bad."

"We are agreed on that," Margaret answered. "If I am going to have a premonition, I do wish it would be clear and precise, not this vague feeling of a headache coming on. That is a really fine metaphor! It is exactly what I feel!"

"I suppose we will discover what it is when we get to Comyn Castle." He sounded impatient and worried. "And I certainly hope it is not something of my mother's doing!"

"How could she be doing anything? By now, she is miles away, at Arilinn, with Liriel and poor little Domenic."

Mikhail gave her a look of surprise. "You really haven't grasped what it means to live in a telepathic community, have you?"

"What do you mean?"

"If I know my mother, and believe me, I do, she has been burning up the relays sending messages to Regis. She doesn't need to be present, physically, though that is preferable. She can manage quite nicely without coming anywhere near Thendara!"

Margaret was near despair at this. What could she do? Nothing! It was frustrating and frightening. There were people who were going to decide her life, and she would have no say in the matter.

Chiya, *stop fussing!*

How can I do that, Father, when it seems as if . . .

I know how it feels—more exactly than you can imagine! But Javanne will not meddle in your life. Can you trust me to make things right for you?

I can try—but it isn't easy!

No, it isn't. Just believe that Regis will not be stampeded into any decisions that affect the realm without careful consideration. He has managed to keep Darkover on her present course for all these years, and he is not about to be overset by his sister, or anyone else.

Beneath these comforting words, Margaret sensed Lew Alton's concern about his wife, and she felt terrible for worrying about herself. Why couldn't she just think about Dio, and force her mind away from the man riding beside her. Where was her discipline? If only she did not sense how well she and Mikhail suited each other! It was not fair.

Mikhail shook his head. "Tell me, cousin, if you can, about that niggling worry you have at the back of your mind."

"Why?"

"Well, I know you have some of the Aldaran Gift. There is something in the past that is disturbing you, and I would like to know what it is."

"I never wanted any of this. Why couldn't I be like Ariel and not have telepathy or anything else! I don't really understand why I have it and, say, Rafaella does not, since her sister had enough to end up in a Tower."

Mikhail became thoughtful. "That is something we have wondered about for years—centuries, probably. You know that we have, to a degree, bred to preserve the Gifts."

"Yes, I know, and I think it is a sad thing, because it reduces human beings to animals, like horses or cattle."

"But you have no objection to Terranan genetic engineering for the purpose of healthy teeth or good eyesight?"

"Ouch! You have me there. No, I don't because, I suppose, those sorts of things are good for the entire species, not just a few."

He gave a little chuckle. "I see—we of the Domains are selfish. Well, it is not the first time that charge has been leveled against us, and will not be the last. But, despite our knowledge and our efforts, we have never been able to be certain how the process works. It seems that the tendency is a return to an untalented individual, so that those with the Gifts have become prized, perhaps overmuch, as we have seen in Ariel's misery."

"Poor woman. She must have felt like a tone-deaf woman in a family of superb musicians." Margaret shook her head. "But except for that sudden vision about Domenic, and the other one . . ."

"What other one?"

"About Alanna Alar, your niece to be."

"Ah—and here I thought you were just being kind to my sister, and telling her what she wanted to hear, based on Liri's knowledge that she was carrying a girl at last. I did not realize that you got a strong impression of her future."

"I did, and I do not like it, because . . . well, I would rather not say. I don't like the idea of knowing the future because I think we always imagine it in terms of what we know, and then when we get to the real future, we try to make it fit into our interpretation of the idea, instead of dealing with the reality. I have read a good many things that various prophets wrote down, and they are full of ambiguities and subject to the sort of beliefs that lead to wars. I don't want the Alton Gift, but I really, really don't want the ability to pierce the veil of the future!"

Mikhail shook his head. "But, you were ready to rush up to the door of Hali Tower just yesterday, and you know, in your heart, that someday you will enter it."

"That's different!" she tried to explain. "That is my future, and only I will have to cope with it—if it ever

comes to be. But I refuse to make predictions about the
life of an unborn child! It's wrong! It's cruel!"

"This has nothing to do with Ariel's daughter, does
it?"

"No, it doesn't." She paused, gathering her thoughts.
"I believe Ashara Alton foresaw me, not me particularly, but the possibility of Marguerida Alton in some
hazy future. At least, when Istvana told me she had
overshadowed other women, I leaped to the premise that
she was anticipating my existence—which she somehow
knew was a threat to her own." She shuddered at the
mention of the name, but refused to let her fears overwhelm her. The bulk of the Castle was much closer now,
visible above the houses along the street, and she had a
much clearer view of the tower where Ashara had continued to reside long after her death.

Now she realized what had been bothering her as they
rode closer. She shook her head, trying to clear her
mind. Margaret remembered how the Tower had looked,
and how it had given her the shivers when she saw it on
her first visit. It had been a fine building of white stones,
like the rest of Comyn Castle. *Now* what stood there
was a blackened ruin, the top blasted off as if by lightning. None of the roofs nearby showed any sign of having been burned or damaged. What had happened?

Mikhail followed her eyes, and his mouth sagged for
a second. "Ashara's Tower . . ."

"It looks like it was burned in a fire. I wonder how
it . . ."

"I don't. Wonder, I mean. I think when you pulled
the keystone out of the Tower in the overworld, you
also seared the physical one on Darkover. And a good
thing, too!"

"But, Mikhail—someone could have been killed! If I
had ever guessed the kind of damage I could do, I don't
know if I would have been so willing to . . ."

"Dear cousin, you did what you had to do. No one
blames you for it." He smiled at her, and her heart
warmed. "Now, you were saying something a moment
ago, before we observed the ruins of the Old Tower,
about Ashara. About interpreting the future. Please,
go on."

Margaret clenched the reins a little tighter in her

hand. "Her name still makes me feel helpless, you know. Sometimes I am not really sure she is gone for good, no matter what anyone says." She forced herself to breathe slowly, to become calm again. "I still don't know exactly what happened, but I am sure she made Dyan Ardais bring me to her. It is all rather vague and misty in my mind. When she saw me, I think she knew I was the one that she feared. And she moved to make sure I would never realize the Alton Gift. She must have been a remarkable woman—not admirable, but so powerful."

He nodded. "By all accounts, she was that and a great deal more. I understand your objections to the Aldaran Gift a little better now. They make sense. But you have enough of it that you are getting hints or something."

"What I have is the same feeling of foreboding that I had when I was on my way to Darkover. This is stronger, perhaps—it is all so subjective, and I have a lively imagination. I think maybe that you can't ever really see your own future clearly, and that is what causes problems—when you try to manipulate it for your own purposes."

"But, Marguerida, everyone tries to manipulate things to their own advantage!"

"I don't!"

"Of course you do! Otherwise you and my mother would not be at loggerheads! I know what you want—I want it, too. And both of us are going to do everything we can to make certain that it comes out our way. You can't deny that!"

Caught again, Margaret smiled at him. "No, I can't. Or, rather, I could, but it would be disingenuous. And while there are plenty of people I would gladly dissemble for, you are not one of them."

"I know. From the first time we met, I knew that we could never lie to each other, not really." His voice was warm and tender, and she knew he had spoken rather than used telepathy because that was too intimate now. She was grateful for his politeness, but also touched by his checked passion.

"What sort of ability do you have?"

"I have *laran,* of course, but I do not have any of the Gifts. I am just an ordinary telepath, good enough to sit on the Telepathic Council which has been our ruling body for most of my life. Liriel has the greatest ability, which is why she is a good technician, and Mother has it, and Rafael and Gabe, though theirs, like my father's, is very modest."

"Oh. When we went into the overworld to find Donal, it seemed to me that you were quite able, but I just don't know enough to judge. Everyone has made such a fuss over the Alton Gift that I haven't paid attention to any others. I know there is a Hastur Gift—Lady Marilla tried to explain it to me, but it didn't make much sense at the time. Don't you have it?"

"Lord, no!" He seemed shocked and rather upset. "Sorry. I didn't mean to snap at you. I admit I rather expected to have it when I got older, and I was really disappointed when it failed to materialize. The Hastur Gift is that of the living matrix—the full gift lets one work without a physical matrix."

Margaret stared at him, then looked at her left hand for a moment. "But I haven't used a crystal, and I don't think I even could."

"Yes, I know. Liriel tried to explain it to me—your shadow matrix—but it just gave me a headache, since the description was extremely technical. She did say it was different from the Hastur Gift, though. She and Jeff sent word to Arilinn about it, and the Archivist there is apparently going slightly mad trying to find any reference to such a thing in the past."

"Tell me more about this Telepathic Council, will you? Uncle Rafe mentioned it, but somehow it never got explained, or else I didn't understand."

"For centuries Darkover was governed by the Comyn Council, which was made up of one member, male except for the Aillard representative, from each of the Domains, plus *leroni* from the Towers. The Aldarans were originally part of it, and then we threw them out. It is a long, involved story, full of betrayal, and I will tell it to you some other time. The Council sat in summer, and made decisions about trade with the Terranan and a great many other things. But when your grandfather, Kennard, left and took your father with him, the Council ceased to function, and a few years after the Sharra Rebellion, it ceased to exist. Regis created the Telepathic Council to take its place, but, truthfully, no one has ever been happy with it. It is less exclusive than the Comyn

Council was, but because there are now many voices where there had been few, it accomplishes less. More, the people are not happy with it."

"The people?" Margaret glanced at craftsmen in their shops along the street, and saw women and men who were involved with the daily business of living. She hadn't thought about them a great deal, for those she had encountered had seemed both content and able-bodied. There were no beggars in Thendara to be seen, and no obvious evidence of aristocratic abuse, though she was sure there were instances of it. Human nature was still a long way from perfection. "How do you know what they think?"

"By listening. As Dyan Ardais' paxman, I hear things which would never come to his ears, and as the least son of my father, I have heard more than you might imagine from farmers and craftsmen and others. Many of them have no interest in anything beyond their own lives, of course, but those who do feel that the Telepathic Council does not serve Darkover well any longer."

"What do they want instead?"

"That I cannot answer. There are a few, with Terranan educations, among the Domain families who think that something like the Federation government would be good, but what I have heard from the ordinary folk is that they would prefer to restore the Comyn Council."

"Isn't that trying to turn back time, Mikhail?"

"Perhaps. But we are not Terra, and we have no tradition of anything like a democratic system here. Elections would be very difficult with a populace that is unlettered, don't you think?"

"I had not considered the problem, but I can see you have given it a great deal of thought, Mik."

"Yes, I have. At first I did it because, as Regis' titular heir, it was my duty. Now I do it because it interests me greatly. And I have had a lot of time to think about it, about the future of Darkover, even if I cannot see into it."

"Perhaps it is just as well, don't you think? Not to see into the future?"

"I think I do not need to see into it—because, as Uncle Jeff said, I am riding into it, whether I want to or not."

26

◆

The sun was lowering behind them, turning the white stones of Comyn Castle a wonderful pink as they finally left the crooked streets of Thendara. Guardsmen in the blue and silver colors of the Hasturs stood on either side of the gates, and they saluted as Lew rode beneath the carved lintel and into the outer court. This was a different entrance than the one Rafe Scott had taken Margaret through on her earlier visit, and she looked around with interest.

The pleasant and pungent smell of horses rose in the air, and several hostlers and grooms sprang forward. On one side, Margaret could see a large stabling facility, and on the other what she suspected were barracks. A set of steps stood at the end of the courtyard, and on it waited a lad of thirteen or fourteen. He was dressed in blue tunic and gray trousers, and Margaret wondered who he was, for he did not look like a servant.

A groom helped Margaret to dismount, and she found she was very glad to be on firm ground once again. She watched the groom lead the horse away, and wondered how she was going to get it back to Rafaella. Then she thought of the lovely Dorilys, back at Armida, and gave a little sigh. She was tired, and there were too many things going on in her mind.

The lad, bright-haired and rather slight, came down the steps and bowed to Lew, then to Margaret. He gave Mikhail part of a grin, then seemed to remember he was being formal. "I am Danilo Hastur, heir to Hastur," he said courteously, as if he had practiced the words while he waited. "My father sends you welcome, and regrets he cannot be present to greet you. He is presently occupied with matters of state, but wishes you to join us at dinner." His voice cracked once while he spoke, and he turned very pink.

So, this boy was the one who had taken Mikhail's place. He appeared bright but tense, and unsure of himself. Margaret wondered if the burden of Hastur weighed heavily on his small shoulders.

Margaret glanced up at the Tower she had spied from a distance, at the place where Ashara had maintained an earthly presence for so many centuries. It was ruined, like Hali, broken and blackened. She felt a surge of guilty pleasure, and felt secretly glad she had destroyed it—although she desperately hoped no one had been injured. Yet another of Ashara Alton's ties to the real world had been severed.

Before she could continue her thoughts, Margaret found her father's hand lightly on her elbow. "Come along. We will go to the Alton Suite. I want a bath, and I am sure you do, too." *And I want to see Dio right away!*

She felt suddenly very fatigued, and more than a little anxious. Now that she had a chance to see her stepmother, she discovered she was extremely reluctant to do so. She did not want to see Diotima sick! She didn't want her to die, like Ivor!

Lew was quiet and brooding, like his former self, but Margaret knew that he was desperately worried. Obediently, she followed him into the castle and through several corridors and up three flights of stairs. Lew was half a corridor ahead of her when they finally arrived at their goal. Despite all the twisting and turning, she did not feel at all lost or disoriented. Deep in the recesses of her mind, there remained a map of the maze that was Comyn Castle, and she was certain she could have found her way to the Alton Suite blindfolded.

Lew Alton opened the tall double doors, and walked into the room beyond. It was what Margaret had now come to think of as a typical sitting or living room, with lots of patterned rugs, hangings on the walls, and large couches. On one of these, Dio lay dozing, covered with a light blanket. The first sight of her stepmother made her throat close up and her breath catch. Nothing Lew had said had prepared her for the reality.

She was so pale she was almost colorless, and her

golden hair was brittle and lifeless. Her once-pretty hands rested on her lap, limp and shrunken. She stirred a little as they came in, but did not wake until Lew bent down and brushed a sunken cheek with his lips.

"I was dreaming of you," Dio whispered from between cracked lips.

"I hope it was a nice dream." Lew tried to sound casual, but instead sounded worried and tired.

"Nicer than some I have had. Your hair was dark, and you shone like Aldones himself."

"How romantic of you, after all these years, my dearest. Look who I have brought with me!"

Margaret swallowed the cold terror in her throat and moved closer. She bent down and touched Dio's hands. They were icy and the skin beneath her fingers was flaky and dry. "Hello, Dio." She felt awkward and very young as she looked down at the only mother she had ever really known.

"Marja!" A weak smile touched her lips. "How wonderful to have you here. I have been longing to see you. When did you arrive?" *How lovely she is now! My beautiful daughter, my little girl—well, woman, isn't she?*

"More than a month ago. It seems like a lifetime, really. Father found me at Armida, and Lady Javanne was not pleased to see him walk in from the storm."

"Storm? Have you been having adventures without me again?" Dio sounded like an echo of her usual self, as if she were trying to conceal her illness. "Every time I left you alone, Marja, you got into some mischief. Remember the time you built that tree house with the children from . . . I can't recall their names . . . and you stole the wood from the lumberyard."

"What's this? I never heard anything about a tree house," Lew said. His features were stern, as if he were fighting despair with all of his tremendous will.

"Of course you didn't! We hushed up the whole thing, didn't we, Marja? It was rather fun. And it was a very well-made tree house." A spasm of coughing choked off her words, and Margaret looked at her father, terrified. Her pulse quickened with fear. But Lew did not appear to be very disturbed by Dio's coughing.

"A good thing we made it sturdy, since you came to tea with us," Margaret answered, forcing a cheerfulness into her voice that she was far from feeling. How could her father bear it? Her new-found respect for her estranged father increased as she watched him behave as if everything were quite normal. She bit her lip, then continued. "I was so startled when you hiked your skirts up and climbed up to the platform as if you had done it a hundred times. And the Weevus children thought you were wonderful, and one of them, Daren, wanted to come and live with us and have you for a mother. He had a perfectly nice mother, but she wasn't the sort who climbed trees."

"What else has been going on behind my back?" Lew asked, sounding very amused, though she caught an undercurrent of pain in his voice.

"Lots of things. We didn't want to bother you with them." Dio gave her husband a feeble smile. "You've filled out nicely since you left us, *chiya*. You were such a slender girl, all legs and eyes, and now you are a woman." This speech seemed to exhaust her, and her hand in Margaret's felt limp.

"Next time you build a tree house, Marja, you'd better invite me for tea as well. I can manage the climb, I believe." *I should have prepared her better for Dio— what a selfish fool I can be! But I couldn't! Still, she is handling herself wonderfully. How the gods have favored me in my child. How could I have let her leave me—set herself apart for all these years?*

Stop whipping yourself Father. The past is past—we have to deal with the present! "Absolutely, Father. I saw a tree at Armida that would be perfect, and I can't imagine why there isn't one there already."

He gave a sharp snort of laughter. "I cannot wait to see the expression on Javanne's face. Now—how are you today, dearest?"

"Much the same, though one of Regis' Healers gave me something that eased the spasms, and I have been able to rest a little. They wish me to get strong enough to be moved to Arilinn for treatment."

"Then that is what we will do, Dio. We will get you strong."

"You always think that you can make things right, and that is why I love you."

Margaret was embarrassed at this open display of

deep affection, and felt excluded by its intimacy. She
wondered if she would ever say such tender words to
any man, and found that she wanted to more than she
could have imagined. "I think I'd like to have a bath,"
she said, to conceal her feelings, "and get ready for dinner. Regis has asked us to dine with him, which sounds
terribly formal." She made a gesture at her rather
worn clothing.

"It is as formal as anything gets on Darkover, but
don't worry, Marja." Lew nodded as he spoke. "Your
rooms are through that door. One of the servants should
have brought your things by now."

Margaret could not think of anything to say, so she
withdrew. What was wrong with Dio, she wondered, and
why hadn't she been treated with Terran medical technology? Or perhaps she had, and it had not worked. She
needed to ask someone, but she didn't want to disturb
her father.

After several frustrating minutes, she remembered
Regis Hastur's consort, who had been so kind and
friendly on her previous visit. *Lady Linnea?*

You needn't shout! There was no anger in the answering thought, just good humor and with it welcome! *What
is it, Marguerida?* The calm and serenity in Linnea's
thoughts eased her fears a little.

*My mother, Dio, is so very ill, and I wondered what can
be done here on Darkover that can't be done by Terranan
medicine. It will just kill Father if she doesn't get better!*

*A good question. The Terrans are very good with their
machines and all, but a trained* leronis *can work what
you might think were miracles.*

How?

Remember when you were monitored?

How did Linnea know that? It didn't matter. *Yes.*

*Dio is being monitored in the same way, right down to
her cells. And what can be perceived can be affected,
you see?*

Sort of. It's rather hard to believe.

*You don't have to believe, Marguerida. Now, don't
worry. Diotima is in the best hands, and everything that
can be done will be.*

The mental contact was withdrawn gently, and Margaret took several shaky breaths and tried to ignore the

sense of despair that filled her. Looking around the
room, she noticed her still-packed bags, and started to
undo the clasps when a plump maid came in. The girl
moved to help her, but Margaret waved her back, eager
to have something to do to keep her mind and hands
busy.

It was all very well to be told not to worry, but she
could not help it. Ivor's death was still too fresh in her
mind, in her heart, and the idea that Dio might perish
was more than she could bear. She could not stop thinking about it, no matter how hard she tried. While they
had been traveling, she had managed to deny her fears,
but now she had actually seen Dio, it was quite impossible. And duty demanded she do exactly that. It was, she
decided, the hardest thing she had ever had to do, and
her admiration for her father, who had probably had to
do many things that he hadn't wished to, increased
again. He really was not the man she remembered, and
she was eager, she discovered, to know the Lew Alton
he now was. But he did not really know *her* either. They
would have to start all over, fresh but still burdened by
the past. In her present mood, that was enough to blurr
her eyes with tears.

She blinked away the wetness, angry at herself, and
concentrated on her unpacking again. Beneath her precious recording equipment Margaret found the green
spider-silk dress which Manuella had sent as a gift, quite
crushed but still beautiful. She had completely forgotten
about it during her journey, and now she shook it out
and wondered if it was appropriate for a formal dinner.

"Can you get the wrinkles out of this?" she asked
the maid.

"Certainly, *domna*. It would be my pleasure. How
lovely it is." The maid held it up. "MacEwan's work?"

"How did you know?"

"No one has his hand with the cloth. He is the finest
master tailor in Thendara. I will make it right while
you bathe."

When she undressed, Margaret spent a few minutes
looking at her left hand. For the most part, she ignored
it, and the glove which concealed the peculiar lines on
it, but she tried to see if the lines were different. Was

she going to have to wear a leather glove on her hand for the rest of her life?

The lines did look a little different today, and she wondered if it was something to do with her second foray into the overworld. A matrix stone was a focus for innate talents, from what Liriel and Istvana had told her. Kept in a silken bag, it did not function except when taken out and used. So it was different, very different from having the shadow of a matrix stone engraved in the flesh. And it was not quite like anything anyone knew about.

If her father were not so distracted with Dio, she might like to talk to him about it. But she really didn't want to bother him now. Well, she couldn't do anything about it right then anyway. She let it go with difficulty, found herself thinking about Mikhail instead, and decided that this subject was even more hazardous to her peace of mind than trying to figure out telepathy with insufficient information.

A steaming, scented bath did a great deal toward restoring her energy and settling Margaret's mind. It was with great reluctance that she quitted the tub, dried her body carefully, slipped on a soft robe that was hanging, ready for her, and put the glove back on. It was so stiff now that she hated having it against her skin, but she dared not risk touching someone without its protective covering.

When she got back to her bedroom, she found the maid singing quietly to herself as she smoothed the bedding and patted the pillow into shape. The song distracted her from worrying about Dio, thinking about Mikhail, or the other things her ever-active mind seemed determined to bother her with. "What's that you are singing . . . I am sorry, I did not even ask your name."

"I am Piedra, *domna*. It's not much—just an old lullaby my mother always sang to me. I always sing it when I make the bed. It is quite foolish, but I believe that people sleep more soundly when I leave a lullaby on their pillow."

"That sounds very sensible to me," Margaret answered. "Will you sing it all the way through for me? I'd like to hear all the words." She reached down and picked up her recorder, checked to make sure the batteries had not failed, and turned it on. She wanted something safe around her, and music was the surest thing she knew. Music did not lie or die; it simply was.

The maid looked mildly startled, then amused. "If you like, *domna*." She began to sing, a very slight soprano with no training, but sweet and simple, like the song itself. The words were charming, all about various birds and animals going to sleep, and Margaret suspected it had an endless number of verses. She had heard similar things on other worlds, but none, she decided, was prettier than this.

When Piedra was finished, Margaret thanked her. She got out her Terran underwear, which was clean, and put on the soft cotton things. Then she pulled the spider-silk dress over her head and let it settle across her shoulders. It fit nicely, and Piedra's nimble fingers fastened the many buttons that ran along the spine. She sat Margaret down and undid her hair from the knot she had put it in for bathing, and gave it a long, careful brushing, so that Margaret relaxed with the gentle movements and almost forgot about her worries for a time.

The maid pinned and dressed her hair, slipped the butterfly clasp into place, and grinned broadly. "You have lovely hair, *domna*."

"Really? I never thought so—it's so fine and flyaway." She studied the woman in the mirror, and saw a stranger. Margaret was not vain, and rarely looked at herself more than to be sure she hadn't left toothpaste on her lips or that there were no dust marks on her cheeks. She had hated mirrors for as long as she could remember. Even though Ashara was no longer there to haunt her, she still felt somewhat uneasy looking at her own image.

The person in the mirror was very pale, with golden eyes which seemed enormous and lambent. She realized that her resemblance to Thyra Darriell was very strong, though Thyra's hair was a little darker, and her eyes were amber, not golden like Margaret's. But the delicate bones beneath her fair skin were like her long dead mother's, and she could only be grateful she had not inherited her frightening instability.

She did not know the beautiful, aristocratic woman in the mirror at all. Margaret looked at her gloved hand against the soft silk of the gown and down at her stockinged feet peeking out from beneath the embroidered hem. She was going to look very odd, wearing a leather glove and one of her two pairs of boots to a formal dinner. Well, there were her beloved bedroom slippers, so worn and disgusting that she should have replaced them ages ago. Boots had been acceptable at Armida, but this was Comyn Castle. Odd—she wanted so much to reflect well on her father. She had never wanted that before, and after a second, she decided she liked it. "I don't have anything for my feet."

Piedra looked pleased. "I noticed you didn't have anything proper when I put your clothes away, so I went and borrowed something for you. I hope you do not mind."

"Mind? Certainly not. But where did you find any shoes?"

Piedra shook her head, and her cheeks turned rosy. "Comyn Castle is full of things—like an attic, *domna*—that are left and forgotten or just plain discarded. It is shocking! The staff has to keep it all clean and dusted, so I know more about closets than I wish to. And in the Aillard Suite there is an entire cabinet full of old shoes and slippers. Jerana Aillard left them. She was said to have been very vain, and to have loved fancy shoes. I think they will fit."

Like a conjurer, the maid produced a pair of silvery slippers adorned with a pattern of feathers. They fit well enough, being of a soft leather that gave. "She must have been a very tall woman for her shoes to fit me."

"I don't know, *domna*. All I have heard is that she drove the staff mad with her demands when she was here, which was a great deal of the time, since she was married to Aran Elhalyn, who was keeping the throne warm just then. It was all long before my time. Pardon, *domna,* are you going to wear that glove? It doesn't quite go with the dress."

It was tactfully said, but it confirmed all her doubts. "Well, I have to keep my hand covered, and I just don't have anything else with me. If I had known that I would be attending state dinners, I would have made arrangements, of course." She envisioned herself with baggage filled with pretty gowns and fine slippers and all the rest. The image was so ridiculous that she laughed out loud.

"I'll go find you something nicer, then. I confess that I rather enjoy an excuse to rummage about in the closets—it is ever so much more fun than just dusting things. And sweeping carpets! Ugh. Just thinking about it makes me sneeze!"

Piedra left the room, and Margaret wriggled her toes in the shoes of a long-dead woman. A queen, it seemed. She wondered if she would ever be able to keep the intricacies of Darkovan families straight. The Elhalyns. Mikhail had mentioned them as the real kings of Darkover. But she really didn't want to think about Darkovan history just then, so she put her recorder back in its case to keep busy.

The maid returned with several long boxes in her arms. She was grinning, and was clearly enjoying herself immensely helping Margaret get ready for dinner. She put the boxes down and started to take out sets of gloves—long ones and short ones, leather ones and cloth ones. There must have been three dozen pairs.

"More loot from the Aillard Suite?"

"Loot? Well, I never thought about it like that, but, yes, I suppose it is. Hmm. These silk ones are a good color match, if they will fit you."

Margaret took the offered gloves and tried on the right one, to see if they fit. The gloves were long, almost elbow high, and were made of the same fine silk as her gown, but in some other weave, so they stretched over her fingers. There was fine embroidery, tiny silver feathers, around the open end, and she was almost sorry that the sleeve of her gown would hide it. But the glove fit perfectly, and she was happy to remove the leather one on her left hand, and replace it with the lighter one.

As soon as the silk slipped over the lines in her palm, Margaret felt something change. The sense of energy moving back and forth across her skin lessened, and she realized that this material was a better shield than leather. She noticed she had been unconsciously resisting the energy, and that now she no longer needed to. It was such a relief that she nearly cried, but instead she pulled herself together, thanked Piedra again and went back to the sitting room to find her father.

Lew's hair was still a little damp from bathing, and he had put on a bronze-colored tunic and brown trousers.

The fabric was old, she thought. The clothes must have been waiting for him all those years. And they still fit perfectly! Margaret thought he looked very handsome, except for the worry lines between his eyebrows. He looked at her, in her unaccustomed finery, and nodded his approval. "You look quite wonderful in that gown. Where did you get it—in one of the closets?"

"I feel pretty wonderful, too, which is strange. I've felt a lot of things since I got here, but wonderful was not one of them. And this dress is funny—it was a gift from Manuella MacEwan when I left Thendara what seems like ages ago. She insisted I would need something dressy, and that I would end up at the Castle, and I thought she was crazy. But, then, I've been thinking everyone on Darkover was crazy from time to time."

"Who is Manuella?"

"She is the wife of master tailor Aaron MacEwan, in Threadneedle Street. She was very kind to me, and I intend to take them all my business from now on. Even if the Altons have patronized some other tailor since time immemorial!

Lew chuckled. "That's the spirit! Fly in the face of tradition. I always wanted to, and I had so few opportunities. I believe that my father Kennard frequented some other tailor, for anything that was not made on the estate, but damn if I can recall the name just now."

The couch where Diotima had been resting was vacant now. "Where is Dio?"

"The Healer and I got her into bed and she is sleeping."

"What exactly is wrong with her, Father?" Margaret didn't want to ask the question, but she could not help herself.

"That is a good question, Marja. She has a disease which in the past was called 'cancer,' and which used to kill millions of people every year on old Terra. But genetic engineering fixed that, and now no one really knows how to treat the condition. In the past they used radiation, and even some things that were poison, in very small amounts, which could at times be worse than the disease itself. Today, there is hardly anyone who has a clue how to use such methods, though they did try. Dio said that if she were going to die, she wanted to do it under the sun of Darkover and nowhere else. So, I brought her home. What else could I do?" *She must not die! Not yet. I need her so much!*

"I am glad you did, even though I suspect you think you should have remained in the Senate or something else self-sacrificing."

Lew stared at her, then gave a little laugh. "You always could see right through me, just like . . . I have something for you." He turned to a table and picked up a small box. "This belonged to my mother, Yllana Aldaran. Dio has never worn it, for she does not wear much jewelry. But I think it was meant for you." He held the box out and Margaret took it.

It was a jeweler's box, old velvet rubbed and worn. Inside there was an enormous pearl in the shape of a single drop, a black tear resting on the pale satin which lined the box. It hung from a slender silver chain, and it was beautiful. Margaret held her breath for a moment, then took it out. "Why is it supposed to be mine?"

"Well, your name means 'pearl,' you know. Here, let me help you. You will ruin that fine hairdo otherwise." He stood behind her, and drew the chain over her shoulders, shifted her hair aside gently, and fixed the clasp. She could feel his breath against her hair, and she began to understand why Darkovan women kept the napes of their necks well covered.

As if Lew, too, was aware of their physical closeness, he stepped away quickly. Margaret pulled her hair back into place, and looked down at the great black pearl resting just above the curve of her breasts. It lay gracefully on the shining green cloth of her gown, as if it liked being worn once more. She put the box down. "Thank you. It is the most beautiful thing I ever saw."

"It becomes you," he answered. "But, why are you wearing Aillard feathers on your feet?"

"Am I? I didn't have any shoes, only boots, so Piedra went and borrowed these from a closet. She says Comyn Castle is like a big attic. These belonged to someone called Jerana a long time ago. I am wearing her gloves, too—they also have feathers embroidered on them, but you can't see them under my sleeves. I was just surprised there was anything large enough to fit my big feet. Otherwise I would have had to go stocking-footed or wear

my old slippers. I hope it is all right to borrow them—
I mean, no one will mind, will they?"

"Walking in a queen's shoes," he mused softly. "No,
they won't mind. Come, let's go down to dinner. I am
hungry. And I want to find out what Regis has been up
to while I was away. I hope there is some smoked rabbit-
horn. They never export it, and I have been longing for
some for twenty years and more."

Margaret gave her father a curious glance. She had
never known him to show any interest in food except to
fill his stomach, and he had eaten platters of Thetan
oysters or slabs of seagrass bread with equal indiffer-
ence. She did not doubt that he was sincere, but it was
a side of Lew she had never seen before, and it made
him more human. She was going to have to get to know
who he really was, and her heart warmed at the prospect. He gave her his arm, and she rested a gloved hand
on his sleeve, feeling almost giddy as they went into
the corridor.

The dining room was a comfortable chamber, with a
long table set between two roaring fireplaces. The chairs
had high backs, and were carved with the figure of a tall
tree painted silver against the dark wood. One servant
was walking around with a tray of goblets, offering wine
to people, and another had a platter of small appetizers,
little puffs of pastry filled with spiced meat.

Jeff was near the door when they came in, talking
to Gabriel Lanart. Mikhail's father looked at Lew and
Margaret and scowled. She suspected that Jeff and Gabriel had been discussing the Alton Domain, and that
Gabriel had not liked what he heard one bit. Then Lady
Linnea came forward, greeted Margaret with honest affection, and gave Lew one of her charming smiles.

"This is a wonderful moment for me. I am glad to
have you back on Darkover, Lew, even if the circumstances are less than happy ones. How is Diotima?"

"As the healers say, she is resting comfortably. That
is to say she is in a deep sleep from drugs and knows
no pain for the moment."

"Good. She has not really slept since you left for
Armida four days ago."

Lew nodded. "I never wanted to be in two places at

once so much as these past few days." He glanced toward the table, which was almost groaning with various dishes being set out by the servants.

"He is looking to see if there is smoked rabbit-horn," Margaret said impishly.

"Of course there is," Lady Linnea answered. "Regis told me how fond you were of it." She saw that Linnea was also wearing a spider-silk gown, blue with silver embroidery, and felt relieved that she was properly dressed for the occasion. Linnea wore no gloves, of course, since she did not need any, but otherwise Margaret thought she was dressed enough like the consort so she would not stand out.

Margaret heard a slight gasp behind her, and turned. Mikhail, dressed in the blue and silver of the Hastur house, was staring at her, his mouth a little agape. *Damn her for being so beautiful!*

Before she could speak to him, Regis entered the dining room, followed by Danilo Syrtis-Ardais and the young heir Dani. Regis appeared both worried and elated, as he nodded to everyone. He seemed somehow different than he had been at their first meeting, as if some burden had been lifted from his shoulders and he did not quite know how to behave in its absence.

He made a waving gesture, and everyone moved to the table. It was rather warm in the room, and Margaret was glad of her pretty gown, which was lighter than her other clothes. Then Regis came toward her, reaching for her hand and smiling. "Kinswoman, I welcome you to Comyn Castle again. You look quite lovely, and less confused than on your previous visit."

"Thank you, Lord Regis, but I am not less confused, just more used to being confused."

He laughed warmly. "That's good. Confusion is natural, but being at ease with it is difficult. And you, Lew, are looking less like one of Zandru's demons than when you appeared at the door a few days ago."

"*Bredhu*, I have my daughter and my wife as safe as I can make them, and I am content. You look rather smug yourself. Been into the cream pitcher again?"

Regis laughed again, and Margaret guessed this was some old joke, from when they had been boys and foster-brothers. The Regent just shook his head and did not reply, but she thought that if he had been a cat, there would have been feathers in his mouth.

When everyone was seated, Regis smiled. "It seems that fortune smiles upon us, for Lew Alton has returned at last, even though the circumstances which brought him home are sad. We must all hope that our *leroni* can do what Terran medicine has been unable to, Lew. But now the Domains are once more as they should be, and we will meet in the Crystal Chamber the day after tomorrow to reform the Comyn Council."

This announcement made both Lew and *Dom* Gabriel look up sharply. Margaret could almost hear the wheels grinding away in her uncle's mind. Lew's face was unreadable, though, and she guessed he must have had a lot of practice during his years in the Senate.

"It is strange how often sorrow brings us together." Regis continued, as if he had not said anything momentous. "Jeff here has told me of young Domenic Alar's terrible accident, and I have communicated with my sister. She has arrived safely at Arilinn, and everything that can be done is being done. We must hope he can be restored to full health." He paused and sighed. "At least he is not lost, as my older children were lost, not to chance, but to deliberate evil, to assassins, when the World Wreckers came to loot Darkover. Time has not blunted my sorrow, even though those times brought me together with my Linnea." He gave his lady a smile down the length of the table, and she returned it, so they looked quite young in their affection.

Margaret had seen something like that look pass between Dio and her father, and once more she felt the absence of any strong attachment in her own life. She had not really been aware of it while Ivor lived, but his death had left a vacant place in her heart, and she had felt a real hunger for something she did not have a name for. Well, it did have a name, of course, but she was afraid to let her mind express it, because, if the stormy look on *Dom* Gabriel's face was anything to judge by, she was going to be deeply disappointed, and probably frustrated as well.

Then she realized that Mikhail was almost staring at her, rudely by Darkovan standards, as if he were trying to attract her attention. *See—I told you something was up! There hasn't been a Council meeting in years!*

If you are so smart, tell me what it is going to be about, Margaret answered. *And I thought you said there was that Telepathic Council.*

I don't know, but Uncle Regis is more excited than I have ever seen him before, so it must be important. The Telepathic Council doesn't meet, cousin, it just is.

Oh. I can see how that might not be very satisfactory. Is he excited? He doesn't look it.

You don't know him like I do. Trust me, Regis is excited, and something very big is about to happen.

I do trust you, Mikhail. For no reason at all, I trust you completely.

Then Margaret noticed *Dom* Gabriel glaring at her, as he sat beside Lady Linnea, across the table from her, and colored to the roots of her hair, as if she had been doing something wrong. She liked Mikhail—more than liked him—but she did not like his father, and she wished she could.

"A Council meeting?" *Dom* Gabriel asked gruffly.

"Yes," Regis answered calmly. "But since this is a festive occasion, with the return of Lew and the presence of his daughter, I think we should keep to matters that will not disrupt our digestions. I know you will agree, Gabriel." It was lightly said, but there was no mistaking the authority in Regis' voice.

For a moment, *Dom* Gabriel looked as if he would argue the matter. Then Linnea passed him a platter of vegetables, and he shrugged and served himself.

Margaret was relieved, for she was tired and the thought of an argument was repulsive. She glanced up, found Mikhail watching her covertly, and bent her eyes to her food again. Lady Linnea asked her about her music research, and Margaret told her about the singers she had met in the hills.

How well she handles herself, even with my father scowling at her! This made her look up again, and Mikhail smiled at her so broadly that Margaret thought her heart would explode. She almost choked on her mouthful.

Behave yourself—everyone at the table will notice you looking at me!

As you wish, cousin, but it is not easy!

In spite of herself, Margaret smiled. It was wonderful to bask in his admiration, to sense his strong feelings about her. But it also made her uneasy, made her want to withdraw. The tension of her accustomed behavior and the newly discovered longing for closeness warred, and her throat closed up a little. Her appetite diminished, and she noticed Lady Linnea watching her carefully.

Margaret took several deep breaths, schooled herself with discipline, and applied herself to her excellent dinner. She tried not to think about the handsome young man who glanced at her from time to time, or anything else disturbing. Regis guided the general conversation toward matters of weather and crops, and since she knew nothing about these things, she was able to listen without feeling quite so overwhelmed. But Margaret was extremely glad when the meal was over, and she could return to her room.

She undressed, with the help of Piedra, and got into a clean nightgown that had been provided for her. Margaret settled into the huge bed, exhausted. But sleep eluded her. She was worried about Dio, and she wondered what the meeting that Regis had announced would be about. At last, however, her body surrendered, and she fell into a dreamless slumber.

27

$\blacklozenge$

When Margaret finally woke up the following morning, she could sense the bustle of Comyn Castle around her, and realized she must have slept very late. She lay in the huge bed and tried to make sense of the past few days, and particularly of the dinner party the evening before. There had been currents and cross-currents, most of which she had been too tired to analyze, and besides, it was very distracting to try to think straight with Mikhail just a few seats away, sending her occasional thoughts that upset what little emotional balance remained to her.

It was clear that *Dom* Gabriel had been surprised by Regis' announcement, and that it had some great significance to him. Her father, on the other hand, had not seemed very startled, and looked as if he had anticipated the move. It was all too complex, and even though she knew that the event would probably impact on her directly, Margaret just wished it would go away.

She got up, bathed again, and dressed in her now clean garments. She sorted through the boxes of gloves that Piedra had left the night before until she found a pair of short, silk ones that would fit. Then she went in search of Dio, and hardly noticed that her stomach was growling with hunger.

The Alton Suite consisted of many groupings of rooms stretching out on both sides of the sitting room she had first entered, and Margaret found that she knew its layout without asking. She knocked on any door that was shut, then walked in if there was no answer. At last she found Diotima in a bedroom at the other end of the suite from her own. She was dozing in the middle of an enormous bed, her small figure dwarfed by the expanse of linens, and shadowed by the hangings around it.

Margaret swallowed hard. She felt small and helpless and frightened, and she mustn't. Dio was an empath, and anything Margaret felt, her stepmother might pick up. That would not do her any good, and Margaret began to wonder at the wisdom of her coming.

There was a stir in the corner of the room, and a woman stood up from the shadows. She was of moderate height, and perhaps sixty, by the wrinkles around her eyes and mouth. She moved toward Margaret without making a sound on the thick carpet.

"Domna?" She spoke in a whisper.

"I came to see how my mother was faring."

"She is the same—not better but not worse. Would you like to sit with her a while? I am sure that would be a comfort."

Margaret was not certain, since her own lively fears were plaguing her mind. "Yes, I would."

"Then I will leave you with her for a time. I will be in the next room, if I am needed. Just call out."

"But what is your name?"

"I am Katerina di Asturien, and I am a Healer."

"Thank you. I'll just sit with her."

Margaret drew up a chair beside the bed and sat down. She could hear Dio's breathing, soft and not labored, and that reassured her a little. She let her mind wander, then decided that she needed to concentrate on good things, so she thought of Thetis, and the warm wind off the sea, and the smell of the azurines that grew around the front door of the house. She realized with a small pang that she would probably never see that place again, and she had a deep longing for the sea and the smell of it. One of the songs the islanders sang came back to her, about homecoming after a long ocean voyage in a small canoe, and she hummed it under her breath, because it was gentle and comforting.

Dio stirred. "I dreamed I was back on Thetis," she muttered fretfully, her small hands plucking at the sheet across her breasts. "I smelled the nightblooms in flower, and the salt of the sea."

"I was thinking about home, Dio, and you must have felt me."

"Marja! You really are here. I was almost afraid I had

dreamed you, though Lew assured me I hadn't. My mouth is so dry," she complained.

There was a pitcher of some rosy-colored liquid beside the bed, and a glass. Margaret filled it halfway, then knelt on the huge bed with care, and lifted her mother's head, and held the glass to her lips. Dio drank thirstily, then rested her head against Margaret's shoulder.

"Why are you wearing gloves in the house," Dio asked suddenly.

"It is a very long story," Margaret answered gently, setting the glass back on the table, and scooting around so she could continue to support Dio. It felt very peculiar to hold her mother in her arms, to be the comforter rather than the one being comforted. Margaret did not want to let go and, more, she wanted to will her stepmother into health. "I will tell you another time, when you are not so weary."

"I may not have another time, *chiya.*"

"Don't say that!" *You simply cannot die!*

Everyone dies, Marguerida. It is one of the only things which is certain. And, at least, you are reconciled with your father, which has been the wish of my heart for decades.

Diotima Ridenow-Alton—if you die, I will never speak to you again!

That's true enough, though I still speak to my father from time to time, and I think he can hear me—wherever he is now. But, tell me of your adventures—you don't want me to perish from curiosity, do you?

It was immensely reassuring to be teased, so Margaret settled herself into a more comfortable position, and began to tell her mother everything that had happened to her since she arrived. She was not halfway through with the narrative when she felt Dio fall asleep in her arms, a deep and restful sleep that seemed normal and much better than how she had been when Margaret came into the room. Her arm went numb, but she refused to move, to disturb the woman, and she thought of all the good things she could think of, hoping vainly that some of it would trickle into Dio's mind and help her in her illness.

Lew found them there late that afternoon. Margaret felt the flood of emotion from her father, the joy and terror all mixed together in a profound stew of feelings. She just lifted her head from watching Dio and smiled at him, ignoring the tears on his cheeks, and those on her own as well.

The next morning, Margaret followed her father into the Crystal Chamber. It was nearly midday, and the meal she had eaten earlier seemed to lie like lead in her belly. She did not want to be there, and could not understand why she needed to be present. Or, rather, she believed she understood all too well, and did not want to sit around and listen while a bunch of near strangers made decisions about her future.

Despite her agitation and simmering anger, she almost gasped when they entered. Nothing in her memories quite prepared her for the sight. It was a great circular room, high up in the Castle, and the walls were pierced with enormous windows of colored glass, so it appeared to be ablaze with light. There was a round table in the middle of the room, and the colors of the glass made wonderful patterns across the wood. She knew she had never been in the room before, but it felt familiar all the same. Lew had assured her that the room was built long after Ashara was dead, so she guessed she had picked up the sense of familiarity from him, not from the long-gone Keeper. Still, the feeling of knowing a place she had never been in before bothered her, and increased her unease.

There was something a little uncanny about the chamber, and Margaret wondered what it was. She looked around, at the chairs carved with the devices of the Domains, and found nothing there to disturb her. Then she looked up at the vaulted ceiling, painted with a design of the four moons and several stars, and realized that it was more than just a ceiling. There was something hidden behind the designs which brought gooseflesh to her skin.

The entire room smelled good, of furniture wax and swept carpets. From what Mikhail had told her, Margaret knew it had not been used for its original purpose for a long time. So, why was she so uneasy?

"Why does this room feel so strange?" Margaret whispered to her father.

He looked at her for a second. "There are dampers, telepathic dampers, all around the room, which is why it has not been used for years. They were put into place to keep any Altons past or present from using the Gift to force agreement from the rest of the Council."

"Oh, I see. You couldn't use this room for a meeting of a Telepathic Council, because it wouldn't work. I don't like it."

"Neither of us does, Marja. I have no happy memories of this room."

Dom Gabriel entered the chamber, frowned at them, and headed for the carved chair with the Alton device on it, the crag with an eagle perched on it which her father had told her was the sign of their family. He pulled the chair back with a sharp jerk, and banged it against his knee. Then he sat down and rested his arms on the shining surface of the table, almost daring them to question his right to the Alton Domain.

It was clear that the tallest-backed seats were for the heads of the Domains, but there were plenty of lesser chairs, and she wondered if she should take one, or remove herself to one of the others ranged along the walls of the huge room. She did not know her place, and it had been so many years since she had experienced that sense of dislocation that she found herself starting to shrink back into childhood invisibility. Lew seemed to sense her withdrawal, and gave her a quick and comforting pat on her shoulder, then nodded toward the table. It was clear he knew her place, even if she didn't, and that made her less hesitant.

Margaret remembered the previous afternoon, when Lew had found her holding her stepmother, and how the tears had run into the scar on his face. They had left Dio in the care of the Healer soon after, and gone back into the sitting room. There, for the first time in her adult life, they had talked, clumsily at first, then with more ease. It had been a wonderful time, both painful and healing. And, as they spoke, something within her seemed to melt, a cold, stony place in her heart that she had barely known existed until it was gone. Whatever happened now, Margaret knew that her father loved her, had always loved her, and that she could trust him as she had always wished to. It was a strange sensation, disquieting and new, and she treasured it even as she feared that it was unreal.

There was a stir at the entrance, and Lady Javanne Hastur came into the room, wearing her traveling clothes and looking very out of sorts. Her usually carefully applied cosmetics were a little smeared, and her usually carefully coifed hair was almost bedraggled. Instead of smelling of perfumes, the distinct odor of horse sweat rose around her.

Then young Dyan Ardais came in with Lady Marilla beside him. Dyan appeared apprehensive, but Marilla was all smiles. She came up to Margaret. "How good to see you up and about and looking fit," she began, enveloping her in a gentle embrace. She smelled of scent, some flowery combination that Margaret liked.

When she looked over Lady Marilla's shoulder, she saw Mikhail, wearing the Hastur colors and looking very handsome beneath the shining windows. Her cousin gave her a wink, and Margaret grinned at him. She wished they were anywhere but this room, because it had become a habit between them to have private little conversations, and she enjoyed them.

Margaret wondered when Dyan and his mother had arrived, for she had not seen them the previous evening, when the company had again gathered for a meal. It was, she knew, several days hard riding from Ardais to Thendara, and she realized that they must have been sent for, that Regis must have planned this meeting even before she had left Armida. And Javanne must have ridden from Arilinn Tower as soon as she delivered her grandson into the care of the healers there.

Then she began to ponder why they were gathered in the Crystal Chamber, rather than one of the many large rooms she knew existed in Comyn Castle. There was clearly some significance to the choice of that room over all the others in the Castle. There had to be a reason for their presence. Margaret felt as if she had the pieces of a puzzle staring her in the face, but could not make any sense of them yet. She still did not understand the way things worked, but she suspected she was about to find out more about the governing of Darkover than she ever wanted to know.

Margaret noticed that her aunt was staring at Dyan

Ardais and Lady Marilla very hard, and almost wished she could hear what the older woman was thinking. There was suspicion in it, and something else as well. It occurred to her that Javanne had not expected the Ardais folk, and that their presence was troubling for some reason. Regis must not have told his sister that he was reconvening the Comyn Council. He was playing his cards very close to his chest, Margaret decided, even with his sister. Javanne had come, no doubt, expecting something more along the lines of a family gathering to decide Margaret's fate, and likely to propose that Mikhail be sent off to become Senator in place of Herm Aldaran. She held back a chuckle, and saw that Mikhail was also suppressing his easy laugh.

Regis and Lady Linnea came into the room then, and looked around. He saw Gabriel sitting in the Alton chair and a curious expression came into his face. He did not appear angry, but rather he was vastly amused. His ever-present shadow, Danilo Syrtis-Ardais, stood behind him, and Margaret wondered if Regis and Linnea ever had any privacy at all, let alone enough to get their children. *What a vulgar mind I have,* she thought, glad that in this room no one could eavesdrop on her thoughts.

Regis took his place in a tall chair with the silver tree carved on it, and his sister Javanne slipped into the one beside it. As a Hastur, Margaret assumed this was the correct place for her aunt, and looked at her father for some cue as to where she should sit, since it was quite clear that he intended her to take a place at the table, not along the wall.

Dyan, a little reluctantly, sat in the Ardais chair. Then Mikhail held another chair and helped Lady Marilla into it. It was one of the tallest chairs, one that signified a Domain holder, and Margaret remembered that Marilla had called herself Aillard, not Ardais, when they had met what seemed like ages before. When he had the woman seated, Mikhail retreated to stand behind Dyan's chair, mimicking Danilo's posture perfectly.

Lew, beside her, appeared lost in thought for a moment. Then he took her arm in a light hold and guided her to a chair two seats away from *Dom* Gabriel. It had a figure carved on the back of it, but she didn't have time to really take a look. Then he seated himself between her and her uncle, placed his single hand on the surface of the table, and looked smug.

Dom Gabriel opened his mouth in protest, but a look from his wife silenced him. Instead, he swore under his breath, and looked daggers at everyone. He clearly did not know quite what to make of the situation either, and she was sure he did not like it at all.

Regis cleared his throat. Before he began to speak, he looked toward the door of the chamber, as if he was expecting someone else, then gave a little shrug. "When Lew Alton left Darkover, the Comyn lay in ruins. The Aillard and Elhalyn lines were almost extinct, and Dyan Ardais was dead, his son still in swaddling bands. That left the Aldarans, who have not had a place here in generations, and we Hasturs, and the Ridenows. *Dom* Gabriel was entrusted with the Alton Domain, by the decision of Jeff Kerwin to remain at Arilinn." He gave a little sigh, as if thinking of these events caused him some pain.

"Then we suffered through a very troubled time, when the World Wreckers came, and many fine people were assassinated for no better reason than that they were perceived as a threat to the aims of the Wreckers. My own children were killed, as were those of other people, slain by stealth, in a cowardly way, that I have never really forgiven. We survived, but we lost good people, people we needed to govern."

He gave a long sigh, and Linnea patted his hand. In turn, he gave his consort a look of gratitude, and such abiding affection that Margaret was simultaneously embarrassed and envious. "After the defeat of the World Wreckers, we tried to reorganize things, and we used the vehicle of the Telepathic Council. It was the best solution we had at the time, and the Terrans did not interfere. And so things have remained for a generation. The Telepathic Council is not perfect, but it has met our needs adequately." Javanne stirred impatiently beside him, and her brows knitted.

"However, ten days ago I received a delegation, a most surprising collection of men from the city guilds and people from the countryside. They have demanded that the local government shall be given over again to what is left of the Comyn Council. They feel, rather strongly, that the Telepathic Council is not sufficiently Darkovan, that it is too Terran and does not truly represent our needs. It was a remarkable occasion, perhaps the most remarkable in a reign that has not been wanting in momentous events." He paused, as if reflecting on the meeting. "They were thinking of themselves and their children after them. We have no history of democracy on Darkover, but it seems that exposure to the Terranan have given the people some ideas of their own."

"They demanded of you!" *Dom* Gabriel's face turned an unlovely red. "That is outrageous! I hope you sent them off with a . . ."

"But what is left of the Council?" asked Javanne, her eyes narrowing thoughtfully as she interrupted her husband before be made a complete fool of himself. "Prince Derik Elhalyn died without children."

"True," Regis answered. "Derik left no heirs of his body, and his sister's children were either babies or not yet even born. Priscilla Elhalyn is a very retiring woman, and she has kept herself and her children away from Thendara for what I am sure are very good reasons to her mind. But her eldest is now a bit younger than Dyan, and although they do not bear the Elhalyn name, they do possess the bloodline. And since the Elhalyn have always granted their women *comynara* status, I think a case could be made for restoring the line through one of these children—we will have to test them and see which is the most stable. I requested Priscilla to join us, but she demurred." He sighed. "Perhaps I was insufficiently persuasive. However, we can manage without her, I believe."

This created a stir, and several voices were heard exclaiming. Under cover of this noise, Margaret asked her father very quietly, "What's wrong with these Elhalyn people? Why shouldn't they be stable?"

"Too much inbreeding leads to a great many problems," he whispered back.

She nodded. In their desire to preserve *laran,* the chief families of Darkover had not really taken into consideration the long term effects of their breeding programs. Margaret still didn't really understand why the Elhalyns were so important, nor why Regis was so determined to revive that particular line. But she had taken his measure in the past two days, and she had a great deal of respect for his calm sensibility. Darkover had been fortunate to have this man to guide them after the Sharra Rebellion.

The door of the chamber opened, and a complete stranger entered. He was tall, rufus-haired, and Margaret knew he must be a Ridenow from his distinctive eyes. He was rather too young to be one of Diotima's brothers, but perhaps he was related to Istvana instead.

"Forgive my lateness. My horse went lame and it took me longer than it should have." He made a bow toward Regis, who did not appear to be at all surprised at this latest arrival, although it was clear that Javanne and Gabriel were. If anything, Regis appeared relieved. Then Lady Javanne gave her brother a look of betrayal, and Margaret wondered if she had come to Thendara expecting to lead a meeting of her own.

From the expression on her father's face, he was startled as well, though he did not look displeased. "Who is he," she whispered.

"I am not sure, *chiya,* except that he must be one of Dio's kin. He has the look of Lord Edric Serrais, so I think he might be a son. But now I know why Regis has been stalking about the corridors of Comyn Castle looking as if he had cream on his mustache." Lew leaned back in his chair, clearly amused at the presence of the newcomer. "The old devil is even cleverer than I thought."

Dom Gabriel heard this remark, and gave Lew an unreadable look. Then he looked across the table at his wife. Margaret followed his eyes, and saw her aunt's face narrow with calculation.

Regis rose, smiling. "Welcome, Lord Ridenow. I am pleased that you managed to arrive, for we have only just begun. Lew, I don't think you know Francisco Ridenow, though I have written of him to you from time to time."

"Of course! I should have known." Lew stood up and greeted the newcomer with every appearance of delight, as if they were friends already, or, perhaps, allies. He drew Francisco to the table. "This is my daughter, Marguerida Alton." Margaret pushed her chair back clumsily, made a slight bow that did not quite become a curtsy, and smiled at the man. Close-up, he looked a little younger than herself and was quite handsome.

There was a pause, while Francisco got himself seated, and Margaret and Lew returned to their chairs. She turned to Mikhail, and found him looking very stern. Then she realized he was watching *Dom* Francisco with a wary eye, and wondered if he were jealous. It gave her a funny feeling, a kind of warmth in her chest that was not unpleasant, but very new. No one had ever been jealous on her account before, and she wasn't sure how to react.

"I have been speaking of the recent past, Francisco, mostly for the benefit of Marguerida, who does not know our history." He gave Lew a piercing look at this remark, and her father's cheeks reddened slightly. "After the Sharra Rebellion, I was the only adult heir to Hastur still alive, and next after me, my sister's sons. At the time I had not found Linnea and had only nedestro sons of my own, so I designated Mikhail as my heir," Regis said.

He cleared his throat again, and Lady Linnea, beside him, coiled her fingers into his, a gesture so tender and intimate that it was almost shocking. "There things have stood for twenty years, and while I was not certain it was the best situation, I was not impelled to rush into any decisions. It has been hard on Mikhail, for I have not formalized things, so he remains heir designate, even though I now have two sons to take my place. I can only say that, having lost my older children to fate, I was not eager to make little Dani my heir. I learned that life was much more chancy than I ever imagined, and it left a mark on me."

"You are going to name Dani as your heir, then," Javanne asked, her face almost cheerful.

Regis turned his head and gave her a curious look, as if she were a stranger, and not a very nice one. Javanne's expression changed, and the pleasure she had showed a moment before vanished. "I thought a great deal about the delegation I had received, and also about the changes that were taking place in the Federation. They did not bode well for Darkover, for it seemed that with the Expansionists in power, it was likely that we were going to face the challenge of more plunderers, more

World Wreckers. This was Lew's opinion, but it confirmed my own, from other sources of information. And it seemed to me that reconvening the Comyn Council at this point in time would be a step forward, not a regression. But one of the things the common folk's delegation were particularly insistent on was restoring the Elhalyn to the throne. Since this was an idea very dear to my heart, I was inclined to agree." He smiled charmingly, and Margaret remembered that one of the things that the Hasturs supposedly had as part of their Gift was the ability to manipulate people. That explained why he had chosen to meet in the Crystal Chamber; if the dampers kept the Alton Gift from being used, then it logically kept Regis' Gifts in check as well.

Still, she was somewhat puzzled. Regis was king in everything but name, and he seemed to want to abdicate the position. She did not know a great deal about power, other than the vicious, petty games that academics played, but she knew enough to realize this was an unprecedented move for him to make. The only satisfaction she had was the certainty that everyone else at the table was almost as puzzled as she was.

"So, we have an Ardais, and I am sure young Dyan will serve ably. Lady Marilla is a Lindir and one of the last of the Aillards, but we all know how able she is. I trust we can pry her away from her kilns from time to time, to join us in our necessary deliberations." He gave Marilla a smile that was very charming, and Margaret watched the woman relax beneath it. "*Dom* Francisco is willing to serve for the Ridenows. We will find an Elhalyn to serve on the Council, though it may take time."

"But, Regis," *Dom* Gabriel protested, despite the fact that Javanne was signaling him to keep quiet while she evaluated the new situation, "what is your purpose in all this?"

"My purpose is to give Darkover the best people she has to offer, to lead her into the future. And that future is not in my hands, or yours, old friend, but in the hands of these youngsters—in the hands of Mikhail, Dyan, Francisco, and Marguerida. I will not live forever, nor will Lew nor Javanne nor you—and we cannot go on behaving as if we will. That has been the mistake I have made in not taking matters into hand before."

"Mikhail? What has he to say in any of this—he will not be inheriting Hastur." *Dom* Gabriel was clearly angry, as if it were the fault of his younger son that all of these changes were being proposed. "He is merely a younger son, paxman to Dyan Ardais, and nothing more!"

"And you would have me waste all his training and his intelligence, then?"

"Training? You mean that Terranan education you gave him? I think that makes him unsuited to have anything to do with governing Darkover—he is corrupted!" *Dom* Gabriel brought his fist down on the table as he spoke. "It is clear you have plans for him, and whatever they are, I will not allow them."

"Gabriel, be quiet!" Javanne snapped these words out. "There is a use to which Mikhail can be put, and I know what it is. Regis, I want you to send Mikhail to take Lew's seat in the Senate. He has always wanted to travel to the stars, and now would be a perfect time! We simply cannot allow an Aldaran to sit in the Senate—they cannot be trusted, and you know it. I am sure Lew acted as he thought best, but he was wrong."

The expression on Mikhail's face was a combination of alarm and anger. Margaret didn't blame him at all. She had told him of his mother's scheme, but neither of them had really given it a great deal of credence. And he did not want to leave Darkover now, she knew. How sad, she reflected, that having wished to travel to the stars all his life, he might now have the opportunity when he no longer wanted it. Now she realized that Javanne and Gabriel felt they had lost Mikhail long ago to what they saw as frightening and dangerous Terranan ideas, ideas that had been encouraged by Regis. She tried not to feel frightened or sad at the idea, but she knew him well enough now to realize that if Regis wanted it, he would go. Mikhail would put Darkover before his personal happiness, and her own, for that was the sort of man he was. She loved him for that, she decided, even if it meant her life would be ruined just when it was truly starting.

"No!" Regis shook his head. "That will not fit in with the plan I have, and Mikhail does not have the experience he needs to take a Senatorial seat. Herm Aldaran will remain in that position. I sent him to the lower house six years ago with the intention that he would someday take Lew's place, though I did not expect it to be so soon."

"But," *Dom* Gabriel protested, "this is outrageous! I never approved of that appointment, and I still don't! I think you have lost your mind, Regis."

Remarkably, Regis kept his temper and answered calmly. "No, I have not. I made the decision after much consideration, because Herm is a canny politician, and because he understands what must be done to protect our world." He paused, took a deep breath, and looked to Lady Linnea for support. "More, it is my intention to invite the Aldarans to return to the Comyn Council in the near future. We cannot allow ourselves to be divided when we will need every resource to keep Darkover whole!"

Several voices were raised in protest, the loudest being *Dom* Gabriel's. "Are you mad? No one will sit at Council with a damned Aldaran—not me, not anyone."

"Nonsense. What harm the Aldarans did is generations past, and we must heal the wound, not keep it open and bleeding. We will have foes enough from the Expansionist forces to keep us busy without having another one lurking at our backs. With the Aldarans here, we can keep an eye on them!"

"If you imagine you can force me to be party to this nonsense, then you are deluded. In fact," *Dom* Gabriel went on, "It seems to me that you are no longer fit to guide Darkover, Regis! Dani is too young to take on your responsibilities . . . but another regent can be appointed." He drew his shoulders up, puffed out his large chest, and continued. "With the guidance of older men, such as myself I am sure . . ."

Dyan Ardais stirred in his chair. His hand went to the pommel of his small sword. "That sounds very close to treason to my ears, *Dom* Gabriel," the young man snarled, startling many people present. "I am loyal to Regis, to Hastur, to Darkover. I will not sit here silently and let you speak so."

"Be quiet, puppy! You are only looking out for Mikhail's interests, and I know it, even if you don't. He has charmed you, like he does everyone. I know he is dangerous, and cannot be trusted! He thinks too much!"

"And that is exactly what Darkover needs—thought-ful men." Regis' face was flushed with rage, but his voice was calm and even. Behind him, Danilo was tense, ready to leap to the defense of his liege, and the Guardsmen standing at the doorway were alert. Margaret wondered if blood had ever been spilled in that room before, and hoped her uncle's would not be the first. A glance at Mikhail's face told her that his thoughts were running in the same direction, that it was tearing him apart to see his father and his uncle ready to go at each other. If it had not been so serious, if there had not been so many swords and knives in the room, it would almost have been ludicrous, the idea of two men in their early fifties getting into a brawl. But it was serious, and she knew it.

More, Margaret understood that she was right in the middle of it—that as heir to the Alton Domain, she was not some observer but an actual player in a game that she did not fully understand. And a deadly game, if the expressions on the faces of the men were anything to judge by. She could not sit there, passively, silently, any longer. She gave Lew a quick glance out of the corner of her eyes, and saw him give her a little nod, as if he were following her thoughts, even though the room itself prevented it.

"I know I haven't any business speaking, but—"

"Then keep quiet," Javanne hissed.

"No, I will not. First, as a University-trained re-searcher, I have to say that I do not think that Regis has completely revealed his plans, and that theorizing with incomplete data is always foolish."

"Listen to her!" *Dom* Gabriel was so red faced now that his ears were nearly purple. "A 'University-trained researcher,' indeed! This woman doesn't know her place, which is to do as she is told, and be quiet the rest of the time. She is unfit to inherit the Alton Domain! She is too Terranan, too independent! Why, she is little bet-ter than a Renunciate!"

For some reason this last, which Gabriel clearly in-tended as an ultimate insult, made Margaret laugh. Ev-eryone looked at her, even Mikhail, as if she had lost her mind. "I would be proud to be a Renunciate, were it not for the fact that I don't wish to be one." She understood her uncle better now. He had a vast sense of inferiority, for reasons she did not know, and he had lived for decades with a managing woman who probably rarely did what he wanted. Suddenly Margaret knew that he found her behavior too similar to his wife's, and that he wanted more than anything to control her, if only because he could not control Javanne, and never had been able to. That explained his immediate opposition to any match between her and Mikhail—he could not control Mik either.

"You cannot have it both ways, Uncle," she went on as calmly as she was able. "Either I am important or I am not. I cannot only be important to suit you, and keep quiet the rest of the time."

Gabriel rounded on Lew. "This is all your fault!"

Lew smiled slowly. "Very likely. I did not try to make her meek and biddable—there was always too much of myself and her mother in her for that." There was an emotion in his voice, as if for the first time he could think of Thyra without pain or regret, could see that she had been something more than the woman he remembered. "But I believe she is right. Regis has something else he wants to say. I confess I am looking forward to it."

"And so am I," Dyan chimed in, clearly ready to cast his lot with Lew Alton.

"Well," Francisco Ridenow added, "thus far I have not heard anything that disturbs me, so I hope Lord Regis will continue with his revelations."

Lady Marilla cleared her throat. "Like *Dom* Gabriel, I cannot like the idea of any Aldaran sitting in this chamber. But I also can see some wisdom in keeping them under our eye, rather than permitting them to do whatever they wish behind our backs. I have thought a great deal about this, since Marguerida asked me about them some time back, and I decided that perhaps I was prejudiced by the past—that I do not know these people and that perhaps they are not really the monsters we imagine them to be."

"This is still not a full Council, so nothing we say will carry any weight," Javanne put in. She sniffed and gave

Lady Marilla a glance of open contempt. "It is only a lot of heated air. It will all come to nothing." She seemed quite sure of herself. It seemed likely that she believed she could influence her brother in private.

"How very disloyal of you, Javanne," Regis said dryly. "It would be shocking, if I did not know you so well." He gave a little sigh. "Decision has never been my strong suit, for I always see too many possibilities. But I have thought long on this matter, and I do not think I will be swayed by any arguments now. Even my sister will acknowledge that it took me a long while to make up my mind, but now that I have, I will stand by my choices."

He looked at Linnea for support, then continued. "There are still several matters to be resolved. One is the disposition of the Alton Domain, and that lies at the heart of the predicament. It is not that we have too few legitimate claimants, but that we have too many. *Dom* Gabriel feels he has a rightful claim on it, because he has held the position for years. I do not know how Lew feels. But since he has returned, his claim is the most valid."

"I have no desire to reclaim the Alton Domain. I have a wife who is very ill, and all I want is to get her well, not sit in Council meetings until my bottom gets numb. I had enough of that while I served in the Senate to last several lifetimes!" Lew's single hand roamed restlessly across the table top, back and forth, as if he was trying to put his finger on something which remained elusive.

"And Marguerida's claim?"

"She is my daughter, my only living child. And since I did not designate Gabriel as my heir before I departed, my sense is that she remains the most legitimate person to hold the Domain."

"She does not follow our ways!" Gabriel roared. "She must be made to resign the Domain into my hands, or the hands of my sons! I will not permit anything else!"

Margaret looked at her Aunt Javanne, and was met with a hard-eyed glare. It must have been hard for her, all these years, married to Gabriel, trying to be a proper Darkovan woman, when she clearly had drive and ambition. Javanne must have hated being able only to manipulate her husband, instead of sitting in a place of power.

And Mikhail was too much like Javanne, Margaret guessed. He could not be manipulated, controlled, or bullied either.

She gave Mikhail a glance, and he smiled at her, as if he knew her thoughts despite the dampers in the chamber. Suddenly the matter of the Alton Domain seemed irrelevant. Uncle Gabriel was a good man, in his stubborn, slow way, and he had kept her lands well. On the other hand, she realized she had a responsibility, a duty to fulfill. Her father had never asked anything of her, not really, but he clearly wanted her to inherit his estates, and she knew she would not fail him. She was just afraid that the cost was going to be one she did not wish to pay. *Funny,* she thought. *I never believed there would be any man who would be a light in my life, and now there is, and he cannot have me, nor I him. Life is not fair!*

"The crux of the matter is that the people will have—demand to have—a Comyn Council again. So the Heirships must be settled, clearly defined, or else we will spend all our energy squabbling and have none left for our real business—which is to serve the people of Darkover as well as we are able. I may be Regent, but I know that I am a servant of the people I rule, and I never want to forget that!" Regis' voice rang out against the great windows, echoing, and bringing everyone back to attention.

There was a rather shocked silence at this statement, and *Dom* Gabriel looked as if he had had the wind knocked out of him. Javanne, on the other hand, looked very thoughtful, and Margaret did not doubt that she was looking for ways to turn this new political situation to her advantage.

"Serve the people?" Gabriel sounded as if he suspected a trap in that.

Regis ignored his brother-in-law. "First among the Domains comes the Elhalyn of Hastur, but those among them are too young to govern wisely and have had no experience with ruling, they will need guidance. Danilo—my son by Linnea—will be heir to Hastur of Hastur, but again he is too young to have a seat at Council." He paused, and Margaret saw something in his face, a shadow of doubt or worry. She remembered the tense young man who had greeted them on their return to Thendara. She noticed that Regis had very carefully not declared his eldest son the heir, but put it off to some vague future, and she wondered if there was something amiss with Danilo Hastur. "Mikhail is my next heir, after Danilo, and I am minded to appoint him to the Regency of the Elhalyn Domain. Your good sense and Terran education will stand you in good stead for this task, Mikhail, until we can be sure that the eldest living son of Derik's sister is sound of mind. We cannot risk another Derik. In another year he will be of an age to rule, but there will be no talk of crowning for some time to come."

Javanne stared at her brother, and Margaret did not blame her. It sounded as if he were perfectly prepared to abdicate his position in favor of a young man who had never been trained to rule. It was a bold move, and a dangerous one, to surrender his power so quickly.

Mikhail looked as if he had been struck with an ax. "Lord of Light," he whispered. "Me, a Regent!"

Regis heard him and gave a slight smile. "It is completely appropriate. Your grandmother was Alanna Elhalyn."

"I never thought of that," Mikhail muttered.

"Why Mikhail and not Gabriel or Rafael?" asked Javanne, her cheeks full of color. She glared at her brother, then at her son, as if they were some sort of monsters.

"Mikhail has been trained to rule, and he can give the correct guidance. Gabe and Rafael are good men, sister, but they are not suited to the task I have in mind."

Mikhail looked very distressed, almost as upset as his mother. "I am sworn to Hastur, Regis. If I take on the Elhalyn Domain, it alters everything. My loyalties will have to be to them, and . . ." He tried to shrug it off. "Well, Priscilla's son Alan will be old enough to be crowned soon. But, frankly, he is a little odd. It is the second son, Vincent, who . . ." Like a sleepwalker Mikhail moved from his place behind Dyan's chair. He went to a chair almost opposite Regis, a chair marked with the silver tree of Hastur but with a crown above it, and sat down. "Now that I no longer want the crown that

Regis swore to me, I have the burden of a crown I never sought," he whispered.

This turn of events was puzzling to Margaret. She was not sure why Regis was so bent on restoring the traditional kings of Darkover—the little she had heard made her think they were a strange family—nor why he should appoint Mikhail, except that his grandmother had been an Elhalyn. By that logic, Javanne would be just as good a candidate for the role of regent, and she would love it! Maybe there was some custom that prevented a woman from being regent.

Gabriel growled. "That is ridiculous. Mikhail will fill Alan's head with a lot of Terranan nonsense, if he isn't already ruined."

Lew stirred. "Gabriel, you are still living in the past. We have to try to adapt, both of us. The old Darkover that we grew up in is gone. Forever, I suspect. Even restoring the Elhalyn line to the throne will not bring it back. Regis has made several remarkable proposals, and I think we need time to digest them. May I suggest we adjourn, and let our tempers cool."

"You can suggest anything you like—but I will oppose all of these matters—Aldarans in the Comyn Council and Mikhail sitting for Elhalyn! I will take it to the Cortes, and they will see the . . ."

"I would not recommend you oppose me, *Dom* Gabriel," Regis said formally. He looked at Margaret. "I have the best interests of Darkover in mind, and opposition will only lay us open to the schemes of our enemies. And, if you do, then I will remove you from the Council."

There was no mistaking his tone. A silence settled across the room, while everyone digested this threat. Margaret looked from face to face, trying to judge the mood. But most of all, her eyes were drawn to Mikhail. *Well,* she thought, *at least he won't be leaving Darkover.*

28

◆

Gabriel stormed out of the Crystal Chamber, nearly knocking over one of the Guardsmen as he went to the door. Javanne started to follow him, but her brother grasped her wrist in a hard grip. "We must talk, sister," he said, his face unsmiling. "We must talk about loyalty."

Javanne looked surprised now, as if Regis were a complete stranger. "Loyalty?"

"Precisely. Come along." Regis rose, slipped his arm into Javanne's, and started toward the door. Danilo had to step back quickly to avoid being hit with the chair, but he fell in smoothly behind Regis. Then Lady Linnea stood up slowly, her face grave, and the four of them left the chamber.

"Well," Francisco Ridenow announced, "this was not quite what I expected when Regis asked me to come here. I thought it was going to be dull." He chuckled and turned to Lew. "Is it always this heated?"

Lew shook his head. "Believe me, this was rather tame compared to a few previous occasions!"

"I see." He gazed at Mikhail, whose head was in his hands, then at Lady Marilla and Dyan Ardaisi. "It has given me quite an appetite, you know. As well as a great deal to think about. Aldarans in the Crystal Chamber? Who would have believed that?"

"I would," Dyan Ardais said suddenly.

"Really?"

"I know what they did, the deals they made with the Terranan, in the past, but I have always thought that it was a bad idea to let them get up to new mischief behind our backs."

"There is a certain wisdom in that," Francisco agreed. He studied Dyan and Lady Marilla, then looked at Mikhail again. "But I am too hungry to think properly. Nothing more is going to be settled today, is it? Then I say we should go find some food, and perhaps some wine as well. Perhaps a great deal of wine."

Despite the air of tension and uncertainty in the room, everyone laughed. Dyan helped his mother to her feet, and Francisco rose. They walked to the door, paused to see if the last three occupants would follow them, then left.

"He seems a cheerful sort," Margaret told her father. "Can we get out of here—this room makes my skin crawl. Come on, Mikhail—don't just sit there like the end of the world has come." She spoke with more heartiness than she felt, for she could not imagine why he was so upset. When she had first met him, he had expressed his frustration at being only a paxman, when he had been trained to be a king. Now he would be regent for this Alan Elhalyn, or one of his younger brothers, and he didn't appear pleased at all.

Mikhail looked up, and seemed to compose himself a little. "You are right. The end of the world has not come—it has only been turned upside down! Regis never gave me a hint of his plans! It changes everything, and I am not quite sure . . . oh, to hell with it. Mother will never let him . . ."

Lew looked at Mikhail. "I think that we should leave now." He glanced toward the two Guardsmen still standing near the door, trying to look as if they had not been listening, as if what had been said would not be the talk of the barracks in a few hours. "There is a little terrace that I rather liked when I was younger. Let's go sit and enjoy the sun and clear our minds."

"Very well." Mikhail stood, then looked at the carving on the back of his chair for a long moment. He shook his head. "My father will never forgive me for this, never."

"Why?" Margaret walked over to her cousin. "I don't see that this should be anything for him to be angry about, except that he seems to enjoy being upset about anything he didn't think of! Will one of you please explain to me why this decision is so dreadful. You said you wanted something more meaningful than being a paxman, Mik—and this sounds like an important thing your uncle has asked you to do."

They left the Crystal Chamber and Lew led them down the corridor and out onto a small terrace that overlooked the city of Thendara, glowing ruddily in the early afternoon sun. Margaret stretched her arms over her head and smelled the clear air, glad to be out of doors.

"Regis has just reshaped things in a way I never anticipated, nor Mikhail either, and we are both rather surprised." Lew spoke quietly. "She's very beautiful, isn't she?"

"Who," Margaret asked.

"Thendara. I have seen a great many cities, *chiya*, but the view over Thendara remains my favorite. I never thought I would stand here again and look across it."

Mikhail was leaning against the balistrade, and some of the tension that had gripped him left his shoulders. He still didn't look happy, but he seemed to Margaret to be less distressed, and that was enough for the moment. "I do not want to be a crown on a stick, hung in the marketplace for men to bow down to."

"And just what does that mean," Margaret asked him.

"Regis once told me that if I wished to live my own life, I should have arranged to be born to other parents." He laughed a little at this ironic jest. "I didn't understand him at the time. No one chooses his own life, really. Do they, Uncle Lew?"

"Well, no. I did not choose to be the many things I have become—or at least it has always seemed to me that I was forced into situations that were not precisely what I would have chosen. That, I believe, is hindsight. When I did the things I did, it certainly seemed right at the time. But, Mikhail, I do know how you feel right now."

"Well, I don't," Margaret snapped, her patience worn thin.

Lew smiled at her. "For generations the Elhalyn have been our kings, but the power behind the throne has always been a Hastur. What Regis has done, by nominating Mikhail to the Regency of Elhalyn, is to make him a kingmaker. What it means, I believe, is that while young Danilo will be Regis' heir, the real power will be in Mikhail's hands. He does not know if they are capable hands, but he believes that they are. It is a bold move, one that I confess I admire."

Mikhail gave a sharp, barking laugh. "That is easy for

you to say—your entire life has not just been disarranged!" Mikhail turned and looked at her. "My life is no longer my own. So I cannot say to you what I should have said sooner—that I wish we could have wed. Then you could have been a queen, though to me you are already more than that."

Margaret felt her face flame. She turned to her father, but he seemed to be miles away, deep in some thoughts of his own. "I don't think I would make a very good queen, Mik. I would be breaking rules right and left all the time. But I do wish you had spoken, because . . . it would have meant a lot to me. I take it that you being regent for the Elhalyn makes a difference?" She was holding back her disappointment with great difficulty.

"In the past," Lew answered, "it would have done so. Now, I am not sure. As the holder of the Alton Domain, an alliance with the regent of Elhalyn would have been an extremely powerful combination, one that the other Domains would have viewed with suspicion."

"Well, what if you reclaim the Domain, and leave me out of it? I don't want the thing, you know!"

"That, I think, would not be in the best interests of Darkover."

"I see. I am supposed to put my personal happiness aside for the sake of the planet?" Margaret was simmering with rage and rebellion now, feeling very much as she had during her adolescence.

Lew chuckled, then reached over and patted her cheek gently. "No, *chiya,* I would not ask you to do that."

"Then, what?"

"Anyone but a complete fool can see that you and Mikhail are in love, my Marja. And I want you both to be happy, because that will serve Darkover as well as your own needs."

"My mother and father will never permit that," Mikhail protested.

"Hmm. If my guess is correct, Regis is bending his charm to persuade Javanne to his ideas even as we speak. You see, power is being redistributed, and there will be a great deal of resistance, of course. But I believe, in the long term, something will be worked out that will satisfy everyone. Well, not *Dom* Gabriel, perhaps."

"Are you telling me to be patient, Father?"

"Yes. You must go to a Tower, to Arilinn or Neskaya, for some training."

"Mik says that takes years and years. By the time I am done, I'll be a dried-up old prune! And that isn't what I want! Everyone seems bent on deciding my life without consulting me. The only person on Darkover who has ever asked me what I want is Mikhail."

"All right, my Marja, what do you want?" Lew moved his handless arm toward her a little in a gesture of affection.

"I want . . . to marry Mikhail, if he will have me."

Of course I will have you! There is nothing I want more than that!

Well, then, that is settled, isn't it?

It's not that simple, Marguerida. I only wish it were. Aldones, how I love you!

"Nothing else?" Lew interrupted.

"Yes, there is more! The level of illiteracy on Darkover is unforgivable! It isn't healthy, and it's not safe. People here need to be more informed about the Federation, about the danger from people like the Expansionists. As long as the Comyn make all the decisions for an uninformed populace, then I think Darkover is at risk."

"Well said, daughter! And, absolutely right. So, would you establish schools or just set aside our feudal ways in a sweep of the hand?" He was teasing her now, and she was torn between wanting to enjoy it and the desire to shake him.

"I have no desire to disrupt Darkovan culture wholesale. But, if I am really to be the heir to a Domain, then I want Darkover to be in the strongest possible position as regards the Federation. I don't want to dwindle into a mere wife, or end up an aging intrigant, like Javanne!"

"She would be deeply hurt by that estimation," Lew answered cheerfully. "And you are quite correct. We must prepare Darkover for the future—*without* discarding our customs right and left. I am proud of you, daughter, prouder than I ever imagined I would be."

Margaret felt as if all the air had gone from her lungs at this sudden praise. She looked at Lew, tears forming in her eyes, and found him smiling at her. "Thank you.

I have waited a long time to hear that. I never knew how much I needed to hear it until you said it."

I never knew how much I wanted to say that I was proud of you—so both of us are pleased. Now, I am going to go talk to Dio. See if you can't persuade Mikhail out of his dumps, will you? You have chosen a fine man, Marguerida—a man who is almost good enough for you!

With that, Lew Alton turned and left the terrace. Margaret moved closer to her cousin, leaning against the ballustrade, their shoulders almost touching. Gently, she put her right hand over his left one, feeling the warmth of his skin on hers.

"Don't despair, Mik—it feels awful."

"I'm being a fool, aren't I?"

"No. You are just behaving like any man who has had the rug yanked out from under his feet."

He chuckled. "Dead on the mark! Do you know, I am very angry with Regis for just springing it on me—he didn't even ask me first!" Mikhail twined his fingers into hers, as Lady Linnea had claimed Regis' in the Crystal Chamber an hour before.

She remembered how envious she had been of that small movement, that tenderness and intimacy. Margaret felt herself no longer envious, just content to stand beside Mikhail and look out at the city. They stood quietly for a long time, neither speaking nor moving,

"Do you think this mess will get worked out?" he asked at last.

"If my father can manage it, yes. And if he can't, there is always mushroom farming!"

Mikhail turned and put his arms around her, his breath brushing her cheeks. He reached up and touched one of the tendrils of copper hair that curled over her brow. "Do you know how glad I am that I have resisted all the comely lasses of Darkover, and that I love you very much."

She felt breathless again, and cold for a second. The intensity of his feelings was frightening after a lifetime of deliberate isolation. Margaret glanced toward the blackened ruins of the Old Tower, where Ashara had captured her two decades before, then looked back at Mikhail. Her chill vanished, as if the last ice in her heart were melting under the sun of Darkover. She was home, at last; the exile she had never known she had was gone forever. "I think I do."

Mikhail Hastur looked into her eyes, then bent forward and pressed his lips to hers. It was a tender kiss, passionate but gentle, and it burned like lightning through the very core of her being. She knew that she would never have another moment as wonderful as this. No matter what happened, she would have this, and with that she was content.

EXILE'S SONG

A Novel of Darkover

by **Marion Zimmer Bradley**

Margaret Alton is the daughter of Lew Alton, Darkover's Senator to the Terran Federation, but her morose, uncommunicative father is secretive about the obscure planet of her birth. So when her university job sends her to Darkover, she has only fleeting, haunting memories of a tumultuous childhood. But once in the light of the Red Sun, as her veiled and mysterious heritage becomes manifest, she finds herself trapped by a destiny more terrifying than any nightmare!

- A direct sequel to *The Heritage of Hastur* and *Sharra's Exile*
- With cover art by Romas Kukalis

☐ **Hardcover Edition**   UE2705-$21.95